THE EYE OF THE WORLD

TOR
fantasy

THE EYE OF THE WORLD

ROBERT JORDAN

A TOM DOHERTY ASSOCIATES BOOK
NEW YORK

THE EYE OF THE WORLD

A TOR BOOK

Published by Tom Doherty Associates, Inc.
49 West 24 Street
New York, NY 10010

Maps by John M. Ford
Interior illustrations by Matthew C. Nielsen
Cover illustrations by Darryl Sweet

ISBN # 0-312-85009-3

To Harriet
Heart of my heart,
Light of my life,
Forever.

CONTENTS

PROLOGUE

Dragonmount

The palace still shook occasionally as the earth rumbled in memory, groaned as if it would deny what had happened. Bars of sunlight cast through rents in the walls made motes of dust glitter where they yet hung in the air. Scorch-marks marred the walls, the floors, the ceilings. Broad black smears crossed the blistered paints and gilt of once-bright murals, soot overlaying crumbling friezes of men and animals which seemed to have attempted to walk before the madness grew quiet. The dead lay everywhere, men and women and children, struck down in attempted flight by the lightnings that had flashed down every corridor, or seized by the fires that had stalked them, or sunken into stone of the palace, the stones that had flowed and sought, almost alive, before stillness came again. In odd counterpoint, colorful tapestries and paintings, masterworks all, hung undisturbed except where bulging walls had pushed them awry. Finely carved furnishings, inlaid with ivory and gold, stood untouched except where rippling floors had toppled them. The mind-twisting had struck at the core, ignoring peripheral things.

Lews Therin Telamon wandered the palace, deftly keeping his balance when the earth heaved. "Ilyena! My love, where are you?" The edge of his pale gray cloak trailed through blood as he stepped across the body of a woman, her golden-haired beauty marred by the horror of her last moments, her still-open eyes frozen in disbelief. "Where are you, my wife? Where is everyone hiding?"

His eyes caught his own reflection in a mirror hanging askew from bubbled marble. His clothes had been regal once, in gray and scarlet and gold; now the finely-woven cloth, brought by merchants from across the World Sea, was torn and dirty, thick with the same dust that covered his hair and skin. For a moment he fingered the symbol on his cloak, a circle half white and half black, the colors separated by a sinuous line. It meant something, that symbol. But the embroidered circle could not hold his attention long. He gazed at his own image with as much wonder. A tall man just into his middle years, handsome once, but now with hair already more white than brown and a face lined by strain and worry, dark eyes that had seen too much. Lews Therin began to chuckle, then threw back his head; his laughter echoed down the lifeless halls.

"Ilyena, my love! Come to me, my wife. You must see this."

Behind him the air rippled, shimmered, solidified into a man who looked around, his mouth twisting briefly with distaste. Not so tall as Lews Therin, he was clothed all in black, save for the snow-white lace at his throat and the silverwork on the turned-down tops of his thigh-high boots. He stepped carefully, handling his cloak fastidiously to avoid brushing the dead. The floor trembled with aftershocks, but his attention was fixed on the man staring into the mirror and laughing.

"Lord of the Morning," he said, "I have come for you."

The laughter cut off as if it had never been, and Lews Therin turned, seeming unsurprised. "Ah, a guest. Have you the Voice, stranger? It will soon be time for the Singing, and here all are welcome to take part. Ilyena, my love, we have a guest. Ilyena, where are you?"

The black-clad man's eyes widened, darted to the body of the golden-haired woman, then back to Lews Therin. "Shai'tan take you, does the taint already have you so far in its grip?"

"That name. Shai—" Lews Therin shuddered and raised a hand as though to ward off something. "You mustn't say that name. It is dangerous."

"So you remember that much, at least. Dangerous for you, fool, not for me. What else do you remember? Remember, you Light-blinded idiot! I will not let it end with you swaddled in unawareness! Remember!"

For a moment Lews Therin stared at his raised hand, fascinated by the patterns of grime. Then he wiped his hand on his even dirtier coat and turned his attention back to the other man. "Who are you? What do you want?"

The black-clad man drew himself up arrogantly. "Once I was called Elan Morin Tedronai, but now—"

"Betrayer of Hope." It was a whisper from Lews Therin. Memory stirred, but he turned his head, shying away from it.

"So you do remember some things. Yes, Betrayer of Hope. So have men named me, just as they named you Dragon, but unlike you I embrace the name. They gave me the name to revile me, but I will yet make them kneel and worship it. What will you do with your name? After this day, men will call you Kinslayer. What will you do with that?"

Lews Therin frowned down the ruined hall. "Ilyena should be here to offer a guest welcome," he murmured absently, then raised his voice. "Ilyena, where are you?" The floor shook; the golden-haired woman's body shifted as if in answer to his call. His eyes did not see her.

Elan Morin grimaced. "Look at you," he said scornfully. "Once you stood first among the Servants. Once you wore the Ring of Tamyrlin, and sat in the High Seat. Once you summoned the Nine Rods of Dominion. Now look at you! A pitiful, shattered wretch. But it is not enough. You humbled me in the Hall of Servants. You defeated me at the Gates of Paaran Disen. But I am the greater, now. I will not let you die without knowing that. When you die, your last thought will be the full knowledge of your defeat, of how complete and utter it is. If I let you die at all."

"I cannot imagine what is keeping Ilyena. She will give me the rough side of her tongue if she thinks I have been hiding a guest from her. I hope you enjoy conversation, for she surely does. Be forewarned. Ilyena will ask you so many questions you may end up telling her everything you know."

Tossing back his black cloak, Elan Morin flexed his hands. "A pity for you," he mused, "that one of your Sisters is not here. I was never very skilled at Healing, and I follow a different power now. But even one of them could only give you a few lucid minutes, if you did not destroy her first. What I can do will serve as well, for my purposes." His sudden smile was cruel. "But I fear Shai'tan's healing is different from the sort you know. Be healed, Lews Therin!" He extended his hands, and the light dimmed as if a shadow had been laid across the sun.

Pain blazed in Lews Therin, and he screamed, a scream that came from his depths, a scream he could not stop. Fire seared his marrow; acid rushed along his veins. He toppled backwards, crashing to the marble floor; his head struck the stone and rebounded. His heart pounded, trying to beat its way out of his chest, and every pulse gushed new flame through him. Helplessly he convulsed, thrashing, his skull a sphere of purest agony on the point of bursting. His hoarse screams reverberated through the palace.

Slowly, ever so slowly, the pain receded. The outflowing seemed to take a thousand years and left him twitching weakly, sucking breath through a raw throat. Another thousand years seemed to pass before he could manage to heave himself over, muscles like jellyfish, and shakily push himself up on hands and knees. His eyes fell on the golden-haired woman, and the scream that was ripped out of him dwarfed every sound he had made before. Tottering, almost falling, he scrabbled brokenly across the floor to her. It took every bit of his strength to pull her up into his arms. His hands shook as he smoothed her hair back from her staring face.

"Ilyena! Light help me, Ilyena!" His body curved around hers protectively, his sobs the full-throated cries of a man who had nothing left to live for. "Ilyena, no! *No!*"

"You can have her back, Kinslayer. The Great Lord of the Dark can make her live again, if you will serve him. If you will serve me."

Lews Therin raised his head, and the black-clad man took an involuntary step back from that gaze. "Ten years, Betrayer," Lews Therin said softly, the soft sound of steel being bared. "Ten years your foul master has wracked the world. And now this. I will. . . ."

"Ten years! You pitiful fool! This war has not lasted ten years, but since the beginning of time. You and I have fought a thousand battles with the turning of the Wheel, a thousand times a thousand, and we will fight until time dies and the Shadow is triumphant!" He finished in a shout, with a raised fist, and it was Lews Therin's turn to pull back, breath catching at the glow in the Betrayer's eyes.

Carefully Lews Therin laid Ilyena down, fingers gently brushing her hair. Tears blurred his vision as he stood, but his voice was iced iron. "For what else you have done, there can be no forgiveness, Betrayer, but for Ilyena's death I will destroy you beyond anything your master can repair. Prepare to—"

"Remember, you fool! Remember your futile attack on the Great Lord of the Dark! Remember his counterstroke! Remember! Even now the Hundred Companions are tearing the world apart, and every day a hundred men more join them. What hand slew Ilyena Sunhair, Kinslayer? Not mine. Not mine. What hand struck down every life that bore a drop of your blood, everyone who loved you, everyone you loved? Not mine, Kinslayer. Not mine. Remember, and know the price of opposing Shai'tan!"

Sudden sweat made tracks down Lews Therin's face through the dust and dirt. He remembered, a cloudy memory like a dream of a dream, but he knew it true.

His howl beat at the walls, the howl of a man who had discovered his soul damned by his own hand, and he clawed at his face as if to tear away the sight of what he had done. Everywhere he looked his eyes found the dead. Torn they were, or broken or burned, or half-consumed by stone. Everywhere lay lifeless faces he knew, faces he loved. Old servants and friends of his childhood, faithful companions through the long years of battle. And his children. His own sons and daughters, sprawled like broken dolls, play stilled forever. All slain by his hand. His children's faces accused him, blank eyes asking why, and his tears were no answer. The Betrayer's laughter flogged him, drowned out his howls. He could not bear the faces, the pain. He could not bear to remain any longer. Desperately he reached out to the True Source, to tainted *Saidin,* and he Traveled.

The land around him was flat and empty. A river flowed nearby, straight and broad, but he could sense there were no people within a hundred leagues. He was alone, as alone as a man could be while still alive, yet he could not escape memory. The eyes pursued him through the endless caverns of his mind. He could not hide from them. His children's eyes. Ilyena's eyes. Tears glistened on his cheeks as he turned his face to the sky.

"Light, forgive me!" He did not believe it could come, forgiveness. Not for what he had done. But he shouted to the sky anyway, begged for what he could not believe he could receive. "Light, forgive me!"

He was still touching *Saidin,* the male half of the power that drove the universe, that turned the Wheel of Time, and he could feel the oily taint fouling its surface, the taint of the Shadow's counterstroke, the taint that doomed the world. Because of him. Because in his pride he had believed that men could match the Creator, could mend what the Creator had made and they had broken. In his pride he had believed.

He drew on the True Source deeply, and still more deeply, like a man dying of thirst. Quickly he had drawn more of the One Power than he could channel unaided; his skin felt as if it were aflame. Straining, he forced himself to draw more, tried to draw it all.

"Light, forgive me! Ilyena!"

The air turned to fire, the fire to light liquefied. The bolt that struck from the heavens would have seared and blinded any eye that glimpsed it, even for an instant. From the heavens it came, blazed through Lews Therin Telamon, bored into the bowels of the earth. Stone turned to vapor at its touch. The earth thrashed and quivered like a living thing in agony. Only a heartbeat did the shining bar exist, connecting ground and sky, but even after it vanished the earth yet heaved like the sea in a storm. Molten rock fountained five hundred feet into the air, and the groaning ground rose, thrusting the burning spray ever upward, ever higher. From north and south, from east and west, the wind howled in, snapping trees like twigs, shrieking and blowing as if to aid the growing mountain ever skyward. Ever skyward.

At last the wind died, the earth stilled to trembling mutters. Of Lews Therin Telamon, no sign remained. Where he had stood a mountain now rose miles into the sky, molten lava still gushing from its broken peak. The broad, straight river had been pushed into a curve away from the mountain, and there it split to form a long island in its midst. The shadow of the mountain almost reached the island; it lay dark across the land like the ominous hand of prophecy. For a time the dull, protesting rumbles of the earth were the only sound.

On the island, the air shimmered and coalesced. The black-clad man stood staring at the fiery mountain rising out of the plain. His face twisted in rage and contempt. "You cannot escape so easily, Dragon. It is not done between us. It will not be done until the end of time."

Then he was gone, and the mountain and the island stood alone. Waiting.

And the Shadow fell upon the Land, and the World was riven stone from stone. The oceans fled, and the mountains were swallowed up, and the nations were scattered to the eight corners of the World. The moon was as blood, and the sun was as ashes. The seas boiled, and the living envied the dead. All was shattered, and all but memory lost, and one memory above all others, of him who brought the Shadow and the Breaking of the World. And him they named Dragon.

> (from *Aleth nin Taerin alta Camora,*
> *The Breaking of the World.*
> Author unknown, the Fourth Age)

And it came to pass in those days, as it had come before and would come again, that the Dark lay heavy on the land and weighed down the hearts of men, and the green things failed, and hope died. And men cried out to the Creator, saying, O Light of the Heavens, Light of the World, let the Promised One be born of the mountain, according to the prophecies, as he was in ages past and will be in ages to come. Let the Prince of the Morning sing to the land that green things will grow and the valleys give forth lambs. Let the arm of the Lord of the Dawn shelter us from the Dark, and the great sword of justice defend us. Let the Dragon ride again on the winds of time.

> (from *Charal Drianaan te Calamon,*
> *The Cycle of the Dragon.*
> Author unknown, the Fourth Age)

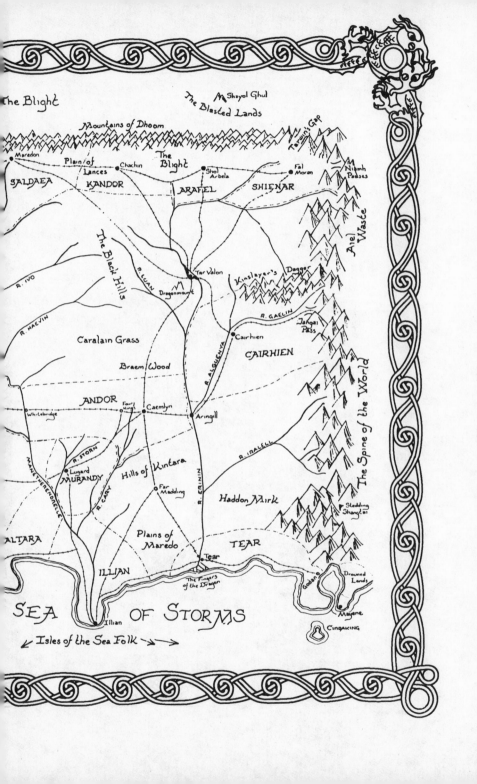

CHAPTER
1

An Empty Road

The Wheel of Time turns, and Ages come and pass, leaving memories that become legend. Legend fades to myth, and even myth is long forgotten when the Age that gave it birth comes again. In one Age, called the Third Age by some, an Age yet to come, an Age long past, a wind rose in the Mountains of Mist. The wind was not the beginning. There are neither beginnings nor endings to the turning of the Wheel of Time. But it was *a* beginning.

Born below the ever cloud-capped peaks that gave the mountains their name, the wind blew east, out across the Sand Hills, once the shore of a great ocean, before the Breaking of the World. Down it flailed into the Two Rivers, into the tangled forest called the Westwood, and beat at two men walking with a cart and horse down the rock-strewn track called the Quarry Road. For all that spring should have come a good month since, the wind carried an icy chill as if it would rather bear snow.

Gusts plastered Rand al'Thor's cloak to his back, whipped the earth-colored wool around his legs, then streamed it out behind him. He wished his coat were heavier, or that he had worn an extra shirt. Half the time when he tried to tug the cloak back around him it caught on the quiver swinging at his hip. Trying to hold the cloak one-handed did not do much good anyway; he had his bow in the other, an arrow nocked and ready to draw.

As a particularly strong blast tugged the cloak out of his hand, he glanced at his father over the back of the shaggy brown mare. He felt a little foolish about wanting to reassure himself that Tam was still there, but it was that kind of day. The wind howled when it rose, but aside from that, quiet lay heavy on the land. The soft creak of the axle sounded loud by comparison. No birds sang in the forest, no squirrels chittered from a branch. Not that he expected them, really; not this spring.

Only trees that kept leaf or needle through the winter had any green about them. Snarls of last year's bramble spread brown webs over stone outcrops under the trees. Nettles numbered most among the few weeds; the rest were the sorts with sharp burrs or thorns, or stinkweed, which left a rank smell on the unwary boot that crushed it. Scattered white patches of snow still dotted the ground where tight clumps of trees kept deep shade. Where sunlight did reach, it held neither strength nor warmth. The pale sun sat above the trees to the east, but its light was crisply dark, as if mixed with shadow. It was an awkward morning, made for unpleasant thoughts.

Without thinking he touched the nock of the arrow; it was ready to draw to his cheek in one smooth movement, the way Tam had taught him. Winter had been bad enough on the farms, worse than even the oldest folk remembered, but it must have been harsher still in the mountains, if the number of wolves driven down into the Two Rivers was any guide. Wolves raided the sheep pens and chewed their way into barns to get the cattle and horses. Bears had been after the sheep, too, where a bear had not been seen in years. It was no longer safe to be out after dark. Men were the prey as often as sheep, and the sun did not always have to be down.

Tam was taking steady strides on the other side of Bela, using his spear as a walking staff, ignoring the wind that made his brown cloak flap like a banner. Now and again he touched the mare's flank lightly, to remind her to keep moving. With his thick chest and broad face, he was a pillar of reality in that morning, like a stone in the middle of a drifting dream. His sun-roughened cheeks might be lined and his hair have only a sprinkling of black among the gray, but there was a solidness to him, as though a flood could wash around him without uprooting his feet. He stumped down the road now impassively. Wolves and bears were all very well, his manner said, things that any man who kept sheep must be aware of, but they had best not try to stop Tam al'Thor getting to Emond's Field.

With a guilty start Rand returned to watching his side of the road, Tam's matter-of-factness reminding him of his task. He was a head taller than his father, taller than anyone else in the district, and had little of Tam in him physically, except perhaps for a breadth of shoulder. Gray eyes and the reddish tinge to his hair came from his mother, so Tam said. She had been an outlander, and Rand remembered little of her aside from a smiling face, though he did put flowers on her grave every year, at Bel Tine, in the spring, and at Sunday, in the summer.

Two small casks of Tam's apple brandy rested in the lurching cart, and eight larger barrels of apple cider, only slightly hard after a winter's curing. Tam delivered the same every year to the Winespring Inn for use during Bel Tine, and he had declared that it would take more than wolves or a cold wind to stop him this spring. Even so they had not been to the village for weeks. Not even Tam traveled much these days. But Tam had given his word about the brandy and cider, even if he had waited to make delivery until the day before Festival. Keeping his word was important to Tam. Rand was just glad to get away from the farm, almost as glad as about the coming of Bel Tine.

As Rand watched his side of the road, the feeling grew in him that he was being watched. For a while he tried to shrug it off. Nothing moved or made a sound among the trees, except the wind. But the feeling not only persisted, it grew stronger. The hairs on his arms stirred; his skin prickled as if it itched on the inside.

He shifted his bow irritably to rub at his arms, and told himself to stop letting fancies take him. There was nothing in the woods on his side of the road, and Tam would have spoken if there had been anything on the other. He glanced over his shoulder . . . and blinked. Not more than twenty spans back down the road a cloaked figure on horseback followed them, horse and rider alike black, dull and ungleaming.

It was more habit than anything else that kept him walking backward alongside the cart even while he looked.

The rider's cloak covered him to his boot tops, the cowl tugged well forward so no part of him showed. Vaguely Rand thought there was something odd about the horseman, but it was the shadowed opening of the hood that fascinated him. He could see only the vaguest outlines of a face, but he had the feeling he was looking right into the rider's eyes. And he could not look away. Queasiness settled in his stomach. There was only shadow to see in the hood, but he felt hatred as sharply as if he could see a snarling face, hatred for everything that lived. Hatred for him most of all, for him above all things.

Abruptly a stone caught his heel and he stumbled, breaking his eyes away from the dark horseman. His bow dropped to the road, and only an outthrust hand grabbing Bela's harness saved him from falling flat on his back. With a startled snort the mare stopped, twisting her head to see what had caught her.

Tam frowned over Bela's back at him. "Are you all right, lad?"

"A rider," Rand said breathlessly, pulling himself upright. "A stranger, following us."

"Where?" The older man lifted his broad-bladed spear and peered back warily.

"There, down the. . . ." Rand's words trailed off as he turned to point. The road behind was empty. Disbelieving, he stared into the forest on both sides of the road. Bare-branched trees offered no hiding place, but there was not a glimmer of horse or horseman. He met his father's questioning gaze. "He was there. A man in a black cloak, on a black horse."

"I wouldn't doubt your word, lad, but where has he gone?"

"I don't know. But he was there." He snatched up the fallen bow and arrow, hastily checked the fletching before renocking, and half drew before letting the bowstring relax. There was nothing to aim at. "He was."

Tam shook his grizzled head. "If you say so, lad. Come on, then. A horse leaves hoofprints, even on this ground." He started toward the rear of the cart, his cloak whipping in the wind. "If we find them, we'll know for a fact he was there. If not . . . well, these are days to make a man think he's seeing things."

Abruptly Rand realized what had been odd about the horseman, aside from his being there at all. The wind that beat at Tam and him had not so much as shifted a fold of that black cloak. His mouth was suddenly dry. He must have imagined it. His father was right; this was a morning to prickle a man's imagination. But he did not believe it. Only, how did he tell his father that the man who had apparently vanished into air wore a cloak the wind did not touch?

With a worried frown he peered into the woods around them; it looked different than it ever had before. Almost since he was old enough to walk, he had run loose in the forest. The ponds and streams of the Riverwood, beyond the last farms east of Emond's Field, were where he had learned to swim. He had explored into the Sand Hills—which many in the Two Rivers said was bad luck—and once he had even gone to the very foot of the Mountains of Mist, him and his closest friends, Mat Cauthon and Perrin Aybara. That was a lot further afield than most people in Emond's Field ever went; to them a journey to the next village, up to Watch Hill or down to Deven Ride, was a big event. Nowhere in all of that had he found a place that made him afraid. Today, though, the Westwood was not the place he remembered. A man who could disappear so suddenly could reappear just as suddenly, maybe even right beside them.

"No, father, there's no need." When Tam stopped in surprise, Rand covered his flush by tugging at the hood of his cloak. "You're probably right. No point looking for what isn't there, not when we can use the time getting on to the village and out of this wind."

"I could do with a pipe," Tam said slowly, "and a mug of ale where it's warm." Abruptly he gave a broad grin. "And I expect you're eager to see Egwene."

Rand managed a weak smile. Of all things he might want to think about right then, the Mayor's daughter was far down the list. He did not need any more confusion. For the past year she had been making him increasingly jittery whenever they were together. Worse, she did not even seem to be aware of it. No, he certainly did not want to add Egwene to his thoughts.

He was hoping his father had not noticed he was afraid when Tam said, "Remember the flame, lad, and the void."

It was an odd thing Tam had taught him. Concentrate on a single flame and feed all your passions into it—fear, hate, anger—until your mind became empty. Become one with the void, Tam said, and you could do anything. Nobody else in Emond's Field talked that way. But Tam won the archery competition at Bel Tine every year with his flame and his void. Rand thought he might have a chance at placing this year himself, if he could manage to hold onto the void. For Tam to bring it up now meant he *had* noticed, but he said nothing more about it.

Tam clucked Bela into motion once more, and they resumed their journey, the older man striding along as if nothing untoward had happened and nothing untoward could. Rand wished he could imitate him. He tried forming the emptiness in his mind, but it kept slipping away into images of the black-cloaked horseman.

He wanted to believe that Tam was right, that the rider had just been his imagination, but he could remember that feeling of hatred too well. There *had* been someone. And that someone had meant him harm. He did not stop looking back until the high-peaked, thatched roofs of Emond's Field surrounded him.

The village lay close onto the Westwood, the forest gradually thinning until the last few trees stood actually among the stout frame houses. The land sloped gently down to the east. Though not without patches of woods, farms and hedge-bordered fields and pastures quilted the land beyond the village all the way to the Riverwood and its tangle of streams and ponds. The land to the west was just as fertile, and the pastures there lush in most years, but only a handful of farms could be found in the Westwood. Even those few dwindled to none miles short of the Sand Hills, not to mention the Mountains of Mist, which rose above the Westwood treetops, distant but in plain sight from Emond's Field. Some said the land was too rocky, as if there were not rocks everywhere in the Two Rivers, and others said it was hard-luck land. A few muttered that there was no point getting any closer to the mountains than needs be. Whatever the reasons, only the hardiest men farmed in the Westwood.

Small children and dogs dodged around the cart in whooping swarms once it passed the first row of houses. Bela plodded on patiently, ignoring the yelling youngsters who tumbled under her nose, playing tag and rolling hoops. In the last months there had been little of play or laughter from the children; even when the weather had slackened enough to let children out, fear of wolves kept them in. It seemed the approach of Bel Tine had taught them how to play again.

Festival had affected the adults as well. Broad shutters were thrown back, and in almost every house the goodwife stood in a window, apron tied about her and long-braided hair done up in a kerchief, shaking sheets or hanging mattresses over the windowsills. Whether or not leaves had appeared on the trees, no woman would let Bel Tine come before her spring cleaning was done. In every yard rugs hung from stretched lines, and children who had not been quick enough to run free in the streets instead vented their frustration on the carpets with wicker beaters. On roof after roof the goodman of the house clambered about, checking the thatch to see if the winter's damage meant calling on old Cenn Buie, the thatcher.

Several times Tam paused to engage one man or another in brief conversation. Since he and Rand had not been off the farm for weeks, everyone wanted to catch up on how things were out that way. Few Westwood men had been in. Tam spoke of damage from winter storms, each one worse than the one before, and stillborn lambs, of brown fields where crops should be sprouting and pastures greening, of ravens flocking in where songbirds had come in years before. Grim talk, with preparations for Bel Tine going on all around them, and much shaking of heads. It was the same on all sides.

Most of the men rolled their shoulders and said, "Well, we'll survive, the Light willing." Some grinned and added, "And if the Light doesn't will, we'll still survive."

That was the way of most Two Rivers people. People who had to watch the hail beat their crops or the wolves take their lambs, and start over, no matter how many years it happened, did not give up easily. Most of those who did were long since gone.

Tam would not have stopped for Wit Congar if the man had not come out into the street so they had to halt or let Bela run over him. The Congars—and the Coplins; the two families were so intermarried no one really knew where one family let off and the other began—were known from Watch Hill to Deven Ride, and maybe as far as Taren Ferry, as complainers and troublemakers.

"I have to get this to Bran al'Vere, Wit," Tam said, nodding to the barrels in the cart, but the scrawny man held his ground with a sour expression on his face. He had been sprawled on his front steps, not up on his roof, though the thatch looked as if it badly needed Master Buie's attention. He never seemed ready to start over, or to finish what he started the first time. Most of the Coplins and Congars were like that, those who were not worse.

"What are we going to do about Nynaeve, al'Thor?" Congar demanded. "We can't have a Wisdom like that for Emond's Field."

Tam sighed heavily. "It's not our place, Wit. The Wisdom is women's business."

"Well, we'd better do something, al'Thor. She said we'd have a mild winter. And a good harvest. Now you ask her what she hears on the wind, and she just scowls at you and stomps off."

"If you asked her the way you usually do, Wit," Tam said patiently, "you're lucky she didn't thump you with that stick she carries. Now if you don't mind, this brandy—"

"Nynaeve al'Meara is just too young to be Wisdom, al'Thor. If the Women's Circle won't do something, then the Village Council has to."

"What business of yours is the Wisdom, Wit Congar?" roared a woman's voice. Wit flinched as his wife marched out of the house. Daise Congar was twice as wide as Wit, a hard-faced woman without an ounce of fat on her. She glared at him with her fists on her hips. "You try meddling in Women's Circle business, and see how you like eating your own cooking. Which you won't do in my kitchen. And washing your own clothes and making your own bed. Which won't be under my roof."

"But, Daise," Wit whined, "I was just. . . ."

"If you'll pardon me, Daise," Tam said. "Wit. The Light shine on you both." He got Bela moving again, leading her around the scrawny fellow. Daise was concentrating on her husband now, but any minute she could realize whom it was Wit had been talking to.

That was why they had not accepted any of the invitations to stop for a bite to eat or something hot to drink. When they saw Tam, the goodwives of Emond's Field went on point like hounds spotting a rabbit. There was not a one of them who did not know just the perfect wife for a widower with a good farm, even if it was in the Westwood.

Rand stepped along just as quickly as Tam, perhaps even more so. He was sometimes cornered when Tam was not around, with no way to escape outside of rudeness. Herded onto a stool by the kitchen fire, he would be fed pastries or honeycakes or meatpies. And always the goodwife's eyes weighed and measured him as neatly as any merchant's scales and tapes while she told him that what he was eating was not nearly so good as her widowed sister's cooking, or her next-to-eldest cousin's. Tam was certainly not getting any younger, she would say. It was good that he had loved his wife so—it boded well for the next woman in his life—but he had mourned long enough. Tam needed a good woman. It was a simple fact, she would say, or something very close, that a man just could not do without a woman to take care of him and keep him out of trouble. Worst of all were those who paused thoughtfully at about that point, then asked with elaborate casualness exactly how old *he* was now.

Like most Two Rivers folk, Rand had a strong stubborn streak. Outsiders sometimes said it was the prime trait of people in the Two Rivers, that they could give mules lessons and teach stones. The goodwives were fine and kindly women for the most part, but he hated being pushed into anything, and they made him feel as if he were being prodded with sticks. So he walked fast, and wished Tam would hurry Bela along.

Soon the street opened onto the Green, a broad expanse in the middle of the village. Usually covered with thick grass, the Green this spring showed only a few fresh patches among the yellowish brown of dead grass and the black of bare earth. A double handful of geese waddled about, beadily eyeing the ground but not finding anything worth pecking, and someone had tethered a milkcow to crop the sparse growth.

Toward the west end of the Green, the Winespring itself gushed out of a low stone outcrop in a flow that never failed, a flow strong enough to knock a man down and sweet enough to justify its name a dozen times over. From the spring the rapidly widening Winespring Water ran swiftly off to the east, willows dotting its banks all the way to Master Thane's mill and beyond, until it split into dozens of streams in the swampy depths of the Waterwood. Two low, railed footbridges crossed the clear stream at the Green, and one bridge, wider than the others and stout enough to bear wagons. The Wagon Bridge marked where the North Road, coming down from Taren Ferry and Watch Hill, became the Old Road, leading to Deven Ride. Outsiders sometimes found it funny that the road had one name to the north and another to the south, but that was the way it had always been, as far as anyone in Emond's Field knew, and that was that. It was a good enough reason for Two Rivers people.

On the far side of the bridges, the mounds were already building for the Bel Tine fires, three careful stacks of logs almost as big as houses. They had to be on cleared dirt, of course, not on the Green, even sparse as it was. What of Festival did not take place around the fires would happen on the Green.

Near the Winespring a score of older women sang softly as they erected the Spring Pole. Shorn of its branches, the straight, slender trunk of a fir tree stood ten feet high even in the hole they had dug for it. A knot of girls too young to wear their hair braided sat cross-legged and watched enviously, occasionally singing snatches of the song the women sang.

Tam clucked at Bela as if to make her speed her pace, though she ignored it, and Rand studiously kept his eyes from what the women were doing. In the morning the men would pretend to be surprised to find the Pole, then at noon the unmarried women would dance the Pole, entwining it with long, colored ribbons while the unmarried men sang. No one knew when the custom began or why—it was another thing that was the way it had always been—but it was an excuse to sing and dance, and nobody in the Two Rivers needed much excuse for that.

The whole day of Bel Tine would be taken up with singing and dancing and feasting, with time out for footraces, and contests in almost everything. Prizes would be given not only in archery, but for the best with the sling, and the quarterstaff. There would be contests at solving riddles and puzzles, at the rope tug, and lifting and tossing weights, prizes for the best singer, the best dancer and the best fiddle player, for the quickest to shear a sheep, even the best at bowls, and at darts.

Bel Tine was supposed to come when spring had well and truly arrived, the first lambs born and the first crop up. Even with the cold hanging on, though, no one had any idea of putting it off. Everyone could use a little singing and dancing. And to top everything, if the rumors could be believed, a grand display of fireworks was planned for the Green—if the first peddler of the year appeared in time, of course. That had been causing considerable talk; it was ten years since the last such display, and that was still talked about.

The Winespring Inn stood at the east end of the Green, hard beside the Wagon Bridge. The first floor of the inn was river rock, though the foundation was of older stone some said came from the mountains. The whitewashed second story—where Brandelwyn al'Vere, the innkeeper and Mayor of Emond's Field for the past twenty years, lived in the back with his wife and daughters—jutted out over the lower floor all the way around. Red roof tile, the only such roof in the village, glittered in the weak sunlight, and smoke drifted from three of the inn's dozen tall chimneys.

At the south end of the inn, away from the stream, stretched the remains of a much larger stone foundation, once part of the inn—or so it was said. A huge oak grew in the middle of it now, with a bole thirty paces around and spreading branches as thick as a man. In the summer, Bran al'Vere set tables and benches under those branches, shady with leaves then, where people could enjoy a cup and a cooling breeze while they talked or perhaps set out a board for a game of stones.

"Here we are, lad." Tam reached for Bela's harness, but she stopped in front of the inn before his hand touched leather. "Knows the way better than I do," he chuckled.

As the last creak of the axle faded, Bran al'Vere appeared from the inn, seeming as always to step too lightly for a man of his girth, nearly double that of anyone else in the village. A smile split his round face, which was topped by a sparse fringe of gray hair. The innkeeper was in his shirtsleeves despite the chill, with a spotless white apron wrapped around him. A silver medallion in the form of a set of balance scales hung on his chest.

The medallion, along with the full-size set of scales used to weigh the coins of the merchants who came down from Baerlon for wool or tabac, was the symbol of the Mayor's office. Bran only wore it for dealing with the merchants and for festivals, feastdays, and weddings. He had it on a day early now, but that night was Winternight, the night before Bel Tine, when everyone would visit back and forth almost the whole night long, exchanging small gifts, having a bite to eat and a touch to drink at every house. *After the winter,* Rand thought, *he probably considers Winternight excuse enough not to wait until tomorrow.*

"Tam," the Mayor shouted as he hurried toward them. "The Light shine on me, it's good to see you at last. And you, Rand. How are you, my boy?"

"Fine, Master al'Vere," Rand said. "And you, sir?" But Bran's attention was already back on Tam.

"I was almost beginning to think you wouldn't be bringing your brandy this year. You've never waited so late before."

"I've no liking for leaving the farm these days, Bran," Tam replied. "Not with the wolves the way they are. And the weather."

Bran harrumphed. "I could wish somebody wanted to talk about something besides the weather. Everyone complains about it, and folk who should know better expect me to set it right. I've just spent twenty minutes explaining to Mistress al'Donel that I can do nothing about the storks. Though what she expected me to do. . . ." He shook his head.

"An ill omen," a scratchy voice announced, "no storks nesting on the rooftops at Bel Tine." Cenn Buie, as gnarled and dark as an old root, marched up to Tam and Bran and leaned on his walking staff, near as tall as he was and just as gnarled. He tried to fix both men at once with a beady eye. "There's worse to come, you mark my words."

"Have you become a soothsayer, then, interpreting omens?" Tam asked dryly. "Or do you listen to the wind, like a Wisdom? There's certainly enough of it. Some originating not far from here."

"Mock if you will," Cenn muttered, "but if it doesn't warm enough for crops to sprout soon, more than one root cellar will come up empty before there's a harvest. By next winter there may be nothing left alive in the Two Rivers but wolves and ravens. If it is next winter at all. Maybe it will still be this winter."

"Now what is that supposed to mean?" Bran said sharply.

Cenn gave them a sour look. "I've not much good to say about Nynaeve al'Meara. You know that. For one thing, she's too young to— No matter. The Women's Circle seems to object to the Village Council even talking about their business, though they interfere in ours whenever they want to, which is most of the time, or so it seems to—"

"Cenn," Tam broke in, "is there a point to this?"

"This is the point, al'Thor. Ask the Wisdom when the winter will end, and she walks away. Maybe she doesn't want to tell us what she hears on the wind. Maybe what she hears is that the winter won't end. Maybe it's just going to go on being winter until the Wheel turns and the Age ends. There's your point."

"Maybe sheep will fly," Tam retorted, and Bran threw up his hands.

"The Light protect me from fools. You sitting on the Village Council, Cenn, and now you're spreading that Coplin talk. Well, you listen to me. We have enough problems without. . . ."

A quick tug at Rand's sleeve and a voice pitched low, for his ear alone, distracted him from the older men's talk. "Come on, Rand, while they're arguing. Before they put you to work."

Rand glanced down, and had to grin. Mat Cauthon crouched beside the cart so Tam and Bran and Cenn could not see him, his wiry body contorted like a stork trying to bend itself double.

Mat's brown eyes twinkled with mischief, as usual. "Dav and I caught a big old badger, all grouchy at being pulled out of his den. We're going to let it loose on the Green and watch the girls run."

Rand's smile broadened; it did not sound as much like fun to him as it would have a year or two back, but Mat never seemed to grow up. He took a quick look at his father—the men had their heads together still, all three talking at once—then lowered his own voice. "I promised to unload the cider. I can meet you later, though."

Mat rolled his eyes skyward. "Toting barrels! Burn me, I'd rather play stones with my baby sister. Well, I know of better things than a badger. We have strangers in the Two Rivers. Last evening—"

For an instant Rand stopped breathing. "A man on horseback?" he asked intently. "A man in a black cloak, on a black horse? And his cloak doesn't move in the wind?"

Mat swallowed his grin, and his voice dropped to an even hoarser whisper. "You saw him, too? I thought I was the only one. Don't laugh, Rand, but he scared me."

"I'm not laughing. He scared me, too. I could swear he hated me, that he wanted to kill me." Rand shivered. Until that day he had never thought of anyone wanting to kill him, really wanting to kill him. That sort of thing just did not happen in the Two Rivers. A fistfight, maybe, or a wrestling match, but not killing.

"I don't know about hating, Rand, but he was scary enough anyway. All he did was sit on his horse looking at me, just outside the village, but I've never been so frightened in my life. Well, I looked away, just for a moment—it wasn't easy, mind you—then when I looked back he'd vanished. Blood and ashes! Three days, it's been, and I can hardly stop thinking about him. I keep looking over my shoulder." Mat attempted a laugh that came out as a croak. "Funny how being scared takes you. You think strange things. I actually thought—just for a minute, mind—it might be the Dark One." He tried another laugh, but no sound at all came out this time.

Rand took a deep breath. As much to remind himself as for any other reason, he said by rote, "The Dark One and all of the Forsaken are bound in Shayol Ghul, beyond the Great Blight, bound by the Creator at the moment of Creation, bound until the end of time. The hand of the Creator shelters the world, and the Light shines on us all." He drew another breath and went on. "Besides, if he was free, what would the Shepherd of the Night be doing in the Two Rivers watching farmboys?"

"I don't know. But I do know that rider was . . . evil. Don't laugh. I'll take oath on it. Maybe it was the Dragon."

"You're just full of cheerful thoughts, aren't you?" Rand muttered. "You sound worse than Cenn."

"My mother always said the Forsaken would come for me if I didn't mend my ways. If I ever saw anybody who looked like Ishamael, or Aginor, it was him."

"Everybody's mother scared them with the Forsaken," Rand said dryly, "but most grow out of it. Why not the Shadowman, while you're about it?"

Mat glared at him. "I haven't been so scared since. . . . No, I've never been that scared, and I don't mind admitting it."

"Me, either. My father thinks I was jumping at shadows under the trees."

Mat nodded glumly and leaned back against the cart wheel. "So does my da. I told Dav, and Elam Dowtry. They've been watching like hawks ever since, but they haven't seen anything. Now Elam thinks I was trying to trick him. Dav thinks he's down from Taren Ferry—a sheepstealer, or a chickenthief. A chickenthief!" He lapsed into affronted silence.

"It's probably all foolishness anyway," Rand said finally. "Maybe he is just a sheepstealer." He tried to picture it, but it was like picturing a wolf taking the cat's place in front of a mouse hole.

"Well, I didn't like the way he looked at me. And neither did you, not if how you jumped at me is any guide. We ought to tell someone."

"We already have, Mat, both of us, and we weren't believed. Can you imagine trying to convince Master al'Vere about this fellow, without him seeing him? He'd send us off to Nynaeve to see if we were sick."

"There are two of us, now. Nobody could believe we both imagined it."

Rand rubbed the top of his head briskly, wondering what to say. Mat was something of a byword around the village. Few people had escaped his pranks. Now his name came up whenever a washline dropped the laundry in the dirt or a loose saddle girth deposited a farmer in the road. Mat did not even have to be anywhere around. His support might be worse than none.

After a moment Rand said, "Your father would believe you put me up to it, and mine. . . ." He looked over the cart to where Tam and Bran and Cenn had been talking, and found himself staring his father in the eyes. The Mayor was still lecturing Cenn, who took it now in sullen silence.

"Good morning, Matrim," Tam said brightly, hefting one of the brandy casks up onto the side of the cart. "I see you've come to help Rand unload the cider. Good lad."

Mat leaped to his feet at the first word and began backing away. "Good morning to you, Master al'Thor. And to you, Master al'Vere. Master Buie. May the Light shine on you. My da sent me to—"

"No doubt he did," Tam said. "And no doubt, since you are a lad who does his chores right off, you've finished the task already. Well, the quicker you lads get the cider into Master al'Vere's cellar, the quicker you can see the gleeman."

"Gleeman!" Mat exclaimed, stopping dead in his footsteps, at the same instant that Rand asked, "When will he get here?"

Rand could remember only two gleemen coming into the Two Rivers in his whole life, and for one of those he had been young enough to sit on Tam's shoulders to watch. To have one there actually during Bel Tine, with his harp and his flute and his stories and all. . . . Emond's Field would still be talking about this Festival ten years off, even if there were not any fireworks.

"Foolishness," Cenn grumbled, but fell silent at a look from Bran that had all the weight of the Mayor's office in it.

Tam leaned against the side of the cart, using the brandy cask as a prop for his arm. "Yes, a gleeman, and already here. According to Master al'Vere, he's in a room in the inn right now."

"Arrived in the dead of night, he did." The innkeeper shook his head in disapproval. "Pounded on the front door till he woke the whole family. If not for Festival, I'd have told him to stable his own horse and sleep in the stall with it, gleeman or not. Imagine coming in the dark like that."

Rand stared wonderingly. No one traveled beyond the village by night, not these days, certainly not alone. The thatcher grumbled under his breath again, too low this time for Rand to understand more than a word or two. "Madman" and "unnatural."

"He doesn't wear a black cloak, does he?" Mat asked suddenly.

Bran's belly shook with his chuckle. "Black! His cloak is like every gleeman's cloak I've ever seen. More patches than cloak, and more colors than you can think of."

Rand startled himself by laughing out loud, a laugh of pure relief. The menacing black-clad rider as a gleeman was a ridiculous notion, but. . . . He clapped a hand over his mouth in embarrassment.

"You see, Tam," Bran said. "There's been little enough laughter in this village since winter came. Now even the gleeman's cloak brings a laugh. That alone is worth the expense of bringing him down from Baerlon."

"Say what you will," Cenn spoke up suddenly. "I still say it's a foolish waste of money. And those fireworks you all insisted on sending off for."

"So there are fireworks," Mat said, but Cenn went right on.

"They should have been here a month ago with the first peddler of the year, but there hasn't been a peddler, has there? If he doesn't come by tomorrow, what are we going to do with them? Hold another Festival just to set them off? That's if he even brings them, of course."

"Cenn"—Tam sighed—"you've as much trust as a Taren Ferry man."

"Where is he, then? Tell me that, al'Thor."

"Why didn't you tell us?" Mat demanded in an aggrieved voice. "The whole village would have had as much fun with the waiting as with the gleeman. Or almost, anyway. You can see how everybody's been over just a rumor of fireworks."

"I can see," Bran replied with a sidelong look at the thatcher. "And if I knew for sure how that rumor started . . . if I thought, for instance, that somebody had been complaining about how much things cost where people could hear him when the things are supposed to be secret. . . ."

Cenn cleared his throat. "My bones are too old for this wind. If you don't mind, I'll just see if Mistress al'Vere won't fix me some mulled wine to take the chill off. Mayor. Al'Thor." He was headed for the inn before he finished, and as the door swung shut behind him, Bran sighed.

"Sometimes I think Nynaeve is right about. . . . Well, that's not important now. You young fellows think for a minute. Everyone's excited about the fireworks, true, and that's only at a rumor. Think how they'll be if the peddler doesn't get here in time, after all their anticipating. And with the weather the way it is, who knows when he will come. They'd be fifty times as excited about a gleeman."

"And feel fifty times as bad if he hadn't come," Rand said slowly. "Even Bel Tine might not do much for people's spirits after that."

"You have a head on your shoulders when you choose to use it," Bran said. "He'll follow you on the Village Council one day, Tam. Mark my words. He couldn't do much worse right now than someone I could name."

"None of this is unloading the cart," Tam said briskly, handing the first cask of brandy to the Mayor. "I want a warm fire, my pipe, and a mug of your good ale." He hoisted the second brandy cask onto his shoulder. "I'm sure Rand will thank you for your help, Matrim. Remember, the sooner the cider is in the cellar. . . ."

As Tam and Bran disappeared into the inn, Rand looked at his friend. "You don't have to help. Dav won't keep that badger long."

"Oh, why not?" Mat said resignedly. "Like your da said, the quicker it's in the cellar. . . ." Picking up one of the casks of cider in both arms, he hurried toward the inn in a half trot. "Maybe Egwene is around. Watching you stare at her like a poleaxed ox will be as good as a badger any day."

Rand paused in the act of putting his bow and quiver in the back of the cart. He really had managed to put Egwene out of his mind. That was unusual in itself. But she would likely be around the inn somewhere. There was not much chance he could avoid her. Of course, it had been weeks since he saw her last.

"Well?" Mat called from the front of the inn. "I didn't say I would do it by myself. You aren't on the Village Council yet."

With a start, Rand took up a cask and followed. Perhaps she would not be there after all. Oddly, that possibility did not make him feel any better.

CHAPTER
2

Strangers

When Rand and Mat carried the first barrels through the common room, Master al'Vere was already filling a pair of mugs with his best brown ale, his own make, from one of the casks racked against one wall. Scratch, the inn's yellow cat, crouched atop it with his eyes closed and his tail wrapped around his feet. Tam stood in front of the big fireplace of river rock, thumbing a long-stemmed pipe full of tabac from a polished canister the innkeeper always kept on the plain stone mantel. The fireplace stretched half the length of the big, square room, with a lintel as high as a man's shoulder, and the crackling blaze on the hearth vanquished the chill outside.

At that time of the busy day before Festival, Rand expected to find the common room empty except for Bran and his father and the cat, but four more members of the Village Council, including Cenn, sat in high-backed chairs in front of the fire, mugs in hand and blue-gray pipesmoke wreathing their heads. For once none of the stones boards were in use, and all of Bran's books stood idle on the shelf opposite the fireplace. The men did not even talk, peering silently into their ale or tapping pipestems against their teeth in impatience, as they waited for Tam and Bran to join them.

Worry was not uncommon for the Village Council these days, not in Emond's Field, and likely not in Watch Hill, or Deven Ride. Or even Taren Ferry, though who knew what Taren Ferry folk really thought about anything?

Only two of the men before the fire, Haral Luhhan, the blacksmith, and Jon Thane, the miller, so much as glanced at the boys as they entered. Master Luhhan, though, made it more than a glance. The blacksmith's arms were as big as most men's legs, roped with heavy muscle, and he still wore his long leather apron as if he had hurried to the meeting straight from the forge. His frown took them both in, then he straightened around in his chair deliberately, turning his attention back to an over-studious tamping of his pipe with a thick thumb.

Curious, Rand slowed, then barely bit back a yelp as Mat kicked his ankle. His friend nodded insistently toward the doorway at the back of the common room and hurried on without waiting. Limping slightly, Rand followed less quickly.

"What was that about?" he demanded as soon as he was in the hall that led to the kitchen. "You almost broke my—"

"It's old Luhhan," Mat said, peering past Rand's shoulder into the common room. "I think he suspects I was the one who—" He cut off abruptly as Mistress al'Vere bustled out of the kitchen, the aroma of fresh-baked bread wafting ahead of her.

The tray in her hands carried some of the crusty loaves for which she was famous around Emond's Field, as well as plates of pickles and cheese. The food reminded Rand abruptly that he had eaten only an end of bread before leaving the farm that morning. His stomach gave an embarrassing rumble.

A slender woman, with her thick braid of graying hair pulled over one shoulder, Mistress al'Vere smiled in a motherly fashion that took in both of them. "There is more of this in the kitchen, if you two are hungry, and I never knew boys your age who weren't. Or any other age, for that matter. If you prefer, I'm baking honeycakes this morning."

She was one of the few married women in the area who never tried to play matchmaker with Tam. Toward Rand her motherliness extended to warm smiles and a quick snack whenever he came by the inn, but she did as much for every young man in the area. If she occasionally looked at him as if she wanted to do more, at least she took it no further than looks, for which he was deeply grateful.

Without waiting for a reply she swept on into the common room. Immediately there was the sound of chairs scraping on the floor as the men got to their feet, and exclaimings over the smell of the bread. She was easily the best cook in Emond's Field, and not a man for miles around but eagerly leaped at a chance to put his feet under her table.

"Honeycakes," Mat said, smacking his lips.

"After," Rand told him firmly, "or we'll never get done."

A lamp hung over the cellar stairs, just beside the kitchen door, and another made a bright pool in the stone-walled room beneath the inn, banishing all but a little dimness in the furthest corners. Wooden racks along the walls and across the floor held casks of brandy and cider, and larger barrels of ale and wine, some with taps driven in. Many of the wine barrels were marked with chalk in Bran al'Vere's hand, giving the year they had been bought, what peddler had brought them, and in which city they had been made, but all of the ale and brandy was the make of Two Rivers farmers or of Bran himself. Peddlers, and even merchants, sometimes brought brandy or ale from outside, but it was never as good and cost the earth, besides, and nobody ever drank it more than once.

"Now," Rand said, as they set their casks in the racks, "what did you do that you have to avoid Master Luhhan?"

Mat shrugged. "Nothing, really. I told Adan al'Caar and some of his snot-nosed friends—Ewin Finngar and Dag Coplin—that some farmers had seen ghost hounds, breathing fire and running through the woods. They ate it up like clotted cream."

"And Master Luhhan is mad at you for that?" Rand said doubtfully.

"Not exactly." Mat paused, then shook his head. "You see, I covered two of his dogs with flour, so they were all white. Then I let them loose near Dag's house. How was I to know they'd run straight home? It really isn't my fault. If Mistress Luhhan hadn't left the door open they couldn't have gotten inside. It isn't like I intended to get flour all over her house." He gave a bark of laughter. "I hear she chased old Luhhan and the dogs, all three, out of the house with a broom."

Rand winced and laughed at the same time. "If I were you, I'd worry more about Alsbet Luhhan than about the blacksmith. She's almost as strong, and her temper is a lot worse. No matter, though. If you walk fast, maybe he won't notice you." Mat's expression said he did not think Rand was funny.

When they went back through the common room, though, there was no need for Mat to hurry. The six men had their chairs in a tight knot before the fireplace. With his back to the fire, Tam was speaking in a low voice, and the others were leaning forward to listen, so intent on his words they would likely not have noticed if a flock of sheep had been driven through. Rand wanted to move closer, to hear what they were talking about, but Mat plucked at his sleeve and gave him an agonized look. With a sigh he followed Mat out to the cart.

On their return to the hallway they found a tray by the top of the steps, and hot honeycakes filling the hall with their sweet aroma. There were two mugs, as well, and a pitcher of steaming mulled cider. Despite his own admonition about waiting until later Rand found himself making the last two trips between cart and cellar while trying to juggle a cask and a piping honeycake.

Setting his final cask in the racks, he wiped crumbs from his mouth while Mat was unburdening himself, then said, "Now for the glee—"

Feet clattered on the stairs, and Ewin Finngar half fell into the cellar in his haste, his pudgy face shining with eagerness to impart his news. "There are strangers in the village." He caught his breath and gave Mat a wry look. "I haven't seen any ghost hounds, but I hear somebody floured Master Luhhan's dogs. I hear Mistress Luhhan has ideas who to look for, too."

The years separating Rand and Mat from Ewin, only fourteen, were usually more than enough for them to give short shrift to anything he had to say. This time they exchanged one startled glance, then both were talking at once.

"In the village?" Rand asked. "Not in the woods?"

Right on top of him Mat added, "Was his cloak black? Could you see his face?"

Ewin looked uncertainly from one of them to the other, then spoke quickly when Mat took a threatening step. "Of course I could see his face. And his cloak is green. Or maybe gray. It changes. It seems to fade into wherever he's standing. Sometimes you don't see him even when you look right at him, not unless he moves. And hers is blue, like the sky, and ten times fancier than any feastday clothes I ever saw. She's ten times prettier than anybody I ever saw, too. She's a high-born lady, like in the stories. She must be."

"Her?" Rand said. "Who are you talking about?" He stared at Mat, who had put both hands on top of his head and squeezed his eyes shut.

"They're the ones I meant to tell you about," Mat muttered, "before you got me off onto—" He cut off, opening his eyes for a sharp glance at Ewin. "They arrived last evening," Mat went on after a moment, "and took rooms here at the inn. I saw them ride in. Their horses, Rand. I never saw horses so tall, or so sleek. They look like they could run forever. I think he works for her."

"In service," Ewin broke in. "They call it being in service, in the stories."

Mat continued as if Ewin had not spoken. "Anyway, he defers to her, does what she says. Only he isn't like a hired man. A soldier, maybe. The way he wears his sword, it's part of him, like his hand or his foot. He makes the merchants' guards look like cur dogs. And her, Rand. I never even imagined anyone like her. She's out of a gleeman's story. She's like . . . like. . . ." He paused to give Ewin a sour look. ". . . like a high-born lady," he finished with a sigh.

"But who are they?" Rand asked. Except for merchants, once a year to buy tabac and wool, and the peddlers, outsiders never came into the Two Rivers, or as good as never. Maybe at Taren Ferry, but not this far south. Most of the merchants and peddlers had been coming for years, too, so they did not really count as strangers. Just outsiders. It was a good five years since the last time a real stranger appeared in Emond's Field, and he had been trying to hide from some sort of trouble up in Baerlon that nobody in the village understood. He had not stayed long. "What do they want?"

"What do they want?" Mat exclaimed. "I don't care what they want. Strangers, Rand, and strangers like you never even dreamed of. Think of it!"

Rand opened his mouth, then closed it without speaking. The black-cloaked rider had him as nervous as a cat in a dog run. It just seemed like an awful coincidence, three strangers around the village at the same time. Three if this fellow's cloak that changed colors never changed to black.

"Her name is Moiraine," Ewin said into the momentary silence. "I heard him say it. Moiraine, he called her. The Lady Moiraine. His name is Lan. The Wisdom may not like her, but I do."

"What makes you think Nynaeve dislikes her?" Rand said.

"She asked the Wisdom for directions this morning," Ewin said, "and called her 'child.'" Rand and Mat both whistled softly through their teeth, and Ewin tripped over his tongue in his haste to explain. "The Lady Moiraine didn't know she was the Wisdom. She apologized when she found out. She did. And asked some questions about herbs, and about who is who around Emond's Field, just as respectfully as any woman in the village—more so than some. She's always asking questions, about how old people are, and how long they've lived where they live, and . . . oh, I don't know what all. Anyway, Nynaeve answered like she'd bitten a green sweetberry. Then, when the Lady Moiraine walked away, Nynaeve stared after her like, like . . . well, it wasn't friendly, I can tell you that."

"Is that all?" Rand said. "You know Nynaeve's temper. When Cenn Buie called her a child last year, she thumped him on the head with her stick, and he's on the Village Council, and old enough to be her grandfather, besides. She flares up at anything, and never stays angry past turning around."

"That's too long for me," Ewin muttered.

"I don't care who Nynaeve thumps"—Mat chortled—"so long as it isn't me. This is going to be the best Bel Tine ever. A gleeman, a lady—who could ask for more? Who needs fireworks?"

"A gleeman?" Ewin said, his voice rising sharply.

"Come on, Rand," Mat went on, ignoring the younger boy. "We're done here. You have to see this fellow."

He bounded up the stairs, with Ewin scrambling behind him calling, "Is there really a gleeman, Mat? This isn't like the ghost hounds, is it? Or the frogs?"

Rand paused long enough to turn down the lamp, then hurried after them.

In the common room Rowan Hurn and Samel Crawe had joined the others in front of the fire, so that the entire Village Council was there. Bran al'Vere spoke now, his normally bluff voice pitched so low that only a rumbling murmur traveled beyond the close-gathered chairs. The Mayor emphasized his words by tapping a thick forefinger into the palm of his other hand, and eyed each man in turn. They all nodded in agreement with whatever he was saying, though Cenn more reluctantly than the rest.

The way the men all but huddled together spoke more plainly than a painted sign. Whatever they were talking about, it was for the Village Council alone, at least for now. They would not appreciate Rand trying to listen in. Reluctantly he pulled himself away. There was still the gleeman. And these strangers.

Outside, Bela and the cart were gone, taken away by Hu or Tad, the inn's stablemen. Mat and Ewin stood glaring at one another a few paces from the front door of the inn, their cloaks whipping in the wind.

"For the last time," Mat barked, "I am *not* playing a trick on you. There *is* a gleeman. Now go away. Rand, will you tell this woolhead I am telling the truth so he'll leave me alone?"

Pulling his cloak together, Rand stepped forward to support Mat, but words died as the hairs stirred on the back of his neck. He was being watched again. It was far from the feeling the hooded rider had given him, but neither was it pleasant, especially so soon after that encounter.

A quick look about the Green showed him only what he had seen before—children playing, people preparing for Festival, and no one more than glancing in his direction. The Spring Pole stood alone, now, waiting. Bustle and childish shouts filled the side streets. All was as it should be. Except that he was being watched.

Then something led him to turn around, to raise his eyes. On the edge of the inn's tile roof perched a large raven, swaying a little in the gusting wind from the mountains. Its head was cocked to one side, and one beady, black eye was focused . . . on him, he thought. He swallowed, and suddenly anger flickered in him, hot and sharp.

"Filthy carrion eater," he muttered.

"I am tired of being stared at," Mat growled, and Rand realized his friend had stepped up beside him and was frowning at the raven, too.

They exchanged a glance, then as one their hands darted for rocks.

The two stones flew true . . . and the raven stepped aside; the stones whistled through the space where it had been. Fluffing its wings once, it cocked its head again, fixing them with a dead black eye, unafraid, giving no sign that anything had happened.

Rand stared at the bird in consternation. "Did you ever see a raven do that?" he asked quietly.

Mat shook his head without looking away from the raven. "Never. Nor any other bird, either."

"A vile bird," came a woman's voice from behind them, melodious despite echoes of distaste, "to be mistrusted in the best of times."

With a shrill cry the raven launched itself into the air so violently that two black feathers drifted down from the roof's edge.

Startled, Rand and Mat twisted to follow the bird's swift flight, over the Green and toward the cloud-tipped Mountains of Mist, tall beyond the Westwood, until it dwindled to a speck in the west, then vanished from view.

Rand's gaze fell to the woman who had spoken. She, too, had been watching the flight of the raven, but now she turned back, and her eyes met his. He could only stare. This had to be the Lady Moiraine, and she was everything that Mat and Ewin had said, everything and more.

When he had heard she called Nynaeve child, he had pictured her as old, but she was not. At least, he could not put any age to her at all. At first he thought she was as young as Nynaeve, but the longer he looked the more he thought she was older than that. There was a maturity about her large, dark eyes, a hint of knowing that no one could have gotten young. For an instant he thought those eyes were

Her smile did fade then, slowly, as if something had been recalled to her. For a moment she merely looked at him. "I am a student of history," she said at last, "a collector of old stories. This place you call the Two Rivers has always interested me. Sometimes I study the stories of what happened here long ago, here and at other places."

"Stories?" Rand said. "What ever happened in the Two Rivers to interest someone like—I mean, what could have happened here?"

"And what else would you call it beside the Two Rivers?" Mat added. "That's what it has always been called."

"As the Wheel of Time turns," Moiraine said, half to herself and with a distant look in her eyes, "places wear many names. Men wear many names, many faces. Different faces, but always the same man. Yet no one knows the Great Pattern the Wheel weaves, or even the Pattern of an Age. We can only watch, and study, and hope."

Rand stared at her, unable to say a word, even to ask what she meant. He was not sure she had meant for them to hear. The other two were just as tongue-tied, he noticed. Ewin's mouth hung open.

Moiraine focused on them again, and all three gave a little shake as if waking up. "Later we will talk," she said. None of them said a word. "Later." She moved on toward the Wagon Bridge, appearing to glide over the ground rather than walk, her cloak spreading on either side of her like wings.

As she left, a tall man Rand had not noticed before moved away from the front of the inn and followed her, one hand resting on the long hilt of a sword. His clothes were a dark grayish green that would have faded into leaf or shadow, and his cloak swirled through shades of gray and green and brown as it shifted in the wind. It almost seemed to disappear at times, that cloak, fading into whatever lay beyond it. His hair was long, and gray at the temples, held back from his face by a narrow leather headband. That face was made from stony planes and angles, weathered but unlined despite the gray in his hair. When he moved, Rand could think of nothing but a wolf.

In passing the three youths his gaze ran over them, eyes as cold and blue as a midwinter dawn. It was as if he were weighing them in his mind, and there was no sign on his face of what the scales told him. He quickened his pace until he caught up to Moiraine, then slowed to walk by her shoulder, bending to speak to her. Rand let out a breath he had not realized he had been holding.

"That was Lan," Ewin said throatily, as if he, too, had been holding his breath. It had been that kind of look. "I'll bet he's a Warder."

"Don't be a fool." Mat laughed, but it was a shaky laugh. "Warders

are just in stories. Anyway, Warders have swords and armor covered
in gold and jewels, and spend all their time up north, in the Great
Blight, fighting evil and Trollocs and such.''

"He *could* be a Warder,'' Ewin insisted.

"Did you see any gold or jewels on him?'' Mat scoffed. "Do we
have Trollocs in the Two Rivers? We have sheep. I wonder what could
ever have happened here to interest someone like her.''

"Something could have,'' Rand answered slowly. "They say the inn's
been here for a thousand years, maybe more.''

"A thousand years of sheep,'' Mat said.

"A silver penny!'' Ewin burst out. "She gave me a whole silver
penny! Think what I can buy when the peddler comes.''

Rand opened his hand to look at the coin she had given him, and
almost dropped it in surprise. He did not recognize the fat silver coin
with the raised image of a woman balancing a single flame on her upturned hand, but he had watched while Bran al'Vere weighed out the
coins merchants brought from a dozen lands, and he had an idea of
its value. That much silver would buy a good horse anywhere in the
Two Rivers, with some left over.

He looked at Mat and saw the same stunned expression he knew
must be on his own face. Tilting his hand so Mat could see the coin
but not Ewin, he raised a questioning eyebrow. Mat nodded, and for
a minute they stared at one another in perplexed wonder.

"What kind of chores does she have?'' Rand asked finally.

"I don't know,'' Mat said firmly, "and I don't care. I won't spend
it, either. Even when the peddler comes.'' With that he thrust his coin
into his coat pocket.

Nodding, Rand slowly did the same with his. He was not sure why,
but somehow what Mat said seemed right. The coin should not be
spent. Not when it came from her. He could not think of anything else
silver was good for, but. . . .

"Do you think I should keep mine, too?'' Anguished indecision
painted Ewin's face.

"Not unless you want to,'' Mat said.

"I think she gave it to you to spend,'' Rand said.

Ewin looked at his coin, then shook his head and stuffed the silver
penny into his pocket. "I'll keep it,'' he said mournfully.

"There's still the gleeman,'' Rand said, and the younger boy
brightened.

"If he ever wakes up,'' Mat added.

"Rand,'' Ewin asked, "*is* there a gleeman?''

"You'll see," Rand answered with a laugh. It was clear Ewin would not believe until he set eyes on the gleeman. "He has to come down sooner or later."

Shouting drifted across the Wagon Bridge, and when Rand looked to see what was causing it, his laughter became wholehearted. A milling crowd of villagers, from gray-haired oldsters to toddlers barely able to walk, escorted a tall wagon toward the bridge, a huge wagon drawn by eight horses, the outside of its rounded canvas cover hung about with bundles like bunches of grapes. The peddler had come at last. Strangers and a gleeman, fireworks and a peddler. It was going to be the best Bel Tine ever.

CHAPTER
3

The Peddler

Clusters of pots clattered and banged as the peddler's wagon rumbled over the heavy timbers of the Wagon Bridge. Still surrounded by a cloud of villagers and farmers come for Festival, the peddler reined his horses to a stop in front of the inn. From every direction people streamed to swell the numbers around the great wagon, its wheels taller than any of the people with their eyes fastened to the peddler above them on the wagon seat.

The man on the wagon was Padan Fain, a pale, skinny fellow with gangly arms and a massive beak of a nose. Fain, always smiling and laughing as if he knew a joke that no one else knew, had driven his wagon and team into Emond's Field every spring for as long as Rand could remember.

The door of the inn flew open even as the team halted in a jangle of harness, and the Village Council appeared, led by Master al'Vere and Tam. They marched out deliberately, even Cenn Buie, amid all the excited shouting of the others for pins or lace or books or a dozen other things. Reluctantly the crowd parted to let them to the fore, everyone closing in quickly behind and never stopping their calling to the peddler. Most of all, the villagers called for news.

In the eyes of the villagers, needles and tea and the like were no more than half the freight in a peddler's wagon. Every bit as important was word of outside, news of the world beyond the Two Rivers. Some peddlers simply told what they knew, throwing it out in a heap, a pile of rubbish with which they could not be bothered. Others had to have every word dragged out of them, speaking grudgingly, with a bad grace. Fain, however, spoke freely if often teasingly, and spun out the telling, making a show to rival a gleeman. He enjoyed being the center of attention, strutting around like an under-sized rooster, with every eye on him. It occurred to Rand that Fain might not be best pleased to find a real gleeman in Emond's Field.

The peddler gave the Council and villagers alike exactly the same attention as he fussed with tying his reins off just so, which was to say hardly any attention at all. He nodded casually at no one in particular. He smiled without speaking, and waved absently to people with whom he was particularly friendly, though his friendliness had always been of a peculiarly distant kind, backslapping without ever getting close.

The demands for him to speak grew louder, but Fain waited, fiddling with small tasks about the driver's seat, for the crowd and the anticipation to reach the size he wanted. The Council alone kept silent. They maintained the dignity befitting their position, but increasing clouds of pipesmoke rising above their heads showed the effort of it.

Rand and Mat edged into the crowd, getting as close to the wagon as they could. Rand would have stopped halfway, but Mat wriggled through the press, pulling Rand behind him, until they were right behind the Council.

"I had been thinking you were going to stay out on the farm through the whole Festival," Perrin Aybara shouted at Rand over the clamor. Half a head shorter than Rand, the curly-haired blacksmith's apprentice was so stocky as to seem a man and a half wide, with arms and shoulders thick enough to rival those of Master Luhhan himself. He could easily have pushed through the throng, but that was not his way. He picked his path carefully, offering apologies to people who had only half a mind to notice anything but the peddler. He made the apologies anyway, and tried not to jostle anyone as he worked through the crowd to Rand and Mat. "Imagine it," he said when he finally reached them. "Bel Tine and a peddler, both together. I'll bet there really are fireworks."

"You don't know a quarter of it." Mat laughed.

Perrin eyed him suspiciously, then looked a question at Rand.

"It's true," Rand shouted, then gestured at the growing mass of people, all giving voice. "Later. I'll explain later. Later, I said!"

At that moment Padan Fain stood up on the wagon seat, and the crowd quieted in an instant. Rand's last words exploded into utter silence, catching the peddler with an arm raised dramatically and his mouth open. Everybody turned to stare at Rand. The bony little man on the wagon, prepared to have everyone hanging on his first words, gave Rand a sharp, searching look.

Rand's face reddened, and he wished he were Ewin's size so he did not stand out so clearly. His friends shifted uncomfortably, too. It had only been the year before that Fain had taken notice of them for the first time, acknowledging them as men. Fain did not usually have time for anyone too young to buy a good deal of things off his wagon. Rand hoped he had not been relegated to a child again in the peddler's eyes.

With a loud harrumph, Fain tugged at his heavy cloak. "No, not later," the peddler declaimed, once more throwing up a hand grandly. "I will be telling you now." As he spoke he made broad gestures, casting his words over the crowd. "You are thinking you have had troubles in the Two Rivers, are you? Well, all the world has troubles, from the Great Blight south to the Sea of Storms, from the Aryth Ocean in the west to the Aiel Waste in the east. And even beyond. The winter was harsher than you've ever seen before, cold enough to jell your blood and crack your bones? Ahhh! Winter was cold and harsh everywhere. In the Borderlands they'd be calling your winter spring. But spring does not come, you say? Wolves have killed your sheep? Perhaps wolves have attacked men? Is that the way of it? Well, now. Spring is late everywhere. There are wolves everywhere, all hungry for any flesh they can sink a tooth into, be it sheep or cow or man. But there are things worse than wolves or winter. There are those who would be glad to have only your little troubles." He paused expectantly.

"What could be worse than wolves killing sheep, and men?" Cenn Buie demanded. Others muttered in support.

"Men killing men." The peddler's reply, in portentous tones, brought shocked murmurs that increased as he went on. "It is war I mean. There is war in Ghealdan, war and madness. The snows of the Dhallin Forest are red with the blood of men. Ravens and the cries of ravens fill the air. Armies march to Ghealdan. Nations, great houses and great men, send their soldiers to fight."

"War?" Master al'Vere's mouth fit awkwardly around the unfamiliar word. No one in the Two Rivers had ever had anything to do with a war. "Why are they having a war?"

Fain grinned, and Rand had the feeling he was mocking the villagers' isolation from the world, and their ignorance. The peddler leaned forward as if he were about to impart a secret to the Mayor, but his whisper was meant to carry and did. "The standard of the Dragon has been raised, and men flock to oppose. And to support."

One long gasp left every throat together, and Rand shivered in spite of himself.

"The Dragon!" someone moaned. "The Dark One's loose in Ghealdan!"

"Not the Dark One," Haral Luhhan growled. "The Dragon's not the Dark One. And this is a false Dragon, anyway."

"Let's hear what Master Fain has to say," the Mayor said, but no one would be quieted that easily. People cried out from every side, men and women shouting over one another.

"Just as bad as the Dark One!"

"The Dragon broke the world, didn't he?"

"He started it! He caused the Time of Madness!"

"You know the prophecies! When the Dragon is reborn, your worst nightmares will seem like your fondest dreams!"

"He's just another false Dragon. He must be!"

"What difference does that make? You remember the last false Dragon. He started a war, too. Thousands died, isn't that right, Fain? He laid siege to Illian."

"It's evil times! No one claiming to be the Dragon Reborn for twenty years, and now three in the last five years. Evil times! Look at the weather!"

Rand exchanged looks with Mat and Perrin. Mat's eyes shone with excitement, but Perrin wore a worried frown. Rand could remember every tale he had heard about the men who named themselves the Dragon Reborn, and if they had all proven themselves false Dragons by dying or disappearing without fulfilling any of the prophecies, what they had done was bad enough. Whole nations torn by battle, and cities and towns put to the torch. The dead fell like autumn leaves, and refugees clogged the roads like sheep in a pen. So the peddlers said, and the merchants, and no one in the Two Rivers with any sense doubted it. The world would end, so some said, when the real Dragon was born again.

"Stop this!" the Mayor shouted. "Be quiet! Stop working yourselves to a lather out of your own imaginations. Let Master Fain tell us about this false Dragon." The people began to quieten, but Cenn Buie refused to be silent.

"*Is* this a false Dragon?" the thatcher asked sourly.

Master al'Vere blinked as if taken by surprise, then snapped, "Don't be an old fool, Cenn!" But Cenn had kindled the crowd again.

"He can't be the Dragon Reborn! Light help us, he can't be!"

"You old fool, Buie! You *want* bad luck, don't you?"

"Be naming the Dark One, next! You're taken by the Dragon, Cenn Buie! Trying to bring us all harm!"

Cenn looked around defiantly, trying to stare down the glowers, and raised his voice. "I didn't hear Fain say this was a false Dragon. Did you? Use your eyes! Where are the crops that should be knee high or better? Why is it still winter when spring should be here a month?" There were angry shouts for Cenn to hold his tongue. "I will not be silent! I've no liking for this talk, either, but I won't hide my head under a basket till a Taren Ferry man comes to cut my throat. And I won't dangle on Fain's pleasure, not this time. Speak it out plain, peddler. What have you heard? Eh? Is this man a false Dragon?"

If Fain was perturbed by the news he brought or the upset he had caused, he gave no sign of it. He merely shrugged and laid a skinny finger alongside his nose. "As to that, now, who can say until it is over and done?" He paused with one of his secretive grins, running his eyes over the crowd as if imagining how they would react and finding it funny. "I do know," he said, too casually, "that he can wield the One Power. The others couldn't. But he can channel. The ground opens beneath his enemies' feet, and strong walls crumble at his shout. Lightning comes when he calls and strikes where he points. That I've heard, and from men I believe."

A stunned silence fell. Rand looked at his friends. Perrin seemed to be seeing things he did not like, but Mat *still* looked excited.

Tam, his face only a little less composed than usual, drew the Mayor close, but before he could speak Ewin Finngar burst out.

"He'll go mad and die! In the stories, men who channel the Power always go mad, and then waste away and die. Only women can touch it. Doesn't he know that?" He ducked under a cuff from Master Buie.

"Enough of that from you, boy." Cenn shook a gnarled fist in Ewin's face. "Show a proper respect and leave this to your elders. Get away with you!"

"Hold steady, Cenn," Tam growled. "The boy is just curious. There's no need of this foolishness from you."

"Act your age," Bran added. "And for once remember you're a member of the Council."

Cenn's wrinkled face grew darker with every word from Tam and the Mayor, until it was almost purple. "You know what kind of women he's talking about. Stop frowning at me, Luhhan, and you, too, Crawe. This is a decent village of decent folk, and it's bad enough to have Fain here talking about false Dragons using the Power without this Dragon-possessed fool of a boy bringing Aes Sedai into it. Some things just shouldn't be talked about, and I don't care if you will be letting that fool gleeman tell any kind of tale he wants. It isn't right or decent."

"I never saw or heard or smelled anything that couldn't be talked about," Tam said, but Fain was not finished.

"The Aes Sedai are already into it," the peddler spoke up. "A party of them has ridden south from Tar Valon. Since he can wield the Power, none but Aes Sedai can defeat him, for all the battles they fight, or deal with him once he's defeated. If he is defeated."

Someone in the crowd moaned aloud, and even Tam and Bran exchanged uneasy frowns. Huddles of villagers clumped together, and some pulled their cloaks tighter around themselves, though the wind had actually lessened.

"Of course, he'll be defeated," someone shouted.

"They're always beaten in the end, false Dragons."

"He has to be defeated, doesn't he?"

"What if he isn't?"

Tam had finally managed to speak quietly into the Mayor's ear, and Bran, nodding from time to time and ignoring the hubbub around them, waited until he was finished before raising his own voice.

"All of you listen. Be quiet and listen!" The shouting died to a murmur again. "This goes beyond mere news from outside. It must be discussed by the Village Council. Master Fain, if you will join us inside the inn, we have questions to ask."

"A good mug of hot mulled wine would not go far amiss with me just now," the peddler replied with a chuckle. He jumped down from the wagon, dusted his hands on his coat, and cheerfully righted his cloak. "Will you be looking after my horses, if you please?"

"I want to hear what he has to say!" More than one voice was raised in protest.

"You can't take him off! My wife sent me to buy pins!" That was Wit Congar; he hunched his shoulders at the stares some of the others gave him, but he held his ground.

"We've a right to ask questions, too," somebody back in the crowd shouted. "I—"

"Be silent!" the Mayor roared, producing a startled hush. "When the Council has asked its questions, Master Fain will be back to tell you all his news. And to sell you his pots and pins. Hu! Tad! Stable Master Fain's horses."

Tam and Bran moved in on either side of the peddler, the rest of the Council gathered behind them, and the whole cluster swept into the Winespring Inn, firmly shutting the door in the faces of those who tried to crowd inside after them. Pounding on the door brought only a single shout from the Mayor.

"Go home!"

People milled around in front of the inn muttering about what the peddler had said, and what it meant, and what questions the Council was asking, and why they should be allowed to listen and ask questions of their own. Some peered in through the front windows of the inn, and a few even questioned Hu and Tad, though it was far from clear what they were supposed to know. The two stolid stablemen just grunted in reply and went on methodically removing the team's harness. One by one they led Fain's horses away and, when the last was gone, did not return.

Rand ignored the crowd. He took a seat on the edge of the old stone foundation, gathered his cloak around him, and stared at the inn door. Ghealdan. Tar Valon. The very names were strange and exciting. They were places he knew only from peddlers' news, and tales told by merchants' guards. Aes Sedai and wars and false Dragons: those were the stuff of stories told late at night in front of the fireplace, with one candle making strange shapes on the wall and the wind howling against the shutters. On the whole, he believed he would rather have blizzards and wolves. Still, it must be different out there, beyond the Two Rivers, like living in the middle of a gleeman's tale. An adventure. One long adventure. A whole lifetime of it.

Slowly the villagers dispersed, still muttering and shaking their heads. Wit Congar paused to stare into the now-abandoned wagon as though he might find another peddler hidden inside. Finally only a few of the younger folk were left. Mat and Perrin drifted over to where Rand sat.

"I don't see how the gleeman could beat this," Mat said excitedly. "I wonder if we might get to see this false Dragon?"

Perrin shook his shaggy head. "I don't want to see him. Somewhere else, maybe, but not in the Two Rivers. Not if it means war."

"Not if it means Aes Sedai here, either," Rand added. "Or have you forgotten who caused the Breaking? The Dragon may have started it, but it was Aes Sedai who actually broke the world."

"I heard a story once," Mat said slowly, "from a wool-buyer's guard. He said the Dragon would be reborn in mankind's greatest hour of need, and save us all."

"Well, he was a fool if he believed that," Perrin said firmly. "And you were a fool to listen." He did not sound angry; he was slow to anger. But he sometimes got exasperated with Mat's quicksilver fancies, and there was a touch of that in his voice. "I suppose he claimed we'd all live in a new Age of Legends afterwards, too."

"I didn't say I believed it," Mat protested. "I just heard it. Nynaeve did, too, and I thought she was going to skin me and the guard both. He said—the guard did—that a lot of people do believe, only they're afraid to say so, afraid of the Aes Sedai or the Children of the Light. He wouldn't say any more after Nynaeve lit into us. She told the merchant, and he said it was the guard's last trip with him."

"A good thing, too," Perrin said. "The Dragon going to save us? Sounds like Coplin talk to me."

"What kind of need would be great enough that we'd want the Dragon to save us from it?" Rand mused. "As well ask for help from the Dark One."

"He didn't say," Mat replied uncomfortably. "And he didn't mention any new Age of Legends. He said the world would be torn apart by the Dragon's coming."

"That would surely save us," Perrin said dryly. "Another Breaking."

"Burn me!" Mat growled. "I'm only telling you what the guard said."

Perrin shook his head. "I just hope the Aes Sedai and this Dragon, false or not, stay where they are. Maybe that way the Two Rivers will be spared."

"You think they're really Darkfriends?" Mat was frowning thoughtfully.

"Who?" Rand asked.

"Aes Sedai."

Rand glanced at Perrin, who shrugged. "The stories," he began slowly, but Mat cut him off.

"Not all the stories say they serve the Dark One, Rand."

"Light, Mat," Rand said, "they caused the Breaking. What more do you want?"

"I suppose." Mat sighed, but the next moment he was grinning again. "Old Bili Congar says they don't exist. Aes Sedai. Darkfriends.

Says they're just stories. He says he doesn't believe in the Dark One, either."

Perrin snorted. "Coplin talk from a Congar. What else can you expect?"

"Old Bili named the Dark One. I'll bet you didn't know that."

"Light!" Rand breathed.

Mat's grin broadened. "It was last spring, just before the cutworm got into his fields and nobody else's. Right before everybody in his house came down with yelloweye fever. I heard him do it. He still says he doesn't believe, but whenever I ask him to name the Dark One now, he throws something at me."

"You are just stupid enough to do that, aren't you, Matrim Cauthon?" Nynaeve al'Meara stepped into their huddle, the dark braid pulled over her shoulder almost bristling with anger. Rand scrambled to his feet. Slender and barely taller than Mat's shoulder, at the moment the Wisdom seemed taller than any of them, and it did not matter that she was young and pretty. "I suspected something of the sort about Bili Congar at the time, but I thought you at least had more sense than to try taunting him into such a thing. You may be old enough to be married, Matrim Cauthon, but in truth you shouldn't be off your mother's apron strings. The next thing, you'll be naming the Dark One yourself."

"No, Wisdom," Mat protested, looking as if he would rather be anywhere else than there. "It was old Bil—I mean, Master Congar, not me! Blood and ashes, I—"

"Watch your tongue, Matrim!"

Rand stood up straighter, though her glare was not directed at him. Perrin looked equally abashed. Later one or another of them would almost certainly complain about being scolded by a woman not all that much older than themselves—someone always did after one of Nynaeve's scoldings, if never in her hearing—but the gap in ages always seemed more than wide enough when face to face with her. Especially if she was angry. The stick in her hand was thick at one end and a slender switch at the other, and she was liable to give a flail to anybody she thought was acting the fool—head or hands or legs—no matter their age or position.

The Wisdom so held his attention that at first Rand failed to see she was not alone. When he realized his mistake, he began to think about leaving no matter what Nynaeve would say or do later.

Egwene stood a few paces behind the Wisdom, watching intently. Of a height with Nynaeve, and with the same dark coloring, she could at that moment have been a reflection of Nynaeve's mood, arms crossed beneath her breasts, mouth tight with disapproval. The hood of her soft gray cloak shaded her face, and her big brown eyes held no laughter now.

If there was any fairness, he thought that being two years older than her should give him some advantage, but that was not the way of it. At the best of times he was never very nimble with his tongue when talking to any of the village girls, not like Perrin, but whenever Egwene gave him that intent look, with her eyes as wide as they would go, as if every last ounce of her attention was on him, he just could not seem to make the words go where he wanted. Perhaps he could get away as soon as Nynaeve finished. But he knew he would not, even if he did not understand why.

"If you are done staring like a moonstruck lamb, Rand al'Thor," Nynaeve said, "perhaps you can tell me why you were talking about something even you three great bullcalves ought to have sense enough to keep out of your mouths."

Rand gave a start and pulled his eyes away from Egwene; she had grown a disconcerting smile when the Wisdom began speaking. Nynaeve's voice was tart, but she had the beginnings of a knowing smile on her face, too—until Mat laughed aloud. The Wisdom's smile vanished, and the look she gave Mat cut his laughter off in a strangled croak.

"Well, Rand?" Nynaeve said.

Out of the corner of his eye he saw Egwene still smiling. *What does she think is so funny?* "It was natural enough to talk of it, Wisdom," he said hurriedly. "The peddler—Padan Fain . . . ah . . . Master Fain—brought news of a false Dragon in Ghealdan, and a war, and Aes Sedai. The Council thought it was important enough to talk to him. What else would we be talking about?"

Nynaeve shook her head. "So that's why the peddler's wagon stands abandoned. I heard people rushing to meet it, but I couldn't leave Mistress Ayellin till her fever broke. The Council is questioning the peddler about what's happening in Ghealdan, are they? If I know them, they're asking all the wrong questions and none of the right ones. It will take the Women's Circle to find out anything useful." Settling her cloak firmly on her shoulders she disappeared into the inn.

Egwene did not follow the Wisdom. As the inn door closed behind Nynaeve, the younger woman came to stand in front of Rand. The frowns were gone from her face, but her unblinking stare made him uneasy. He looked to his friends, but they moved away, grinning broadly as they abandoned him.

"You shouldn't let Mat get you mixed up in his foolishness, Rand," Egwene said, as solemn as a Wisdom herself, then abruptly she giggled. "I haven't seen you look like that since Cenn Buie caught you and Mat up in his apple trees when you were ten."

He shifted his feet and glanced at his friends. They stood not far away, Mat gesturing excitedly as he talked.

"Will you dance with me tomorrow?" That was not what he had meant to say. He did want to dance with her, but at the same time he wanted nothing so little as the uncomfortable way he was sure to feel while he was with her. The way he felt right then.

The corners of her mouth quirked up in a small smile. "In the afternoon," she said. "I will be busy in the morning."

From the others came Perrin's exclamation. "A gleeman!"

Egwene turned toward them, but Rand put a hand on her arm. "Busy? How?"

Despite the chill she pushed back the hood of her cloak and with apparent casualness pulled her hair forward over her shoulder. The last time he had seen her, her hair had hung in dark waves below her shoulders, with only a red ribbon keeping it back from her face; now it was worked into a long braid.

He stared at that braid as if it were a viper, then stole a glance at the Spring Pole, standing alone on the Green now, ready for tomorrow. In the morning unmarried women of marriageable age would dance the Pole. He swallowed hard. Somehow, it had never occurred to him that she would reach marriageable age at the same time that he did.

"Just because someone is old enough to marry," he muttered, "doesn't mean they should. Not right away."

"Of course not. Or ever, for that matter."

Rand blinked. "Ever?"

"A Wisdom almost never marries. Nynaeve has been teaching me, you know. She says I have a talent, that I can learn to listen to the wind. Nynaeve says not all Wisdoms can, even if they say they do."

"Wisdom!" he hooted. He failed to notice the dangerous glint in her eye. "Nynaeve will be Wisdom here for another fifty years at least. Probably more. Are you going to spend the rest of your life as her apprentice?"

"There are other villages," she replied heatedly. "Nynaeve says the villages north of the Taren always choose a Wisdom from away. They think it stops her from having favorites among the village folk."

His amusement melted as fast as it had come. "Outside the Two Rivers? I'd never see you again."

"And you wouldn't like that? You have not given any sign lately that you'd care one way or another."

"No one ever leaves the Two Rivers," he went on. "Maybe somebody from Taren Ferry, but they're all strange anyway. Hardly like Two Rivers folk at all."

Egwene gave an exasperated sigh. "Well, maybe I'm strange, too. Maybe I want to see some of the places I hear about in the stories. Have you ever thought of that?"

"Of course I have. I daydream sometimes, but I know the difference between daydreams and what's real."

"And I do not?" she said furiously, and promptly turned her back on him.

"That wasn't what I meant. I was talking about me. Egwene?"

She jerked her cloak around her, a wall to shut him off, and stiffly walked a few paces away. He rubbed his head in frustration. How to explain? This was not the first time she had squeezed meanings from his words that he never knew was in them. In her present mood, a misstep would only make matters worse, and he was fairly sure that nearly anything he said would be a misstep.

Mat and Perrin came back then. Egwene ignored their coming. They looked at her hesitantly, then crowded close to Rand.

"Moiraine gave Perrin a coin, too," Mat said. "Just like ours." He paused before adding, "And he saw the rider."

"Where?" Rand demanded. "When? Did anybody else see him? Did you tell anyone?"

Perrin raised broad hands in a slowing gesture. "One question at a time. I saw him on the edge of the village, watching the smithy, just at twilight yesterday. Gave me the shivers, he did. I told Master Luhhan, only nobody was there when he looked. He said I was seeing shadows. But he carried his biggest hammer around with him while we were banking the forge-fire and putting the tools up. He's never done that before."

"So he believed you," Rand said, but Perrin shrugged.

"I don't know. I asked him why he was carrying the hammer if all I saw was shadows, and he said something about wolves getting bold enough to come into the village. Maybe he thought that's what I saw, but he ought to know I can tell the difference between a wolf and a man on horseback, even at dusk. I know what I saw, and nobody is going to make me believe different."

"I believe you," Rand said. "Remember, I saw him, too." Perrin gave a satisfied grunt, as if he had not been sure of that.

"What *are* you talking about?" Egwene demanded suddenly.

Rand suddenly wished he had spoken more quietly. He would have if he had realized she was listening. Mat and Perrin, grinning like fools, fell all over themselves telling her of their encounters with the black-cloaked rider, but Rand kept silent. He was sure he knew what she would say when they were done.

"Nynaeve was right," Egwene announced to the sky when the two youths fell silent. "None of you is ready to be off leading strings. People do ride horses, you know. That doesn't make them monsters out of a gleeman's tale." Rand nodded to himself; it was just as he had thought. She rounded on him. "And you've been spreading these tales. Sometimes you have no sense, Rand al'Thor. The winter has been frightening enough without you going about scaring the children."

Rand gave a sour grimace. "I haven't spread anything, Egwene. But I saw what I saw, and it was no farmer out looking for a strayed cow."

Egwene drew a deep breath and opened her mouth, but whatever she had been going to say vanished as the door of the inn opened and a man with shaggy white hair came hurrying out as if pursued.

CHAPTER
4

The Gleeman

The door of the inn banged shut behind the white-haired man, and he spun around to glare at it. Lean, he would have been tall if not for a stoop to his shoulders, but he moved in a spry fashion that belied his apparent age. His cloak seemed a mass of patches, in odd shapes and sizes, fluttering with every breath of air, patches in a hundred colors. It was really quite thick, Rand saw, despite what Master al'Vere had said, with the patches merely sewn on like decorations.

"The gleeman!" Egwene whispered excitedly.

The white-haired man whirled, cloak flaring. His long coat had odd, baggy sleeves and big pockets. Thick mustaches, as snowy as the hair on his head, quivered around his mouth, and his face was gnarled like a tree that had seen hard times. He gestured imperiously at Rand and the others with a long-stemmed pipe, ornately carved, that trailed a wisp of smoke. Blue eyes peered out from under bushy white brows, drilling into whatever he looked at.

Rand stared at the man's eyes almost as much as at the rest of him.

Everybody in the Two Rivers had dark eyes, and so did most of the merchants, and their guards, and everyone else he had ever seen. The Congars and the Coplins had made fun of him for his gray eyes, until the day he finally punched Ewal Coplin in the nose; the Wisdom had surely gotten onto him for that. He wondered if there was a place where nobody had dark eyes. *Maybe Lan comes from there, too.*

"What sort of place is this?" the gleeman demanded in a deep voice that sounded in some way larger than that of an ordinary man. Even in the open air it seemed to fill a great room and resonate from the walls. "The yokels in that village on the hill tell me I can get here before dark, neglecting to say that that was only if I left well before noon. When I finally do arrive, chilled to the bone and ready for a warm bed, your innkeeper grumbles about the hour as if I were a wandering swineherd and your Village Council hadn't begged me to display my art at this festival of yours. And he never even told me he was the Mayor." He slowed for a breath, taking them all in with a glare, but he was off again on the instant. "When I came downstairs to smoke my pipe before the fire and have a mug of ale, every man in the common room stares at me as if I were his least favorite brother-in-law seeking to borrow money. One old grandfather starts ranting at me about the kind of stories I should or should not tell, then a girl-child shouts at me to get out, and threatens me with a great club when I don't move quickly enough for her. Who ever heard of treating a gleeman so?"

Egwene's face was a study, her goggle-eyed amaze at a gleeman in the flesh marred by a desire to defend Nynaeve.

"Your pardon, Master Gleeman," Rand said. He knew he was grinning foolishly, himself. "That was our Wisdom, and—"

"That pretty little slip of a girl?" the gleeman exclaimed. "A village Wisdom? Why, at her age she should better be flirting with the young men than foretelling the weather and curing the sick."

Rand shifted uncomfortably. He hoped Nynaeve never overheard the man's opinion. At least, not until he had done with his performing. Perrin winced at the gleeman's words, and Mat whistled soundlessly, as if both had had the same thought as he had.

"The men were the Village Council," Rand went on. "I'm sure they intended no discourtesy. You see, we just learned there's a war in Ghealdan, and a man claiming to be the Dragon Reborn. A false Dragon. Aes Sedai are riding there from Tar Valon. The Council is trying to decide if we might be in danger here."

"Old news, even in Baerlon," the gleeman said dismissively, "and that is the last place in the world to hear anything." He paused, looking around the village, and dryly added, "Almost the last place." Then his eyes fell on the wagon in front of the inn, standing alone now, with its shafts on the ground. "So. I thought I recognized Padan Fain in there." His voice was still deep, but the resonance had gone, replaced by scorn. "Fain was always one to carry bad news quickly, and the worse, the faster. There's more raven in him than man."

"Master Fain has come often to Emond's Field, Master Gleeman," Egwene said, a hint of disapproval finally breaking through her delight. "He is always full of laughter, and he brings much more good news than bad."

The gleeman eyed her for a moment, then smiled broadly. "Now you're a lovely lass. You should have rose buds in your hair. Unfortunately, I cannot pull roses from the air, not this year, but how would you like to stand beside me tomorrow for a part of my performance? Hand me my flute when I want it, and certain other apparatus. I always choose the prettiest girl I can find as my assistant."

Perrin snickered, and Mat, who had been snickering, laughed out loud. Rand blinked in surprise; Egwene was glaring at him, and he had not even smiled. She straightened around and spoke in a too-calm voice.

"Thank you, Master Gleeman. I would be happy to assist you."

"Thom Merrilin," the gleeman said. They stared. "My name is Thom Merrilin, not Master Gleeman." He hitched the multi-hued cloak up on his shoulders, and abruptly his voice once more seemed to reverberate in a great hall. "Once a Court-bard, I am now indeed risen to the exalted rank of Master Gleeman, yet my name is plain Thom Merrilin, and gleeman is the simple title in which I glory." And he swept a bow so elaborate with flourishes of his cloak that Mat clapped and Egwene murmured appreciatively.

"Master . . . ah . . . Master Merrilin," Mat said, unsure exactly what form of address to take out of what Thom Merrilin had said, "what *is* happening in Ghealdan? Do you know anything about this false Dragon? Or the Aes Sedai?"

"Do I look like a peddler, boy?" the gleeman grumbled, tapping out his pipe on the heel of his palm. He made the pipe disappear somewhere inside his cloak, or his coat; Rand was not sure where it had gone or how. "I am a gleeman, not a newsmonger. And I make a point of never knowing anything about Aes Sedai. Much safer that way."

"But the war," Mat began eagerly, only to be cut off by Master Merrilin.

"In wars, boy, fools kill other fools for foolish causes. That's enough for anyone to know. I am here for my art." Suddenly he thrust a finger at Rand. "You, lad. You're a tall one. Not with your full growth on you yet, but I doubt there's another man in the district with your height. Not many in the village with eyes that color, either, I'll wager. The point is, you're an axe handle across the shoulders and as tall as an Aielman. What's your name, lad?"

Rand gave it hesitantly, not sure whether or not the man was making fun of him, but the gleeman had already turned his attention to Perrin. "And you have almost the size of an Ogier. Close enough. How are you called?"

"Not unless I stand on my own shoulders." Perrin laughed. "I'm afraid Rand and I are just ordinary folk, Master Merrilin, not made-up creatures from your stories. I'm Perrin Aybara."

Thom Merrilin tugged at one of his mustaches. "Well, now. Made-up creatures from my stories. Is that what they are? You lads are widely traveled, then, it seems."

Rand kept his mouth shut, certain they were the butt of a joke, now, but Perrin spoke up.

"We've all of us been as far as Watch Hill, and Deven Ride. Not many around here have gone as far." He was not boasting; Perrin seldom did. He was just telling the truth.

"We've all seen the Mire, too," Mat added, and he did sound boastful. "That's the swamp at the far end of the Waterwood. Nobody at all goes there—it's full of quicksands and bogs—except us. And nobody goes to the Mountains of Mist, either, but we did, once. To the foot of them, anyway."

"As far as that?" the gleeman murmured, brushing at his mustaches now continually. Rand thought he was hiding a smile, and he saw that Perrin was frowning.

"It's bad luck to enter the mountains," Mat said, as if he had to defend himself for not going further. "Everybody knows that."

"That's just foolishness, Matrim Cauthon," Egwene cut in angrily. "Nynaeve says. . . ." She broke off, her cheeks turning pink, and the look she gave Thom Merrilin was not as friendly as it had been. "It is not right to make. . . . It isn't. . . ." Her face went redder, and she fell silent. Mat blinked, as if he was just getting a suspicion of what had been going on.

"You're right, child," the gleeman said contritely. "I apologize humbly. I am here to entertain. Aah, my tongue has always gotten me into trouble."

"Maybe we haven't traveled as far as you," Perrin said flatly, "but what does how tall Rand is have to do with anything?"

"Just this, lad. A little later I will let you try to pick me up, but you won't be able to lift my feet from the ground. Not you, nor your tall friend there—Rand, is it?—nor any other man. Now what do you think of that?"

Perrin snorted a laugh. "I think I can lift you right now." But when he stepped forward Thom Merrilin motioned him back.

"Later, lad, later. When there are more folk to watch. An artist needs an audience."

A score of folk had gathered on the Green since the gleeman appeared from the inn, young men and women down to children who peeked, wide-eyed and silent, from behind the older onlookers. All looked as if they were waiting for miraculous things from the gleeman. The white-haired man looked them over—he appeared to be counting them—then gave a slight shake of his head and sighed.

"I suppose I had better give you a small sample. So you can run tell the others. Eh? Just a taste of what you'll see tomorrow at your festival."

He took a step back, and suddenly leaped into the air, twisting and somersaulting to land facing them atop the old stone foundation. More than that, three balls—red, white, and black—began dancing between his hands even as he landed.

A soft sound came from the watchers, half astonishment, half satisfaction. Even Rand forgot his irritation. He flashed Egwene a grin and got a delighted one in return, then both turned to stare unabashedly at the gleeman.

"You want stories?" Thom Merrilin declaimed. "I have stories, and I will give them to you. I will make them come alive before your eyes." A blue ball joined the others from somewhere, then a green one, and a yellow. "Tales of great wars and great heroes, for the men and boys. For the women and girls, the entire *Aptarigine Cycle*. Tales of Artur Paendrag Tanreall, Artur Hawkwing, Artur the High King, who once ruled all the lands from the Aiel Waste to the Aryth Ocean, and even beyond. Wondrous stories of strange people and strange lands, of the Green Man, of Warders and Trollocs, of Ogier and Aiel. *The Thousand Tales of Anla, the Wise Counselor*. 'Jaem the Giant-Slayer.' *How Susa Tamed Jain Farstrider*. 'Mara and the Three Foolish Kings.'"

"Tell us about Lenn," Egwene called. "How he flew to the moon in the belly of an eagle made of fire. Tell about his daughter Salya walking among the stars."

Rand looked at her out of the corner of his eye, but she seemed intent on the gleeman. She had never liked stories about adventures and long journeys. Her favorites were always the funny ones, or stories about women outwitting people who were supposed to be smarter than everyone else. He was sure she had asked for tales about Lenn and Salya to put a burr under his shirt. Surely she could see the world outside was no place for Two Rivers folk. Listening to tales of adventures, even dreaming about them, was one thing; having them take place around you would be something else again.

"Old stories, those," Thom Merrilin said, and abruptly he was juggling three colored balls with each hand. "Stories from the Age before the Age of Legends, some say. Perhaps even older. But I have *all* stories, mind you now, of Ages that were and will be. Ages when men ruled the heavens and the stars, and Ages when man roamed as brother to the animals. Ages of wonder, and Ages of horror. Ages ended by fire raining from the skies, and Ages doomed by snow and ice covering land and sea. I have all stories, and I will tell all stories. Tales of Mosk the Giant, with his Lance of Fire that could reach around the world, and his wars with Alsbet, the Queen of All. Tales of Materese the Healer, Mother of the Wondrous Ind."

The balls now danced between Thom's hands in two intertwining circles. His voice was almost a chant, and he turned slowly as he spoke, as if surveying the onlookers to gauge his effect. "I will tell you of the end of the Age of Legends, of the Dragon, and his attempt to free the Dark One into the world of men. I will tell of the Time of Madness, when Aes Sedai shattered the world; of the Trolloc Wars, when men battled Trollocs for rule of the earth; of the War of the Hundred Years, when men battled men and the nations of our day were wrought. I will tell the adventures of men and women, rich and poor, great and small, proud and humble. *The Siege of the Pillars of the Sky*. 'How Goodwife Karil Cured Her Husband of Snoring.' *King Darith and the Fall of the House of—*"

Abruptly the flow of words and the juggling alike stopped. Thom simply snatched the balls from the air and stopped talking. Unnoticed by Rand, Moiraine had joined the listeners. Lan was at her shoulder, though he had to look twice to see the man. For a moment Thom looked at Moiraine sideways, his face and body still except for making the balls disappear into his capacious coat sleeves. Then he bowed to her, holding his cloak wide. "Your pardon, but you are surely not from this district?"

"Lady!" Ewin hissed fiercely. "The Lady Moiraine."

Thom blinked, then bowed again, more deeply. "Your pardon again
. . . ah, Lady. I meant no disrespect."

Moiraine made a small waving-away gesture. "None was perceived,
Master Bard. And my name is simply Moiraine. I am indeed a stranger
here, a traveler like yourself, far from home and alone. The world can
be a dangerous place when one is a stranger."

"The Lady Moiraine collects stories," Ewin put in. "Stories about
things that happened in the Two Rivers. Though I don't know what
ever happened here to make a story of."

"I trust you will like my stories, as well . . . Moiraine." Thom
watched her with obvious wariness. He looked not best pleased to find
her there. Suddenly Rand wondered what sort of entertainment a lady
like her might be offered in a city like Baerlon, or Caemlyn. Surely it
could not be anything better than a gleeman.

"That is a matter of taste, Master Bard," Moiraine replied. "Some
stories I like, and some I do not."

Thom's bow was his deepest yet, bending his long body parallel to
the ground. "I assure you, none of my stories will displease. All will
please and entertain. And you do me too much honor. I am a simple
gleeman; that and nothing more."

Moiraine answered his bow with a gracious nod. For an instant she
seemed even more the lady Ewin had named her, accepting an offering
from one of her subjects. Then she turned away, and Lan followed, a
wolf heeling a gliding swan. Thom stared after them, bushy brows
drawn down, stroking his long mustaches with a knuckle, until they
were halfway up the Green. *He's not pleased at all,* Rand thought.

"Are you going to juggle some more, now?" Ewin demanded.

"Eat fire," Mat shouted. "I want to see you eat fire."

"The harp!" a voice cried from the crowd. "Play the harp!" Someone else called for the flute.

At that moment the door of the inn opened and the Village Council
trundled out, Nynaeve in their midst. Padan Fain was not with them,
Rand saw; apparently the peddler had decided to remain in the warm
common room with his mulled wine.

Muttering about "a strong brandy," Thom Merrilin abruptly jumped
down from the old foundation. He ignored the cries of those who had
been watching him, pressing inside past the Councilors before they
were well out of the doorway.

"Is he supposed to be a gleeman or a king?" Cenn Buie asked in
annoyed tones. "A waste of good money, if you ask me."

Bran al'Vere half turned after the gleeman, then shook his head.
"That man may be more trouble than he's worth."

Nynaeve, busy gathering her cloak around her, sniffed loudly. "Worry about the gleeman if you want, Brandelwyn al'Vere. At least he is in Emond's Field, which is more than you can say for this false Dragon. But as long as you are worrying, there are others here who *should* excite your worry."

"If you please, Wisdom," Bran said stiffly, "kindly leave who should worry me to my deciding. Mistress Moiraine and Master Lan are guests in my inn, and decent, respectable folk, so I say. Neither of *them* has called me a fool in front of the whole Council. Neither of *them* has told the Council it hasn't a full set of wits among them."

"It seems my estimate was too high by half," Nynaeve retorted. She strode away without a backward glance, leaving Bran's jaw working as he searched for a reply.

Egwene looked at Rand as if she were going to speak, then darted after the Wisdom instead. Rand knew there must be some way to stop her from leaving the Two Rivers, but the only way he could think of was not one he was prepared to take, even if she was willing. And she had as much as said she was not willing at all, which made him feel even worse.

"That young woman wants a husband," Cenn Buie growled, bouncing on his toes. His face was purple, and getting darker. "She lacks proper respect. We're the Village Council, not boys raking her yard, and—"

The Mayor breathed heavily through his nose, and suddenly rounded on the old thatcher. "Be quiet, Cenn! Stop acting like a black-veiled Aiel!" The skinny man froze on his toes in astonishment. The Mayor never let his temper get the best of him. Bran glared. "Burn me, but we have better things to be about than this foolishness. Or do you intend to prove Nynaeve right?" With that he stumped back into the inn and slammed the door behind him.

The Council members glanced at Cenn, then moved off in their separate directions. All but Haral Luhhan, who accompanied the stony-visaged thatcher, talking quietly. The blacksmith was the only one who could ever get Cenn to see reason.

Rand went to meet his father, and his friends trailed after him.

"I've never seen Master al'Vere so mad," was the first thing Rand said, getting him a disgusted look from Mat.

"The Mayor and the Wisdom seldom agree," Tam said, "and they agreed less than usual today. That's all. It's the same in every village."

"What about the false Dragon?" Mat asked, and Perrin added eager murmurs. "What about the Aes Sedai?"

Tam shook his head slowly. "Master Fain knew little more than he had already told. At least, little of interest to us. Battles won or lost. Cities taken and retaken. All in Ghealdan, thank the Light. It hasn't spread, or had not the last Master Fain knew."

"Battles interest me," Mat said, and Perrin added, "What did he say about them?"

"Battles don't interest me, Matrim," Tam said. "But I'm sure he will be glad to tell you all about them later. What does interest me is that we shouldn't have to worry about them here, as far as the Council can tell. We can see no reason for Aes Sedai to come here on their way south. And as for the return journey, they aren't likely to want to cross the Forest of Shadows and swim the White River."

Rand and the others chuckled at the idea. There were three reasons why no one came into the Two Rivers except from the north, by way of Taren Ferry. The Mountains of Mist, in the west, were the first, of course, and the Mire blocked the east just as effectively. To the south was the White River, which got its name from the way rocks and boulders churned its swift waters to froth. And beyond the White lay the Forest of Shadows. Few Two Rivers folk had ever crossed the White, and fewer still returned if they did. It was generally agreed, though, that the Forest of Shadows stretched south for a hundred miles or more without a road or a village, but with plenty of wolves and bears.

"So that's an end to it for us," Mat said. He sounded at least a little disappointed.

"Not quite," Tam said. "Day after tomorrow we will send men to Deven Ride and Watch Hill, and Taren Ferry, too, to arrange for a watch to be kept. Riders along the White and the Taren, both, and patrols between. It should be done today, but only the Mayor agrees with me. The rest can't see asking anyone to spend Bel Tine off riding across the Two Rivers."

"But I thought you said we didn't have to worry," Perrin said, and Tam shook his head.

"I said should not, boy, not did not. I've seen men die because they were sure that what should not happen, would not. Besides, the fighting will stir up all sorts of people. Most will just be trying to find safety, but others will be looking for a way to profit from the confusion. We'll offer any of the first a helping hand, but we must be ready to send the second type on their way."

Abruptly Mat spoke up. "Can we be part of it? I want to, anyway. You know I can ride as well as anyone in the village."

"You want a few weeks of cold, boredom, and sleeping rough?"

Tam chuckled. "Likely that's all there will be to it. I hope that's all. We're well out of the way even for refugees. But you can speak to Master al'Vere if your mind is made up. Rand, it's time for us to be getting back to the farm."

Rand blinked in surprise. "I thought we were staying for Winternight."

"Things need seeing to at the farm, and I need you with me."

"Even so, we don't have to leave for hours yet. And I want to volunteer for the patrols, too."

"We are going now," his father replied in a tone that brooked no argument. In a softer voice he added, "We'll be back tomorrow in plenty of time for you to speak to the Mayor. And plenty of time for Festival, too. Five minutes, now, then meet me in the stable."

"Are you going to join Rand and me on the watch?" Mat asked Perrin as Tam left. "I'll bet there's nothing like this ever happened in the Two Rivers before. Why, if we get up to the Taren, we might even see soldiers, or who knows what. Even Tinkers."

"I expect I will," Perrin said slowly, "if Master Luhhan doesn't need me, that is."

"The war is in Ghealdan," Rand snapped. With an effort he lowered his voice. "The war is in Ghealdan, and the Aes Sedai are the Light knows where, but none of it is here. The man in the black cloak is, or have you forgotten him already?" The others exchanged embarrassed looks.

"Sorry, Rand," Mat muttered. "But a chance to do something besides milk my da's cows doesn't come along very often." He straightened under their startled stares. "Well, I do milk them, and every day, too."

"The black rider," Rand reminded them. "What if he hurts somebody?"

"Maybe he's a refugee from the war," Perrin said doubtfully.

"Whatever he is," Mat said, "the watch will find him."

"Maybe," Rand said, "but he seems to disappear when he wants to. It might be better if they knew to look for him."

"We'll tell Master al'Vere when we volunteer for the patrols," Mat said, "he'll tell the Council, and they'll tell the watch."

"The Council!" Perrin said incredulously. "We'd be lucky if the Mayor didn't laugh out loud. Master Luhhan and Rand's father already think the two of us are jumping at shadows."

Rand sighed. "If we're going to do it, we might as well do it now. He won't laugh any louder today than he will tomorrow."

"Maybe," Perrin said with a sidelong glance at Mat, "we should try finding some others who've seen him. We'll see just about everybody in the village tonight." Mat's scowl deepened, but he still did not say anything. All of them understood that Perrin meant they should find witnesses who were more reliable than Mat. "He won't laugh any louder tomorrow," Perrin added when Rand hesitated. "And I'd just as soon have somebody else with us when we go to him. Half the village would suit me fine."

Rand nodded slowly. He could already hear Master al'Vere laughing. More witnesses certainly could not hurt. And if three of them had seen the fellow, others had to have, too. They must have. "Tomorrow, then. You two find whoever you can tonight, and tomorrow we go to the Mayor. After that. . . ." They looked at him silently, no one raising the question of what happened if they could not find anyone else who had seen the black-cloaked man. The question was clear in their eyes, though, and he had no answer. He sighed heavily. "I'd better go, now. My father will be wondering if I fell into a hole."

Followed by their goodbyes, he trotted around to the stableyard where the high-wheeled cart stood propped on its shafts.

The stable was a long, narrow building, topped by a high-peaked, thatched roof. Stalls, their floors covered with straw, filled both sides of the dim interior, lit only by the open double-doors at either end. The peddler's team munched their oats in eight stalls, and Master al'Vere's massive Dhurrans, the team he hired out when farmers had hauling beyond the abilities of their own horses, filled six more, but only three others were occupied. Rand thought he could match up horse and rider with no trouble. The tall, deep-chested black stallion that swung up its head fiercely had to be Lan's. The sleek white mare with an arched neck, its quick steps as graceful as a girl dancing, even in the stall, could only belong to Moiraine. And the third unfamiliar horse, a rangy, slab-sided gelding of a dusty brown, fit Thom Merrilin perfectly.

Tam stood in the rear of the stable, holding Bela by a lead rope and speaking quietly to Hu and Tad. Before Rand had taken two steps into the stable his father nodded to the stablemen and brought Bela out, wordlessly gathering up Rand as he went.

They harnessed the shaggy mare in silence. Tam appeared so deep in thought that Rand held his tongue. He did not really look forward to trying to convince his father about the black-cloaked rider, much less the Mayor. Tomorrow would have to be time enough, when Mat and the rest had found others who had seen the man. If they found others.

As the cart lurched into motion, Rand took his bow and quiver from the back, awkwardly belting the quiver at his waist as he half trotted alongside. When they reached the last row of houses in the village, he nocked an arrow, carrying it half raised and partly drawn. There was nothing to see except mostly leafless trees, but his shoulders tightened. The black rider could be on them before either of them knew it. There might not be time to draw the bow if he was not already halfway to it.

He knew he could not keep up the tension on the bowstring for long. He had made the bow himself, and Tam was one of the few others in the district who could even draw it all the way to the cheek. He cast around for something to take his mind off thinking about the dark rider. Surrounded by the forest, their cloaks flapping in the wind, it was not easy.

"Father," he said finally, "I don't understand why the Council had to question Padan Fain." With an effort he took his eyes off the woods and looked across Bela at Tam. "It seems to me, the decision you reached could have been made right on the spot. The Mayor frightened everybody half out of their wits, talking about Aes Sedai and the false Dragon here in the Two Rivers."

"People are funny, Rand. The best of them are. Take Haral Luhhan. Master Luhhan is a strong man, and a brave one, but he can't bear to see butchering done. Turns pale as a sheet."

"What does that have to do with anything? Everybody knows Master Luhhan can't stand the sight of blood, and nobody but the Coplins and the Congars thinks anything of it."

"Just this, lad. People don't always think or behave the way you might believe they would. Those folk back there . . . let the hail beat their crops into the mud, and the wind take off every roof in the district, and the wolves kill half their livestock, and they'll roll up their sleeves and start from scratch. They'll grumble, but they won't waste any time with it. But you give them just the thought of Aes Sedai and a false Dragon in Ghealdan, and soon enough they'll start thinking that Ghealdan is not that far the other side of the Forest of Shadows, and a straight line from Tar Valon to Ghealdan wouldn't pass that much to the east of us. As if the Aes Sedai wouldn't take the road through Caemlyn and Lugard instead of traveling cross-country! By tomorrow morning half the village would have been sure the entire war was about to descend on us. It would take weeks to undo. A fine Bel Tine that would make. So Bran gave them the idea before they could get it for themselves.

"They've seen the Council take the problem under consideration, and by now they'll be hearing what we decided. They chose us for the Village Council because they trust we can reason things out in the best way for everybody. They trust our opinions. Even Cenn's, which doesn't say much for the rest of us, I suppose. At any rate, they will hear there isn't anything to worry about, and they'll believe it. It is not that they couldn't reach the same conclusion, or would not, eventually, but this way we won't have Festival ruined, and nobody has to spend weeks worrying about something that isn't likely to happen. If it does, against all odds . . . well, the patrols will give us enough warning to do what we can. I truly don't think it will come to that, though."

Rand puffed out his cheeks. Apparently, being on the Council was more complicated than he had believed. The cart rumbled on along the Quarry Road.

"Did anyone besides Perrin see this strange rider?" Tam asked.

"Mat did, but—" Rand blinked, then stared across Bela's back at his father. "You believe me? I have to go back. I have to tell them." Tam's shout halted him as he turned to run back to the village.

"Hold, lad, hold! Do you think I waited this long to speak for no reason?"

Reluctantly Rand kept on beside the cart, still creaking along behind patient Bela. "What made you change your mind? Why can't I tell the others?"

"They'll know soon enough. At least, Perrin will. Mat, I'm not sure of. Word must be gotten to the farms as best it can, but in another hour there won't be anyone in Emond's Field above sixteen, those who can be responsible about it, at least, who doesn't know a stranger is skulking around and likely not the sort you would invite to Festival. The winter has been bad enough without this to scare the young ones."

"Festival?" Rand said. "If you had seen him you wouldn't want him closer than ten miles. A hundred, maybe."

"Perhaps so," Tam said placidly. "He could be just a refugee from the troubles in Ghealdan, or more likely a thief who thinks the pickings will be easier here than in Baerlon or Taren Ferry. Even so, no one around here has so much they can afford to have it stolen. If the man is trying to escape the war . . . well, that's still no excuse for scaring people. Once the watch is mounted, it should either find him or frighten him off."

"I hope it frightens him off. But why do you believe me now, when you didn't this morning?"

"I had to believe my own eyes then, lad, and I saw nothing." Tam shook his grizzled head. "Only young men see this fellow, it seems. When Haral Luhhan mentioned Perrin jumping shadows, though, it all came out. Jon Thane's oldest son saw him, too, and so did Samel Crawe's boy, Bandry. Well, when four of you say you've seen a thing—and solid lads, all—we start thinking maybe it's there whether we can see it or not. All except Cenn, of course. Anyway, that's why we're going home. With both of us away, this stranger could be up to any kind of mischief there. If not for Festival, I wouldn't come back tomorrow, either. But we can't make ourselves prisoners in our own homes just because this fellow is lurking about."

"I didn't know about Ban or Lem," Rand said. "The rest of us were going to the Mayor tomorrow, but we were worried he wouldn't believe us, either."

"Gray hairs don't mean our brains have curdled," Tam said dryly. "So you keep a sharp eye. Maybe I'll catch sight of him, too, if he shows up again."

Rand settled down to do just that. He was surprised to realize that his step felt lighter. The knots were gone from his shoulders. He was still scared, but it was not so bad as it had been. Tam and he were just as alone on the Quarry Road as they had been that morning, but in some way he felt as if the entire village were with them. That others knew and believed made all the difference. There was nothing the black-cloaked horseman could do that the people of Emond's Field could not handle together.

CHAPTER
5

Winternight

T he sun stood halfway down from its noonday high by the time
the cart reached the farmhouse. It was not a big house, not
nearly so large as some of the sprawling farmhouses to the east,
dwellings that had grown over the years to hold entire families. In the
Two Rivers that often included three or four generations under one
roof, including aunts, uncles, cousins, and nephews. Tam and Rand
were considered out of the ordinary as much for being two men living
alone as for farming in the Westwood.

Here most of the rooms were on one floor, a neat rectangle with no
wings or additions. Two bedrooms and an attic storeroom fitted up
under the steeply sloped thatch. If the whitewash was all but gone
from the stout wooden walls after the winter storms, the house was
still in a tidy state of repair, the thatch tightly mended and the doors
and shutters well-hung and snug-fitting.

House, barn, and stone sheep pen formed the points of a triangle
around the farmyard, where a few chickens had ventured out to scratch
at the cold ground. An open shearing shed and a stone dipping trough

stood next to the sheep pen. Hard by the fields between the farmyard and the trees loomed the tall cone of a tight-walled curing shed. Few farmers in the Two Rivers could make do without both wool and tabac to sell when the merchants came.

When Rand took a look in the stone pen, the heavy-horned herd ram looked back at him, but most of the black-faced flock remained placidly where they lay, or stood with their heads in the feed trough. Their coats were thick and curly, but it was still too cold for shearing.

"I don't think the black-cloaked man came here," Rand called to his father, who was walking slowly around the farmhouse, spear held at the ready, examining the ground intently. "The sheep wouldn't be so settled if that one had been around."

Tam nodded but did not stop. When he had made a complete circuit of the house, he did the same around the barn and the sheep pen, still studying the ground. He even checked the smokehouse and the curing shed. Drawing a bucket of water from the well, he filled a cupped hand, sniffed the water, and gingerly touched it with the tip of his tongue. Abruptly he barked a laugh, then drank it down in a quick gulp.

"I suppose he didn't," he told Rand, wiping his hand on his coat front. "All this about men and horses I can't see or hear just makes me look crossways at everything." He emptied the well water into another bucket and started for the house, the bucket in one hand and his spear in the other. "I'll start some stew for supper. And as long as we're here, we might as well get caught up on a few chores."

Rand grimaced, regretting Winternight in Emond's Field. But Tam was right. Around a farm the work never really got done; as soon as one thing was finished two more always needed doing. He hesitated about it, but kept his bow and quiver close at hand. If the dark rider did appear, he had no intention of facing him with nothing but a hoe.

First was stabling Bela. Once he had unharnessed her and put her into a stall in the barn next to their cow, he set his cloak aside and rubbed the mare down with handfuls of dry straw, then curried her with a pair of brushes. Climbing the narrow ladder to the loft, he pitched down hay for her feed. He fetched a scoopful of oats for her as well, though there was little enough left and might be no more for a long while unless the weather warmed soon. The cow had been milked that morning before first light, giving a quarter of her usual yield; she seemed to be drying up as the winter hung on.

Enough feed had been left to see the sheep for two days—they should have been in the pasture by now, but there was none worth calling it so—but he topped off their water. Whatever eggs had been laid needed to be gathered, too. There were only three. The hens seemed to be getting cleverer at hiding them.

He was taking a hoe to the vegetable garden behind the house when Tam came out and settled on a bench in front of the barn to mend harness, propping his spear beside him. It made Rand feel better about the bow lying on his cloak a pace from where he stood.

Few weeds had pushed above ground, but more weeds than anything else. The cabbages were stunted, barely a sprout of the beans or peas showed, and there was not a sign of a beet. Not everything had been planted, of course; only part, in hopes the cold might break in time to make a crop of some kind before the cellar was empty. It did not take long to finish hoeing, which would have suited him just fine in years past, but now he wondered what they would do if nothing came up this year. Not a pleasant thought. And there was still firewood to split.

It seemed to Rand like years since there had *not* been firewood to split. But complaining would not keep the house warm, so he fetched the axe, propped up bow and quiver beside the chopping block, and got to work. Pine for a quick, hot flame, and oak for long burning. Before long he was warm enough to put his coat aside. When the pile of split wood grew big enough, he stacked it against the side of the house, beside other stacks already there. Most reached all the way to the eaves. Usually by this time of year the woodpiles were small and few, but not this year. Chop and stack, chop and stack, he lost himself in the rhythm of the axe and the motions of stacking wood. Tam's hand on his shoulder brought him back to where he was, and for a moment he blinked in surprise.

Gray twilight had come on while he worked, and already it was fading quickly toward night. The full moon stood well above the treetops, shimmering pale and bulging as if about to fall on their heads. The wind had grown colder without his noticing, too, and tattered clouds scudded across the darkling sky.

"Let's wash up, lad, and see about some supper. I've already carried in water for hot baths before sleep."

"Anything hot sounds good to me," Rand said, snatching up his cloak and tossing it round his shoulders. Sweat soaked his shirt, and the wind, forgotten in the heat of swinging the axe, seemed to be trying to freeze it now that he had stopped work. He stifled a yawn, shivering as he gathered the rest of his things. "And sleep, too, for that. I might just sleep right through Festival."

"Would you care to make a small wager about that?" Tam smiled, and Rand had to grin back. He would not miss Bel Tine if he had had no sleep in a week. No one would.

Tam had been extravagant with the candles, and a fire crackled in the big stone fireplace, so that the main room had a warm, cheerful feel to it. A broad oaken table was the main feature of the room other than the fireplace, a table long enough to seat a dozen or more, though there had seldom been so many around it since Rand's mother died. A few cabinets and chests, most of them skillfully made by Tam himself, lined the walls, and high-backed chairs stood around the table. The cushioned chair that Tam called his reading chair sat angled before the flames. Rand preferred to do his reading stretched out on the rug in front of the fire. The shelf of books by the door was not nearly as long as the one at the Winespring Inn, but books were hard to come by. Few peddlers carried more than a handful, and those had to be stretched out among everyone who wanted them.

If the room did not look quite so freshly scrubbed as most farm wives kept their homes—Tam's piperack and *The Travels of Jain Farstrider* sat on the table, while another wood-bound book rested on the cushion of his reading chair; a bit of harness to be mended lay on the bench by the fireplace, and some shirts to be darned made a heap on a chair—if not quite so spotless, it was still clean and neat enough, with a lived-in look that was almost as warming and comforting as the fire. Here, it was possible to forget the chill beyond the walls. There was no false Dragon here. No wars or Aes Sedai. No men in black cloaks. The aroma from the stewpot hanging over the fire permeated the room, and filled Rand with ravenous hunger.

His father stirred the stewpot with a long-handled wooden spoon, then took a taste. "A little while longer."

Rand hurried to wash his face and hands; there was a pitcher and basin on the washstand by the door. A hot bath was what he wanted, to take away the sweat and soak the chill out, but that would come when there had been time to heat the big kettle in the back room.

Tam rooted around in a cabinet and came up with a key as long as his hand. He twisted it in the big iron lock on the door. At Rand's questioning look he said, "Best to be safe. Maybe I'm taking a fancy, or maybe the weather is blacking my mood, but. . . ." He sighed and bounced the key on his palm. "I'll see to the back door," he said, and disappeared toward the back of the house.

Rand could not remember either door ever being locked. No one in the Two Rivers locked doors. There was no need. Until now, at least. From overhead, from Tam's bedroom, came a scraping, as of some-

thing being dragged across the floor. Rand frowned. Unless Tam had
suddenly decided to move the furniture around, he could only be pulling out the old chest he kept under his bed. Another thing that had
never been done in Rand's memory.

He filled a small kettle with water for tea and hung it from a hook
over the fire, then set the table. He had carved the bowls and spoons
himself. The front shutters had not yet been closed, and from time to
time he peered out, but full night had come and all he could see were
moon shadows. The dark rider could be out there easily enough, but
he tried not to think about that.

When Tam came back, Rand stared in surprise. A thick belt slanted
around Tam's waist, and from the belt hung a sword, with a bronze
heron on the black scabbard and another on the long hilt. The only
men Rand had ever seen wearing swords were the merchants' guards.
And Lan, of course. That his father might own one had never even
occurred to him. Except for the herons, the sword looked a good deal
like Lan's sword.

"Where did that come from?" he asked. "Did you get it from a
peddler? How much did it cost?"

Slowly Tam drew the weapon; firelight played along the gleaming
length. It was nothing at all like the plain, rough blades Rand had seen
in the hands of merchants' guards. No gems or gold adorned it, but it
seemed grand to him, nonetheless. The blade, very slightly curved and
sharp on only one edge, bore another heron etched into the steel.
Short quillons, worked to look like braid, flanked the hilt. It seemed
almost fragile compared with the swords of the merchants' guards;
most of those were double-edged, and thick enough to chop down a
tree.

"I got it a long time ago," Tam said, "a long way from here. And
I paid entirely too much; two coppers is too much for one of these.
Your mother didn't approve, but she was always wiser than I. I was
young then, and it seemed worth the price at the time. She always
wanted me to get rid of it, and more than once I've thought she was
right, that I should just give it away."

Reflected fire made the blade seem aflame. Rand started. He had
often daydreamed about owning a sword. "Give it away? How could
you give a sword like that away?"

Tam snorted. "Not much use in herding sheep, now is it? Can't plow
a field or harvest a crop with it." For a long minute he stared at the
sword as if wondering what he was doing with such a thing. At last he
let out a heavy sigh. "But if I am not just taken by a black fancy, if

our luck runs sour, maybe in the next few days we'll be glad I tucked it in that old chest, instead." He slid the sword smoothly back into its sheath and wiped his hand on his shirt with a grimace. "The stew should be ready. I'll dish it out while you fix the tea."

Rand nodded and got the tea canister, but he wanted to know everything. Why would Tam have bought a sword? He could not imagine. And where had Tam come by it? How far away? No one ever left the Two Rivers; or very few, at least. He had always vaguely supposed his father must have gone outside—his mother had been an outlander—but a sword . . . ? He had a lot of questions to ask once they had settled at the table.

The tea water was boiling fiercely, and he had to wrap a cloth around the kettle's handle to lift it off the hook. Heat soaked through immediately. As he straightened from the fire, a heavy thump at the door rattled the lock. All thoughts of the sword, or the hot kettle in his hand, flew away.

"One of the neighbors," he said uncertainly. "Master Dautry wanting to borrow. . . ." But the Dautry farm, their nearest neighbor, was an hour away even in the daylight, and Oren Dautry, shameless borrower that he was, was still not likely to leave his house by dark.

Tam softly placed the stew-filled bowls on the table. Slowly he moved away from the table. Both of his hands rested on his sword hilt. "I don't think—" he began, and the door burst open, pieces of the iron lock spinning across the floor.

A figure filled the doorway, bigger than any man Rand had ever seen, a figure in black mail that hung to his knees, with spikes at wrists and elbows and shoulders. One hand clutched a heavy, scythe-like sword; the other hand was flung up before his eyes as if to shield them from the light.

Rand felt the beginnings of an odd sort of relief. Whoever this was, it was not the black-cloaked rider. Then he saw the curled ram's horns on the head that brushed the top of the doorway, and where mouth and nose should have been was a hairy muzzle. He took in all of it in the space of one deep breath that he let out in a terrified yell as, without thinking, he hurled the hot kettle at that half-human head.

The creature roared, part scream of pain, part animal snarl, as boiling water splashed over its face. Even as the kettle struck, Tam's sword flashed. The roar abruptly became a gurgle, and the huge shape toppled back. Before it finished falling, another was trying to claw its way past. Rand glimpsed a misshapen head topped by spike-like horns before Tam struck again, and two huge bodies blocked the door. He realized his father was shouting at him.

"Run, lad! Hide in the woods!" The bodies in the doorway jerked as others outside tried to pull them clear. Tam thrust a shoulder under the massive table; with a grunt he heaved it over atop the tangle. "There are too many to hold! Out the back! Go! Go! I'll follow!"

Even as Rand turned away, shame filled him that he obeyed so quickly. He wanted to stay and help his father, though he could not imagine how, but fear had him by the throat, and his legs moved on their own. He dashed from the room, toward the back of the house, as fast as he had ever run in his life. Crashes and shouts from the front door pursued him.

He had his hands on the bar across the back door when his eye fell on the iron lock that was never locked. Except that Tam had done just that tonight. Letting the bar stay where it was, he darted to a side window, flung up the sash and threw back the shutters. Night had replaced twilight completely. The full moon and drifting clouds made dappled shadows chase one another across the farmyard.

Shadows, he told himself. Only shadows. The back door creaked as someone outside, or something, tried to push it open. His mouth went dry. A crash shook the door in its frame and lent him speed; he slipped through the window like a hare going to ground, and cowered against the side of the house. Inside the room, wood splintered like thunder.

He forced himself up to a crouch, made himself peer inside, just with one eye, just at the corner of the window. In the dark he could not make out much, but more than he really wanted to see. The door hung askew, and shadowed shapes moved cautiously into the room, talking in low, guttural voices. Rand understood none of what was said; the language sounded harsh, unsuited to a human tongue. Axes and spears and spiked things dully reflected stray glimmers of moonlight. Boots scraped on the floor, and there was a rhythmic click, as of hooves, as well.

He tried to work moisture back into his mouth. Drawing a deep, ragged breath, he shouted as loudly as he could. "They're coming in the back!" The words came out in a croak, but at least they came out. He had not been sure they would. "I'm outside! Run, father!" With the last word he was sprinting away from the farmhouse.

Coarse-voiced shouts in the strange tongue raged from the back room. Glass shattered, loud and sharp, and something thudded heavily to the ground behind him. He guessed one of them had broken through the window rather than try to squeeze through the opening, but he did not look back to see if he was right. Like a fox running from hounds he darted into the nearest moon-cast shadows as if headed for the woods, then dropped to his belly and slithered back to the barn and its larger, deeper shadows. Something fell across his shoulders, and he thrashed about, not sure if he was trying to fight or escape, until he realized he was grappling with the new hoe handle Tam had been shaping.

Idiot! For a moment he lay there, trying to stop panting. *Coplin fool idiot!* At last he crawled on along the back of the barn, dragging the hoe handle with him. It was not much, but it was better than nothing. Cautiously he looked around the corner at the farmyard and the house.

Of the creature that had jumped out after him there was no sign. It could be anywhere. Hunting him, surely. Even creeping up on him at that very moment.

Frightened bleats filled the sheep pen to his left; the flock milled as if trying to find an escape. Shadowed shapes flickered in the lighted front windows of the house, and the clash of steel on steel rang through the darkness. Suddenly one of the windows burst outward in a shower of glass and wood as Tam leaped through it, sword still in hand. He landed on his feet, but instead of running away from the house he dashed toward the back of it, ignoring the monstrous things scrambling after him through the broken window and the doorway.

Rand stared in disbelief. Why was he not trying to get away? Then he understood. Tam had last heard his voice from the rear of the house. "Father!" he shouted. "I'm over here!"

In mid-stride Tam whirled, not running toward Rand, but at an angle away from him. "Run, lad!" he shouted, gesturing with the sword as if to someone ahead of him. "Hide!" A dozen huge forms streamed after him, harsh shouts and shrill howls shivering the air.

Rand pulled back into the shadows behind the barn. There he could not be seen from the house, in case any of the creatures were still inside. He was safe; for the moment, at least. But not Tam. Tam, who was trying to lead those things away from him. His hands tightened on the hoe handle, and he had to clench his teeth to stop a sudden laugh. A hoe handle. Facing one of those creatures with a hoe handle would not be much like playing at quarterstaffs with Perrin. But he could not let Tam face what was chasing him alone.

"If I move like I was stalking a rabbit," he whispered to himself, "they'll never hear me, or see me." The eerie cries echoed in the darkness, and he tried to swallow. "More like a pack of starving wolves." Soundlessly he slipped away from the barn, toward the forest, gripping the hoe handle so hard that his hands hurt.

At first, when the trees surrounded him, he took comfort from them.

They helped hide him from whatever the creatures were that had attacked the farm. As he crept through the woods, though, moon shadows shifted, and it began to seem as if the darkness of the forest changed and moved, too. Trees loomed malevolently; branches writhed toward him. But were they just trees and branches? He could almost hear the growling chuckles stifled in their throats while they waited for him. The howls of Tam's pursuers no longer filled the night, but in the silence that replaced them he flinched every time the wind scraped one limb against another. Lower and lower he crouched, and moved more and more slowly. He hardly dared to breathe for fear he might be heard.

Suddenly a hand closed over his mouth from behind, and an iron grip seized his wrist. Frantically he clawed over his shoulder with his free hand for some hold on the attacker.

"Don't break my neck, lad," came Tam's hoarse whisper.

Relief flooded him, turning his muscles to water. When his father released him he fell to his hands and knees, gasping as if he had run for miles. Tam dropped down beside him, leaning on one elbow.

"I wouldn't have tried that if I had thought how much you've grown in the last few years," Tam said softly. His eyes shifted constantly as he spoke, keeping a sharp watch on the darkness. "But I had to make sure you didn't speak out. Some Trollocs can hear like a dog. Maybe better."

"But Trollocs are just. . . ." Rand let the words trail off. Not just a story, not after tonight. Those things could be Trollocs or the Dark One himself for all he knew. "Are you sure?" he whispered. "I mean . . . Trollocs?"

"I'm sure. Though what brought them to the Two Rivers. . . . I never saw one before tonight, but I've talked with men who have, so I know a little. Maybe enough to keep us alive. Listen closely. A Trolloc can see better than a man in the dark, but bright lights blind them, for a time at least. That may be the only reason we got away from so many. Some can track by scent or sound, but they're said to be lazy. If we can keep out of their hands long enough, they should give up."

That made Rand feel only a little better. "In the stories they hate men, and serve the Dark One."

"If anything belongs in the Shepherd of the Night's flocks, lad, it is Trollocs. They kill for the pleasure of killing, so I've been told. But that's the end of my knowledge, except that they cannot be trusted unless they're afraid of you, and then not far."

Rand shivered. He did not think he would want to meet anyone a Trolloc was afraid of. "Do you think they're still hunting for us?"

"Maybe, maybe not. They don't seem very smart. Once we got into the forest, I sent the ones after me off toward the mountains without much trouble." Tam fumbled at his right side, then put his hand close to his face. "Best act as if they are, though."

"You're hurt."

"Keep your voice down. It's just a scratch, and there is nothing to be done about it now, anyway. At least the weather seems to be warming." He lay back with a heavy sigh. "Perhaps it won't be too bad spending the night out."

In the back of his mind Rand had just been thinking fond thoughts of his coat and cloak. The trees cut the worst of the wind, but what gusted through still sliced like a frozen knife. Hesitantly he touched Tam's face, and winced. "You're on fire. I have to get you to Nynaeve."

"In a bit, lad."

"We don't have any time to waste. It's a long way in the dark." He scrambled to his feet and tried to pull his father up. A groan barely stifled by Tam's clenched teeth made Rand hastily ease him back down.

"Let me rest a while, boy. I'm tired."

Rand pounded his fist on his thigh. Snug in the farmhouse, with a fire and blankets, plenty of water and willowbark, he might have been willing to wait for daybreak before hitching Bela and taking Tam into the village. Here was no fire, no blankets, no cart, and no Bela. But those things were still back at the house. If he could not carry Tam to them, perhaps he could bring some of them, at least, to Tam. If the Trollocs were gone. They had to go sooner or later.

He looked at the hoe handle, then dropped it. Instead he drew Tam's sword. The blade gleamed dully in the pale moonlight. The long hilt felt odd in his hand; the weight and heft were strange. He slashed at the air a few times before stopping with a sigh. Slashing at air was easy. If he had to do it against a Trolloc he was surely just as likely to run instead, or freeze stiff so he could not move at all until the Trolloc swung one of those odd swords and. . . . *Stop it! It's not helping anything!*

As he started to rise, Tam caught his arm. "Where are you going?"

"We need the cart," he said gently. "And blankets." He was shocked at how easily he pulled his father's hand from his sleeve. "Rest, and I'll be back."

"Careful," Tam breathed.

He could not see Tam's face in the moonlight, but he could feel his eyes on him. "I will be." *As careful as a mouse exploring a hawk's nest,* he thought.

As silently as another shadow, he slid into the darkness. He thought of all the times he had played tag in the woods with his friends as children, stalking one another, straining not to be heard until he put a hand on someone's shoulder. Somehow he could not make this seem the same.

Creeping from tree to tree, he tried to make a plan, but by the time he reached the edge of the woods he had made and discarded ten. Everything depended on whether or not the Trollocs were still there. If they were gone, he could simply walk up to the house and take what he needed. If they were still there. . . . In that case, there was nothing for it but go back to Tam. He did not like it, but he could do Tam no good by getting killed.

He peered toward the farm buildings. The barn and the sheep pen were only dark shapes in the moonlight. Light spilled from the front windows of the house, though, and through the open front door. *Just the candles father lit, or are there Trollocs waiting?*

He jumped convulsively at a nighthawk's reedy cry, then sagged against a tree, shaking. This was getting him nowhere. Dropping to his belly, he began to crawl, holding the sword awkwardly before him. He kept his chin in the dirt all the way to the back of the sheep pen.

Crouched against the stone wall, he listened. Not a sound disturbed the night. Carefully he eased up enough to look over the wall. Nothing moved in the farmyard. No shadows flickered against the lit windows of the house, or in the doorway. *Bela and the cart first, or the blankets and other things.* It was the light that decided him. The barn was dark. Anything could be waiting inside, and he would have no way of knowing until it was too late. At least he would be able to see what was inside the house.

As he started to lower himself again, he stopped suddenly. There was *no* sound. Most of the sheep might have settled down already and gone back to sleep, though it was not likely, but a few were always awake even in the middle of the night, rustling about, bleating now and again. He could barely make out the shadowy mounds of sheep on the ground. One lay almost beneath him.

Trying to make no noise, he hoisted himself onto the wall until he could stretch out a hand to the dim shape. His fingers touched curly wool, then wetness; the sheep did not move. Breath left him in a rush as he pushed back, almost dropping the sword as he fell to the ground outside the pen. *They kill for fun.* Shakily he scrubbed the wetness from his hand in the dirt.

Fiercely he told himself that nothing had changed. The Trollocs had done their butchery and gone. Repeating that in his mind, he crawled on across the farmyard, keeping as low as he could, but trying to watch every direction, too. He had never thought he would envy an earthworm.

At the front of the house he lay close beside the wall, beneath the broken window, and listened. The dull thudding of blood in his ears was the loudest sound he heard. Slowly he reared up and peered inside.

The stewpot lay upside down in the ashes on the hearth. Splintered, broken wood littered the room; not a single piece of furniture remained whole. Even the table rested at an angle, two legs hacked to rough stubs. Every drawer had been pulled out and smashed; every cupboard and cabinet stood open, many doors hanging by one hinge. Their contents were strewn over the wreckage, and everything was dusted with white. Flour and salt, to judge from the slashed sacks tossed down by the fireplace. Four twisted bodies made a tangle in the remnants of the furnishings. Trollocs.

Rand recognized one by its ram's horns. The others were much the same, even in their differences, a repulsive melange of human faces distorted by muzzles, horns, feathers, and fur. Their hands, almost human, only made it worse. Two wore boots; the others had hooves. He watched without blinking until his eyes burned. None of the Trollocs moved. They had to be dead. And Tam was waiting.

He ran in through the front door and stopped, gagging at the stench. A stable that had not been mucked out in months was the only thing he could think of that might come close to matching it. Vile smears defiled the walls. Trying to breathe through his mouth, he hurriedly began poking through the mess on the floor. There had been a waterbag in one of the cupboards.

A scraping sound behind him sent a chill to his marrow, and he spun, almost falling over the remains of the table. He caught himself, and moaned behind teeth that would have chattered had he not had them clenched until his jaw ached.

One of the Trollocs was getting to its feet. A wolf's muzzle jutted out below sunken eyes. Flat, emotionless eyes, and all too human. Hairy, pointed ears twitched incessantly. It stepped over one of its dead companions on sharp goat hooves. The same black mail the others wore rasped against leather trousers, and one of the huge, scythe-curved swords swung at its side.

It muttered something, guttural and sharp, then said, "Others go away. Narg stay. Narg smart." The words were distorted and hard to understand, coming from a mouth never meant for human speech. Its tone was meant to be soothing, he thought, but he could not take his eyes off the stained teeth, long and sharp, that flashed every time the creature spoke. "Narg know some come back sometime. Narg wait. You no need sword. Put sword down."

Until the Trolloc spoke Rand had not realized that he held Tam's sword wavering before him in both hands, its point aimed at the huge creature. It towered head and shoulders above him, with a chest and arms to dwarf Master Luhhan.

"Narg no hurt." It took a step closer, gesturing. "You put sword down." The dark hair on the backs of its hands was thick, like fur.

"Stay back," Rand said, wishing his voice were steadier. "Why did you do this? Why?"

"*Vlja daeg roghda!*" The snarl quickly became a toothy smile. "Put sword down. Narg no hurt. Myrddraal want talk you." A flash of emotion crossed the distorted face. Fear. "Others come back, you talk Myrddraal." It took another step, one big hand coming to rest on its own sword hilt. "You put sword down."

Rand wet his lips. Myrddraal! The worst of the stories was walking tonight. If a Fade was coming, it made a Trolloc pale by comparison. He had to get away. But if the Trolloc drew that massive blade he would not have a chance. He forced his lips into a shaky smile. "All right." Grip tightening on the sword, he let both hands drop to his sides. "I'll talk."

The wolf-smile became a snarl, and the Trolloc lunged for him. Rand had not thought anything that big could move so fast. Desperately he brought his sword up. The monstrous body crashed into him, slamming him against the wall. Breath left his lungs in one gasp. He fought for air as they fell to the floor together, the Trolloc on top. Frantically he struggled beneath the crushing weight, trying to avoid thick hands groping for him, and snapping jaws.

Abruptly the Trolloc spasmed and was still. Battered and bruised, half suffocated by the bulk on top of him, for a moment Rand could only lie there in disbelief. Quickly he came to his senses, though, enough to writhe out from under the body, at least. And body it was. The bloodied blade of Tam's sword stood out from the center of the Trolloc's back. He had gotten it up in time after all. Blood covered

Rand's hands, as well, and made a blackish smear across the front of his shirt. His stomach churned, and he swallowed hard to keep from being sick. He shook as hard as he had in the worst of his fear, but this time in relief at still being alive.

Others come back, the Trolloc had said. The other Trollocs would be returning to the farmhouse. And a Myrddraal, a Fade. The stories said Fades were twenty feet tall, with eyes of fire, and they rode shadows like horses. When a Fade turned sideways, it disappeared, and no wall could stop them. He had to do what he had come for, and get away quickly.

Grunting with the effort he heaved the Trolloc's body over to get to the sword—and almost ran when open eyes stared at him. It took him a minute to realize they were staring through the glaze of death.

He wiped his hands on a tattered rag—it had been one of Tam's shirts only that morning—and tugged the blade free. Cleaning the sword, he reluctantly dropped the rag on the floor. There was no time for neatness, he thought with a laugh that he had to clamp his teeth shut to stop. He did not see how they could ever clean the house well enough for it to be lived in again. The horrible stench had probably already soaked right into the timbers. But there was no time to think of that. *No time for neatness. No time for anything, maybe.*

He was sure he was forgetting any number of things they would need, but Tam was waiting, and the Trollocs were coming back. He gathered what he could think of on the run. Blankets from the bedrooms upstairs, and clean cloths to bandage Tam's wound. Their cloaks and coats. A waterbag that he carried when he took the sheep to pasture. A clean shirt. He did not know when he would have time to change, but he wanted to get out of his blood-smeared shirt at the first opportunity. The small bags of willowbark and their other medicines were part of a dark, muddy-looking pile he could not bring himself to touch.

One bucket of the water Tam had brought in still stood by the fireplace, miraculously unspilled and untouched. He filled the waterbag from it, gave his hands a hasty wash in the rest, and made one more quick search for anything he might have forgotten. He found his bow among the wreckage, broken cleanly in two at the thickest point. He shuddered as he let the pieces fall. What he had gathered already would have to do, he decided. Quickly he piled everything outside the door.

The last thing before leaving the house, he dug a shuttered lantern from the mess on the floor. It still held oil. Lighting it from one of the candles, he closed the shutters—partly against the wind, but mostly to keep from drawing attention—and hurried outside with the lantern in one hand and the sword in the other. He was not sure what he would find in the barn. The sheep pen kept him from hoping too much. But he needed the cart to get Tam to Emond's Field, and for the cart he needed Bela. Necessity made him hope a little.

The barn doors stood open, one creaking on its hinges as it shifted in the wind. The interior looked as it always had, at first. Then his eyes fell on empty stalls, the stall doors ripped from their hinges. Bela and the cow were gone. Quickly he went to the back of the barn. The cart lay on its side, half the spokes broken out of its wheels. One shaft was only a foot-long stump.

The despair he had been holding at bay filled him. He was not sure he could carry Tam as far as the village even if his father could bear to be carried. The pain of it might kill Tam more quickly than the fever. Still, it was the only chance left. He had done all he could do here. As he turned to go, his eyes fell on the hacked-off cart shaft lying on the straw-strewn floor. Suddenly he smiled.

Hurriedly he set the lantern and the sword on the straw-covered floor, and in the next instant he was wrestling with the cart, tipping it back over to fall upright with a snap of more breaking spokes, then throwing his shoulder into it to heave it over on the other side. The undamaged shaft stood straight out. Snatching up the sword he hacked at the well-seasoned ash. To his pleased surprise great chips flew with his strokes, and he cut through as quickly as he could have with a good axe.

When the shaft fell free, he looked at the sword blade in wonder. Even the best-sharpened axe would have dulled chopping through that hard, aged wood, but the sword looked as brightly sharp as ever. He touched the edge with his thumb, then hastily stuck it in his mouth. The blade was still razor-sharp.

But he had no time for wonder. Blowing out the lantern—there was no need to have the barn burn down on top of everything else—he gathered up the shafts and ran back to get what he had left at the house.

Altogether it made an awkward burden. Not a heavy one, but hard to balance and manage, the cart shafts shifting and twisting in his arms as he stumbled across the plowed field. Once back in the forest they were even worse, catching on trees and knocking him half off his feet. They would have been easier to drag, but that would leave a clear trail behind him. He intended to wait as long as possible before doing that.

Tam was right where he had left him, seemingly asleep. He hoped it was sleep. Suddenly fearful, he dropped his burdens and put a hand to his father's face. Tam still breathed, but the fever was worse.

The touch roused Tam, but only into a hazy wakefulness. "Is that you, boy?" he breathed. "Worried about you. Dreams of days gone. Nightmares." Murmuring softly, he drifted off again.

"Don't worry," Rand said. He lay Tam's coat and cloak over him to keep off the wind. "I'll get you to Nynaeve just as quick as I can." As he went on, as much to reassure himself as for Tam's benefit, he peeled off his bloodstained shirt, hardly even noticing the cold in his haste to be rid of it, and hurriedly pulled on the clean one. Throwing his old shirt away made him feel as if he had just had a bath. "We'll be safe in the village in no time, and the Wisdom will set everything right. You'll see. Everything's going to be all right."

That thought was like a beacon as he pulled on his coat and bent to tend Tam's wound. They would be safe once they reached the village, and Nynaeve would cure Tam. He just had to get him there.

CHAPTER 6

The Westwood

In the moonlight Rand could not really see what he was doing, but Tam's wound seemed to be only a shallow gash along the ribs, no longer than the palm of his hand. He shook his head in disbelief. He had seen his father take more of an injury than that and not even stop work except to wash it off. Hastily he searched Tam from head to foot for something bad enough to account for the fever, but the one cut was all he could find.

Small as it was, that lone cut was still grave enough; the flesh around it burned to the touch. It was even hotter than the rest of Tam's body, and the rest of him was hot enough to make Rand's jaws clench. A scalding fever like that could kill, or leave a man a husk of what he had once been. He soaked a cloth with water from the skin and laid it across Tam's forehead.

He tried to be gentle about washing and bandaging the gash on his father's ribs, but soft groans still interrupted Tam's low muttering. Stark branches loomed around them, threatening as they shifted as in the wind. Surely the Trollocs would go on their way when they failed to find Tam and him, when they came back to the farmhouse and found it still empty. He tried to make himself believe it, but the wanton destruction at the house, the senselessness of it, left little room for belief of that sort. Believing they would give up short of killing everyone and everything they could find was dangerous, a foolish chance he could not afford to take.

Trollocs. Light above, Trollocs! Creatures out of a gleeman's tale coming out of the night to bash in the door. And a Fade. Light shine on me, a Fade!

Abruptly he realized he was holding the untied ends of the bandage in motionless hands. *Frozen like a rabbit that's seen a hawk's shadow,* he thought scornfully. With an angry shake of his head he finished tying the bandage around Tam's chest.

Knowing what he had to do, even getting on with it, did not stop him being afraid. When the Trollocs came back they would surely begin searching the forest around the farm for some trace of the people who had escaped them. The body of the one he had killed would tell them those people were not far off. Who knew what a Fade would do, or could do? On top of that, his father's comment about Trollocs' hearing was as loud in his mind as if Tam had just said it. He found himself resisting the urge to put a hand over Tam's mouth, to still his groans and murmurs. *Some track by scent. What can I do about that? Nothing.* He could not waste time worrying over problems he could do nothing about.

"You have to keep quiet," he whispered in his father's ear. "The Trollocs will be back."

Tam spoke in hushed, hoarse tones. "You're still lovely, Kari. Still lovely as a girl."

Rand grimaced. His mother had been dead fifteen years. If Tam believed she was still alive, then the fever was even worse than Rand had thought. How could he be kept from speaking, now that silence might mean life?

"Mother wants you to be quiet," Rand whispered. He paused to clear his throat of a sudden tightness. She had had gentle hands; he remembered that much. "Kari wants you to be quiet. Here. Drink."

Tam gulped thirstily from the waterskin, but after a few swallows he turned his head aside and began murmuring softly again, too low for Rand to understand. He hoped it was too low to be heard by hunting Trollocs, too.

Hastily he got on with what was needed. Three of the blankets he wove around and between the shafts cut from the cart, contriving a makeshift litter. He would only be able to carry one end, letting the other drag on the ground, but it would have to do. From the last blanket he cut a long strip with his belt knife, then tied one end of the strip to each of the shafts.

As gently as he could, he lifted Tam onto the litter, wincing with every moan. His father had always seemed indestructible. Nothing could harm him; nothing could stop him, or even slow him down. For him to be in this condition almost robbed Rand of what courage he had managed to gather. But he had to keep on. That was all that kept him moving. He had to.

When Tam finally lay on the litter, Rand hesitated, then took the sword belt from his father's waist. When he fastened it around himself, it felt odd there; it made him feel odd. Belt and sheath and sword together only weighed a few pounds, but when he sheathed the blade it seemed to drag at him like a great weight.

Angrily he berated himself. This was no time or place for foolish fancies. It was only a big knife. How many times had he daydreamed about wearing a sword and having adventures? If he could kill one Trolloc with it, he could surely fight off any others as well. Only, he knew all too well that what had happened in the farmhouse had been the purest luck. And his daydream adventures had never included his teeth chattering, or running for his life through the night, or his father at the point of death.

Hastily he tucked the last blanket around Tam, and laid the waterskin and the rest of the cloths beside his father on the litter. With a deep breath he knelt between the shafts and lifted the strip of blanket over his head. It settled across his shoulders and under his arms. When he gripped the shafts and straightened, most of the weight was on his shoulders. It did not seem like very much. Trying to keep a smooth pace, he set out for Emond's Field, the litter scraping along behind him.

He had already decided to make his way to the Quarry Road and follow that to the village. The danger would almost certainly be greater along the road, but Tam would receive no help at all if he got them lost trying to find his way through the woods and the dark.

In the darkness he was almost out onto the Quarry Road before he knew it. When he realized where he was, his throat tightened like a fist. Hurriedly he turned the litter around and dragged it back into the trees a way, then stopped to catch his breath and let his heart stop pounding. Still panting, he turned east, toward Emond's Field.

Traveling through the trees was more difficult than taking Tam down the road, and the night surely did not help, but going out onto the road itself would be madness. The idea was to reach the village *without* meeting any Trollocs; without even seeing any, if he had his wish. He had to assume the Trollocs were still hunting them, and sooner or later they would realize the two had set off for the village. That was the most likely place to go, and the Quarry Road the most likely route. In truth, he found himself closer to the road than he liked. The night and the shadows under the trees seemed awfully bare cover in which to hide from the eyes of anyone traveling along it.

Moonlight filtering through bare branches gave only enough illumination to fool his eyes into thinking they saw what was underfoot. Roots threatened to trip him at every step, old brambles snagged his legs, and sudden dips or rises in the ground had him half falling as his foot met nothing but air where he expected firm earth, or stumbling when his toe struck dirt while still moving forward. Tam's mutterings broke into a sharp groan whenever one of the shafts bumped too quickly over root or rock.

Uncertainty made him peer into the darkness until his eyes burned, listen as he had never listened before. Every scrape of branch against branch, every rustle of pine needles, brought him to a halt, ears straining, hardly daring to breathe for fear he might not hear some warning sound, for fear he might hear that sound. Only when he was sure it was just the wind would he go on.

Slowly weariness crept into his arms and legs, driven home by a night wind that mocked his cloak and coat. The weight of the litter, so little at the start, now tried to pull him to the ground. His stumbles were no longer all from tripping. The almost constant struggle not to fall took as much out of him as did the actual work of pulling the litter. He had been up before dawn to begin his chores, and even with the trip to Emond's Field he had done almost a full day's work. On any normal night he would be resting before the fireplace, reading one of Tam's small collection of books before going to bed. The sharp chill soaked into his bones, and his stomach reminded him that he had had nothing to eat since Mistress al'Vere's honeycakes.

He muttered to himself, angry at not taking some food at the farm. A few minutes more could not have made any difference. A few minutes to find some bread and cheese. The Trollocs would not have come back in just a few minutes more. Or just the bread. Of course, Mistress al'Vere would insist on putting a hot meal in front of him once they reached the inn. A steaming plate of her thick lamb stew, probably. And some of that bread she had been baking. And lots of hot tea.

"They came over the Dragonwall like a flood," Tam said suddenly, in a strong, angry voice, "and washed the land with blood. How many died for Laman's sin?"

Rand almost fell from surprise. Wearily he lowered the litter to the ground and untangled himself. The strip of blanket left a burning groove in his shoulders. Shrugging to work the knots out, he knelt beside Tam. Fumbling for the waterbag, he peered through the trees, trying vainly in the dim moonlight to see up and down the road, not twenty paces away. Nothing moved there but shadows. Nothing but shadows.

"There isn't any flood of Trollocs, father. Not now, anyway. We'll be safe in Emond's Field soon. Drink a little water."

Tam brushed aside the waterbag with an arm that seemed to have regained all of its strength. He seized Rand's collar, pulling him close enough to feel the heat of his father's fever in his own cheek. "They called them savages," Tam said urgently. "The fools said they could be swept aside like rubbish. How many battles lost, how many cities burned, before they faced the truth? Before the nations stood together against them?" He loosed his hold on Rand, and sadness filled his voice. "The field at Marath carpeted with the dead, and no sound but the cries of ravens and the buzzing of flies. The topless towers of Cairhien burning in the night like torches. All the way to the Shining Walls they burned and slew before they were turned back. All the way to—"

Rand clamped a hand over his father's mouth. The sound came again, a rhythmic thudding, directionless in the trees, fading then growing stronger again as the wind shifted. Frowning, he turned his head slowly, trying to decide from where it came. A flicker of motion caught the corner of his eye, and in an instant he was crouched over Tam. He was startled to feel the hilt of the sword clutched tight in his hand, but most of him concentrated on the Quarry Road as if the road were the only real thing in the entire world.

Wavering shadows to the east slowly resolved themselves into a horse and rider followed up the road by tall, bulky shapes trotting to keep up with the animal. The pale light of the moon glittered from spearheads and axe blades. Rand never even considered that they might be villagers coming to help. He knew what they were. He could feel it, like grit scraping his bones, even before they drew close enough for moonlight to reveal the hooded cloak swathing the horseman, a cloak that hung undisturbed by the wind. All of the shapes appeared black in the night, and the horse's hooves made the same sounds that any other's would, but Rand knew this horse from any other.

Behind the dark rider came nightmare forms with horns and muzzles and beaks, Trollocs in a double file, all in steps, boots and hooves striking the ground at the same instant as if obeying a single mind. Rand counted twenty as they ran past. He wondered what kind of man would dare turn his back on so many Trollocs. Or on one, for that matter.

The trotting column disappeared westward, thumping footfalls fading into the darkness, but Rand remained where he was, not moving a muscle except to breathe. Something told him to be certain, absolutely certain, they were gone before he moved. At long last he drew a deep breath and began to straighten.

This time the horse made no sound at all. In eerie silence the dark rider returned, his shadowy mount stopping every few steps as it walked slowly back down the road. The wind gusted higher, moaning through the trees; the horseman's cloak lay still as death. Whenever the horse halted, that hooded head swung from side to side as the rider peered into the forest, searching. Exactly opposite Rand the horse stopped again, the shadowed opening of the hood turning toward where he crouched above his father.

Rand's hand tightened convulsively on the sword hilt. He felt the gaze, just as he had that morning, and shivered again from the hatred even if he could not see it. That shrouded man hated everyone and everything, everything that lived. Despite the cold wind, sweat beaded on Rand's face.

Then the horse was moving on, a few soundless steps and stops, until all Rand could see was a barely distinguishable blur in the night far down the road. It could have been anything, but he had not taken his eyes off it for a second. If he lost it, he was afraid the next time he saw the black-cloaked rider might be when that silent horse was on top of him.

Abruptly the shadow was rushing back, passing him in a silent gallop. The rider looked only ahead of him as he sped westward into the night, toward the Mountains of Mist. Toward the farm.

Rand sagged, gulping air and scrubbing cold sweat off his face with his sleeve. He did not care any more about why the Trollocs had come. If he never found out why, that would be fine, just as long as it was all ended.

With a shake he gathered himself, hastily checking his father. Tam was still murmuring, but so softly Rand could not make out the words. He tried to give him a drink, but the water spilled over his father's chin. Tam coughed and choked on the trickle that made it into his mouth, then began muttering again as if there had not been any interruption.

Rand splashed a little more water on the cloth on Tam's forehead, pushed the waterbag back on the litter, and scrambled between the shafts again.

He started out as if he had had a good night's sleep, but the new strength did not last long. Fear masked his tiredness in the beginning, but though the fear remained, the mask melted away quickly. Soon he was back to stumbling forward, trying to ignore hunger and aching muscles. He concentrated on putting one foot in front of the other without tripping.

In his mind he pictured Emond's Field, shutters thrown back and the houses lit for Winternight, people shouting greetings as they passed back and forth on their visits, fiddles filling the streets with "Jaem's Folly" and "Heron on the Wing." Haral Luhhan would have one too many brandies and start singing "The Wind in the Barley" in a voice like a bullfrog—he always did—until his wife managed to shush him, and Cenn Buie would decide to prove he could still dance as well as ever, and Mat would have something planned that would not quite happen the way he intended, and everybody would know he was responsible even if no one could prove it. He could almost smile thinking about how it would be.

After a time Tam spoke up again.

"*Avendesora*. It's said it makes no seed, but they brought a cutting to Cairhien, a sapling. A royal gift of wonder for the King." Though he sounded angry, he was barely loud enough for Rand to understand. Anyone who could hear him would be able to hear the litter scraping across the ground, too. Rand kept on, only half listening. "They never make peace. Never. But they brought a sapling, as a sign of peace. A hundred years it grew. A hundred years of peace with those who make no peace with strangers. Why did he cut it down? Why? Blood was the price for *Avendoraldera*. Blood the price for Laman's pride." He faded off into muttering once more.

Tiredly Rand wondered what fever-dream Tam could be having now. *Avendesora*. The Tree of Life was supposed to have all sorts of miraculous qualities, but none of the stories mentioned any sapling, or any "they." There was only the one, and that belonged to the Green Man.

Only that morning he might have felt foolish at musing over the Green Man and the Tree of Life. They were only stories. *Are they?*

Trollocs were just stories this morning. Maybe all the stories were as real as the news the peddlers and merchants brought, all the gleeman's tales and all the stories told at night in front of the fireplace. Next he might actually meet the Green Man, or an Ogier giant, or a wild, black-veiled Aielman.

Tam was talking again, he realized, sometimes only murmuring, sometimes loud enough to understand. From time to time he stopped to pant for breath, then went on as if he thought he had been speaking the whole time.

". . . battles are always hot, even in the snow. Sweat heat. Blood heat. Only death is cool. Slope of the mountain . . . only place didn't stink of death. Had to get away from smell of it . . . sight of it. . . . heard a baby cry. Their women fight alongside the men, sometimes, but why they had let her come, I don't . . . gave birth there alone, before she died of her wounds. . . . covered the child with her cloak, but the wind . . . blown the cloak away. . . . child, blue with the cold. Should have been dead, too. . . . crying there. Crying in the snow. I couldn't just leave a child. . . . no children of our own. . . . always knew you wanted children. I knew you'd take it to your heart, Kari. Yes, lass. Rand is a good name. A good name."

Suddenly Rand's legs lost the little strength they had. Stumbling, he fell to his knees. Tam moaned with the jolt, and the strip of blanket cut into Rand's shoulders, but he was not aware of either. If a Trolloc had leaped up in front of him right then, he would just have stared at it. He looked over his shoulder at Tam, who had sunk back into wordless murmurs. *Fever-dreams,* he thought dully. Fevers always brought bad dreams, and this was a night for nightmares even without a fever.

"You are my father," he said aloud, stretching back a hand to touch Tam, "and I am—" The fever was worse. Much worse.

Grimly he struggled to his feet. Tam murmured something, but Rand refused to listen to any more. Throwing his weight against the improvised harness he tried to put all of his mind into taking one leaden step after another, into reaching the safety of Emond's Field. But he could not stop the echo in the back of his mind. *He's my father. It was just a fever-dream. He's my father. It was just a fever-dream. Light, who am I?*

CHAPTER
7

Out of the Woods

G ray first light came while Rand still trudged through the forest. At first he did not really see. When he finally did, he stared at the fading darkness in surprise. No matter what his eyes told him, he could hardly believe he had spent all night trying to travel the distance from the farm to Emond's Field. Of course, the Quarry Road by day, rocks and all, was a far cry from the woods by night. On the other hand, it seemed days since he had seen the black-cloaked rider on the road, weeks since he and Tam had gone in for their supper. He no longer felt the strip of cloth digging into his shoulders, but then he felt nothing in his shoulders except numbness, nor in his feet, for that matter. In between, it was another matter. His breath came in labored pants that had long since set his throat and lungs to burning, and hunger twisted his stomach into queasy sickness.

Tam had fallen silent some time before. Rand was not sure how long it had been since the murmurs ceased, but he did not dare halt now to check on Tam. If he stopped he would never be able to force himself to start out again. Anyway, whatever Tam's condition, he could do nothing beyond what he was doing. The only hope lay ahead, in the village. He tried wearily to increase his pace, but his wooden legs continued their slow plod. He barely even noticed the cold, or the wind.

Vaguely he caught the smell of woodsmoke. At least he was almost there if he could smell the village chimneys. A tired smile had only begun on his face, though, when it turned to a frown. Smoke lay heavy in the air—too heavy. With the weather, a fire might well be blazing on every hearth in the village, but the smoke was still too strong. In his mind he saw again the Trollocs on the road. Trollocs coming from the east, from the direction of Emond's Field. He peered ahead, trying to make out the first houses, and ready to shout for help at the first sight of anyone, even Cenn Buie or one of the Coplins. A small voice in the back of his head told him to hope someone there could still give help.

Suddenly a house became visible through the last bare-branched trees, and it was all he could do to keep his feet moving. Hope turning to sharp despair, he staggered into the village.

Charred piles of rubble stood in the places of half the houses of Emond's Field. Soot-coated brick chimneys thrust like dirty fingers from heaps of blackened timbers. Thin wisps of smoke still rose from the ruins. Grimy-faced villagers, some yet in their night clothes, poked through the ashes, here pulling free a cookpot, there simply prodding forlornly at the wreckage with a stick. What little had been rescued from the flames dotted the streets; tall mirrors and polished sideboards and highchests stood in the dust among chairs and tables buried under bedding, cooking utensils, and meager piles of clothing and personal belongings.

The destruction seemed scattered at random through the village. Five houses marched untouched in one row, while in another place a lone survivor stood surrounded by desolation.

On the far side of the Winespring Water, the three huge Bel Tine bonfires roared, tended by a cluster of men. Thick columns of black smoke bent northward with the wind, flecked by careless sparks. One of Master al'Vere's Dhurran stallions was dragging something Rand could not make out over the ground toward the Wagon Bridge, and the flames.

Before he was well out of the trees, a sooty-faced Haral Luhhan hurried to him, clutching a woodsman's axe in one thick-fingered hand. The burly blacksmith's ash-smeared nightshirt hung to his boots, the angry red welt of a burn across his chest showing through a ragged tear. He dropped to one knee beside the litter. Tam's eyes were closed, and his breathing came low and hard.

"Trollocs, boy?" Master Luhhan asked in a smoke-hoarse voice. "Here, too. Here, too. Well, we may have been luckier than anyone has a right to be, if you can credit it. He needs the Wisdom. Now where in the Light is she? Egwene!"

Egwene, running by with her arms full of bedsheets torn into bandages, looked around at them without slowing. Her eyes stared at something in the far distance; dark circles made them appear even larger than they actually were. Then she saw Rand and stopped, drawing a shuddering breath. "Oh, no, Rand, not your father? Is he . . . ? Come, I'll take you to Nynaeve."

Rand was too tired, too stunned, to speak. All through the night Emond's Field had been a haven, where he and Tam would be safe. Now all he could seem to do was stare in dismay at her smoke-stained dress. He noticed odd details as if they were very important. The buttons down the back of her dress were done up crookedly. And her hands were clean. He wondered why her hands were clean when smudges of soot marked her cheeks.

Master Luhhan seemed to understand what had come over him. Laying his axe across the shafts, the blacksmith picked up the rear of the litter and gave it a gentle push, prodding him to follow Egwene. He stumbled after her as if walking in his sleep. Briefly he wondered how Master Luhhan knew the creatures were Trollocs, but it was a fleeting thought. If Tam could recognize them, there was no reason why Haral Luhhan could not.

"All the stories are real," he muttered.

"So it seems, lad," the blacksmith said. "So it seems."

Rand only half heard. He was concentrating on following Egwene's slender shape. He had pulled himself together just enough to wish she would hurry, though in truth she was keeping her pace to what the two men could manage with their burden. She led them halfway down the Green, to the Calder house. Char blackened the edges of its thatch, and smut stained the whitewashed walls. Of the houses on either side only the foundation stones were left, and two piles of ash and burned timbers. One had been the house of Berin Thane, one of the miller's brothers. The other had been Abell Cauthon's. Mat's father. Even the chimneys had toppled.

"Wait here," Egwene said, and gave them a look as if expecting an answer. When they only stood there, she muttered something under her breath, then dashed inside.

"Mat," Rand said. "Is he . . . ?"

"He's alive," the blacksmith said. He set down his end of the litter

and straightened slowly. "I saw him a little while ago. It's a wonder
any of us are alive. The way they came after my house, and the forge,
you'd have thought I had gold and jewels in there. Alsbet cracked
one's skull with a frying pan. She took one look at the ashes of our
house this morning and set out hunting around the village with the
biggest hammer she could dig out of what's left of the forge, just in
case any of them hid instead of running away. I could almost pity the
thing if she finds one." He nodded to the Calder house. "Mistress
Calder and a few others took in some of those who were hurt, the
ones with no home of their own still standing. When the Wisdom's
seen Tam, we'll find him a bed. The inn, maybe. The Mayor offered
it already, but Nynaeve said the hurt folk would heal better if there
weren't so many of them together."

Rand sank to his knees. Shrugging out of his blanket harness, he
wearily busied himself with checking Tam's covers. Tam never moved
or made a sound, even when Rand's wooden hands jostled him. But
he was still breathing, at least. *My father. The other was just the fever
talking.* "What if they come back?" he said dully.

"The Wheel weaves as the Wheel wills," Master Luhhan said uneasily. "If they come back. . . . Well, they're gone, now. So we pick up
the pieces, build up what's been torn down." He sighed, his face going
slack as he knuckled the small of his back. For the first time Rand
realized that the heavyset man was as tired as he was himself, if not
more so. The blacksmith looked at the village, shaking his head. "I
don't suppose today will be much of a Bel Tine. But we'll make it
through. We always have." Abruptly he took up his axe, and his face
firmed. "There's work waiting for me. Don't you worry, lad. The Wisdom will take good care of him, and the Light will take care of us
all. And if the Light doesn't, well, we'll just take care of ourselves.
Remember, we're Two Rivers folk."

Still on his knees, Rand looked at the village as the blacksmith
walked away, really looked for the first time. Master Luhhan was right,
he thought, and was surprised that he was not surprised by what he
saw. People still dug in the ruins of their homes, but even in the short
time he had been there more of them had begun to move with a sense
of purpose. He could almost feel the growing determination. But he
wondered. They had seen Trollocs; had they seen the black-cloaked
rider? Had they felt his hatred?

Nynaeve and Egwene appeared from the Calder house, and he
sprang to his feet. Or rather, he tried to spring to his feet; it was more
of a stumbling lurch that almost put him on his face in the dust.

The Wisdom dropped to her knees beside the litter without giving him so much as a glance. Her face and dress were even dirtier than Egwene's, and the same dark circles lined her eyes, though her hands, too, were clean. She felt Tam's face and thumbed open his eyelids. With a frown she pulled down the coverings and eased the bandage aside to look at the wound. Before Rand could see what lay underneath she had replaced the wadded cloth. Sighing, she smoothed the blanket and cloak back up to Tam's neck with a gentle touch, as if tucking a child in for the night.

"There's nothing I can do," she said. She had to put her hands on her knees to straighten up. "I'm sorry, Rand."

For a moment he stood, not understanding, as she started back to the house, then he scrambled after her and pulled her around to face him. "He's dying," he cried.

"I know," she said simply, and he sagged with the matter-of-factness of it.

"You have to do something. You have to. You're the Wisdom."

Pain twisted her face, but only for an instant, then she was all hollow-eyed resolve again, her voice emotionless and firm. "Yes, I am. I know what I can do with my medicines, and I know when it's too late. Don't you think I would do something if I could? But I can't. I can't, Rand. And there are others who need me. People I *can* help."

"I brought him to you as quickly as I could," he mumbled. Even with the village in ruins, there had been the Wisdom for hope. With that gone, he was empty.

"I know you did," she said gently. She touched his cheek with her hand. "It isn't your fault. You did the best anyone could. I am sorry, Rand, but I have others to tend to. Our troubles are just beginning, I'm afraid."

Vacantly he stared after her until the door of the house closed behind her. He could not make any thought come except that she would not help.

Suddenly he was knocked back a step as Egwene cannoned into him, throwing her arms around him. Her hug was hard enough to bring a grunt from him any other time; now he only looked silently at the door behind which his hopes had vanished.

"I'm so sorry, Rand," she said against his chest. "Light, I wish there was something I could do."

Numbly he put his arms around her. "I know. I . . . I have to do something, Egwene. I don't know what, but I can't just let him. . . ." His voice broke, and she hugged him harder.

"Egwene!" At Nynaeve's shout from the house, Egwene jumped. "Egwene, I need you! And wash your hands again!"

She pushed herself free from Rand's arms. "She needs my help, Rand."

"Egwene!"

He thought he heard a sob as she spun away from him. Then she was gone, and he was left alone beside the litter. For a moment he looked down at Tam, feeling nothing but hollow helplessness. Suddenly his face hardened. "The Mayor will know what to do," he said, lifting the shafts once more. "The Mayor will know." Bran al'Vere always knew what to do. With weary obstinacy he set out for the Winespring Inn.

Another of the Dhurran stallions passed him, its harness straps tied around the ankles of a big shape draped with a dirty blanket. Arms covered with coarse hair dragged in the dirt behind the blanket, and one corner was pushed up to reveal a goat's horn. The Two Rivers was no place for stories to become horribly real. If Trollocs belonged anywhere it was in the world outside, for places where they had Aes Sedai and false Dragons and the Light alone knew what else come to life out of the tales of gleemen. Not the Two Rivers. Not Emond's Field.

As he made his way down the Green, people called to him, some from the ruins of their homes, asking if they could help. He heard them only as murmurs in the background, even when they walked alongside him for a distance as they spoke. Without really thinking about it he managed words that said he needed no help, that everything was being taken care of. When they left him, with worried looks, and sometimes a comment about sending Nynaeve to him, he noticed that just as little. All he let himself be aware of was the purpose he had fixed in his head. Bran al'Vere could do something to help Tam. What that could be he tried not to dwell on. But the Mayor would be able to do something, to think of something.

The inn had almost completely escaped the destruction that had taken half the village. A few scorch marks marred its walls, but the red roof tiles glittered in the sunlight as brightly as ever. All that was left of the peddler's wagon, though, were blackened iron wheel-rims leaning against the charred wagon box, now on the ground. The big round hoops that had held up the canvas cover slanted crazily, each at a different angle.

Thom Merrilin sat cross-legged on the old foundation stones, carefully snipping singed edges from the patches on his cloak with a pair of small scissors. He set down cloak and scissors when Rand drew near. Without asking if Rand needed or wanted help, he hopped down and picked up the back of the litter.

"Inside? Of course, of course. Don't you worry, boy. Your Wisdom will take care of him. I've watched her work, since last night, and she has a deft touch and a sure skill. It could be a lot worse. Some died last night. Not many, perhaps, but any at all are too many for me. Old Fain just disappeared, and that's the worst of all. Trollocs will eat anything. You should thank the Light your father's still here, and alive for the Wisdom to heal."

Rand blotted out the words—*He* is *my father!*—reducing the voice to meaningless sound that he noticed no more than a fly's buzzing. He could not bear any more sympathy, any more attempts to boost his spirits. Not now. Not until Bran al'Vere told him how to help Tam.

Suddenly he found himself facing something scrawled on the inn door, a curving line scratched with a charred stick, a charcoal teardrop balanced on its point. So much had happened that it hardly surprised him to find the Dragon's Fang marked on the door of the Winespring Inn. Why anyone would want to accuse the innkeeper or his family of evil, or bring the inn bad luck, was beyond him, but the night had convinced him of one thing. Anything was possible. Anything at all.

At a push from the gleeman he lifted the latch, and went in.

The common room was empty except for Bran al'Vere, and cold, too, for no one had found time to lay a fire. The Mayor sat at one of the tables, dipping his pen in an inkwell with a frown of concentration on his face and his gray-fringed head bent over a sheet of parchment. Nightshirt tucked hastily into his trousers and bagging around his considerable waist, he absently scratched at one bare foot with the toes of the other. His feet were dirty, as if he had been outside more than once without bothering about boots, despite the cold. "What's your trouble?" he demanded without looking up. "Be quick with it. I have two dozen things to do right this minute, and more that should have been done an hour ago. So I have little time or patience. Well? Out with it!"

"Master al'Vere?" Rand said. "It's my father."

The Mayor's head jerked up. "Rand? Tam!" He threw down the pen and knocked over his chair as he leaped up. "Perhaps the Light hasn't abandoned us altogether. I was afraid you were both dead. Bela galloped into the village an hour after the Trollocs left, lathered and blowing as if she'd run all the way from the farm, and I thought. . . . No time for that, now. We'll take him upstairs." He seized the rear of the litter, shouldering the gleeman out of the way. "You go get the Wisdom, Master Merrilin. And tell her I said hurry, or I'll know the reason why! Rest easy, Tam. We'll soon have you in a good, soft bed. Go, gleeman, go!"

Thom Merrilin vanished through the doorway before Rand could speak. "Nynaeve wouldn't do anything. She said she couldn't help him. I knew . . . I hoped you'd think of something."

Master al'Vere looked at Tam more sharply, then shook his head. "We will see, boy. We will see." But he no longer sounded confident. "Let's get him into a bed. He can rest easy, at least."

Rand let himself be prodded toward the stairs at the back of the common room. He tried hard to keep his certainty that somehow Tam would be all right, but it had been thin to begin with, he realized, and the sudden doubt in the Mayor's voice shook him.

On the second floor of the inn, at the front, were half a dozen snug, well-appointed rooms with windows overlooking the Green. Mostly they were used by the peddlers, or people down from Watch Hill or up from Deven Ride, but the merchants who came each year were often surprised to find such comfortable rooms. Three of them were taken now, and the Mayor hurried Rand to one of the unused ones.

Quickly the down comforter and blankets were stripped back on the wide bed, and Tam was transferred to the thick feather mattress, with goose-down pillows tucked under his head. He made no sound beyond hoarse breathing as he was moved, not even a groan, but the Mayor brushed away Rand's concern, telling him to set a fire to take the chill off the room. While Rand dug wood and kindling from the woodbox next to the fireplace, Bran threw back the curtains on the window, letting in the morning light, then began to gently wash Tam's face. By the time the gleeman returned, the blaze on the hearth was warming the room.

"She will not come," Thom Merrilin announced as he stalked into the room. He glared at Rand, his bushy white brows drawing down sharply. "You didn't tell me she had seen him already. She almost took my head off."

"I thought . . . I don't know . . . maybe the Mayor could do something, could make her see. . . ." Hands clenched in anxious fists, Rand turned from the fireplace to Bran. "Master al'Vere, what can I do?" The rotund man shook his head helplessly. He laid a freshly dampened cloth on Tam's forehead and avoided meeting Rand's eye. "I can't just watch him die, Master al'Vere. I have to do something." The gleeman shifted as if to speak. Rand rounded on him eagerly. "Do you have an idea? I'll try anything."

"I was just wondering," Thom said, tamping his long-stemmed pipe with his thumb, "if the Mayor knew who scrawled the Dragon's Fang on his door." He peered into the bowl, then looked at Tam and replaced the unlit pipe between his teeth with a sigh. "Someone seems not to like him anymore. Or maybe it's his guests they don't like."

Rand gave him a disgusted look and turned away to stare into the fire. His thoughts danced like the flames, and like the flames they concentrated fixedly on one thing. He would not give up. He could not just stand there and watch Tam die. *My father,* he thought fiercely. *My father.* Once the fever was gone, that could be cleared up as well. But the fever first. Only, how?

Bran al'Vere's mouth tightened as he looked at Rand's back, and the glare he directed at the gleeman would have given a bear pause, but Thom just waited expectantly as if he had not noticed it.

"It's probably the work of one of the Congars, or a Coplin," the Mayor said finally, "though the Light alone knows which. They're a large brood, and if there's ill to be said of someone, or even if there isn't, they'll say it. They make Cenn Buie sound honey-tongued."

"That wagonload who came in just before dawn?" the gleeman asked. "They hadn't so much as smelled a Trolloc, and all they wanted to know was when Festival was going to start, as if they couldn't see half the village in ashes."

Master al'Vere nodded grimly. "One branch of the family. But none of them are very different. That fool Darl Coplin spent half the night demanding I put Mistress Moiraine and Master Lan out of the inn, out of the village, as if there would be any village at all left without them."

Rand had only half listened to the conversation, but this last tugged him to speak. "What did they do?"

"Why, she called ball lightning out of a clear night sky," Master al'Vere replied. "Sent it darting straight at the Trollocs. You've seen trees shattered by it. The Trollocs stood it no better."

"Moiraine?" Rand said incredulously, and the Mayor nodded.

"Mistress Moiraine. And Master Lan was a whirlwind with that sword of his. His sword? The man himself is a weapon, and in ten places at once, or so it seemed. Burn me, but I still wouldn't believe it if I couldn't step outside and see. . . ." He rubbed a hand over his bald head. "Winternight visits just beginning, our hands full of presents and honeycakes and our heads full of wine, then the dogs snarling, and suddenly the two of them burst out of the inn, running through the village, shouting about Trollocs. I thought they'd had too much wine. After all . . . Trollocs? Then, before anyone knew what was happening, those . . . those things were right in the streets with us, slashing at people with their swords, torching houses, howling to freeze a man's blood." He made a sound of disgust in his throat. "We just ran like chickens with a fox in the henyard till Master Lan put some backbone into us."

"No need to be so hard," Thom said. "You did as well as anyone could. Not every Trolloc lying out there fell to the two of them."

"Umm . . . yes, well." Master al'Vere gave himself a shake. "It's still almost too much to believe. An Aes Sedai in Emond's Field. And Master Lan is a Warder."

"An Aes Sedai?" Rand whispered. "She can't be. I talked to her. She isn't. . . . She doesn't. . . ."

"Did you think they wore signs?" the Mayor said wryly. "'Aes Sedai' painted across their backs, and maybe, 'Danger, stay away'?" Suddenly he slapped his forehead. "Aes Sedai. I'm an old fool, and losing my wits. There's a chance, Rand, if you're willing to take it. I can't tell you to do it, and I don't know if I'd have the nerve, if it were me."

"A chance?" Rand said. "I'll take any chance, if it'll help."

"Aes Sedai can heal, Rand. Burn me, lad, you've heard the stories. They can cure where medicines fail. Gleeman, you should have remembered that better than I. Gleemen's tales are full of Aes Sedai. Why didn't you speak up, instead of letting me flail around?"

"I'm a stranger here," Thom said, looking longingly at his unlit pipe, "and Goodman Coplin isn't the only one who wants nothing to do with Aes Sedai. Best the idea came from you."

"An Aes Sedai," Rand muttered, trying to make the woman who had smiled at him fit the stories. Help from an Aes Sedai was sometimes worse than no help at all, so the stories said, like poison in a pie, and their gifts always had a hook in them, like fishbait. Suddenly the coin in his pocket, the coin Moiraine had given him, seemed like a burning coal. It was all he could do not to rip it out of his coat and throw it out the window.

"Nobody wants to get involved with Aes Sedai, lad," the Mayor said slowly. "It is the only chance I can see, but it's still no small decision. I cannot make it for you, but I have seen nothing but good from Mistress Moiraine . . . Moiraine Sedai, I should call her, I suppose. Sometimes"—he gave a meaningful look at Tam—"you have to take a chance, even if it's a poor one."

"Some of the stories are exaggerated, in a way," Thom added, as if the words were being dragged from him. "Some of them. Besides, boy, what choice do you have?"

"None," Rand sighed. Tam still had not moved a muscle; his eyes were sunken as if he had been sick a week. "I'll . . . I'll go find her."

"The other side of the bridges," the gleeman said, "where they are . . . disposing of the dead Trollocs. But be careful, boy. Aes Sedai do what they do for reasons of their own, and they aren't always the reasons others think."

The last was a shout that followed Rand through the door. He had to hold onto the sword hilt to keep the scabbard from tangling in his legs as he ran, but he would not take the time to remove it. He clattered down the stairs and dashed out of the inn, tiredness forgotten for the moment. A chance for Tam, however small, was enough to overcome a night without sleep, for a time at least. That the chance came from an Aes Sedai, or what the price of it might be, he did not want to consider. And as for actually facing an Aes Sedai. . . . He took a deep breath and tried to move faster.

The bonfires stood well beyond the last houses to the north, on the Westwood side of the road to Watch Hill. The wind still carried the oily black columns of smoke away from the village, but even so a sickly sweet stink filled the air, like a roast left hours too long on the spit. Rand gagged at the smell, then swallowed hard when he realized its source. A fine thing to do with Bel Tine fires. The men tending the fires had cloths tied over their noses and mouths, but their grimaces made it plain the vinegar dampening the cloths was not enough. Even if it did kill the stench, they still knew the stench was there, and they still knew what they were doing.

Two of the men were untying the harness straps of one of the big Dhurrans from a Trolloc's ankles. Lan, squatting beside the body, had tossed back the blanket enough to reveal the Trolloc's shoulders and goat-snouted head. As Rand trotted up the Warder unfastened a metal badge, a blood-red enameled trident, from one spiked shoulder of the Trolloc's shirt of black mail.

"Ko'bal," he announced. He bounced the badge on his palm and snatched it out of the air with a growl. "That makes seven bands so far."

Moiraine, seated cross-legged on the ground a short distance off, shook her head tiredly. A walking staff, covered from end to end in carved vines and flowers, lay across her knees, and her dress had the rumpled look of having been worn too long. "Seven bands. Seven! That many have not acted together since the Trolloc Wars. Bad news piles on bad news. I am afraid, Lan. I thought we had gained a march, but we may be further behind than ever."

Rand stared at her, unable to speak. An Aes Sedai. He had been trying to convince himself that she would not look any different now that he knew who . . . what he was looking at, and to his surprise she did not. She was no longer quite so pristine, not with wisps of her hair sticking out in all directions and a faint streak of soot across her nose, yet not really different, either. Surely there must be something about an Aes Sedai to mark her for what she was. On the other hand, if outward appearance reflected what was inside, and if the stories were true, then she should look closer to a Trolloc than to a more than handsome woman whose dignity was not dented by sitting in the dirt. And she could help Tam. Whatever the cost, there was that before anything else.

He took a deep breath. "Mistress Moiraine . . . I mean, Moiraine Sedai." Both turned to look at him, and he froze under her gaze. Not the calm, smiling gaze he remembered from the Green. Her face was tired, but her dark eyes were a hawk's eyes. Aes Sedai. Breakers of the world. Puppeteers who pulled strings and made thrones and nations dance in designs only the women from Tar Valon knew.

"A little more light in the darkness," the Aes Sedai murmured. She raised her voice. "How are your dreams, Rand al'Thor?"

He stared at her. "My dreams?"

"A night like that can give a man bad dreams, Rand. If you have nightmares, you must tell me of it. I can help with bad dreams, sometimes."

"There's nothing wrong with my. . . . It's my father. He's hurt. It's not much more than a scratch, but the fever is burning him up. The Wisdom won't help. She says she can't. But the stories—" She raised an eyebrow, and he stopped and swallowed hard. *Light, is there a story with an Aes Sedai where she isn't a villain?* He looked at the Warder, but Lan appeared more interested in the dead Trolloc than in anything Rand might say. Fumbling his way under her eyes, he went on. "I . . . ah . . . it's said Aes Sedai can heal. If you can help him . . . anything you can do for him . . . whatever the cost. . . . I mean. . . ." He took a deep breath and finished up in a rush. "I'll pay any price in my power if you help him. Anything."

"Any price," Moiraine mused, half to herself. "We will speak of prices later, Rand, if at all. I can make no promises. Your Wisdom knows what she is about. I will do what I can, but it is beyond my power to stop the Wheel from turning."

"Death comes sooner or later to everyone," the Warder said grimly, "unless they serve the Dark One, and only fools are willing to pay that price."

Moiraine made a clucking sound. "Do not be so gloomy, Lan. We have some reason to celebrate. A small one, but a reason." She used the staff to pull herself to her feet. "Take me to your father, Rand. I will help him as much as I am able. Too many here have refused to let me help at all. They have heard the stories, too," she added dryly.

"He's at the inn," Rand said. "This way. And thank you. Thank you!"

They followed, but his pace took him quickly ahead. He slowed impatiently for them to catch up, then darted ahead again and had to wait again.

"Please hurry," he urged, so caught up in actually getting help for Tam that he never considered the temerity of prodding an Aes Sedai. "The fever is burning him up."

Lan glared at him. "Can't you see she's tired? Even with an *angreal,* what she did last night was like running around the village with a sack of stones on her back. I don't know that you are worth it, sheepherder, no matter what she says."

Rand blinked and held his tongue.

"Gently, my friend," Moiraine said. Without slowing her pace, she reached up to pat the Warder's shoulder. He towered over her protectively, as if he could give her strength just by being close. "You think only of taking care of me. Why should he not think the same of his father?" Lan scowled, but fell silent. "I am coming as quickly as I can, Rand, I promise you."

The fierceness of her eyes, or the calm of her voice—not gentle, exactly; more firmly in command—Rand did not know which to believe. Or perhaps they did go together. Aes Sedai. He was committed, now. He matched his stride to theirs, and tried not to think of what the price might be that they would talk about later.

CHAPTER
8

A Place of Safety

While he was still coming through the door Rand's eyes went to his father—his father no matter what *anyone* said. Tam had not moved an inch; his eyes were still shut, and his breath came in labored gasps, low and rasping. The white-haired gleeman cut off a conversation with the Mayor—who was bent over the bed again, tending Tam—and gave Moiraine an uneasy look. The Aes Sedai ignored him. Indeed, she ignored everyone except for Tam, but at him she stared with an intent frown.

Thom stuck his unlit pipe between his teeth, then snatched it out again and glowered at it. "Man cannot even smoke in peace," he muttered. "I had better make sure some farmer doesn't steal my cloak to keep his cow warm. At least I can have my pipe out there." He hurried out of the room.

Lan stared after him, his angular face as expressionless as a rock. "I do not like that man. There is something about him I don't trust. I did not see a hair of him last night."

"He was there," Bran said, watching Moiraine uncertainly. "He must have been. His cloak did not get singed in front of the fireplace."

Rand did not care if the gleeman had spent the night hiding in the stable. "My father?" he said to Moiraine pleadingly.

Bran opened his mouth, but before he could speak Moiraine said, "Leave me with him, Master al'Vere. There is nothing you can do here now except get in my way."

For a minute Bran hesitated, torn between dislike of being ordered about in his own inn and reluctance to disobey an Aes Sedai. Finally, he straightened to clap Rand on the shoulder. "Come along, boy. Let us leave Moiraine Sedai to her . . . ah . . . her. . . . There's plenty you can give me a hand with downstairs. Before you know it Tam will be shouting for his pipe and a mug of ale."

"Can I stay?" Rand spoke to Moiraine, though she did not really seem to be aware of anyone besides Tam. Bran's hand tightened, but Rand ignored him. "Please? I'll keep out of your way. You won't even know I am here. He's my father," he added with a fierceness that startled him and widened the Mayor's eyes in surprise. Rand hoped the others put it down to tiredness, or the strain of dealing with an Aes Sedai.

"Yes, yes," Moiraine said impatiently. She had tossed her cloak and staff carelessly across the only chair in the room, and now she pushed up the sleeves of her gown, baring her arms to her elbows. Her attention never really left Tam, even while she spoke. "Sit over there. And you, too, Lan." She gestured vaguely in the direction of a long bench against the wall. Her eyes traveled slowly from Tam's feet to his head, but Rand had the prickly feeling that she was looking *beyond* him in some fashion. "You may talk if you wish," she went on absently, "but do it quietly. Now, you go, Master al'Vere. This is a sickroom, not a gathering hall. See that I am not disturbed."

The Mayor grumbled under his breath, though not loudly enough to catch her attention, of course, squeezed Rand's shoulder again, then obediently, if reluctantly, closed the door behind him.

Muttering to herself, the Aes Sedai knelt beside the bed and rested her hands lightly on Tam's chest. She closed her eyes, and for a long time she neither moved nor made a sound.

In the stories Aes Sedai wonders were always accompanied by flashes and thunderclaps, or other signs to indicate mighty works and great powers. *The* Power. The One Power, drawn from the True Source that drove the Wheel of Time. That was not something Rand wanted to think about, the Power involved with Tam, himself in the same room where the Power might be used. In the same village was bad enough. For all he could tell, though, Moiraine might just as well have gone to sleep. But he thought Tam's breathing sounded easier. She must be doing something. So intent was he that he jumped when Lan spoke softly.

"That is a fine weapon you wear. Is there by chance a heron on the blade, as well?"

For a moment Rand stared at the Warder, not grasping what it was he was talking about. He had completely forgotten Tam's sword in the lather of dealing with an Aes Sedai. It did not seem so heavy anymore. "Yes, there is. What is she doing?"

"I'd not have thought to find a heron-mark sword in a place like this," Lan said.

"It belongs to my father." He glanced at Lan's sword, the hilt just visible at the edge of his cloak; the two swords did look a good deal alike, except that no herons showed on the Warder's. He swung his eyes back to the bed. Tam's breathing did sound easier; the rasp was gone. He was sure of it. "He bought it a long time ago."

"Strange thing for a sheepherder to buy."

Rand spared a sidelong look for Lan. For a stranger to wonder about the sword was prying. For a Warder to do it. . . . Still, he felt he had to say something. "He never had any use for it, that I know of. He said it *had* no use. Until last night, anyway. I didn't even know he had it till then."

"He called it useless, did he? He must not always have thought so." Lan touched the scabbard at Rand's waist briefly with one finger. "There are places where the heron is a symbol of the master swordsman. That blade must have traveled a strange road to end up with a sheepherder in the Two Rivers."

Rand ignored the unspoken question. Moiraine still had not moved. *Was* the Aes Sedai doing anything? He shivered and rubbed his arms, not sure he really wanted to know what she was doing. An Aes Sedai.

A question of his own popped into his head then, one he did not want to ask, one he needed an answer to. "The Mayor—" He cleared his throat, and took a deep breath. "The Mayor said the only reason there's anything left of the village is because of you and her." He made himself look at the Warder. "If you had been told about a man in the woods . . . a man who made people afraid just by looking at them . . . would that have warned you? A man whose horse doesn't make any noise? And the wind doesn't touch his cloak? Would you have known what was going to happen? Could you and Moiraine Sedai have stopped it if you'd known about him?"

"Not without half a dozen of my sisters," Moiraine said, and Rand started. She still knelt by the bed, but she had taken her hands from Tam and half turned to face the two of them on the bench. Her voice never raised, but her eyes pinned Rand to the wall. "Had I known when I left Tar Valon that I would find Trollocs and Myrddraal here, I would have brought half a dozen of them, a dozen, if I had to drag them by the scruffs of their necks. By myself, a month's warning would have made little difference. Perhaps none. There is only so much one person can do, even calling on the One Power, and there were probably well over a hundred Trollocs scattered around this district last night. An entire fist."

"It would still have been good to know," Lan said sharply, the sharpness directed at Rand. "When did you see him, exactly, and where?"

"That's of no consequence now," Moiraine said. "I will not have the boy thinking he is to blame for something when he is not. I am as much to blame. That accursed raven yesterday, the way it behaved, should have warned me. And you, too, my old friend." Her tongue clicked angrily. "I was overconfident to the point of arrogance, sure that the Dark One's touch could not have spread so far. Nor so heavily, not yet. So sure."

Rand blinked. "The raven? I don't understand."

"Carrion eaters." Lan's mouth twisted in distaste. "The Dark One's minions often find spies among creatures that feed on death. Ravens and crows, mainly. Rats, in the cities, sometimes."

A quick shiver ran through Rand. Ravens and crows as spies of the Dark One? There were ravens and crows everywhere now. The Dark One's touch, Moiraine had said. The Dark One was always there—he knew that—but if you tried to walk in the Light, tried to live a good life, and did not name him, he could not harm you. That was what everybody believed, what everybody learned with his mother's milk. But Moiraine seemed to be saying. . . .

His glance fell on Tam, and everything else was pushed right out of his head. His father's face was noticeably less flushed than it had been, and his breathing sounded almost normal. Rand would have leaped up if Lan had not caught his arm. "You've done it."

Moiraine shook her head and sighed. "Not yet. I hope it is only not yet. Trolloc weapons are made at forges in the valley called Thakan'dar, on the very slopes of Shayol Ghul itself. Some of them take a taint from that place, a stain of evil in the metal. Those tainted blades make wounds that will not heal unaided, or cause deadly fevers, strange sicknesses that medicines cannot touch. I have soothed your father's pain, but the mark, the taint, is still in him. Left alone, it will grow again, and consume him."

"But you won't leave it alone." Rand's words were half plea, half command. He was shocked to realize he had spoken to an Aes Sedai like that, but she seemed not to notice his tone.

"I will not," she agreed simply. "I am very tired, Rand, and I have had no chance to rest since last night. Ordinarily it would not matter, but for this kind of hurt. . . . This"—she took a small bundle of white silk from her pouch—"is an *angreal.*" She saw his expression. "You know of *angreal,* then. Good."

Unconsciously he leaned back, further away from her and what she held. A few stories mentioned *angreal,* those relics of the Age of Legends that Aes Sedai used to perform their greatest wonders. He was startled to see her unwrap a smooth ivory figurine, age-darkened to deep brown. No longer than her hand, it was a woman in flowing robes, with long hair falling about her shoulders.

"We have lost the making of these," she said. "So much is lost, perhaps never to be found again. So few remain, the Amyrlin Seat almost did not allow me to take this one. It is well for Emond's Field, and for your father, that she did give her permission. But you must not hope too much. Now, even with it, I can do little more than I could have without it yesterday, and the taint is strong. It has had time to fester."

"You can help him," Rand said fervently. "I know you can."

Moiraine smiled, a bare curving of her lips. "We shall see." Then she turned back to Tam. One hand she laid on his forehead; the other cupped the ivory figure. Eyes closed, her face took on a look of concentration. She scarcely seemed to breathe.

"That rider you spoke of," Lan said quietly, "the one who made you afraid—that was surely a Myrddraal."

"A Myrddraal!" Rand exclaimed. "But Fades are twenty feet tall and. . . ." The words faded away under the Warder's mirthless grin.

"Sometimes, sheepherder, stories make things larger than truth. Believe me, the truth is big enough with a Halfman. Halfman, Lurk, Fade, Shadowman; the name depends on the land you're in, but they all mean Myrddraal. Fades are Trolloc spawn, throwbacks almost to the human stock the Dreadlords used to make the Trollocs. Almost. But if the human strain is made stronger, so is the taint that twists the Trollocs. Halfmen have powers of a kind, the sort that stem from the Dark One. Only the weakest Aes Sedai would fail to be a match for a Fade, one against one, but many a good man and true has fallen to them. Since the wars that ended the Age of Legends, since the Forsaken were bound, they have been the brain that tells the Trolloc fists where to strike. In the days of the Trolloc Wars, Halfmen led the Trollocs in battle, under the Dreadlords."

"He scared me," Rand said faintly. "He just looked at me, and. . . ." He shivered.

"No need for shame, sheepherder. They scare me, too. I've seen men who have been soldiers all their lives freeze like a bird facing a snake when they confronted a Halfman. In the north, in the Borderlands along the Great Blight, there is a saying. The look of the Eyeless is fear."

"The Eyeless?" Rand said, and Lan nodded.

"Myrddraal see like eagles, in darkness or in light, but they have no eyes. I can think of few things more dangerous than facing a Myrddraal. Moiraine Sedai and I both tried to kill the one that was here last night, and we failed every time. Halfmen have the Dark One's own luck."

Rand swallowed. "A Trolloc said the Myrddraal wanted to talk to me. I didn't know what it meant."

Lan's head jerked up; his eyes were blue stones. "You *talked* to a Trolloc?"

"Not exactly," Rand stammered. The Warder's gaze held him like a trap. "It talked to me. It said it wouldn't hurt me, that the Myrddraal wanted to talk to me. Then it tried to kill me." He licked his lips and rubbed his hand along the nobby leather of the sword hilt. In short, choppy sentences he explained about returning to the farmhouse. "I killed it, instead," he finished. "By accident, really. It jumped at me, and I had the sword in my hand."

Lan's face softened slightly, if rock could be said to soften. "Even so, that is something to speak of, sheepherder. Until last night there were few men south of the Borderlands who could say they had seen a Trolloc, much less killed one."

"And fewer still who have slain a Trolloc alone and unaided," Moiraine said wearily. "It is done, Rand. Lan, help me up."

The Warder sprang to her side, but he was no quicker than Rand darting to the bed. Tam's skin was cool to the touch, though his face had a pale, washed-out look, as if he had spent far too long out of the sun. His eyes were still closed, but he drew the deep breaths of normal sleep.

"He will be all right now?" Rand asked anxiously.

"With rest, yes," Moiraine said. "A few weeks in bed, and he will
be as good as ever." She walked unsteadily, despite holding Lan's arm.
He swept her cloak and staff from the chair cushion for her to sit, and
she eased herself down with a sigh. With a slow care she rewrapped
the *angreal* and returned it to her pouch.

Rand's shoulders shook; he bit his lip to keep from laughing. At the
same time he had to scrub a hand across his eyes to clear away tears.
"Thank you."

"In the Age of Legends," Moiraine went on, "some Aes Sedai could
fan life and health to flame if only the smallest spark remained. Those
days are gone, though—perhaps forever. So much was lost; not just
the making of *angreal*. So much that could be done which we dare not
even dream of, if we remember it at all. There are far fewer of us
now. Some talents are all but gone, and many that remain seem
weaker. Now there must be both will and strength for the body to
draw on, or even the strongest of us can do nothing in the way of
Healing. It is fortunate that your father is a strong man, both in body
and spirit. As it is, he used up much of his strength in the fight for
life, but all that is left now is for him to recuperate. That will take
time, but the taint is gone."

"I can never repay you," he told her without taking his eyes from
Tam, "but anything I can do for you, I will. Anything at all." He
remembered the talk of prices, then, and his promise. Kneeling beside
Tam he meant it even more than before, but it still was not easy to
look at her. "Anything. As long as it does not hurt the village, or my
friends."

Moiraine raised a hand dismissively. "If you think it is necessary. I
would like to talk with you, anyway. You will no doubt leave at the
same time we do, and we can speak at length then."

"Leave!" he exclaimed, scrambling to his feet. "Is it really that bad?
Everyone looked to me as if they were ready to start rebuilding. We
are pretty settled folk in the Two Rivers. Nobody ever leaves."

"Rand—"

"And where would we go? Padan Fain said the weather is just as
bad everywhere else. He's . . . he was . . . the peddler. The
Trollocs. . . ." Rand swallowed, wishing Thom Merrilin had not told
him what Trollocs ate. "The best I can see to do is stay right here
where we belong, in the Two Rivers, and put things back together.
We have crops in the ground, and it has to warm enough for the shearing, soon. I don't know who started this talk about leaving—one of
the Coplins, I'll bet—but whoever it was—"

"Sheepherder," Lan broke in, "you talk when you should be listening."

He blinked at both of them. He had been half babbling, he realized, and he had rambled on while she tried to talk. While an Aes Sedai tried to talk. He wondered what to say, how to apologize, but Moiraine smiled while he was still thinking.

"I understand how you feel, Rand," she said, and he had the uncomfortable feeling that she really did. "Think no more of it." Her mouth tightened, and she shook her head. "I have handled this badly, I see. I should have rested, first, I suppose. It is you who will be leaving, Rand. You who must leave, for the sake of your village."

"Me?" He cleared his throat and tried again. "Me?" It sounded a little better this time. "Why do I have to go? I don't understand any of this. I don't want to go anywhere."

Moiraine looked at Lan, and the Warder unfolded his arms. He looked at Rand from under his leather headband, and Rand had the feeling of being weighed on invisible scales again. "Did you know," Lan said suddenly, "that some homes were not attacked?"

"Half the village is in ashes," he protested, but the Warder waved it away.

"Some houses were only torched to create confusion. The Trollocs ignored them afterwards, and the people who fled from them as well, unless they actually got in the way of the true attack. Most of the people who've come in from the outlying farms never saw a hair of a Trolloc, and that only at a distance. Most never knew there was any trouble until they saw the village."

"I did hear about Darl Coplin," Rand said slowly. "I suppose it just didn't sink in."

"Two farms were attacked," Lan went on. "Yours and one other. Because of Bel Tine everyone who lived at the second farm was already in the village. Many people were saved because the Myrddraal was ignorant of Two Rivers customs. Festival and Winternight made its task all but impossible, but it did not know that."

Rand looked at Moiraine, leaning back in the chair, but she said nothing, only watched him, a finger laid across her lips. "Our farm, and who else's?" he asked finally.

"The Aybara farm," Lan replied. "Here in Emond's Field, they struck first at the forge, and the blacksmith's house, and Master Cauthon's house."

Rand's mouth was suddenly dry. "That's crazy," he managed to get out, then jumped as Moiraine straightened.

"Not crazy, Rand," she said. "Purposeful. The Trollocs did not come to Emond's Field by happenstance, and they did not do what they did for the pleasure of killing and burning, however much that delighted them. They knew what, or rather who, they were after. The Trollocs came to kill or capture young men of a certain age who live near Emond's Field."

"My age?" Rand's voice shook, and he did not care. "Light! Mat. What about Perrin?"

"Alive and well," Moiraine assured him, "if a trifle sooty."

"Ban Crawe and Lem Thane?"

"Were never in any danger," Lan said. "At least, no more than anyone else."

"But they saw the rider, the Fade, too, and they're the same age as I am."

"Master Crawe's house was not even damaged," Moiraine said, "and the miller and his family slept through half the attack before the noise woke them. Ban is ten months older than you, and Lem eight months younger." She smiled dryly at his surprise. "I told you I asked questions. And I also said young men of a *certain* age. You and your two friends are within weeks of one another. It was you three the Myrddraal sought, and none others."

Rand shifted uneasily, wishing she would not look at him like that, as if her eyes could pierce his brain and read what lay in every corner of it. "What would they want with us? We're just farmers, shepherds."

"That is a question that has no answer in the Two Rivers," Moiraine said quietly, "but the answer is important. Trollocs where they have not been seen in almost two thousand years tells us that much."

"Lots of stories tell about Trolloc raids," Rand said stubbornly. "We just never had one here before. Warders fight Trollocs all the time."

Lan snorted. "Boy, I expect to fight Trollocs along the Great Blight, but not here, nearly six hundred leagues to the south. That was as hot a raid last night as I'd expect to see in Shienar, or any of the Borderlands."

"In one of you," Moiraine said, "or all three, there is something the Dark One fears."

"That . . . that's impossible." Rand stumbled to the window and stared out at the village, at the people working among the ruins. "I don't care what's happened, that is just impossible." Something on the Green caught his eye. He stared, then realized it was the blackened stump of the Spring Pole. A fine Bel Tine, with a peddler, and a glee-man, and strangers. He shivered, and shook his head violently. "No.

No, I'm a shepherd. The Dark One can't be interested in me."

"It took a great deal of effort," Lan said grimly, "to bring so many Trollocs so far without raising a hue and cry from the Borderlands to Caemlyn and beyond. I wish I knew how they did it. Do you really believe they went to all that bother just to burn a few houses?"

"They will be back," Moiraine added.

Rand had his mouth open to argue with Lan, but that brought him up short. He spun to face her. "Back? Can't you stop them? You did last night, and you were surprised, then. Now you know they are here."

"Perhaps," Moiraine replied. "I could send to Tar Valon for some of my sisters; they might have time to make the journey before we need them. The Myrddraal knows *I* am here, too, and it probably will not attack—not openly, at least—lacking reinforcements, more Myrddraal and more Trollocs. With enough Aes Sedai and enough Warders, the Trollocs can be beaten off, though I cannot say how many battles it will take."

A vision danced in his head, of Emond's Field all in ashes. All the farms burned. And Watch Hill, and Deven Ride, and Taren Ferry. All ashes and blood. "No," he said, and felt a wrenching inside as if he had lost his grip on something. "That's why I have to leave, isn't it? The Trollocs won't come back if I am not here." A last trace of obstinacy made him add, "If they really are after me."

Moiraine's eyebrows raised as if she were surprised that he was not convinced, but Lan said, "Are you willing to bet your village on it, sheepherder? Your whole Two Rivers?"

Rand's stubbornness faded. "No," he said again, and felt that emptiness inside again, too. "Perrin and Mat have to go, too, don't they?" Leaving the Two Rivers. Leaving his home and his father. At least Tam would get better. At least he would be able to hear him say all that on the Quarry Road had been nonsense. "We could go to Baerlon, I suppose, or even Caemlyn. I've heard there are more people in Caemlyn than in the whole Two Rivers. We'd be safe there." He tried out a laugh that sounded hollow. "I used to daydream about seeing Caemlyn. I never thought it would come about like this."

There was a long silence, then Lan said, "I would not count on Caemlyn for safety. If the Myrddraal want you badly enough, they will find a way. Walls are a poor bar to a Halfman. And you would be a fool not to believe they want you very badly indeed."

Rand thought his spirits had sunk as low as they possibly could, but at that they slid deeper.

"There is a place of safety," Moiraine said softly, and Rand's ears pricked up to listen. "In Tar Valon you would be among Aes Sedai and Warders. Even during the Trolloc Wars the forces of the Dark One feared to attack the Shining Walls. The one attempt was their greatest defeat until the very end. And Tar Valon holds all the knowledge we Aes Sedai have gathered since the Time of Madness. Some fragments even date from the Age of Legends. In Tar Valon, if anywhere, you will be able to learn why the Myrddraal want you. Why the Father of Lies wants you. That I can promise."

A journey all the way to Tar Valon was almost beyond thinking. A journey to a place where he would be surrounded by Aes Sedai. Of course, Moiraine had healed Tam—or it looked as if she had, at least—but there were all those stories. It was uncomfortable enough to be in a room with one Aes Sedai, but to be in a city full of them. . . . And she still had not demanded her price. There was always a price, so the stories said.

"How long will my father sleep?" he asked at last. "I . . . I have to tell him. He shouldn't just wake and find me gone." He thought he heard Lan give a sigh of relief. He looked at the Warder curiously, but Lan's face was as expressionless as ever.

"It is unlikely he will wake before we depart," Moiraine said. "I mean to go soon after full dark. Even a single day of delay could be fatal. It will be best if you leave him a note."

"In the night?" Rand said doubtfully, and Lan nodded.

"The Halfman will discover we are gone soon enough. There is no need to make things any easier for it than we must."

Rand fussed with his father's blankets. It was a very long way to Tar Valon. "In that case. . . . In that case, I had better go find Mat and Perrin."

"I will attend to that." Moiraine got to her feet briskly and donned her cloak with suddenly restored vigor. She put a hand on his shoulder, and he tried very hard not to flinch. She did not press hard, but it was an iron grip that held him as surely as a forked stick held a snake. "It will be best if we keep all of this just among us. Do you understand? The same ones who put the Dragon's Fang on the inn door might make trouble if they knew."

"I understand." He drew a relieved breath when she took her hand away.

"I will have Mistress al'Vere bring you something to eat," she went on just as if she had not noticed his reaction. "Then you need to sleep. It will be a hard journey tonight even if you are rested."

The door closed behind them, and Rand stood looking down at Tam—looking at Tam, but seeing nothing. Not until that very minute had he realized that Emond's Field was a part of him as much as he was a part of it. He realized it now because he knew that was what he had felt tearing loose. He was apart from the village, now. The Shepherd of the Night wanted him. It was impossible—he was only a farmer—but the Trollocs had come, and Lan was right about one thing. He could not risk the village on the chance Moiraine was wrong. He could not even tell anyone; the Coplins really would make trouble about something like that. He had to trust an Aes Sedai.

"Don't wake him, now," Mistress al'Vere said, as the Mayor shut the door behind his wife and himself. The cloth-covered tray she carried gave off delicious, warm smells. She set it on the chest against the wall, then firmly moved Rand away from the bed.

"Mistress Moiraine told me what he needs," she said softly, "and it does not include you falling on top of him from exhaustion. I've brought you a bite to eat. Don't let it get cold, now."

"I wish you wouldn't call her that," Bran said peevishly. "Moiraine Sedai is proper. She might get mad."

Mistress al'Vere gave him a pat on the cheek. "You just leave me to worry about that. She and I had a long talk. And keep your voice down. If you wake Tam, you'll have to answer to me *and* Moiraine Sedai." She put an emphasis on Moiraine's title that made Bran's insistence seem foolish. "The two of you keep out of my way." With a fond smile for her husband, she turned to the bed and Tam.

Master al'Vere gave Rand a frustrated look. "She's an Aes Sedai. Half the women in the village act as if she sits in the Women's Circle, and the rest as if she were a Trolloc. Not a one of them seems to realize you have to be careful around Aes Sedai. The men may keep looking at her sideways, but at least they aren't doing anything that might provoke her."

Careful, Rand thought. It was not too late to start being careful. "Master al'Vere," he said slowly, "do you know how many farms were attacked?"

"Only two that I've heard of so far, including your place." The Mayor paused, frowning, then shrugged. "It doesn't seem enough, with what happened here. I should be glad of it, but. . . . Well, we'll probably hear of more before the day is out."

Rand sighed. No need to ask which farms. "Here in the village, did they. . . . I mean, was there anything to show what they were after?"

"After, boy? I don't know that they were after anything, except maybe killing us all. It was just the way I said. The dogs barking, and Moiraine Sedai and Lan running through the streets, then somebody shouted that Master Luhhan's house and the forge were on fire. Abell Cauthon's house flared up—odd that; it's nearly in the middle of the village. Anyway, the next thing the Trollocs were all among us. No, I don't think they were *after* anything." He gave an abrupt bark of a laugh, and cut it short with a wary look at his wife. She did not look around from Tam. "To tell the truth," he went on more quietly, "they seemed almost as confused as we were. I doubt they expected to find an Aes Sedai here, or a Warder."

"I suppose not," Rand said, grimacing.

If Moiraine had told the truth about that, she probably had told the truth about the rest, too. For a moment he thought about asking the Mayor's advice, but Master al'Vere obviously knew little more about Aes Sedai than anyone else in the village. Besides, he was reluctant to tell even the Mayor what was going on—what Moiraine said was going on. He was not sure if he was more afraid of being laughed at or being believed. He rubbed a thumb against the hilt of Tam's sword. His father had been out into the world; he must know more about Aes Sedai than the Mayor did. But if Tam really had been out of the Two Rivers, then maybe what he had said in the Westwood. . . . He scrubbed both hands through his hair, scattering that line of thought.

"You need sleep, lad," the Mayor said.

"Yes, you do," Mistress al'Vere added. "You're almost falling down where you stand."

Rand blinked at her in surprise. He had not even realized she had left his father. He did need sleep; just the thought set off a yawn.

"You can take the bed in the next room," the Mayor said. "There's already a fire laid."

Rand looked at his father; Tam was still deep in sleep, and that made him yawn again. "I'd rather stay in here, if you don't mind. For when he wakes up."

Sickroom matters were in Mistress al'Vere's province, and the Mayor left it to her. She hesitated only a moment before nodding. "But you let him wake on his own. If you bother his sleep. . . ." He tried to say he would do as she ordered, but the words got tangled in yet another yawn. She shook her head with a smile. "You will be asleep yourself in no time at all. If you must stay, curl up next to the fire. And drink a little of that beef broth before you doze off."

"I will," Rand said. He would have agreed to anything that kept him in that room. "And I won't wake him."

"See that you do not," Mistress al'Vere told him firmly, but not in an unkindly way. "I'll bring you up a pillow and some blankets."

When the door finally closed behind them, Rand dragged the lone chair in the room over beside the bed and sat down where he could watch Tam. It was all very well for Mistress al'Vere to talk about sleep—his jaws cracked as he stifled a yawn—but he could not sleep yet. Tam might wake at any time, and maybe only stay awake a short while. Rand had to be waiting when he did.

He grimaced and twisted in the chair, absently shifting the sword hilt out of his ribs. He still felt backward about telling anyone what Moiraine had said, but this was Tam, after all. This was. . . . Without realizing it he set his jaw determinedly. *My father. I can tell my father anything.*

He twisted a little more in the chair and put his head against the chairback. Tam was his father, and nobody could tell him what to say or not say to his father. He just had to stay awake until Tam woke up. He just had to. . . .

CHAPTER
9

Tellings of the Wheel

Rand's heart pounded as he ran, and he stared in dismay at the barren hills surrounding him. This was not just a place where spring was late in coming; spring had never come here, and never would come. Nothing grew in the cold soil that crunched under his boots, not so much as a bit of lichen. He scrambled past boulders, twice as tall as he was; dust coated the stone as if never a drop of rain had touched it. The sun was a swollen, blood-red ball, more fiery than on the hottest day of summer and bright enough to sear his eyes, but it stood stark against a leaden cauldron of a sky where clouds of sharp black and silver roiled and boiled on every horizon. For all the swirling clouds, though, no breath of breeze stirred across the land, and despite the sullen sun the air burned cold like the depths of winter.

Rand looked over his shoulder often as he ran, but he could not see his pursuers. Only desolate hills and jagged black mountains, many topped by tall plumes of dark smoke rising to join the milling clouds. If he could not see his hunters, though, he could hear them, howling behind him, guttural voices shouting with the glee of the chase, howling with the joy of blood to come. Trollocs. Coming closer, and his strength was almost gone.

With desperate haste he scrambled to the top of a knife-edged ridge, then dropped to his knees with a groan. Below him a sheer rock wall fell away, a thousand-foot cliff plummeting into a vast canyon. Steamy mists covered the canyon floor, their thick gray surface rolling in grim waves, rolling and breaking against the cliff beneath him, but more slowly than any ocean wave had ever moved. Patches of fog glowed red for an instant as if great fires had suddenly flared beneath, then died. Thunder rumbled in the depths of the valley, and lightning crackled through the gray, sometimes striking up at the sky.

It was not the valley itself that sapped his strength and filled the empty spaces left with helplessness. From the center of the furious vapors a mountain thrust upward, a mountain taller than any he had ever seen in the Mountains of Mist, a mountain as black as the loss of all hope. That bleak stone spire, a dagger stabbing at the heavens, was the source of his desolation. He had never seen it before, but he knew it. The memory of it flashed away like quicksilver when he tried to touch it, but the memory was there. He knew it was there.

Unseen fingers touched him, pulled at his arms and legs, trying to draw him to the mountain. His body twitched, ready to obey. His arms and legs stiffened as if he thought he could dig his fingers and toes into the stone. Ghostly strings entwined around his heart, pulling him, calling him to the spire mountain. Tears ran down his face, and he sagged to the ground. He felt his will draining away like water out of a holed bucket. Just a little longer, and he would go where he was called. He would obey, do as he was told. Abruptly he discovered another emotion: anger. Push him, pull him, he was not a sheep to be prodded into a pen. The anger squeezed itself into one hard knot, and he clung to it as he would have clung to a raft in a flood.

Serve me, a voice whispered in the stillness of his mind. A familiar voice. If he listened hard enough he was sure he would know it. *Serve me.* He shook his head to try to get it out of his head. *Serve me!* He shook his fist at the black mountain. "The Light consume you, Shai'tan!"

Abruptly the smell of death lay thick around him. A figure loomed over him, in a cloak the color of dried blood, a figure with a face. . . . He did not want to see the face that looked down at him. He did not want to think of that face. It hurt to think of it, turned his mind to embers. A hand reached toward him. Not caring if he fell over the edge, he threw himself away. He had to get away. Far away. He fell, flailing at the air, wanting to scream, finding no breath for screaming, no breath at all.

Abruptly he was no longer in the barren land, no longer falling. Winter-brown grass flattened under his boots; it seemed like flowers. He almost laughed to see scattered trees and bushes, leafless as they were, dotting the gently rolling plain that now surrounded him. In the distance reared a single mountain, its peak broken and split, but this mountain brought no fear or despair. It was just a mountain, though oddly out of place there, with no other in sight.

A broad river flowed by the mountain, and on an island in the middle of that river was a city such as might live in a gleeman's tale, a city surrounded by high walls gleaming white and silver beneath the warm sun. With mingled relief and joy he started for the walls, for the safety and serenity he somehow knew he would find behind them.

As he came closer he made out soaring towers, many joined by wondrous walkways that spanned the open air. High bridges arched from both banks of the river to the island city. Even at a distance he could see lacy stonework on those spans, seemingly too delicate to withstand the swift waters that rushed beneath them. Beyond those bridges lay safety. Sanctuary.

Of a sudden a chill ran along his bones; an icy clamminess settled on his skin, and the air around him turned fetid and dank. Without looking back he ran, ran from the pursuer whose freezing fingers brushed his back and tugged at his cloak, ran from the light-eating figure with the face that. . . . He could not remember the face, except as terror. He did not want to remember the face. He ran, and the ground passed beneath his feet, rolling hills and flat plain . . . and he wanted to howl like a dog gone mad. The city was receding before him. The harder he ran, the further away drifted the white shining walls and haven. They grew smaller, and smaller, until only a pale speck remained on the horizon. The cold hand of his pursuer clutched at his collar. If those fingers touched him he knew he would go mad. Or worse. Much worse. Even as that surety came to him he tripped and fell . . .

"Noooo!" he screamed.

. . . and grunted as paving stones smacked the breath out of him. Wonderingly he got to his feet. He stood on the approaches to one of the marvelous bridges he had seen rearing over the river. Smiling people walked by on either side of him, people dressed in so many colors they made him think of a field of wildflowers. Some of them spoke to him, but he could not understand, though the words sounded as if he should. But the faces were friendly, and the people gestured him on-ward, over the bridge with its intricate stonework, onward toward the shining, silver-streaked walls and the towers beyond. Toward the safety he knew waited there.

He joined the throng streaming across the bridge and into the city through massive gates set in tall, pristine walls. Within was a wonder-land where the meanest structure seemed a palace. It was as though the builders had been told to take stone and brick and tile and create beauty to take the breath of mortal men. There was no building, no monument that did not make him stare with goggling eyes. Music drifted down the streets, a hundred different songs, but all blending with the clamor of the crowds to make one grand, joyous harmony. The scents of sweet perfumes and sharp spices, of wondrous foods and myriad flowers, all floated in the air, as if every good smell in the world were gathered there.

The street by which he entered the city, broad and paved with smooth, gray stone, stretched straight before him toward the center of the city. At its end loomed a tower larger and taller than any other in the city, a tower as white as fresh-fallen snow. That tower was where safety lay, and the knowledge he sought. But the city was such as he had never dreamed of seeing. Surely it would not matter if he delayed just a short time in going to the tower? He turned aside onto a nar-rower street, where jugglers strolled among hawkers of strange fruits.

Ahead of him down the street was a snow-white tower. The same tower. In just a little while, he thought, and rounded another corner. At the far end of this street, too, lay the white tower. Stubbornly he turned another corner, and another, and each time the alabaster tower met his eyes. He spun to run away from it . . . and skidded to a halt. Before him, the white tower. He was afraid to look over his shoulder, afraid it would be there, too.

The faces around him were still friendly, but shattered hope filled them now, hope he had broken. Still the people gestured him forward, pleading gestures. Toward the tower. Their eyes shone with desperate need, and only he could fulfill it, only he could save them.

Very well, he thought. The tower was, after all, where he wanted to go.

Even as he took his first step forward disappointment faded from those about him, and smiles wreathed every face. They moved with him, and small children strewed his path with flower petals. He looked over his shoulder in confusion, wondering who the flowers were meant for, but behind him were only more smiling people gesturing him on.

They must be for me, he thought, and wondered why that suddenly did not seem strange at all. But wonderment lasted only a moment before melting away; all was as it should be.

First one, then another of the people began to sing, until every voice was lifted in a glorious anthem. He still could not understand the words, but a dozen interweaving harmonies shouted joy and salvation. Musicians capered through the on-flowing crowd, adding flutes and harps and drums in a dozen sizes to the hymn, and all the songs he had heard before blended in without seam. Girls danced around him, laying garlands of sweet-smelling blossoms across his shoulders, twining them about his neck. They smiled at him, their delight growing with every step he took. He could not help but smile back. His feet itched to join in their dance, and even as he thought of it he was dancing, his steps fitting as if he had known it all from birth. He threw back his head and laughed; his feet were lighter than they had ever been, dancing with. . . . He could not remember the name, but it did not seem important.

It is your destiny, a voice whispered in his head, and the whisper was a thread in the paean.

Carrying him like a twig on the crest of a wave, the crowd flowed into a huge square in the middle of the city, and for the first time he saw that the white tower rose from a great palace of pale marble, sculpted rather than built, curving walls and swelling domes and delicate spires fingering the sky. The whole of it made him gasp in awe. Broad stairs of pristine stone led up from the square, and at the foot of those stairs the people halted, but their song rose ever higher. The swelling voices buoyed his feet. *Your destiny,* the voice whispered, insistent now, eager.

He no longer danced, but neither did he stop. He mounted the stairs without hesitation. This was where he belonged.

Scrollwork covered the massive doors at the top of the stairs, carvings so intricate and delicate that he could not imagine a knife blade fine enough to fit. The portals swung open, and he went in. They closed behind him with an echoing crash like thunder.

"We have been waiting for you," the Myrddraal hissed.

Rand sat bolt upright, gasping for breath and shivering, staring. Tam was still asleep on the bed. Slowly his breathing slowed. Half-consumed logs blazed in the fireplace with a good bed of coals built up around the fire-irons; someone had been there to tend it while he slept. A blanket lay at his feet, where it had fallen when he woke. The makeshift litter was gone, too, and his and Tam's cloaks had been hung by the door.

He wiped cold sweat from his face with a hand that was none too steady and wondered if naming the Dark One in a dream brought his attention the same way that naming him aloud did.

Twilight darkened the window; the moon was well up, round and fat, and evening stars sparkled above the Mountains of Mist. He had slept the day away. He rubbed a sore spot on his side. Apparently he had slept with the sword hilt jabbing him in the ribs. Between that and an empty stomach and the night before, it was no wonder he had had nightmares.

His belly rumbled, and he got up stiffly and made his way to the table where Mistress al'Vere had left the tray. He twitched aside the white napkin. Despite the time he had slept, the beef broth was still warm, and so was the crusty bread. Mistress al'Vere's hand was plain; the tray had been replaced. Once she decided you needed a hot meal, she did not give up till it was inside you.

He gulped down some broth, and it was all he could do to put some meat and cheese between two pieces of bread before stuffing it in his mouth. Taking big bites, he went back to the bed.

Mistress al'Vere had apparently seen to Tam, as well. Tam had been undressed, his clothes now clean and neatly folded on the bedside table, and a blanket was drawn up under his chin. When Rand touched his father's forehead, Tam opened his eyes.

"There you are, boy. Marin said you were here, but I couldn't even sit up to see. She said you were too tired for her to wake just so I could look at you. Even Bran can't get around her when she has her mind set."

Tam's voice was weak, but his gaze was clear and steady. *The Aes Sedai was right,* Rand thought. With rest he would be as good as ever.

"Can I get you something to eat? Mistress al'Vere left a tray."

"She fed me already . . . if you can call it that. Wouldn't let me have anything but broth. How can a man avoid bad dreams with nothing but broth in his. . . ." Tam fumbled a hand from under the cover and toched the sword at Rand's waist. "Then it wasn't a dream. When Marin told me I was sick, I thought I had been. . . . But you're all right. That is all that matters. What of the farm?"

Rand took a deep breath. "The Trollocs killed the sheep. I think they took the cow, too, and the house needs a good cleaning." He managed a weak smile. "We were luckier than some. They burned half the village."

He told Tam everything that had happened, or at least most of it. Tam listened closely, and asked sharp questions, so he found himself having to tell about returning to the farmhouse from the woods, and that brought in the Trolloc he had killed. He had to tell how Nynaeve had said Tam was dying to explain why the Aes Sedai had tended him instead of the Wisdom. Tam's eyes widened at that, an Aes Sedai in Emond's Field. But Rand could see no need to go over every step of the journey from the farm, or his fears, or the Myrddraal on the road. Certainly not his nightmares as he slept by the bed. Especially he saw no reason to mention Tam's ramblings under the fever. Not yet. Moiraine's story, though: there was no avoiding that.

"Now that's a tale to make a gleeman proud," Tam muttered when he was done. "What would Trollocs want with you boys? Or the Dark One, Light help us?"

"You think she was lying? Master al'Vere said she was telling the truth about only two farms being attacked. And about Master Luhhan's house, and Master Cauthon's."

For a moment Tam lay silent before saying, "Tell me what she said. Her exact words, mind, just as she said them."

Rand struggled. Who ever remembered the *exact* words they heard? He chewed at his lip and scratched his head, and bit by bit he brought it out, as nearly as he could remember. "I can't think of anything else," he finished. "Some of it I'm not too sure she didn't say a little differently, but it's close, anyway."

"It's good enough. It has to be, doesn't it? You see, lad, Aes Sedai are tricksome. They don't lie, not right out, but the truth an Aes Sedai tells you is not always the truth you think it is. You take care around her."

"I've heard the stories," Rand retorted. "I'm not a child."

"So you're not, so you're not." Tam sighed heavily, then shrugged in annoyance. "I should be going along with you, just the same. The world outside the Two Rivers is nothing like Emond's Field."

That was an opening to ask about Tam going outside and all the rest of it, but Rand did not take it. His mouth fell open, instead. "Just like that? I thought you would try to talk me out of it. I thought you'd have a hundred reasons I should not go." He realized he had been hoping Tam would have a hundred reasons, and good ones.

"Maybe not a hundred," Tam said with a snort, "but a few did come to mind. Only they don't count for much. If Trollocs are after you, you will be safer in Tar Valon than you could ever be here. Just remember to be wary. Aes Sedai do things for their own reasons, and those are not always the reasons you think."

"The gleeman said something like that," Rand said slowly.

"Then he knows what he's talking about. You listen sharp, think deep, and guard your tongue. That's good advice for any dealings beyond the Two Rivers, but most especially with Aes Sedai. And with Warders. Tell Lan something, and you've as good as told Moiraine. If he's a Warder, then he's bonded to her as sure as the sun rose this morning, and he won't keep many secrets from her, if any."

Rand knew little about the bonding between Aes Sedai and Warders, though it played a big part in every story about Warders he had ever heard. It was something to do with the Power, a gift to the Warder, or maybe some sort of exchange. The Warders got all sorts of benefits, according to the stories. They healed more quickly than other men, and could go longer without food or water or sleep. Supposedly they could sense Trollocs, if they were close enough, and other creatures of the Dark One, too, which explained how Lan and Moiraine had tried to warn the village before the attack. As to what the Aes Sedai got out of it, the stories were silent, but he was not about to believe they did not get something.

"I'll be careful," Rand said. "I just wish I knew why. It doesn't make any sense. Why me? Why us?"

"I wish I knew, too, boy. Blood and ashes, I wish I knew." Tam sighed heavily. "Well, no use trying to put a broken egg back in the shell, I suppose. How soon do you have to go? I'll be back on my feet in a day or two, and we can see about starting a new flock. Oren Dautry has some good stock he might be willing to part with, with the pastures all gone, and so does Jon Thane."

"Moiraine . . . the Aes Sedai said you had to stay in bed. She said weeks." Tam opened his mouth, but Rand went on. "And she talked to Mistress al'Vere."

"Oh. Well, maybe I can talk Marin around." Tam did not sound hopeful of it, though. He gave Rand a sharp look. "The way you avoided answering means you have to leave soon. Tomorrow? Or tonight?"

"Tonight," Rand said quietly, and Tam nodded sadly.

"Yes. Well, if it must be done, best not to delay. But we will see about this 'weeks' business." He plucked at his blankets with more irritation than strength. "Perhaps I'll follow in a few days anyway. Catch you up on the road. We will see if Marin can keep me in bed when I want to get up."

There was a tap at the door, and Lan stuck his head into the room. "Say your goodbyes quickly, sheepherder, and come. There may be trouble."

"Trouble?" Rand said, and the Warder growled at him impatiently. "Just hurry!"

Hastily Rand snatched up his cloak. He started to undo the sword belt, but Tam spoke up.

"Keep it. You will probably have more need of it than I, though, the Light willing, neither of us will. Take care, lad. You hear?"

Ignoring Lan's continued growls, Rand bent to grab Tam in a hug. "I will come back. I promise you that."

"Of course you will." Tam laughed. He returned the hug weakly, and ended by patting Rand on the back. "I know that. And I'll have twice as many sheep for you to tend when you return. Now go, before that fellow does himself an injury."

Rand tried to hang back, tried to find the words for the question he did not want to ask, but Lan entered the room to catch him by the arm and pull him into the hall. The Warder had donned a dull gray-green tunic of overlapping metal scales. His voice rasped with irritation.

"We have to hurry. Don't you understand the word *trouble*?"

Outside the room Mat waited, cloaked and coated and carrying his bow. A quiver hung at his waist. He was rocking anxiously on his heels, and he kept glancing off toward the stairs with what seemed to be equal parts impatience and fear. "This isn't much like the stories, Rand, is it?" he said hoarsely.

"What kind of trouble?" Rand demanded, but the Warder ran ahead of him instead of answering, taking the steps down two at a time. Mat dashed after him with quick gestures for Rand to follow.

Shrugging into his cloak, he caught up to them downstairs. Only a feeble light filled the common room; half the candles had burned out and most of the rest were guttering. It was empty except for the three of them. Mat stood next to one of the front windows, peeping out as if trying not to be seen. Lan held the door open a crack and peered into the inn yard.

Wondering what they could be watching, Rand went to join him. The Warder muttered at him to take a care, but he did open the door a trifle wider to make room for Rand to look, too.

At first he was not sure exactly what he was seeing. A crowd of village men, some three dozen or so, clustered near the burned-out husk of the peddler's wagon, night pushed back by the torches some of them carried. Moiraine faced them, her back to the inn, leaning with seeming casualness on her walking staff. Hari Coplin stood in the front of the crowd with his brother, Darl, and Bili Congar. Cenn Buie

was there, as well, looking uncomfortable. Rand was startled to see
Hari shake his fist at Moiraine.

"Leave Emond's Field!" the sour-faced farmer shouted. A few
voices in the crowd echoed him, but hesitantly, and no one pushed
forward. They might be willing to confront an Aes Sedai from within
a crowd, but none of them wanted to be singled out. Not by an Aes
Sedai who had every reason to take offense.

"You brought those monsters!" Darl roared. He waved a torch over
his head, and there were shouts of, "You brought them!" and "It's
your fault!" led by his cousin Bili.

Hari elbowed Cenn Buie, and the old thatcher pursed his lips and
gave him a sidelong glare. "Those things . . . those Trollocs didn't
appear until after you came," Cenn muttered, barely loud enough to
be heard. He swung his head from side to side dourly as if wishing he
were somewhere else and looking for a way to get there. "You're an
Aes Sedai. We want none of your sort in the Two Rivers. Aes Sedai
bring trouble on their backs. If you stay, you will only bring more."

His speech brought no response from the gathered villagers, and
Hari scowled in frustration. Abruptly he snatched Darl's torch and
shook it in her direction. "Get out!" he shouted. "Or we'll burn you
out!"

Dead silence fell, except for the shuffling of a few feet as men drew
back. Two Rivers folk could fight back if they were attacked, but violence was far from common, and threatening people was foreign to
them, beyond the occasional shaking of a fist. Cenn Buie, Bili Congar,
and the Coplins were left out front alone. Bili looked as if he wanted
to back away, too.

Hari gave an uneasy start at the lack of support, but he recovered
quickly. "Get out!" he shouted again, echoed by Darl and, more
weakly, by Bili. Hari glared at the others. Most of the crowd failed to
meet his eye.

Suddenly Bran al'Vere and Haral Luhhan moved out of the shadows, stopping apart from both the Aes Sedai and the crowd. In one
hand the Mayor casually carried the big wooden maul he used to drive
spigots into casks. "Did someone suggest burning my inn?" he asked
softly.

The two Coplins took a step back, and Cenn Buie edged away from
them. Bili Congar dived into the crowd. "Not that," Darl said quickly.
"We never said that, Bran . . . ah, Mayor."

Bran nodded. "Then perhaps I heard you threatening to harm guests
in my inn?"

"She's an Aes Sedai," Hari began angrily, but his words cut off as Haral Luhhan moved.

The blacksmith simply stretched, thrusting thick arms over his head, tightening massive fists until his knuckles cracked, but Hari looked at the burly man as if one of those fists had been shaken under his nose. Haral folded his arms across his chest. "Your pardon, Hari. I did not mean to cut you off. You were saying?"

But Hari, shoulders hunched as though he were trying to draw into himself and disappear, seemed to have nothing more to say.

"I'm surprised at you people," Bran rumbled. "Paet al'Caar, your boy's leg was broken last night, but I saw him walking on it today—because of her. Eward Candwin, you were lying on your belly with a gash down your back like a fish for cleaning, till she laid hands on you. Now it looks as if it happened a month ago, and unless I misdoubt there'll barely be a scar. And you, Cenn." The thatcher started to fade back into the crowd, but stopped, held uncomfortably by Bran's gaze. "I'd be shocked to see any man on the Village Council here, Cenn, but you most of all. Your arm would still be hanging useless at your side, a mass of burns and bruises, if not for her. If you have no gratitude, have you no shame?"

Cenn half lifted his right hand, then looked away from it angrily. "I cannot deny what she did," he muttered, and he did sound ashamed. "She helped me, and others," he went on in a pleading tone, "but she's an Aes Sedai, Bran. If those Trollocs didn't come because of her, why did they come? We want no part of Aes Sedai in the Two Rivers. Let them keep their troubles away from us."

A few men, safely back in the crowd, shouted then. "We want no Aes Sedai troubles!" "Send her away!" "Drive her out!" "Why did they come if not because of her?"

A scowl grew on Bran's face, but before he could speak Moiraine suddenly whirled her vine-carved staff above her head, spinning it with both hands. Rand's gasp echoed that of the villagers, for a hissing white flame flared from each end of the staff, standing straight out like spearpoints despite the rod's whirling. Even Bran and Haral edged away from her. She snapped her arms down straight out before her, the staff parallel to the ground, but the pale fire still jetted out, brighter than the torches. Men shied away, held up hands to shield their eyes from the pain of that brilliance.

"Is this what Aemon's blood has come to?" The Aes Sedai's voice was not loud, but it overwhelmed every other sound. "Little people squabbling for the right to hide like rabbits? You have forgotten who you were, forgotten what you were, but I had hoped some small part was left, some memory in blood and bone. Some shred to steel you for the long night coming."

No one spoke. The two Coplins looked as if they never wanted to open their mouths again.

Bran said, "Forgotten who we were? We are who we always have been. Honest farmers and shepherds and craftsmen. Two Rivers folk."

"To the south," Moiraine said, "lies the river you call the White River, but far to the east of here men call it still by its rightful name. Manetherendrelle. In the Old Tongue, Waters of the Mountain Home. Sparkling waters that once coursed through a land of bravery and beauty. Two thousand years ago Manetherendrelle flowed by the walls of a mountain city so lovely to behold that Ogier stonemasons came to stare in wonder. Farms and villages covered this region, and that you call the Forest of Shadows, as well, and beyond. But all of those folk thought of themselves as the people of the Mountain Home, the people of Manetheren.

"Their King was Aemon al Caar al Thorin, Aemon son of Caar son of Thorin, and Eldrene ay Ellan ay Carlan was his Queen. Aemon, a man so fearless that the greatest compliment for courage any could give, even among his enemies, was to say a man had Aemon's heart. Eldrene, so beautiful that it was said the flowers bloomed to make her smile. Bravery and beauty and wisdom and a love that death could not sunder. Weep, if you have a heart, for the loss of them, for the loss of even their memory. Weep, for the loss of their blood."

She fell silent then, but no one spoke. Rand was as bound as the others in the spell she had created. When she spoke again, he drank it in, and so did the rest.

"For nearly two centuries the Trolloc Wars had ravaged the length and breadth of the world, and wherever battles raged, the Red Eagle banner of Manetheren was in the forefront. The men of Manetheren were a thorn to the Dark One's foot and a bramble to his hand. Sing of Manetheren, that would never bend knee to the Shadow. Sing of Manetheren, the sword that could not be broken.

"They were far away, the men of Manetheren, on the Field of Bekkar, called the Field of Blood, when news came that a Trolloc army was moving against their home. Too far to do else but wait to hear of their land's death, for the forces of the Dark One meant to make an end of them. Kill the mighty oak by hacking away its roots. Too far to do else but mourn. But they were the men of the Mountain Home.

"Without hesitation, without thought for the distance they must travel, they marched from the very field of victory, still covered in dust and sweat and blood. Day and night they marched, for they had seen the horror a Trolloc army left behind it, and no man of them could sleep while such a danger threatened Manetheren. They moved as if their feet had wings, marching further and faster than friends hoped or enemies feared they could. At any other day that march alone would have inspired songs. When the Dark One's armies swooped down upon the lands of Manetheren, the men of the Mountain Home stood before it, with their backs to the Tarendrelle."

Some villager raised a small cheer then, but Moiraine kept on as if she had not heard. "The host that faced the men of Manetheren was enough to daunt the bravest heart. Ravens blackened the sky; Trollocs blackened the land. Trollocs and their human allies. Trollocs and Darkfriends in tens of tens of thousands, and Dreadlords to command. At night their cookfires outnumbered the stars, and dawn revealed the banner of Ba'alzamon at their head. Ba'alzamon, Heart of the Dark. An ancient name for the Father of Lies. The Dark One could not have been free of his prison at Shayol Ghul, for if he had been, not all the forces of humankind together could have stood against him, but there was power there. Dreadlords, and some evil that made that light-destroying banner seem no more than right and sent a chill into the souls of the men who faced it.

"Yet, they knew what they must do. Their homeland lay just across the river. They must keep that host, and the power with it, from the Mountain Home. Aemon had sent out messengers. Aid was promised if they could hold for but three days at the Tarendrelle. Hold for three days against odds that should overwhelm them in the first hour. Yet somehow, through bloody assault and desperate defense, they held through an hour, and the second hour, and the third. For three days they fought, and though the land became a butcher's yard, no crossing of the Tarendrelle did they yield. By the third night no help had come, and no messengers, and they fought on alone. For six days. For nine. And on the tenth day Aemon knew the bitter taste of betrayal. No help was coming, and they could hold the river crossings no more."

"What did they do?" Hari demanded. Torchfires flickered in the chill night breeze, but no one made a move to draw a cloak tighter.

"Aemon crossed the Tarendrelle," Moiraine told them, "destroying the bridges behind him. And he sent word throughout his land for the people to flee, for he knew the powers with the Trolloc horde would find a way to bring it across the river. Even as the word went out, the Trolloc crossing began, and the soldiers of Manetheren took up the

fight again, to buy with their lives what hours they could for their people to escape. From the city of Manetheren, Eldrene organized the
flight of her people into the deepest forests and the fastness of the
mountains.

"But some did not flee. First in a trickle, then a river, then a flood,
men went, not to safety, but to join the army fighting for their land.
Shepherds with bows, and farmers with pitchforks, and woodsmen with
axes. Women went, too, shouldering what weapons they could find and
marching side by side with their men. No one made that journey who
did not know they would never return. But it was their land. It had
been their fathers', and it would be their children's, and they went to
pay the price of it. Not a step of ground was given up until it was
soaked in blood, but at the last the army of Manetheren was driven
back, back to here, to this place you now call Emond's Field. And
here the Trolloc hordes surrounded them."

Her voice held the sound of cold tears. "Trolloc dead and the
corpses of human renegades piled up in mounds, but always more
scrambled over those charnel heaps in waves of death that had no end.
There could be but one finish. No man or woman who had stood beneath the banner of the Red Eagle at that day's dawning still lived
when night fell. The sword that could not be broken was shattered.

"In the Mountains of Mist, alone in the emptied city of Manetheren,
Eldrene felt Aemon die, and her heart died with him. And where her
heart had been was left only a thirst for vengeance, vengeance for her
love, vengeance for her people and her land. Driven by grief she
reached out to the True Source, and hurled the One Power at the
Trolloc army. And there the Dreadlords died wherever they stood,
whether in their secret councils or exhorting their soldiers. In the passing of a breath the Dreadlords and the generals of the Dark One's
host burst into flame. Fire consumed their bodies, and terror consumed
their just-victorious army.

"Now they ran like beasts before a wildfire in the forest, with no
thought for anything but escape. North and south they fled. Thousands
drowned attempting to cross the Tarendrelle without the aid of the
Dreadlords, and at the Manetherendrelle they tore down the bridges
in their fright at what might be following them. Where they found
people, they slew and burned, but to flee was the need that gripped
them. Until, at last, no one of them remained in the lands of Manetheren. They were dispersed like dust before the whirlwind. The final
vengeance came more slowly, but it came, when they were hunted
down by other peoples, by other armies in other lands. None was left
alive of those who did murder at Aemon's Field.

"But the price was high for Manetheren. Eldrene had drawn to herself more of the One Power than any human could ever hope to wield unaided. As the enemy generals died, so did she die, and the fires that consumed her consumed the empty city of Manetheren, even the stones of it, down to the living rock of the mountains. Yet the people had been saved.

"Nothing was left of their farms, their villages, or their great city. Some would say there was nothing left for them, nothing but to flee to other lands, where they could begin anew. They did not say so. They had paid such a price in blood and hope for their land as had never been paid before, and now they were bound to that soil by ties stronger than steel. Other wars would wrack them in years to come, until at last their corner of the world was forgotten and at last they had forgotten wars and the ways of war. Never again did Manetheren rise. Its soaring spires and splashing fountains became as a dream that slowly faded from the minds of its people. But they, and their children, and their children's children, held the land that was theirs. They held it when the long centuries had washed the why of it from their memories. They held it until, today, there is you. Weep for Manetheren. Weep for what is lost forever."

The fires on Moiraine's staff winked out, and she lowered it to her side as if it weighed a hundred pounds. For a long moment the moan of the wind was the only sound. Then Paet al'Caar shouldered past the Coplins.

"I don't know about your story," the long-jawed farmer said. "I'm no thorn to the Dark One's foot, nor ever likely to be, neither. But my Wil is walking because of you, and for that I am ashamed to be here. I don't know if you can forgive me, but whether you will or no, I'll be going. And for me, you can stay in Emond's Field as long as you like."

With a quick duck of his head, almost a bow, he pushed back through the crowd. Others began to mutter then, offering shamefaced penitence before they, too, slipped away one by one. The Coplins, sour-mouthed and scowling once more, looked at the faces around them and vanished into the night without a word. Bili Congar had disappeared even before his cousins.

Lan pulled Rand back and shut the door. "Let's go, boy." The Warder started for the back of the inn. "Come along, both of you. Quickly!"

Rand hesitated, exchanging a wondering glance with Mat. While Moiraine had been telling the story, Master al'Vere's Dhurrans could not have dragged him away, but now something else held his feet. This was the real beginning, leaving the inn and following the Warder into the night. . . . He shook himself, and tried to firm his resolve. He had no choice but to go, but he would come back to Emond's Field, however far or long this journey was.

"What are you waiting for?" Lan asked from the door that led out of the back of the common room. With a start Mat hurried to him.

Trying to convince himself that he was beginning a grand adventure, Rand followed them through the darkened kitchen and out into the stableyard.

CHAPTER
10

Leavetaking

A single lantern, its shutters half closed, hung from a nail on a stall post, casting a dim light. Deep shadows swallowed most of the stalls. As Rand came through the doors from the stableyard, hard on the heels of Mat and the Warder, Perrin leaped up in a rustle of straw from where he had been sitting with his back against a stall door. A heavy cloak swathed him.

Lan barely paused to demand, "Did you look the way I told you, blacksmith?"

"I looked," Perrin replied. "There's nobody here but us. Why would anybody hide—"

"Care and a long life go together, blacksmith." The Warder ran a quick eye around the shadowed stable and the deeper shadows of the hayloft above, then shook his head. "No time," he muttered, half to himself. "Hurry, she says."

As if to suit his words, he strode quickly to where the five horses stood tethered, bridled and saddled at the back of the pool of light. Two were the black stallion and white mare that Rand had seen before. The others, if not quite so tall or so sleek, certainly appeared to be among the best the Two Rivers had to offer. With hasty care Lan began examining cinches and girth straps, and the leather ties that held saddlebags, waterskins, and blanketrolls behind the saddles.

Rand exchanged shaky smiles with his friends, trying hard to look as if he really was eager to be off.

For the first time Mat noticed the sword at Rand's waist, and pointed to it. "You becoming a Warder?" He laughed, then swallowed it with a quick glance at Lan. The Warder apparently took no notice. "Or at least a merchant's guard," Mat went on with a grin that seemed only a little forced. He hefted his bow. "An honest man's weapon isn't good enough for him."

Rand thought about flourishing the sword, but Lan being there stopped him. The Warder was not even looking in his direction, but he was sure the man was aware of everything that went on around him. Instead he said with exaggerated casualness, "It might be useful," as if wearing a sword were nothing out of the ordinary.

Perrin moved, trying to hide something under his cloak. Rand glimpsed a wide leather belt encircling the apprentice blacksmith's waist, with the handle of an axe thrust through a loop on the belt.

"What do you have there?" he asked.

"Merchant's guard, indeed," Mat hooted.

The shaggy-haired youth gave Mat a frown that suggested he had already had more than his fair share of joking, then sighed heavily and tossed back his cloak to uncover the axe. It was no common woodsman's tool. A broad half-moon blade on one side of the head and a curved spike on the other made it every bit as strange for the Two Rivers as Rand's sword. Perrin's hand rested on it with a sense of familiarity, though.

"Master Luhhan made it about two years ago, for a wool-buyer's guard. But when it was done the fellow wouldn't pay what he had agreed, and Master Luhhan would not take less. He gave it to me when"—he cleared his throat, then shot Rand the same warning frown he'd given Mat—"when he found me practicing with it. He said I might as well have it since he couldn't make anything useful from it."

"Practicing," Mat snickered, but held up his hands soothingly when Perrin raised his head. "As you say. It's just as well one of us knows how to use a real weapon."

"That bow is a real weapon," Lan said suddenly. He propped an arm across the saddle of his tall black and regarded them gravely. "So are the slings I've seen you village boys with. Just because you never used them for anything but hunting rabbits or chasing a wolf away from the sheep makes no difference. Anything can be a weapon, if the man or woman who holds it has the nerve and will to make it so. Trollocs aside, you had better have that clear in your minds before we leave the Two Rivers, before we leave Emond's Field, if you want to reach Tar Valon alive."

His face and voice, cold as death and hard as a rough-hewn gravestone, stifled their smiles and their tongues. Perrin grimaced and pulled his cloak back over the axe. Mat stared at his feet and stirred the straw on the stable floor with his toe. The Warder grunted and went back to his checking, and the silence lengthened.

"It isn't much like the stories," Mat said, finally.

"I don't know," Perrin said sourly. "Trollocs, a Warder, an Aes Sedai. What more could you ask?"

"Aes Sedai," Mat whispered, sounding as if he were suddenly cold.

"Do you believe her, Rand?" Perrin asked. "I mean, what would Trollocs want with us?"

As one, they glanced at the Warder. Lan appeared absorbed in the white mare's saddle girth, but the three of them moved back toward the stable door, away from Lan. Even so, they huddled together and spoke softly.

Rand shook his head. "I don't know, but she had it right about our farms being the only ones attacked. And they attacked Master Luhhan's house and the forge first, here in the village. I asked the Mayor. It's as easy to believe they are after us as anything else I can think of." Suddenly he realized they were both staring at him.

"You asked the Mayor?" Mat said incredulously. "She said not to tell anybody."

"I didn't tell him why I was asking," Rand protested. "Do you mean you didn't talk to anybody at all? You didn't let anybody know you're going?"

Perrin shrugged defensively. "Moiraine Sedai said not anybody."

"We left notes," Mat said. "For our families. They'll find them in the morning. Rand, my mother thinks Tar Valon is the next thing to Shayol Ghul." He gave a little laugh to show he did not share her opinion. It was not very convincing. "She'd try to lock me in the cellar if she believed I was even thinking of going there."

"Master Luhhan is stubborn as stone," Perrin added, "and Mistress Luhhan is worse. If you'd seen her digging through what's left of the house, saying she hoped the Trollocs did come back so she could get her hands on them. . . ."

"Burn me, Rand," Mat said, "I know she's an Aes Sedai and all, but the Trollocs were really here. She said not to tell anybody. If an Aes Sedai doesn't know what to do about something like this, who does?"

"I don't know." Rand rubbed at his forehead. His head hurt; he could not get that dream out of his mind. "My father believes her. At least, he agreed that we had to go."

Suddenly Moiraine was in the doorway. "You talked to your father about this journey?" She was clothed in dark gray from head to foot, with a skirt divided for riding astride, and the serpent ring was the only gold she wore now.

Rand eyed her walking staff; despite the flames he had seen, there was no sign of charring, or even soot. "I couldn't go off without letting him know."

She eyed him for a moment with pursed lips before turning to the others. "And did you also decide that a note was not enough?" Mat and Perrin talked on top of each other, assuring her they had only left notes, the way she had said. Nodding, she waved them to silence, and gave Rand a sharp look. "What is done is already woven in the Pattern. Lan?"

"The horses are ready," the Warder said, "and we have enough provisions to reach Baerlon with some to spare. We can leave at any time. I suggest now."

"Not without me." Egwene slipped into the stable, a shawl-wrapped bundle in her arms. Rand nearly fell over his own feet.

Lan's sword had come half out of its sheath; when he saw who it was he shoved the blade back, his eyes suddenly flat. Perrin and Mat began babbling to convince Moiraine they had not told Egwene about leaving. The Aes Sedai ignored them; she simply looked at Egwene, tapping her lips thoughtfully with one finger.

The hood of Egwene's dark brown cloak was pulled up, but not enough to hide the defiant way she faced Moiraine. "I have everything I need here. Including food. And I will not be left behind. I'll probably never get another chance to see the world outside the Two Rivers."

"This isn't a picnic trip into the Waterwood, Egwene," Mat growled. He stepped back when she looked at him from under lowered brows.

"Thank you, Mat. I wouldn't have known. Do you think you three are the only ones who want to see what's outside? I've dreamed about it as long as you have, and I don't intend to miss this chance."

"How did you find out we were leaving?" Rand demanded. "Anyway, you can't go with us. We aren't leaving for the fun of it. The

Trollocs are after us." She gave him a tolerant look, and he flushed and stiffened indignantly.

"First," she told him patiently, "I saw Mat creeping about, trying hard not to be noticed. Then I saw Perrin attempting to hide that absurd great axe under his cloak. I knew Lan had bought a horse, and it suddenly occurred to me to wonder why he needed another. And if he could buy one, he could buy others. Putting that with Mat and Perrin sneaking about like bull calves pretending to be foxes . . . well, I could see only one answer. I don't know if I'm surprised or not to find you here, Rand, after all your talk about daydreams. With Mat and Perrin involved, I suppose I should have known you would be in it, too."

"I have to go, Egwene," Rand said. "All of us do, or the Trollocs will come back."

"The Trollocs!" Egwene laughed incredulously. "Rand, if you've decided to see some of the world, well and good, but please spare me any of your nonsensical tales."

"It's true," Perrin said as Mat began, "The Trollocs—"

"Enough," Moiraine said quietly, but it cut their talk as sharply as a knife. "Did anyone else notice all of this?" Her voice was soft, but Egwene swallowed and drew herself up before answering.

"After last night, all they can think about is rebuilding, that and what to do if it happens again. They couldn't see anything else unless it was pushed under their noses. And I told no one what I suspected. No one."

"Very well," Moiraine said after a moment. "You may come with us."

A startled expression darted across Lan's face. It was gone in an instant, leaving him outwardly calm, but furious words erupted from him. "No, Moiraine!"

"It is part of the Pattern, now, Lan."

"It is ridiculous!" he retorted. "There's no reason for her to come along, and every reason for her not to."

"There *is* a reason for it," Moiraine said calmly. "A part of the Pattern, Lan." The Warder's stony face showed nothing, but he nodded slowly.

"But, Egwene," Rand said, "the Trollocs will be chasing us. We won't be safe until we get to Tar Valon."

"Don't try to frighten me off," she said. "I am going."

Rand knew that tone of voice. He had not heard it since she decided that climbing the tallest trees was for children, but he remembered it well. "If you think being chased by Trollocs will be fun," he began, but Moiraine interrupted.

"We have no time for this. We must be as far away as possible by daybreak. If she is left behind, Rand, she could rouse the village before we have gone a mile, and that would surely warn the Myrddraal."

"I would not do that," Egwene protested.

"She can ride the gleeman's horse," the Warder said. "I'll leave him enough to buy another."

"That will not be possible," came Thom Merrilin's resonant voice from the hayloft. Lan's sword left its sheath this time, and he did not put it back as he stared up at the gleeman.

Thom tossed down a blanketroll, then slung his cased flute and harp across his back and shouldered bulging saddlebags. "This village has no use for me, now, while on the other hand, I have never performed in Tar Valon. And though I usually journey alone, after last night I have no objections at all to traveling in company."

The Warder gave Perrin a hard look, and Perrin shifted uncomfortably. "I didn't think of looking in the loft," he muttered.

As the long-limbed gleeman scrambled down the ladder from the loft, Lan spoke, stiffly formal. "Is this part of the Pattern, too, Moiraine Sedai?"

"Everything is a part of the Pattern, my old friend," Moiraine replied softly. "We cannot pick and choose. But we shall see."

Thom put his feet on the stable floor and turned from the ladder, brushing straw from his patch-covered cloak. "In fact," he said in more normal tones, "you might say that I insist on traveling in company. I have given many hours over many mugs of ale to thinking of how I might end my days. A Trolloc's cookpot was not one of the thoughts." He looked askance at the Warder's sword. "There's no need for that. I am not a cheese for slicing."

"Master Merrilin," Moiraine said, "we must go quickly, and almost certainly in great danger. The Trollocs are still out there, and we go by night. Are you sure that you want to travel with us?"

Thom eyed the lot of them with a quizzical smile. "If it is not too dangerous for the girl, it can't be too dangerous for me. Besides, what gleeman would not face a little danger to perform in Tar Valon?"

Moiraine nodded, and Lan scabbarded his sword. Rand suddenly wondered what would have happened if Thom had changed his mind, or if Moiraine had not nodded. The gleeman began saddling his horse as if similar thoughts had never crossed his mind, but Rand noticed that he eyed Lan's sword more than once.

"Now," Moiraine said. "What horse for Egwene?"

"The peddler's horses are as bad as the Dhurrans," the Warder replied sourly. "Strong, but slow plodders."

"Bela," Rand said, getting a look from Lan that made him wish he had kept silent. But he knew he could not dissuade Egwene; the only thing left was to help. "Bela may not be as fast as the others, but she's strong. I ride her sometimes. She can keep up."

Lan looked into Bela's stall, muttering under his breath. "She might be a little better than the others," he said finally. "I don't suppose there is any other choice."

"Then she will have to do," Moiraine said. "Rand, find a saddle for Bela. Quickly, now! We have tarried too long already."

Rand hurriedly chose a saddle and blanket in the tack room, then fetched Bela from her stall. The mare looked back at him in sleepy surprise when he put the saddle on her back. When he rode her, it was barebacked; she was not used to a saddle. He made soothing noises while he tightened the girth strap, and she accepted the oddity with no more than a shake of her mane.

Taking Egwene's bundle from her, he tied it on behind the saddle while she mounted and adjusted her skirts. They were not divided for riding astride, so her wool stockings were bared to the knee. She wore the same soft leather shoes as all the other village girls. They were not at all suited for journeying to Watch Hill, much less Tar Valon.

"I still think you shouldn't come," he said. "I wasn't making it up about the Trollocs. But I promise I will take care of you."

"Perhaps I'll take care of you," she replied lightly. At his exasperated look she smiled and bent down to smooth his hair. "I know you'll look after me, Rand. We will look after each other. But now you had better look after getting on your horse."

All of the others were already mounted and waiting for him, he realized. The only horse left riderless was Cloud, a tall gray with a black mane and tail that belonged to Jon Thane, or had. He scrambled into the saddle, though not without difficulty as the gray tossed his head and pranced sideways as Rand put his foot in the stirrup, and his scabbard caught in his legs. It was not chance that his friends had not chosen Cloud. Master Thane often raced the spirited gray against merchants' horses, and Rand had never known him to lose, but he had never known Cloud to give anyone an easy ride, either. Lan must have given a huge price to make the miller sell. As he settled in the saddle Cloud's dancing increased, as if the gray were eager to run. Rand gripped the reins firmly and tried to think that he would have no trouble. Perhaps if he convinced himself, he could convince the horse, too.

An owl hooted in the night outside, and the village people jumped before they realized what it was. They laughed nervously and exchanged shamefaced looks.

"Next thing, field mice will chase us up a tree," Egwene said with an unsteady chuckle.

Lan shook his head. "Better if it had been wolves."

"Wolves!" Perrin exclaimed, and the Warder favored him with a flat stare.

"Wolves don't like Trollocs, blacksmith, and Trollocs don't like wolves, or dogs, either. If I heard wolves I would be sure there were no Trollocs waiting out there for us." He moved into the moonlit night, walking his tall black slowly.

Moiraine rode after him without a moment's hesitation, and Egwene kept hard to the Aes Sedai's side. Rand and the gleeman brought up the rear, following Mat and Perrin.

The back of the inn was dark and silent, and dappled moon shadows filled the stableyard. The soft thuds of the hooves faded quickly, swallowed by the night. In the darkness the Warder's cloak made him a shadow, too. Only the need to let him lead the way kept the others from clustering around him. Getting out of the village without being seen was going to be no easy task, Rand decided as he neared the gate. At least, without being seen by villagers. Many windows in the village emitted pale yellow light, and although those glows seemed very small in the night now, shapes moved frequently within them, the shapes of villagers watching to see what this night brought. No one wanted to be caught by surprise again.

In the deep shadows beside the inn, just on the point of leaving the stableyard, Lan abruptly halted, motioning sharply for silence.

Boots rattled on the Wagon Bridge, and here and there on the bridge moonlight glinted off metal. The boots clattered across the bridge, grated on gravel, and approached the inn. No sound at all came from those in the shadow. Rand suspected his friends, at least, were too frightened to make a noise. Like him.

The footsteps halted before the inn in the grayness just beyond the dim light from the common-room windows. It was not until Jon Thane stepped forward, a spear propped on his stout shoulder, an old jerkin sewn all over with steel disks straining across his chest, that Rand saw them for what they were. A dozen men from the village and the surrounding farms, some in helmets or pieces of armor that had lain dust-covered in attics for generations, all with a spear or a woodaxe or a rusty bill.

The miller peered into a common-room window, then turned with a curt, "It looks right here." The others formed in two ragged ranks behind him, and the patrol marched into the night as if stepping to three different drums.

"Two Dha'vol Trollocs would have them all for breakfast," Lan muttered when the sound of their boots had faded, "but they have eyes and ears." He turned his stallion back. "Come."

Slowly, quietly, the Warder took them back across the stableyard, down the bank through the willows and into the Winespring Water. So close to the Winespring itself the cold, swift water, gleaming as it swirled around the horses' legs, was deep enough to lap against the soles of the riders' boots.

Climbing out on the far bank, the line of horses wound its way under the Warder's deft direction, keeping away from any of the village houses. From time to time Lan stopped, signing them all to be quiet, though no one else heard or saw anything. Each time he did, however, another patrol of villagers and farmers soon passed. Slowly they moved toward the north edge of the village.

Rand peered at the high-peaked houses in the dark, trying to impress them on his memory. *A fine adventurer I am,* he thought. He was not even out of the village yet, and already he was homesick. But he did not stop looking.

They passed beyond the last farmhouses on the outskirts of the village and into the countryside, paralleling the North Road that led to Taren Ferry. Rand thought that surely no night sky elsewhere could be as beautiful as the Two Rivers sky. The clear black seemed to reach to forever, and myriad stars gleamed like points of light scattered through crystal. The moon, only a thin slice less than full, appeared almost close enough to touch, if he stretched, and. . . .

A black shape flew slowly across the silvery ball of the moon. Rand's involuntary jerk on the reins halted the gray. A bat, he thought weakly, but he knew it was not. Bats were a common sight of an evening, darting after flies and bitemes in the twilight. The wings that carried this creature might have the same shape, but they moved with the slow, powerful sweep of a bird of prey. And it was hunting. The way it cast back and forth in long arcs left no doubt of that. Worst of all was the size. For a bat to seem so large against the moon it would have had to be almost within arm's reach. He tried to judge in his mind how far away it must be, and how big. The body of it had to be as large as a man, and the wings. . . . It crossed the face of the moon again, wheeling suddenly downward to be engulfed by the night.

He did not realize that Lan had ridden back to him until the Warder caught his arm. "What are you sitting here and staring at, boy? We have to keep moving." The others waited behind Lan.

Half expecting to be told he was letting fear of the Trollocs overcome his sense, Rand told what he had seen. He hoped that Lan would dismiss it as a bat, or a trick of his eyes.

Lan growled a word, sounding as if it left a bad taste in his mouth. "Draghkar." Egwene and the other Two Rivers folk stared at the sky nervously in all directions, but the gleeman groaned softly.

"Yes," Moiraine said. "It is too much to hope otherwise. And if the Myrddraal has a Draghkar at his command, then he will soon know where we are, if he does not already. We must move more quickly than we can cross-country. We may still reach Taren Ferry ahead of the Myrddraal, and he and his Trollocs will not cross as easily as we."

"A Draghkar?" Egwene said. "What is it?"

It was Thom Merrilin who answered her hoarsely. "In the war that ended the Age of Legends, worse than Trollocs and Halfmen were created."

Moiraine's head jerked toward him as he spoke. Not even the dark could hide the sharpness of her look.

Before anyone could ask the gleeman for more, Lan began giving directions. "We take to the North Road, now. For your lives, follow my lead, keep up and keep together."

He wheeled his horse about, and the others galloped wordlessly after him.

CHAPTER 11

The Road to Taren Ferry

O n the hard-packed dirt of the North Road the horses stretched out, manes and tails streaming back in the moonlight as they raced northward, hooves pounding a steady rhythm. Lan led the way, black horse and shadow-clad rider all but invisible in the cold night. Moiraine's white mare, matching the stallion stride for stride, was a pale dart speeding through the dark. The rest followed in a tight line, as if they were all tied to a rope with one end in the Warder's hands.

Rand galloped last in line, with Thom Merrilin just ahead and the others less distinct beyond. The gleeman never turned his head, reserving his eyes for where they ran, not what they ran from. If Trollocs appeared behind, or the Fade on its silent horse, or that flying creature, the Draghkar, it would be up to Rand to sound an alarm.

Every few minutes he craned his neck to peer behind while he clung to Cloud's mane and reins. The Draghkar. . . . Worse than Trollocs and Fades, Thom had said. But the sky was empty, and only darkness and shadows met his eyes on the ground. Shadows that could hide an army.

Now that the gray had been let loose to run, the animal sped through the night like a ghost, easily keeping pace with Lan's stallion. And Cloud wanted to go faster. He wanted to catch the black, strained to catch the black. Rand had to keep a firm hand on the reins to hold him back. Cloud lunged against his restraint as if the gray thought this were a race, fighting him for mastery with every stride. Rand clung to saddle and reins with every muscle taut. Fervently he hoped his mount did not detect how uneasy he was. If Cloud did, he would lose the one real edge he held, however precariously.

Lying low on Cloud's neck, Rand kept a worried eye on Bela and on her rider. When he had said the shaggy mare could stay with the others, he had not meant on the run. She kept up now only by running as he had not thought she could. Lan had not wanted Egwene in their number. Would he slow for her if Bela began to flag? Or would he try to leave her behind? The Aes Sedai and the Warder thought Rand and his friends were important in some way, but for all of Moiraine's talk of the Pattern, he did not think they included Egwene in that importance.

If Bela fell back, he would fall back, too, whatever Moiraine and Lan had to say about it. Back where the Fade and the Trollocs were. Back where the Draghkar was. With all his heart and desperation he silently shouted at Bela to run like the wind, silently tried to will strength into her. *Run!* His skin prickled, and his bones felt as if they were freezing, ready to split open. *The Light help her, run!* And Bela ran.

On and on they sped, northward into the night, time fading into an indistinct blur. Now and again the lights of farmhouses flashed into sight, then disappeared as quickly as imagination. Dogs' sharp challenges faded swiftly behind, or cut off abruptly as the dogs decided they had been chased away. They raced through darkness relieved only by watery pale moonlight, a darkness where trees along the road loomed up without warning, then were gone. For the rest, murk surrounded them, and only a solitary night-bird's cry, lonely and mournful, disturbed the steady pounding of hooves.

Abruptly Lan slowed, then brought the file of horses to a stop. Rand was not sure how long they had been moving, but a soft ache filled his legs from gripping the saddle. Ahead of them in the night, lights sparkled, as if a tall swarm of fireflies held one place among the trees.

Rand frowned at the lights in puzzlement, then suddenly gasped with surprise. The fireflies were windows, the windows of houses covering the sides and top of a hill. It was Watch Hill. He could hardly believe they had come so far. They had probably made the journey as fast as it had ever been traveled. Following Lan's example, Rand and Thom Merrilin dismounted. Cloud stood head down, sides heaving. Lather, almost indistinguishable from the horse's smoky sides, flecked the gray's neck and shoulders. Rand thought that Cloud would not be carrying anyone further that night.

"Much as I would like to put all these villages behind me," Thom announced, "a few hours rest would not go amiss right now. Surely we have enough of a lead to allow that?"

Rand stretched, knuckling the small of his back. "If we're stopping the rest of the night in Watch Hill, we may as well go on up."

A vagrant gust of wind brought a fragment of song from the village, and smells of cooking that made his mouth water. They were still celebrating in Watch Hill. There had been no Trollocs to disturb their Bel Tine. He looked for Egwene. She was leaning against Bela, slumped with weariness. The others were climbing down as well, with many a sigh and much stretching of aching muscles. Only the Warder and the Aes Sedai showed no visible sign of fatigue.

"I could do with some singing," Mat put in tiredly. "And maybe a hot mutton pie at the White Boar." Pausing, he added, "I've never been further than Watch Hill. The White Boar's not nearly as good as the Winespring Inn."

"The White Boar isn't so bad," Perrin said. "A mutton pie for me, too. And lots of hot tea to take the chill off my bones."

"We cannot stop until we are across the Taren," Lan said sharply. "Not for more than a few minutes."

"But the horses," Rand protested. "We'll run them to death if we try to go any further tonight. Moiraine Sedai, surely you—"

He had vaguely noticed her moving among the horses, but he had not paid any real attention to what she did. Now she brushed past him to lay her hands on Cloud's neck. Rand fell silent. Suddenly the horse tossed his head with a soft whicker, nearly pulling the reins from Rand's hands. The gray danced a step sideways, as restive as if he had spent a week in a stable. Without a word Moiraine went to Bela.

"I did not know she could do that," Rand said softly to Lan, his cheeks hot.

"You, of all people, should have suspected it," the Warder replied. "You watched her with your father. She will wash all the fatigue away. First from the horses, then from the rest of you."

"The rest of us. Not you?"

"Not me, sheepherder. I don't need it, not yet. And not her. What she can do for others, she cannot do for herself. Only one of us will ride tired. You had better hope she does not grow too tired before we reach Tar Valon."

"Too tired for what?" Rand asked the Warder.

"You were right about your Bela, Rand," Moiraine said from where she stood by the mare. "She has a good heart, and as much stubbornness as the rest of you Two Rivers folk. Strange as it seems, she may be the least weary of all."

A scream ripped the darkness, a sound like a man dying under sharp knives, and wings swooped low above the party. The night deepened in the shadow that swept over them. With panicked cries the horses reared wildly.

The wind of the Draghkar's wings beat at Rand with a feel like the touch of slime, like chittering in the dank dimness of a nightmare. He had no time even to feel the fear of it, for Cloud exploded into the air with a scream of his own, twisting desperately as if attempting to shake off some clinging thing. Rand, hanging onto the reins, was jerked off his feet and dragged across the ground, Cloud screaming as though the big gray felt wolves tearing at his hocks.

Somehow he maintained his grip on the reins; using the other hand as much as his legs he scrambled onto his feet, taking leaping, staggering steps to keep from being pulled down again. His breath came in ragged pants of desperation. He could not let Cloud get away. He threw out a frantic hand, barely catching the bridle. Cloud reared, lifting him into the air; Rand clung helplessly, hoping against hope that the horse would quieten.

The shock of landing jarred Rand to his teeth, but suddenly the gray was still, nostrils flaring and eyes rolling, stiff-legged and trembling. Rand was trembling as well, and all but hanging from the bridle. *That jolt must have shaken the fool animal, too,* he thought. He took three or four deep, shaky breaths. Only then could he look around and see what had happened to the others.

Chaos reigned among the party. They clutched reins against jerking heads, trying with little success to calm the rearing horses that dragged them about in a milling mass. Only two seemingly had no trouble at all with their mounts. Moiraine sat straight in her saddle, the white mare stepping delicately away from the confusion as if nothing at all out of the ordinary had happened. On foot, Lan scanned the sky, sword in one hand and reins in the other; the sleek black stallion stood quietly beside him.

Sounds of merrymaking no longer came from Watch Hill. Those in the village must have heard the cry, too. Rand knew they would listen awhile, and perhaps watch for what had caused it, then return to their jollity. They would soon forget the incident, its memory submerged by song and food and dance and fun. Perhaps when they heard the news of what had happened in Emond's Field some would remember, and wonder. A fiddle began to play, and after a moment a flute joined in. The village was resuming its celebration.

"Mount!" Lan commanded curtly. Sheathing his sword, he leaped onto the stallion. "The Draghkar would not have showed itself unless it had already reported our whereabouts to the Myrddraal." Another strident shriek drifted down from far above, fainter but no less harsh. The music from Watch Hill silenced raggedly once more. "It tracks us now, marking us for the Halfman. He won't be far."

The horses, fresh now as well as fear-struck, pranced and backed away from those trying to mount. A cursing Thom Merrilin was the first into his saddle, but the others were up soon after. All but one.

"Hurry, Rand!" Egwene shouted. The Draghkar gave shrill voice once more, and Bela ran a few steps before she could rein the mare in. "Hurry!"

With a start Rand realized that instead of trying to mount Cloud he had been standing there staring at the sky in a vain attempt to locate the source of those vile shrieks. More, all unaware, he had drawn Tam's sword as if to fight the flying thing.

His face reddened, making him glad for the night to hide him. Awkwardly, with one hand occupied by the reins, he resheathed the blade, glancing hastily at the others. Moiraine, Lan, and Egwene all were looking at him, though he could not be sure how much they could see in the moonlight. The rest seemed too absorbed with keeping their horses under control to pay him any mind. He put a hand on the pommel and reached the saddle in one leap, as if he had been doing the like all his life. If any of his friends had noticed the sword, he would surely hear about it later. There would be time enough to worry about it then.

As soon as he was in the saddle they were all off at a gallop again, up the road and by the dome-like hill. Dogs barked in the village; their passage was not entirely unnoticed. *Or maybe the dogs smelled Trollocs,* Rand thought. The barking and the village lights alike vanished quickly behind them.

They galloped in a knot, horses all but jostling together as they ran. Lan ordered them to spread out again, but no one wanted to be even a little alone in the night. A scream came from high overhead. The Warder gave up and let them run clustered.

Rand was close behind Moiraine and Lan, the gray straining in an effort to force himself between the Warder's black and the Aes Sedai's trim mare. Egwene and the gleeman raced on either flank of him, while Rand's friends crowded in behind. Cloud, spurred by the Draghkar's cries, ran beyond anything Rand could do to slow him even had he wished to, yet the gray could not gain so much as a step on the other two horses.

The Draghkar's shriek challenged the night.

Stout Bela ran with neck outstretched and tail and mane streaming in the wind of her running, matching the larger horses' every stride. *The Aes Sedai must have done something more than simply ridding her of fatigue.*

Egwene's face in the moonlight was smiling in excited delight. Her braid streamed behind like the horses' manes, and the gleam in her eyes was not all from the moon, Rand was sure. His mouth dropped open in surprise, until a swallowed biteme set him off into a fit of coughing.

Lan must have asked a question, for Moiraine suddenly shouted over the wind and the pounding of hooves. "I cannot! Most especially not from the back of a galloping horse. They are not easily killed, even when they can be seen. We must run, and hope."

They galloped through a tatter of fog, thin and no higher than the horses' knees. Cloud sped through it in two strides, and Rand blinked, wondering if he had imagined it. Surely the night was too cold for fog. Another patch of ragged gray whisked by them to one side, larger than the first. It had been growing, as if the mist oozed from the ground. Above them, the Draghkar screamed in rage. Fog enveloped the riders for a brief moment and was gone, came again and vanished behind. The icy mist left a chill dampness on Rand's face and hands. Then a wall of pale gray loomed before them, and they were suddenly enshrouded. The thickness of it muffled the sound of their hooves to dullness, and the cries from overhead seemed to come through a wall. Rand could only just make out the shapes of Egwene and Thom Merrilin on either side of him.

Lan did not slow their pace. "There is still only one place we can be going," he called, his voice sounding hollow and directionless.

"Myrddraal are sly," Moiraine replied. "I will use its own slyness against it." They galloped on silently.

Slaty mist obscured both sky and ground, so that the riders, themselves turned to shadow, appeared to float through night clouds. Even the legs of their own horses seemed to have vanished.

Rand shifted in his saddle, shrinking away from the icy fog. Knowing that Moiraine could do things, even seeing her do them, was one thing; having those things leave his skin damp was something else again. He realized he was holding his breath, too, and called himself nine kinds of idiot. He could not ride all the way to Taren Ferry without breathing. She had used the One Power on Tam, and he seemed all right. Still, he had to make himself let that breath go and inhale. The air was heavy, but if colder it was otherwise no different than that on any other foggy night. He told himself that, but he was not sure he believed it.

Lan encouraged them to keep close, now, to stay where each could see the outlines of others in that damp, frosty grayness. Yet the Warder still did not slacken his stallion's dead run. Side by side, Lan and Moiraine led the way through the fog as if they could see clearly what lay ahead. The rest could only trust and follow. And hope.

The shrill cries that had hounded them faded as they galloped, and then were gone, but that gave small comfort. Forest and farmhouses, moon and road were shrouded and hidden. Dogs still barked, hollow and distant in the gray haze, when they passed farms, but there was no other sound save the dull drumming of their horses' hooves. Nothing in that featureless ashen fog changed. Nothing gave any hint of the passage of time except the growing ache in thigh and back.

It had to have been hours, Rand was sure. His hands had clutched his reins until he was not sure he could release them, and he wondered if he would ever walk properly again. He glanced back only once. Shadows in the fog raced behind him, but he could not even be certain of their number. Or even that they really were his friends. The chill and damp soaked through his cloak and coat and shirt, soaked into his bones, so it seemed. Only the rush of air past his face and the gather and stretch of the horse beneath him told him he was moving at all. It must have been hours.

"Slow," Lan called suddenly. "Draw rein."

Rand was so startled that Cloud forced between Lan and Moiraine, forging ahead for half a dozen strides before he could pull the big gray to a halt and stare.

Houses loomed in the fog on all sides, houses strangely tall to Rand's eye. He had never seen this place before, but he had often heard descriptions. That tallness came from high redstone foundations, necessary when the spring melt in the Mountains of Mist made the Taren overflow its banks. They had reached Taren Ferry.

Lan trotted the black warhorse past him. "Don't be so eager, sheepherder."

Discomfited, Rand fell into place without explaining as the party moved deeper into the village. His face was hot, and for the moment the fog was welcome.

A lone dog, unseen in the cold mist, barked at them furiously, then ran away. Here and there a light appeared in a window as some early-riser stirred. Other than the dog, no sound save the muted clops of their horses' hooves disturbed the last hour of the night.

Rand had met few people from Taren Ferry. He tried to recall what little he knew about them. They seldom ventured down into what they called "the lower villages," with their noses up as if they smelled something bad. The few he had met bore strange names, like Hilltop and Stoneboat. One and all, Taren Ferry folk had a reputation for slyness and trickery. If you shook hands with a Taren Ferry man, people said, you counted your fingers afterwards.

Lan and Moiraine stopped before a tall, dark house that looked exactly like any other in the village. Fog swirled around the Warder like smoke as he leaped from his saddle and mounted the stairs that rose to the front door, as high above the street as their heads. At the top of the stairs Lan hammered with his fist on the door.

"I thought he wanted quiet," Mat muttered.

Lan's pounding went on. A light appeared in the window of the next house, and someone shouted angrily, but the Warder kept on with his drumming.

Abruptly the door was flung back by a man in a nightshirt that flapped about his bare ankles. An oil lamp in one hand illumined a narrow face with pointed features. He opened his mouth angrily, then let it stay open as his head swiveled to take in the fog, eyes bulging. "What's this?" he said. "What's this?" Chill gray tendrils curled into the doorway, and he hurriedly stepped back away from them.

"Master Hightower," Lan said. "Just the man I need. We want to cross over on your ferry."

"He never even saw a high tower," Mat snickered. Rand made shushing motions at his friend. The sharp-faced fellow raised his lamp higher and peered down at them suspiciously.

After a minute Master Hightower said crossly, "The ferry goes over in daylight. Not in the night. Not ever. And not in this fog, neither. Come back when the sun's up and the fog's gone."

He started to turn away, but Lan caught his wrist. The ferryman opened his mouth angrily. Gold glinted in the lamplight as the Warder counted out coins one by one into the other's palm. Hightower licked his lips as the coins clinked, and by inches his head moved closer to his hand, as if he could not believe what he was seeing.

"And as much again," Lan said, "when we are safely on the other side. But we leave now."

"Now?" Chewing his lower lip, the ferrety man shifted his feet and peered out at the mist-laden night, then nodded abruptly. "Now it is. Well, let loose my wrist. I have to rouse my haulers. You don't think I pull the ferry across myself, do you?"

"I will wait at the ferry," Lan said flatly. "For a little while." He released his hold on the ferryman.

Master Hightower jerked the handful of coins to his chest and, nodding agreement, hastily shoved the door closed with his hip.

CHAPTER 12

Across the Taren

Lan came down the stairs, telling the company to dismount and
lead their horses after him through the fog. Again they had to
trust that the Warder knew where he was going. The fog
swirled around Rand's knees, hiding his feet, obscuring everything
more than a yard away. The fog was not as heavy as it had been outside the town, but he could barely make out his companions.

Still no human stirred in the night except for them. A few more
windows than before showed a light, but the thick mist turned most of
them to dim patches, and as often as not that hazy glow, hanging in
the gray, was all that was visible. Other houses, revealing a little more,
seemed to float on a sea of cloud or to thrust abruptly out of the mist
while their neighbors remained hidden, so that they could have stood
alone for miles around.

Rand moved stiffly from the ache of the long ride, wondering if
there was any way he could walk the rest of the way to Tar Valon.
Not that walking was much better than riding at that moment, of
course, but even so his feet were almost the only part of him that was
not sore. At least he was used to walking.

Only once did anyone speak loudly enough for Rand to hear clearly. "You must handle it," Moiraine said in answer to something unheard from Lan. "He will remember too much as it is, and no help for it. If I stand out in his thoughts. . . ."

Rand grumpily shifted his now-sodden cloak on his shoulders, keeping close with the others. Mat and Perrin grumbled to themselves, muttering under their breaths, with bitten-off exclamations whenever one stubbed a toe on something unseen. Thom Merrilin grumbled, too, words like "hot meal" and "fire" and "mulled wine" reaching Rand, but neither the Warder nor the Aes Sedai took notice. Egwene marched along without a word, her back straight and her head high. It was a somewhat painfully hesitant march, to be sure, for she was as unused to riding as the rest.

She was getting her adventure, he thought glumly, and as long as it lasted he doubted if she would notice little things like fog or damp or cold. There must be a difference in what you saw, it seemed to him, depending on whether you sought adventure or had it forced on you. The stories could no doubt make galloping through a cold fog, with a Draghkar and the Light alone knew what else chasing you, sound thrilling. Egwene might be feeling a thrill; he only felt cold and damp and glad to have a village around him again, even if it was Taren Ferry.

Abruptly he walked into something large and warm in the murk: Lan's stallion. The Warder and Moiraine had stopped, and the rest of the party did the same, patting their mounts as much to comfort themselves as the animals. The fog was a little thinner here, enough for them to see one another more clearly than they had in a long while, but not enough to make out much more. Their feet were still hidden by low billows like gray floodwater. The houses seemed to have all been swallowed.

Cautiously Rand led Cloud forward a little way and was surprised to hear his boots scrape on wooden planks. The ferry landing. He backed up carefully, making the gray back as well. He had heard what the Taren Ferry landing was like—a bridge that led nowhere except to the ferryboat. The Taren was supposed to be wide and deep, with treacherous currents that could pull under the strongest swimmer. Much wider than the Winespring Water, he supposed. With the fog added in. . . . It was a relief when he felt dirt under his feet again.

A fierce "Hsst!" from Lan, as sharp as the fog. The Warder gestured at them as he dashed to Perrin's side and threw back the stocky youth's cloak, exposing the great axe. Obediently, if still not understanding, Rand tossed his own cloak over his shoulder to show his sword. As

Lan moved swiftly back to his horse, bobbing lights appeared in the mist, and muffled footsteps approached.

Six stolid-faced men in rough clothes followed Master Hightower. The torches they carried burned away a patch of fog around them. When they stopped, all of the party from Emond's Field could be plainly seen, the lot of them surrounded by a gray wall that seemed thicker for the torchlight reflected from it. The ferryman examined them, his narrow head tilted, nose twitching like a weasel sniffing the breeze for a trap.

Lan leaned against his saddle with apparent casualness, but one hand rested ostentatiously on the long hilt of his sword. There was an air about him of a metal spring, compressed, waiting.

Rand hurriedly copied the Warder's pose—at least insofar as putting his hand on his sword. He did not think he could achieve that deadly-seeming slouch. *They'd probably laugh if I tried.*

Perrin eased his axe in its leather loop and planted his feet deliberately. Mat put a hand to his quiver, though Rand was not sure what condition his bowstring was in after being out in all this damp. Thom Merrilin stepped forward grandly and held up one empty hand, turning it slowly. Suddenly he gestured with a flourish, and a dagger twirled between his fingers. The hilt slapped into his palm, and, abruptly nonchalant, he began trimming his fingernails.

A low, delighted laugh floated from Moiraine. Egwene clapped as if watching a performance at Festival, then stopped and looked abashed, though her mouth twitched with a smile just the same.

Hightower seemed far from amused. He stared at Thom, then cleared his throat loudly. "There was mention made of more gold for the crossing." He looked around at them again, a sullen, sly look. "What you gave me before is in a safe place now, hear? It's none of it where you can get at it."

"The rest of the gold," Lan told him, "goes into your hand when we are on the other side." The leather purse hanging at his waist clinked as he gave it a little shake.

For a moment the ferryman's eyes darted, but at last he nodded. "Let's be about it, then," he muttered, and stalked out onto the landing followed by his six helpers. The fog burned away around them as they moved; gray tendrils closed in behind, quickly filling where they had been. Rand hurried to keep up.

The ferry itself was a wooden barge with high sides, boarded by a ramp that could be raised to block off the end. Ropes as thick as a man's wrist ran along each side of it, ropes fastened to massive posts at the end of the landing and disappearing into the night over the river. The ferryman's helpers stuck their torches in iron brackets on the ferry's sides, waited while everyone led their horses aboard, then pulled up the ramp. The deck creaked beneath hooves and shuffling feet, and the ferry shifted with the weight.

Hightower muttered half under his breath, growling for them to keep the horses still and stay to the center, out of the haulers' way. He shouted at his helpers, chivvying them as they readied the ferry to cross, but the men moved at the same reluctant speed whatever he said, and he was halfhearted about it, often cutting off in mid-shout to hold his torch high and peer into the fog. Finally he stopped shouting altogether and went to the bow, where he stood staring into the mist that covered the river. He did not move until one of the haulers touched his arm; then he jumped, glaring.

"What? Oh. You, is it? Ready? About time. Well, man, what are you waiting for?" He waved his arms, heedless of the torch and the way the horses whickered and tried to move back. "Cast off! Give way! Move!" The man slouched off to comply, and Hightower peered once more into the fog ahead, rubbing his free hand uneasily on his coat front.

The ferry lurched as its moorings were loosed and the strong current caught it, then lurched again as the guide-ropes held it. The haulers, three to a side, grabbed hold of the ropes at the front of the ferry and laboriously began walking toward the back, muttering uneasily as they edged out onto the gray-cloaked river.

The landing disappeared as mist surrounded them, tenuous streamers drifting across the ferry between the flickering torches. The barge rocked slowly in the current. Nothing except the steady tread of the haulers, forward to take hold of the ropes and back down again pulling, gave a hint of any other movement. No one spoke. The villagers kept as close to the center of the ferry as they could. They had heard the Taren was far wider than the streams they were used to; the fog made it infinitely vaster in their minds.

After a time Rand moved closer to Lan. Rivers a man could not wade or swim or even see across were nervous-making to someone who had never seen anything broader or deeper than a Waterwood pond. "Would they really have tried to rob us?" he asked quietly. "He acted more as if he were afraid we would rob him."

The Warder eyed the ferryman and his helpers—none appeared to be listening—before answering just as softly. "With the fog to hide them . . . well, when what they do is hidden, men sometimes deal with strangers in ways they wouldn't if there were other eyes to see. And the quickest to harm a stranger are the soonest to think a stranger will harm them. This fellow . . . I believe he might sell his mother to Trollocs for stew meat if the price was right. I'm a little surprised you ask. I heard the way people in Emond's Field speak of those from Taren Ferry."

"Yes, but. . . . Well, everyone says they. . . . But I never thought they would actually. . . ." Rand decided he had better stop thinking that he knew anything at all of what people were like beyond his own village. "He might tell the Fade we crossed on the ferry," he said at last. "Maybe he'll bring the Trollocs over after us."

Lan chuckled dryly. "Robbing a stranger is one thing, dealing with a Halfman something else again. Can you really see him ferrying Trollocs over, especially in this fog, no matter how much gold was offered? Or even talking to a Myrddraal, if he had any choice? Just the thought of it would keep him running for a month. I don't think we have to worry very much about Darkfriends in Taren Ferry. Not here. We are safe . . . for a time, at least. From this lot, anyway. Watch yourself."

Hightower had turned from peering into the fog ahead. Pointed face pushed forward and torch held high, he stared at Lan and Rand as if seeing them clearly for the first time. Deck-planks creaked under the haulers' feet and the occasional stamp of a hoof. Abruptly the ferryman twitched as he realized they were watching him watching them. With a leap he spun back to looking for the far bank, or whatever it was he sought in the fog.

"Say no more," Lan said, so softly Rand almost could not understand. "These are bad days to speak of Trollocs, or Darkfriends, or the Father of Lies, with strange ears to hear. Such talk can bring worse than the Dragon's Fang scrawled on your door."

Rand felt no desire to go on with his questions. Gloom settled on him even more than it had before. Darkfriends! As if Fades and Trollocs and Draghkar were not enough to worry about. At least you could tell a Trolloc at sight.

Abruptly pilings loomed shadowy in the mist before them. The ferry thudded against the far bank, and then the haulers were hurrying to lash the craft fast and let down the ramp at that end with a thump, while Mat and Perrin announced loudly that the Taren was not half as wide as they had heard. Lan led his stallion down the ramp, followed by Moiraine and the others. As Rand, the last, took Cloud down behind Bela, Master Hightower called out angrily.

"Here, now! Here! Where's my gold?"

"It shall be paid." Moiraine's voice came from somewhere in the mist. Rand's boots clumped from the ramp to a wooden landing. "And a silver mark for each of your men," the Aes Sedai added, "for the quick crossing."

The ferryman hesitated, face pushed forward as if he smelled danger, but at the mention of silver the haulers roused themselves. Some paused to seize a torch, but they all thumped down the ramp before Hightower could open his mouth. With a sullen grimace, the ferryman followed his crew.

Cloud's hooves clumped hollowly in the fog as Rand made his way carefully along the landing. The gray mist was as thick here as over the river. At the foot of the landing, the Warder was handing out coins, surrounded by the torches of Hightower and his fellows. Everyone else except Moiraine waited just beyond in an anxious cluster. The Aes Sedai stood looking at the river, though what she could see was beyond Rand. With a shiver he hitched up his cloak, sodden as it was. He was really out of the Two Rivers, now, and it seemed much farther away than the width of a river.

"There," Lan said, handing a last coin to Hightower. "As agreed." He did not put up his purse, and the ferrety-faced man eyed it greedily.

With a loud creak, the landing shivered. Hightower jerked upright, head swiveling back toward the mist-cloaked ferry. The torches remaining on board were a pair of dim, fuzzy points of light. The landing groaned, and with a thunderous crack of snapping wood, the twin glows lurched, then began to revolve. Egwene cried out wordlessly, and Thom cursed.

"It's loose!" Hightower screamed. Grabbing his haulers, he pushed them toward the end of the landing. "The ferry's loose, you fools! Get it! Get it!"

The haulers stumbled a few steps under Hightower's shoves, then stopped. The faint lights on the ferry spun faster, then faster still. The fog above them swirled, sucked into a spiral. The landing trembled. The cracking and splintering of wood filled the air as the ferry began breaking apart.

"Whirlpool," one of the haulers said, his voice filled with awe.

"No whirlpools on the Taren." Hightower sounded empty. "Never been a whirlpool. . . ."

"An unfortunate occurrence." Moiraine's voice was hollow in the fog that made her a shadow as she turned from the river.

"Unfortunate," Lan agreed in a flat tone. "It seems you'll be carrying no one else across the river for a time. An ill thing that you lost your craft in our service." He delved again into his purse, ready in his hand. "This should repay you."

For a moment Hightower stared at the gold, glinting in Lan's hand in the torchlight, then his shoulders hunched and his eyes darted to the others he had carried across. Made indistinct by the fog, the Emond's Fielders stood silently. With a frightened, inarticulate cry, the ferryman snatched the coins from Lan, whirled, and ran into the mist. His haulers were only half a step behind him, their torches quickly swallowed as they vanished upriver.

"There is nothing further to hold us here," the Aes Sedai said as if nothing out of the ordinary had happened. Leading her white mare, she started away from the landing, up the bank.

Rand stood staring at the hidden river. *It could have been happenstance. No whirlpools, he said, but it.* . . . Abruptly he realized everyone else had gone. Hurriedly he scrambled up the gently sloping bank.

In the space of three paces the heavy mist faded away to nothing. He stopped dead and stared back. Along a line running down the shore thick gray hung on one side, on the other shone a clear night sky, still dark though the sharpness of the moon hinted at dawn not far off.

The Warder and the Aes Sedai stood conferring beside their horses a short distance beyond the border of the fog. The others huddled a little apart; even in the moonlit darkness their nervousness was palpable. All eyes were on Lan and Moiraine, and all but Egwene were leaning back as if torn between losing the pair and getting too close. Rand trotted the last few spans to Egwene's side, leading Cloud, and she grinned at him. He did not think the shine in her eyes was all from moonlight.

"It follows the river as if drawn with a pen," Moiraine was saying in satisfied tones. "There are not ten women in Tar Valon who could do that unaided. Not to mention from the back of a galloping horse."

"I don't mean to complain, Moiraine Sedai," Thom said, sounding oddly diffident for him, "but would it not have been better to cover us a little further? Say to Baerlon? If that Draghkar looks on this side of the river, we'll lose everything we have gained."

"Draghkar are not very smart, Master Merrilin," the Aes Sedai said dryly. "Fearsome and deadly dangerous, and with sharp eyes, but little intelligence. It will tell the Myrddraal that this side of the river is clear, but the river itself is cloaked for miles in both directions. The Myrddraal will know the extra effort that cost me. He will have to consider that we may be escaping down the river, and that will slow him. He will have to divide his efforts. The fog should hold long enough that he will never be sure that we did not travel at least partway by boat. I could have extended the fog a little way toward Baerlon, instead, but then the Draghkar could search the river in a matter of hours, and the Myrddraal would know exactly where we were headed."

Thom made a puffing sound and shook his head. "I apologize, Aes Sedai. I hope I did not offend."

"Ah, Moi . . . ah, Aes Sedai." Mat stopped to swallow audibly. "The ferry . . . ah . . . did you . . . I mean . . . I don't understand why. . . ." He trailed off weakly, and there was a silence so deep that the loudest sound Rand heard was his own breathing.

Finally Moiraine spoke, and her voice filled the empty silence with sharpness. "You all want explanations, but if I explained my every action to you, I would have no time for anything else." In the moonlight, the Aes Sedai seemed taller, somehow, almost looming over them. "Know this. I intend to see you safely in Tar Valon. That is the one thing you need to know."

"If we keep standing here," Lan put in, "the Draghkar will not need to search the river. If I remember correctly. . . ." He led his horse on up the riverbank.

As if the Warder's movement had loosened something in his chest, Rand drew a deep breath. He heard others doing the same, even Thom, and remembered an old saying. Better to spit in a wolf's eye than to cross an Aes Sedai. Yet the tension had lessened. Moiraine was not looming over anyone; she barely reached his chest.

"I don't suppose we could rest a bit," Perrin said hopefully, ending with a yawn. Egwene, slumped against Bela, sighed tiredly.

It was the first sound even approaching a complaint that Rand had heard from her. *Maybe now she realizes this isn't some grand adventure after all.* Then he guiltily remembered that, unlike him, she had not slept the day away. "We do need to rest, Moiraine Sedai," he said. "After all, we have ridden all night."

"Then I suggest we see what Lan has for us," Moiraine said. "Come."

She led them on up the bank, into the woods beyond the river. Bare branches thickened the shadows. A good hundred spans from the Taren they came to a dark mound beside a clearing. Here a long-ago flood had undermined and toppled an entire stand of leatherleafs, washing them together into a great, thick tangle, an apparently solid mass of trunks and branches and roots. Moiraine stopped, and suddenly a light appeared low to the ground, coming from under the heap of trees.

Thrusting a stub of a torch ahead of him, Lan crawled out from under the mound and straightened. "No unwelcome visitors," he told Moiraine. "And the wood I left is still dry, so I started a small fire. We will rest warm."

"You expected us to stop here?" Egwene said in surprise.

"It seemed a likely place," Lan replied. "I like to be prepared, just in case."

Moiraine took the torch from him. "Will you see to the horses? When you are done I will do what I can about everyone's tiredness. Right now I want to talk to Egwene. Egwene?"

Rand watched the two women crouch down and disappear under the great pile of tree trunks. There was a low opening, barely big enough to crawl into. The light of the torch vanished.

Lan had included feedbags and a small quantity of oats in the supplies, but he stopped the others from unsaddling their horses. Instead he produced the hobbles he had also packed. "They would rest easier without the saddles, but if we must leave quickly, there may be no time to replace them."

"They don't look to me like they need any rest," Perrin said as he attempted to slip a feedbag over his mount's muzzle. The horse tossed its head before allowing him to put the straps in place. Rand was having difficulties with Cloud, too, taking three tries before he could get the canvas bag over the gray's nose.

"They do," Lan told them. He straightened from hobbling his stallion. "Oh, they can still run. They will run at their fastest, if we let them, right up to the second they drop dead from exhaustion they never even felt. I would rather Moiraine Sedai had not had to do what she did, but it was necessary." He patted the stallion's neck, and the horse bobbed his head as if acknowledging the Warder's touch. "We must go slowly with them for the next few days, until they recover. More slowly than I would like. But with luck it will be enough."

"Is that . . . ?" Mat swallowed audibly. "Is that what she meant? About our tiredness?"

Rand patted Cloud's neck and stared at nothing. Despite what she had done for Tam, he had no desire for the Aes Sedai to use the Power on him. *Light, she as much as admitted sinking the ferry.*

"Something like it." Lan chuckled wryly. "But you will not have to worry about running yourself to death. Not unless things get a lot worse than they are. Just think of it as an extra night's sleep."

The shrill scream of the Draghkar suddenly echoed from above the fog-covered river. Even the horses froze. Again it came, closer now, and again, piercing Rand's skull like needles. Then the cries were fading, until they had faded away entirely.

"Luck," Lan breathed. "It searches the river for us." He gave a quick shrug and abruptly sounded matter-of-fact. "Let's get inside. I could do with some hot tea and something to fill my belly."

Rand was the first to crawl on hands and knees through the opening in the tangle of trees and down a short tunnel. At the end of it, he stopped, still crouching. Ahead was an irregularly shaped space, a woody cave easily large enough to hold them all. The roof of tree trunks and branches came too low to allow any but the women to stand. Smoke from a small fire on a bed of river stones drifted up and through; the draft was enough to keep the space free of smoke, but the interweaving was too thick to let out even a glimmer of the flames. Moiraine and Egwene, their cloaks thrown aside, sat cross-legged, facing one another beside the fire.

"The One Power," Moiraine was saying, "comes from the True Source, the driving force of Creation, the force the Creator made to turn the Wheel of Time." She put her hands together in front of her and pushed them against each other. "*Saidin,* the male half of the True Source, and *Saidar,* the female half, work against each other and at the same time together to provide that force. *Saidin*"—she lifted one hand, then let it drop—"is fouled by the touch of the Dark One, like water with a thin slick of rancid oil floating on top. The water is still pure, but it cannot be touched without touching the foulness. Only *Saidar* is still safe to be used." Egwene's back was to Rand. He could not see her face, but she was leaning forward eagerly.

Mat poked Rand from behind and muttered something, and he moved on into the tree cavern. Moiraine and Egwene ignored his entry. The other men crowded in behind him, tossing off damp cloaks, settling around the fire, and holding hands out to the warmth. Lan, the last to enter, pulled waterbags and leather sacks from a nook in the wall, took out a kettle, and began to prepare tea. He paid no attention to what the women were saying, but Rand's friends began to stop toasting their hands and stare openly. Thom pretended that all of his interest was engaged in loading his thickly carved pipe, but the way he leaned toward the women gave him away. Moiraine and Egwene acted as if they were alone.

"No," Moiraine said in answer to a question Rand had missed, "the True Source cannot be used up, any more than the river can be used up by the wheel of a mill. The Source is the river; the Aes Sedai, the waterwheel."

"And you really think I can learn?" Egwene asked. Her face shone
with eagerness. Rand had never seen her look so beautiful, or so far
away from him. "I can become an Aes Sedai?"

Rand jumped up, cracking his head against the low roof of logs.
Thom Merrilin grabbed his arm, yanking him back down.

"Don't be a fool," the gleeman murmured. He eyed the women—neither seemed to have noticed—and the look he gave Rand
was sympathetic. "It's beyond you now, boy."

"Child," Moiraine said gently, "only a very few can learn to touch
the True Source and use the One Power. Some of those can learn to
a greater degree, some to a lesser. You are one of the bare handful
for whom there is no need to learn. At least, touching the Source will
come to you whether you want it or not. Without the teaching you can
receive in Tar Valon, though, you will never learn to channel it fully,
and you may not survive. Men who have the ability to touch *Saidin*
born in them die, of course, if the Red Ajah does not find them and
gentle them. . . ."

Thom growled deep in his throat, and Rand shifted uncomfortably.
Men like those of whom the Aes Sedai spoke were rare—he had only
heard of three in his whole life, and thank the Light never in the Two
Rivers—but the damage they did before the Aes Sedai found them
was always bad enough for the news to carry, like the news of wars,
or earthquakes that destroyed cities. He had never really understood
what the Ajahs did. According to the stories they were societies among
the Aes Sedai that seemed to plot and squabble among themselves
more than anything else, but the stories were clear on one point. The
Red Ajah held its prime duty to be the prevention of another Breaking
of the World, and they did it by hunting down every man who even
dreamed of wielding the One Power. Mat and Perrin looked as if they
suddenly wished they were back home in their beds.

". . . but some of the women die, too. It is hard to learn without a
guide. The women we do not find, those who live, often become . . .
well, in this part of the world they might become Wisdoms of their
villages." The Aes Sedai paused thoughtfully. "The old blood is strong
in Emond's Field, and the old blood sings. I knew you for what you
were the moment I saw you. No Aes Sedai can stand in the presence
of a woman who can channel, or who is close to her change, and not
feel it." She rummaged in the pouch at her belt and produced the
small blue gem on a gold chain that she had earlier worn in her hair.
"You are very close to your change, your first touching. It will be
better if I guide you through it. That way you will avoid the . . . un-

pleasant effects that come to those who must find their own way."

Egwene's eyes widened as she looked at the stone, and she wet her lips repeatedly. "Is . . . does that have the Power?"

"Of course not," Moiraine snapped. "*Things* do not have the Power, child. Even an *angreal* is only a tool. This is just a pretty blue stone. But it can give off light. Here."

Egwene's hands trembled as Moiraine laid the stone on her fingertips. She started to pull back, but the Aes Sedai held both her hands in one of hers and gently touched the other to the side of Egwene's head.

"Look at the stone," the Aes Sedai said softly. "It is better this way than fumbling alone. Clear your mind of everything but the stone. Clear your mind, and let yourself drift. There is only the stone and emptiness. I will begin it. Drift, and let me guide you. No thoughts. Drift."

Rand's fingers dug into his knees; his jaws clenched until they hurt. *She has to fail. She has to.*

Light bloomed in the stone, just one flash of blue and then gone, no brighter than a firefly, but he flinched as if it had been blinding. Egwene and Moiraine stared into the stone, faces empty. Another flash came, and another, until the azure light pulsed like the beating of a heart. *It's the Aes Sedai,* he thought desperately. *Moiraine's doing it. Not Egwene.*

One last, feeble flicker, and the stone was merely a bauble again. Rand held his breath.

For a moment Egwene continued to stare at the small stone, then she looked up at Moiraine. "I . . . I thought I felt . . . something, but. . . . Perhaps you're mistaken about me. I am sorry I wasted your time."

"I have wasted nothing, child." A small smile of satisfaction flitted across Moiraine's lips. "That last light was yours alone."

"It was?" Egwene exclaimed, then slid immediately back into glumness. "But it was barely there at all."

"Now you are behaving like a foolish village girl. Most who come to Tar Valon must study for many months before they can do what you just did. You may go far. Perhaps even the Amyrlin Seat, one day, if you study hard and work hard."

"You mean . . . ?" With a cry of delight Egwene threw her arms around the Aes Sedai. "Oh, thank you. Rand, did you hear? I'm going to be an Aes Sedai!"

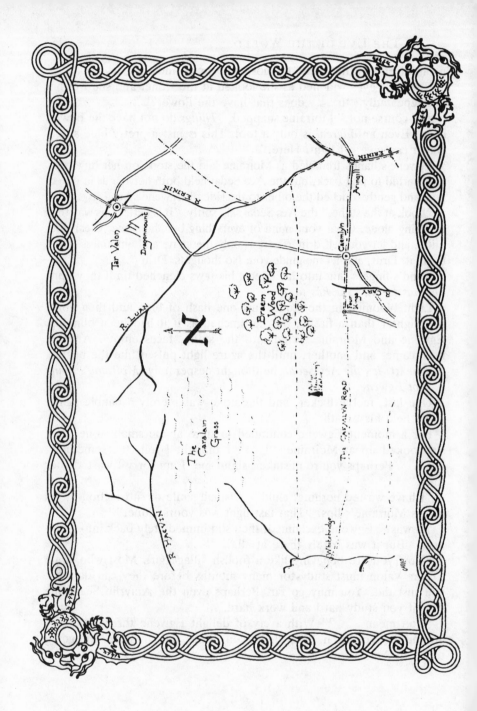

CHAPTER
13

Choices

Before they went to sleep Moiraine knelt by each in turn and laid her hands on their heads. Lan grumbled that he had no need and she should not waste her strength, but he did not try to stop her. Egwene was eager for the experience, Mat and Perrin clearly frightened of it, and frightened to say no. Thom jerked away from the Aes Sedai's hands, but she seized his gray head with a look that allowed no nonsense. The gleeman scowled through the entire thing. She smiled mockingly once she took her hands away. His frown deepened, but he did look refreshed. They all did.

Rand had drawn back into a niche in the uneven wall where he hoped he would be overlooked. His eyes wanted to slide closed once he leaned back against the timber jumble, but he forced himself to watch. He pushed a fist against his mouth to stifle a yawn. A little sleep, an hour or two, and he would be just fine. Moiraine did not forget him, though.

He flinched at the coolness of her fingers on his face, and said, "I don't—" His eyes widened in wonder. Tiredness drained out of him like water running downhill; aches and soreness ebbed to dim memories and vanished. He stared at her with his mouth hanging open. She only smiled and withdrew her hands.

"It is done," she said, and as she stood with a weary sigh he was reminded that she could not do the same for herself. Indeed, she only drank a little tea, refusing the bread and cheese Lan tried to press on her, before curling up beside the fire. She seemed to fall asleep the instant she wrapped her cloak around her.

The others, all save Lan, were dropping asleep wherever they could find a space to stretch out, but Rand could not imagine why. He felt as if he had already had a full night in a good bed. No sooner did he lean back against the log wall, though, than sleep rolled him under. When Lan poked him awake an hour later he felt as though he had had three days rest.

The Warder awakened them all, except Moiraine, and he sternly hushed any sound that might disturb her. Even so, he allowed them only a short stay in the snug cave of trees. Before the sun was twice its own height above the horizon, all traces that anyone had ever stopped there had been cleared away and they were all mounted and moving north toward Baerlon, riding slowly to conserve the horses. The Aes Sedai's eyes were shadowed, but she sat her saddle upright and steady.

Fog still hung thick over the river behind them, a gray wall resisting the efforts of the feeble sun to burn it away and hiding the Two Rivers from view. Rand watched over his shoulder as he rode, hoping for one last glimpse, even of Taren Ferry, until the fogbank was lost to sight.

"I never thought I'd ever be this far from home," he said when the trees at last hid both the fog and the river. "Remember when Watch Hill seemed a long way?" *Two days ago, that was. It seems like forever.*

"In a month or two, we'll be back," Perrin said in a strained voice. "Think what we'll have to tell."

"Even Trollocs can't chase us forever," Mat said. "Burn me, they can't." He straightened around with a heavy sigh, slumping in his saddle as if he did not believe a word that had been said.

"Men!" Egwene snorted. "You get the adventure you're always prating about, and already you're talking about home." She held her head high, yet Rand noticed a tremor to her voice, now that nothing more was to be seen of the Two Rivers.

Neither Moiraine nor Lan made any attempt to reassure them, not a word to say that of course they would come back. He tried not to think on what that might mean. Even rested, he was full enough of doubts without searching out more. Hunching in his saddle he began a waking dream of tending the sheep alongside Tam in a pasture with deep, lush grass and larks singing of a spring morning. And a trip into Emond's Field, and Bel Tine the way it had been, dancing on the Green with never a care beyond whether he might stumble in the steps. He managed to lose himself in it for a long time.

The journey to Baerlon took almost a week. Lan muttered about the laggardness of their travel, but it was he who set the pace and forced the rest to keep it. With himself and his stallion, Mandarb—he said it meant "Blade" in the Old Tongue—he was not so sparing. The Warder covered twice as much ground as they did, galloping ahead, his color-shifting cloak swirling in the wind, to scout what lay before them, or dropping behind to examine their backtrail. Any others who tried to move at more than a walk, though, got cutting words on taking care of their animals, biting words on how well they would do afoot if the Trollocs did appear. Not even Moiraine was proof against his tongue if she let the white mare pick up its step. Aldieb, the mare was called; in the Old Tongue, "Westwind," the wind that brought the spring rains.

The Warder's scouting never turned up any sign of pursuit, or ambush. He spoke only to Moiraine of what he saw, and that quietly, so it could not be overheard, and the Aes Sedai informed the rest of them of what she thought they needed to know. In the beginning, Rand looked over his shoulder as much as he did ahead. He was not the only one. Perrin fingered his axe often, and Mat rode with an arrow nocked to his bow, in the beginning. But the land behind remained empty of Trollocs or figures in black cloaks, the sky remained empty of Draghkar. Slowly, Rand began to think perhaps they really had escaped.

No very great cover was to be had, even in the thickest parts of the woods. Winter clung as hard north of the Taren as it did in the Two Rivers. Stands of pine or fir or leatherleaf, and here and there a few spicewoods or laurels, dotted a forest of otherwise bare, gray branches. Not even the elders showed a leaf. Only scattered green sprigs of new growth stood out against brown meadows beaten flat by the winter's snows. Here, too, much of what did grow was stinging nettles and coarse thistle and stinkweed. On the bare dirt of the forest floor some of the last snow still hung on, in shady patches and in drifts beneath the low branches of evergreens. Everyone kept their cloaks drawn well about them, for the thin sunlight had no warmth to it and the night cold pierced deep. No more birds flew here than in the Two Rivers, not even ravens.

There was nothing leisurely about the slowness of their movement. The North Road—Rand continued to think of it that way, though he suspected it might have a different name here, north of the Taren—still ran almost due north, but at Lan's insistence their path snaked this way and that through the forest as often as it ran along the hard-packed dirt road. A village, or a farm, or any sign of men or civilization sent them circling for miles to avoid it, though there were few enough of any of those. The whole first day Rand saw no evidence aside from the road that men had ever been in that woods. It came to him that even when he had gone to the foot of the Mountains of Mist he might not have been as far from a human habitation as he was that day.

The first farm he saw—a large frame house and tall barn with high-peaked, thatched roofs, a curl of smoke rising from a stone chimney—was a shock.

"It's no different from back home," Perrin said, frowning at the distant buildings, barely visible through the trees. People moved around the farmyard, as yet unaware of the travelers.

"Of course it is," Mat said. "We're just not close enough to see."

"I tell you, it's no different," Perrin insisted.

"It must be. We're north of the Taren, after all."

"Quiet, you two," Lan growled. "We don't want to be seen, remember? This way." He turned west, to circle the farm through the trees.

Looking back, Rand thought Perrin was right. The farm looked much the same as any around Emond's Field. There was a small boy toting water from the well, and older boys tending sheep behind a rail fence. It even had a curing shed, for tabac. But Mat was right, too. *We're north of the Taren. It must be different.*

Always they halted while light still clung to the sky, to choose a spot sloped for drainage and sheltered from the wind that seldom died completely, only changed direction. Their fire was always small and hidden from only a few yards off, and once tea was brewed, the flames were doused and the coals buried.

At their first stop, before the sun sank, Lan began teaching the boys what to do with the weapons they carried. He started with the bow. After watching Mat put three arrows into a knot the size of a man's head, on the fissured trunk of a dead leatherleaf, at a hundred paces, he told the others to take their turns. Perrin duplicated Mat's feat, and Rand, summoning the flame and the void, the empty calm that let the bow become a part of him, or him of it, clustered his three where the points almost touched one another. Mat gave him a congratulatory clap on the shoulder.

"Now if you all had bows," the Warder said dryly when they started grinning, "and if the Trollocs agreed not to come so close you couldn't use them. . . ." The grins faded abruptly. "Let me see what I can teach you in case they do come that close."

He showed Perrin a bit of how to use that great-bladed axe; raising an axe to someone, or something, that had a weapon was not at all like chopping wood or flailing around in pretend. Setting the big apprentice blacksmith to a series of exercises, block, parry, and strike, he did the same for Rand and his sword. Not the wild leaping about and slashing that Rand had in mind whenever he thought about using it, but smooth motions, one flowing into another, almost a dance.

"Moving the blade is not enough," Lan said, "though some think it is. The mind is part of it, most of it. Blank your mind, sheepherder. Empty it of hate or fear, of everything. Burn them away. You others listen to this, too. You can use it with the axe or the bow, with a spear, or a quarterstaff, or even your bare hands."

Rand stared at him. "The flame and the void," he said wonderingly. "That's what you mean, isn't it? My father taught me about that."

The Warder gave him an unreadable look in return. "Hold the sword as I showed you, sheepherder. I cannot make a mud-footed villager into a blademaster in an hour, but perhaps I can keep you from slicing off your own foot."

Rand sighed and held the sword upright before him in both hands. Moiraine watched without expression, but the next evening she told Lan to continue the lessons.

The meal at evening was always the same as at midday and breakfast, flatbread and cheese and dried meat, except that evenings they had hot tea to wash it down instead of water. Thom entertained them, evenings. Lan would not let the gleeman play harp or flute—no need to rouse the countryside, the Warder said—but Thom juggled and told stories. "Mara and the Three Foolish Kings," or one of the hundreds about Anla the Wise Counselor, or something filled with glory and adventure, like *The Great Hunt of the Horn*, but always with a happy ending and a joyous homecoming.

Yet if the land was peaceful around them, if no Trollocs appeared among the trees, no Draghkar among the clouds, it seemed to Rand that they managed to raise their tension themselves, whenever it was in danger of vanishing.

There was the morning that Egwene awoke and began unbraiding her hair. Rand watched her from the corner of his eye as he made up his blanketroll. Every night when the fire was doused, everyone took to their blankets except for Egwene and the Aes Sedai. The two women always went aside from the others and talked for an hour or two, returning when the others were asleep. Egwene combed her hair out—one hundred strokes; he counted—while he was saddling Cloud, tying his saddlebags and blanket behind the saddle. Then she tucked the comb away, swept her loose hair over her shoulder, and pulled up the hood of her cloak.

Startled, he asked, "What are you doing?" She gave him a sidelong look without answering. It was the first time he had spoken to her in two days, he realized, since the night in the log shelter on the bank of the Taren, but he did not let that stop him. "All your life you've waited to wear your hair in a braid, and now you're giving it up? Why? Because she doesn't braid hers?"

"Aes Sedai don't braid their hair," she said simply. "At least, not unless they want to."

"You aren't an Aes Sedai. You're Egwene al'Vere from Emond's Field, and the Women's Circle would have a fit if they could see you now."

"Women's Circle business is none of yours, Rand al'Thor. And I *will* be an Aes Sedai. Just as soon as I reach Tar Valon."

He snorted. "As soon as you reach Tar Valon. Why? Light, tell me that. You're no Darkfriend."

"Do you think Moiraine Sedai is a Darkfriend? Do you?" She squared around to face him with her fists clenched, and he almost thought she was going to hit him. "After she saved the village? After she saved your father?"

"I don't know what she is, but whatever she is, it doesn't say anything about the rest of them. The stories—"

"Grow up, Rand! Forget the stories and use your eyes."

"My eyes saw her sink the ferry! Deny that! Once you get an idea in your head, you won't budge even if somebody points out you're trying to stand on water. If you weren't such a Light-blinded fool, you'd see—!"

"Fool, am I? Let me tell you a thing or two, Rand al'Thor! You are the muliest, most wool-headed—!"

"You two trying to wake everybody inside ten miles?" the Warder asked.

Standing there with his mouth open, trying to get a word in edgewise, Rand suddenly realized he had been shouting. They both had.

Egwene's face went scarlet to her eyebrows, and she spun away with a muttered, "Men!" that seemed as much for the Warder as for him.

Warily, Rand looked around the camp. Everybody was looking at him, not just the Warder. Mat and Perrin, with their faces white. Thom, tensed as if ready to run or fight. Moiraine. The Aes Sedai's face was expressionless, but her eyes seemed to bore into his head. Desperately, he tried to recall exactly what he had said, about Aes Sedai and Darkfriends.

"It is time to be going," Moiraine said. She turned to Aldieb, and Rand shivered as if he had been let out of a trap. He wondered if he had been.

Two nights later, with the fire burning low, Mat licked the last crumbs of cheese from his fingers and said, "You know, I think we've lost them for good." Lan was off in the night, taking a last look around. Moiraine and Egwene had gone aside for one of their conversations. Thom was half dozing over his pipe, and the young men had the fire to themselves.

Perrin, idly poking the embers with a stick, answered. "If we've lost them, why does Lan keep scouting?" Nearly asleep, Rand rolled over, his back to the fire.

"We lost them back at Taren Ferry." Mat lay back with his fingers laced behind his head, staring at the moon-filled sky. "If they were even really after us."

"You think that Draghkar was chasing us because it liked us?" Perrin asked.

"I say, stop worrying about Trollocs and such," Mat went on as if Perrin had not spoken, "and start thinking about seeing the world. We're out where the stories come from. What do you think a real city is like?"

"We're going to Baerlon," Rand said sleepily, but Mat snorted.

"Baerlon's all very well, but I've seen that old map Master al'Vere has. If we turn south once we reach Caemlyn, the road leads all the way to Illian, and beyond."

"What's so special about Illian?" Perrin said, yawning.

"For one thing," Mat replied, "Illian isn't full of Aes Se—"

A silence fell, and Rand was suddenly wide awake. Moiraine had come back early. Egwene was with her, but it was the Aes Sedai, standing at the edge of the firelight, who held their attention. Mat lay there on his back, his mouth still open, staring at her. Moiraine's eyes caught the light like dark, polished stones. Abruptly Rand wondered how long she had been standing there.

"The lads were just—" Thom began, but Moiraine spoke right over the top of him.

"A few days respite, and you are ready to give up." Her calm, level voice contrasted sharply with her eyes. "A day or two of quiet, and already you have forgotten Winternight."

"We haven't forgotten," Perrin said. "It's just—" Still not raising her voice, the Aes Sedai treated him as she had the gleeman.

"Is that the way you all feel? You are all eager to run off to Illian and forget about Trollocs, and Halfmen, and Draghkar?" She ran her eyes over them—that stony glint playing against the everyday tone of voice made Rand uneasy—but she gave no one a chance to speak. "The Dark One is after you three, one or all, and if I let you go running off wherever you want to go, he will take you. Whatever the Dark One wants, I oppose, so hear this and know it true. Before I let the Dark One have you, I will destroy you myself."

It was her voice, so matter-of-fact, that convinced Rand. The Aes Sedai would do exactly what she said, if she thought it was necessary. He had a hard time sleeping that night, and he was not the only one. Even the gleeman did not begin snoring till long after the last coals died. For once, Moiraine offered no help.

Those nightly talks between Egwene and the Aes Sedai were a sore point for Rand. Whenever they disappeared into the darkness, aside from the rest for privacy, he wondered what they were saying, what they were doing. What was the Aes Sedai doing to Egwene?

One night, he waited until the other men had all settled down, Thom snoring like a saw cutting an oak knot. Then he slipped away, clutching his blanket around him. Using every bit of skill he had gained stalking rabbits, he moved with the moon shadows until he was crouched at the base of a tall leatherleaf tree, thick with tough, broad leaves, close enough to hear Moiraine and Egwene, where they sat on a fallen log with a small lantern for light.

"Ask," Moiraine was saying, "and if I can tell you now, I will. Understand, there is much for which you are not yet ready, things you cannot learn until you have learned other things which require still others to be learned before them. But ask what you will."

"The Five Powers," Egwene said slowly. "Earth, Wind, Fire, Water, and Spirit. It doesn't seem fair that men should have been strongest in wielding Earth and Fire. Why should they have had the strongest Powers?"

Moiraine laughed. "Is that what you think, child? Is there a rock so hard that wind and water cannot wear it away, a fire so strong that water cannot quench it or wind snuff it out?"

Egwene was silent for a time, digging her toe into the forest floor.

"They . . . they were the ones who . . . who tried to free the Dark One and the Forsaken, weren't they? The male Aes Sedai?" She took a deep breath and picked up speed. "The women were not part of it. It was the men who went mad and broke the world."

"You are afraid," Moiraine said grimly. "If you had remained in Emond's Field, you would have become Wisdom, in time. That was Nynaeve's plan, was it not? Or, you would have sat in the Women's Circle and managed the affairs of Emond's Field while the Village Council thought it was doing so. But you did the unthinkable. You left Emond's Field, left the Two Rivers, seeking adventure. You wanted to do it, and at the same time you are afraid of it. And you are stubbornly refusing to let your fear best you. You would not have asked me how a woman becomes an Aes Sedai, otherwise. You would not have thrown custom and convention over the fence, otherwise."

"No," Egwene protested. "I'm not afraid. I do want to become an Aes Sedai."

"Better for you if you were afraid, but I hope you hold to that conviction. Few women these days have the ability to become initiates, much less have the wish to." Moiraine's voice sounded as if she had begun musing to herself. "Surely never before two in one village. The old blood is indeed still strong in the Two Rivers."

In the shadows, Rand shifted. A twig snapped under his foot. He froze instantly, sweating and holding his breath, but neither of the women looked around.

"Two?" Egwene exclaimed. "Who else? Is it Kari? Kari Thane? Lara Ayellan?"

Moiraine gave an exasperated click of her tongue, then said sternly, "You must forget I said that. Her road lies another way, I fear. Concern yourself with your own circumstances. It is not an easy road you have chosen."

"I will not turn back," Egwene said.

"Be that as it may. But you still want reassurance, and I cannot give it to you, not in the way you want."

"I don't understand."

"You want to know that Aes Sedai are good and pure, that it was those wicked men of the legends who caused the Breaking of the World, not the women. Well, it was the men, but they were no more wicked than any men. They were insane, not evil. The Aes Sedai you will find in Tar Valon are human, no different from any other women except for the ability that sets us apart. They are brave and cowardly, strong and weak, kind and cruel, warm-hearted and cold. Becoming an Aes Sedai will not change you from what you are."

Egwene drew a heavy breath. "I suppose I was afraid of that, that I'd be changed by the Power. That and the Trollocs. And the Fade. And. . . . Moiraine Sedai, in the name of the Light, why did the Trollocs come to Emond's Field?"

The Aes Sedai's head swung, and she looked straight at Rand's hiding place. His breath seized in his throat; her eyes were as hard as when she had threatened them, and he had the feeling they could penetrate the leatherleaf's thick branches. *Light, what will she do if she finds me listening?*

He tried to melt back into the deeper shadows. With his eyes on the women, a root snagged his foot, and he barely caught himself from tumbling into dead brush that would have pointed him out with a crackle of snapping branches like fireworks. Panting, he scrambled away on all fours, keeping silent as much by luck as by anything he did. His heart pounded so hard he thought that might give him away itself. *Fool! Eavesdropping on an Aes Sedai!*

Back where the others were sleeping, he managed to slip in among them silently. Lan moved as he dropped to the ground and jerked his blanket up, but the Warder settled back with a sigh. He had only been rolling over in his sleep. Rand let out a long, silent breath.

A moment later Moiraine appeared out of the night, stopping where she could study the slumbering shapes. Moonlight made a nimbus around her. Rand closed his eyes and breathed evenly, all the while listening hard for footsteps coming closer. None did. When he opened his eyes again, she was gone.

When finally sleep came, it was fitful and filled with sweaty dreams where all the men in Emond's Field claimed to be the Dragon Reborn and all the women had blue stones in their hair like the one Moiraine wore. He did not try to overhear Moiraine and Egwene again.

On into the sixth day the slow journey stretched. The warmthless sun slid slowly toward the treetops, while a handful of thin clouds drifted high to the north. The wind gusted higher for a moment, and Rand pulled his cloak back up onto his shoulders, muttering to himself. He wondered if they would ever get to Baerlon. The distance they had traveled from the river already was more than enough to take him from Taren Ferry to the White River, but Lan always said it was just a short journey whenever he was asked, hardly worth calling a journey at all. It made him feel lost.

Lan appeared ahead of them in the woods, returning from one of his forays. He reined in and rode beside Moiraine, his head bent close to hers.

Rand grimaced, but he did not ask any questions. Lan simply refused to acknowledge all such questions aimed at him.

Only Egwene, among the others, even appeared to notice Lan's return, so used to this arrangement had they become, and she kept back, too. The Aes Sedai might have begun acting as if Egwene were in charge of the Emond's Fielders, but that gave her no say when the Warder made his reports. Perrin was carrying Mat's bow, wrapped in the thoughtful silence that seemed to take them all more and more as they got further from the Two Rivers. The horses' slow walk allowed Mat to practice juggling three small stones under Thom Merrilin's watchful eye. The gleeman had given lessons each night, too, as well as Lan.

Lan finished whatever he had been telling Moiraine, and she twisted in her saddle to look back at the others. Rand tried not to stiffen when her eyes moved across him. Did they linger on him a moment longer than on anyone else? He had the queasy feeling that she knew who had been listening in the darkness that night.

"Hey, Rand," Mat called, "I can juggle four!" Rand waved in reply without looking around. "I told you I'd get to four before you. I— Look!"

They had topped a low hill, and below them, a scant mile away through the stark trees and the stretching shadows of evening, lay Baerlon. Rand gasped, trying to smile and gape at the same time.

A log wall, nearly twenty feet tall, surrounded the town, with wooden watchtowers scattered along its length. Within, rooftops of slate and tile glinted with the sinking sun, and feathers of smoke drifted upward from chimneys. Hundreds of chimneys. There was not a thatched roof to be seen. A broad road ran east from the town, and another west, each with at least a dozen wagons and twice as many ox-carts trudging toward the palisade. Farms lay scattered about the town, thickest to the north while only a few broke the forest to the south, but they might as well not have existed so far as Rand was concerned. *It's bigger than Emond's Field and Watch Hill and Deven Ride all put together! And maybe Taren Ferry, too.*

"So that's a city," Mat breathed, leaning forward across his horse's neck to stare.

Perrin could only shake his head. "How can so many people live in one place?"

Egwene simply stared.

Thom Merrilin glanced at Mat, then rolled his eyes and blew out his mustaches. "City!" he snorted.

"And you, Rand?" Moiraine said. "What do you think of your first sight of Baerlon?"

"I think it's a long way from home," he said slowly, bringing a sharp laugh from Mat.

"You have further to go yet," Moiraine said. "Much further. But there is no other choice, except to run and hide and run again for the rest of your lives. And short lives they would be. You must remember that, when the journey becomes hard. You have no choice."

Rand exchanged glances with Mat and Perrin. By their faces, they were thinking the same thing he was. How could she talk as if they had any choice after what she had said? *The Aes Sedai's made our choices.*

Moiraine went on as if their thoughts were not plain. "The danger begins again here. Watch what you say within those walls. Above all, do not mention Trollocs, or Halfmen, or any such. You must not even think of the Dark One. Some in Baerlon have even less love for Aes Sedai than do the people of Emond's Field, and there may even be Darkfriends." Egwene gasped, and Perrin muttered under his breath. Mat's face paled, but Moiraine went on calmly. "We must attract as little attention as possible." Lan was exchanging his cloak of shifting grays and greens for one of dark brown, more ordinary, though of fine cut and weave. His color-changing cloak made a large bulge in one of his saddlebags. "We do not go by our own names here," Moiraine continued. "Here I am known as Alys, and Lan is Andra. Remember that. Good. Let us be within the walls before night catches us. The gates of Baerlon are closed from sundown to sunrise."

Lan led the way down the hill and through the woods toward the log wall. The road passed half a dozen farms—none lay close, and none of the people finishing their chores seemed to notice the travelers—ending at heavy wooden gates bound with wide straps of black iron. They were closed tight, even if the sun was not down yet.

Lan rode close to the wall and gave a tug to a frayed rope hanging down beside the gates. A bell clanged on the other side of the wall. Abruptly a wizened face under a battered cloth cap peered down suspiciously from atop the wall, glaring between the cut-off ends of two of the logs, a good three spans over their heads.

"What's all this, eh? It's too late in the day to be opening this gate. Too late, I say. Go around to the Whitebridge Gate if you want to—" Moiraine's mare moved out to where the man atop the wall had a clear view of her. Suddenly his wrinkles deepened in a gap-toothed smile, and he seemed to quiver between speaking and doing his duty. "I didn't know it was you, mistress. Wait. I'll be right down. Just wait. I'm coming. I'm coming."

The head dipped out of sight, but Rand could still hear muffled shouts for them to stay where they were, that he was coming. With great creaks of disuse, the right-hand gate slowly swung outward. It stopped when open just wide enough for one horse to pass through at a time, and the gatekeeper poked his head into the gap, flashed his half-toothless smile at them again and darted back out of the way. Moiraine followed Lan through, with Egwene right behind her.

Rand trotted Cloud after Bela and found himself in a narrow street fronted by high wooden fences and warehouses, tall and windowless, broad doors closed up tight. Moiraine and Lan were already on foot, speaking to the wrinkle-faced gatekeeper, so Rand dismounted, too.

The little man, in a much-mended cloak and coat, held his cloth cap crumpled in one hand and ducked his head whenever he spoke. He peered at those dismounting behind Lan and Moiraine, and shook his head. "Downcountry folk." He grinned. "Why, Mistress Alys, you taken up collecting downcountry folk with hay in their hair?" His look took in Thom Merrilin, then. "You ain't a sheepfarmer. I remember letting you go through some days back, I do. Didn't like your tricks downcountry, eh, gleeman?"

"I hope you remembered to forget letting us through, Master Avin," Lan said, pressing a coin into the man's free hand. "And letting us back in, too."

"No need for that, Master Andra. No need for that. You give me plenty when you went out. Plenty." Just the same, Avin made the coin disappear as deftly as if he were a gleeman, too. "I ain't told nobody, and I won't, neither. Especially not them Whitecloaks," he finished with a scowl. He pursed up his lips to spit, then glanced at Moiraine and swallowed, instead.

Rand blinked, but kept his mouth shut. The others did, too, though it appeared to be an effort for Mat. *Children of the Light,* Rand thought wonderingly. Stories told about the Children by peddlers and merchants and merchants' guards varied from admiration to hatred, but all agreed the Children hated Aes Sedai as much as they did Dark-friends. He wondered if this was more trouble already.

"The Children are in Baerlon?" Lan demanded.

"They surely are." The gatekeeper bobbed his head. "Came the same day you left, as I recall. Ain't nobody here likes them at all. Most don't let on, of course."

"Have they said why they are here?" Moiraine asked intently.

"Why they're here, mistress?" Avin was so astonished he forgot to duck his head. "Of course, they said why— Oh, I forgot. You been downcountry. Likely you ain't heard nothing but sheep bleating. They say they're here because of what's going on down in Ghealdan. The Dragon, you know—well, him as calls himself Dragon. They say the fellow's stirring up evil—which I expect he is—and they're here to stamp it out, only he's down there in Ghealdan, not here. Just an excuse to meddle in other people's business, is what I figure. There's already been the Dragon's Fang on some people's doors." This time he did spit.

"Have they caused much trouble, then?" Lan said, and Avin shook his head vigorously.

"Not that they don't want to, I expect, only the Governor don't trust them no more than I do. He won't let but maybe ten or so inside the walls at one time, and ain't they mad about that. The rest have a camp a little ways north, I hear. Bet they got the farmers looking over their shoulders. The ones that do come in, they just stalk around in those white cloaks, looking down their noses at honest folk. Walk in the Light, they say, and it's an order. Near come to blows more than once with the wagoneers and miners and smelters and all, and even the Watch, but the Governor wants it all peaceful, and that's how it's been so far. If they're hunting evil, I say why aren't they up in Saldaea? There's some kind of trouble up there, I hear. Or down in Ghealdan? There's been a big battle down there, they say. Real big."

Moiraine drew a soft breath. "I had heard that Aes Sedai were going to Ghealdan."

"Yes, they did, mistress." Avin's head started bobbing again. "They went to Ghealdan, all right, and that's what started this battle, or so I hear. They say some of those Aes Sedai are dead. Maybe all of them. I know some folks don't hold with Aes Sedai, but I say, who else is going to stop a false Dragon? Eh? And those damned fools who think they can be men Aes Sedai or some such. What about them? Course, some say—not the Whitecloaks, mind, and not me, but some folks—that maybe this fellow really is the Dragon Reborn. He can do things, I hear. Use the One Power. There's thousands following him."

"Don't be a fool," Lan snapped, and Avin's face folded into a hurt look.

"I'm only saying what I heard, ain't I? Just what I heard, Master Andra. They say, some do, that he's moving his army east and south, toward Tear." His voice became heavy with meaning. "They say he's named them the People of the Dragon."

"Names mean little," Moiraine said calmly. If anything she had
heard disturbed her, she gave no outward sign of it now. "You could
call your mule People of the Dragon, if you wanted."

"Not likely, mistress." Avin chuckled. "Not with the Whitecloaks
around, for sure. I don't expect anybody else would look kindly on a
name like that, neither. I see what you mean, but . . . oh, no, mistress.
Not *my* mule."

"No doubt a wise decision," Moiraine said. "Now we must be off."

"And don't you worry, mistress," Avin said, with a deep bob of his
head, "I ain't seen nobody." He darted to the gate and began tugging
it closed with quick jerks. "Ain't seen nobody, and ain't seen nothing." The gate thudded shut, and he pulled down the locking bar with
a rope. "In fact, mistress, this gate ain't been open in days."

"The Light illumine you, Avin," Moiraine said.

She led them away from the gate, then. Rand looked back, once,
and Avin was still standing in front of the gate. He seemed to be polishing a coin with an edge of his cloak and chuckling.

The way led through dirt streets barely the width of two wagons,
empty of people, all lined with warehouses and occasional high,
wooden fences. Rand walked a time beside the gleeman. "Thom, what
was all that about Tear, and the People of the Dragon? Tear is a city
all the way down on the Sea of Storms, isn't it?"

"The Karaethon Cycle," Thom said curtly.

Rand blinked. *The Prophecies of the Dragon.* "Nobody tells the . . .
those stories in the Two Rivers. Not in Emond's Field, anyway. The
Wisdom would skin them alive, if they did."

"I suppose she would, at that," Thom said dryly. He glanced at
Moiraine up ahead with Lan, saw she could not overhear, and went
on. "Tear is the greatest port on the Sea of Storms, and the Stone of
Tear is the fortress that guards it. The Stone is said to be the first
fortress built after the Breaking of the World, and in all this time it
has never fallen, though more than one army has tried. One of the
Prophecies says that the Stone of Tear will never fall until the People
of the Dragon come to the Stone. Another says the Stone will never
fall till the Sword That Cannot Be Touched is wielded by the Dragon's
hand." Thom grimaced. "The fall of the Stone will be one of the major
proofs that the Dragon has been reborn. May the Stone stand till I am
dust."

"The sword that cannot be touched?"

"That's what it says. I don't know whether it really is a sword. Whatever it is, it lies in the Heart of the Stone, the central citadel of the

fortress. None but the Great Lords of Tear can enter there, and they never speak of what lies inside. Certainly not to gleemen, anyway."

Rand frowned. "The Stone cannot fall until the Dragon wields the sword, but how can he, unless the Stone has already fallen? Is the Dragon supposed to be a Great Lord of Tear?"

"Not much chance of that," the gleeman said dryly. "Tear hates anything to do with the Power even more than Amador, and Amador is the stronghold of the Children of the Light."

"Then how can the Prophecy be fulfilled?" Rand asked. "I'd like it well enough if the Dragon was never reborn, but a prophecy that cannot be fulfilled doesn't make much sense. It sounds like a story meant to make people think the Dragon never will be reborn. Is that it?"

"You ask an awful lot of questions, boy," Thom said. "A prophecy that was easily fulfilled would not be worth much, now would it?" Suddenly his voice brightened. "Well, we're here. Wherever here is."

Lan had stopped by a section of head-high wooden fence that looked no different from any other they had passed. He was working the blade of his dagger between two of the boards. Abruptly he gave a grunt of satisfaction, pulled, and a length of the fence swung out like a gate. In fact it was a gate, Rand saw, though one meant to be opened only from the other side. The metal latch that Lan had lifted with his dagger showed that.

Moiraine went through immediately, drawing Aldieb behind her. Lan motioned the others to follow, and brought up the rear, closing the gate behind him.

On the other side of the fence Rand found himself in the stableyard of an inn. A loud bustle and clatter came from the building's kitchen, but what struck him was its size: it covered more than twice as much ground as the Winespring Inn, and was four stories high besides. Well over half the windows were aglow in the deepening twilight. He wondered at this city, that could have so many strangers in it.

No sooner had they come well into the stableyard than three men in dirty canvas aprons appeared at the huge stable's broad, arched doors. One, a wiry fellow and the only one without a manure fork in his hands, came forward waving his arms.

"Here! Here! You can't come in that way! You'll have to go round the front!"

Lan's hand went to his purse again, but even as it did another man, as big around as Master al'Vere, came hurrying out of the inn. Puffs of hair stuck out above his ears, and his sparkling white apron was as good as a sign proclaiming him the innkeeper.

"It's all right, Mutch," the newcomer said. "It's all right. These folk are expected guests. Take care of their horses, now. Good care."

Mutch sullenly knuckled his forehead, then motioned his two companions to come help. Rand and the others hurriedly got their saddlebags and blanketrolls down while the innkeeper turned to Moiraine. He gave her a deep bow, and spoke with a genuine smile.

"Welcome, Mistress Alys. Welcome. It's good to be seeing you, you and Master Andra, both. Very good. Your fine conversation has been missed. Yes, it has. I must say I worried, you going downcountry and all. Well, I mean, at a time like this, with the weather all crazy and wolves howling right up to the walls in the night." Abruptly he slapped both hands against his round belly and shook his head. "Here I go on like this, chattering away, instead of taking you inside. Come. Come. Hot meals and warm beds, that's what you'll be wanting. And the best in Baerlon are right here. The very best."

"And hot baths, too, I trust, Master Fitch?" Moiraine said, and Egwene echoed her fervently. "Oh, yes."

"Baths?" the innkeeper said. "Why, just the best and the hottest in Baerlon. Come. Welcome to the Stag and Lion. Welcome to Baerlon."

CHAPTER 14

The Stag and Lion

Inside, the inn was every bit as busy as the sounds coming from it had indicated and more. The party from Emond's Field followed Master Fitch through the back door, soon weaving around and between a constant stream of men and women in long aprons, platters of food and trays of drink held high. The bearers murmured quick apologies when they got in anyone's way, but they never slowed by a step. One of the men took hurried orders from Master Fitch and disappeared at a run.

"The inn is near full, I'm afraid," the innkeeper told Moiraine. "Almost to the rafters. Every inn in the town is the same. With the winter we just had . . . well, as soon as it cleared enough for them to get down out of the mountains we were inundated—yes, that's the word—inundated by men from the mines and smelters, all telling the most horrible tales. Wolves, and worse. The kind of tales men tell when they've been cooped up all winter. I can't think there's anyone left up there at all, we have that many here. But never fear. Things may be a little crowded, but I'll do my best by you and Master Andra.

And your friends, too, of course." He glanced curiously once or twice at Rand and the others; except for Thom their clothes named them country folk, and Thom's gleeman's cloak made him a strange traveling companion as well for "Mistress Alys" and "Master Andra." "I will do my best, you may rest assured."

Rand stared at the bustle around them and tried to avoid being stepped on, though none of the help really seemed to be in any danger of that. He kept thinking of how Master al'Vere and his wife tended the Winespring Inn with sometimes a little assistance from their daughters.

Mat and Perrin craned their necks in interest toward the common room, from which rolled a wave of laughter and singing and jovial shouting whenever the wide door at the end of the hall swung open. Muttering about finding out the news, the Warder grimly disappeared through that swinging door, swallowed by a wave of merriment.

Rand wanted to follow him, but he wanted a bath even more. He could have done with people and laughing right then, but the common room would appreciate his presence more when he was clean. Mat and Perrin apparently felt the same; Mat was scratching surreptitiously.

"Master Fitch," Moiraine said, "I understand there are Children of the Light in Baerlon. Is there likely to be trouble?"

"Oh, never you worry about them, Mistress Alys. They're up to their usual tricks. Claim there's an Aes Sedai in the town." Moiraine lifted an eyebrow, and the innkeeper spread his plump hands. "Don't you worry. They've tried it before. There's no Aes Sedai in Baerlon, and the Governor knows it. The Whitecloaks think if they show an Aes Sedai, some woman they claim is an Aes Sedai, people will let all of them inside the walls. Well, I suppose some would. Some would. But most people know what the Whitecloaks are up to, and they support the Governor. No one wants to see some harmless old woman hurt just so the Children can have an excuse for whipping up a frenzy."

"I am glad to hear it," Moiraine said dryly. She put a hand on the innkeeper's arm. "Is Min still here? I wish to talk with her, if she is."

Master Fitch's answer was lost to Rand in the arrival of attendants to lead them to the baths. Moiraine and Egwene vanished behind a plump woman with a ready smile and an armload of towels. The gleeman and Rand and his friends found themselves following a slight, dark-haired fellow, Ara by name.

Rand tried asking Ara about Baerlon, but the man barely said two words together except to say Rand had a funny accent, and then the first sight of the bath chamber drove all thoughts of talk right out of Rand's head. A dozen tall, copper bathtubs sat in a circle on the tiled

floor, which sloped down slightly to a drain in the center of the big
stone-walled room. A thick towel, neatly folded, and a large cake of
yellow soap sat on a stool behind each tub, and big black iron caul-
drons of water stood heating over fires along one wall. On the opposite
wall logs blazing in a deep fireplace added to the general warmth.

"Almost as good as the Winespring Inn back home," Perrin said
loyally, if not exactly with a great attention to truth.

Thom barked a laugh, and Mat sniggered, "Sounds like we brought
a Coplin with us and didn't know it."

Rand shrugged out of his cloak and stripped off his clothes while
Ara filled four of the copper tubs. None of the others was far behind
Rand in choosing a bathtub. Once their clothes were all in piles on
the stools, Ara brought them each a large bucket of hot water and a
dipper. That done, he sat on a stool by the door, leaning back against
the wall with his arms crossed, apparently lost in his own thoughts.

There was little in the way of conversation while they lathered and
sluiced away a week of grime with dippers of steaming water. Then it
was into the tubs for a long soak; Ara had made the water hot enough
that settling in was a slow process of luxuriant sighs. The air in the
room went from warm to misty and hot. For a long time there was no
sound except the occasional long, relaxing exhalation as tight muscles
loosened and a chill that they had come to think permanent was drawn
out of their bones.

"Need anything else?" Ara asked suddenly. He did not have much
room to talk about people's accents; he and Master Fitch both sounded
as if they had a mouth full of mush. "More towels? More hot water?"

"Nothing," Thom said in his reverberant voice. Eyes closed, he gave
an indolent wave of his hand. "Go and enjoy the evening. At a later
time I will see that you receive more than adequate recompense for
your services." He settled lower in the tub, until the water covered
everything but his eyes and nose.

Ara's eyes went to the stools behind the tubs, where their clothes
and belongings were stacked. He glanced at the bow, but lingered
longest over Rand's sword and Perrin's axe. "Is there trouble downcountry, too?" he said abruptly. "In the Rivers, or whatever you call
it?"

"The Two Rivers," Mat said, pronouncing each separate word dis-
tinctly. "It's the Two Rivers. As for trouble, why—"

"What do you mean, too?" Rand asked. "Is there some kind of
trouble here?"

Perrin, enjoying his soak, murmured, "Good! Good!" Thom raised
himself back up a little, and opened his eyes.

"Here?" Ara snorted. "Trouble? Miners having fistfights in the streets in the dark of the morning aren't trouble. Or. . . ." He stopped and eyed them a moment. "I meant the Ghealdan kind of trouble," he said finally. "No, I suppose not. Nothing but sheep downcountry, is there? No offense. I just meant it's quiet down there. Still, it's been a strange winter. Strange things in the mountains. I heard the other day there were Trollocs up in Saldaea. But that's the Borderlands then, isn't it?" He finished with his mouth still open, then snapped it shut, appearing surprised that he had said so much.

Rand had tensed at the word *Trollocs,* and tried to hide it by wringing his washcloth out over his head. As the fellow went on he relaxed, but not everyone kept his mouth shut.

"Trollocs?" Mat chortled. Rand splashed water at him, but Mat just wiped it off of his face with a grin. "You just let me tell you about Trollocs."

For the first time since climbing into his tub, Thom spoke. "Why don't you not? I am a little tired of hearing my own stories back from you."

"He's a gleeman," Perrin said, and Ara gave him a scornful look.

"I saw the cloak. You going to perform?"

"Just a minute," Mat protested. "What's this about me telling Thom's stories? Are you all—?"

"You just don't tell them as well as Thom," Rand cut him off hastily, and Perrin hopped in. "You keep adding in things, trying to make it better, and they never do."

"And you get it all mixed up, too," Rand added. "Best leave it to Thom."

They were all talking so fast that Ara stared at them with his mouth hanging open. Mat stared, too, as if everyone else had suddenly gone crazy. Rand wondered how to shut him up short of jumping on him.

The door banged open to admit Lan, brown cloak slung over one shoulder, along with a gust of cooler air that momentarily thinned the mist.

"Well," the Warder said, rubbing his hands, "this is what I have been waiting for." Ara picked up a bucket, but Lan waved it away. "No, I will see to myself." Dropping his cloak on one of the stools, he bundled the bath attendant out of the room, despite the fellow's protests, and shut the door firmly after him. He waited there a moment, his head cocked to listen, and when he turned back to the rest of them his voice was stony and his eyes stabbed at Mat. "It's a good thing I got back when I did, farmboy. Don't you listen to what you are told?"

"I didn't do anything," Mat protested. "I was just going to tell him

about the Trollocs, not about. . . ." He stopped, and leaned back from
the Warder's eyes, flat against the back of the tub.

"Don't talk about Trollocs," Lan said grimly. "Don't even think
about Trollocs." With an angry snort he began filling himself a bathtub. "Blood and ashes, you had better remember, the Dark One has
eyes and ears where you least expect. And if the Children of the Light
heard Trollocs were after you, they'd be burning to get their hands on
you. To them, it would be as much as naming you Darkfriend. It may
not be what you are used to, but until we get where we are going,
keep your trust small unless Mistress Alys or I tell you differently."
At his emphasis on the name Moiraine was using, Mat flinched.

"There was something that fellow wouldn't tell us," Rand said.
"Something he thought was trouble, but he wouldn't say what it was."

"Probably the Children," Lan said, pouring more hot water into his
tub. "Most people consider them trouble. Some don't, though, and he
did not know you well enough to risk it. You might have gone running
to the Whitecloaks, for all he knew."

Rand shook his head; this place already sounded worse than Taren
Ferry could possibly be.

"He said there were Trollocs in . . . in Saldaea, wasn't it?" Perrin
said.

Lan hurled his empty bucket to the floor with a crash. "You will
talk about it, won't you? There are always Trollocs in the Borderlands,
blacksmith. Just you put it in the front of your mind that we want no
more attention than mice in a field. Concentrate on that. Moiraine
wants to get you all to Tar Valon alive, and I will do it if it can be
done, but if you bring any harm to her. . . ."

The rest of their bathing was done in silence, and dressing afterwards, too.

When they left the bath chamber, Moiraine was standing at the end
of the hall with a slender girl not much taller than herself. At least,
Rand thought it was a girl, though her dark hair was cut short and she
wore a man's shirt and trousers. Moiraine said something, and the girl
looked at the men sharply, then nodded to Moiraine and hurried away.

"Well, now," Moiraine said as they drew closer, "I am sure a bath
has given you all an appetite. Master Fitch has given us a private dining room." She talked on inconsequentially as she turned to lead the
way, about their rooms and the crowding in the town, and how the
innkeeper hoped Thom would favor the common room with some music and a story or two. She never mentioned the girl, if girl it had been.

The private dining room had a polished oak table with a dozen chairs around it, and a thick rug on the floor. As they entered, Egwene, freshly gleaming hair combed out around her shoulders, turned from warming her hands at the fire crackling on the hearth. Rand had had plenty of time for thought during the long silence in the bath chamber. Lan's constant admonitions not to trust anyone, and especially Ara being afraid to trust them, had made him think of just how alone they really were. It seemed they could not trust anyone but themselves, and he was still not too sure how far they could trust Moiraine, or Lan. Just themselves. And Egwene was still Egwene. Moiraine said it would have happened to her anyway, this touching the True Source. She had no control over it, and that meant it was not her fault. And she was still Egwene.

He opened his mouth to apologize, but Egwene stiffened and turned her back before he could get a word out. Staring sullenly at her back, he swallowed what he had been going to say. *All right, then. If she wants to be like that, there's nothing I can do.*

Master Fitch bustled in then, followed by four women in white aprons as long as his, with a platter holding three roast chickens and others bearing silver, and pottery dishes, and covered bowls. The women began setting the table immediately, while the innkeeper bowed to Moiraine.

"My apologies, Mistress Alys, for making you wait like this, but with so many people in the inn, it's a wonder anybody gets served at all. I am afraid the food isn't what it should be, either. Just the chickens, and some turnips and henpeas, with a little cheese for after. No, it just isn't what it should be. I truly do apologize."

"A feast." Moiraine smiled. "For these troubled times, a feast indeed, Master Fitch."

The innkeeper bowed again. His wispy hair, sticking out in all directions as if he constantly ran his hands through it, made the bow comical, but his grin was so pleasant that anyone who laughed would be laughing with him, not at him. "My thanks, Mistress Alys. My thanks." As he straightened he frowned and wiped an imagined bit of dust from the table with a corner of his apron. "It isn't what I would have laid before you a year ago, of course. Not nearly. The winter. Yes. The winter. My cellars are emptying out, and the market is all but bare. And who can blame the farm folk? Who? There's certainly no telling when they'll harvest another crop. No telling at all. It's the wolves get the mutton and beef that should go on people's tables, and. . . ."

Abruptly he seemed to realize that this was hardly the conversation to settle his guests to a comfortable meal. "How I do run on. Full of old wind, that's me. Old wind. Mari, Cinda, let these good people eat in peace." He made shooing gestures at the women and, as they scurried from the room, swung back to bow to Moiraine yet again. "I hope you enjoy your meal, Mistress Alys. If there's anything else you need, just speak it, and I will fetch it. Just you speak it. It is a pleasure serving you and Master Andra. A pleasure." He gave one more deep bow and was gone, closing the door softly behind him.

Lan had slouched against the wall through all of this as if half asleep. Now he leaped up and was at the door in two long strides. Pressing an ear to a door panel, he listened intently for a slow count of thirty, then snatched open the door and stuck his head into the hall. "They're gone," he said at last, closing the door. "We can talk safely."

"I know you say not to trust anyone," Egwene said, "but if you suspect the innkeeper, why stay here?"

"I suspect him no more than anyone else," Lan replied. "But then, until we reach Tar Valon, I suspect everyone. There, I'll suspect only half."

Rand started to smile, thinking the Warder was making a joke. Then he realized there was not a trace of humor on Lan's face. He really would suspect people in Tar Valon. Was anywhere safe?

"He exaggerates," Moiraine told them soothingly. "Master Fitch is a good man, honest and trustworthy. But he does like to talk, and with the best will in the world he might let something slip to the wrong ear. And I have never yet stopped at an inn where half the maids did not listen at doors and spend more time gossiping than making beds. Come, let us be seated before our meal gets cold."

They took places around the table, with Moiraine at the head and Lan at the foot, and for a while everyone was too busy filling their plates for talk. It might not have been a feast, but after close to a week of flatbread and dried meat, it tasted like one.

After a time, Moiraine asked, "What did you learn in the common room?" Knives and forks stilled, suspended in mid-air, and all eyes turned to the Warder.

"Little that's good," Lan replied. "Avin was right, at least as far as talk has it. There was a battle in Ghealdan, and Logain was the victor. A dozen different stories are floating about, but they all agree on that."

Logain? That must be the false Dragon. It was the first time Rand had heard a name put to the man. Lan sounded almost as if he knew him.

"The Aes Sedai?" Moiraine asked quietly, and Lan shook his head.

"I don't know. Some say they were all killed, some say none." He snorted. "Some even say they went over to Logain. There's nothing reliable, and I did not care to show too much interest."

"Yes," Moiraine said. "Little that is good." With a deep breath she brought her attention back to the table. "And what of our own circumstances?"

"There, the news is better. No odd happenings, no strangers around who might be Myrddraal, certainly no Trollocs. And the Whitecloaks are busy trying to make trouble for Governor Adan because he won't cooperate with them. They will not even notice us unless we advertise ourselves."

"Good," Moiraine said. "That agrees with what the bath maid said. Gossip does have its points. Now," she addressed the entire company, "we have a long journey still ahead of us, but the last week has not been easy, either, so I propose to remain here tonight and tomorrow night, and leave early the following morning." All the younger folk grinned; a city for the first time. Moiraine smiled, but she still said, "What does Master Andra say to that?"

Lan eyed the grinning faces flatly. "Well enough, if they remember what I've told them for a change."

Thom snorted through his mustaches. "These country folk loose in a . . . a city." He snorted again and shook his head.

With the crowding at the inn there were only three rooms to be had, one for Moiraine and Egwene, and two to take the men. Rand found himself sharing with Lan and Thom, on the fourth floor at the back, close up under the overhanging eaves, with a single small window that overlooked the stableyard. Full night had fallen, and light from the inn made a pool outside. It was a small room to begin, and an extra bed set up for Thom made it smaller, though all three were narrow. And hard, Rand found when he threw himself down on his. Definitely not the best room.

Thom stayed only long enough to uncase his flute and harp, then left already practicing grand poses. Lan went with him.

It was strange, Rand thought as he shifted uncomfortably on the bed. A week ago he would have been downstairs like a falling rock for just the chance he might see a gleeman perform, for just the rumor of it. But he had heard Thom tell his stories every night for a week, and Thom would be there tomorrow night, and the next, and the hot bath had loosened kinks in muscles that he had thought would be there forever, and his first hot meal in a week oozed lethargy into him. Sleepily he wondered if Lan really did know the false Dragon, Logain. A muffled shout came from belowstairs, the common room greeting Thom's arrival, but Rand was already asleep.

*   *   *

The stone hallway was dim and shadowy, and empty except for Rand. He could not tell where the light came from, what little there was of it; the gray walls were bare of candles or lamps, nothing at all to account for the faint glow that seemed to just be there. The air was still and dank, and somewhere in the distance water dripped with a steady, hollow plonk. Wherever this was, it was not the inn. Frowning, he rubbed at his forehead. Inn? His head hurt, and thoughts were hard to hold on to. There had been something about . . . an inn? It was gone, whatever it was.

He licked his lips and wished he had something to drink. He was awfully thirsty, dry-as-dust thirsty. It was the dripping sound that decided him. With nothing to choose by except his thirst, he started toward that steady *plonk—plonk—plonk*.

The hallway stretched on, without any crossing corridor and without the slightest change in appearance. The only features at all were the rough doors set at regular intervals in pairs, one on either side of the hall, the wood splintered and dry despite the damp in the air. The shadows receded ahead of him, staying the same, and the dripping never came any closer. After a long time he decided to try one of those doors. It opened easily, and he stepped through into a grim, stone-walled chamber.

One wall opened in a series of arches onto a gray stone balcony, and beyond that was a sky such as he had never seen. Striated clouds in blacks and grays, reds and oranges, streamed by as if storm winds drove them, weaving and interweaving endlessly. *No one* could ever have seen a sky like that; it could not exist.

He pulled his eyes away from the balcony, but the rest of the room was no better. Odd curves and peculiar angles, as if the chamber had been melted almost haphazardly out of the stone, and columns that seemed to grow out of the gray floor. Flames roared on the hearth like a forge-fire with the bellows pumping, but gave no heat. Strange oval stones made the fireplace; they just looked like stones, wet-slick despite the fire, when he looked straight at them, but when he glimpsed them from the corner of his eye they seemed to be faces instead, the faces of men and women writhing in anguish, screaming silently. The high-backed chairs and the polished table in the middle of the room were perfectly ordinary, but that in itself emphasized the rest. A single mirror hung on the wall, but that was not ordinary at all. When he looked at it he saw only a blur where his reflection should have been. Everything else in the room was shown true, but not him.

A man stood in front of the fireplace. He had not noticed the man when he first came in. If he had not known it was impossible, he would have said no one had been there until he actually looked at the man. Dressed in dark clothes of a fine cut, he seemed in the prime of his maturity, and Rand supposed women would have found him good-looking.

"Once more we meet face-to-face," the man said and, just for an instant, his mouth and eyes became openings into endless caverns of flame.

With a yell Rand hurled himself backwards out of the room, so hard that he stumbled across the hall and banged into the door there, knocking it open. He twisted and grabbed at the doorhandle to keep from falling to the floor—and found himself staring wide-eyed into a stone room with an impossible sky through the arches leading to a balcony, and a fireplace. . . .

"You cannot get away from me that easily," the man said.

Rand twisted, scrambling back out of the room, trying to regain his feet without slowing down. This time there was no corridor. He froze half crouched not far from the polished table, and looked at the man by the fireplace. It was better than looking at the fireplace stones, or at the sky.

"This is a dream," he said as he straightened. Behind him he heard the click of the door closing. "It's some kind of nightmare." He shut his eyes, thinking about waking up. When he was a child the Wisdom had said if you could do that in a nightmare, it would go away. *The . . . Wisdom? What?* If only his thoughts would stop sliding away. If only his head would stop hurting, then he could think straight.

He opened his eyes again. The room was still as it had been, the balcony, the sky. The man by the fireplace.

"Is it a dream?" the man said. "Does it matter?" Once again, for a moment, his mouth and eyes became peepholes into a furnace that seemed to stretch forever. His voice did not change; he did not seem to notice it happening at all.

Rand jumped a little this time, but he managed to keep from yelling. *This is a dream. It has to be.* All the same, he stepped backwards all the way to the door, never taking his eyes off the fellow by the fire, and tried the handle. It did not move; the door was locked.

"You seem thirsty," the man by the fire said. "Drink."

On the table was a goblet, shining gold and ornamented with rubies and amethysts. It had not been there before. He wished he could stop jumping. It was only a dream. His mouth felt like dust.

"I am, a little," he said, picking up the goblet. The man leaned forward intently, one hand on the back of a chair, watching him. The smell of spiced wine drove home to Rand just how thirsty he was, as if he had had nothing to drink in days. *Have I?*

With the wine halfway to his mouth, he stopped. Whispers of smoke were rising from the chairback between the man's fingers. And those eyes watched him so sharply, flickering rapidly in and out of flames.

Rand licked his lips and put the wine back on the table, untasted. "I'm not as thirsty as I thought." The man straightened abruptly, his face without expression. His disappointment could not have been more plain if he had cursed. Rand wondered what was in the wine. But that was a stupid question, of course. This was all a dream. *Then why won't it stop?* "What do you want?" he demanded. "Who are you?"

Flames rose in the man's eyes and mouth; Rand thought he could hear them roar. "Some call me Ba'alzamon."

Rand found himself facing the door, jerking frantically at the handle. All thought of dreams had vanished. The Dark One. The doorhandle would not budge, but he kept twisting.

"Are you the one?" Ba'alzamon said suddenly. "You cannot hide it from me forever. You cannot even hide yourself from me, not on the highest mountain or in the deepest cave. I know you down to the smallest hair."

Rand turned to face the man—to face Ba'alzamon. He swallowed hard. A nightmare. He reached back to give the doorhandle one last pull, then stood up straighter.

"Are you expecting glory?" Ba'alzamon said. "Power? Did they tell you the Eye of the World would serve you? What glory or power is there for a puppet? The strings that move you have been centuries weaving. Your father was chosen by the White Tower, like a stallion roped and led to his business. Your mother was no more than a brood mare to their plans. And those plans lead to your death."

Rand's hands knotted in fists. "My father is a good man, and my mother was a good woman. Don't you talk about them!"

The flames laughed. "So there is some spirit in you after all. Perhaps you *are* the one. Little good it will do you. The Amyrlin Seat will use you until you are consumed, just as Davian was used, and Yurian Stonebow, and Guaire Amalasan, and Raolin Darksbane. Just as Logain is being used. Used until there is nothing left of you."

"I don't know. . . ." Rand swung his head from side to side. That one moment of clear thinking, born in anger, was gone. Even as he groped for it again he could not remember how he had reached it the first time. His thoughts spun around and around. He seized one like a raft in the whirlpool. He forced the words out, his voice strengthening the further he went. "You . . . are bound . . . in Shayol Ghul. You and all the Forsaken . . . bound by the Creator until the end of time."

"The end of time?" Ba'alzamon mocked. "You live like a beetle under a rock, and you think your slime is the universe. The death of time will bring me power such as you could not dream of, worm."

"You are bound—"

"Fool, I have never been bound!" The fires of his face roared so hot that Rand stepped back, sheltering behind his hands. The sweat on his palms dried from the heat. "I stood at Lews Therin Kinslayer's shoulder when he did the deed that named him. It was I who told him to kill his wife, and his children, and all his blood, and every living person who loved him or whom he loved. It was I who gave him the moment of sanity to know what he had done. Have you ever heard a man scream his soul away, worm? He could have struck at me, then. He could not have won, but he could have tried. Instead he called down his precious One Power upon himself, so much that the earth split open and reared up Dragonmount to mark his tomb.

"A thousand years later I sent the Trollocs ravening south, and for three centuries they savaged the world. Those blind fools in Tar Valon said I was beaten in the end, but the Second Covenant, the Covenant of the Ten Nations, was shattered beyond remaking, and who was left to oppose me then? I whispered in Artur Hawkwing's ear, and the length and breadth of the land Aes Sedai died. I whispered again, and the High King sent his armies across the Aryth Ocean, across the World Sea, and sealed two dooms. The doom of his dream of one land and one people, and a doom yet to come. At his deathbed I was there when his councilors told him only Aes Sedai could save his life. I spoke, and he ordered his councilors to the stake. I spoke, and the High King's last words were to cry that Tar Valon must be destroyed.

"When men such as these could not stand against me, what chance do you have, a toad crouching beside a forest puddle. You will serve me, or you will dance on Aes Sedai strings until you die. And then you *will* be mine. The dead belong to me!"

"No," Rand muttered, "this is a dream. It is a dream!"

"Do you think you are safe from me in your dreams? Look!" Ba'alzamon pointed commandingly, and Rand's head turned to follow, although he did not turn it; he did not want to turn.

The goblet was gone from the table. Where it had been, crouched a large rat, blinking at the light, sniffing the air warily. Ba'alzamon crooked his finger, and with a squeak the rat arched its back, forepaws lifting into the air while it balanced awkwardly on its hind feet. The finger curved more, and the rat toppled over, scrabbling frantically, pawing at nothing, squealing shrilly, its back bending, bending, bending. With a sharp snap like the breaking of a twig, the rat trembled violently and was still, lying bent almost double.

Rand swallowed. "Anything can happen in a dream," he mumbled. Without looking he swung his fist back against the door again. His hand hurt, but he still did not wake up.

"Then go to the Aes Sedai. Go to the White Tower and tell them. Tell the Amyrlin Seat of this . . . dream." The man laughed; Rand felt the heat of the flames on his face. "That is one way to escape them. They will not use you, then. No, not when they know that I know. But will they let you live, to spread the tale of what they do? Are you a big enough fool to believe they will? The ashes of many like you are scattered on the slopes of Dragonmount."

"This is a dream," Rand said, panting. "It's a dream, and I am going to wake up."

"Will you?" Out of the corner of his eye he saw the man's finger move to point at him. "Will you, indeed?" The finger crooked, and Rand screamed as he arched backwards, every muscle in his body forcing him further. "Will you ever wake again?"

Convulsively Rand jerked up in the darkness, his hands tightening on cloth. A blanket. Pale moonlight shone through the single window. The shadowed shapes of the other two beds. A snore from one of them, like canvas ripping: Thom Merrilin. A few coals gleamed among the ashes on the hearth.

It had been a dream, then, like that nightmare in the Winespring Inn the day of Bel Tine, everything that he had heard and done all jumbled in together with old tales and nonsense from nowhere. He pulled the blanket up around his shoulders, but it was not cold that made him shake. His head hurt, too. Perhaps Moiraine could do something to stop these dreams. *She said she could help with nightmares.*

With a snort he lay back. Were the dreams really bad enough for him to ask the help of an Aes Sedai? On the other hand, could anything he did now get him in any deeper? He had left the Two Rivers, come away with an Aes Sedai. But there had not been any choice, of course. So did he have any choice but to trust her? An Aes Sedai? It was as bad as the dreams, thinking about it. He huddled under his blanket, trying to find the calmness of the void the way Tam had taught him, but sleep was a long time returning.

CHAPTER
15

Strangers and Friends

Sunlight streaming across his narrow bed finally woke Rand out of a deep but restless sleep. He pulled a pillow over his head, but it did not really shut out the light, and he did not really want to go back to sleep. There had been more dreams after the first. He could not remember any but the first, but he knew he wanted no more.

With a sigh he tossed the pillow aside and sat up, wincing as he stretched. All the aches he thought had soaked out in the bath were back. And his head still hurt, too. It did not surprise him. A dream like that was enough to give anybody a headache. The others had already faded, but not that one.

The other beds were empty. Light poured in through the window at a steep angle; the sun stood well above the horizon. By this hour back on the farm he would have already fixed something to eat and been well into his chores. He scrambled out of bed, muttering angrily to himself. A city to see, and they did not even wake him. At least someone had seen that there was water in the pitcher, and still warm, too.

He washed and dressed quickly, hesitating a moment over Tam's sword. Lan and Thom had left their saddlebags and blanketrolls behind in the room, of course, but the Warder's sword was nowhere to be seen. Lan had worn his sword in Emond's Field even before there was any hint of trouble. He thought he would take the older man's lead. Telling himself it was not because he had often daydreamed about walking the streets of a real city wearing a sword, he belted it on and tossed his cloak over his shoulder like a sack.

Taking the stairs two at a time, he hurried down to the kitchen. That was surely the quickest place to get a bite, and on his only day in Baerlon he did not want to waste any more time than he already had. *Blood and ashes, but they could have waked me.*

Master Fitch was in the kitchen, confronting a plump woman whose arms were covered in flour to her elbows, obviously the cook. Rather, she was confronting him, shaking her finger under his nose. Serving maids and scullions, potboys and spitboys, hurried about their tasks, elaborately ignoring what was going on in front of them.

". . . my Cirri is a good cat," the cook was saying sharply, "and I won't hear a word otherwise, do you hear? Complaining about him doing his job too well, that's what you're doing, if you ask me."

"I have had complaints," Master Fitch managed to get in. "Complaints, mistress. Half the guests—"

"I won't hear of it. I just won't hear of it. If they want to complain about my cat, let *them* do the cooking. My poor old cat, who's just doing his job, and me, we'll go somewhere where we're appreciated, see if we don't." She untied her apron and started to lift it over her head.

"No!" Master Fitch yelped, and leaped to stop her. They danced in a circle with the cook trying to take her apron off and the innkeeper trying to put it back on her. "No, Sara," he panted. "There's no need for this. No need, I say! What would I do without you? Cirri's a fine cat. An excellent cat. He's the best cat in Baerlon. If anyone else complains, I'll tell them to be thankful the cat is doing his job. Yes, thankful. You mustn't go. Sara? Sara!"

The cook stopped their circling and managed to snatch her apron free of him. "All right, then. All right." Clutching the apron in both hands, she still did not retie it. "But if you expect me to have anything ready for midday, you'd best get out of here and let me get to it. This may be your inn, but it's my kitchen. Unless you want to do the cooking?" She made as if to hand the apron to him.

Master Fitch stepped back with his hands spread wide. He opened his mouth, then stopped, looking around for the first time. The kitchen help still studiously ignored the cook and the innkeeper, and Rand began an intensive search of his coat pockets, though except for the coin Moiraine had given him there was nothing in them but a few coppers and a handful of odds and ends. His pocket knife and sharpening stone. Two spare bowstrings and a piece of string he had thought might be useful.

"I am sure, Sara," Master Fitch said carefully, "that everything will be up to your usual excellence." With that he took one last suspicious look at the kitchen help, then left with as much dignity as he could manage.

Sara waited until he was gone before briskly tying her apron strings again, then fastened her eye on Rand. "I suppose you want something to eat, eh? Well, come on in." She gave him a quick grin. "I don't bite, I don't, no matter what you may have seen as you shouldn't. Ciel, get the lad some bread and cheese and milk. That's all there is right now. Sit yourself, lad. Your friends have all gone out, except one lad I understand wasn't feeling well, and I expect you'll be wanting to do the same."

One of the serving maids brought a tray while Rand took a stool at the table. He began eating as the cook went back to kneading her bread dough, but she was not finished talking.

"You mustn't take any mind of what you saw, now. Master Fitch is a good enough man, though the best of you aren't any bargains. It's the folk complaining as has him on edge, and what do they have to complain about? Would they rather find live rats than dead ones? Though it isn't like Cirri to leave his handiwork behind. And over a dozen? Cirri wouldn't let so many get into the inn, he wouldn't. It's a clean place, too, and not one to be so troubled. And all with backs broken." She shook her head at the strangeness of it all.

The bread and cheese turned to ashes in Rand's mouth. "Their backs were broken?"

The cook waved a floury hand. "Think on happier things, that's my way of looking. There's a gleeman, you know. In the common room right this minute. But then, you came with him, didn't you? You are one of those as came with Mistress Alys last evening, aren't you? I thought you were. I won't get much chance to see this gleeman myself, I'm thinking, not with the inn as full as it is, and most of them riffraff down from the mines." She gave the dough an especially heavy thump. "Not the sort we'd let in most times, only the whole town is filled up with them. Better than some they could be, though, I suppose. Why, I haven't seen a gleeman since before the winter, and. . . ."

Rand ate mechanically, not tasting anything, not listening to what the cook said. Dead rats, with their backs broken. He finished his breakfast hastily, stammered his thanks, and hurried out. He had to talk to someone.

The common room of the Stag and Lion shared little except its purpose with the same room at the Winespring Inn. It was twice as wide and three times as long, and colorful pictures of ornate buildings with gardens of tall trees and bright flowers were painted high on the walls. Instead of one huge fireplace, a hearth blazed on each wall, and scores of tables filled the floor, with almost every chair, bench, or stool taken.

Every man among the crowd of patrons with pipes in their teeth and mugs in their fists leaned forward with his attention on one thing: Thom, standing atop a table in the middle of the room, his many-colored cloak tossed over a nearby chair. Even Master Fitch held a silver tankard and a polishing cloth in motionless hands.

". . . prancing, silver hooves and proud, arched necks," Thom proclaimed, while somehow seeming not only to be riding a horse, but to be one of a long procession of riders. "Silken manes flutter with tossed heads. A thousand streaming banners whip rainbows against an endless sky. A hundred brazen-throated trumpets shiver the air, and drums rattle like thunder. Wave on wave, cheers roll from watchers in their thousands, roll across the rooftops and towers of Illian, crash and break unheard around the thousand ears of riders whose eyes and hearts shine with their sacred quest. The Great Hunt of the Horn rides forth, rides to seek the Horn of Valere that will summon the heroes of the Ages back from the grave to battle for the Light. . . ."

It was what the gleeman had called Plain Chant, those nights beside the fire on the ride north. Stories, he said, were told in three voices, High Chant, Plain Chant, and Common, which meant simply telling it the way you might tell your neighbor about your crop. Thom told stories in Common, but he did not bother to hide his contempt for the voice.

Rand closed the door without going in and slumped against the wall. He would get no advice from Thom. Moiraine—what *would* she do if she knew?

He became aware of people staring at him as they passed, and realized he was muttering under his breath. Smoothing his coat, he straightened. He had to talk to somebody. The cook had said one of the others had not gone out. It was an effort not to run.

When he rapped on the door of the room where the other boys had slept and poked his head in, only Perrin was there, lying on his bed

and still not dressed. He twisted his head on the pillow to look at
Rand, then closed his eyes again. Mat's bow and quiver were propped
in the corner.

"I heard you weren't feeling well," Rand said. He came in and sat
on the next bed. "I just wanted to talk. I. . . ." He did not know how
to bring it up, he realized. "If you're sick," he said, half standing,
"maybe you ought to sleep. I can go."

"I don't know if I'll ever sleep again." Perrin sighed. "I had a bad
dream, if you must know, and couldn't get back to sleep. Mat will be
quick enough to tell you. He laughed this morning, when I told them
why I was too tired to go out with him, but he dreamed, too. I listened
to him for most of the night, tossing and muttering, and you can't tell
me he got a good night's sleep." He threw a thick arm across his eyes.
"Light, but I'm tired. Maybe if I just stay here for an hour or two, I'll
feel like getting up. Mat will never let me hear the end of it if I miss
seeing Baerlon because of a dream."

Rand slowly lowered himself to the bed again. He licked his lips,
then said quickly, "Did he kill a rat?"

Perrin lowered his arm and stared at him. "You, too?" he said finally. When Rand nodded, he said, "I wish I was back home. He
told me . . . he said. . . . What are we going to do? Have you told
Moiraine?"

"No. Not yet. Maybe I won't. I don't know. What about you?"

"He said. . . . Blood and ashes, Rand, I don't know." Perrin raised
up on his elbow abruptly. "Do you think Mat had the same dream?
He laughed, but it sounded forced, and he looked funny when I said
I couldn't sleep because of a dream."

"Maybe he did," Rand said. Guiltily, he felt relieved he was not the
only one. "I was going to ask Thom for advice. He's seen a lot of the
world. You . . . you don't think we should tell Moiraine, do you?"

Perrin fell back on his pillow. "You've heard the stories about Aes
Sedai. Do you think we can trust Thom? If we can trust anybody.
Rand, if we get out of this alive, if we ever get back home, and you
hear me say anything about leaving Emond's Field, even to go as far
as Watch Hill, you kick me. All right?"

"That's no way to talk," Rand said. He put on a smile, as cheerful
as he could make it. "Of course we'll get home. Come on, get up.
We're in a city, and we have a whole day to see it. Where are your
clothes?"

"You go. I just want to lie here awhile." Perrin put his arm back
across his eyes. "You go ahead. I'll catch you up in an hour or two."

"It's your loss," Rand said as he got up. "Think of what you might miss." He stopped at the door. "Baerlon. How many times have we talked about seeing Baerlon one day?" Perrin lay there with his eyes covered and did not say a word. After a minute Rand stepped out and closed the door behind him.

In the hallway he leaned against the wall, his smile fading. His head still hurt; it was worse, not better. He could not work up much enthusiasm for Baerlon, either, not now. He could not summon enthusiasm about anything.

A chambermaid came by, her arms full of sheets, and gave him a concerned look. Before she could speak he moved off down the hall, shrugging into his cloak. Thom would not be finished in the common room for hours yet. He might as well see what he could. Perhaps he could find Mat, and see if Ba'alzamon had been in his dreams, too. He went downstairs more slowly this time, rubbing his temple.

The stairs ended near the kitchen, so he took that way out, nodding to Sara but hurrying on when she seemed about to take up where she had left off. The stableyard was empty except for Mutch, standing in the stable door, and one of the other ostlers carrying a sack on his shoulder into the stable. Rand nodded to Mutch, too, but the stableman gave him a truculent look and went inside. He hoped the rest of the city was more like Sara and less like Mutch. Ready to see what a city was like, he picked up his step.

At the open stableyard gates, he stopped and stared. People packed the street like sheep in a pen, people swathed to the eyes in cloaks and coats, hats pulled down against the cold, weaving in and out at a quick step as though the wind whistling over the rooftops blew them along, elbowing past one another with barely a word or a glance. *All strangers,* he thought. *None of them know each other.*

The smells were strange, too, sharp and sour and sweet all mixed in a hodgepodge that had him rubbing his nose. Even at the height of Festival he had never seen so many people so jammed together. Not even half so many. And this was only one street. Master Fitch and the cook said the whole city was full. The whole city . . . like this?

He backed slowly away from the gate, away from the street full of people. It really was not right to go off and leave Perrin sick in bed. And what if Thom finished his storytelling while Rand was off in the city? The gleeman might go out himself, and Rand needed to talk to someone. Much better to wait a bit. He breathed a sigh of relief as he turned his back on the swarming street.

Going back inside the inn did not appeal to him, though, not with his headache. He sat on an upended barrel against the back of the inn and hoped the cold air might help his head.

Mutch came to the stable door from time to time to stare at him, and even across the stableyard he could make out the fellow's disapproving scowl. Was it country people the man did not like? Or had he been embarrassed by Master Fitch greeting them after he had tried to chase them off for coming in the back way? *Maybe he's a Darkfriend,* he thought, expecting to chuckle at the idea, but it was not a funny thought. He rubbed his hand along the hilt of Tam's sword. There was not much left that was funny at all.

"A shepherd with a heron-mark sword," said a low, woman's voice. "That's almost enough to make me believe anything. What trouble are you in, downcountry boy?"

Startled, Rand jumped to his feet. It was the crop-haired young woman who had been with Moiraine when he came out of the bath chamber, still dressed in a boy's coat and breeches. She was a little older than he was, he thought, with dark eyes even bigger than Egwene's, and oddly intent.

"You are Rand, aren't you?" she went on. "My name is Min."

"I'm not in trouble," he said. He did not know what Moiraine had told her, but he remembered Lan's admonition not to attract any notice. "What makes you think I'm in trouble? The Two Rivers is a quiet place, and we're all quiet people. No place for trouble, unless it has to do with crops, or sheep."

"Quiet?" Min said with a faint smile. "I've heard men talk about you Two Rivers folk. I've heard the jokes about wooden-headed sheepherders, and then there are men who have actually been downcountry."

"Wooden-headed?" Rand said, frowning. "What jokes?"

"The ones who know," she went on as if he had not spoken, "say you walk around all smiles and politeness, just as meek and soft as butter. On the surface, anyway. Underneath, they say, you're all as tough as old oak roots. Prod too hard, they say, and you dig up stone. But the stone isn't buried very deep in you, or in your friends. It's as if a storm has scoured away almost all the covering. Moiraine didn't tell me everything, but I see what I see."

Old oak roots? Stone? It hardly sounded like the sort of thing the merchants or their people would say. That last made him jump, though.

He looked around quickly; the stableyard was empty, and the nearest windows were closed. "I don't know anybody named—what was it again?"

"Mistress Alys, then, if you prefer," Min said with an amused look that made his cheeks color. "There's no one close enough to hear."

"What makes you think Mistress Alys has another name?"

"Because she told me," Min said, so patiently that he blushed again. "Not that she had a choice, I suppose. I saw she was . . . different . . . right away. When she stopped here before, on her way downcountry. She knew about me. I've talked to . . . others like her before."

"'Saw'?" Rand said.

"Well, I don't suppose you'll go running to the Children. Not considering who your traveling companions are. The Whitecloaks wouldn't like what I do any more than they like what she does."

"I don't understand."

"She says I see pieces of the Pattern." Min gave a little laugh and shook her head. "Sounds too grand, to me. I just see things when I look at people, and sometimes I know what they mean. I look at a man and a woman who've never even talked to one another, and I know they'll marry. And they do. That sort of thing. She wanted me to look at you. All of you together."

Rand shivered. "And what did you see?"

"When you're all in a group? Sparks swirling around you, thousands of them, and a big shadow, darker than midnight. It's so strong, I almost wonder why everybody can't see it. The sparks are trying to fill the shadow, and the shadow is trying to swallow the sparks." She shrugged. "You are all tied together in something dangerous, but I can't make any more of it."

"All of us?" Rand muttered. "Egwene, too? But they weren't after— I mean—"

Min did not seem to notice his slip. "The girl? She's part of it. And the gleeman. All of you. You're in love with her." He stared at her. "I can tell that even without seeing any images. She loves you, too, but she's not for you, or you for her. Not the way you both want."

"What's that supposed to mean?"

"When I look at her, I see the same as when I look at . . . Mistress Alys. Other things, things I don't understand, too, but I know what *that* means. She won't refuse it."

"This is all foolishness," Rand said uncomfortably. His headache was fading to numbness; his head felt packed with wool. He wanted to get away from this girl and the things she saw. And yet. . . . "What do you see when you look at . . . the rest of us?"

"All sorts of things," Min said, with a grin as if she knew what he really wanted to ask. "The War . . . ah . . . Master Andra has seven ruined towers around his head, and a babe in a cradle holding a sword, and. . . ." She shook her head. "Men like him—you understand?—always have so many images they crowd one another. The strongest images around the gleeman are a man—not him—juggling fire, and the White Tower, and that doesn't make any sense at all for a man. The strongest things I see about the big, curly-haired fellow are a wolf, and a broken crown, and trees flowering all around him. And the other one—a red eagle, an eye on a balance scale, a dagger with a ruby, a horn, and a laughing face. There are other things, but you see what I mean. This time I can't make up or down out of any of it." She waited then, still grinning, until he finally cleared his throat and asked.

"What about me?"

Her grin stopped just short of outright laughter. "The same kind of things as the rest. A sword that isn't a sword, a golden crown of laurel leaves, a beggar's staff, you pouring water on sand, a bloody hand and a white-hot iron, three women standing over a funeral bier with you on it, black rock wet with blood—"

"All right," he broke in uneasily. "You don't have to list it all."

"Most of all, I see lightning around you, some striking at you, some coming out of you. I don't know what any of it means, except for one thing. You and I will meet again." She gave him a quizzical look, as if she did not understand that either.

"Why shouldn't we?" he said. "I'll be coming back this way on my way home."

"I suppose you will, at that." Suddenly her grin was back, wry and mysterious, and she patted his cheek. "But if I told you everything I saw, you'd be as curly-haired as your friend with the shoulders."

He jerked back from her hand as if it were red-hot. "What do you mean? Do you see anything about rats? Or dreams?"

"Rats! No, no rats. As for dreams, maybe it's your idea of a dream, but I never thought it was mine."

He wondered if she was crazy, grinning like that. "I have to go," he said, edging around her. "I . . . I have to meet my friends."

"Go, then. But you won't escape."

He didn't exactly break into a run, but every step he took was quicker than the step before.

"Run, if you want," she called after him. "You can't escape from me."

Her laughter sped him across the stableyard and out into the street, into the hubbub of people. Her last words were too close to what Ba'alzamon had said. He blundered into people as he hurried through the crowd, earning hard looks and hard words, but he did not slow down until he was several streets away from the inn.

After a time he began to pay attention again to where he was. His head felt like a balloon, but he stared and enjoyed anyway. He thought Baerlon was a grand city, if not exactly in the same way as cities in Thom's stories. He wandered up broad streets, most paved with flagstone, and down narrow, twisting lanes, wherever chance and the shifting of the crowd took him. It had rained during the night, and the streets that were unpaved had already been churned to mud by the crowds, but muddy streets were nothing new to him. None of the streets in Emond's Field was paved.

There certainly were no palaces, and only a few houses were very much bigger than those back home, but every house had a roof of slate or tile as fine as the roof of the Winespring Inn. He supposed there would be a palace or two in Caemlyn. As for inns, he counted nine, not one smaller than the Winespring and most as large as the Stag and Lion, and there were plenty of streets he had not seen yet.

Shops dotted every street, with awnings out front sheltering tables covered with goods, everything from cloth to books to pots to boots. It was as if a hundred peddlers' wagons had spilled out their contents. He stared so much that more than once he had to hurry on at the suspicious look of a shopkeeper. He had not understood the first shopkeeper's stare. When he did understand, he started to get angry until he remembered that here he was the stranger. He could not have bought much, anyway. He gasped when he saw how many coppers were exchanged for a dozen discolored apples or a handful of shriveled turnips, the sort that would be fed to the horses in the Two Rivers, but people seemed eager to pay.

There were certainly more than enough people, to his estimation. For a while the sheer number of them almost overwhelmed him. Some wore clothes of finer cut than anyone in the Two Rivers—almost as fine as Moiraine's—and quite a few had long, fur-lined coats that flapped around their ankles. The miners everybody at the inn kept talking about, they had the hunched look of men who grubbed underground. But most of the people did not look any different from those he had grown up with, not in dress or in face. He had expected they would, somehow. Indeed, some of them had so much the look of the Two Rivers in their faces that he could imagine they belonged to one family or another that he knew around Emond's Field. A toothless, gray-haired fellow with ears like jug handles, sitting on a bench outside one of the inns and peering mournfully into an empty tankard, could easily have been Bili Congar's close cousin. The lantern-jawed tailor sewing in front of his shop might have been Jon Thane's brother, even to the same bald spot on the back of his head. A near mirror image of Samel Crawe pushed past Rand as he turned a corner, and. . . .

In disbelief he stared at a bony little man with long arms and a big nose, shoving hurriedly through the crowd in clothes that looked like a bundle of rags. The man's eyes were sunken and his dirty face gaunt, as if he had not eaten or slept in days, but Rand could swear. . . . The ragged man saw him then, and froze in mid-step, heedless of people who all but stumbled over him. The last doubt in Rand's mind vanished.

"Master Fain!" he shouted. "We all thought you were—"

As quick as a blink the peddler darted away, but Rand dodged after him, calling apologies over his shoulder to the people he bumped. Through the crowd he just caught sight of Fain dashing into an alleyway, and he turned after.

A few steps into the alleyway the peddler had stopped in his tracks. A tall fence made it into a dead end. As Rand skidded to a halt, Fain rounded on him, crouching warily and backing away. He flapped grimy hands at Rand to stay back. More than one rip showed in his coat, and his cloak was worn and tattered as if it had seen much harder use than it was meant for.

"Master Fain?" Rand said hesitantly. "What is the matter? It's me, Rand al'Thor, from Emond's Field. We all thought the Trollocs had taken you."

Fain gestured sharply and, still in a crouch, ran a few crabbed steps toward the open end of the alley. He did not try to pass Rand, or even come close to him. "Don't!" he rasped. His head shifted constantly as he tried to see everything in the street beyond Rand. "Don't mention"—his voice dropped to a hoarse whisper, and he turned his head away, watching Rand with quick, sidelong glances—"*them.* There be Whitecloaks in the town."

"They have no reason to bother us," Rand said. "Come back to the Stag and Lion with me. I'm staying there with friends. You know most of them. They'll be glad to see you. We all thought you were dead."

"Dead?" the peddler snapped indignantly. "Not Padan Fain. Padan Fain knows which way to jump and where to land." He straightened his rags as if they were feastday clothes. "Always have, and always will. I'll live a long time. Longer than—" Abruptly his face tightened and his hands clutched hold of his coat front. "They burned my wagon, and all my goods. Had no cause to be doing that, did they? I couldn't get to my horses. *My* horses, but that fat old innkeeper had them locked up in his stable. I had to step quick not to get my throat slit, and what did it get me? All that I've got left is what I stand up in. Now, is that fair? Is it, now?"

"Your horses are safe in Master al'Vere's stable. You can get them anytime. If you come to the inn with me, I'm sure Moiraine will help you get back to the Two Rivers."

"Aaaaah! She's . . . she's the Aes Sedai, is she?" A guarded look came over Fain's face. "Maybe, though. . . ." He paused, licking his lips nervously. "How long will you be at this—What was it? What did you call it?—the Stag and Lion?"

"We leave tomorrow," Rand said. "But what does that have to do with—?"

"You just don't know," Fain whined, "standing there with a full belly and a good night's sleep in a soft bed. I've hardly slept a wink since that night. My boots are all worn out with running, and as for what I've had to eat. . . ." His face twisted. "I don't want to be within miles of an Aes Sedai," he spat the last words, "not miles and miles, but I may have to. I've no choice, have I? The thought of her eyes on me, of her even knowing where I am. . . ." He reached toward Rand as if he wanted to grab his coat, but his hands stopped short, fluttering, and he actually took a step back. "Promise me you won't tell her. She frightens me. There's no need to be telling her, no reason for an Aes Sedai to even be knowing I'm alive. You have to promise. You have to!"

"I promise," Rand said soothingly. "But there's no reason for you to be afraid of her. Come with me. The least you'll get is a hot meal."

"Maybe. Maybe." Fain rubbed his chin pensively. "Tomorrow, you say? In that time. . . . You won't forget your promise? You won't be letting her . . . ?"

"I won't let her hurt you," Rand said, wondering how he could stop an Aes Sedai, whatever she wanted to do.

"She won't hurt me," Fain said. "No, she won't. I won't be letting her." Like a flash he hared past Rand into the crowd.

"Master Fain!" Rand called. "Wait!"

He dashed out of the alley just in time to catch sight of a ragged coat disappearing around the next corner. Still calling, he ran after it, darted around the corner. He only had time to see a man's back before he crashed into it and they both went down in a heap in the mud.

"Can't you watch where you're going?" came a mutter from under him, and Rand scrambled up in surprise.

"Mat?"

Mat sat up with a baleful glare and began scraping mud off his cloak with his hands. "You must really be turning into a city man. Sleep all morning and run right over people." Climbing to his feet, he stared at his muddy hands, then muttered and wiped them off on his cloak. "Listen, you'll never guess who I thought I just saw."

"Padan Fain," Rand said.

"Padan Fa— How did you know?"

"I was talking to him, but he ran off."

"So the Tro—" Mat stopped to look around warily, but the crowd was passing them by with never a glance. Rand was glad he had learned a little caution. "So they didn't get him. I wonder why he left Emond's Field, without a word like that? Probably started running then, too, and didn't stop until he got here. But why was he running just now?"

Rand shook his head and wished he had not. It felt as though it might fall off. "I don't know, except that he's afraid of M . . . Mistress Alys." All this watching what you said was not easy. "He doesn't want her to know he's here. He made me promise I wouldn't tell her."

"Well, his secret is safe with me," Mat said. "I wish she didn't know where I was, either."

"Mat?" People still streamed by without paying them any heed, but Rand lowered his voice anyway, and leaned closer. "Mat, did you have a nightmare last night? About a man who killed a rat?"

Mat stared at him without blinking. "You, too?" he said finally. "And Perrin, I suppose. I almost asked him this morning, but. . . . He must have. Blood and ashes! Now somebody's making us dream things. Rand, I wish *nobody* knew where I was."

"There were dead rats all over the inn this morning." He did not feel as afraid at saying it as he would have earlier. He did not feel much of anything. "Their backs were broken." His voice rang in his own ears. If he was getting sick, he might have to go to Moiraine. He was surprised that even the thought of the One Power being used on him did not bother him.

Mat took a deep breath, hitching his cloak, and looked around as if searching for somewhere to go. "What's happening to us, Rand? What?"

"I don't know. I'm going to ask Thom for advice. About whether to tell . . . anyone else."

"No! Not her. Maybe him, but not her."

The sharpness of it took Rand by surprise. "Then you believed him?" He did not need to say which "him" he meant; the grimace on Mat's face said he understood.

"No," Mat said slowly. "It's the chances, that's all. If we tell her, and he was lying, then maybe nothing happens. Maybe. But maybe just him being in our dreams is enough for. . . . I don't know." He stopped to swallow. "If we don't tell her, maybe we'll have some more dreams. Rats or no rats, dreams are better than. . . . Remember the ferry? I say we keep quiet."

"All right." Rand remembered the ferry—and Moiraine's threat, too—but somehow it seemed a long time ago. "All right."

"Perrin won't say anything, will he?" Mat went on, bouncing on his toes. "We have to get back to him. If he tells her, she'll figure it out about all of us. You can bet on it. Come on." He started off briskly through the crowd.

Rand stood there looking after him until Mat came back and grabbed him. At the touch on his arm he blinked, then followed his friend.

"What's the matter with you?" Mat asked. "You going to sleep again?"

"I think I have a cold," Rand said. His head was as tight as a drum, and almost as empty.

"You can get some chicken soup when we get back to the inn," Mat said. He kept up a constant chatter as they hunted through the packed streets. Rand made an effort to listen, and even to say something now and then, but it *was* an effort. He was not tired; he did not want to sleep. He just felt as if he were drifting. After a while he found himself telling Mat about Min.

"A dagger with a ruby, eh?" Mat said. "I like that. I don't know about the eye, though. Are you sure she wasn't making it up? It seems to me she would know what it all means if she really is a soothsayer."

"She didn't say she's a soothsayer," Rand said. "I believe she does see things. Remember, Moiraine was talking to her when we finished our baths. And she knows who Moiraine is."

Mat frowned at him. "I thought we weren't supposed to use that name."

"No," Rand muttered. He rubbed his head with both hands. It was so hard to concentrate on anything.

"I think maybe you really are sick," Mat said, still frowning. Suddenly he pulled Rand to a stop by his coat sleeve. "Look at them."

Three men in breastplates and conical steel caps, burnished till they shone like silver, were making their way down the street toward Rand

and Mat. Even the mail on their arms gleamed. Their long cloaks, pristine white and embroidered on the left breast with a golden sunburst, just cleared the mud and puddles of the street. Their hands rested on their sword hilts, and they looked around them as if looking at things that had wriggled out from under a rotting log. Nobody looked back, though. Nobody even seemed to notice them. Just the same, the three did not have to push through the crowd; the bustle parted to either side of the white-cloaked men as if by happenstance, leaving them to walk in a clear space that moved with them.

"Do you suppose they're Children of the Light?" Mat asked in a loud voice. A passerby looked hard at Mat, then quickened his pace.

Rand nodded. Children of the Light. Whitecloaks. Men who hated Aes Sedai. Men who told people how to live, causing trouble for those who refused to obey. If burned farms and worse could be called as mild as trouble. *I should be afraid,* he thought. *Or curious.* Something, at any rate. Instead he stared at them passively.

"They don't look like so much to me," Mat said. "Full of themselves, though, aren't they?"

"They don't matter," Rand said. "The inn. We have to talk to Perrin."

"Like Eward Congar. He always has his nose in the air, too." Suddenly Mat grinned, a twinkle in his eye. "Remember when he fell off the Wagon Bridge and had to tramp home dripping wet? That took him down a peg for a month."

"What does that have to do with Perrin?"

"See that?" Mat pointed to a cart resting on its shafts in an alleyway just ahead of the Children. A single stake held a dozen stacked barrels in place on the flat bed. "Watch." Laughing, he darted into a cutler's shop to their left.

Rand stared after him, knowing he should do something. That look in Mat's eyes always meant one of his tricks. But oddly, he found himself looking forward to whatever Mat was going to do. Something told him that feeling was wrong, that it was dangerous, but he smiled in anticipation anyway.

In a minute Mat appeared above him, climbing half out of an attic window onto the tile roof of the shop. His sling was in his hands, already beginning to whirl. Rand's eyes went back to the cart. Almost immediately there was a sharp crack, and the stake holding the barrels broke just as the Whitecloaks came abreast of the alley. People jumped out of the way as the barrels rolled down the cart shafts with an empty rumble and jounced into the street, splashing mud and muddy water in every direction. The three Children jumped no less quickly than anyone else, their superior looks replaced by surprise. Some passersby fell down, making more splashes, but the three moved agilely, avoiding the barrels with ease. They could not avoid the flying mud that splattered their white cloaks, though.

A bearded man in a long apron hurried out of the alley, waving his arms and shouting angrily, but one look at the three trying vainly to shake the mud from their cloaks and he vanished back into the alley even faster than he had come out. Rand glanced up at the shop roof; Mat was gone. It had been an easy shot for any Two Rivers lad, but the effect was certainly all that could be hoped for. He could not help laughing; the humor seemed to be wrapped in wool, but it was still funny. When he turned back to the street, the three Whitecloaks were staring straight at him.

"You find something funny, yes?" The one who spoke stood a little in front of the others. He wore an arrogant, unblinking look, with a light in his eyes as if he knew something important, something no one else knew.

Rand's laughter cut off short. He and the Children were alone with the mud and the barrels. The crowd that had been all around them had found urgent business up or down the street.

"Does fear of the Light hold your tongue?" Anger made the Whitecloak's narrow face seem even more pinched. He glanced dismissively at the sword hilt sticking out from Rand's cloak. "Perhaps you are responsible for this, yes?" Unlike the others he had a golden knot beneath the sunburst on his cloak.

Rand moved to cover the sword, but instead swept his cloak back over his shoulder. In the back of his head was a frantic wonder at what he was doing, but it was a distant thought. "Accidents happen," he said. "Even to the Children of the Light."

The narrow-faced man raised an eyebrow. "You are that dangerous, youngling?" He was not much older than Rand.

"Heron-mark, Lord Bornhald," one of the others said warningly.

The narrow-faced man glanced at Rand's sword hilt again—the bronze heron was plain—and his eyes widened momentarily. Then his gaze rose to Rand's face, and he sniffed dismissively. "He is too young. You are not from this place, yes?" he said coldly to Rand. "You come from where?"

"I just arrived in Baerlon." A tingling thrill ran along Rand's arms and legs. He felt flushed, almost warm. "You wouldn't know of a good inn, would you?"

"You avoid my questions," Bornhald snapped. "What evil is in you that you do not answer me?" His companions moved up to either side of him, faces hard and expressionless. Despite the mudstains on their cloaks, there was nothing funny about them now.

The tingling filled Rand; the heat had grown to a fever. He wanted to laugh, it felt so good. A small voice in his head shouted that something was wrong, but all he could think of was how full of energy he felt, nearly bursting with it. Smiling, he rocked on his heels and waited for what was going to happen. Vaguely, distantly, he wondered what it would be.

The leader's face darkened. One of the others drew his sword enough for an inch of steel to show and spoke in a voice quivering with anger. "When the Children of the Light ask questions, you gray-eyed bumpkin, we expect answers, or—" He cut off as the narrow-faced man threw an arm across his chest. Bornhald jerked his head up the street.

The Town Watch had arrived, a dozen men in round steel caps and studded leather jerkins, carrying quarterstaffs as if they knew how to use them. They stood watching, silently, from ten paces off.

"This town has lost the Light," growled the man who had half drawn his sword. He raised his voice to shout at the Watch. "Baerlon stands in the Shadow of the Dark One!" At a gesture from Bornhald he slammed his blade back into its scabbard.

Bornhald turned his attention back to Rand. The light of knowing burned in his eyes. "Darkfriends do not escape us, youngling, even in a town that stands in the Shadow. We will meet again. You may be sure of it!"

He spun on his heel and strode away, his two companions close behind, as if Rand had ceased to exist. For the moment, at least. When they reached the crowded part of the street, the same seemingly accidental pocket as before opened around them. The Watchmen hesitated, eyeing Rand, then shouldered their quarterstaffs and followed the white-cloaked three. They had to push their way into the crowd, shouting, "Make way for the Watch!" Few did make way, except grudgingly.

Rand still rocked on his heels, waiting. The tingle was so strong that he almost quivered; he felt as if he were burning up.

Mat came out of the shop, staring at him. "You aren't sick," he said finally. "You are crazy!"

Rand drew a deep breath, and abruptly it was all gone like a pricked bubble. He staggered as it vanished, the realization of what he had just done flooding in on him. Licking his lips, he met Mat's stare. "I think we had better go back to the inn, now," he said unsteadily.

"Yes," Mat said. "Yes. I think we better had."

The street had begun to fill up again, and more than one passerby stared at the two boys and murmured something to a companion. Rand was sure the story would spread. A crazy man had tried to start a fight with three Children of the Light. That was something to talk about. *Maybe the dreams* are *driving me crazy.*

The two lost their way several times in the haphazard streets, but after a while they fell in with Thom Merrilin, making a grand procession all by himself through the throng. The gleeman said he was out to stretch his legs and for a bit of fresh air, but whenever anyone looked twice at his colorful cloak he would announce in a resounding voice, "I am at the Stag and Lion, tonight only."

It was Mat who began disjointedly telling Thom about the dream and their worry over whether or not to tell Moiraine, but Rand joined in, for there were differences in exactly how they remembered it. *Or maybe each dream* was *a little different,* he thought. The major part of the dreams was the same, though.

They had not gone far in the telling before Thom started paying full attention. When Rand mentioned Ba'alzamon, the gleeman grabbed them each by a shoulder with a command to hold their tongues, raised on tiptoe to look over the heads of the crowd, then hustled them out of the press to a dead-end alley that was empty except for a few crates and a slat-ribbed, yellow dog huddled out of the cold.

Thom stared out at the crowd, looking for anyone stopping to listen, before turning his attention to Rand and Mat. His blue eyes bored into theirs, between flickering away to watch the mouth of the alley. "Don't ever say that name where strangers can hear." His voice was low, but urgent. "Not even where a stranger *might* hear. It is a very dangerous name, even where Children of the Light are not wandering the streets."

Mat snorted. "I could tell you about Children of the Light," he said with a wry look at Rand.

Thom ignored him. "If only one of you had had this dream. . . ." He tugged at his mustache furiously. "Tell me everything you can remember about it. Every detail." He kept up his wary watch while he listened.

". . . he named the men he said had been used," Rand said finally. He thought he had told everything else. "Guaire Amalasan. Raolin Darksbane."

"Davian," Mat added before he could go on. "And Yurian Stonebow."

"And Logain," Rand finished.

"Dangerous names," Thom muttered. His eyes seemed to drill at them even more intently than before. "Nearly as dangerous as that other, one way and another. All dead, now, except for Logain. Some long dead. Raolin Darksbane nearly two thousand years. But dangerous just the same. Best you don't say them aloud even when you're alone. Most people wouldn't recognize a one of them, but if the wrong person overhears. . . ."

"But who were they?" Rand said.

"Men," Thom murmured. "Men who shook the pillars of heaven and rocked the world on its foundations." He shook his head. "It doesn't matter. Forget about them. They are dust now."

"Did the . . . were they used, like he said?" Mat asked. "And killed?"

"You might say the White Tower killed them. You might say that." Thom's mouth tightened momentarily, then he shook his head again. "But used . . . ? No, I cannot see that. The Light knows the Amyrlin Seat has enough plots going, but I can't see that."

Mat shivered. "He said so many things. Crazy things. All that about Lews Therin Kinslayer, and Artur Hawkwing. And the Eye of the World. What in the Light is that supposed to be?"

"A legend," the gleeman said slowly. "Maybe. As big a legend as the horn of Valere, at least in the Borderlands. Up there, young men go hunting the Eye of the World the way young men from Illian hunt the horn. Maybe a legend."

"What do we do, Thom?" Rand said. "Do we tell her? I don't want any more dreams like that. Maybe she could do something."

"Maybe we wouldn't like what she did," Mat growled.

Thom studied them, considering and stroking his mustache with a knuckle. "I say hold your peace," he said finally. "Don't tell anyone, for the time, at least. You can always change your mind, if you have to, but once you tell, it's done, and you're tied up worse than ever with . . . with her." Suddenly he straightened, his stoop almost disappearing. "The other lad! You say he had the same dream? Does he have sense enough to keep his mouth shut?"

"I think so," Rand said at the same time that Mat said, "We were going back to the inn to warn him."

"The Light send we're not too late!" Cloak flapping around his ankles, patches fluttering in the wind, Thom strode out of the alley, looking back over his shoulder without stopping. "Well? Are your feet pegged to the ground?"

Rand and Mat hurried after him, but he did not wait for them to catch up. This time he did not pause for people who looked at his cloak, or those who hailed him as a gleeman, either. He clove through the crowded streets as if they were empty, Rand and Mat half running to follow in his wake. In much less time than Rand expected they were hurrying up to the Stag and Lion.

As they started in, Perrin came speeding out, trying to throw his cloak around his shoulders as he ran. He nearly fell in his effort not to carom into them. "I was coming looking for you two," he panted when he had caught his balance.

Rand grabbed him by the arm. "Did you tell anyone about the dream?"

"Say that you didn't," Mat demanded.

"It's very important," Thom said.

Perrin looked at them in confusion. "No, I haven't. I didn't even get out of bed until less than an hour ago." His shoulders slumped. "I've given myself a headache trying not to think about it, much less talk about it. Why did you tell him?" He nodded at the gleeman.

"We had to talk to somebody or go crazy," Rand said.

"I will explain later," Thom added with a significant look at the people passing in and out of the Stag and Lion.

"All right," Perrin replied slowly, still looking confused. Suddenly he slapped his head. "You almost made me forget why I was looking for you, not that I don't wish I could. Nynaeve is inside."

"Blood and ashes!" Mat yelped. "How did she get here? Moiraine. . . . The ferry. . . ."

Perrin snorted. "You think a little thing like a sunken ferry could stop her? She rooted Hightower out—I don't know how he got back over the river, but she said he was hiding in his bedroom and didn't want to go near the river—anyway, she bullied him into finding a boat big enough for her and her horse and rowing her across. Himself. She only gave him time to find one of his haulers to work another set of oars."

"Light!" Mat breathed.

"What is she doing here?" Rand wanted to know. Mat and Perrin both gave him a scornful look.

"She came after us," Perrin said. "She's with . . . with Mistress Alys right now, and it's cold enough in there to snow."

"Couldn't we just go somewhere else for a while?" Mat asked. "My da says, only a fool puts his hand in a hornet nest until he absolutely has to."

Rand cut in. "She can't make us go back. Winternight should have been enough to make her see that. If she doesn't, we will have to make her."

Mat's eyebrows lifted higher with every word, and when Rand finished he let out a low whistle. "You ever try to make Nynaeve see something she doesn't want to see? I have. I say we stay away till night, and sneak in then."

"From my observation of the young woman," Thom said, "I don't think she will stop until she has had her say. If she is not allowed to have it soon, she might keep on until she attracts attention none of us wants."

That brought them all up short. They exchanged glances, drew deep breaths, and marched inside as if to face Trollocs.

CHAPTER
16

The Wisdom

Perrin led the way into the depths of the inn. Rand was so intent on what he intended to say to Nynaeve that he did not see Min until she seized his arm and pulled him to one side. The others kept on a few steps down the hall before realizing he had stopped, then they halted, too, half impatient to go on, half reluctant to do so.

"We don't have time for that, boy," Thom said gruffly.

Min gave the white-haired gleeman a sharp look. "Go juggle something," she snapped, drawing Rand further away from the others.

"I really don't have time," Rand told her. "Certainly not for any more fool talk about escaping and the like." He tried to get his arm loose, but every time he pulled free, she grabbed it again.

"And I don't have time for your foolishness, either. Will you be still!" She gave the others a quick look, then moved closer, lowering her voice. "A woman arrived a little while ago—shorter than I, young, with dark eyes and dark hair in a braid down to her waist. She's part of it, right along with the rest of you."

For a minute Rand just stared at her. *Nynaeve? How can she be involved? Light, how can I be involved?* "That's . . . impossible."

"You know her?" Min whispered.

"Yes, and she can't be mixed in . . . in whatever it is you. . . ."

"The sparks, Rand. She met Mistress Alys coming in, and there were sparks, with just the two of them. Yesterday I couldn't see sparks without at least three or four of you together, but today it's all sharper, and more furious." She looked at Rand's friends, waiting impatiently, and shivered before turning back to him. "It's almost a wonder the inn doesn't catch fire. You're all in more danger today than yesterday. Since she came."

Rand glanced at his friends. Thom, his brows drawn down in a bushy V, was leaning forward on the point of taking some action to hurry him along. "She won't do anything to hurt us," he told Min. "I have to go, now." He succeeded in getting his arm back, this time.

Ignoring her squawk, he joined the others, and they started off again down the corridor. Rand looked back once. Min shook her fist at him and stamped her foot.

"What did she have to say?" Mat asked.

"Nynaeve is part of it," Rand said without thinking, then shot Mat a hard look that caught him with his mouth open. Then understanding slowly spread across Mat's face.

"Part of what?" Thom said softly. "Does that girl know something?"

While Rand was still trying to gather in his head what to say, Mat spoke up. "Of course she's part of it," he said grumpily. "Part of the same bad luck we've been having since Winternight. Maybe having the Wisdom show up is no great affair to you, but I'd as soon have the Whitecloaks here, myself."

"She saw Nynaeve arrive," Rand said. "Saw her talking to Mistress Alys, and thought she might have something to do with us." Thom gave him a sidelong look and ruffled his mustaches with a snort, but the others seemed to accept Rand's explanation. He did not like keeping secrets from his friends, but Min's secret could be as dangerous for her as any of theirs was for them.

Perrin stopped suddenly in front of a door, and despite his size he seemed oddly hesitant. He drew a deep breath, looked at his companions, took another breath, then slowly opened the door and went in. One by one the rest of them followed. Rand was the last, and he closed the door behind him with the utmost reluctance.

It was the room where they had eaten the night before. A blaze crackled on the hearth, and a polished silver tray sat in the middle of the table holding a gleaming silver pitcher and cups. Moiraine and

Nynaeve sat at opposite ends of the table, neither taking her eyes from the other. All the other chairs were empty. Moiraine's hands rested on the table, as still as her face. Nynaeve's braid was thrown over her shoulder, the end gripped in one fist; she kept giving it little tugs the way she did when she was being even more stubborn than usual with the Village Council. *Perrin was right.* Despite the fire it seemed freezing cold, and all coming from the two women at the table.

Lan was leaning against the mantel, staring into the flames and rubbing his hands for warmth. Egwene, her back flat against the wall, had her cloak on with the hood pulled up. Thom, Mat, and Perrin stopped uncertainly in front of the door.

Shrugging uncomfortably, Rand walked to the table. *Sometimes you have to grab the wolf by the ears,* he reminded himself. But he remembered another old saying, too. *When you have a wolf by the ears, it's as hard to let go as to hold on.* He felt Moiraine's eyes on him, and Nynaeve's, and his face became hot, but he sat down anyway, halfway between the two.

For a minute the room was as still as a carving, then Egwene and Perrin, and finally Mat, made their reluctant way to the table and took seats—toward the middle, with Rand. Egwene tugged her hood further forward, enough to half hide her face, and they all avoided looking at anyone.

"Well," Thom snorted, from his place beside the door. "At least that much is done."

"Since everyone is here," Lan said, leaving the fireplace and filling one of the silver cups with wine, "perhaps you will finally take this." He proffered the cup to Nynaeve; she looked at it suspiciously. "There is no need to be afraid," he said patiently. "You saw the innkeeper bring the wine, and neither of us has had a chance to put anything in it. It is quite safe."

The Wisdom's mouth tightened angrily at the word *afraid,* but she took the cup with a murmured, "Thank you."

"I am interested," he said, "in how you found us."

"So am I." Moiraine leaned forward intently. "Perhaps you are willing to speak now that Egwene and the boys have been brought to you?"

Nynaeve sipped the wine before answering the Aes Sedai. "There was nowhere for you to go except Baerlon. To be safe, though, I followed your trail. You certainly cut back and forth enough. But then, I suppose you would not care to risk meeting decent people."

"You . . . followed our trail?" Lan said, truly surprised for the first time that Rand could remember. "I must be getting careless."

"You left very little trace, but I can track as well as any man in the Two Rivers, except perhaps Tam al'Thor." She hesitated, then added, "Until my father died, he took me hunting with him, and taught me what he would have taught the sons he never had." She looked at Lan challengingly, but he only nodded with approval.

"If you can follow a trail I have tried to hide, he taught you well. Few can do that, even in the Borderlands."

Abruptly Nynaeve buried her face in her cup. Rand's eyes widened. She was blushing. Nynaeve never showed herself even the least bit disconcerted. Angry, yes; outraged, often; but never out of countenance. But she was certainly red-cheeked now, and trying to hide in the wine.

"Perhaps now," Moiraine said quietly, "you will answer a few of my questions. I have answered yours freely enough."

"With a great sackful of gleeman's tales," Nynaeve retorted. "The only *facts* I can see are that four young people have been carried off, for the Light alone knows what reason, by an Aes Sedai."

"You have been told that isn't known here," Lan said sharply. "You must learn to guard your tongue."

"Why should I?" Nynaeve demanded. "Why should I help hide you, or what you are? I've come to take Egwene and the boys back to Emond's Field, not help you spirit them away."

Thom broke in, in a scornful voice. "If you want them to see their village again—or you, either—you had better be more careful. There are those in Baerlon who would kill her"—he jerked his head toward Moiraine—"for what she is. Him, too." He indicated Lan, then abruptly moved forward to put his fists on the table. He loomed over Nynaeve, and his long mustaches and thick eyebrows suddenly seemed threatening.

Her eyes widened, and she started to lean back, away from him; then her back stiffened defiantly. Thom did not appear to notice; he went right on in an ominously soft voice. "They'd swarm over this inn like murderous ants on a rumor, a whisper. Their hate is that strong, their desire to kill or take any like these two. And the girl? The boys? You? You are all associated with them, enough for the Whitecloaks, anyway. You wouldn't like the way they ask questions, especially when the White Tower is involved. Whitecloak Questioners assume you're guilty before they start, and they have only one sentence for that kind of guilt. They don't care about finding the truth; they think they know that already. All they go after with their hot irons and pincers is a confession. Best you remember some secrets are too dangerous for saying aloud, even when you think you know who hears." He straightened with a muttered, "I seem to tell that to people often of late."

"Well put, gleeman," Lan said. The Warder had that weighing look in his eyes again. "I'm surprised to find you so concerned."

Thom shrugged. "It's known I arrived with you, too. I don't care for the thought of a Questioner with a hot iron telling me to repent my sins and walk in the Light."

"That," Nynaeve put in sharply, "is just one more reason for them to come home with me in the morning. Or this afternoon, for that matter. The sooner we're away from you and on our way back to Emond's Field, the better."

"We can't," Rand said, and was glad that his friends all spoke up at the same time. That way Nynaeve's glare had to be spread around; she spared no one as it was. But he had spoken first, and they all fell silent, looking at him. Even Moiraine sat back in her chair, watching him over steepled fingers. It was an effort for him to meet the Wisdom's eyes. "If we go back to Emond's Field, the Trollocs will come back, too. They're . . . hunting us. I don't know why, but they are. Maybe we can find out why in Tar Valon. Maybe we can find out how to stop it. It's the only way."

Nynaeve threw up her hands. "You sound just like Tam. He had himself carried to the village meeting and tried to convince everybody. He'd already tried with the Village Council. The Light knows how your . . . Mistress Alys"—she invested the name with a wagonload of scorn—"managed to make him believe; he has a mite of sense, usually, more than most men. In any case, the Council is a pack of fools most of the time, but not foolish enough for that, and neither was anyone else. They agreed you had to be found. Then Tam wanted to be the one to come after you, and him not able to stand by himself. Foolishness must run in your family."

Mat cleared his throat, then mumbled, "What about my da? What did he say?"

"He's afraid you'll try your tricks with outlanders and get your head thumped. He seemed more afraid of that than of . . . Mistress Alys, here. But then, he was never much brighter than you."

Mat seemed unsure how to take what she had said, or how to reply, or even whether to reply.

"I expect," Perrin began hesitantly. "I mean, I suppose Master Luhhan was not too pleased about my leaving, either."

"Did you expect him to be?" Nynaeve shook her head disgustedly and looked at Egwene. "Maybe I should not be surprised at this hare-brained idiocy from you three, but I thought others had more judgment."

Egwene sat back so she was shielded by Perrin. "I left a note," she said faintly. She tugged at the hood of her cloak as if she was afraid her unbound hair showed. "I explained everything." Nynaeve's face darkened.

Rand sighed. The Wisdom was on the point of one of her tongue-lashings, and it looked as if it might be a first-rate one. If she took a position in the heat of anger—if she said she intended to see them back in Emond's Field no matter what anybody said, for instance—she would be nearly impossible to budge. He opened his mouth.

"A note!" Nynaeve began, just as Moiraine said, "You and I must still talk, Wisdom."

If Rand could have stopped himself, he would have, but the words poured out as if it were a floodgate he had opened instead of his mouth. "All this is very well, but it doesn't change anything. We can't go back. We have to go on." He spoke more slowly toward the end, and his voice sank, so he finished in a whisper, with the Wisdom and the Aes Sedai both looking at him. It was the sort of look he received if he came on women talking Women's Circle business, the sort that said he had stepped in where he did not belong. He sat back, wishing he was somewhere else.

"Wisdom," Moiraine said, "you must believe that they are safer with me than they would be back in the Two Rivers."

"Safer!" Nynaeve tossed her head dismissively. "You are the one who brought them here, where the Whitecloaks are. The same Whitecloaks who, if the gleeman tells the truth, may harm them because of *you*. Tell me how they are safer, Aes Sedai."

"There are many dangers from which I cannot protect them," Moiraine agreed, "any more than you can protect them from being struck by lightning if they go home. But it is not lightning of which they must be afraid, nor even Whitecloaks. It is the Dark One, and minions of the Dark One. From those things I *can* protect. Touching the True Source, touching *Saidar,* gives me that protection, as it does to every Aes Sedai." Nynaeve's mouth tightened skeptically. Moiraine's grew tighter, too, with anger, but she went on, her voice hard on the edge of patience. "Even those poor men who find themselves wielding the Power for a short time gain that much, though sometimes touching *Saidin* protects, and sometimes the taint makes them more vulnerable. But I, or any Aes Sedai, can extend my protection to those

close by me. No Fade can harm them as long as they are as close to
me as they are right now. No Trolloc can come within a quarter of a
mile without Lan knowing it, feeling the evil of it. Can you offer them
half as much if they return to Emond's Field with you?"

"You stand up straw men," Nynaeve said. "We have a saying in the
Two Rivers. 'Whether the bear beats the wolf or the wolf beats the
bear, the rabbit always loses.' Take your contest somewhere else and
leave Emond's Field folk out of it."

"Egwene," Moiraine said after a moment, "take the others and
leave the Wisdom alone with me for a while." Her face was impassive;
Nynaeve squared herself at the table as if getting ready for an all-in
wrestling match.

Egwene bounced to her feet, her desire to be dignified obviously
warring with her desire to avoid a confrontation with the Wisdom over
her unbraided hair. She had no difficulty gathering up everyone by
eye, though. Mat and Perrin scraped back their chairs hurriedly, making polite murmurs while trying not to actually run on their way out.
Even Lan started for the door at a signal from Moiraine, drawing
Thom with him.

Rand followed, and the Warder shut the door behind them, then
took up guard across the hallway. Under Lan's eyes the others moved
on down the hall a short distance; they were not to be allowed even
the slightest chance of eavesdropping. When they had gone far enough
to suit him, Lan leaned back against the wall. Even without his color-
shifting cloak, he was so still that it would be easy not to notice him
until you were right on him.

The gleeman muttered something about better things to do with his
time and left with a stern, "Remember what I said," over his shoulder
to the boys. No one else seemed inclined to leave.

"What did he mean?" Egwene asked absently, her eyes on the door
that hid Moiraine and Nynaeve. She kept fiddling with her hair as if
torn between continuing to hide the fact that it was no longer braided
and pushing back the hood of her cloak.

"He gave us some advice," Mat said.

Perrin gave him a sharp look. "He said not to open our mouths until
we were sure what we were going to say."

"That sounds like good advice," Egwene said, but clearly she was
not really interested.

Rand was engrossed in his own thoughts. How could Nynaeve possibly be part of it? How could any of them be involved with Trollocs,
and Fades, and Ba'alzamon appearing in their dreams? It was crazy.

He wondered if Min had told Moiraine about Nynaeve. *What are they saying in there?*

He had no idea how long he had been standing there when the door finally opened. Nynaeve stepped out, and gave a start when she saw Lan. The Warder murmured something that made her toss her head angrily, then he slipped past her through the door.

She turned toward Rand, and for the first time he realized the others had all quietly disappeared. He did not want to face the Wisdom alone, but he could not get away now that he had met Nynaeve's eye. *A particularly searching eye,* he thought, puzzled. *What did they say?* He drew himself up as she came closer.

She indicated Tam's sword. "That seems to fit you, now, though I would like it better if it did not. You've grown, Rand."

"In a week?" He laughed, but it sounded forced, and she shook her head as if he did not understand. "Did she convince you?" he asked.

"It really is the only way." He paused, thinking of Min's sparks. "Are you coming with us?"

Nynaeve's eyes opened wide. "Coming with you! Why would I do that? Mavra Mallen came up from Deven Ride to see to things till I return, but she'll be wanting to get back as soon as she can. I still hope to make you see sense and come home with me."

"We can't." He thought he saw something move at the still-open door, but they were alone in the hallway.

"You told me that, and she did, too." Nynaeve frowned. "If *she* wasn't mixed up in it. . . . Aes Sedai are not to be trusted, Rand."

"You sound as if you really do believe us," he said slowly. "What happened at the village meeting?"

Nynaeve looked back at the doorway before answering; there was no movement there now. "It was a shambles, but there is no need for her to know we can't handle our affairs any better than that. And I believe only one thing: you are all in danger as long as you are with her."

"Something happened," he insisted. "Why do you want us to go back if you think there's even a chance we are right? And why you, at all? As soon send the Mayor himself as the Wisdom."

"You *have* grown." She smiled, and for a moment her amusement had him shifting his feet. "I can think of a time when you would not have questioned where I chose to go or what I chose to do, wherever or whatever it was. A time just a week ago."

He cleared his throat and pressed on stubbornly. "It doesn't make sense. Why are you really here?"

She half glanced at the still-empty doorway, then took his arm. "Let's walk while we talk." He let himself be led away, and when they were far enough from the door not to be overheard, she began again. "As I said, the meeting was a shambles. Everybody agreed someone had to be sent after you, but the village split into two groups. One wanted you rescued, though there was considerable argument over how that was to be done considering that you were with a . . . the likes of *her*."

He was glad she was remembering to watch what she said. "The others believed Tam?" he said.

"Not exactly, but they thought you shouldn't be among strangers, either, especially not with someone like *her*. Either way, though, almost every man wanted to be one of the party. Tam, and Bran al'Vere, with the scales of office around his neck, and Haral Luhhan, till Alsbet made him sit down. Even Cenn Buie. The Light save me from men who think with the hair on their chests. Though I don't know as there are any other kind." She gave a hearty sniff, and looked up at him, an accusing glance. "At any rate, I could see it would be another day, perhaps more, before they came to any decision, and somehow . . . somehow I was sure we did not dare wait that long. So I called the Women's Circle together and told them what had to be done. I cannot say they liked it, but they saw the right of it. And that is why I am here; because the men around Emond's Field are stubborn woolheads. They're probably still arguing about who to send, though I left word I would take care of it."

Nynaeve's story explained her presence, but it did nothing to reassure him. She was still determined to bring them back with her.

"What did she say to you in there?" he asked. Moiraine would surely have covered every argument, but if there was one she had missed, he would make it.

"More of the same," Nynaeve replied. "And she wanted to know about you boys. To see if she could reason out why you . . . have attracted the kind of attention you have . . . she *said*." She paused, watching him out of the corner of her eye. "She tried to disguise it, but most of all she wanted to know if any of you was born outside the Two Rivers."

His face was suddenly as taut as a drumhead. He managed a hoarse chuckle. "She does think of some odd things. I hope you assured her we're all Emond's Field born."

"Of course," she replied. There had only been a heartbeat's pause before she spoke, so brief he would have missed it if he had not been watching for it.

He tried to think of something to say, but his tongue felt like a piece of leather. *She knows.* She was the Wisdom, after all, and the Wisdom was supposed to know everything about everyone. *If she knows, it was no fever-dream. Oh, Light help me, father!*

"Are you all right?" Nynaeve asked.

"He said . . . said I . . . wasn't his son. When he was delirious . . . with the fever. He said he found me. I thought it was just. . . ." His throat began to burn, and he had to stop.

"Oh, Rand." She stopped and took his face in both hands. She had to reach up to do it. "People say strange things in a fever. Twisted things. Things that are not true, or real. Listen to me. Tam al'Thor ran away seeking adventure when he was a boy no older than you. I can just remember when he came back to Emond's Field, a grown man with a red-haired, outlander wife and a babe in swaddling clothes. I remember Kari al'Thor cradling that child in her arms with as much love given and delight taken as I have ever seen from any woman with a babe. Her child, Rand. You. Now you straighten up and stop this foolishness."

"Of course," he said. *I was* born *outside the Two Rivers.* "Of course." Maybe Tam had been having a fever-dream, and maybe he had found a baby after a battle. "Why didn't you tell her?"

"It is none of any outlander's business."

"Were any of the others born outside?" As soon as the question was out, he shook his head. "No, don't answer. It's none of my business, either." But it would be nice to know if Moiraine had some special interest in him, over and above what she had in the whole lot of them. *Would it?*

"No, it isn't your business," Nynaeve agreed. "It might not mean anything. She could just be searching blindly for a reason, any reason, why those things are after you. After *all* of you."

Rand managed a grin. "Then you do believe they're chasing us."

Nynaeve shook her head wryly. "You've certainly learned how to twist words since you met her."

"What are you going to do?" he asked.

She studied him; he met her eyes steadily. "Today, I am going to have a bath. For the rest, we will have to see, won't we?"

CHAPTER
17

Watchers and Hunters

After the Wisdom left him, Rand made his way to the common room. He needed to hear people laughing, to forget what Nynaeve had said and the trouble she might cause alike.

The room was crowded indeed, but no one was laughing, though every chair and bench was filled and people lined the walls. Thom was performing again, standing on a table against the far wall, his gestures grand enough to fill the big room. It was *The Great Hunt of the Horn* again, but no one complained, of course. There were so many tales to be told about each of the Hunters, and so many Hunters to tell of, that no two tellings were ever the same. The whole of it in one telling would have taken a week or more. The only sound competing with the gleeman's voice and harp was the crackling of the fires in the fire-places.

"... To the eight corners of the world, the Hunters ride, to the eight pillars of heaven, where the winds of time blow and fate seizes the mighty and the small alike by the forelock. Now, the greatest of the Hunters is Rogosh of Talmour, Rogosh Eagle-eye, famed at the

court of the High King, feared on the slopes of Shayol Ghul. . . ."
The Hunters were always mighty heroes, all of them.

Rand spotted his two friends and squeezed onto a place Perrin made
for him on the end of their bench. Kitchen smells drifting into the
room reminded him that he was hungry, but even the people who had
food in front of them gave it little attention. The maids who should
have been serving stood entranced, clutching their aprons and looking
at the gleeman, and nobody seemed to mind at all. Listening was better than eating, no matter how good the food.

". . . since the day of her birth has the Dark One marked Blaes as
his own, but not of this mind is she—no Darkfriend, Blaes of Ma-
tuchin! Strong as the ash she stands, lithe as the willow branch, beautiful as the rose. Golden-haired Blaes. Ready to die before she yields.
But hark! Echoing from the towers of the city, trumpets blare, brazen
and bold. Her heralds proclaim the arrival of a hero at her court.
Drums thunder and cymbals sing! Rogosh Eagle-eye comes to do
homage . . ."

"The Bargain of Rogosh Eagle-eye" wound its way to an end, but
Thom paused only to wet his throat from a mug of ale before launching
into "Lian's Stand." In turn that was followed by "The Fall of Aleth-
Loriel," and "Gaidal Cain's Sword," and "The Last Ride of Buad of
Albhain." The pauses grew longer as the evening wore on, and when
Thom exchanged the harp for his flute, everyone knew it was the end
of storytelling for the night. Two men joined Thom, with a drum and
a hammered dulcimer, but sitting beside the table while he remained
atop it.

The three young men from Emond's Field began clapping their
hands with the first note of "The Wind That Shakes the Willow," and
they were not the only ones. It was a favorite in the Two Rivers, and
in Baerlon, too, it seemed. Here and there voices even took up the
words, not so off-key as for anyone to hush them.

> "My love is gone, carried away
> by the wind that shakes the willow,
> and all the land is beaten hard
> by the wind that shakes the willow.
> But I will hold her close to me
> in heart and dearest memory,
> and with her strength to steel my soul,
> her love to warm my heart-strings,
> I will stand where we once sang,
> though cold wind shakes the willow."

The second song was not so sad. In fact, "Only One Bucket of Water" seemed even more merry than usual by comparison, which might have been the gleeman's intent. People rushed to clear tables from the floor to make room for dancing, and began kicking up their heels until the walls shook from the stomping and whirling. The first dance ended with laughing dancers leaving the floor holding their sides, and new people taking their places.

Thom played the opening notes of "Wild Geese on the Wing," then paused for people to take their places for the reel.

"I think I'll try a few steps," Rand said, getting to his feet. Perrin popped up right behind him. Mat was the last to move, and so found himself staying behind to guard the cloaks, along with Rand's sword and Perrin's axe.

"Remember I want a turn, too," Mat called after them.

The dancers formed two long lines facing each other, men in one, women in the other. First the drum and then the dulcimer took up the beat, and all the dancers began bending their knees in time. The girl across from Rand, her dark hair in braids that made him think of home, gave him a shy smile, and then a wink that was not shy at all. Thom's flute leaped into the tune, and Rand moved forward to meet the dark-haired girl; she threw back her head and laughed as he spun her around and passed her on to the next man in line.

Everyone in the room was laughing, he thought as he danced around his next partner, one of the serving maids with her apron flapping wildly. The only unsmiling face he saw was on a man huddled by one of the fireplaces, and that fellow had a scar that crossed his whole face from one temple to the opposite jaw, giving his nose a slant and drawing the corner of his mouth down. The man met his gaze and grimaced, and Rand looked away in embarrassment. Maybe with that scar the fellow could not smile.

He caught his next partner as she spun, and whirled her in a circle before passing her on. Three more women danced with him as the music gained speed, then he was back with the first dark-haired girl for a fast promenade that changed the lines about completely. She was still laughing, and she gave him another wink.

The scar-faced man was scowling at him. His step faltered and his cheeks grew hot. He had not meant to embarrass the fellow; he really did not think he had stared. He turned to meet his next partner and forgot all about the man. The next woman to dance into his arms was Nynaeve.

He stumbled through the steps, almost tripping over his own feet,

nearly stepping on hers. She danced gracefully enough to make up for
his clumsiness, smiling the while.

"I thought you were a better dancer," she laughed as they changed
partners.

He had only a moment to gather himself before they changed again,
and he found himself dancing with Moiraine. If he had thought he was
stumble-footed with the Wisdom, it was nothing to how he felt with
the Aes Sedai. She glided across the floor smoothly, her gown swirling
about her; he almost fell twice. She gave him a sympathetic smile,
which made it worse rather than helping. It was a relief to go to his
next partner in the pattern, even if it was Egwene.

He regained some of his poise. After all, he had danced with her
for years. Her hair still hung unbraided, but she had gathered it back
with a red ribbon. *Probably couldn't decide whether to please Moiraine
or Nynaeve,* he thought sourly. Her lips were parted, and she looked
as if she wanted to say something, but she never spoke, and he was
not about to speak first. Not after the way she had cut off his earlier
attempt in the private dining room. They stared at one another soberly
and danced apart without a word.

He was glad enough to return to the bench when the reel was done.
The music for another dance, a jig, began while he was sitting down.
Mat hurried to join in, and Perrin slid onto the bench as he was
leaving.

"Did you see her?" Perrin began before he was even seated. "Did
you?"

"Which one?" Rand asked. "The Wisdom, or Mistress Alys? I
danced with both of them."

"The Ae . . . Mistress Alys, too?" Perrin exclaimed. "I danced with
Nynaeve. I didn't even know she danced. She never does at any of the
dances back home."

"I wonder," Rand said thoughtfully, "what the Women's Circle
would say about the Wisdom dancing? Maybe that's why."

Then the music and the clapping and the singing were too loud for
any further talk. Rand and Perrin joined in the clapping as the dancers
circled the floor. Several times he became aware of the scar-faced man
staring at him. The man had a right to be touchy, with that scar, but
Rand did not see anything he could do now that would not make matters worse. He concentrated on the music and avoided looking at the
fellow.

The dancing and singing went on into the night. The maids finally
did remember their duties; Rand was glad to wolf down some hot stew

and bread. Everyone ate where they sat or stood. Rand joined in three more dances, and he managed his steps better when he found himself dancing with Nynaeve again, and with Moiraine, as well. This time they both complimented him on his dancing, which made him stammer. He danced with Egwene again, too; she stared at him, dark-eyed and always seeming on the point of speaking, but never saying a word. He was just as silent as she, but he was sure he did not scowl at her, no matter what Mat said when he returned to the bench.

Toward midnight Moiraine left. Egwene, after one harried look from the Aes Sedai to Nynaeve, hurried after her. The Wisdom watched them with an unreadable expression, then deliberately joined in another dance before she left, too, with a look as if she had gained a point on the Aes Sedai.

Soon Thom was putting his flute into its case and arguing good-naturedly with those who wanted him to stay longer. Lan came by to gather up Rand and the others.

"We have to make an early start," the Warder said, leaning close to be heard over the noise, "and we will need all the rest we can get."

"There's a fellow been staring at me," Mat said. "A man with a scar across his face. You don't think he could be a . . . one of the *friends* you warned us about?"

"Like this?" Rand said, drawing a finger across his nose to the corner of his mouth. "He stared at me, too." He looked around the room. People were drifting away, and most of those still left clustered around Thom. "He's not here, now."

"I saw the man," Lan said. "According to Master Fitch, he's a spy for the Whitecloaks. He's no worry to us." Maybe he was not, but Rand could see something was bothering the Warder.

Rand glanced at Mat, who had the stiff expression on his face that always meant he was hiding something. *A Whitecloak spy. Could Bornhald want to get back at us that much?* "We're leaving early?" he said. "Really early?" Maybe they could be gone before anything came of it.

"At first light," the Warder replied.

As they left the common room, Mat singing snatches of song under his breath, and Perrin stopping now and again to try out a new step he had learned, Thom joined them in high spirits. Lan's face was expressionless as they headed for the stairs.

"Where is Nynaeve sleeping?" Mat asked. "Master Fitch said we got the last rooms."

"She has a bed," Thom said dryly, "in with Mistress Alys and the girl."

Perrin whistled between his teeth, and Mat muttered, "Blood and ashes! I wouldn't be in Egwene's shoes for all the gold in Caemlyn!"

Not for the first time, Rand wished Mat could think seriously about something for more than two minutes. Their own shoes were not very comfortable right then. "I'm going to get some milk," he said. Maybe it would help him sleep. *Maybe I won't dream tonight.*

Lan looked at him sharply. "There's something wrong tonight. Don't wander far. And remember, we leave whether you are awake enough to sit your saddle or have to be tied on."

The Warder started up the stairs; the others followed him, their jollity subdued. Rand stood in the hall alone. After having so many people around, it was lonely indeed.

He hurried to the kitchen, where a scullery maid was still on duty. She poured a mug of milk from a big stone crock for him.

As he came out of the kitchen, drinking, a shape in dull black started toward him down the length of the hall, raising pale hands to toss back the dark cowl that had hidden the face beneath. The cloak hung motionless as the figure moved, and the face. . . . A man's face, but pasty white, like a slug under a rock, and eyeless. From oily black hair to puffy cheeks was as smooth as an eggshell. Rand choked, spraying milk.

"You are one of them, boy," the Fade said, a hoarse whisper like a file softly drawn across bone.

Dropping the mug, Rand backed away. He wanted to run, but it was all he could do to make his feet take one halting step at a time. He could not break free of that eyeless face; his gaze was held, and his stomach curdled. He tried to shout for help, to scream; his throat was like stone. Every ragged breath hurt.

The Fade glided closer, in no hurry. Its strides had a sinuous, deadly grace, like a viper, the resemblance emphasized by the overlapping black plates of armor down its chest. Thin, bloodless lips curved in a cruel smile, made more mocking by the smooth, pale skin where eyes should have been. The voice made Bornhald's seem warm and soft. "Where are the others? I know they are here. Speak, boy, and I will let you live."

Rand's back struck wood, a wall or a door—he could not make himself look around to see which. Now that his feet had stopped, he could not make them start again. He shivered, watching the Myrddraal slither nearer. His shaking grew harder with every slow stride.

"Speak, I say, or—"

From above came a quick clatter of boots, from the stairs up the hall, and the Myrddraal cut off, whirling. The cloak hung still. For an instant the Fade's head tilted, as if that eyeless gaze could pierce the wooden wall. A sword appeared in a dead-white hand, blade as black as the cloak. The light in the hall seemed to grow dimmer in the presence of that blade. The pounding of boots grew louder, and the Fade spun back to Rand, an almost boneless movement. The black blade rose; narrow lips peeled back in a rictus snarl.

Trembling, Rand knew he was going to die. Midnight steel flashed at his head . . . and stopped.

"You belong to the Great Lord of the Dark." The breathy grating of that voice sounded like fingernails scratched across a slate. "You are his."

Spinning in a black blur, the Fade darted down the hall away from Rand. The shadows at the end of the hall reached out and embraced it, and it was gone.

Lan leaped down the last stairs, landing with a crash, sword in hand.

Rand struggled to find his voice. "Fade," he gasped. "It was. . . ." Abruptly he remembered his sword. With the Myrddraal facing him he had never thought of it. He fumbled the heron-mark blade out now, not caring if it was too late. "It ran that way!"

Lan nodded absently; he seemed to be listening to something else. "Yes. It's going; fading. No time to pursue it, now. We're leaving, sheepherder."

More boots stumbled down the stairs; Mat and Perrin and Thom, hung about with blankets and saddlebags. Mat was still buckling his bedroll, with his bow awkward under his arm.

"Leaving?" Rand said. Sheathing his sword, he took his things from Thom. "Now? In the night?"

"You want to wait for the Halfman to come back, sheepherder?" the Warder said impatiently. "For half a dozen of them? It knows where we are, now."

"I will ride with you again," Thom told the Warder, "if you have no great objections. Too many people remember that I arrived with you. I fear that before tomorrow this will be a bad place to be known as your friend."

"You can ride with us, or ride to Shayol Ghul, gleeman." Lan's scabbard rattled from the force with which he rammed his sword home.

A stableman came darting past them from the rear door, and then Moiraine appeared with Master Fitch, and behind them Egwene, with her bundled shawl in her arms. And Nynaeve. Egwene looked frightened almost to tears, but the Wisdom's face was a mask of cool anger.

"You must take this seriously," Moiraine was telling the innkeeper. "You will certainly have trouble here by morning. Darkfriends, perhaps; perhaps worse. When it comes, quickly make it clear that we are gone. Offer no resistance. Just let whoever it is know that we left in the night, and they should bother you no further. It is us they are after."

"Never you worry about trouble," Master Fitch replied jovially. "Never a bit. If any come around my inn trying to make trouble for my guests . . . well, they'll get short shrift from the lads and I. Short shrift. And they'll hear not a word about where you've gone or when, or even if you were ever here. I've no use for that kind. Not a word will be spoken about you by any here. Not a word!"

"But—"

"Mistress Alys, I really must see to your horses if you're going to leave in good order." He pulled loose from her grip on his sleeve and trotted in the direction of the stables.

Moiraine sighed vexedly. "Stubborn, stubborn man. He will not listen."

"You think Trollocs might come here hunting for us?" Mat asked.

"Trollocs!" Moiraine snapped. "Of course not! There are other things to fear, not the least of which is how we were found." Ignoring Mat's bristle, she went right on. "The Fade cannot believe we will remain here, now that we know it has found us, but Master Fitch takes Darkfriends too lightly. He thinks of them as wretches hiding in the shadows, but Darkfriends can be found in the shops and streets of every city, and in the highest councils, too. The Myrddraal may send them to see if he can learn of our plans." She turned on her heel and left, Lan close behind her.

As they started for the stableyard, Rand fell in beside Nynaeve. She had her saddlebags and blankets, too. "So you're coming after all," he said. *Min was right.*

"*Was* there something down here?" she asked quietly. "*She* said it was—" She stopped abruptly and looked at him.

"A Fade," he answered. He was amazed that he could say it so calmly. "It was in the hall with me, and then Lan came."

Nynaeve shrugged her cloak against the wind as they left the inn. "Perhaps there is something after you. But I came to see you safely back in Emond's Field, all of you, and I will not leave till that is done. I won't leave you alone with *her* sort." Lights moved in the stables where the ostlers were saddling the horses.

"Mutch!" the innkeeper shouted from the stable door where he stood with Moiraine. "Stir your bones!" He turned back to her, appearing to attempt to soothe her rather than really listening when she spoke, though he did it deferentially, with bows interspersed among the orders called to the stablemen.

The horses were led out, the stablemen grumbling softly about the hurry and the lateness. Rand held Egwene's bundle, handing it up to her when she was on Bela's back. She looked back at him with wide, fear-filled eyes. *At least she doesn't think it's an adventure anymore.*

He was ashamed as soon as he thought it. She was in danger because of him and the others. Even riding back to Emond's Field alone would be safer than going on. "Egwene, I. . . ."

The words died in his mouth. She was too stubborn to just turn back, not after saying she was going all the way to Tar Valon. *What about what Min saw? She's part of it. Light, part of what?*

"Egwene," he said, "I'm sorry. I can't seem to think straight anymore."

She leaned down to grip his hand hard. In the light from the stable he could see her face clearly. She did not look as frightened as she had.

Once they were all mounted, Master Fitch insisted on leading them to the gates, the stablemen lighting the way with their lamps. The round-bellied innkeeper bowed them on their way with assurances that he would keep their secrets, and invitations to come again. Mutch watched them leave as sourly as he had watched them arrive.

There was one, Rand thought, who would not give short shrift to anyone, or any kind of shrift. Mutch would tell the first person who asked him when they had gone and everything else he could think of concerning them. A little distance down the street, he looked back. One figure stood, lamp raised high, peering after them. He did not need to see the face to know it was Mutch.

The streets of Baerlon were abandoned at that hour of the night; only a few faint glimmers here and there escaped tightly closed shutters, and the light of the moon in its last quarter waxed and waned with the wind-driven clouds. Now and again a dog barked as they passed an alleyway, but no other sound disturbed the night except their horses' hooves and the wind whistling across the rooftops. The riders held an even deeper silence, huddled in their cloaks and their own thoughts.

The Warder led the way, as usual, with Moiraine and Egwene close behind. Nynaeve kept near the girl, and the others brought up the rear in a tight cluster. Lan kept the horses moving at a brisk walk.

Rand watched the streets around them warily, and he noticed his friends doing the same. Shifting moon shadows recalled the shadows at the end of the hall, the way they had seemed to reach out to the Fade. An occasional noise in the distance, like a barrel toppling, or another dog barking, jerked every head around. Slowly, bit by bit as they made their way through the town, they all bunched their horses closer to Lan's black stallion and Moiraine's white mare.

At the Caemlyn Gate Lan dismounted and hammered with his fist on the door of a small square stone building squatting against the wall. A weary Watchman appeared, rubbing sleepily at his face. As Lan spoke, his sleepiness vanished, and he stared past the Warder to the others.

"You want to leave?" he exclaimed. "Now? In the night? You must be mad!"

"Unless there is some order from the Governor that prohibits our leaving," Moiraine said. She had dismounted as well, but she stayed back from the door, out of the light that spilled into the dark street.

"Not exactly, mistress." The Watchman peered at her, frowning as he tried to make out her face. "But the gates stay shut from sundown to sunup. No one to come in except in daylight. That's the order. Anyway, there're wolves out there. Killed a dozen cows in the last week. Could kill a man just as easy."

"No one to come in, but nothing about leaving," Moiraine said as if that settled the matter. "You see? We are not asking you to disobey the Governor."

Lan pressed something into the Watchman's hand. "For your trouble," he murmured.

"I suppose," the Watchman said slowly. He glanced at his hand; gold glinted before he hastily stuffed it in his pocket. "I suppose leaving wasn't mentioned at that. Just a minute." He stuck his head back inside. "Arin! Dar! Get out here and help me open the gate. There's people want to leave. Don't argue. Just do it."

Two more of the Watch appeared from inside, stopping to stare in sleepy surprise at the party of eight waiting to leave. Under the first Watchman's urgings they shuffled over to heave at the big wheel that raised the thick bar across the gates, then turned their efforts to cranking the gates open. The crank-and-ratchet made a rapid clicking sound, but the well-oiled gates swung outward silently. Before they were even a quarter open, though, a cold voice spoke out of the darkness.

"What is this? Are these gates not ordered closed until sunrise?"

Five white-cloaked men walked into the light from the guardhouse door. Their cowls were drawn up to hide their faces, but each man rested his hand on his sword, and the golden suns on their left breasts were a plain announcement of who they were. Mat muttered under his breath. The Watchmen stopped their cranking and exchanged uneasy looks.

"This is none of your affair," the first Watchman said belligerently. Five white hoods turned to regard him, and he finished in a weaker tone. "The Children hold no sway here. The Governor—"

"The Children of the Light," the white-cloaked man who had first spoken said softly, "hold sway wherever men walk in the Light. Only where the Shadow of the Dark One reigns are the Children denied, yes?" He swung his hood from the Watchman to Lan, then suddenly gave the Warder a second, more wary, look.

The Warder had not moved; in fact, he seemed completely at ease. But not many people could look at the Children so uncaringly. Lan's stony face could as well have been looking at a bootblack. When the Whitecloak spoke again, he sounded suspicious.

"What kind of people want to leave town walls in the night during times like these? With wolves stalking the darkness, and the Dark One's handiwork seen flying over the town?" He eyed the braided leather band that crossed Lan's forehead and held his long hair back. "A northerner, yes?"

Rand hunched lower in his saddle. A Draghkar. It had to be that, unless the man just named anything he did not understand as the Dark One's handiwork. With a Fade at the Stag and Lion, he should have expected a Draghkar, but at the moment he was hardly thinking about it. He thought he recognized the Whitecloak's voice.

"Travelers," Lan replied calmly. "Of no interest to you or yours."

"Everyone is of interest to the Children of the Light."

Lan shook his head slightly. "Are you really after more trouble with the Governor? He has limited your numbers in the town, even had you followed. What will he do when he discovers you're harassing honest citizens at his gates?" He turned to the Watchmen. "Why have you stopped?" They hesitated, put their hands back on the crank, then hesitated again when the Whitecloak spoke.

"The Governor does not know what happens under his nose. There is evil he does not see, or smell. But the Children of the Light see." The Watchmen looked at one another; their hands opened and closed as if regretting the spears left inside the guardhouse. "The Children of the Light smell the evil." The Whitecloak's eyes turned to the people on horseback. "We smell it, and root it out. Wherever it is found."

Rand tried to make himself even smaller, but the movement drew the man's attention.

"What have we here? Someone who does not wish to be seen? What do you—? Ah!" The man brushed back the hood of his white cloak, and Rand was looking at the face he had known would be there. Bornhald nodded with obvious satisfaction. "Clearly, Watchman, I have saved you from a great disaster. These are Darkfriends you were about to help escape from the Light. You should be reported to your Governor for discipline, or perhaps given to the Questioners to discover your true intent this night." He paused, eyeing the Watchman's fear; it seemed to have no effect on him. "You would not wish that, no? Instead, I will take these ruffians to our camp, that they may be questioned in the Light—instead of you, yes?"

"You will take me to your camp, Whitecloak?" Moiraine's voice came suddenly from every direction at once. She had moved back into the night at the Children's approach, and shadows clumped around her. "You will question me?" Darkness wreathed her as she took a step forward; it made her seem taller. "You will bar my way?"

Another step, and Rand gasped. She *was* taller, her head level with his where he sat on the gray's back. Shadows clung about her face like thunderclouds.

"Aes Sedai!" Bornhald shouted, and five swords flashed from their sheaths. "Die!" The other four hesitated, but he slashed at her in the same motion that cleared his sword.

Rand cried out as Moiraine's staff rose to intercept the blade. That delicately carved wood could not possibly stop hard-swung steel. Sword met staff, and sparks sprayed in a fountain, a hissing roar hurling Bornhald back into his white-cloaked companions. All five went down in a heap. Tendrils of smoke rose from Bornhald's sword, on the ground beside him, blade bent at a right angle where it had been melted almost in two.

"You dare attack me!" Moiraine's voice roared like a whirlwind. Shadow spun in on her, draped her like a hooded cloak; she loomed as high as the town wall. Her eyes glared down, a giant staring at insects.

"Go!" Lan shouted. In one lightning move he snatched the reins of Moiraine's mare and leaped into his own saddle. "Now!" he commanded. His shoulders brushed either gate as his stallion tore through the narrow opening like a flung stone.

For a moment Rand remained frozen, staring. Moiraine's head and shoulders stood above the wall, now. Watchmen and Children alike cowered away from her, huddling with their backs against the front of the guardhouse. The Aes Sedai's face was lost in the night, but her eyes, as big as full moons, shone with impatience as well as anger when they touched him. Swallowing hard, he booted Cloud in the ribs and galloped after the others.

Fifty paces from the wall, Lan drew them up, and Rand looked back. Moiraine's shadowed shape towered high over the log palisade, head and shoulders a deeper darkness against the night sky, surrounded by a silver nimbus from the hidden moon. As he watched, mouth hanging open, the Aes Sedai stepped over the wall. The gates began swinging shut frantically. As soon as her feet were on the ground outside, she was suddenly her normal size again.

"Hold the gates!" an unsteady voice shouted inside the wall. Rand thought it was Bornhald. "We must pursue them, and take them!" But the Watchmen did not slow the pace of closing. The gates slammed shut, and moments later the bar crashed into place, sealing them. *Maybe some of those other Whitecloaks aren't as eager to confront an Aes Sedai as Bornhald.*

Moiraine hurried to Aldieb, stroking the white mare's nose once before she tucked her staff under the girth strap. Rand did not need to look this time to know there was not even a nick in the staff.

"You were taller than a giant," Egwene said breathlessly, shifting on Bela's back. No one else spoke, though Mat and Perrin edged their horses away from the Aes Sedai.

"Was I?" Moiraine said absently as she swung into her saddle.

"I saw you," Egwene protested.

"The mind plays tricks in the night; the eye sees what is not there."

"This is no time for games," Nynaeve began angrily, but Moiraine cut her off.

"No time for games indeed. What we gained at the Stag and Lion we may have lost here." She looked back at the gate and shook her head. "If only I could believe the Draghkar was on the ground." With a self-deprecatory sniff she added, "Or if only the Myrddraal were truly blind. If I am wishing, I might as well wish for the truly impossible. No matter. They know the way we must go, but with luck we will stay a step ahead of them. Lan!"

The Warder moved off eastward down the Caemlyn Road, and the rest followed close behind, hooves thudding rhythmically on the hard-packed earth.

They kept to an easy pace, a fast walk the horses could maintain for hours without any Aes Sedai help. Before they had been even one hour on their way, though, Mat cried out, pointing back the way they had come.

"Look there!"

They all drew rein and stared.

Flames lit the night over Baerlon as if someone had built a house-size bonfire, tinting the undersides of the cloud with red. Sparks whipped into the sky on the wind.

"I warned him," Moiraine said, "but he would not take it seriously." Aldieb danced sideways, an echo of the Aes Sedai's frustration. "He would not take it seriously."

"The inn?" Perrin said. "That's the Stag and Lion? How can you be sure?"

"How far do you want to stretch coincidence?" Thom asked. "It could be the Governor's house, but it isn't. And it isn't a warehouse, or somebody's kitchen stove, or your grandmother's haystack."

"Perhaps the Light shines on us a little this night," Lan said, and Egwene rounded on him angrily.

"How can you say that? Poor Master Fitch's inn is burning! People may be hurt!"

"If they have attacked the inn," Moiraine said, "perhaps our exit from the town and my . . . display went unnoticed."

"Unless that's what the Myrddraal wants us to think," Lan added.

Moiraine nodded in the darkness. "Perhaps. In any case, we must press on. There will be little rest for anyone tonight."

"You say that so easily, Moiraine," Nynaeve exclaimed. "What about the people at the inn? People must be hurt, and the innkeeper has lost his livelihood, because of you! For all your talk about walking in the Light you're ready to go on without sparing a thought for him. His trouble is because of you!"

"Because of those three," Lan said angrily. "The fire, the injured, the going on—all because of those three. The fact that the price must be paid is proof that it is worth paying. The Dark One wants those boys of yours, and anything he wants this badly, he must be kept from. Or would you rather let the Fade have them?"

"Be at ease, Lan," Moiraine said. "Be at ease. Wisdom, you think I can help Master Fitch and the people at the inn? Well, you are right." Nynaeve started to say something, but Moiraine waved it away and went on. "I can go back by myself and give some help. Not too much, of course. That would draw attention to those I helped, attention they would not thank me for, especially with the Children of the Light in the town. And that would leave only Lan to protect the rest of you. He is very good, but it will take more than him if a Myrddraal and a fist of Trollocs find you. Of course, we could all return, though I doubt I can get all of us back into Baerlon unnoticed. And that would expose all of you to whomever set that fire, not to mention the Whitecloaks. Which alternative would you choose, Wisdom, if you were I?"

"I would do something," Nynaeve muttered unwillingly.

"And in all probability hand the Dark One his victory," Moiraine replied. "Remember what—who—it is that he wants. We are in a war, as surely as anyone in Ghealdan, though thousands fight there and only eight of us here. I will have gold sent to Master Fitch, enough to rebuild the Stag and Lion, gold that cannot be traced to Tar Valon. And help for any who were hurt, as well. Any more than that will only endanger them. It is far from simple, you see. Lan." The Warder turned his horse and took up the road again.

From time to time Rand looked back. Eventually all he could see was the glow on the clouds, and then even that was lost in the darkness. He hoped Min was all right.

All was still pitch-dark when the Warder finally led them off the packed dirt of the road and dismounted. Rand estimated there were no more than a couple of hours till dawn. They hobbled the horses, still saddled, and made a cold camp.

"One hour," Lan warned as everyone except him was wrapping up in their blankets. He would stand guard while they slept. "One hour, and we must be on our way." Silence settled over them.

After a few minutes Mat spoke in a whisper that barely reached Rand. "I wonder what Dav did with that badger." Rand shook his head silently, and Mat hesitated. Finally he said, "I thought we were safe, you know, Rand. Not a sign of anything since we crossed the Taren, and there we were in a city, with walls around us. I thought we were safe. And then that dream. And a Fade. Are we ever going to be safe again?"

"Not until we get to Tar Valon," Rand said. "That's what she told us."

"Will we be safe then?" Perrin asked softly, and all three of them looked to the shadowy mound that was the Aes Sedai. Lan had melded into the darkness; he could have been anywhere.

Rand yawned suddenly. The others twitched nervously at the sound. "I think we'd better get some sleep," he said. "Staying awake won't answer anything."

Perrin spoke quietly. "She should have done something."

No one answered.

Rand squirmed onto his side to avoid a root, tried his back, then rolled off of a stone onto his belly and another root. It was not a good campsite they had stopped at, not like the spots the Warder had chosen on the way north from the Taren. He fell asleep wondering if the roots digging into his ribs would make him dream, and woke at Lan's touch on his shoulder, ribs aching and grateful that if any dreams had come he did not remember them.

It was still the dark just before dawn, but once the blankets were rolled and strapped behind their saddles Lan had them riding east again. As the sun rose they made a bleary-eyed breakfast on bread and cheese and water, eating while they rode, huddled in their cloaks against the wind. All except Lan, that is. He ate, but he was not bleary-eyed, and he did not huddle. He had changed back into his shifting cloak, and it whipped around him, fluttering through grays and greens, and the only mind he paid it was to keep it clear of his sword-arm. His face remained without expression, but his eyes searched constantly, as if he expected an ambush any moment.

CHAPTER
18

The Caemlyn Road

The Caemlyn Road was not very different from the North Road through the Two Rivers. It was considerably wider, of course, and showed the wear of much more use, but it was still hard-packed dirt, lined on either side by trees that would not have been at all out of place in the Two Rivers, especially since only the evergreens carried a leaf.

The land itself was different, though, for by midday the road entered low hills. For two days the road ran through the hills—cut right through them, sometimes, if they were wide enough to have made the road go much out of its way and not so big as to have made digging through too difficult. As the angle of the sun shifted each day it became apparent that the road, for all it appeared straight to the eye, curved slowly southward as it ran east. Rand had daydreamed over Master al'Vere's old map—half the boys in Emond's Field had daydreamed over it—and as he remembered, the road curved around something called the Hills of Absher until it reached Whitebridge.

From time to time Lan had them dismount atop one of the hills, where he could get a good view of the road both ahead and behind, and the surrounding countryside as well. The Warder would study the view while the others stretched their legs or sat under the trees and ate.

"I used to like cheese," Egwene said on the third day after leaving Baerlon. She sat with her back to the bole of a tree, grimacing over a dinner that was once again the same as breakfast, as supper would be. "Not a chance of tea. Nice hot tea." She pulled her cloak tighter and shifted around the tree in a vain effort to avoid the swirling wind.

"Flatwort tea and andilay root," Nynaeve was saying to Moiraine, "are best for fatigue. They clear the head and dim the burn in tired muscles."

"I am sure they do," the Aes Sedai murmured, giving Nynaeve a sidelong glance.

Nynaeve's jaw tightened, but she continued in the same tone. "Now, if you must go without sleep. . . ."

"No tea!" Lan said sharply to Egwene. "No fire! We can't see them yet, but they are back there, somewhere, a Fade or two and their Trollocs, and they know we are taking this road. No need to tell them exactly where we are."

"I wasn't asking," Egwene muttered into her cloak. "Just regretting."

"If they know we're on the road," Perrin asked, "why don't we go straight across to Whitebridge?"

"Even Lan cannot travel as fast cross-country as by road," Moiraine said, interrupting Nynaeve, "especially not through the Hills of Absher." The Wisdom gave an exasperated sigh. Rand wondered what she was up to; after ignoring the Aes Sedai completely for the first day, Nynaeve had spent the last two trying to talk to her about herbs. Moiraine moved away from the Wisdom as she went on. "Why do you think the road curves to avoid them? And we would have to come back to this road eventually. We might find them ahead of us instead of following."

Rand looked doubtful, and Mat muttered something about "the long way round."

"Have you seen a farm this morning?" Lan asked. "Or even the smoke from a chimney? You haven't, because it's all wilderness from Baerlon to Whitebridge, and Whitebridge is where we must cross the Arinelle. That is the only bridge spanning the Arinelle south of Maradon, in Saldaea."

Thom snorted and blew out his mustaches. "What is to stop them from having someone, something, at Whitebridge already?"

From the west came the keening wail of a horn. Lan's head whipped around to stare back down the road behind them. Rand felt a chill. A part of him remained calm enough to think, ten miles, no more.

"Nothing stops them, gleeman," the Warder said. "We trust to the Light and luck. But now we know for certain there are Trollocs behind us."

Moiraine dusted her hands. "It is time for us to move on." The Aes Sedai mounted her white mare.

That set off a scramble for the horses, speeded by a second winding of the horn. This time others answered, the thin sounds floating out of the west like a dirge. Rand made ready to put Cloud to a gallop right away, and everyone else settled their reins with the same urgency. Everyone except Lan and Moiraine. The Warder and the Aes Sedai exchanged a long look.

"Keep them moving, Moiraine Sedai," Lan said finally. "I will return as soon as I am able. You will know if I fail." Putting a hand on Mandarb's saddle, he vaulted to the back of the black stallion and galloped down the hill. Heading west. The horns sounded again.

"The Light go with you, last Lord of the Seven Towers," Moiraine said almost too softly for Rand to hear. Drawing a deep breath, she turned Aldieb to the east. "We must go on," she said, and started off at a slow, steady trot. The others followed her in a tight file.

Rand twisted once in his saddle to look for Lan, but the Warder was already lost to sight among the low hills and leafless trees. Last Lord of the Seven Towers, she had called him. He wondered what that meant. He had not thought anyone besides himself had heard, but Thom was chewing the ends of his mustaches, and he had a speculative frown on his face. The gleeman seemed to know a great many things.

The horns called and answered once more behind them. Rand shifted in his saddle. They were closer this time; he was sure of it. Eight miles. Maybe seven. Mat and Egwene looked over their shoulders, and Perrin hunched as if he expected something to hit him in the back. Nynaeve rode up to speak to Moiraine.

"Can't we go any faster?" she asked. "Those horns are getting closer."

The Aes Sedai shook her head. "And why do they let us know they are there? Perhaps so we will hurry on without thinking of what might be ahead."

They kept on at the same steady pace. At intervals the horns gave cry behind them, and each time the sound was closer. Rand tried to stop thinking of how close, but the thought came unbidden at every brazen wail. Five miles, he was thinking anxiously, when Lan suddenly burst around the hill behind them at a gallop.

He came abreast of Moiraine, reining in the stallion. "At least three fists of Trollocs, each led by a Halfman. Maybe five."

"If you were close enough to see them," Egwene said worriedly, "they could have seen you. They could be right on your heels."

"He was not seen." Nynaeve drew herself up as everyone looked at her. "I have followed his trail, remember."

"Hush," Moiraine commanded. "Lan is telling us there are perhaps five hundred Trollocs behind us." A stunned silence followed, then Lan spoke again.

"And they are closing the gap. They will be on us in an hour or less."

Half to herself, the Aes Sedai said, "If they had that many before, why were they not used at Emond's Field? If they did not, how did they come here since?"

"They are spread out to drive us before them," Lan said, "with scouts quartering ahead of the main parties."

"Driving us toward what?" Moiraine mused. As if to answer her a horn sounded in the distance to the west, a long moan that was answered this time by others, all ahead of them. Moiraine stopped Aldieb; the others followed her lead, Thom and the Emond's Field folk looking around fearfully. Horns cried out before them, and behind. Rand thought they held a note of triumph.

"What do we do now?" Nynaeve demanded angrily. "Where do we go?"

"All that is left is north or south," Moiraine said, more thinking aloud than answering the Wisdom. "To the south are the Hills of Absher, barren and dead, and the Taren, with no way to cross, and no traffic by boat. To the north, we can reach the Arinelle before nightfall, and there will be a chance of a trader's boat. If the ice has broken at Maradon."

"There is a place the Trollocs will not go," Lan said, but Moiraine's head whipped around sharply.

"No!" She motioned to the Warder, and he put his head close to hers so their talk could not be overheard.

The horns winded, and Rand's horse danced nervously.

"They're trying to frighten us," Thom growled, attempting to steady his mount. He sounded half angry and half as if the Trollocs were succeeding. "They're trying to scare us until we panic and run. They'll have us, then."

Egwene's head swung with every blast of a horn, staring first ahead of them, then behind, as if looking for the first Trollocs. Rand wanted to do the same thing, but he tried to hide it. He moved Cloud closer to her.

"We go north," Moiraine announced.

The horns keened shrilly as they left the road and trotted into the surrounding hills.

The hills were low, but the way was all up and down, with never a flat stretch, beneath bare-branched trees and through dead undergrowth. The horses climbed laboriously up one slope only to canter down the other. Lan set a hard pace, faster than they had used on the road.

Branches lashed Rand across the face and chest. Old creepers and vines caught his arms, and sometimes snagged his foot right out of the stirrup. The keening horns came ever closer, and ever more frequently.

As hard as Lan pushed them, they were not getting farther on very quickly. They traveled two feet up or down for every one forward, and every foot was a scrambling effort. And the horns were coming nearer. *Two miles,* he thought. *Maybe less.*

After a time Lan began peering first one way then another, the hard planes of his face as close to worry as Rand had seen them. Once the Warder stood in his stirrups to stare back the way they had come. All Rand could see were trees. Lan settled back into his saddle and unconsciously pushed back his cloak to clear his sword as he resumed searching the forest.

Rand met Mat's eye questioningly, but Mat only grimaced at the Warder's back and shrugged helplessly.

Lan spoke, then, over his shoulder. "There are Trollocs nearby." They topped a hill and started down the other side. "Some of the scouts, sent ahead of the rest. Probably. If we come on them, stay with me at all costs, and do as I do. We must keep on the way we are going."

"Blood and ashes!" Thom muttered. Nynaeve motioned to Egwene to keep close.

Scattered stands of evergreens provided the only real cover, but Rand tried to peer in every direction at once, his imagination turning gray tree trunks caught out of the corner of his eye into Trollocs. The horns were closer, too. And directly behind them. He was sure of it. Behind and coming closer.

They topped another hill.

Below them, just starting up the slope, marched Trollocs carrying poles tipped with great loops of rope or long hooks. Many Trollocs. The line stretched far to either side, the ends out of sight, but at its center, directly in front of Lan, a Fade rode.

The Myrddraal seemed to hesitate as the humans appeared atop the hill, but in the next instant it produced a sword with the black blade Rand remembered so queasily, and waved it over its head. The line of Trollocs scrambled forward.

Even before the Myrddraal moved, Lan's sword was in his hand. "Stay with me!" he cried, and Mandarb plunged down the slope toward the Trollocs. "For the Seven Towers!" he shouted.

Rand gulped and booted the gray forward; the whole group of them streamed after the Warder. He was surprised to find Tam's sword in his fist. Caught up by Lan's cry, he found his own. "Manetheren! Manetheren!"

Perrin took it up. "Manetheren! Manetheren!"

But Mat shouted, *"Carai an Caldazar! Carai an Ellisande! Al Ellisande!"*

The Fade's head turned from the Trollocs to the riders charging toward him. The black sword froze over its head, and the opening of its cowl swiveled, searching among the oncoming horsemen.

Then Lan was on the Myrddraal, as the human folk fell on the Trolloc line. Warder's blade met black steel from the forges at Thakan'dar with a clang like a great bell, the toll echoing in the hollow, a flash of blue light filling the air like sheet lightning.

Beast-muzzled almost-men swarmed around each of the humans, catchpoles and hooks flailing. Only Lan and the Myrddraal did they avoid; those two fought in a clear circle, black horses matching step for step, swords matching stroke for stroke. The air flashed and pealed.

Cloud rolled his eyes and screamed, rearing and lashing out with his hooves at the snarling, sharp-toothed faces surrounding him. Heavy bodies crowded shoulder-to-shoulder around him. Digging his heels in ruthlessly, Rand forced the gray on regardless, swinging his sword with little of the skill Lan had tried to impart, hacking as if hewing wood. *Egwene!* Desperately he searched for her as he kicked the gray onward, slashing a path through the hairy bodies as though chopping undergrowth.

Moiraine's white mare dashed and cut at the slightest touch of the Aes Sedai's hand on the reins. Her face was as hard as Lan's as her staff lashed out. Flame enveloped Trollocs, then burst with a roar that left misshapen forms unmoving on the ground. Nynaeve and Egwene rode close to the Aes Sedai with frantic urgency, teeth bared almost as fiercely as the Trollocs', belt knives in hand. Those short blades would be no use at all if a Trolloc came close. Rand tried to turn Cloud toward them, but the gray had the bit in his teeth. Screaming and kicking, Cloud struggled forward however hard Rand tugged at the reins.

Around the three women a space opened as Trollocs tried to flee from Moiraine's staff, but as they attempted to avoid her, she sought them out. Fires roared, and the Trollocs howled in rage and fury. Above roar and howl crashed the tolling of the Warder's sword against the Myrddraal's; the air flared blue around them, flared again. Again.

A noose on the end of a pole swept at Rand's head. With an awkward slash, he cut the catchpole in two, then hacked the goat-faced Trolloc that held it. A hook caught his shoulder from behind and tangled in his cloak, jerking him backwards. Frantically, almost losing his sword, he clutched the pommel of his saddle to keep his seat. Cloud twisted, shrieking. Rand hung onto saddle and reins desperately; he could feel himself slipping, inch by inch, falling to the hook. Cloud swung around; for an instant Rand saw Perrin, half out of his saddle, struggling to wrest his axe away from three Trollocs. They had him by one arm and both legs. Cloud plunged, and only Trollocs filled Rand's eyes.

A Trolloc dashed in and seized Rand's leg, forcing his foot free of the stirrup. Panting, he let go of the saddle to stab it. Instantly the hook pulled him out of the saddle, to Cloud's hindquarters; his death-grip on the reins was all that kept him from the ground. Cloud reared and shrieked. And in that same moment the pulling vanished. The Trolloc at his leg threw up its hands and screamed. All of the Trollocs screamed, a howl like all the dogs in the world gone mad.

Around the humans Trollocs fell writhing to the ground, tearing at their hair, clawing their own faces. All of the Trollocs. Biting at the ground, snapping at nothing, howling, howling, howling.

Then Rand saw the Myrddraal. Still upright in the saddle of its madly dancing horse, black sword still flailing, it had no head.

"It won't die until nightfall," Thom had to shout, between heavy breaths, over the unrelenting screams. "Not completely. That is what I've heard, anyway."

"Ride!" Lan shouted angrily. The Warder had already gathered Moiraine and the other two women and had them halfway up the next hill. "This is not all of them!" Indeed, the horns dirged again, above the shrieks of the Trollocs on the ground, to east and west and south.

For a wonder, Mat was the only one who had been unhorsed. Rand trotted toward him, but Mat tossed a noose away from him with a shudder, gathered his bow, and scrambled into his saddle unaided, though rubbing at his throat.

The horns bayed like hounds with the scent of a deer. Hounds closing in. If Lan had set a hard pace before, he doubled it now, till the horses scrabbled uphill faster than they had gone down before, then nearly threw themselves at the other side. But still the horns came ever nearer, until the guttural shouts of pursuit were heard whenever the horns paused, until eventually the humans reached a hilltop just as Trollocs appeared on the next hill behind them. The hilltop blackened with Trollocs, snouted, distorted faces howling, and three Myrddraal overawed them all. Only a hundred spans separated the two parties.

Rand's heart shriveled like an old grape. *Three!*

The Myrddraal's black swords rose as one; Trollocs boiled down the slope, thick, triumphant cries rising, catchpoles bobbing above as they ran.

Moiraine climbed down from Aldieb's back. Calmly she removed something from her pouch, unwrapped it. Rand glimpsed dark ivory. The *angreal.* With *angreal* in one hand and staff in the other, the Aes Sedai set her feet, facing the onrushing Trollocs and the Fades' black swords, raised her staff high, and stabbed it down into the earth.

The ground rang like an iron kettle struck by a mallet. The hollow clang dwindled, faded away. For an instant then, it was silent. Everything was silent. The wind died. The Trolloc cries stilled; even their charge forward slowed and stopped. For a heartbeat, everything waited. Slowly the dull ringing returned, changing to a low rumble, growing until the earth moaned.

The ground trembled beneath Cloud's hooves. This was Aes Sedai work like the stories told about; Rand wished he were a hundred miles away. The tremble became a shaking that set the trees around them quivering. The gray stumbled and nearly fell. Even Mandarb and riderless Aldieb staggered as if drunk, and those who rode had to cling to reins and manes, to anything, to keep their seats.

The Aes Sedai still stood as she had begun, holding the *angreal* and her upright staff thrust into the hilltop, and neither she nor the staff moved an inch, for all that the ground shook and shivered around her. Now the ground rippled, springing out from in front of her staff, lapping toward the Trollocs like ripples on a pond, ripples that grew as they ran, toppling old bushes, flinging dead leaves into the air, growing, becoming waves of earth, rolling toward the Trollocs. Trees in the hollow lashed like switches in the hands of small boys. On the far slope Trollocs fell in heaps, tumbled over and over by the raging earth.

Yet as if the ground were not rearing all around them, the Myrddraal moved forward in a line, their dead-black horses never missing a step, every hoof in unison. Trollocs rolled on the ground all about the black steeds, howling and grabbing at the hillside that heaved them up, but the Myrddraal came slowly on.

Moiraine lifted her staff, and the earth stilled, but she was not done. She pointed to the hollow between the hills, and flame gouted from the ground, a fountain twenty feet high. She flung her arms wide, and the fire raced to left and right as far as the eye could see, spreading into a wall separating humans and Trollocs. The heat made Rand put his hands in front of his face, even on the hilltop. The Myrddraal's black mounts, whatever strange powers they had, screamed at the fire, reared and fought their riders as the Myrddraal beat at them, trying to force them through the flames.

"Blood and ashes," Mat said faintly. Rand nodded numbly.

Abruptly Moiraine wavered and would have fallen had Lan not leaped from his horse to catch her. "Go on," he told the others. The harshness of his voice was at odds with the gentle way he lifted the Aes Sedai to her saddle. "That fire won't burn forever. Hurry! Every minute counts!"

The wall of flame roared as if it would indeed burn forever, but Rand did not argue. They galloped northward as fast as they could make their horses go. The horns in the distance shrilled out disappointment, as if they already knew what had happened, then fell silent.

Lan and Moiraine soon caught up with the others, though Lan led Aldieb by the reins while the Aes Sedai swayed and held the pommel of her saddle with both hands. "I will be all right soon," she said to their worried looks. She sounded tired yet confident, and her gaze was as compelling as ever. "I am not at my strongest when working with Earth and Fire. A small thing."

The two of them moved into the lead again at a fast walk. Rand did not think Moiraine could stay in the saddle at any faster pace. Nynaeve rode foward beside the Aes Sedai, steadying her with a hand. For a time as the party went on across the hills the two women whispered, then the Wisdom delved into her cloak and handed a small packet to Moiraine. Moiraine unfolded it and swallowed the contents. Nynaeve said something more, then fell back with the others, ignoring their questioning looks. Despite their circumstances, Rand thought she had a slight look of satisfaction.

He did not really care what the Wisdom was up to. He rubbed the hilt of his sword continually, and whenever he realized what he was doing, he stared down at it in wonder. *So that's what a battle is like.* He could not remember much of it, not any particular part. Everything ran together in his head, a melted mass of hairy faces and fear. Fear and heat. It had seemed as hot as a midsummer noon while it was going on. He could not understand that. The icy wind was trying to freeze beads of perspiration all over his face and body.

He glanced at his two friends. Mat was scrubbing sweat off his face with the edge of his cloak. Perrin, staring at something in the distance and not liking what he was seeing, appeared unaware of the beads glistening on his forehead.

The hills grew smaller, and the land began to level out, but instead of pressing on, Lan stopped. Nynaeve moved as if to rejoin Moiraine, but the Warder's look kept her away. He and the Aes Sedai rode ahead and put their heads together, and from Moiraine's gestures it became apparent they were arguing. Nynaeve and Thom stared at them, the Wisdom frowning worriedly, the gleeman muttering under his breath and pausing to stare back the way they had come, but everyone else avoided looking at them altogether. Who knew what might come out of an argument between an Aes Sedai and a Warder?

After a few minutes Egwene spoke to Rand quietly, casting an uneasy eye at the still-arguing pair. "Those things you were shouting at the Trollocs." She stopped as if unsure how to proceed.

"What about them?" Rand asked. He felt a little awkward—warcries were all right for Warders; Two Rivers folk did not do things like that, whatever Moiraine said—but if she made fun of him over it. . . . "Mat must have repeated that story ten times."

"And badly," Thom put in. Mat grunted in protest.

"However he told it," Rand said, "we've all heard it any number of times. Besides, we had to shout something. I mean, that's what you do at a time like that. You heard Lan."

"And we have a right," Perrin added thoughtfully. "Moiraine says we're all descended from those Manetheren people. They fought the Dark One, and we're fighting the Dark One. That gives us a right."

Egwene sniffed as if to show what she thought of that. "I wasn't talking about that. What . . . what was it you were shouting, Mat?"

Mat shrugged uncomfortably. "I don't remember." He stared at them defensively. "Well, I don't. It's all foggy. I don't know what it was, or where it came from, or what it means." He gave a self-deprecating laugh. "I don't suppose it means anything."

"I . . . I think it does," Egwene said slowly. "When you shouted, I thought—just for a minute—I thought I understood you. But it's all gone, now." She sighed and shook her head. "Perhaps you're right. Strange what you can imagine at a time like that, isn't it?"

"Carai an Caldazar," Moiraine said. They all twisted to stare at

her. "*Carai an Ellisande. Al Ellisande.* For the honor of the Red Eagle.
For the honor of the Rose of the Sun. The Rose of the Sun. The
ancient warcry of Manetheren, and the warcry of its last king. Eldrene
was called the Rose of the Sun." Moiraine's smile took in Egwene and
Mat both, though her gaze may have rested a moment longer on him
than on her. "The blood of Arad's line is still strong in the Two Rivers.
The old blood still sings."

Mat and Egwene looked at each other, while everyone else looked
at them both. Egwene's eyes were wide, and her mouth kept quirking
into a smile that she bit back every time it began, as if she was not
sure just how to take this talk of the old blood. Mat was sure, from
the scowling frown on his face.

Rand thought he knew what Mat was thinking. The same thing he
was thinking. If Mat was a descendant of the ancient kings of Manetheren, maybe the Trollocs were really after him and not all three of
them. The thought made him ashamed. His cheeks colored, and when
he caught a guilty grimace on Perrin's face, he knew Perrin had been
having the same thought.

"I can't say that I have ever heard the like of this," Thom said after
a minute. He shook himself and became brusque. "Another time I
might even make a story out of it, but right now. . . . Do you intend
to remain here for the rest of the day, Aes Sedai?"

"No," Moiraine replied, gathering her reins.

A Trolloc horn keened from the south as if to emphasize her word.
More horns answered, east and west. The horses whickered and sidled
about nervously.

"They have passed the fire," Lan said calmly. He turned to Moiraine. "You are not strong enough for what you intend, not yet, not
without rest. And neither Myrddraal nor Trolloc will enter that place."

Moiraine raised a hand as if to cut him off, then sighed and let it
fall instead. "Very well," she said irritably. "You are right, I suppose,
but I would rather there was any other choice." She pulled her staff
from under the girth strap of her saddle. "Gather in around me, all of
you. As close as you can. Closer."

Rand urged Cloud nearer the Aes Sedai's mare. At Moiraine's insistence they kept on crowding closer in a circle around her until every
horse had its head stretched over the croup or withers of another. Only
then was the Aes Sedai satisfied. Then, without speaking, she stood in
the stirrups and swung her staff over their heads, stretching to make
certain it covered everyone.

Rand flinched each time the staff passed over him. A tingle ran through him with every pass. He could have followed the staff without seeing it, just by following the shivers as it moved over people. It was no surprise to him that Lan was the only one not affected.

Abruptly Moiraine thrust the staff out to the west. Dead leaves whirled into the air and branches whipped as if a dustdevil ran along the line she pointed to. As the invisible whirlwind vanished from sight she settled back into her saddle with a sigh.

"To the Trollocs," she said, "our scents and our tracks will seem to follow that. The Myrddraal will see through it in time, but by then. . . ."

"By then," Lan said, "we will have lost ourselves."

"Your staff is very powerful," Egwene said, earning a sniff from Nynaeve.

Moiraine made a clicking sound. "I have told you, child, things do not have power. The One Power comes from the True Source, and only a living mind can wield it. This is not even an *angreal*, merely an aid to concentration." Wearily she slid the staff back under her girth strap. "Lan?"

"Follow me," the Warder said, "and keep quiet. It will ruin everything if the Trollocs hear us."

He led the way north again, not at the crashing pace they had been making, but rather in the quick walk with which they had traveled the Caemlyn Road. The land continued to flatten, though the forest remained as thick.

Their path was no longer straight, as it had been before, for Lan chose out a route that meandered over hard ground and rocky outcrops, and he no longer let them force their way through tangles of brush, instead taking the time to make their way around. Now and again he dropped to the rear, intently studying the trail they made. If anyone so much as coughed, it drew a sharp grunt from him.

Nynaeve rode beside the Aes Sedai, concern battling dislike on her face. And there was a hint of something more, Rand thought, almost as if the Wisdom saw some goal in sight. Moiraine's shoulders were slumped, and she held her reins and the saddle with both hands, swaying with every step Aldieb took. It was plain that laying the false trail, small as that might have seemed beside producing an earthquake and a wall of flame, had taken a great deal out of her, strength she no longer had to lose.

Rand almost wished the horns would start again. At least they were a way of telling how far back the Trollocs were. And the Fades.

He kept looking behind them, and so was not the first to see what lay ahead. When he did, he stared, perplexed. A great, irregular mass stretched off to either side out of sight, in most places as high as the trees that grew right up to it, with even taller spires here and there. Leafless vines and creepers covered it all in thick layers. A cliff? *The vines will make climbing easy, but we'll never get the horses up.*

Suddenly, as they rode a little closer, he saw a tower. It was clearly a tower, not some kind of rock formation, with an odd, pointed dome on the top. "A city!" he said. And a city wall, and the spires were guard towers on the wall. His jaw dropped. It had to be ten times as big as Baerlon. Fifty times as big.

Mat nodded. "A city," he agreed. "But what's a city doing in the middle of a forest like this?"

"And without any people," Perrin said. When they looked at him, he pointed to the wall. "Would people let vines grow over everything like that? You know how creepers can tear down a wall. Look how it's fallen."

What Rand saw adjusted itself in his mind again. It was as Perrin said. Under almost every low place in the wall was a brush-covered hill; rubble from the collapsed wall above. No two of the guard towers were the same height.

"I wonder what city it was," Egwene mused. "I wonder what happened to it. I don't remember anything from papa's map."

"It was called Aridhol," Moiraine said. "In the days of the Trolloc Wars, it was an ally of Manetheren." Staring at the massive walls, she seemed almost unaware of the others, even of Nynaeve, who supported her in the saddle with a hand on her arm. "Later Aridhol died, and this place was called by another name."

"What name?" Mat asked.

"Here," Lan said. He stopped Mandarb in front of what had once been a gate wide enough for fifty men to march through abreast. Only the broken, vine-encrusted watchtowers remained; of the gates there was no sign. "We enter here." Trolloc horns shrieked in the distance. Lan peered in the direction of the sound, then looked at the sun, halfway down toward the treetops in the west. "They have discovered it's a false trail. Come, we must find shelter before dark."

"What name?" Mat asked again.

Moiraine answered as they rode into the city. "Shadar Logoth," she said. "It is called Shadar Logoth."

CHAPTER
19

Shadow's Waiting

Broken paving stones crunched under the horses' hooves as Lan led the way into the city. The entire city was broken, what Rand could see of it, and as abandoned as Perrin had said. Not so much as a pigeon moved, and weeds, mainly old and dead, sprouted from cracks in walls as well as pavement. More buildings had roofs fallen in than had them whole. Tumbled walls spilled fans of brick and stone into the streets. Towers stopped, abrupt and jagged, like broken sticks. Uneven rubble hills with a few stunted trees growing on their slopes could have been the remains of palaces or of entire blocks of the city.

Yet what was left standing was enough to take Rand's breath. The largest building in Baerlon would have vanished in the shadows of almost anything here. Pale marble palaces topped with huge domes met him wherever he looked. Every building appeared to have at least one dome; some had four or five, and each one shaped differently. Long walks lined by columns ran hundreds of paces to towers that seemed to reach the sky. At every intersection stood a bronze fountain, or the alabaster spire of a monument, or a statue on a pedestal. If the fountains were dry, most of the spires toppled, and many of the statues broken, what remained was so great that he could only marvel.

And I thought Baerlon was a city! Burn me, but Thom must have been laughing up his sleeve. Moiraine and Lan, too.

He was so caught up in staring that he was taken by surprise when Lan suddenly stopped in front of a white stone building that had once been twice as big as the Stag and Lion in Baerlon. There was nothing to say what it had been when the city lived and was great, perhaps even an inn. Only a hollow shell remained of the upper floors—the afternoon sky was visible through empty window frames, glass and wood alike long since gone—but the ground floor seemed sound enough.

Moiraine, hands still on the pommel, studied the building intently before nodding. "This will do."

Lan leaped from his saddle and lifted the Aes Sedai down in his arms. "Bring the horses inside," he commanded. "Find a room in the back to use for a stable. Move, farmboys. This isn't the village green." He vanished inside carrying the Aes Sedai.

Nynaeve scrambled down and hurried after him, clutching her bag of herbs and ointments. Egwene was right behind her. They left their mounts standing.

"'Bring the horses inside,'" Thom muttered wryly, and puffed out his mustaches. He climbed down, stiff and slow, knuckled his back, and gave a long sigh, then took Aldieb's reins. "Well?" he said, lifting an eyebrow at Rand and his friends.

They hurried to dismount, and gathered up the rest of the horses. The doorway, without anything to say there had ever been a door in it, was more than big enough to get the animals through, even two abreast.

Inside was a huge room, as wide as the building, with a dirty tile floor and a few ragged wall hangings, faded to a dull brown, that looked as if they would fall apart at a touch. Nothing else. Lan had made a place in the nearest corner for Moiraine with his cloak and hers. Nynaeve, muttering about the dust, knelt beside the Aes Sedai, digging in her bag, which Egwene held open.

"I may not like her, it is true," Nynaeve was saying to the Warder as Rand, leading Bela and Cloud, came in behind Thom, "but I help anyone who needs my help, whether I like them or not."

"I made no accusation, Wisdom. I only said, have a care with your herbs."

She gave him a look from the corner of her eye. "The fact is, she needs my herbs, and so do you." Her voice was acerbic to start, and grew more tart as she spoke. "The fact is, she can only do so much, even with her One Power, and she has done about as much as she can without collapsing. The fact is, your sword cannot help her now, Lord of the Seven Towers, but my herbs can."

Moiraine laid a hand on Lan's arm. "Be at ease, Lan. She means no harm. She simply does not know." The Warder snorted derisively.

Nynaeve stopped digging in her bag and looked at him, frowning, but it was to Moiraine she spoke. "There are many things I don't know. What thing is this?"

"For one," Moiraine replied, "all I truly need is a little rest. For another, I agree with you. Your skills and knowledge will be more useful than I thought. Now, if you have something that will help me sleep for an hour and not leave me groggy—?"

"A weak tea of foxtail, marisin, and—"

Rand missed the last of it as he followed Thom into a room behind the first, a chamber just as big and even emptier. Here was only the dust, thick and undisturbed until they came. Not even the tracks of birds or small animals marked the floor.

Rand began to unsaddle Bela and Cloud, and Thom, Aldieb and his gelding, and Perrin, his horse and Mandarb. All but Mat. He dropped his reins in the middle of the room. There were two doorways from the room besides the one by which they had entered.

"Alley," Mat announced, drawing his head back in from the first. They could all see that much from where they were. The second doorway was only a black rectangle in the rear wall. Mat went through slowly, and came out much faster, vigorously brushing old cobwebs out of his hair. "Nothing in there," he said, giving the alleyway another look.

"You going to take care of your horse?" Perrin said. He had already finished his own and was lifting the saddle from Mandarb. Strangely, the fierce-eyed stallion gave him no trouble at all, though he did watch Perrin. "Nobody is going to do it for you."

Mat gave the alley one last look and went to his horse with a sigh.

As Rand laid Bela's saddle on the floor, he noticed that Mat had taken on a glum stare. His eyes seemed a thousand miles away, and he was moving by rote.

"Are you all right, Mat?" Rand said. Mat lifted the saddle from his horse, and stood holding it. "Mat? Mat!"

Mat gave a start and almost dropped the saddle. "What? Oh. I . . . I was just thinking."

"Thinking?" Perrin hooted from where he was replacing Mandarb's bridle with a hackamore. "You were asleep."

Mat scowled. "I was thinking about . . . about what happened back there. About those words I. . . ." Everybody turned to look at him then, not just Rand, and he shifted uneasily. "Well, you heard what Moiraine said. It's as if some dead man was speaking with my mouth. I don't like it." His scowl grew deeper when Perrin chuckled.

"Aemon's warcry, she said—right? Maybe you're Aemon come back again. The way you go on about how dull Emond's Field is, I'd think you would like that—being a king and hero reborn."

"Don't say that!" Thom drew a deep breath; everybody stared at him now. "That is dangerous talk, stupid talk. The dead can be reborn, or take a living body, and it is not something to speak of lightly." He took another breath to calm himself before going on. "The old blood, she said. The blood, not a dead man. I've heard that it can happen, sometimes. Heard, though I never really thought. . . . It was your roots, boy. A line running from you to your father to your grandfather, right on back to Manetheren, and maybe beyond. Well, now you know your family is old. You ought to let it go at that and be glad. Most people don't know much more than that they had a father."

Some of us can't even be sure of that, Rand thought bitterly. *Maybe the Wisdom was right. Light, I hope she was.*

Mat nodded at what the gleeman said. "I suppose I should. Only . . . do you think it has anything to do with what's happened to us? The Trollocs and all? I mean . . . oh, I don't know what I mean."

"I think you ought to forget about it, and concentrate on getting out of here safely." Thom produced his long-stemmed pipe from inside his cloak. "And I think I am going to have a smoke." With a waggle of the pipe in their direction, he disappeared into the front room.

"We are all in this together, not just one of us," Rand told Mat.

Mat gave himself a shake, and laughed, a short bark. "Right. Well, speaking of being in things together, now that we're done with the horses, why don't we go see a little more of this city. A real city, and no crowds to jostle your elbow and poke you in the ribs. Nobody looking down their long noses at us. There's still an hour, maybe two, of daylight left."

"Aren't you forgetting the Trollocs?" Perrin said.

Mat shook his head scornfully. "Lan said they wouldn't come in here, remember? You need to listen to what people say."

"I remember," Perrin said. "And I do listen. This city—Aridhol?—was an ally of Manetheren. See? I listen."

"Aridhol must have been the greatest city in the Trolloc Wars," Rand said, "for the Trollocs to still be afraid of it. They weren't afraid to come into the Two Rivers, and Moiraine said Manetheren was—how did she put it?—a thorn to the Dark One's foot."

Perrin raised his hands. "Don't mention the Shepherd of the Night. Please?"

"What do you say?" Mat laughed. "Let's go."

"We should ask Moiraine," Perrin said, and Mat threw up his hands.

"Ask Moiraine? You think she'll let us out of her sight? And what about Nynaeve? Blood and ashes, Perrin, why not ask Mistress Luhhan while you're about it?"

Perrin nodded reluctant agreement, and Mat turned to Rand with a grin. "What about you? A real city? With palaces!" He gave a sly laugh. "And no Whitecloaks to stare at us."

Rand gave him a dirty look, but he hesitated only a minute. Those palaces were like a gleeman's tale. "All right."

Stepping softly so as not to be heard in the front room, they left by the alley, following it away from the front of the building to a street on the other side. They walked quickly, and when they were a block away from the white stone building Mat suddenly broke into a capering dance.

"Free." He laughed. "Free!" He slowed until he was turning in a circle, staring at everything and still laughing. The afternoon shadows stretched long and jagged, and the sinking sun made the ruined city golden. "Did you ever even dream of a place like this? Did you?"

Perrin laughed, too, but Rand shrugged uncomfortably. This was nothing like the city in his first dream, but just the same. . . . "If we're going to see anything," he said, "we had better get on with it. There isn't much daylight left."

Mat wanted to see everything, it seemed, and he pulled the others along with his enthusiasm. They climbed over dusty fountains with basins wide enough to hold everybody in Emond's Field and wandered in and out of structures chosen at random, but always the biggest they could find. Some they understood, and some not. A palace was plainly a palace, but what was a huge building that was one round, white dome as big as a hill outside and one monstrous room inside? And a walled place, open to the sky and big enough to have held all of Emond's Field, surrounded by row on row on row of stone benches?

Mat grew impatient when they found nothing but dust, or rubble, or colorless rags of wall hangings that crumbled at a touch. Once some wooden chairs stood stacked against a wall; they all fell to bits when Perrin tried to pick one up.

The palaces, with their huge, empty chambers, some of which could have held the Winespring Inn with room to spare on every side and above as well, made Rand think too much of the people who had once filled them. He thought everybody in the Two Rivers could have stood under that round dome, and as for the place with the stone benches. . . . He could almost imagine he could see the people in the shadows, staring in disapproval at the three intruders disturbing their rest.

Finally even Mat tired, grand as the buildings were, and remembered that he had had only an hour's sleep the night before. Everyone began to remember that. Yawning, they sat on the steps of a tall building fronted by row on row of tall stone columns and argued about what to do next.

"Go back," Rand said, "and get some sleep." He put the back of his hand against his mouth. When he could talk again, he said, "Sleep. That's all I want."

"You can sleep anytime," Mat said determinedly. "Look at where we are. A ruined city. Treasure."

"Treasure?" Perrin's jaws cracked. "There isn't any treasure here. There isn't anything but dust."

Rand shaded his eyes against the sun, a red ball sitting close to the rooftops. "It's getting late, Mat. It'll be dark soon."

"There could be treasure," Mat maintained stoutly. "Anyway, I want to climb one of the towers. Look at that one over there. It's whole. I'll bet you could see for miles from up there. What do you say?"

"The towers are not safe," said a man's voice behind them.

Rand leaped to his feet and spun around clutching his sword hilt, and the others were just as quick.

A man stood in the shadows among the columns at the top of the stairs. He took half a step forward, raised his hand to shield his eyes, and stepped back again. "Forgive me," he said smoothly. "I have been quite a long time in the dark inside. My eyes are not yet used to the light."

"Who are you?" Rand thought the man's accent sounded odd, even after Baerlon; some words he pronounced strangely, so Rand could barely understand them. "What are you doing here? We thought the city was empty."

"I am Mordeth." He paused as if expecting them to recognize the name. When none of them gave any sign of doing so, he muttered something under his breath and went on. "I could ask the same questions of you. There has been no one in Aridhol for a long time. A long, long time. I would not have thought to find three young men wandering its streets."

"We're on our way to Caemlyn," Rand said. "We stopped to take shelter for the night."

"Caemlyn," Mordeth said slowly, rolling the name around his tongue, then shook his head. "Shelter for the night, you say? Perhaps you will join me."

"You still haven't said what you're doing here," Perrin said.

"Why, I am a treasure hunter, of course."

"Have you found any?" Mat demanded excitedly.

Rand thought Mordeth smiled, but in the shadows he could not be sure. "I have," the man said. "More than I expected. Much more. More than I can carry away. I never expected to find three strong, healthy young men. If you will help me move what I *can* take to where my horses are, you may each have a share of the rest. As much as you can carry. Whatever I leave will be gone, carried off by some other treasure hunter, before I can return for it."

"I told you there must be treasure in a place like this," Mat exclaimed. He darted up the stairs. "We'll help you carry it. Just take us to it." He and Mordeth moved deeper into the shadows among the columns.

Rand looked at Perrin. "We can't leave him." Perrin glanced at the sinking sun, and nodded.

They went up the stairs warily, Perrin easing his axe in its belt loop. Rand's hand tightened on his sword. But Mat and Mordeth were waiting among the columns, Mordeth with arms folded, Mat peering impatiently into the interior.

"Come," Mordeth said. "I will show you the treasure." He slipped inside, and Mat followed. There was nothing for the others to do but go on.

The hall inside was shadowy, but almost immediately Mordeth turned aside and took some narrow steps that wound around and down through deeper and deeper dark until they fumbled their way in pitch-blackness. Rand felt along the wall with one hand, unsure there would be a step below until his foot met it. Even Mat began to feel uneasy, judging by his voice when he said, "It's awfully dark down here."

"Yes, yes," Mordeth replied. The man seemed to be having no trouble at all with the dark. "There are lights below. Come."

Indeed the winding stairs abruptly gave way to a corridor dimly lit by scattered, smoky torches set in iron sconces on the walls. The flickering flames and shadows gave Rand his first good look at Mordeth, who hurried on without pausing, motioning them to follow.

There was something odd about him, Rand thought, but he could not pick out what it was, exactly. Mordeth was a sleek, somewhat overfed man, with drooping eyelids that made him seem to be hiding behind something and staring. Short, and completely bald, he walked as if he were taller than any of them. His clothes were certainly like nothing Rand had ever seen before, either. Tight black breeches and soft red boots with the tops turned down at his ankles. A long, red vest thickly embroidered in gold, and a snowy white shirt with wide sleeves, the points of his cuffs hanging almost to his knees. Certainly not the kind of clothes in which to hunt through a ruined city in search of treasure. But it was not that which made him seem strange, either.

Then the corridor ended in a tile-walled room, and he forgot about any oddities Mordeth might have. His gasp was an echo of his friends'. Here, too, light came from a few torches staining the ceiling with their smoke and giving everyone more than one shadow, but that light was reflected a thousand times by the gems and gold piled on the floor, mounds of coins and jewelry, goblets and plates and platters, gilded, gem-encrusted swords and daggers, all heaped together carelessly in waist-high mounds.

With a cry Mat ran forward and fell to his knees in front of one of the piles. "Sacks," he said breathlessly, pawing through the gold. "We'll need sacks to carry all of this."

"We can't carry it all," Rand said. He looked around helplessly; all the gold the merchants brought to Emond's Field in a year would not have made the thousandth part of just one of those mounds. "Not now. It's almost dark."

Perrin pulled an axe free, carelessly tossing back the gold chains that had been tangled around it. Jewels glittered along its shiny black handle, and delicate gold scrollwork covered the twin blades. "Tomorrow, then," he said, hefting the axe with a grin. "Moiraine and Lan will understand when we show them this."

"You are not alone?" Mordeth said. He had let them rush past him into the treasure room, but now he followed. "Who else is with you?"

Mat, wrist deep in the riches before him, answered absently. "Moiraine and Lan. And then there's Nynaeve, and Egwene, and Thom. He's a gleeman. We're going to Tar Valon."

Rand caught his breath. Then the silence from Mordeth made him look at the man.

Rage twisted Mordeth's face, and fear, too. His lips pulled back from his teeth. "Tar Valon!" He shook clenched fists at them. "Tar Valon! You said you were going to this . . . this . . . Caemlyn! You lied to me!"

"If you still want," Perrin said to Mordeth, "we'll come back tomorrow and help you." Carefully he set the axe back on the heap of gem-encrusted chalices and jewelry. "If you want."

"No. That is. . . ." Panting, Mordeth shook his head as if he could not decide. "Take what you want. Except. . . . Except. . . ."

Suddenly Rand realized what had been nagging at him about the man. The scattered torches in the hallway had given each of them a ring of shadows, just as the torches in the treasure room did. Only. . . . He was so shocked he said it out loud. "You don't have a shadow."

A goblet fell from Mat's hand with a crash.

Mordeth nodded, and for the first time his fleshy eyelids opened all the way. His sleek face suddenly appeared pinched and hungry. "So." He stood straighter, seeming taller. "It is decided." Abruptly there was no seeming to it. Like a balloon Mordeth swelled, distorted, head pressed against the ceiling, shoulders butting the walls, filling the end of the room, cutting off escape. Hollow-cheeked, teeth bared in a rictus snarl, he reached out with hands big enough to engulf a man's head.

With a yell Rand leaped back. His feet tangled in a gold chain, and he crashed to the floor, the wind knocked out of him. Struggling for breath, he struggled at the same time for his sword, fighting his cloak, which had become wrapped around the hilt. The yells of his friends filled the room, and the clash of gold platters and goblets clattering across the floor. Suddenly an agonized scream shivered in Rand's ears.

Almost sobbing, he managed to inhale at last, just as he got the sword out of its sheath. Cautiously, he got to his feet, wondering which of his friends had given that scream. Perrin looked back at him wide-eyed from across the room, crouched and holding his axe back as if about to chop down a tree. Mat peered around the side of a treasure pile, clutching a dagger snatched from the trove.

Something moved in the deepest part of the shadows left by the torches, and they all jumped. It was Mordeth, clutching his knees to his chest and huddled as deep into the furthest corner as he could get.

"He tricked us," Mat panted. "It was some kind of trick."

Mordeth threw back his head and wailed; dust sifted down as the walls trembled. "You are all dead!" he cried. "All dead!" And he leaped up, diving across the room.

Rand's jaw dropped, and he almost dropped the sword as well. As Mordeth dove through the air, he stretched out and thinned, like a tendril of smoke. As thin as a finger he struck a crack in the wall tiles and vanished into it. A last cry hung in the room as he vanished, fading slowly away after he was gone.

"You are all dead!"

"Let's get out of here," Perrin said faintly, firming his grip on his axe while he tried to face every direction at once. Gold ornaments and gems scattered unnoticed under his feet.

"But the treasure," Mat protested. "We *can't* just leave it now."

"I don't want anything of his," Perrin said, still turning one way after another. He raised his voice and shouted at the walls. "It's your treasure, you hear? We are not taking any of it!"

Rand stared angrily at Mat. "Do you want him coming after us? Or are you going to wait here stuffing your pockets until he comes back with ten more like him?"

Mat just gestured to all the gold and jewels. Before he could say anything, though, Rand seized one of his arms and Perrin grabbed the other. They hustled him out of the room, Mat struggling and shouting about the treasure.

Before they had gone ten steps down the hall, the already dim light behind them began to fail. The torches in the treasure room were going out. Mat stopped shouting. They hastened their steps. The first torch outside the room winked out, then the next. By the time they reached the winding stairs there was no need to drag Mat any longer. They were all running, with the dark closing in behind them. Even the pitch-black of the stairs only made them hesitate an instant, then they sped upwards, shouting at the top of their lungs. Shouting to scare anything that might be waiting; shouting to remind themselves they were still alive.

They burst out into the hall above, sliding and falling on the dusty marble, scrambling out through the columns, to tumble down the stairs and land in a bruised heap in the street.

Rand untangled himself and picked Tam's sword up from the pavement, looking around uneasily. Less than half of the sun still showed above the rooftops. Shadows reached out like dark hands, made blacker by the remaining light, nearly filling the street. He shivered. The shadows looked like Mordeth, reaching.

"At least we're out of it." Mat got up from the bottom of the pile, dusting himself off in a shaky imitation of his usual manner. "And at least I—"

"Are we?" Perrin said.

Rand knew it was not his imagination this time. The back of his neck prickled. Something was watching them from the darkness in the columns. He spun around, staring at the buildings across the way. He could feel eyes on him from there, too. His grip tightened on his sword hilt, though he wondered what good it would be. Watching eyes seemed to be everywhere. The others looked around warily; he knew they could feel it, too.

"We stay in the middle of the street," he said hoarsely. They met his eyes; they looked as frightened as he felt. He swallowed hard. "We stay in the middle of the street, keep out of shadows as much as we can, and walk fast."

"Walk very fast," Mat agreed fervently.

The watchers followed them. Or else there were lots of watchers, lots of eyes staring out of almost every building. Rand could not see anything move, hard as he tried, but he could feel the eyes, eager, hungry. He did not know which would be worse. Thousands of eyes, or just a few, following them.

In the stretches where the sun still reached them, they slowed, just a little, squinting nervously into the darkness that always seemed to lay ahead. None of them was eager to enter the shadows; no one was really sure something might not be waiting. The watchers' anticipation was a palpable thing whenever shadows stretched across the street, barring their way. They ran through those dark places shouting. Rand thought he could hear dry, rustling laughter.

At last, with twilight falling, they came in sight of the white stone building they had left what seemed like days ago. Suddenly the watching eyes departed. Between one step and the next, they vanished in a blink. Without a word Rand broke into a trot, followed by his friends, then a full run that only ended when they hared through the doorway and collapsed, panting.

A small fire burned in the middle of the tile floor, the smoke vanishing through a hole in the ceiling in a way that reminded Rand unpleasantly of Mordeth. Everyone except Lan was there, gathered around the flames, and their reactions varied considerably. Egwene, warming her hands at the fire, gave a start as the three burst into the room, clutching her hands to her throat; when she saw who it was, a relieved sigh spoiled her attempt at a withering look. Thom merely muttered something around his pipestem, but Rand caught the word "fools" before the gleeman went back to poking the flames with a stick.

"You wool-headed witlings!" the Wisdom snapped. She bristled
from head to foot; her eyes glittered, and bright spots of red burned
on her cheeks. "Why under the Light did you run off like that? Are
you all right? Have you no sense at all? Lan is out looking for you
now, and you'll be luckier than you deserve if he does not pound some
sense into the lot of you when he gets back."

The Aes Sedai's face betrayed no agitation at all, but her hands had
loosed a white-knuckled grip on her dress at the sight of them. Whatever Nynaeve had given her must have helped, for she was on her feet.
"You should not have done what you did," she said in a voice as clear
and serene as a Waterwood pond. "We will speak of it later. Something happened out there, or you would not be falling all over one
another like this. Tell me."

"You said it was safe," Mat complained, scrambling to his feet.
"You said Aridhol was an ally of Manetheren, and Trollocs wouldn't
come into the city, and—"

Moiraine stepped forward so suddenly that Mat cut off with his
mouth open, and Rand and Perrin paused in getting up, halfway
crouched or on their knees. "Trollocs? Did you see Trollocs inside the
walls?"

Rand swallowed. "Not Trollocs," he said, and all three began talking excitedly, all at the same time.

Everyone began in a different place. Mat started with finding the
treasure, sounding almost as if he had done it alone, while Perrin began explaining why they had gone off in the first place without telling
anyone. Rand jumped right to what he thought was important, meeting the stranger among the columns. But they were all so excited that
nobody told anything in the order it happened; whenever one of them
thought of something, he blurted it out with no regard for what came
before or after, or for who was saying what. The watchers. They all
babbled about the watchers.

It made the whole tale close to incoherent, but their fear came
through. Egwene began casting uneasy glances at the empty windows
fronting the street. Out there the last remnants of twilight were fading;
the fire seemed very small and dim. Thom took his pipe from between
his teeth and listened with his head cocked, frowning. Moiraine's eyes
showed concern, but not an undue amount. Until. . . .

Suddenly the Aes Sedai hissed, and grabbed Rand's elbow in a tight
grip. "Mordeth! Are you sure of that name? Be very sure, all of you.
Mordeth?"

They murmured a chorused "Yes," taken aback by the Aes Sedai's
intensity.

"Did he touch you?" she asked them all. "Did he give you anything, or did you do anything for him? I must know."

"No," Rand said. "None of us. None of those things."

Perrin nodded agreement, and added, "All he did was try to kill us. Isn't that enough? He swelled up until he filled half the room, shouted that we were all dead men, then vanished." He moved his hand to demonstrate. "Like smoke." Egwene gave a squeak.

Mat twisted away petulantly. "Safe, you said! All that talk about Trollocs not coming here. What were we supposed to think?"

"Apparently you did not think at all," she said, coolly composed once more. "Anyone who thinks would be wary of a place that Trollocs are afraid to enter."

"Mat's doing," Nynaeve said, certainty in her voice. "He's always talking some mischief or other, and the others lose the little wits they were born with when they're around him."

Moiraine nodded briefly, but her eyes remained on Rand and his two friends. "Late in the Trolloc Wars, an army camped within these ruins—Trollocs, Darkfriends, Myrddraal, Dreadlords, thousands in all. When they did not come out, scouts were sent inside the walls. The scouts found weapons, bits of armor, and blood splattered everywhere. And messages scratched on walls in the Trolloc tongue, calling on the Dark One to aid them in their last hour. Men who came later found no trace of the blood or the messages. They had been scoured away. Halfmen and Trollocs remember still. That is what keeps them outside this place."

"And this is where you picked for us to hide?" Rand said in disbelief. "We'd be safer out there trying to outrun them."

"If you had not gone running off," Moiraine said patiently, "you would know that I set wards around this building. A Myrddraal would not even know these wards were there, for it is a different kind of evil they are meant to stop, but what resides in Shadar Logoth will not cross them, or even come too near. In the morning it will be safe for us to go; these things cannot stand the light of the sun. They will be hiding deep in the earth."

"Shadar Logoth?" Egwene said uncertainly. "I thought you said this city was called Aridhol."

"Once it was called Aridhol," Moiraine replied, "and was one of the Ten Nations, the lands that made the Second Covenant, the lands that stood against the Dark One from the first days after the Breaking of the World. In the days when Thorin al Toren al Ban was King of Manetheren, the King of Aridhol was Balwen Mayel, Balwen Iron-hand. In a twilight of despair during the Trolloc Wars, when it seemed the Father of Lies must surely conquer, the man called Mordeth came to Balwen's court."

"The same man?" Rand exclaimed, and Mat said, "It couldn't be!" A glance from Moiraine silenced them. Stillness filled the room except for the Aes Sedai's voice.

"Before Mordeth had been long in the city he had Balwen's ear, and soon he was second only to the King. Mordeth whispered poison in Balwen's ear, and Aridhol began to change. Aridhol drew in on itself, hardened. It was said that some would rather see Trollocs come than the men of Aridhol. The victory of the Light is all. That was the battlecry Mordeth gave them, and the men of Aridhol shouted it while their deeds abandoned the Light.

"The story is too long to tell in full, and too grim, and only fragments are known, even in Tar Valon. How Thorin's son, Caar, came to win Aridhol back to the Second Covenant, and Balwen sat his throne, a withered shell with the light of madness in his eyes, laughing while Mordeth smiled at his side and ordered the deaths of Caar and the embassy as Friends of the Dark. How Prince Caar came to be called Caar One-Hand. How he escaped the dungeons of Aridhol and fled alone to the Borderlands with Mordeth's unnatural assassins at his heels. How there he met Rhea, who did not know who he was, and married her, and set the skein in the Pattern that led to his death at her hands, and hers by her own hand before his tomb, and the fall of Aleth-loriel. How the armies of Manetheren came to avenge Caar and found the gates of Aridhol torn down, no living thing inside the walls, but something worse than death. No enemy had come to Aridhol but Aridhol. Suspicion and hate had given birth to something that fed on that which created it, something locked in the bedrock on which the city stood. Mashadar waits still, hungering. Men spoke of Aridhol no more. They named it Shadar Logoth, the Place Where the Shadow Waits, or more simply, Shadow's Waiting.

"Mordeth alone was not consumed by Mashadar, but he was snared by it, and he, too, has waited within these walls through the long centuries. Others have seen him. Some he has influenced through gifts that twist the mind and taint the spirit, the taint waxing and waning until it rules . . . or kills. If ever he convinces someone to accompany him to the walls, to the boundary of Mashadar's power, he will be able to consume the soul of that person. Mordeth will leave, wearing the body of the one he worse than killed, to wreak his evil on the world again."

"The treasure," Perrin mumbled when she stopped. "He wanted us to help carry the treasure to his horses." His face was haggard. "I'll bet they were supposed to be outside the city somewhere." Rand shivered.

"But we are safe, now, aren't we?" Mat asked. "He didn't give us anything, and he didn't touch us. We're safe, aren't we, with the wards you set?"

"We are safe," Moiraine agreed. "He cannot cross the ward lines, nor can any other denizen of this place. And they must hide from the sunlight, so we can leave safely once it is day. Now, try to sleep. The wards will protect us until Lan returns."

"He has been gone a long time." Nynaeve looked worriedly at the night outside. Full dark had fallen, as black as pitch.

"Lan will be well," Moiraine said soothingly, and spread her blankets beside the fire while she spoke. "He was pledged to fight the Dark One before he left the cradle, a sword placed in his infant hands. Besides, I would know the minute of his death and the way of it, just as he would know mine. Rest, Nynaeve. All will be well." But as she was rolling herself into her blankets, she paused, staring at the street as if she, too, would have liked to know what kept the Warder.

Rand's arms and legs felt like lead and his eyes wanted to slide shut on their own, yet sleep did not come quickly, and once it did, he dreamed, muttering and kicking off his blankets. When he woke, it was suddenly, and he looked around for a moment before he remembered where he was.

The moon was up, the last thin sliver before the new moon, its faint light defeated by the night. Everyone else was still asleep, though not all soundly. Egwene and his two friends twisted and murmured inaudibly. Thom's snores, soft for once, were broken from time to time by half-formed words. There was still no sign of Lan.

Suddenly he felt as if the wards were no protection at all. Anything at all could be out there in the dark. Telling himself he was being foolish, he added wood to the last coals of the fire. The blaze was too small to give much warmth, but it gave more light.

He had no idea what had awakened him from his unpleasant dream. He had been a little boy again, carrying Tam's sword and with a cradle strapped to his back, running through empty streets, pursued by Mordeth, who shouted that he only wanted his hand. And there had been an old man who watched them and cackled with mad laughter the whole time.

He gathered his blankets and lay back, staring at the ceiling. He wanted very much to sleep, even if he had more dreams like the last one, but he could not make his eyes close.

Suddenly the Warder trotted silently out of the darkness into the room. Moiraine came awake and sat up as if he had rung a bell. Lan opened his hand; three small objects fell to the tiles in front of her with the clink of iron. Three blood-red badges in the shape of horned skulls.

"There are Trollocs inside the walls," Lan said. "They will be here in little more than an hour. And the Dha'vol are the worst of them." He began waking the others.

Moiraine smoothly began folding her blankets. "How many? Do they know we are here?" She sounded as if there were no urgency at all.

"I don't think they do," Lan replied. "There are well over a hundred, frightened enough to kill anything that moves, including one another. The Halfmen are having to drive them—four just to handle one fist—and even the Myrddraal seem to want nothing more than to pass through the city and out as quickly as possible. They are not going out of their way to search, and they're so slipshod that if they were not heading nearly straight for us I would say we had nothing to worry about." He hesitated.

"There is something else?"

"Only this," Lan said slowly. "The Myrddraal forced the Trollocs into the city. What forced the Myrddraal?"

Everyone had been listening in silence. Now Thom cursed under his breath, and Egwene breathed a question. "The Dark One?"

"Don't be a fool, girl," Nynaeve snapped. "The Dark One is bound in Shayol Ghul by the Creator."

"For the time being, at least," Moiraine agreed. "No, the Father of Lies is not out there, but we must leave in any case."

Nynaeve eyed her narrowly. "Leave the protection of the wards, and cross Shadar Logoth in the night."

"Or stay here and face the Trollocs," Moiraine said. "To hold them off here would require the One Power. It would destroy the wards and attract the very thing the wards are meant to protect against. Besides, as well build a signal fire atop one of those towers for every Halfman within twenty miles. To leave is not what I would choose to do, but we are the hare, and it is the hounds who dictate the chase."

"What if there are more outside the walls?" Mat asked. "What are we going to do?"

"We will use my original plan," Moiraine said. Lan looked at her. She held up a hand and added, "Which I was too tired to carry out before. But I am rested, now, thanks to the Wisdom. We will make for the river. There, with our backs guarded by the water, I can raise a smaller ward that will hold the Trollocs and Halfmen back until we can make rafts and cross over. Or better yet, we may even be able to hail a trader's boat coming down from Saldaea."

The faces of the Emond's Fielders looked blank. Lan noticed.

"Trollocs and Myrddraal loathe deep water. Trollocs are terrified of it. Neither can swim. A Halfman will not wade anything more than waist deep, especially if it's moving. Trollocs won't do even that if they can find any way to avoid it."

"So once we get across the river we're safe," Rand said, and the Warder nodded.

"The Myrddraal will find it almost as hard to make the Trollocs build rafts as it was to drive them into Shadar Logoth, and if they try to make them cross the Arinelle that way, half will run away and the rest probably drown."

"Get to your horses," Moiraine said. "We are not across the river yet."

CHAPTER
20

Dust on the Wind

As they left the white stone building on their nervously shifting horses, the icy wind came in gusts, moaning across the roof-tops, whipping cloaks like banners, driving thin clouds across the thin sliver of the moon. With a quiet command to stay close, Lan led off down the street. The horses danced and tugged at the reins, eager to be away.

Rand looked up warily at the buildings they passed, looming now in the night with their empty windows like eye sockets. Shadows seemed to move. Occasionally there was a clatter—rubble toppled by the wind. *At least the eyes are gone.* His relief was momentary. Why *are they gone?*

Thom and the Emond's Fielders made a cluster with him, all keeping close enough to touch one another. Egwene's shoulders were hunched, as if she were trying to ease Bela's hooves to the pavement. Rand did not even want to breathe. Sound might attract attention.

Abruptly he realized that a distance had opened ahead of them, separating them from the Warder and the Aes Sedai. The two were indistinct shapes a good thirty paces ahead.

"We're falling behind," he murmured, and booted Cloud to a quicker step. A thin tendril of silver-gray fog drifted low across the street ahead of him.

"Stop!" It was a strangled shout from Moiraine, sharp and urgent, but pitched not to carry far.

Uncertain, he pulled up short. The splinter of fog lay completely across the street now, slowly fattening as if more were oozing out of the buildings on either side of the street. It was as thick as a man's arm now. Cloud whickered and tried to back further away as Egwene and Thom and the others came up on him. Their horses, too, tossed their heads and bridled against coming too near the fog.

Lan and Moiraine rode slowly toward the fog, grown to as big around as a leg, stopping on the other side, well back. The Aes Sedai studied the branch of mist that separated them. Rand shrugged at a sudden itch of fear between his shoulder blades. A faint light accompanied the fog, growing as the foggy tentacle became fatter, but still only a little more than the moonlight. The horses shifted uneasily, even Aldieb and Mandarb.

"What is it?" Nynaeve asked.

"The evil of Shadar Logoth," Moiraine replied. "Mashadar. Unseeing, unthinking, moving through the city as aimlessly as a worm burrows through the earth. If it touches you, you will die." Rand and the others let their horses dance a few quick steps back, but not too far. As much as Rand would have given to be free of the Aes Sedai, she was as safe as home compared to what lay around them.

"Then how do we join you?" Egwene said. "Can you kill it . . . clear a way?"

Moiraine's laugh was bitter and short. "Mashadar is vast, girl, as vast as Shadar Logoth itself. The whole White Tower could not kill it. If I damaged it enough to let you pass, drawing that much of the One Power would pull the Halfmen like a trumpet call. And Mashadar would rush in to heal whatever harm I did, rush in and perhaps catch us in its net."

Rand exchanged looks with Egwene, then asked her question again. Moiraine sighed before answering.

"I do not like it, but what must be done, must be done. This thing will not be above ground everywhere. Other streets will be clear. See that star?" She twisted in her saddle to point to a red star low in the eastern sky. "Keep on toward that star, and it will bring you to the river. Whatever happens, keep moving toward the river. Go as quickly as you can, but above all make no noise. There are still the Trollocs, remember. And four Halfmen."

"But how will we find you again?" Egwene protested.

"I will find you," Moiraine said. "Be assured, I can find you. Now be off. This thing is utterly mindless, but it can sense food." Indeed, ropes of silver-gray had lifted from the larger body. They drifted, wavering, like the tentacles of a hundredarms on the bottom of a Waterwood pond.

When Rand looked up from the thick trunk of opaque mist, the Warder and the Aes Sedai were gone. He licked his lips and met his companions' eyes. They were as nervous as he was. And something worse: they all seemed to be waiting for someone else to move first. Night and ruins surrounded them. The Fades were out there, somewhere, and the Trollocs, maybe around the next corner. The tentacles of fog drifted nearer, halfway to them now, and no longer wavering. They had chosen their intended prey. Suddenly he missed Moiraine very much.

Everyone was still staring, wondering which way to go. He turned Cloud, and the gray broke into a half trot, tugging against the reins to go faster. As if moving first had made him the leader, everyone followed.

With Moiraine gone, there was no one to protect them should Mordeth appear. And the Trollocs. And. . . . Rand forced himself to stop thinking. He would follow the red star. He could hold onto that thought.

Three times they had to backtrack from a street blocked from side to side by a hill of stone and brick the horses could never have crossed. Rand could hear the others breathing, short and sharp, just shy of panic. He gritted his teeth to stop his own panting. *You have to at least make them think you're not afraid. You're doing a good job, woolhead! You'll get everybody out safely.*

They rounded the next corner. A wall of fog bathed the broken pavement with a light as bright as a full moon. Streamers as thick as their horses broke off toward them. Nobody waited. Wheeling, they galloped away in a tight knot with no heed for the clatter of hooves they raised.

Two Trollocs stepped into the street before them, not ten spans away.

For an instant the humans and the Trollocs just stared at one another, each more surprised than the other. Another pair of Trollocs appeared, and another, and another, colliding with the ones in front, folding into a shocked mass at the sight of the humans. Only for an instant did they remain frozen, though. Guttural howls echoed from the buildings, and the Trollocs bounded forward. The humans scattered like quail.

Rand's gray reached full gallop in three strides. "This way!" he shouted, but he heard the same cry from five throats. A hasty glance over his shoulder showed him his companions disappearing in as many directions, Trollocs pursuing them all.

Three Trollocs ran at his own heels, catchpoles waving in the air. His skin crawled as he realized they were matching Cloud stride for stride. He dropped low on Cloud's neck and urged the gray on, chased by thick cries.

The street narrowed ahead, broken-topped buildings leaning out drunkenly. Slowly the empty windows filled with a silvery glow, a dense mist bulging outward. Mashadar.

Rand risked a glance over his shoulder. The Trollocs still ran less than fifty paces back; the light from the fog was enough to see them clearly. A Fade rode behind them now, and they seemed to flee the Halfman as much as to pursue Rand. Ahead of Rand, half a dozen gray tendrils wavered from the windows, a dozen, feeling the air. Cloud tossed his head and screamed, but Rand dug his heels in brutally, and the horse lunged forward wildly.

The tendrils stiffened as Rand galloped between them, but he crouched low on Cloud's back and refused to look at them. The way beyond was clear. *If one of them touches me. . . . Light!* He booted Cloud harder, and the horse leaped forward into the welcome shadows. With Cloud still running, he looked back as soon as the glow of Mashadar began to lessen.

The waving gray tentacles of Mashadar blocked half the street, and the Trollocs were balking, but the Fade snatched a whip from its saddlebow, cracking it over the heads of the Trollocs with a sound like a lightning bolt, popping sparks in the air. Crouching, the Trollocs lurched after Rand. The Halfman hesitated, black cowl studying Mashadar's reaching arms, before it, too, spurred forward.

The thickening tentacles of fog swung uncertainly for a moment, then struck like vipers. At least two latched to each Trolloc, bathing them in gray light; muzzled heads went back to scream, but fog rolled over open mouths, and in, eating the howls. Four leg-thick tentacles whipped around the Fade, and the Halfman and its black horse twitched as if dancing, till the cowl fell back, baring that pale, eyeless face. The Fade shrieked.

There was no sound from that cry, any more than from the Trollocs, but something came through, a piercing whine just beyond hearing, like all the hornets in the world, digging into Rand's ears with all the fear that could exist. Cloud convulsed, as if he, too, heard, and ran harder than ever. Rand hung on, panting, his throat as dry as sand.

After a time he realized he could no longer hear the silent shriek of the Fade dying, and suddenly the clatter of his gallop seemed as loud as shouts. He reined Cloud hard, stopping beside a jagged wall, right where two streets met. A nameless monument reared in the darkness before him.

Slumped in the saddle, he listened, but there was nothing to hear except the blood pounding in his ears. Cold sweat beaded on his face, and he shivered as the wind flailed his cloak.

Finally he straightened. Stars spangled the sky where the clouds did not hide them, but the red star low in the east was easy to mark. *Is anybody else alive to see it?* Were they free, or in the Trollocs' hands? *Egwene, Light blind me, why didn't you follow me?* If they were alive and free, they would be following that star. If not. . . . The ruins were vast; he could search for days without finding anyone, if he could keep away from the Trollocs. And the Fades, and Mordeth, and Mashadar. Reluctantly he decided to make for the river.

He gathered the reins. On the crossing street, one stone fell against another with a sharp click. He froze, not even breathing. He was hidden in the shadows, one step from the corner. Frantically he thought of backing up. What was behind him? What would make a noise and give him away? He could not remember, and he was afraid to take his eyes from the corner of the building.

Darkness bulked at that corner, with the longer darkness of a shaft sticking out of it. Catchpole! Even as the thought flashed into Rand's head, he dug his heels into Cloud's ribs and his sword flew from the scabbard; a wordless shout accompanied his charge, and he swung the sword with all of his might. Only a desperate effort stopped the blade short. With a yelp Mat tumbled back, half falling off his horse and nearly dropping his bow.

Rand drew a deep breath and lowered his sword. His arm shook. "Have you seen anybody else?" he managed.

Mat swallowed hard before pulling himself awkwardly back into his saddle. "I . . . I. . . . Just Trollocs." He put a hand to his throat, and licked his lips. "Just Trollocs. You?"

Rand shook his head. "They must be trying to reach the river. We better do the same." Mat nodded silently, still feeling his throat, and they started toward the red star.

Before they had covered a hundred spans the keening cry of a

Trolloc horn rose behind them in the depths of the city. Another answered, from outside the walls.

Rand shivered, but he kept to his slow pace, watching the darkest places and avoiding them when he could. After one jerk at his reins as if he might gallop off, Mat did the same. Neither horn sounded again, and it was in silence that they came to an opening in the vine-shrouded wall where a gate had once been. Only the towers remained, standing broken-topped against the black sky.

Mat hesitated at the gateway, but Rand said softly, "Is it any safer in here than out there?" He did not slow the gray, and after a moment Mat followed him out of Shadar Logoth, trying to look every way at once. Rand let out a slow breath; his mouth was dry. *We're going to make it. Light, we're going to make it!*

The walls vanished behind, swallowed by the night and the forest. Listening for the slightest sound, Rand kept the red star dead ahead.

Suddenly Thom galloped by from behind, slowing only long enough to shout, "Ride, you fools!" A moment later hunting cries and crashes in the brush behind him announced the presence of Trollocs on his trail.

Rand dug in his heels, and Cloud sprang after the gleeman's gelding. *What happens when we get to the river without Moiraine? Light, Egwene!*

Perrin sat his horse in the shadows, watching the open gateway, some little distance off yet, and absently ran his thumb along the blade of his axe. It seemed to be a clear way out of the ruined city, but he had sat there for five minutes studying it. The wind tossed his shaggy curls and tried to carry his cloak away, but he pulled the cloak back around him without really noticing what he was doing.

He knew that Mat, and almost everyone else in Emond's Field, considered him slow of thought. It was partly because he was big and usually moved carefully—he had always been afraid he might accidentally break something or hurt somebody, since he was so much bigger than the boys he grew up with—but he really did prefer to think things all the way through if he could. Quick thinking, careless thinking, had put Mat into hot water one time after another, and Mat's quick thinking usually managed to get Rand, or him, or both, in the cookpot alongside Mat, too.

His throat tightened. *Light, don't think about being in a cookpot.* He tried to order his thoughts again. Careful thought was the way.

There had been some sort of square in front of the gate once, with a huge fountain in its middle. Part of the fountain was still there, a cluster of broken statues standing in a big, round basin, and so was the open space around it. To reach the gate he would have to ride nearly a hundred spans with only the night to shield him from searching eyes. That was not a pleasant thought, either. He remembered those unseen watchers too well.

He considered the horns he had heard in the city a little while earlier. He had almost turned back, thinking some of the others might have been taken, before realizing that he could not do anything alone if they had been captured. *Not against—what did Lan say—a hundred Trollocs and four Fades. Moiraine Sedai said get to the river.*

He went back to consideration of the gate. Careful thought had not given him much, but he had made his decision. He rode out of the deeper shadow into the lesser darkness.

As he did, another horse appeared from the far side of the square and stopped. He stopped, too, and felt for his axe; it gave him no great sense of comfort. If that dark shape was a Fade. . . .

"Rand?" came a soft, hesitant call.

He let out a long, relieved breath. "It's Perrin, Egwene," he called back, just as softly. It still sounded too loud in the darkness.

The horses came together near the fountain.

"Have you seen anybody else?" they both asked at the same time, and both answered by shaking their heads.

"They'll be all right," Egwene muttered, patting Bela's neck. "Won't they?"

"Moiraine Sedai and Lan will look after them," Perrin replied. "They will look after all of us once we get to the river." He hoped it was so.

He felt a great relief once they were beyond the gate, even if there *were* Trollocs in the forest. Or Fades. He stopped that line of thought. The bare branches were not enough to keep him from guiding on the red star, and they were beyond Mordeth's reach now. That one had frightened him worse than the Trollocs ever had.

Soon they would reach the river and meet Moiraine, and she would put them beyond the Trollocs' reach as well. He believed it because he needed to believe. The wind scraped branches together and rustled the leaves and needles on the evergreens. A nighthawk's lonely cry drifted in the dark, and he and Egwene moved their horses closer together as though they were huddling for warmth. They were very much alone.

A Trolloc horn sounded somewhere behind them, quick, wailing blasts, urging the hunters to hurry, hurry. Then thick, half-human howls rose on their trail, spurred on by the horn. Howls that grew sharper as they caught the human scent.

Perrin put his horse to a gallop, shouting, "Come on!" Egwene came, both of them booting their horses, heedless of noise, heedless of the branches that slapped at them.

As they raced through the trees, guided as much by instinct as by the dim moonlight, Bela fell behind. Perrin looked back. Egwene kicked the mare and flailed her with the reins, but it was doing no good. By their sounds, the Trollocs were coming closer. He drew in enough not to leave her behind.

"Hurry!" he shouted. He could make out the Trollocs now, huge dark shapes bounding through the trees, bellowing and snarling to chill the blood. He gripped the haft of his axe, hanging at his belt, until his knuckles hurt. "Hurry, Egwene! Hurry!"

Suddenly his horse screamed, and he was falling, tumbling out of the saddle as the horse dropped away beneath him. He flung out his hands to brace himself and splashed headfirst into icy water. He had ridden right off the edge of a sheer bluff into the Arinelle.

The shock of freezing water ripped a gasp from him, and he swallowed more than a little before he managed to fight his way to the surface. He felt more than heard another splash, and thought that Egwene must have come right after him. Panting and blowing, he treaded water. It was not easy to keep afloat; his coat and cloak were already sodden, and his boots had filled. He looked around for Egwene, but saw only the glint of moonlight on the black water, ruffled by the wind.

"Egwene? Egwene!"

A spear flashed right in front of his eyes and threw water in his face. Others splashed into the river around him, too. Guttural voices raised in argument on the riverbank, and the Trolloc spears stopped coming, but he gave up on calling for the time being.

The current washed him downriver, but the thick shouts and snarls followed along the bank, keeping pace. Undoing his cloak, he let the river take it. A little less weight to drag him down. Doggedly, he set out swimming for the far bank. There were no Trollocs there. He hoped.

He swam the way they did back home, in the ponds in the Waterwood, stroking with both hands, kicking with both feet, keeping his head out of the water. At least, he tried to keep his head out of the water; it was not easy. Even without the cloak, his coat and boots each seemed to weigh as much as he did. And the axe dragged at his waist, threatening to roll him over if it did not pull him under. He thought about letting the river have that, too; he thought about it more than once. It would be easy, much easier than struggling out of his boots, for instance. But every time he thought of it, he thought of crawling out on the far bank to find Trollocs waiting. The axe would not do him much good against half a dozen Trollocs—or even against one, maybe—but it was better than his bare hands.

After a while he was not even certain he would be able to lift the axe if Trollocs were there. His arms and legs became leaden; it was an effort to move them, and his face no longer came as far out of the river with each stroke. He coughed from water that went up his nose. *A day at the forge has no odds on this,* he thought wearily, and just then his kicking foot struck something. It was not until he kicked it again that he realized what it was. The bottom. He was in the shallows. He was across the river.

Sucking air through his mouth, he got to his feet, splashing about as his legs almost gave way. He fumbled his axe out of its loop as he floundered ashore, shivering in the wind. He did not see any Trollocs. He did not see Egwene, either. Just a few scattered trees along the riverbank, and a moonlight ribbon on the water.

When he had his breath again, he called their names again and again. Faint shouts from the far side answered him; even at that distance he could make out the harsh voices of Trollocs. His friends did not answer, though.

The wind surged, its moan drowning out the Trollocs, and he shivered. It was not cold enough to freeze the water soaking his clothes, but it felt as if it was; it sliced to the bone with an icy blade. Hugging himself was only a gesture that did not stop the shivering. Alone, he climbed tiredly up the riverbank to find shelter against the wind.

Rand patted Cloud's neck, soothing the gray with whispers. The horse tossed his head and danced on quick feet. The Trollocs had been left behind—or so it seemed—but Cloud had the smell of them thick in his nostrils. Mat rode with an arrow nocked, watching for surprises out of the night, while Rand and Thom peered through the branches, searching for the red star that was their guide. Keeping it in view had been easy enough, even with all the branches overhead, so long as they were riding straight toward it. But then more Trollocs had appeared, ahead, and they went galloping off to the side with both packs howling after them. The Trollocs could keep up with a horse, but only for a hundred paces or so, and finally they left the pursuit and the howls behind. But with all the twists and turns, they had lost the guiding star.

"I still say it's over there," Mat said, gesturing off to his right. "We were going north at the end, and that means east is that way."

"There it is," Thom said abruptly. He pointed through the tangled branches to their left, straight at the red star. Mat mumbled something under his breath.

Out of the corner of his eye Rand caught the movement as a Trolloc leaped out from behind a tree without a sound, swinging its catchpole. Rand dug his heels in, and the gray bounded forward just as two more plunged from the shadows after the first. A noose brushed the back of Rand's neck, sending a shiver down his spine.

An arrow took one of the bestial faces in the eye, then Mat swung in beside him as their horses pounded through the trees. They were running toward the river, he realized, but he was not sure it was going to do any good. The Trollocs sped after them, almost close enough to reach out and grab the streaming tails of their horses. Half a step gained, and the catchpoles could drag them both out of their saddles.

He leaned low on the gray's neck to put that much more distance between his own neck and the nooses. Mat's face was nearly buried in his horse's mane. But Rand wondered where Thom was. Had the gleeman decided he was better off on his own, since all three Trollocs had fastened on the boys?

Suddenly Thom's gelding galloped out of the night, hard behind the Trollocs. The Trollocs had only time enough to look back in surprise before the gleeman's hands whipped back and then forward. Moonlight flashed off steel. One Trolloc tumbled forward, rolling over and over before landing in a heap, while a second dropped to its knees with a scream, clawing at its back with both hands. The third snarled, baring a muzzleful of sharp teeth, but as its companions toppled it whirled away into the darkness. Thom's hand made the whip-like motion again, and the Trolloc shrieked, but the shrieks faded into the distance as it ran.

Rand and Mat pulled up and stared at the gleeman.

"My best knives," Thom muttered, but he made no effort to get down and retrieve them. "That one will bring others. I hope the river isn't too far. I hope. . . ." Instead of saying what else he hoped, he shook his head and set off at a quick canter. Rand and Mat fell in behind him.

Soon they reached a low bank where trees grew right to the edge of the night-black water, its moon-streaked surface riffled by the wind. Rand could not see the far side at all. He did not like the idea of crossing on a raft in the dark, but he liked the idea of staying on this side even less. *I'll swim if I have to.*

Somewhere away from the river a Trolloc horn brayed, sharp, quick, and urgent in the darkness. It was the first sound from the horns since they had left the ruins. Rand wondered if it meant some of the others had been captured.

"No use staying here all night," Thom said. "Pick a direction. Upriver, or down?"

"But Moiraine and the others could be anywhere," Mat protested. "Any way we choose could just take us further away."

"So it could." Clucking to his gelding, Thom turned downriver, heading along the bank. "So it could." Rand looked at Mat, who shrugged, and they turned after him.

For a time nothing changed. The bank was higher in some places, lower in others, the trees grew thicker, or thinned out in small clearings, but the night and the river and the wind were all the same, cold and black. And no Trollocs. That was one change Rand was glad to forgo.

Then he saw a light ahead, just a single point. As they drew closer he could see that the light was well above the river, as if it were in a tree. Thom quickened the pace and began to hum under his breath.

Finally they could make out the source of the light, a lantern hoisted atop one of the masts of a large trader's boat, tied up for the night beside a small clearing in the trees. The boat, a good eighty feet long, shifted slightly with the current, tugging against the mooring ropes tied to trees. The rigging hummed and creaked in the wind. The lantern doubled the moonlight on the deck, but no one was in sight.

"Now that," Thom said as he dismounted, "is better than an Aes Sedai's raft, isn't it?" He stood with his hands on his hips, and even in the dark his smugness was apparent. "It doesn't look as if this vessel is made to carry horses, but considering the danger he's in, which we are going to warn him of, the captain may be reasonable. Just let me do all the talking. And bring your blankets and saddlebags, just in case."

Rand climbed down and began untying the things behind his saddle. "You don't mean to leave without the others, do you?"

Thom had no chance to say what he meant to do. Into the clearing burst two Trollocs, howling and waving their catchpoles, with four more right behind. The horses reared and whinnied. Shouts in the distance said more Trollocs were on the way.

"Onto the boat!" Thom shouted. "Quick! Leave all that! Run!"
Suiting his own words, he ran for the boat, patches flapping and instrument cases on his back banging together. "You on the boat!" he shouted. "Wake up, you fools! Trollocs!"

Rand jerked his blanketroll and saddlebags free of the last thong and was right on the gleeman's heels. Tossing his burdens over the rail, he vaulted after them. He just had time to see a man curled up on the deck, beginning to sit up as if he had only that moment awakened, when his feet came down right on top of the fellow. The man grunted loudly, Rand stumbled, and a hooked catchpole slammed into the railing just where he had come over. Shouts rose all over the boat, and feet pounded along the deck.

Hairy hands caught the railing beside the catchpole, and a goat-horned head lifted above it. Off balance, stumbling, Rand still managed to draw his sword and swing. With a scream the Trolloc dropped away.

Men ran everywhere on the boat, shouting, hacking mooring lines with axes. The boat lurched and swung as if eager to be off. Up in the bow three men struggled with a Trolloc. Someone thrust over the side with a spear, though Rand could not see what he was stabbing at. A bowstring snapped, and snapped again. The man Rand had stepped on scrabbled away from him on hands and knees, then flung up his hands when he saw Rand looking at him.

"Spare me!" he cried. "Take whatever you want, take the boat, take everything, but spare me!"

Suddenly something slammed across Rand's back, smashing him to the deck. His sword skittered away from his outstretched hand. Open-mouthed, gasping for a breath that would not come, he tried to reach the sword. His muscles responded with agonized slowness; he writhed like a slug. The fellow who wanted to be spared gave one frightened, covetous look at the sword, then vanished into the shadows.

Painfully Rand managed to look over his shoulder, and knew his luck had run out. A wolf-muzzled Trolloc stood balanced on the railing, staring down at him and holding the splintered end of the catchpole that had knocked the wind out of him. Rand struggled to reach the sword, to move, to get away, but his arms and legs moved jerkily, and only half as he wanted. They wobbled and went in odd directions. His chest felt as if it were strapped with iron bands; silver spots swam in his eyes. Frantically he hunted for some way to escape. Time seemed to slow as the Trolloc raised the jagged pole as if to spear him with it. To Rand the creature appeared to be moving as if in a dream. He watched the thick arm go back; he could already feel the broken haft ripping through his spine, feel the pain of it tearing him open. He thought his lungs would burst. *I'm going to die! Light help me, I'm going to . . . !* The Trolloc's arm started forward, driving the splintered shaft, and Rand found the breath for one yell. "No!"

Suddenly the ship lurched, and a boom swung out of the shadows to catch the Trolloc across the chest with a crunch of breaking bones, sweeping it over the side.

For a moment Rand lay panting and staring up at the boom swinging back and forth above him. *That has to have used up my luck,* he thought. *There can't be any more after that.*

Shakily he got to his feet and picked up his sword, for once holding it in both hands the way Lan had taught him, but there was nothing left on which to use it. The gap of black water between the boat and the bank was widening quickly; the cries of the Trollocs were fading behind in the night.

As he sheathed his sword and slumped against the railing, a stocky man in a coat that hung to his knees strode up the deck to glare at him. Long hair that fell to his thick shoulders and a beard that left his upper lip bare framed a round face. Round but not soft. The boom swung out again, and the bearded man spared part of his glare for that as he caught it; it made a crisp *splat* against his broad palm.

"Gelb!" he bellowed. "Fortune! Where do you be, Gelb?" He spoke so fast, with all the words running together, that Rand could barely understand him. "You can no hide from me on my own ship! Get Floran Gelb out here!"

A crewman appeared with a bull's-eye lantern, and two more pushed a narrow-faced man into the circle of light it cast. Rand recognized the fellow who had offered him the boat. The man's eyes shifted from side to side, never meeting those of the stocky man. The captain, Rand thought. A bruise was coming up on Gelb's forehead where one of Rand's boots had caught him.

"Were you no supposed to secure this boom, Gelb?" the captain asked with surprising calm, though just as fast as before.

Gelb looked truly surprised. "But I did. Tied it down tight. I admit I'm a little slow about things now and then, Captain Domon, but I get them done."

"So you be slow, do you? No so slow at sleeping. Sleeping when you should be standing watch. We could be murdered to a man, for all of you."

"No, Captain, no. It was him." Gelb pointed straight at Rand. "I was on guard, just like I was supposed to be, when he sneaked up and hit me with a club." He touched the bruise on his head, winced, and glared at Rand. "I fought him, but then the Trollocs came. He's in league with them, Captain. A Darkfriend. In league with the Trollocs."

"In league with my aged grandmother!" Captain Domon roared. "Did I no warn you the last time, Gelb? At Whitebridge, off you do go! Get out of my sight before I put you off now." Gelb darted out of the lantern light, and Domon stood opening and closing his hands while he stared at nothing. "These Trollocs do be following me. Why will they no leave me be? Why?"

Rand looked over the rail and was shocked to find the riverbank no longer in sight. Two men manned the long steering oar that stuck out over the stern, and there were six sweeps working to a side now, pulling the ship like a waterbug further out into the river.

"Captain," Rand said, "we have friends back there. If you go back and pick them up, I am sure they'll reward you."

The captain's round face swung toward Rand, and when Thom and Mat appeared he included them in his expressionless stare as well.

"Captain," Thom began with a bow, "allow me to—"

"You come below," Captain Domon said, "where I can see what manner of thing be hauled up on my deck. Come. Fortune desert me, somebody secure this horn-cursed boom!" As crewmen rushed to take the boom, he stumped off toward the stern of the boat. Rand and his two companions followed.

Captain Domon had a tidy cabin in the stern, reached by climbing down a short ladder, where everything gave the impression of being in its proper place, right down to the coats and cloaks hanging from pegs on the back of the door. The cabin stretched the width of the ship, with a broad bed built against one side and a heavy table built out from the other. There was only one chair, with a high back and sturdy arms, and the captain took that himself, motioning the others to find places on various chests and benches that were the only other furnishings. A loud harrumph stopped Mat from sitting on the bed.

"Now," said the captain when they were all seated. "My name be Bayle Domon, captain and owner of the *Spray*, which be this ship. Now who be you, and where be you going out here in the middle of nowhere, and why should I no throw you over the side for the trouble you've brought me?"

Rand still had as much trouble as before in following Domon's rapid speech. When he worked out the last part of what the captain had said he blinked in surprise. *Throw us over the side?*

Mat hurriedly said, "We didn't mean to cause you any trouble. We're on our way to Caemlyn, and then to—"

"And then where the wind takes us," Thom interrupted smoothly. "That's how gleemen travel, like dust on the wind. I am a gleeman, you understand, Thom Merrilin by name." He shifted his cloak so the multihued patches stirred, as if the captain could have missed them. "These two country louts want to become my apprentices, though I am not yet sure I want them." Rand looked at Mat, who grinned.

"That be all very well, man," Captain Domon said placidly, "but it tells me nothing. Less. Fortune prick me, that place be on no road to Caemlyn from anywhere I ever heard tell of."

"Now that is a story," Thom said, and he straightaway began to unfold it.

According to Thom, he had been trapped by the winter snows in a mining town in the Mountains of Mist beyond Baerlon. While there he heard legends of a treasure dating from the Trolloc Wars, in the lost ruin of a city called Aridhol. Now it just so happened that he had earlier learned the location of Aridhol from a map given him many years ago by a dying friend in Illian whose life he had once saved, a man who expired breathing that the map would make Thom rich, which Thom never believed until he heard the legends. When the snows melted enough, he set out with a few companions, including his two would-be apprentices, and after a journey of many hardships they actually found the ruined city. But it turned out the treasure had belonged to one of the Dreadlords themselves, and Trollocs had been sent to fetch it back to Shayol Ghul. Almost every danger they really had faced—Trollocs, Myrddraal, Draghkar, Mordeth, Mashadar—assailed them at one point or another of the story, though the way Thom told it they all seemed to be aimed at him personally, and to have been handled by him with the greatest adroitness. With much derring-do, mostly by Thom, they escaped, pursued by Trollocs, though they became separated in the night, until finally Thom and his two companions sought refuge on the last place left to them, Captain Domon's most welcome ship.

As the gleeman finished up, Rand realized his mouth had been hanging open for some time and shut it with a click. When he looked at Mat, his friend was staring wide-eyed at the gleeman.

Captain Domon drummed his fingers on the arm of his chair. "That be a tale many folk would no believe. Of course, I did see the Trollocs, did I no."

"Every word true," Thom said blandly, "from one who lived it."

"Happen you have some of this treasure with you?"

Thom spread his hands regretfully. "Alas, what little we managed to carry away was with our horses, which bolted when those last Trollocs appeared. All I have left are my flute and my harp, a few coppers, and the clothes on my back. But believe me, you want no part of that treasure. It has the taint of the Dark One. Best to leave it to the ruins and the Trollocs."

"So you've no money to pay your passage. I'd no let my own brother sail with me if he could no pay his passage, especially if he brought Trollocs behind him to hack up my railings and cut up my rigging. Why should I no let you swim back where you came from, and be rid of you?"

"You wouldn't just put us ashore?" Mat said. "Not with Trollocs there?"

"Who said anything about shore?" Domon replied dryly. He studied them a moment, then spread his hands flat on the table. "Bayle Domon be a reasonable man. I'd no toss you over the side if there be a way out of it. Now, I see one of your apprentices has a sword. I need a good sword, and fine fellow that I be, I'll let you have passage far as Whitebridge for it."

Thom opened his mouth, and Rand spoke up quickly, "No!" Tam had not given it to him to trade away. He ran his hand down the hilt, feeling the bronze heron. As long as he had it, it was as if Tam were with him.

Domon shook his head. "Well, if it be no, it be no. But Bayle Domon no give free passage, not to his own mother."

Reluctantly Rand emptied his pocket. There was not much, a few coppers and the silver coin Moiraine had given him. He held it out to the captain. After a second, Mat sighed and did the same. Thom glared, but a smile replaced it so quickly that Rand was not sure it had been there at all.

Captain Domon deftly plucked the two fat silver coins out of the boys' hands and produced a small set of scales and a clinking bag from a brass-bound chest behind his chair. After careful weighing, he dropped the coins in the bag and returned them each some smaller silver and copper. Mostly copper. "As far as Whitebridge," he said, making a neat entry in a leather-bound ledger.

"That's a dear passage just to Whitebridge," Thom grumbled.

"Plus damages to my vessel," the captain answered placidly. He put the scales and the bag back in the chest and closed it in a satisfied way. "Plus a bit for bringing Trollocs down on me so I must run downriver in the night when there be shallows aplenty to pile me up."

"What about the others?" Rand asked. "Will you take them, too? They should have reached the river by now, or they soon will, and they'll see that lantern on your mast."

Captain Domon's eyebrows rose in surprise. "Happen you think we be standing still, man? Fortune prick me, we be three, four miles downriver from where you came aboard. Trollocs make those fellows put their backs into the oars—they know Trollocs better than they like—and the current helps, too. But it makes no nevermind. I'd no put in again tonight if my old grandmother was on the riverbank. I may no put in again at all until I reach Whitebridge. I've had my fill of Trollocs dogging my heels long before tonight, and I'll have no more can I help it."

Thom leaned forward interestedly. "You have had encounters with Trollocs before? Lately?"

Domon hesitated, eyeing Thom narrowly, but when he spoke he merely sounded disgusted. "I wintered in Saldaea, man. Not my choice, but the river froze early and the ice broke up late. They say you can see the Blight from the highest towers in Maradon, but I've no mind for that. I've been there before, and there always be talk of Trollocs attacking a farm or the like. This winter past, though, there be farms burning every night. Aye, and whole villages, too, betimes. They even came right up to the city walls. And if that no be bad enough, the people be all saying it meant the Dark One be stirring, that the Last Days be come." He gave a shiver, and scratched at his head as if the thought made his scalp itch. "I can no wait to get back where people think Trollocs be just tales, the stories I tell be traveler's lies."

Rand stopped listening. He stared at the opposite wall and thought about Egwene and the others. It hardly seemed right for him to be safe on the *Spray* while they were still back there in the night somewhere. The captain's cabin did not seem so comfortable as before.

He was surprised when Thom pulled him to his feet. The gleeman pushed Mat and him toward the ladder with apologies over his shoulder to Captain Domon for the country louts. Rand climbed up without a word.

Once they were on deck Thom looked around quickly to make sure he would not be overheard, then growled, "I could have gotten us passage for a few songs and stories if you two hadn't been so quick to show silver."

"I'm not so sure," Mat said. "He sounded serious about throwing us in the river to me."

Rand walked slowly to the rail and leaned against it, staring back up the night-shrouded river. He could not see anything but black, not even the riverbank. After a minute Thom put a hand on his shoulder, but he did not move.

"There isn't anything you can do, lad. Besides, they're likely safe with the . . . with Moiraine and Lan by this time. Can you think of any better than those two for getting the lot of them clear?"

"I tried to talk her out of coming," Rand said.

"You did what you could, lad. No one could ask more."

"I told her I'd take care of her. I should have tried harder." The creak of the sweeps and the hum of the rigging in the wind made a mournful tune. "I should have tried harder," he whispered.

CHAPTER
21

Listen to the Wind

S unrise creeping across the River Arinelle found its way into the hollow not far from the riverbank where Nynaeve sat with her back against the trunk of a young oak, breathing the deep breath of sleep. Her horse slept, too, head down and legs spraddled in the manner of horses. The reins were wrapped around her wrist. As sunlight fell on the horse's eyelids, the animal opened its eyes and raised its head, jerking the reins. Nynaeve came awake with a start.

For a moment she stared, wondering where she was, then stared around even more wildly when she remembered. But there were only the trees, and her horse, and a carpet of old, dry leaves across the bottom of the hollow. In the deepest dimness, some of last year's shadowshand mushrooms made rings on a fallen log.

"The Light preserve you, woman," she murmured, sagging back, "if you can't stay awake one night." She untied the reins and massaged her wrist as she stood. "You could have awakened in a Trolloc cookpot."

The dead leaves rustled as she climbed to the lip of the hollow and peeped over. No more than a handful of ash trees stood between her and the river. Their fissured bark and bare branches made them seem dead. Beyond, the wide blue-green water flowed by. Empty. Empty of anything. Scattered clumps of evergreens, willows and firs, dotted the far bank, and there seemed to be fewer trees altogether than on her side. If Moiraine or any of the younglings were over there, they were well hidden. Of course, there was no reason they had to have crossed, or tried to cross, in sight of where she was. They could be anywhere ten miles upriver or down. *If they're alive at all, after last night.*

Angry with herself for thinking of the possibility, she slid back down into the hollow. Not even Winternight, or the battle before Shadar Logoth, had prepared her for last night, for that thing, Mashadar. All that frantic galloping, wondering if anyone else was still alive, wondering when she was going to come face-to-face with a Fade, or Trollocs. She had heard Trollocs growling and shouting in the distance, and the quivering shrieks of Trolloc horns had chilled her deeper than the wind ever could, but aside from that first encounter in the ruins she saw Trollocs only once, and that once she was outside. Ten or so of them seemed to spring out of the ground not thirty spans in front of her, bounding toward her on the instant, howling and shouting, brandishing hooked catchpoles. Yet as she pulled her horse around, they fell silent, lifting muzzles to sniff at the air. She watched, too astonished to run, as they turned their backs and vanished into the night. And that had been the most frightening of all.

"They know the smell of who they want," she told her horse, standing in the hollow, "and it is not me. The Aes Sedai is right, it seems, the Shepherd of the Night swallow her up."

Reaching a decision, she set out downriver, leading her horse. She moved slowly, keeping a wary watch on the forest around her; just because the Trollocs had not wanted her last night did not mean they would let her go if she stumbled on them again. As much attention as she gave the woods, she gave even more to the ground in front of her. If the others had crossed below her during the night, she should see some signs of them, signs she might miss from horseback. She might even come on them all still on this side. If she found neither, the river would take her to Whitebridge eventually, and there was a road from Whitebridge to Caemlyn, and all the way to Tar Valon if need be.

The prospect was almost enough to daunt her. Before this she had been no further from Emond's Field than had the boys. Taren Ferry had seemed strange to her; Baerlon would have had her staring in wonder if she had not been so set on finding Egwene and the others. But she allowed none of that to weaken her resolve. Sooner or later she would find Egwene and the boys. Or find a way to make the Aes Sedai answer for whatever had happened to them. One or the other, she vowed.

At intervals she found tracks, plenty of them, but usually her best efforts could not say whether those who made them had been searching or chasing or pursued. Some had been made by boots that could have belonged to humans or Trollocs either one. Others were hoofprints, like goats or oxen; those were Trollocs for sure. But never a clear sign that she could definitely say came from any of those she sought.

She had covered perhaps four miles when the wind brought her a whiff of woodsmoke. It came from further downriver, and not too far, she thought. She hesitated only a moment before tying her horse to a fir tree, well back from the river in a small, thick stand of evergreens that should keep the animal hidden. The smoke could mean Trollocs, but the only way to find out was to look. She tried not to think about the use Trollocs might be making of a fire.

Crouching, she slipped from tree to tree, mentally cursing the skirts she had to hold up out of the way. Dresses were not made for stalking. The sound of a horse slowed her, and when she finally peered cautiously around the trunk of an ash, the Warder was dismounting from his black warhorse in a small clearing on the bank. The Aes Sedai sat on a log beside a small fire where a kettle of water was just coming to a boil. Her white mare browsed behind her among sparse weeds. Nynaeve remained where she was.

"They are all gone," Lan announced grimly. "Four Halfmen started south about two hours before dawn, as near as I can tell—they don't leave much trace behind—but the Trollocs have vanished. Even the corpses, and Trollocs are not known for carrying off their dead. Unless they're hungry."

Moiraine tossed a handful of something into the boiling water and moved the kettle from the fire. "One could always hope they had gone back into Shadar Logoth and been consumed by it, but that would be too much to wish for."

The delicious odor of tea drifted to Nynaeve. *Light, don't let my stomach grumble.*

"There was no clear sign of the boys, or any of the others. The tracks are too muddled to tell anything." In her concealment, Nynaeve smiled; the Warder's failure was a slight vindication of her own. "But this other is important, Moiraine," Lan went on, frowning. He waved away the Aes Sedai's offer of tea and began marching up and down in front of the fire, one hand on his sword hilt and his cloak changing colors as he turned. "I could accept Trollocs in the Two Rivers, even a hundred Trollocs. But this? There must have been almost a thousand in the hunt for us yesterday."

"We were very lucky that not all stayed to search Shadar Logoth. The Myrddraal must have doubted we would hide there, but they also feared to return to Shayol Ghul leaving even the slightest chance uncovered. The Dark One was never a lenient master."

"Don't try to evade it. You know what I am saying. If those thousand were here to be sent into the Two Rivers, why were they not? There is only one answer. They were sent only after we crossed the Taren, when it was known that one Myrddraal and a hundred Trollocs were no longer enough. How? How were they sent? If a thousand Trollocs can be brought so far south from the Blight, so quickly, unseen—not to mention being taken off the same way—can ten thousand be sent into the heart of Saldaea, or Arafel, or Shienar? The Borderlands could be overrun in a year."

"The whole world will be overrun in five if we do not find those boys," Moiraine said simply. "The question worries me, also, but I have no answers. The Ways are closed, and there has not been an Aes Sedai powerful enough to Travel since the Time of Madness. Unless one of the Forsaken is loose—the Light send it is not so, yet or ever—there is still no one who can. In any case, I do not think all the Forsaken together could move a thousand Trollocs. Let us deal with the problems that face us here and now; everything else must wait."

"The boys." It was not a question.

"I have not been idle while you were away. One is across the river, and alive. As for the others, there was a faint trace downriver, but it faded away as I found it. The bond had been broken for hours before I began my search."

Crouched behind her tree, Nynaeve frowned in puzzlement.

Lan stopped his pacing. "You think the Halfmen heading south have them?"

"Perhaps." Moiraine poured herself a cup of tea before going on. "But I will not admit the possibility of them being dead. I cannot. I dare not. You know how much is at stake. I must have those young men. That Shayol Ghul will hunt them, I expect. Opposition from within the White Tower, even from the Amyrlin Seat, I accept. There are always Aes Sedai who will accept only one solution. But. . . ."

Suddenly she put her cup down and sat up straight, grimacing. "If you watch the wolf too hard," she muttered, "a mouse will bite you on the ankle." And she looked right at the tree behind which Nynaeve was hiding. "Mistress al'Meara, you may come out now, if you wish."

Nynaeve scrambled to her feet, hastily dusting dead leaves from her dress. Lan had spun to face the tree as soon as Moiraine's eyes moved; his sword was in his hand before she finished speaking Nynaeve's name. Now he sheathed it again with more force than was strictly necessary. His face was almost as expressionless as ever, but Nynaeve thought there was a touch of chagrin about the set of his mouth. She felt a stab of satisfaction; the Warder had not known she was there, at least.

Satisfaction lasted only a moment, though. She fastened her eyes on Moiraine and walked toward her purposefully. She wanted to remain cold and calm, but her voice quivered with anger. "What have you meshed Egwene and the boys in? What filthy Aes Sedai plots are you planning to use them in?"

The Aes Sedai picked up her cup and calmly sipped her tea. When Nynaeve was close, though, Lan put out an arm to bar her way. She tried to brush the obstruction aside, and was surprised when the Warder's arm moved no more than an oak branch would have. She was not frail, but his muscles were like iron.

"Tea?" Moiraine offered.

"No, I don't want any tea. I would not drink your tea if I was dying of thirst. You won't use any Emond's Field folk in your dirty Aes Sedai schemes."

"You have very little room to talk, Wisdom." Moiraine showed more interest in her hot tea than in anything she was saying. "You can wield the One Power yourself, after a fashion."

Nynaeve pushed at Lan's arm again; it still did not move, and she decided to ignore it. "Why don't you try claiming I am a Trolloc?"

Moiraine's smile was so knowing that Nynaeve wanted to hit her. "Do you think I can stand face-to-face with a woman who can touch the True Source and channel the One Power, even if only now and then, without knowing what she is? Just as you sensed the potential in Egwene. How do you think I knew you were behind that tree? If I had not been distracted, I would have known the moment you came close. You certainly are not a Trolloc, for me to feel the evil of the Dark One. So what did I sense, Nynaeve al'Maera, Wisdom of Emond's Field and unknowing wielder of the One Power?"

Lan was looking down at Nynaeve in a way she did not like; surprised and speculative, it seemed to her, though nothing had changed about his face but his eyes. Egwene *was* special; she had always known that. Egwene would make a fine Wisdom. *They're working together,* she thought, *trying to put me off balance.* "I won't listen to any more of this. You—"

"You must listen," Moiraine said firmly. "I had my suspicions in Emond's Field even before I met you. People told me how upset the Wisdom was that she had not predicted the hard winter and the lateness of spring. They told me how good she was at foretelling weather, at telling the crops. They told me how wonderful her cures were, how she sometimes healed injuries, that should have been crippling, so well there was barely a scar, and not a limp or a twinge. The only ill word I heard about you was from a few who thought you too young for the responsibility, and that only strengthened my suspicions. So much skill so young."

"Mistress Barran taught me well." She tried looking at Lan, but his eyes still made her uncomfortable, so she settled for staring over the Aes Sedai's head at the river. *How dare the village gossip in front of an outlander!* "Who said I was too young?" she demanded.

Moiraine smiled, refusing to be diverted. "Unlike most women who claim to listen to the wind, you actually can, sometimes. Oh, it has nothing to do with the wind, of course. It is of Air and Water. It is not something you needed to be taught; it was born into you, just as it was born into Egwene. But you have learned to handle it, which she still has to learn. Two minutes after I came face-to-face with you, I knew. Do you remember how I suddenly asked you if you were the Wisdom? Why, do you think? There was nothing to distinguish you from any other pretty young woman getting ready for Festival. Even looking for a young Wisdom I expected someone half again your age."

Nynaeve remembered that meeting all too well; this woman, more self-possessed than anyone in the Women's Circle, in a dress more beautiful than any she had ever seen, addressing her as a child. Then Moiraine had suddenly blinked as if surprised and out of a clear sky asked. . . .

She licked lips gone abruptly dry. They were both looking at her, the Warder's face as unreadable as a stone, the Aes Sedai's sympathetic yet intent. Nynaeve shook her head. "No! No, it's impossible. I would know. You are just trying to trick me, and it will not work."

"Of course you do not know," Moiraine said soothingly. "Why should you even suspect? All of your life you have heard about listening to the wind. In any case, you would as soon announce to all of

Emond's Field that you were a Darkfriend as admit to yourself, even in the deepest recesses of your mind, that you have anything to do with the One Power, or the dreaded Aes Sedai." Amusement flitted across Moiraine's face. "But I can tell you how it began."

"I don't want to hear any more of your lies," she said, but the Aes Sedai went right on.

"Perhaps as much as eight or ten years ago—the age varies, but always comes young—there was something you wanted more than anything else in the world, something you needed. And you got it. A branch suddenly falling where you could pull yourself out of a pond instead of drowning. A friend, or a pet, getting well when everyone thought they would die.

"You felt nothing special at the time, but a week or ten days later you had your first reaction to touching the True Source. Perhaps fever and chills that came on suddenly and put you to bed, then disappeared after only a few hours. None of the reactions, and they vary, lasts more than a few hours. Headaches and numbness and exhilaration all mixed together, and you taking foolish chances or acting giddy. A spell of dizziness, when you tripped and stumbled whenever you tried to move, when you could not say a sentence without your tongue mangling half the words. There are others. Do you remember?"

Nynaeve sat down hard on the ground; her legs would not hold her up. She remembered, but she shook her head anyway. It had to be coincidence. Or else Moiraine had asked more questions in Emond's Field than she had thought. The Aes Sedai had asked a great many questions. It had to be that. Lan offered a hand, but she did not even see it.

"I will go further," Moiraine said when Nynaeve kept silent. "You used the Power to Heal either Perrin or Egwene at some time. An affinity develops. You can sense the presence of someone you have Healed. In Baerlon you came straight to the Stag and Lion, though it was not the nearest inn to any gate by which you could have entered. Of the people from Emond's Field, only Perrin and Egwene were at the inn when you arrived. Was it Perrin, or Egwene? Or both?"

"Egwene," Nynaeve mumbled. She had always taken it for granted that she could sometimes tell who was approaching her even when she could not see them; not until now had she realized that it was always someone on whom her cures had worked almost miraculously well. And she had always known when the medicine would work beyond expectations, always felt the certainty when she said the crops would be especially good, or that the rains would come early or late. That was the way she thought it was supposed to be. Not all Wisdoms could listen to the wind, but the best could. That was what Mistress Barran always said, just as she said Nynaeve would be one of the best.

"She had breakbone fever." She kept her head down and spoke to the ground. "I was still apprentice to Mistress Barran, and she set me to watch Egwene. I was young, and I didn't know the Wisdom had everything well in hand. It's terrible to watch, breakbone fever. The child was soaked with sweat, groaning and twisting until I could not understand why I didn't hear her bones snapping. Mistress Barran had told me the fever would break in another day, two at the most, but I thought she was doing me a kindness. I thought Egwene was dying. I used to look after her sometimes when she was a toddler—when her mother was busy—and I started crying because I was going to have to watch her die. When Mistress Barran came back an hour later, the fever had broken. She was surprised, but she made over me more than Egwene. I always thought she believed I had given the child something and was too frightened to admit it. I always thought she was trying to comfort me, to make sure I knew I hadn't hurt Egwene. A week later I fell on the floor in her sitting room, shaking and burning up by turns. She bundled me into bed, but by suppertime it was gone."

She dropped her head in her hands as she finished speaking. *The Aes Sedai chose a good example,* she thought, *Light burn her! Using the Power like an Aes Sedai. A filthy, Darkfriend Aes Sedai!*

"You were very lucky," Moiraine said, and Nynaeve sat erect. Lan stepped back as if what they talked about was none of his business, and busied himself with Mandarb's saddle, not even glancing at them.

"Lucky!"

"You have managed a crude control over the Power, even if touching the True Source still comes at random. If you had not, it would have killed you eventually. As it will, in all probability, kill Egwene if you manage to stop her from going to Tar Valon."

"If I learned to control it. . . ." Nynaeve swallowed hard. It was like admitting all over again that she could do what the Aes Sedai said. "If I learned to control it, so can she. There is no need for her to go to Tar Valon, and get mixed up in your intrigues."

Moiraine shook her head slowly. "Aes Sedai search for girls who can touch the True Source unguided just as assiduously as we search for men who can do so. It is not a desire to increase our numbers—or at least, not only that—nor is it a fear that those women will misuse the Power. The rough control of the Power they may gain, if the Light shines on them, is rarely enough to do any great damage, especially since the actual touching of the Source is beyond their control without a teacher, and comes only randomly. And, of course, they do not suffer the madness that drives men to evil or twisted things. We want to save their lives. The lives of those who never do manage any control at all."

"The fever and chills I had couldn't kill anyone," Nynaeve insisted. "Not in three or four hours. I had the other things, too, and they couldn't kill anybody, either. And they stopped after a few months. What about that?"

"Those were only reactions," Moiraine said patiently. "Each time, the reaction comes closer to the actual touching of the Source, until the two happen almost together. After that there are no more reactions that can be seen, but it is as if a clock has begun ticking. A year. Two years. I know one woman who lasted five years. Of four who have the inborn ability that you and Egwene have, three die if we do not find them and train them. It is not as horrible a death as the men die, but neither is it pretty, if any death can be called so. Convulsions. Screaming. It takes days, and once it begins there is nothing that can be done to stop it, not by all the Aes Sedai in Tar Valon together."

"You're lying. All those questions you asked in Emond's Field. You found out about Egwene's fever breaking, about my fever and chills, all of it. You made all of this up."

"You know I did not," Moiraine said gently.

Reluctantly, more reluctantly than she had ever done anything in her life, Nynaeve nodded. It had been a last stubborn effort to deny what was plain, and there was never any good in that, however unpleasant it might be. Mistress Barran's first apprentice had died the way the Aes Sedai said when Nynaeve was still playing with dolls, and there had been a young woman in Deven Ride only a few years ago. She had been a Wisdom's apprentice, too, one who could listen to the wind.

"You have great potential, I think," Moiraine continued. "With training you might become even more powerful than Egwene, and I believe she can become one of the most powerful Aes Sedai we have seen in centuries."

Nynaeve pushed herself back from the Aes Sedai as she would have from a viper. "No! I'll have nothing to do with—" *With what? Myself?* She slumped, and her voice became hesitant. "I would ask you not to tell anyone about this. Please?" The word nearly stuck in her throat. She would rather Trollocs had appeared than she had been forced to say please to this woman. But Moiraine only nodded assent, and some of her spirit returned. "None of this explains what you want with Rand, and Mat, and Perrin."

"The Dark One wants them," Moiraine replied. "If the Dark One wants a thing, I oppose it. Can there be a simpler reason, or a better?" She finished her tea, watching Nynaeve over the rim of her cup. "Lan, we must be going. South, I think. I fear the Wisdom will not be accompanying us."

Nynaeve's mouth tightened at the way the Aes Sedai said "Wisdom"; it seemed to suggest she was turning her back on great things in favor of something petty. *She doesn't want me along. She's trying to put my back up so I'll go back home and leave them alone with her.* "Oh, yes, I will be going with you. You cannot keep me from it."

"No one will try to keep you from it," Lan said as he rejoined them. He emptied the tea kettle over the fire and stirred the ashes with a stick. "A part of the Pattern?" he said to Moiraine.

"Perhaps so," she replied thoughtfully. "I should have spoken to Min again."

"You see, Nynaeve, you are welcome to come." There was a hesitation in the way Lan said her name, a hint of an unspoken "Sedai" after it.

Nynaeve bristled, taking it for mockery, and bristled, too, at the way they spoke of things in front of her—things she knew nothing about—without the courtesy of an explanation, but she would not give them the satisfaction of asking.

The Warder went on preparing for departure, his economical motions so sure and swift that he was quickly done, saddlebags, blankets, and all fastened behind the saddles of Mandarb and Aldieb.

"I will fetch your horse," he told Nynaeve as he finished with the last saddle tie.

He started up the riverbank, and she allowed herself a small smile. After the way she had watched him undiscovered, he was going to try to find her horse unaided. He would learn that she left little in the way of tracks when she was stalking. It would be a pleasure when he came back empty-handed.

"Why south?" she asked Moiraine. "I heard you say one of the boys is across the river. And how do you know?"

"I gave each of the boys a token. It created a bond of sorts between them and me. So long as they are alive and have those coins in their possession, I will be able to find them." Nynaeve's eyes turned in the direction the Warder had gone, and Moiraine shook her head. "Not like that. It only allows me to discover if they still live, and find them should we become separated. Prudent, do you not think, under the circumstances?"

"I don't like anything that connects you with anyone from Emond's Field," Nynaeve said stubbornly. "But if it will help us find them. . . ."

"It will. I would gather the young man across the river first, if I could." For a moment frustration tinged the Aes Sedai's voice. "He is only a few miles from us. But I cannot afford to take the time. He should make his way down to Whitebridge safely now that the Trollocs have gone. The two who went downriver may need me more. They have lost their coins, and Myrddraal are either pursuing them or else trying to intercept us all at Whitebridge." She sighed. "I must take care of the greatest need first."

"The Myrddraal could have . . . could have killed them," Nynaeve said.

Moiraine shook her head slightly, denying the suggestion as if it were too trivial to be considered. Nynaeve's mouth tightened. "Where is Egwene, then? You haven't even mentioned her."

"I do not know," Moiraine admitted, "but I hope that she is safe."

"You don't know? You hope? All that talk about saving her life by taking her to Tar Valon, and she could be dead for all you know!"

"I could look for her and allow the Myrddraal more time before I arrive to help the two young men who went south. It is them the Dark One wants, not her. They would not bother with Egwene, so long as their true quarry remains uncaught."

Nynaeve remembered her own encounter, but she refused to admit the sense of what Moiraine said. "So the best you have to offer is that she may be alive, if she was lucky. Alive, maybe alone, frightened, even hurt, days from the nearest village or help except for us. And you intend to leave her."

"She may just as easily be safe with the boy across the river. Or on her way to Whitebridge with the other two. In any case, there are no longer Trollocs here to threaten her, and she is strong, intelligent, and quite capable of finding her way to Whitebridge alone, if need be. Would you rather stay on the chance that she may need help, or do you want to try to help those we know are in need? Would you have me search for her and let the boys—and the Myrddraal who are surely pursuing them—go? As much as I hope for Egwene's safety, Nynaeve, I fight against the Dark One, and for now that sets my path."

Moiraine's calm never slipped while she laid out the horrible alternatives; Nynaeve wanted to scream at her. Blinking back tears, she turned her face so the Aes Sedai could not see. *Light, a Wisdom is supposed to look after* all *of her people. Why do I have to choose like this?*

"Here is Lan," Moiraine said, rising and settling her cloak about her shoulders.

To Nynaeve it was only a tiny blow as the Warder led her horse out of the trees. Still, her lips thinned when he handed her the reins. It would have been a small boost to her spirits if there had been even a trace of gloating on his face instead of that insufferable stony calm. His eyes widened when he saw her face, and she turned her back on him to wipe tears from her cheeks. *How dare he mock my crying!*

"Are you coming, Wisdom?" Moiraine asked coolly.

She took one last, slow look at the forest, wondering if Egwene was out there, before sadly mounting her horse. Lan and Moiraine were already in their saddles, turning their horses south. She followed, stiff-backed, refusing to let herself look back; instead she kept her eyes on Moiraine. The Aes Sedai was so confident in her power and her plans, she thought, but if they did not find Egwene and the boys, all of them, alive and unharmed, not all of her power would protect her. Not all her Power. *I can use it, woman! You told me so yourself. I can use it against you!*

CHAPTER
22

A Path Chosen

In a small copse of trees, beneath a pile of cedar branches roughly cut in the dark, Perrin slept long after sunrise. It was the cedar needles, pricking him through his still-damp clothes, that finally pricked through his exhaustion as well. Deep in a dream of Emond's Field, of working at Master Luhhan's forge, he opened his eyes and stared, uncomprehending, at the sweet-smelling branches interwoven over his face, sunlight trickling through.

Most of the branches fell away as he sat up in surprise, but some hung haphazardly from his shoulders, and even his head, making him appear something like a tree himself. Emond's Field faded as memory rushed back, so vivid that for a moment the night before seemed more real than anything around him now.

Panting, frantic, he scrabbled his axe out of the pile. He clutched it in both hands and peered around cautiously, holding his breath. Nothing moved. The morning was cold and still. If there were Trollocs on the east bank of the Arinelle, they were not moving, at least not close to him. Taking a deep, calming breath, he lowered the axe to his knees, and waited a moment for his heart to stop pounding.

The small stand of evergreens surrounding him was the first shelter he had found last night. It was sparse enough to give little protection against watching eyes if he stood up. Plucking branches from his head and shoulders, he pushed aside the rest of his prickly blanket, then crawled on hands and knees to the edge of the copse. There he lay studying the riverbank and scratching where the needles had stabbed him.

The cutting wind of the night before had faded to a silent breeze that barely rippled the surface of the water. The river ran by, calm and empty. And wide. Surely too wide and too deep for Fades to cross. The far bank appeared a solid mass of trees as far as he could see upriver and down. Certainly nothing moved in his view over there.

He was not sure how he felt about that. Fades and Trollocs he could do without quite easily, even on the other side of the river, but a whole list of worries would have vanished with the appearance of the Aes Sedai, or the Warder, or, even better, any of his friends. *If wishes were wings, sheep would fly.* That was what Mistress Luhhan always said.

He had not seen a sign of his horse since riding over the bluff—he hoped it had swum out of the river safely—but he was more used to walking than riding anyway, and his boots were stout and well soled. He had nothing to eat, but his sling was still wrapped around his waist, and that or the snarelines in his pocket ought to yield a rabbit in a little time. Everything for making a fire was gone with his saddlebags, but the cedar trees would yield tinder and a firebow with a bit of work.

He shivered as the breeze gusted into his hiding place. His cloak was somewhere in the river, and his coat and everything else he wore were still clammy cold from the soaking in the river. He had been too tired for the cold and damp to bother him last night, but now he was wide awake to every chill. Just the same, he decided against hanging his clothes on the branches to dry. If the day was not precisely cold, it was not even close to warm.

Time was the problem, he thought with a sigh. Dry clothes, with a little time. A rabbit to roast and a fire to roast it over, with a little time. His stomach rumbled, and he tried to forget about eating alto-Gether. There were more important uses for that time. One thing at a time, and the most important first. That was his way.

His eyes followed the strong flow of the Arinelle downriver. He was a stronger swimmer than Egwene. If she had made it across. . . . No, not *if.* The place where she *had* made it across would be downriver.

He drummed on the ground with his fingers, weighing, considering.

His decision made, he wasted no time in picking up his axe and setting off down the river.

This side of the Arinelle lacked the thick forest of the west bank. Clumps of trees spotted across what would be grassland if spring ever came. Some were big enough to be called thickets, with swathes of evergreens among the barren ash and alder and hardgum. Down by the river the stands were smaller and not so tight. They gave poor cover, but they were all the cover there was.

He dashed from growth to growth in a crouch, throwing himself down when he was among the trees to study the riverbanks, the far side as well as his. The Warder said the river would be a barrier to Fades and Trollocs, but would it? Seeing him might be enough to overcome their reluctance to cross deep water. So he watched carefully from behind the trees and ran from one hiding place to the next, fast and low.

He covered several miles that way, in spurts, until suddenly, halfway to the beckoning shelter of a growth of willows, he grunted and stopped dead, staring at the ground. Patches of bare earth spotted the matted brown of last year's grass, and in the middle of one of those patches, right under his nose, was a clear hoofprint. A slow smile spread across his face. Some Trollocs had hooves, but he doubted if any wore horseshoes, especially horseshoes with the double crossbar Master Luhhan added for strength.

Forgetting possible eyes on the other side of the river, he cast about for more tracks. The plaited carpet of dead grass did not take impressions well, but his sharp eyes found them anyway. The scanty trail led him straight away from the river to a dense stand of trees, thick with leatherleaf and cedar that made a wall against wind or prying eyes. The spreading branches of a lone hemlock towered in the middle of it all.

Still grinning, he pushed his way through the interwoven branches, not caring how much noise he made. Abruptly he stepped into a little clearing under the hemlock—and stopped. Behind a small fire, Egwene crouched, her face grim, with a thick branch held like a club and her back against Bela's flank.

"I guess I should have called out," he said with an abashed shrug.

Tossing her club down, she ran to throw her arms around him. "I thought you had drowned. You're still wet. Here, sit by the fire and warm yourself. You lost your horse, didn't you?"

He let her push him to a place by the fire and rubbed his hands over the flames, grateful for the warmth. She produced an oiled paper packet from her saddlebags and gave him some bread and cheese. The package had been so tightly wrapped that even after its dunking the food was dry. *Here you were worrying about her, and she's done better than you did.*

"Bela got me across," Egwene said, patting the shaggy mare. "She headed away from the Trollocs and just towed me along." She paused. "I haven't seen anybody else, Perrin."

He heard the unspoken question. Regretfully eyeing the packet that she was rewrapping, he licked the last crumbs from his fingers before speaking. "I've seen no one but you since last night. No Fades or Trollocs, either; there's that."

"Rand has to be all right," Egwene said, quickly adding, "they all do. They have to. They're probably looking for us right now. They might find us anytime now. Moiraine is an Aes Sedai, after all."

"I keep being reminded of that," he said. "Burn me, I wish I could forget."

"I did not hear you complaining when she stopped the Trollocs from catching us," Egwene said tartly.

"I just wish we could do without her." He shrugged uncomfortably under her steady gaze. "I suppose we can't, though. I've been thinking." Her eyebrows rose, but he was used to surprise whenever he claimed an idea. Even when his ideas were as good as theirs, they always remembered how deliberate he was in thinking of them. "We can wait for Lan and Moiraine to find us."

"Of course," she cut in. "Moiraine Sedai said she would find us if we were separated."

He let her finish, then went on. "Or the Trollocs could find us, first. Moiraine could be dead, too. All of them could be. No, Egwene. I'm sorry, but they could be. I hope they are all safe. I hope they'll walk up to this fire any minute. But hope is like a piece of string when you're drowning; it just isn't enough to get you out by itself."

Egwene closed her mouth and stared at him with her jaw set. Finally, she said, "You want to go downriver to Whitebridge? If Moiraine Sedai doesn't find us here, that's where she will look next."

"I suppose," he said slowly, "that Whitebridge is where we *should* go. But the Fades probably know that, too. That's where they'll be looking, and this time we don't have an Aes Sedai or a Warder to protect us."

"I suppose you're going to suggest running off somewhere, the way Mat wanted to? Hiding somewhere the Fades and Trollocs won't find us? Or Moiraine Sedai, either?"

"Don't think I haven't considered it," he said quietly. "But every time we think we are free, Fades and Trollocs find us again. I don't know if there *is* anyplace we could hide from them. I don't like it much, but we need Moiraine."

"I don't understand then, Perrin. Where do we go?"

He blinked in surprise. She was waiting for his answer. Waiting for *him* to tell her what to do. It had never occurred to him that she would look to him to take the lead. Egwene never liked doing what someone else had planned out, and she never let anybody tell her what to do. Except maybe the Wisdom, and he thought sometimes she balked at that. He smoothed the dirt in front of him with his hand and cleared his throat roughly.

"If this is where we are now, and that is Whitebridge," he stabbed the ground twice with his finger, "then Caemlyn should be somewhere around here." He made a third mark, off to the side.

He paused, looking at the three dots in the dirt. His entire plan was based on what he remembered of her father's old map. Master al'Vere said it was not too accurate, and, anyway, he had never mooned over it as much as Rand and Mat. But Egwene said nothing. When he looked up, she was still watching him with her hands in her lap.

"Caemlyn?" She sounded stunned.

"Caemlyn." He drew a line in the dirt between two of the dots. "Away from the river, and straight across. Nobody would expect that. We'll wait for them in Caemlyn." He dusted his hands and waited. He thought it was a good plan, but surely she would have objections now. He expected she would take charge—she was always bullying him into something—and that was all right with him.

To his surprise, she nodded. "There must be villages. We can ask directions."

"What worries me," Perrin said, "is what we do if the Aes Sedai *doesn't* find us there. Light, who'd ever have thought I'd worry about something like that? What if she doesn't come to Caemlyn? Maybe she thinks we're dead. Maybe she'll take Rand and Mat straight to Tar Valon."

"Moiraine Sedai said she could find us," Egwene said firmly. "If she can find us here, she can find us in Caemlyn, and she will."

Perrin nodded slowly. "If you say so, but if she doesn't appear in Caemlyn in a few days, we go on to Tar Valon and put our case before the Amyrlin Seat." He took a deep breath. *Two weeks ago you'd never even seen an Aes Sedai, and now you're talking about the Amyrlin Seat. Light!* "According to Lan, there's a good road from Caemlyn." He looked at the oiled paper packet beside Egwene and cleared his throat. "What chance of a little more bread and cheese?"

"This might have to last a long time," she said, "unless you have better luck with snares than I did last night. At least the fire was easy." She laughed softly as if she had made a joke, tucking the packet back into her saddlebags.

Apparently there were limits to how much leadership she was willing to accept. His stomach rumbled. "In that case," he said, standing, "we might as well start now."

"But you're still wet," she protested.

"I'll walk myself dry," he said firmly, and began kicking dirt over the fire. If he was the leader, it was time to start leading. The wind from the river was picking up.

CHAPTER
23

Wolfbrother

From the start Perrin knew the journey to Caemlyn was going to be far from comfortable, beginning with Egwene's insistence that they take turns riding Bela. They did not know how far it was, she said, but it was too far for her to be the only one who rode. Her jaw firmed, and her eyes stared at him unblinking.

"I'm too big to ride Bela," he said. "I'm used to walking, and I'd rather."

"And I am not used to walking?" Egwene said sharply.

"That isn't what I—"

"I'm the only one who's supposed to get saddlesore, is that it? And when you walk till your feet are ready to fall off, you'll expect me to look after you."

"Let it be," he breathed when she looked like going on. "Anyway, you'll take the first turn." Her face turned even more stubborn, but he refused to let her get a word in edgewise. "If you won't get in the saddle by yourself, I'll put you there."

She gave him a startled look, and a small smile curved her lips. "In that case. . . ." She sounded as if she were about to laugh, but she climbed up.

He grumbled to himself as he turned away from the river. Leaders in stories never had to put up with this sort of thing.

Egwene did insist on him taking his turns, and whenever he tried to avoid it, she bullied him into the saddle. Blacksmithing did not lend itself to a slender build, and Bela was not very large as horses went. Every time he put his foot in the stirrup the shaggy mare looked at him with what he was sure was reproach. Small things, perhaps, but they irritated. Soon he flinched whenever Egwene announced, "It's your turn, Perrin."

In stories leaders seldom flinched, and they were never bullied. But, he reflected, they never had to deal with Egwene, either.

There were only short rations of bread and cheese to begin with, and what there was gave out by the end of the first day. Perrin set snares along likely rabbit runs—they looked old, but it was worth a chance—while Egwene began laying a fire. When he was done, he decided to try his hand with his sling before the light failed altogether. They had not seen a sign of anything at all alive, but. . . . To his surprise, he jumped a scrawny rabbit almost at once. He was so surprised when it burst from under a bush right beneath his feet that it almost got away, but he fetched it at forty paces, just as it was darting around a tree.

When he came back to the camp with the rabbit, Egwene had broken limbs all laid for the fire, but she was kneeling beside the pile with her eyes closed. "What are you doing? You can't wish a fire."

Egwene gave a jump at his first words, and twisted around to stare at him with a hand to her throat. "You . . . you startled me."

"I was lucky," he said, holding up the rabbit. "Get your flint and steel. We eat well tonight, at least."

"I don't have a flint," she said slowly. "It was in my pocket, and I lost it in the river."

"Then how . . . ?"

"It was so easy back there on the riverbank, Perrin. Just the way Moiraine Sedai showed me. I just reached out, and. . . ." She gestured as if grasping for something, then let her hand fall with a sigh. "I can't find it, now."

Perrin licked his lips uneasily. "The . . . the Power?" She nodded, and he stared at her. "Are you crazy? I mean . . . the One Power! You can't just play around with something like that."

"It was so easy, Perrin. I can do it. I can channel the Power."

He took a deep breath. "I'll make a firebow, Egwene. Promise you won't try this . . . this . . . *thing* again."

"I will not." Her jaw firmed in a way that made him sigh. "Would you give up that axe of yours, Perrin Aybara? Would you walk around with one hand tied behind your back? I won't do it!"

"I'll make the firebow," he said wearily. "At least, don't try it again tonight? Please?"

She acquiesced grudgingly, and even after the rabbit was roasting on a spit over the flames, he had the feeling she felt she could have done it better. She would not give up trying, either, every night, though the best she ever did was a trickle of smoke that vanished almost immediately. Her eyes dared him to say a word, and he wisely kept his mouth shut.

After that one hot meal, they subsisted on coarse wild tubers and a few young shoots. With still no sign of spring, none of it was plentiful, and none of it tasty, either. Neither complained, but not a meal passed without one or the other sighing regretfully, and they both knew it was for the tang of a bit of cheese, or even the smell of bread. A find of mushrooms—Queen's Crowns, the best—one afternoon in a shady part of the forest was enough to seem a great treat. They gobbled them down, laughing and telling stories from back in Emond's Field, stories that began, "Do you remember when—" but the mushrooms did not last long, and neither did the laughter. There was little mirth in hunger.

Whichever was walking carried a sling, ready to let fly at the sight of a rabbit or squirrel, but the only time either hurled a stone was in frustration. The snares they set so carefully each evening yielded nothing at dawn, and they did not dare stay a day in one place to leave the snares out. Neither of them knew how far it was to Caemlyn, and neither would feel safe until they got there, if then. Perrin began to wonder if his stomach could shrink enough to make a hole all the way through his middle.

They made good time, as he saw it, but as they got farther and farther from the Arinelle without seeing a village, or even a farmhouse where they could ask directions, his doubts about his own plan grew. Egwene continued to appear outwardly as confident as when they set out, but he was sure that sooner or later she would say it would have been better to risk the Trollocs than to wander around lost for the rest of their lives. She never did, but he kept expecting it.

Two days from the river the land changed to thickly forested hills, as gripped by the tail end of winter as everywhere else, and a day after that the hills flattened out again, the dense forest broken by glades, often a mile or more across. Snow still lay in hidden hollows, and the air was brisk of a morning, and the wind cold always. Nowhere did they see a road, or a plowed field, or chimney smoke in the distance, or any other sign of human habitation—at least, none where men still dwelt.

Once the remains of tall stone ramparts encircled a hilltop. Parts of roofless stone houses stood inside the fallen circle. The forest had long swallowed it; trees grew right through everything, and spiderwebs of old creeper enveloped the big stone blocks. Another time they came on a stone tower, broken-topped and brown with old moss, leaning on the huge oak whose thick roots were slowly toppling it. But they found no place where men had breathed in living remembrance. Memories of Shadar Logoth kept them away from the ruins and hurried their footsteps until they were once more deep in places that seemed never to have known a human footstep.

Dreams plagued Perrin's sleep, fearful dreams. Ba'alzamon was in them, chasing him through mazes, hunting him, but Perrin never met him face-to-face, so far as he remembered. And their journey had been enough to bring a few bad dreams. Egwene complained of nightmares about Shadar Logoth, especially the two nights after they found the ruined fort and the abandoned tower. Perrin kept his own counsel even when he woke sweating and shaking in the dark. She was looking to him to lead them safely to Caemlyn, not share worries about which they could do nothing.

He was walking at Bela's head, wondering if they would find anything to eat this evening, when he first caught the smell. The mare flared her nostrils and swung her head in the next moment. He seized her bridle before she could whicker.

"That's smoke," Egwene said excitedly. She leaned forward in the saddle, drew a deep breath. "A cookfire. Somebody is roasting dinner. Rabbit."

"Maybe," Perrin said cautiously, and her eager smile faded. He exchanged his sling for the wicked half-moon of the axe. His hands opened and closed uncertainly on the thick haft. It was a weapon, but neither his hidden practice behind the forge nor Lan's teachings had really prepared him to use it as one. Even the battle before Shadar Logoth was too vague in his mind to give him any confidence. He could never quite manage that void that Rand and the Warder talked about, either.

Sunlight slanted through the trees behind them, and the forest was a still mass of dappled shadows. The faint smell of woodsmoke drifted around them, tinged with the aroma of cooking meat. *It could be rabbit,* he thought, and his stomach grumbled. And it could be something else, he reminded himself. He looked at Egwene; she was watching him. There were responsibilities to being leader.

"Wait here," he said softly. She frowned, but he cut her off as she opened her mouth. "And be quiet! We don't know who it is, yet." She nodded. Reluctantly, but she did it. Perrin wondered why that did not work when he was trying to make her take his turn riding. Drawing a deep breath, he started for the source of the smoke.

He had not spent as much time in the forests around Emond's Field as Rand or Mat, but still he had done his share of hunting rabbits. He crept from tree to tree without so much as snapping a twig. It was not long before he was peering around the bole of a tall oak with spreading, serpentine limbs that bent to touch the ground then rose again. Beyond lay a campfire, and a lean, sun-browned man was leaning against one of the limbs not far from the flames.

At least he was not a Trolloc, but he was the strangest fellow Perrin had ever seen. For one thing, his clothes all seemed to be made from animal skins, with the fur still on, even his boots and the odd, flat-topped round cap on his head. His cloak was a crazy quilt of rabbit and squirrel; his trousers appeared to be made from the long-haired hide of a brown and white goat. Gathered at the back of his neck with a cord, his graying brown hair hung to his waist. A thick beard fanned across half his chest. A long knife hung at his belt, almost a sword, and a bow and quiver stood propped against a limb close to hand.

The man leaned back with his eyes closed, apparently asleep, but Perrin did not stir from his concealment. Six sticks slanted over the fellow's fire, and on each stick a rabbit was skewered, roasted brown and now and then dripping juice that hissed in the flames. The smell of them, so close, made his mouth water.

"You done drooling?" The man opened one eye and cocked it at Perrin's hiding place. "You and your friend might as well sit and have a bite. I haven't seen you eat much the last couple of days."

Perrin hesitated, then stood slowly, still gripping his axe tightly. "You've been watching me for two days?"

The man chuckled deep in his throat. "Yes, I been watching you. And that pretty girl. Pushes you around like a bantam rooster, doesn't she? Heard you, mostly. The horse is the only one of you doesn't trample around loud enough to be heard five miles off. You going to ask her in, or are you intending to eat all the rabbit yourself?"

Perrin bristled; he knew he did not make much noise. You could not get close enough to a rabbit in the Waterwood to fetch it with a sling if you made noise. But the smell of rabbit made him remember that Egwene was hungry, too, not to mention waiting to discover if it was a Trolloc fire they had smelled.

He slipped the haft of his axe through the belt loop and raised his voice. "Egwene! It's all right! It *is* rabbit!" Offering his hand, he added in a more normal tone, "My name is Perrin. Perrin Aybara."

The man considered his hand before taking it awkwardly, as if unused to shaking hands. "I'm called Elyas," he said, looking up. "Elyas Machera."

Perrin gasped, and nearly dropped Elyas's hand. The man's eyes were yellow, like bright, polished gold. Some memory tickled at the back of Perrin's mind, then fled. All he could think of right then was that all of the Trollocs' eyes he had seen had been almost black.

Egwene appeared, cautiously leading Bela. She tied the mare's reins to one of the smaller branches of the oak, and made polite sounds when Perrin introduced her to Elyas, but her eyes kept drifting to the rabbits. She did not seem to notice the man's eyes. When Elyas motioned them to the food, she fell to with a will. Perrin hesitated only a minute longer before joining her.

Elyas waited silently while they ate. Perrin was so hungry he tore off pieces of meat so hot he had to juggle them from hand to hand before he could hold them in his mouth. Even Egwene showed little of her usual neatness; greasy juice ran down her chin. Day faded into twilight before they began to slow down, moonless darkness closing in around the fire, and then Elyas spoke.

"What are you doing out here? There isn't a house inside fifty miles in any direction."

"We're going to Caemlyn," Egwene said. "Perhaps you could—" Her eyebrows lifted coolly as Elyas threw back his head and roared with laughter. Perrin stared at him, a rabbit leg half raised to his mouth.

"Caemlyn?" Elyas wheezed when he could talk again. "The path you're following, the line you've taken the last two days, you'll pass a hundred miles or more north of Caemlyn."

"We were going to ask directions," Egwene said defensively. "We just haven't found any villages or farms, yet."

"And none you will," Elyas said, chuckling. "The way you're going, you can travel all the way to the Spine of the World without seeing another human. Of course, if you managed to climb the Spine—it can

be done, some places—you could find people in the Aiel Waste, but
you wouldn't like it there. You'd broil by day, and freeze by night,
and die of thirst anytime. It takes an Aielman to find water in the
Waste, and they don't like strangers much. No, not much, I'd say."
He set off into another, more furious, burst of laughter, this time actually rolling on the ground. "Not much at all," he managed.

Perrin shifted uneasily. *Are we eating with a madman?*

Egwene frowned, but she waited until Elyas's mirth faded a little,
then said, "Perhaps you could show us the way. You seem to know a
good deal more about where places are than we do."

Elyas stopped laughing. Raising his head, he replaced his round fur
cap, which had fallen off while he was rolling about, and stared at her
from under lowered brows. "I don't much like people," he said in a
flat voice. "Cities are full of people. I don't go near villages, or even
farms, very often. Villagers, farmers, they don't like my friends. I
wouldn't even have helped you if you hadn't been stumbling around
as helpless and innocent as newborn cubs."

"But at least you can tell us which way to go," she insisted. "If you
direct us to the nearest village, even if it's fifty miles away, surely
they'll give us directions to Caemlyn."

"Be still," Elyas said. "My friends are coming."

Bela suddenly whinnied in fear, and began jerking to pull her reins
free. Perrin half rose as shapes appeared all around them in the dark-
ening forest. Bela reared and twisted, screaming.

"Quiet the mare," Elyas said. "They won't hurt her. Or you, if
you're still."

Four wolves stepped into the firelight, shaggy, waist-high forms with
jaws that could break a man's leg. As if the people were not there
they walked up to the fire and lay down between the humans. In the
darkness among the trees firelight reflected off the eyes of more
wolves, on all sides.

Yellow eyes, Perrin thought. Like Elyas's eyes. That was what he
had been trying to remember. Carefully watching the wolves among
them, he reached for his axe.

"I would not do that," Elyas said. "If they think you mean harm,
they'll stop being friendly."

They were staring at him, those four wolves, Perrin saw. He had the
feeling that all the wolves, those in the trees, as well, were staring at
him. It made his skin itch. Cautiously he moved his hands away from
the axe. He imagined he could feel the tension ease among the wolves.
Slowly he sat back down; his hands shook until he gripped his knees

to stop them. Egwene was so stiff she almost quivered. One wolf, close
to black with a lighter gray patch on his face, lay nearly touching her.

Bela had ceased her screaming and rearing. Instead she stood
trembling and shifting in an attempt to keep all of the wolves in view,
kicking occasionally to show the wolves that she could, intending to
sell her life dearly. The wolves seemed to ignore her and everyone
else. Tongues lolling out of their mouths, they waited at their ease.

"There," Elyas said. "That's better."

"Are they tame?" Egwene asked faintly, and hopefully, too.
"They're . . . pets?"

Elyas snorted. "Wolves don't tame, girl, not even as well as men.
They're my friends. We keep each other company, hunt together, con-
verse, after a fashion. Just like any friends. Isn't that right, Dapple?"
A wolf with fur that faded through a dozen shades of gray, dark and
light, turned her head to look at him.

"You talk to them?" Perrin marveled.

"It isn't exactly talking," Elyas replied slowly. "The words don't
matter, and they aren't exactly right, either. Her name isn't Dapple.
It's something that means the way shadows play on a forest pool at a
midwinter dawn, with the breeze rippling the surface, and the tang of
ice when the water touches the tongue, and a hint of snow before
nightfall in the air. But that isn't quite it, either. You can't say it in
words. It's more of a feeling. That's the way wolves talk. The others
are Burn, Hopper, and Wind." Burn had an old scar on his shoulder
that might explain his name, but there was nothing about the other
two wolves to give any indication of what their names might mean.

For all the man's gruffness, Perrin thought Elyas was pleased to have
the chance to talk to another human. He seemed eager enough to do
it, at least. Perrin eyed the wolves' teeth glistening in the firelight and
thought it might be a good idea to keep him talking. "How . . . how
did you learn to talk to wolves, Elyas?"

"They found out," Elyas replied, "I didn't. Not at first. That's always the way of it, I understand. The wolves find you, not you them.
Some people thought me touched by the Dark One, because wolves
started appearing wherever I went. I suppose I thought so, too, sometimes. Most decent folk began to avoid me, and the ones who sought
me out weren't the kind I wanted to know, one way or another. Then
I noticed there were times when the wolves seemed to know what I
was thinking, to respond to what was in my head. That was the real
beginning. They were curious about me. Wolves can sense people, usually, but not like this. They were glad to find me. They say it's been

a long time since they hunted with men, and when they say a long time, the feeling I get is like a cold wind howling all the way down from the First Day."

"I never heard of men hunting with wolves," Egwene said. Her voice was not entirely steady, but the fact that the wolves were just lying there seemed to give her heart.

If Elyas heard her, he gave no sign. "Wolves remember things differently from the way people do," he said. His strange eyes took on a faraway look, as if he were drifting off on the flow of memory himself. "Every wolf remembers the history of all wolves, or at least the shape of it. Like I said, it can't be put into words very well. They remember running down prey side-by-side with men, but it was so long ago that it's more like the shadow of a shadow than a memory."

"That's very interesting," Egwene said, and Elyas looked at her sharply. "No, I mean it. It is." She wet her lips. "Could . . . ah . . . could you teach us to talk to them?"

Elyas snorted again. "It can't be taught. Some can do it, some can't. They say he can." He pointed at Perrin.

Perrin looked at Elyas's finger as if it were a knife. *He really is a madman.* The wolves were staring at him again. He shifted uncomfortably.

"You say you're going to Caemlyn," Elyas said, "but that still doesn't explain what you're doing out here, days from anywhere." He tossed back his fur-patch cloak and lay down on his side, propped on one elbow and waiting expectantly.

Perrin glanced at Egwene. Early on they had concocted a story for when they found people, to explain where they were going without bringing them any trouble. Without letting anyone know where they were really from, or where they were really going, eventually. Who knew what careless word might reach a Fade's ear? They had worked on it every day, patching it together, honing out flaws. And they had decided Egwene was the one to tell it. She was better with words than he was, and she claimed she could always tell when he was lying by his face.

Egwene began at once, smoothly. They were from the north, from Saldaea, from farms outside a tiny village. Neither of them had been more than twenty miles from home in their whole lives before this. But they had heard gleemen's stories, and merchants' tales, and they wanted to see some of the world. Caemlyn, and Illian. The Sea of Storms, and maybe even the fabled islands of the Sea Folk.

Perrin listened with satisfaction. Not even Thom Merrilin could have

made a better tale from the little they knew of the world outside the
Two Rivers, or one better suited to their needs.

"From Saldaea, eh?" Elyas said when she was done.

Perrin nodded. "That's right. We thought about seeing Maradon
first. I'd surely like to see the King. But the capital city would be the
first place our fathers would look."

That was his part of it, to make it plain they had never been to
Maradon. That way no one would expect them to know anything about
the city, just in case they ran into someone who really had been there.
It was all a long way from Emond's Field and the events of Win-
ternight. Nobody hearing the tale would have any reason to think of
Tar Valon, or Aes Sedai.

"Quite a story." Elyas nodded. "Yes, quite a story. There's a few
things wrong with it, but the main thing is Dapple says it's all a lump
of lies. Every last word."

"Lies!" Egwene exclaimed. "Why would we lie?"

The four wolves had not moved, but they no longer seemed to be
just lying there around the fire; they crouched, instead, and their yellow eyes watched the Emond's Fielders without blinking.

Perrin did not say anything, but his hand strayed to the axe at his
waist. The four wolves rose to their feet in one quick movement, and
his hand froze. They made no sound, but the thick hackles on their
necks stood erect. One of the wolves back under the trees raised a
growling howl into the night. Others answered, five, ten, twenty, till
the darkness rippled with them. Abruptly they, too, were still. Cold
sweat trickled down Perrin's face.

"If you think. . . ." Egwene stopped to swallow. Despite the chill
in the air there was sweat on her face, too. "If you think we are lying,
then you'll probably prefer that we make our own camp for the night,
away from yours."

"Ordinarily I would, girl. But right now I want to know about the
Trollocs. And the Halfmen." Perrin struggled to keep his face impassive, and hoped he was doing better at it than Egwene. Elyas went on
in a conversational tone. "Dapple says she smelled Halfmen and
Trollocs in your minds while you were telling that fool story. They all
did. You're mixed up with Trollocs, somehow, and the Eyeless.
Wolves hate Trollocs and Halfmen worse than wildfire, worse than
anything, and so do I.

"Burn wants to be done with you. It was Trollocs gave him that
mark when he was a yearling. He says game is scarce, and you're fatter
than any deer he's seen in months, and we should be done with you.

But Burn is always impatient. Why don't you tell me about it? I hope you're not Darkfriends. I don't like killing people after I've fed them. Just remember, they'll know if you lie, and even Dapple is already near as upset as Burn." His eyes, as yellow as the wolves' eyes, blinked no more than theirs did. *They* are *a wolf's eyes*, Perrin thought.

Egwene was looking at him, he realized, waiting for him to decide what they should do. *Light, suddenly I'm the leader again.* They had decided from the first that they could not risk telling the real story to anyone, but he saw no chance for them to get away even if he managed to get his axe out before. . . .

Dapple growled deep in her throat, and the sound was taken up by the other three around the fire, then by the wolves in the darkness. The menacing rumble filled the night.

"All right," Perrin said quickly. "All right!" The growling cut off, sharp and sudden. Egwene unclenched her hands and nodded. "It all started a few days before Winternight," Perrin began, "when our friend Mat saw a man in a black cloak. . . ."

Elyas never changed his expression or the way he lay on his side, but there was something about the tilt of his head that spoke of ears pricking up. The four wolves sat down as Perrin went on; he had the impression they were listening, too. The story was a long one, and he told almost all of it. The dream he and the others had had in Baerlon, though, he kept to himself. He waited for the wolves to make some sign they had caught the omission, but they only watched. Dapple seemed friendly, Burn angry. He was hoarse by the time he finished.

". . . and if she doesn't find us in Caemlyn, we'll go on to Tar Valon. We don't have any choice except to get help from the Aes Sedai."

"Trollocs and Halfmen this far south," Elyas mused. "Now that's something to consider." He rooted behind him and tossed Perrin a hide waterbag, not really looking at him. He appeared to be thinking. He waited until Perrin had drunk and replaced the plug before he spoke again. "I don't hold with Aes Sedai. The Red Ajah, those that like hunting for men who mess with the One Power, they wanted to gentle me, once. I told them to their faces they were Black Ajah; served the Dark One, I said, and they didn't like that at all. They couldn't catch me, though, once I got into the forest, but they did try. Yes, they did. Come to that, I doubt any Aes Sedai would take kindly to me, after that. I had to kill a couple of Warders. Bad business, that, killing Warders. Don't like it."

"This talking to wolves," Perrin said uneasily. "It . . . it has to do with the Power?"

"Of course not," Elyas growled. "Wouldn't have worked on me, gentling, but it made me mad, them wanting to try. This is an old thing, boy. Older than Aes Sedai. Older than anybody using the One Power. Old as humankind. Old as wolves. They don't like that either, Aes Sedai. Old things coming again. I'm not the only one. There are other things, other folk. Makes Aes Sedai nervous, makes them mutter about ancient barriers weakening. Things are breaking apart, they say. They're afraid the Dark One will get loose, is what. You'd think I was to blame, the way some of them looked at me. Red Ajah, anyway, but some others, too. The Amyrlin Seat. . . . Aaaah! I keep clear of them, mostly, and clear of friends of Aes Sedai, as well. You will, too, if you're smart."

"I'd like nothing better than to stay away from Aes Sedai," Perrin said.

Egwene gave him a sharp look. He hoped she would not burst out that she wanted to be an Aes Sedai. But she said nothing, though her mouth tightened, and Perrin went on.

"It isn't as if we have a choice. We've had Trollocs chasing us, and Fades, and Draghkar. Everything but Darkfriends. We can't hide, and we can't fight back alone. So who is going to help us? Who else is strong enough, except Aes Sedai?"

Elyas was silent for a time, looking at the wolves, most often at Dapple or Burn. Perrin shifted nervously and tried not to watch. When he watched he had the feeling that he could almost hear what Elyas and the wolves were saying to one another. Even if it had nothing to do with the Power, he wanted no part of it. *He* had *to be making some crazy joke. I can't talk to wolves.* One of the wolves—Hopper, he thought—looked at him and seemed to grin. He wondered how he had put a name to him.

"You could stay with me," Elyas said finally. "With us." Egwene's eyebrows shot up, and Perrin's mouth dropped open. "Well, what could be safer?" Elyas challenged. "Trollocs will take any chance they get to kill a wolf by itself, but they'll go miles out of their way to avoid a pack. And you won't have to worry about Aes Sedai, either. They don't often come into these woods."

"I don't know." Perrin avoided looking at the wolves to either side of him. One was Dapple, and he could feel her eyes on him. "For one thing, it isn't just the Trollocs."

Elyas chuckled coldly. "I've seen a pack pull down one of the Eyeless, too. Lost half the pack, but they wouldn't give up once they had its scent. Trollocs, Myrddraal, it's all one to the wolves. It's you they really want, boy. They've heard of other men who can talk to wolves, but you're the first they've ever met besides me. They'll accept your friend, too, though, and you'll all be safer here than in any city. There's Darkfriends in cities."

"Listen," Perrin said urgently, "I wish you'd stop saying that. I can't—do that . . . what you do, what you're saying."

"As you wish, boy. Play the goat, if you've a mind to. Don't you want to be safe?"

"I'm not deceiving myself. There's nothing to deceive myself about. All we want—"

"We are going to Caemlyn," Egwene spoke up firmly. "And then to Tar Valon."

Closing his mouth, Perrin met her angry look with one of his own. He knew that she followed his lead when she wanted to and not when she did not, but she could at least let him answer for himself. "What about you, Perrin?" he said, and answered himself. "Me? Well, let me think. Yes. Yes, I think I'll go on." He turned a mild smile on her. "Well, Egwene, that makes both of us. I guess I'm going with you, at that. Good to talk these things out before making a decision, isn't it?" She blushed, but the set of her jaw never lessened.

Elyas grunted. "Dapple said that's what you'd decide. She said the girl's planted firmly in the human world, while you"—he nodded at Perrin—"stand halfway between. Under the circumstances, I suppose we'd better go south with you. Otherwise, you'll probably starve to death, or get lost, or—"

Abruptly Burn stood up, and Elyas turned his head to regard the big wolf. After a moment Dapple rose, too. She moved closer to Elyas, so that she also was meeting Burn's stare. The tableau was frozen for long minutes, then Burn whirled and vanished into the night. Dapple shook herself, then resumed her place, flopping down as if nothing had happened.

Elyas met Perrin's questioning eyes. "Dapple runs this pack," he explained. "Some of the males could best her if they challenged, but she's smarter than any of them, and they all know it. She's saved the pack more than once. But Burn thinks the pack is wasting time with you three. Hating Trollocs is about all there is to him, and if there are Trollocs this far south he wants to be off killing them."

"We quite understand," Egwene said, sounding relieved. "We really can find our own way . . . with some directions, of course, if you'll give them."

Elyas waved a hand. "I said Dapple leads this pack, didn't I? In the morning, I'll start south with you, and so will they." Egwene looked as if that was not the best news she could have heard.

Perrin sat wrapped in his own silence. He could *feel* Burn leaving. And the scarred male was not the only one; a dozen others, all young males, loped after him. He wanted to believe it was all Elyas playing on his imagination, but he could not. Just before the departing wolves faded from his mind, he felt a thought he knew came from Burn, as sharp and clear as if it were his own thought. Hatred. Hatred and the taste of blood.

CHAPTER
24

Flight Down the Arinelle

Water dripped in the distance, hollow splashes echoing and reechoing, losing their source forever. There were stone bridges and railless ramps everywhere, all sprouting off from broad, flat-topped stone spires, all polished and smooth and streaked with red and gold. Level on level, the maze stretched up and down through the murk, without any apparent beginning or end. Every bridge led to a spire, every ramp to another spire, other bridges. Whatever direction Rand looked, as far as his eye could make out in the dimness it was the same, above as well as below. There was not enough light to see clearly, and he was almost glad of it. Some of those ramps led to platforms that had to be directly above the ones below. He could not see the base of any of them. He pressed, seeking freedom, knowing it was an illusion. Everything was illusion.

He knew the illusion; he had followed it too many times not to know. However far he went, up or down or in any direction, there was only the shiny stone. Stone, but the dankness of deep, fresh-turned earth permeated the air, and the sickly sweetness of decay. The smell of a grave opened out of its time. He tried not to breathe, but the smell filled his nostrils. It clung to his skin like oil.

A flicker of motion caught his eye, and he froze where he was, half crouched against the polished guardwall around one of the spire tops. It was no hiding place. From a thousand places a watcher could have seen him. Shadow filled the air, but there were no deeper shadows in which to hide. The light did not come from lamps, or lanterns, or torches; it was simply there, such as it was, as if it seeped out of the air. Enough by which to see, after a fashion; enough by which to be seen. But stillness gave a little protection.

The movement came again, and now it was clear. A man striding up a distant ramp, careless of the lack of railings and the drop to nothing below. The man's cloak rippled with his stately haste, and his head turned, searching, searching. The distance was too far for Rand to see more than the shape in the murk, but he did not need to be closer to know the cloak was the red of fresh blood, that the searching eyes blazed like two furnaces.

He tried tracing the maze with his eyes, to see how many connections Ba'alzamon needed before reaching him, then gave it up as useless. Distances were deceiving here, another lesson he had learned. What seemed far away might be reached by turning a corner; what appeared close could be out of reach altogether. The only thing to do, as it had been from the beginning, was to keep moving. Keep moving, and not think. Thinking was dangerous, he knew.

Yet, as he turned away from Ba'alzamon's distant form, he could not help wondering about Mat. Was Mat somewhere in this maze? *Or are there two mazes, two Ba'alzamons?* His mind skittered away from that; it was too dreadful to dwell on. *Is this like Baerlon? Then why can't he find me?* That was a little better. A small comfort. *Comfort? Blood and ashes, where's the comfort in it?*

There had been two or three close brushes, though he could not remember them clearly, but for a long, long time—how long?—he had run while Ba'alzamon vainly pursued. Was this like Baerlon, or was it only a nightmare, only a dream like other men's dreams?

For an instant, then—just for the length of time it took to take a breath—he knew why it was dangerous to think, what it was dangerous to think about. As it had before, every time he allowed himself to think of what surrounded him as a dream, the air shimmered, clouding his eyes. It turned to jell, holding him. Just for an instant.

The gritty heat prickled his skin, and his throat had long since gone dry as he trotted down the thorn-hedge maze. How long had it been now? His sweat evaporated before it had a chance to bead, and his eyes burned. Overhead—and not too far overhead, at that—boiled furious, steely clouds streaked with black, but not a breath of air stirred in the maze. For a moment he thought it had been different, but the thought evaporated in the heat. He had been here a long time. It was dangerous to think, he knew that.

Smooth stones, pale and rounded, made a sketchy pavement, half buried in the bone-dry dust that rose in puffs at even his lightest step. It tickled his nose, threatening a sneeze that might give him away; when he tried to breathe through his mouth, dust clogged his throat until he choked.

This was a dangerous place; he knew that, too. Ahead of him he could see three openings in the high wall of thorns, then the way curved out of sight. Ba'alzamon could be approaching any one of those corners at that very moment. There had been two or three encounters already, though he could not remember much beyond that they had happened and he had escaped . . . somehow. Dangerous to think too much.

Panting in the heat, he stopped to examine the maze wall. Thickly woven thorn bushes, brown and dead-looking, with cruel black thorns like inch-long hooks. Too tall to see over, too dense to see through. Gingerly he touched the wall, and gasped. Despite all his care, a thorn pierced his finger, burning like a hot needle. He stumbled back, his heels catching on the stones, shaking his hand and scattering thick drops of blood. The burn began to subside, but his whole hand throbbed.

Abruptly he forgot the pain. His heel had overturned one of the smooth stones, kicked it out of the dry ground. He stared at it, and empty eye sockets stared back. A skull. A human skull. He looked along the pathway at all the smooth, pale stones, all exactly alike. He shifted his feet hastily, but he could not move without walking on them, and he could not stay still without standing on them. A stray thought took vague shape, that things might not be what they seemed, but he pushed it down ruthlessly. Thinking was dangerous here.

He took a shaky hold on himself. Staying in one place was dangerous, too. That was one of the things he knew dimly but with certainty. The flow of blood from his finger had dwindled to a slow drip, and the throb was almost gone. Sucking his fingertip, he started down the path in the direction he happened to be facing. One way was as good as another in here.

Now he remembered hearing once that you could get out of a maze by always turning in the same direction. At the first opening in the wall of thorns he turned right, then right again at the next. And found himself face-to-face with Ba'alzamon.

Surprise flitted across Ba'alzamon's face, and his blood-red cloak settled as he stopped short. Flames soared in his eyes, but in the heat of the maze Rand barely felt them.

"How long do you think you can evade me, boy? How long do you think you can evade your fate? You are mine!"

Stumbling back, Rand wondered why he was fumbling at his belt, as if for a sword. "Light help me," he muttered. "Light help me." He could not remember what it meant.

"The Light will not help you, boy, and the Eye of the World will not serve you. You are my hound, and if you will not course at my command, I will strangle you with the corpse of the Great Serpent!"

Ba'alzamon stretched out his hand, and suddenly Rand knew a way to escape, a misty, half-formed memory that screamed danger, but nothing to the danger of being touched by the Dark One.

"A dream!" Rand shouted. "This is a dream!"

Ba'alzamon's eyes began to widen, in surprise or anger or both, then the air shimmered, and his features blurred, and faded.

Rand turned about in one spot, staring. Staring at his own image thrown back at him a thousandfold. Ten thousandfold. Above was blackness, and blackness below, but all around him stood mirrors, mirrors set at every angle, mirrors as far as he could see, all showing him, crouched and turning, staring wide-eyed and frightened.

A red blur drifted across the mirrors. He spun, trying to catch it, but in every mirror it drifted behind his own image and vanished. Then it was back again, but not as a blur. Ba'alzamon strode across the mirrors, ten thousand Ba'alzamons, searching, crossing and recrossing the silvery mirrors.

He found himself staring at the reflection of his own face, pale and shivering in the knife-edge cold. Ba'alzamon's image grew behind his, staring at him; not seeing, but staring still. In every mirror, the flames of Ba'alzamon's face raged behind him, enveloping, consuming, merging. He wanted to scream, but his throat was frozen. There was only one face in those endless mirrors. His own face. Ba'alzamon's face. One face.

Rand jerked, and opened his eyes. Darkness, lessened only slightly by a pale light. Barely breathing, he moved nothing except his eyes. A rough wool blanket covered him to his shoulders, and his head was cradled on his arms. He could feel smooth wooden planks under his hands. Deck planks. Rigging creaked in the night. He let out a long breath. He was on the *Spray*. It was over . . . for another night, at least.

Without thinking he put his finger in his mouth. At the taste of blood, he stopped breathing. Slowly he put his hand close to his face, to where he could see in the dim moonlight, to where he could watch the bead of blood form on his fingertip. Blood from the prick of a thorn.

The *Spray* made haste slowly down the Arinelle. The wind came strong, but from directions that made the sails useless. With all Captain Domon's demand for speed, the vessel crept along. By night a man in the bows cast a tallowed lead by lantern light, calling back the depth to the steersman, while the current carried her downriver against the wind with the sweeps pulled in. There were no rocks to fear in the Arinelle, but shallows and shoals there were aplenty, where a boat could go hard aground to remain, bows and more dug into the mud, until help came. If it was help that came first. By day the sweeps worked from sunrise to sunset, but the wind fought them as if it wanted to push the boat back upriver.

They did not put in to shore, neither by day nor by night. Bayle Domon drove boat and crew alike hard, railing at the contrary winds, cursing the slow pace. He blistered the crew for sluggards at the oars and flayed them with his tongue for every mishandled line, his low, hard voice painting Trollocs ten feet tall among them on the deck, ripping out their throats. For two days that was enough to send every man leaping. Then the shock of the Trolloc attack began to fade, and men began to mutter about an hour to stretch their legs ashore, and about the dangers of running downriver in the dark.

The crew kept their grumbles quiet, watching out of the corners of their eyes to make sure Captain Domon was not close enough to hear, but he seemed to hear everything said on his boat. Each time the grumblings began, he silently brought out the long, scythe-like sword and cruelly hooked axe that had been found on the deck after the attack. He would hang them on the mast for an hour, and those who had been wounded would finger their bandages, and the mutterings quieted . . . for a day or so, at least, until one or another of the crew began thinking once more that surely they had left the Trollocs far behind by now, and the cycle began yet again.

Rand noticed that Thom Merrilin stayed clear of the crew when they began whispering together and frowning, though usually he was slapping backs and telling jokes and exchanging banter in a way that put a grin on even the hardest-working man. Thom watched those secretive mutters with a wary eye while appearing to be absorbed in lighting his long-stemmed pipe, or tuning his harp, or almost anything except paying any mind at all to the crew. Rand did not understand why. It was not the three who had come aboard chased by Trollocs whom the crew seemed to blame, but rather Floran Gelb.

For the first day or two Gelb's wiry figure could almost always be found addressing any crewman he could corner, telling his version of the night Rand and the others came on board. Gelb's manner slid from bluster to whines and back again, and his lip always curled when he pointed to Thom or Mat, or especially Rand, trying to lay the blame on them.

"They're strangers," Gelb pleaded, quietly and with an eye out for the captain. "What do we know of them? The Trollocs came with them, that's what we know. They're in league."

"Fortune, Gelb, stow it," growled a man with his hair in a pigtail and a small blue star tattooed on his cheek. He did not look at Gelb as he coiled a line on deck, working it in with his bare toes. All the sailors went barefoot despite the cold; boots could slip on a wet deck. "You'd call your mother Darkfriend if it'd let you slack. Get away from me!" He spat on Gelb's foot and went back to the line.

All the crew remembered the watch Gelb had not kept, and the pigtailed man's was the politest response he got. No one even wanted to work with him. Gelb found himself relegated to solitary tasks, all of them filthy, such as scrubbing the galley's greasy pots, or crawling into the bilges on his belly to search for leaks among years of slime. Soon he stopped talking to anyone. His shoulders took on a defensive hunch, and injured silence became his stance—the more people watching, the more injured, though it earned him no more than a grunt. When Gelb's eyes fell on Rand, however, or on Mat or Thom, murder flashed across his long-nosed face.

When Rand mentioned to Mat that Gelb would cause them trouble sooner or later, Mat looked around the boat, saying, "Can we trust any of them? Any at all?" Then he went off to find a place where he could be alone, or as alone as he could get on a boat less than thirty paces from its raised bow to the sternpost where the steering oars were mounted. Mat had spent too much time alone since the night at Shadar Logoth; brooding, as Rand saw it.

Thom said, "Trouble won't come from Gelb, boy, if it comes. Not yet, at least. None of the crew will back him, and he hasn't the nerve to try anything alone. But the others, now . . . ? Domon almost seems to think the Trollocs are chasing him, personally, but the rest are beginning to think the danger is past. They might just decide they have had enough. They're on the edge of it, as it is." He hitched his patch-covered cloak, and Rand had the feeling he was checking his hidden knives—his second-best set. "If they mutiny, boy, they won't leave passengers behind to tell the tale. The Queen's Writ might not have much force this far from Caemlyn, but even a village mayor will do something about that." That was when Rand, too, began trying not to be noticed when he watched the crewmen.

Thom did his part in diverting the crew from thoughts of mutiny. He told stories, with all the flourishes, every morning and every night, and in between he played any song they requested. To support the notion that Rand and Mat wanted to be apprentice gleemen, he set aside a time each day for lessons, and that was an entertainment for the crew, as well. He would not let either of them touch his harp, of course, and their sessions with the flute produced pained winces, in the beginning, at least, and laughter from the crew even while they were covering their ears.

He taught the boys some of the easier stories, a little simple tumbling, and, of course, juggling. Mat complained about what Thom demanded of them, but Thom blew out his mustaches and glared right back.

"I don't know how to play at teaching, boy. I either teach a thing, or I don't. Now! Even a country bumpkin ought to be able to do a simple handstand. Up you go."

Crewmen who were not working always gathered, squatting in a circle around the three. Some even tried their hand at the lessons Thom taught, laughing at their own fumblings. Gelb stood alone and watched it all darkly, hating them all.

A good part of each day Rand spent leaning on the railing, staring at the shore. It was not that he really expected to see Egwene or any of the others suddenly appear on the riverbank, but the boat traveled so slowly that he sometimes hoped for it. They could catch up without riding too hard. If they had escaped. If they were still alive.

The river rolled on without any sign of life, nor any boat to be seen except the *Spray*. But that was not to say there was nothing to see, and wonder at. In the middle of the first day, the Arinelle ran between high bluffs that stretched for half a mile on either side. For that whole length the stone had been cut into figures, men and women a hundred feet tall, with crowns proclaiming them kings and queens. No two were alike in that royal procession, and long years separated the first from the last. Wind and rain had worn those at the north end smooth and almost featureless, with faces and details becoming more distinct as they went south. The river lapped around the statues' feet, feet washed to smooth nubs, those that were not gone completely. *How long have they stood there,* Rand wondered. *How long for the river to wear away so much stone?* None of the crew so much as looked up from their work, they had seen the ancient carvings so many times before.

Another time, when the eastward shore had become flat grassland again, broken only occasionally by thickets, the sun glinted off something in the distance. "What can that be?" Rand wondered aloud. "It looks like metal."

Captain Domon was walking by, and he paused, squinting toward the glint. "It do be metal," he said. His words still ran together, but Rand had come to understand without having to puzzle it out. "A tower of metal. I have seen it close up, and I know. River traders use it as a marker. We be ten days from Whitebridge at the rate we go."

"A metal tower?" Rand said, and Mat, sitting cross-legged with his back against a barrel, roused from his brooding to listen.

The captain nodded. "Aye. Shining steel, by the look and feel of it, but no a spot of rust. Two hundred feet high, it be, as big around as a house, with no a mark on it and never an opening to be found."

"I'll bet there's treasure inside," Mat said. He stood up and stared toward the far tower as the river carried the *Spray* beyond it. "A thing like that must have been made to protect something valuable."

"Mayhap, lad," the captain rumbled. "There be stranger things in the world than this, though. On Tremalking, one of the Sea Folk's isles, there be a stone hand fifty feet high sticking out of a hill, clutching a crystal sphere as big as this vessel. There be treasure under that hill if there be treasure anywhere, but the island people want no part of digging there, and the Sea Folk care for naught but sailing their ships and searching for the Coramoor, their Chosen One."

"I'd dig," Mat said. "How far is this . . . Tremalking?" A clump of trees slid in front of the shining tower, but he stared as if he could see it yet.

Captain Domon shook his head. "No, lad, it no be the treasure that makes for seeing the world. If you find yourself a fistful of gold, or some dead king's jewels, all well and good, but it be the strangeness you see that pulls you to the next horizon. In Tanchico—that be a port on the Aryth Ocean—part of the Panarch's Palace were built in the

Age of Legends, so it be said. There be a wall there with a frieze showing animals no man living has ever seen."

"Any child can draw an animal nobody's ever seen," Rand said, and the captain chuckled.

"Aye, lad, so they can. But can a child make the bones of those animals? In Tanchico they have them, all fastened together like the animal was. They stand in a part of the Panarch's Palace where any can enter and see. The Breaking left a thousand wonders behind, and there been half a dozen empires or more since, some rivaling Artur Hawkwing's, every one leaving things to see and find. Lightsticks and razorlace and heartstone. A crystal lattice covering an island, and it hums when the moon is up. A mountain hollowed into a bowl, and in its center, a silver spike a hundred spans high, and any who comes within a mile of it, dies. Rusted ruins, and broken bits, and things found on the bottom of the sea, things not even the oldest books know the meaning of. I've gathered a few, myself. Things you never dreamed of, in more places than you can see in ten lifetimes. That be the strangeness that will draw you on."

"We used to dig up bones in the Sand Hills," Rand said slowly. "Strange bones. There was part of a fish—I think it was a fish—as big as this boat, once. Some said it was bad luck, digging in the hills."

The captain eyed him shrewdly. "You thinking about home already, lad, and you just set out in the world? The world will put a hook in your mouth. You'll set off chasing the sunset, you wait and see . . . and if you ever go back, your village'll no be big enough to hold you."

"No!" He gave a start. How long had it been since he had thought of home, of Emond's Field? And what of Tam? It had to be days. It felt like months. "I will go home, one day, when I can. I'll raise sheep, like . . . like my father, and if I never leave again it will be too soon. Isn't that right, Mat? As soon as we can we're going home and forget all this even exists."

With a visible effort Mat pulled away from staring upriver after the vanished tower. "What? Oh. Yes, of course. We'll go home. Of course." As he turned to go, Rand heard him muttering under his breath. "I'll bet he just doesn't want anybody else going after the treasure." He did not seem to realize he had spoken aloud.

Four days into their trip downriver found Rand atop the mast, sitting on the blunt end with his legs wrapped in the stays. The *Spray* rolled gently on the river, but fifty feet above the water that easy roll made the top of the mast sway back and forth through wide arcs. He threw back his head and laughed into the wind that blew in his face.

The oars were out, and from here the boat looked like some twelve-legged spider creeping down the Arinelle. He had been as high as this before, in trees back in the Two Rivers, but this time there were no branches to block his view. Everything on deck, the sailors at the sweeps, men on their knees scrubbing the deck with smoothstones, men doing things with lines and hatchcovers, looked so odd when seen from right overhead, all squat and foreshortened, that he had spent an hour just staring at them and chuckling.

He still chuckled whenever he looked down at them, but now he was staring at the riverbanks flowing by. That was the way it seemed, as if he were still—except for the swaying back and forth, of course—and the banks slid slowly by, trees and hills marching along to either side. He was still, and the whole world moved past him.

On sudden impulse he unwrapped his legs from the stays bracing the mast and held his arms and legs out to either side, balancing against the sway. For three complete arcs he kept his balance like that, then suddenly it was gone. Arms and legs windmilling, he toppled forward and grabbed the forestay. Legs splayed to either side of the mast, nothing holding him to his precarious perch but his two hands on the stay, he laughed. Gulping huge breaths of the fresh, cold wind, he laughed with the exhilaration of it.

"Lad," came Thom's hoarse voice. "Lad, if you're trying to break your fool neck, don't do it by falling on me."

Rand looked down. Thom clung to the ratlines just below him, staring up the last few feet grimly. Like Rand, the gleeman had left his cloak below. "Thom," he said delightedly. "Thom, when did you come up here?"

"When you wouldn't pay any attention to people shouting at you. Burn me, boy, you've got everybody thinking you've gone mad."

He looked down and was surprised to see all the faces staring up at him. Only Mat, sitting cross-legged up in the bows with his back to the mast, was not looking at him. Even the men at the oars had their eyes raised, letting their stroke go ragged. And no one was berating them for it. Rand twisted his head around to look under his arm at the stern. Captain Domon stood by the steering oar, ham-like fists on his hips, glaring at him atop the mast. He turned back to grin at Thom. "You want me to come down, then?"

Thom nodded vigorously. "I would appreciate it greatly."

"All right." Shifting his grip on the forestay, he sprang forward off the mast top. He heard Thom bite off an oath as his fall was cut short and he dangled from the forestay by his hands. The gleeman scowled at him, one hand half stretched out to catch him. He grinned at Thom again. "I'm going down now."

Swinging his legs up, he hooked one knee over the thick line that ran from the mast to the bow, then caught it in the crook of his elbow and let go with his hands. Slowly, then with increasing speed, he slid down. Just short of the bow he dropped to his feet on the deck right in front of Mat, took one step to catch his balance, and turned to face the boat with arms spread wide, the way Thom did after a tumbling trick.

Scattered clapping rose from the crew, but he was looking down at Mat in surprise, and at what Mat held, hidden from everyone else by his body. A curved dagger with a gold scabbard worked in strange symbols. Fine gold wire wrapped the hilt, which was capped by a ruby as big as Rand's thumbnail, and the quillons were golden-scaled serpents baring their fangs.

Mat continued to slide the dagger in and out of its sheath for a moment. Still playing with the dagger he raised his head slowly; his eyes had a faraway look. Suddenly they focused on Rand, and he gave a start and stuffed the dagger under his coat.

Rand squatted on his heels, with his arms crossed on his knees. "Where did you get that?" Mat said nothing, looking quickly to see if anyone else was close by. They were alone, for a wonder. "You didn't take it from Shadar Logoth, did you?"

Mat stared at him. "It's your fault. Yours and Perrin's. The two of you pulled me away from the treasure, and I had it in my hand. Mordeth didn't give it to me. I took it, so Moiraine's warnings about his gifts don't count. You won't tell anybody, Rand. They might try to steal it."

"I won't tell anybody," Rand said. "I think Captain Domon is honest, but I wouldn't put anything past the rest of them, especially Gelb."

"Not anybody," Mat insisted. "Not Domon, not Thom, not anybody. We're the only two left from Emond's Field, Rand. We can't afford to trust anybody else."

"They're alive, Mat. Egwene, and Perrin. I know they're alive." Mat looked ashamed. "I'll keep your secret, though. Just the two of us. At least we don't have to worry about money now. We can sell it for enough to travel to Tar Valon like kings."

"Of course," Mat said after a minute. "If we have to. Just don't tell anybody until I say so."

"I said I wouldn't. Listen, have you had any more dreams since we came on the boat? Like in Baerlon? This is the first chance I've had to ask without six people listening."

Mat turned his head away, giving him a sidelong look. "Maybe."

"What do you mean, maybe? Either you have or you haven't."

"All right, all right, I have. I don't want to talk about it. I don't even want to think about it. It doesn't do any good."

Before either of them could say more Thom came striding up the deck, his cloak over his arm. The wind whipped his white hair about, and his long mustaches seemed to bristle. "I managed to convince the captain you aren't crazy," he announced, "that it was part of your training." He caught hold of the forestay and shook it. "That fool stunt of yours, sliding down the rope, helped, but you are lucky you didn't break your fool neck."

Rand's eyes went to the forestay and followed it up to the top of the mast, and as they did his mouth dropped open. He *had* slid down that. And he had been sitting on top of. . . .

Suddenly he could see himself up there, arms and legs spread wide. He sat down hard, and barely caught himself short of ending up flat on his back. Thom was looking at him thoughtfully.

"I didn't know you had such a good head for heights, lad. We might be able to play in Illian, or Ebou Dar, or even Tear. People in the big cities in the south like tightrope walkers and slackwire artists."

"We're going to—" At the last minute Rand remembered to look around for anyone close enough to overhear. Several of the crew were watching them, including Gelb, glaring as usual, but none could hear what he was saying. "To Tar Valon," he finished. Mat shrugged as if it were all the same to him where they went.

"At the moment, lad," Thom said, settling down beside them, "but tomorrow . . . who knows? That's the way with a gleeman's life." He took a handful of colored balls from one of his wide sleeves. "Since I have you down out of the air, we'll work on the triple crossover."

Rand's gaze drifted to the top of the mast, and he shivered. *What's happening to me? Light, what?* He had to find out. He had to get to Tar Valon before he really did go mad.

CHAPTER
25

The Traveling People

Bela walked along placidly under the weak sun as if the three wolves trotting not far off were only village dogs, but the way she rolled her eyes at them from time to time, showing white all the way around, indicated she felt nothing of the sort. Egwene, on the mare's back, was just as bad. She watched the wolves constantly from the corner of her eye, and sometimes she twisted in the saddle to look around. Perrin was sure she was hunting for the rest of the pack, though she denied it angrily when he suggested as much, denied being afraid of the wolves that paced them, denied worrying about the rest of the pack or what it was up to. She denied, and went right on looking, tight-eyed and wetting her lips uneasily.

The rest of the pack was far distant; he could have told her that. *What good, even if she believed me? Especially if she did.* He was of no mind to open that basket of snakes until he had to. He did not want to think about *how* he knew. The fur-clad man loped ahead of them, sometimes looking almost like a wolf himself, and he never looked around when Dapple, Hopper, and Wind appeared, but he knew, too.

The Emond's Fielders had wakened at dawn that first morning to find Elyas cooking more rabbit and watching them over his full beard without much expression. Except for Dapple, Hopper, and Wind, no wolves were to be seen. In the pale, early daylight, deep shade still lingered under the big oak, and the bare trees beyond looked like fingers stripped to the bone.

"They're around," Elyas answered when Egwene asked where the rest of the pack had gone. "Close enough to help, if need be. Far enough off to avoid any human trouble we get into. Sooner or later there's always trouble when there's two humans together. If we need them, they'll be there."

Something tickled the back of Perrin's mind as he ripped free a bite of roast rabbit. A direction, vaguely sensed. *Of course! That's where they. . . .* The hot juices in his mouth abruptly lost all taste. He picked at the tubers Elyas had cooked in the coals—they tasted something like turnips—but his appetite was gone.

When they had started out Egwene insisted that everyone take a turn riding, and Perrin did not even bother to argue.

"First turn is yours," he told her.

She nodded. "And then you, Elyas."

"My own legs are good enough for me," Elyas said. He looked at Bela, and the mare rolled her eyes as if he were one of the wolves. "Besides, I don't think she wants me riding her."

"That's nonsense," Egwene replied firmly. "There is no point in being stubborn about it. The sensible thing is for everybody to ride sometimes. According to you we have a long way still to go."

"I said no, girl."

She took a deep breath, and Perrin was wondering if she would succeed in bullying Elyas the way she did him, when he realized she was standing there with her mouth open, not saying a word. Elyas was looking at her, just looking, with those yellow wolf's eyes. Egwene stepped back from the raw-boned man, and licked her lips, and stepped back again. Before Elyas turned away, she had backed all the way to Bela and scrambled up onto the mare's back. As the man turned to lead them south, Perrin thought his grin was a good deal like a wolf's, too.

For three days they traveled in that manner, walking and riding south and east all day, stopping only when twilight thickened. Elyas seemed to scorn the haste of city men, but he did not believe in wasting time when there was somewhere to go.

The three wolves were seldom seen. Each night they came to the fire for a time, and sometimes in the day they showed themselves briefly, appearing close at hand when least expected and vanishing in the same manner. Perrin knew they were out there, though, and where. He knew when they were scouting the path ahead and when they were watching the backtrail. He knew when they left the pack's usual hunting grounds, and Dapple sent the pack back to wait for her. Sometimes the three that remained faded from his mind, but long before they were close enough to see again, he was aware of them returning. Even when the trees dwindled to wide-scattered groves separated by great swathes of winter-dead grass, they were as ghosts when they did not want to be seen, but he could have pointed a finger straight at them at any time. He did not know how he knew, and he tried to convince himself that it was just his imagination playing tricks, but it did no good. Just as Elyas knew, he knew.

He tried not thinking about wolves, but they crept into his thoughts all the same. He had not dreamed about Ba'alzamon since meeting Elyas and the wolves. His dreams, as much as he remembered of them on waking, were of everyday things, just as he might have dreamed at home . . . before Baerlon . . . before Winternight. Normal dreams—with one addition. In every dream he remembered there was a point where he straightened from Master Luhhan's forge to wipe the sweat from his face, or turned from dancing with the village girls on the Green, or lifted his head from a book in front of the fireplace, and whether he was outside or under a roof, there was a wolf close to hand. Always the wolf's back was to him, and always he knew—in the dreams it seemed the normal course of things, even at Alsbet Luhhan's dinner table—that the wolf's yellow eyes were watching for what might come, guarding against what might come. Only when he was awake did the dreams seem strange.

Three days they journeyed, with Dapple, Hopper, and Wind bringing them rabbits and squirrels, and Elyas pointing out plants, few of which Perrin recognized, as good to eat. Once a rabbit burst out almost from under Bela's hooves; before Perrin could get a stone in his sling, Elyas skewered it with his long knife at twenty paces. Another time Elyas brought down a fat pheasant, on the wing, with his bow. They ate far better than they had when on their own, but Perrin would as soon have gone back on short rations if it had meant different company. He was not sure how Egwene felt, but he would have been willing to go hungry if he could do it without the wolves. Three days, into the afternoon.

A stand of trees lay ahead, larger than most they had seen, a good four miles across. The sun sat low in the western sky, pushing slanted shadows off to their right, and the wind was picking up. Perrin felt the wolves give over quartering behind them and start forward, not hurrying. They had smelled and seen nothing dangerous. Egwene was taking her turn on Bela. It was time to start looking for a camp for the night, and the big copse would serve the purpose well.

As they came close to the trees, three mastiffs burst from cover, broad-muzzled dogs as tall as the wolves and even heavier, teeth bared in loud, rumbling snarls. They stopped short as soon as they were in the open, but no more than thirty feet separated them from the three people, and their dark eyes kindled with a killing light.

Bela, already on edge from the wolves, whinnied and almost unseated Egwene, but Perrin had his sling whirling around his head in an instant. No need to use the axe on dogs; a stone in the ribs would send the worst dog running.

Elyas waved a hand at him without taking his eyes from the stiff-legged dogs. "Hssst! None of that now!"

Perrin gave him a puzzled frown, but let the sling slow its spin and finally fall to his side. Egwene managed to get Bela under control; she and the mare both watched the dogs warily.

The mastiffs' hackles stood stiff, and their ears were laid back, and their growls sounded like earthquakes. Abruptly Elyas raised one finger shoulder high and whistled, a long, shrill whistle that rose higher and higher and did not end. The growls cut off raggedly. The dogs stepped back, whining and turning their heads as if they wanted to go but were held. Their eyes remained locked to Elyas's finger.

Slowly Elyas lowered his hand, and the pitch of his whistle lowered with it. The dogs followed, until they lay flat on the ground, tongues lolling from their mouths. Three tails wagged.

"See," Elyas said, walking to the dogs. "There's no need for weapons." The mastiffs licked his hands, and he scratched their broad heads and fondled their ears. "They look meaner than they are. They meant to frighten us off, and they wouldn't have bitten unless we tried to go into the trees. Anyway, there's no worry of that, now. We can make the next thicket before full dark."

When Perrin looked at Egwene, her mouth was hanging open. He shut his own mouth with a click of teeth.

Still patting the dogs, Elyas studied the stand of trees. "There'll be Tuatha'an here. The Traveling People." They stared at him blankly, and he added, "Tinkers."

"Tinkers?" Perrin exclaimed. "I've always wanted to see the Tinkers. They camp across the river from Taren Ferry sometimes, but they don't come down into the Two Rivers, as far as I know. I don't know why not."

Egwene sniffed. "Probably because the Taren Ferry folk are as great thieves as the Tinkers. They'd no doubt end up stealing each other blind. Master Elyas, if there really are Tinkers close by, shouldn't we go on? We don't want Bela stolen, and . . . well, we do not have much else, but everybody knows Tinkers will steal anything."

"Including infants?" Elyas asked dryly. "Kidnap children, and all that?" He spat, and she blushed. Those stories about babies were told sometimes, but most often by Cenn Buie or one of the Coplins or Congars. The other tales, everybody knew. "The Tinkers make me sick sometimes, but they don't steal any more than most folks. A good bit less than some I know."

"It will be getting dark soon, Elyas," Perrin said. "We have to camp somewhere. Why not with them, if they'll have us?" Mistress Luhhan had a Tinker-mended pot that she claimed was better than new. Master Luhhan was not too happy about his wife's praise of the Tinker work, but Perrin wanted to see how it was done. Yet there was a reluctance about Elyas that he did not understand. "Is there some reason we shouldn't?"

Elyas shook his head, but the reluctance was still there, in the set of his shoulders and the tightness of his mouth. "May as well. Just don't pay any mind to what they say. Lot of foolishness. Most times the Traveling People do things any which way, but there's times they set a store by formality, so you do what I do. And keep your secrets. No need to tell the world everything."

The dogs trailed along beside them, wagging their tails, as Elyas led the way into the trees. Perrin felt the wolves slow, and knew they would not enter. They were not afraid of the dogs—they were contemptuous of dogs, who had given up freedom to sleep by a fire—but people they avoided.

Elyas walked surely, as if he knew the way, and near the center of the stand the Tinkers' wagons appeared, scattered among the oak and ash.

Like everyone else in Emond's Field, Perrin had heard a good deal about the Tinkers even if he had never seen any, and the camp was just what he expected. Their wagons were small houses on wheels, tall wooden boxes lacquered and painted in bright colors, reds and blues and yellows and greens and some hues to which he could not put a name. The Traveling People were going about work that was disappointingly everyday, cooking, sewing, tending children, mending harness, but their clothes were even more colorful than the wagons—and seemingly chosen at random; sometimes coat and breeches, or dress and shawl, went together in a way that hurt his eyes. They looked like butterflies in a field of wildflowers.

Four or five men in different places around the camp played fiddles and flutes, and a few people danced like rainbow-hued hummingbirds. Children and dogs ran playing among the cookfires. The dogs were mastiffs just like those that had confronted the travelers, but the children tugged at their ears and tails and climbed on their backs, and the massive dogs accepted it all placidly. The three with Elyas, tongues hanging out, looked up at the bearded man as if he were their best friend. Perrin shook his head. They were still big enough to reach a man's throat while barely getting their front feet off the ground.

Abruptly the music stopped, and he realized all the Tinkers were looking at him and his companions. Even the children and dogs stood still and watched, warily, as if on the point of flight.

For a moment there was no sound at all, then a wiry man, grayhaired and short, stepped forward and bowed gravely to Elyas. He wore a high-collared red coat, and baggy, bright green trousers tucked into knee boots. "You are welcome to our fires. Do you know the song?"

Elyas bowed in the same way, both hands pressed to his chest. "Your welcome warms my spirit, Mahdi, as your fires warm the flesh, but I do not know the song."

"Then we seek still," the gray-haired man intoned. "As it was, so shall it be, if we but remember, seek, and find." He swept an arm toward the fires with a smile, and his voice took on a cheerful lightness. "The meal is almost ready. Join us, please."

As if that had been a signal the music sprang up again, and the children took up their laughter and ran with the dogs. Everyone in the camp went back to what they had been doing just as though the newcomers were long-accepted friends.

The gray-haired man hesitated, though, and looked at Elyas. "Your . . . other friends? They will stay away? They frighten the poor dogs so."

"They'll stay away, Raen." Elyas's headshake had a touch of scorn. "You should know that by now."

The gray-haired man spread his hands as if to say nothing was ever certain. As he turned to lead them into the camp, Egwene dismounted and moved close to Elyas. "You two are friends?" A smiling Tinker appeared to take Bela; Egwene gave the reins up reluctantly, after a wry snort from Elyas.

"We know each other," the fur-clad man replied curtly.

"His name is Mahdi?" Perrin said.

Elyas growled something under his breath. "His name's Raen. Mahdi's his title. Seeker. He's the leader of this band. You can call him Seeker if the other sounds odd. He won't mind."

"What was that about a song?" Egwene asked.

"That's why they travel," Elyas said, "or so they say. They're looking for a song. That's what the Mahdi seeks. They say they lost it during the Breaking of the World, and if they can find it again, the paradise of the Age of Legends will return." He ran his eye around the camp and snorted. "They don't even know what the song is; they claim they'll know it when they find it. They don't know how it's supposed to bring paradise, either, but they've been looking near to three thousand years, ever since the Breaking. I expect they'll be looking until the Wheel stops turning."

They reached Raen's fire, then, in the middle of the camp. The Seeker's wagon was yellow trimmed in red, and the spokes of its tall, red-rimmed wheels alternated red and yellow. A plump woman, as gray as Raen but smooth-cheeked still, came out of the wagon and paused on the steps at its back end, straightening a blue-fringed shawl on her shoulders. Her blouse was yellow and her skirt red, both bright. The combination made Perrin blink, and Egwene made a strangled sound.

When she saw the people following Raen, the woman came down with a welcoming smile. She was Ila, Raen's wife, a head taller than her husband, and she soon made Perrin forget about the colors of her clothes. She had a motherliness that reminded him of Mistress al'Vere and had him feeling welcome from her first smile.

Ila greeted Elyas as an old acquaintance, but with a distance that seemed to pain Raen. Elyas gave her a dry grin and a nod. Perrin and Egwene introduced themselves, and she clasped their hands in both of hers with much more warmth than she had shown Elyas, even hugging Egwene.

"Why, you're lovely, child," she said, cupping Egwene's chin and smiling. "And chilled to the bone, too, I expect. You sit close to the fire, Egwene. All of you sit. Supper is almost ready."

Fallen logs had been pulled around the fire for sitting. Elyas refused even that concession to civilization. He lounged on the ground, instead. Iron tripods held two small kettles over the flames, and an oven rested in the edge of the coals. Ila tended them.

As Perrin and the others were taking their places, a slender young man wearing green stripes strolled up to the fire. He gave Raen a hug and Ila a kiss, and ran a cool eye over Elyas and the Emond's Fielders. He was about the same age as Perrin, and he moved as if he were about to begin dancing with his next step.

"Well, Aram"—Ila smiled fondly—"you have decided to eat with your old grandparents for a change, have you?" Her smile slid over to Egwene as she bent to stir a kettle hanging over the cookfire. "I wonder why?"

Aram settled to an easy crouch with his arms crossed on his knees, across the fire from Egwene. "I am Aram," he told her in a low, confident voice. He no longer seemed aware that anyone was there except her. "I have waited for the first rose of spring, and now I find it at my grandfather's fire."

Perrin waited for Egwene to snicker, then saw that she was staring back at Aram. He looked at the young Tinker again. Aram had more than his share of good looks, he admitted. After a minute Perrin knew who the fellow reminded him of. Wil al'Seen, who had all the girls staring and whispering behind his back whenever he came up from Deven Ride to Emond's Field. Wil courted every girl in sight, and managed to convince every one of them that he was just being polite to all the others.

"Those dogs of yours," Perrin said loudly, and Egwene gave a start, "look as big as bears. I'm surprised you let the children play with them."

Aram's smile slipped, but when he looked at Perrin it came back again, even more sure than before. "They will not harm you. They make a show to frighten away danger, and warn us, but they are trained according to the Way of the Leaf."

"The Way of the Leaf?" Egwene said. "What is that?"

Aram gestured to the trees, his eyes fastened intently on hers. "The leaf lives its appointed time, and does not struggle against the wind that carries it away. The leaf does no harm, and finally falls to nourish new leaves. So it should be with all men. And women." Egwene stared back at him, a faint blush rising in her cheeks.

"But what does that mean?" Perrin said. Aram gave him an irritated glance, but it was Raen who answered.

"It means that no man should harm another for any reason whatsoever." The Seeker's eyes flickered to Elyas. "There is no excuse for violence. None. Not ever."

"What if somebody attacks you?" Perrin insisted. "What if somebody hits you, or tries to rob you, or kill you?"

Raen sighed, a patient sigh, as if Perrin was just not seeing what was so clear to him. "If a man hit me, I would ask him why he wanted to do such a thing. If he still wanted to hit me, I would run away, as I would if he wanted to rob or kill me. Much better that I let him take what he wanted, even my life, than that I should do violence. And I would hope that he was not harmed too greatly."

"But you said you wouldn't hurt him," Perrin said.

"I would not, but violence harms the one who does it as much as the one who receives it." Perrin looked doubtful. "You could cut down a tree with your axe," Raen said. "The axe does violence to the tree, and escapes unharmed. Is that how you see it? Wood is soft compared to steel, but the sharp steel is dulled as it chops, and the sap of the tree will rust and pit it. The mighty axe does violence to the helpless tree, and is harmed by it. So it is with men, though the harm is in the spirit."

"But—"

"Enough," Elyas growled, cutting Perrin off. "Raen, it's bad enough you trying to convert village younglings to that nonsense—it gets you in trouble almost everywhere you go, doesn't it?—but I didn't bring this lot here for you to work on them. Leave over."

"And leave them to you?" Ila said, grinding herbs between her palms and letting them trickle into one of the kettles. Her voice was calm, but her hands rubbed the herbs furiously. "Will you teach them your way, to kill or die? Will you lead them to the fate you seek for yourself, dying alone with only the ravens and your . . . your friends to squabble over your body?"

"Be at peace, Ila," Raen said gently, as if he had heard this all and more a hundred times. "He has been welcomed to our fire, my wife."

Ila subsided, but Perrin noticed that she made no apology. Instead she looked at Elyas and shook her head sadly, then dusted her hands and began taking spoons and pottery bowls from a red chest on the side of the wagon.

Raen turned back to Elyas. "My old friend, how many times must I tell you that we do not try to convert anyone. When village people are curious about our ways, we answer their questions. It is most often the young who ask, true, and sometimes one of them will come with us when we journey on, but it is of their own free will."

"You try telling that to some farm wife who's just found out her son or daughter has run off with you Tinkers," Elyas said wryly. "That's why the bigger towns won't even let you camp nearby. Villages put up with you for your mending things, but the cities don't need it, and they don't like you talking their young folks into running off."

"I would not know what the cities allow." Raen's patience seemed inexhaustible. He certainly did not appear to be getting angry at all. "There are always violent men in cities. In any case, I do not think the song could be found in a city."

"I don't mean to offend you, Seeker," Perrin said slowly, "but. . . . Well, I don't look for violence. I don't think I've even wrestled anybody in years, except for feastday games. But if somebody hit me, I'd hit him back. If I didn't, I would just be encouraging him to think he could hit me whenever he wanted to. Some people think they can take advantage of others, and if you don't let them know they can't, they'll just go around bullying anybody weaker than they are."

"Some people," Aram said with a heavy sadness, "can never overcome their baser instincts." He said it with a look at Perrin that made it clear he was not talking about the bullies Perrin spoke of.

"I'll bet you get to run away a lot," Perrin said, and the young Tinker's face tightened in a way that had nothing to do with the Way of the Leaf.

"I think it is interesting," Egwene said, glaring at Perrin, "to meet someone who doesn't believe his muscles can solve every problem."

Aram's good spirits returned, and he stood, offering her his hands with a smile. "Let me show you our camp. There is dancing."

"I would like that." She smiled back.

Ila straightened from taking loaves of bread from the small iron oven. "But supper is ready, Aram."

"I'll eat with mother," Aram said over his shoulder as he drew Egwene away from the wagon by her hand. "We will both eat with mother." He flashed a triumphant smile at Perrin. Egwene was laughing as they ran.

Perrin got to his feet, then stopped. It was not as if she could come to any harm, not if the camp followed this Way of the Leaf as Raen said. Looking at Raen and Ila, both staring dejectedly after their grandson, he said, "I'm sorry. I am a guest, and I shouldn't have—"

"Don't be foolish," Ila said soothingly. "It was his fault, not yours. Sit down and eat."

"Aram is a troubled young man," Raen added sadly. "He is a good boy, but sometimes I think he finds the Way of the Leaf a hard way. Some do, I fear. Please. My fire is yours. Please?"

Perrin sat back down slowly, still feeling awkward. "What happens to somebody who can't follow the Way?" he asked. "A Tinker, I mean."

Raen and Ila exchanged a worried look, and Raen said, "They leave us. The Lost go to live in the villages."

Ila stared in the direction her grandson had gone. "The Lost cannot be happy." She sighed, but her face was placid again when she handed out the bowls and spoons.

Perrin stared at the ground, wishing he had not asked, and there was no more talk while Ila filled their bowls with a thick vegetable stew and handed out thick slices of her crusty bread, nor while they ate. The stew was delicious, and Perrin finished three bowls before he stopped. Elyas, he noted with a grin, emptied four.

After the meal Raen filled his pipe, and Elyas produced his own and stuffed it from Raen's oilskin pouch. When the lighting and tamping and relighting were done, they settled back in silence. Ila took out a bundle of knitting. The sun was only a blaze of red above the treetops to the west. The camp had settled in for the night, but the bustle did not slow, only changed. The musicians who had been playing when they entered the camp had been replaced by others, and even more people than before danced in the light of the fires, their shadows leaping against the wagons. Somewhere in the camp a chorus of male voices rose. Perrin slid down in front of the log and soon felt himself dosing.

After a time Raen said, "Have you visited any of the Tuatha'an, Elyas, since you were with us last spring?"

Perrin's eyes drifted open and half shut again.

"No," Elyas replied around his pipestem. "I don't like being around too many people at once."

Raen chuckled. "Especially people who live in a way so opposite to your own, eh? No, my old friend, don't worry. I gave up years ago hoping you would come to the Way. But I have heard a story since last we met, and if you have not heard it yet, it might interest you. It interests me, and I have heard it again and again, every time we meet others of the People."

"I'll listen."

"It begins in the spring two years ago, with a band of the People who were crossing the Waste by the northern route."

Perrin's eyes shot open. "The Waste? The Aiel Waste? They were crossing the Aiel Waste?"

"Some people can enter the Waste without being bothered," Elyas said. "Gleemen. Peddlers, if they're honest. The Tuatha'an cross the Waste all the time. Merchants from Cairhien used to, before the Tree, and the Aiel War."

"The Aielmen avoid us," Raen said sadly, "though many of us have tried to speak with them. They watch us from a distance, but they will not come near us, nor let us come near them. Sometimes I worry that they might know the song, though I suppose it isn't likely. Among Aiel, men do not sing, you know. Isn't that strange? From the time an Aiel boy becomes a man he will not sing anything but battle chants, or their dirge for the slain. I have heard them singing over their dead, and over those they have killed. That song is one to make the stones weep." Ila, listening, nodded agreement over her knitting.

Perrin did some quick rethinking. He had thought the Tinkers must be afraid all the time, with all this talk of running away, but no one who was afraid would even think of crossing the Aiel Waste. From what he had heard, no one who was sane would try crossing the Waste.

"If this is some story about a song," Elyas began, but Raen shook his head.

"No, my old friend, not a song. I am not sure I know what it is about." He turned his attention to Perrin. "Young Aiel often travel into the Blight. Some of the young men go alone, thinking for some reason that they have been called to kill the Dark One. Most go in small groups. To hunt Trollocs." Raen shook his head sadly, and when he went on his voice was heavy. "Two years ago a band of the People crossing the Waste about a hundred miles south of the Blight found one of these groups."

"Young women," Ila put in, as sorrowful as her husband. "Little more than girls."

Perrin made a surprised sound, and Elyas grinned at him wryly.

"Aiel girls don't have to tend house and cook if they don't want to, boy. The ones who want to be warriors, instead, join one of the war-rior societies, *Far Dareis Mai*, the Maidens of the Spear, and fight right alongside the men."

Perrin shook his head. Elyas chuckled at his expression.

Raen took up the story again, distaste and perplexity mingled in his voice. "The young women were all dead except one, and she was dy-ing. She crawled to the wagons. It was clear she knew they were Tua-tha'an. Her loathing outweighed her pain, but she had a message so important to her that she must pass it on to someone, even us, before she died. Men went to see if they could help any of the others—there was a trail of her blood to follow—but all were dead, and so were three times their number in Trollocs."

Elyas sat up, his pipe almost falling from between his teeth. "A hundred miles into the Waste? Impossible! *Djevik K'Shar*, that's what

Trollocs call the Waste. The Dying Ground. They wouldn't go a hundred miles into the Waste if all the Myrddraal in the Blight were driving them."

"You know an awful lot about Trollocs, Elyas," Perrin said.

"Go on with your story," Elyas told Raen gruffly.

"From trophies the Aiel carried, it was obvious they were coming back from the Blight. The Trollocs had followed, but by the tracks only a few lived to return after killing the Aiel. As for the girl, she would not let anyone touch her, even to tend her wounds. But she seized the Seeker of that band by his coat, and this is what she said, word for word. 'Leafblighter means to blind the Eye of the World, Lost One. He means to slay the Great Serpent. Warn the People, Lost One. Sightburner comes. Tell them to stand ready for He Who Comes With the Dawn. Tell them. . . .' And then she died. Leafblighter and Sightburner," Raen added to Perrin, "are Aiel names for the Dark One, but I don't understand another word of it. Yet she thought it important enough to approach those she obviously despised, to pass it on with her last breath. But to who? We are ourselves, the People, but I hardly think she meant it for us. The Aiel? They would not let us tell them if we tried." He sighed heavily. "She called us the Lost. I never knew before how much they loathe us." Ila set her knitting in her lap and touched his head gently.

"Something they learned in the Blight," Elyas mused. "But none of it makes sense. Slay the Great Serpent? Kill time itself? And blind the Eye of the World? As well say he's going to starve a rock. Maybe she was babbling, Raen. Wounded, dying, she could have lost her grip on what was real. Maybe she didn't even know who those Tuatha'an were."

"She knew what she was saying, and to whom she was saying it. Something more important to her than her own life, and we cannot even understand it. When I saw you walking into our camp, I thought perhaps we would find the answer at last, since you were"—Elyas made a quick motion with his hand, and Raen changed what he had been going to say—"are a friend, and know many strange things."

"Not about this," Elyas said in a tone that put an end to talk. The silence around the campfire was broken only by the music and laughter drifting from other parts of the night-shrouded camp.

Lying with his shoulders propped on one of the logs around the fire, Perrin tried puzzling out the Aiel woman's message, but it made no more sense to him than it had to Raen or Elyas. The Eye of the World. That had been in his dreams, more than once, but he did not want to think about those dreams. Elyas, now. There was a question there he would like answered. What had Raen been about to say about the bearded man, and why had Elyas cut him off? He had no luck with that, either. He was trying to imagine what Aiel girls were like—going into the Blight, where only Warders went that he had ever heard; fighting Trollocs—when he heard Egwene coming back, singing to herself.

Scrambling to his feet, he went to meet her at the edge of the firelight. She stopped short, looking at him with her head tilted to one side. In the dark he could not read her expression.

"You've been gone a long time," he said. "Did you have fun?"

"We ate with his mother," she answered. "And then we danced . . . and laughed. It seems like forever since I danced."

"He reminds me of Wil al'Seen. You always had sense enough not to let Wil put you in his pocket."

"Aram is a gentle boy who is fun to be with," she said in a tight voice. "He makes me laugh."

Perrin sighed. "I'm sorry. I'm glad you had fun dancing."

Abruptly she flung her arms around him, weeping on his shirt. Awkwardly he patted her hair. *Rand would know what to do,* he thought. Rand had an easy way with girls. Not like him, who never knew what to do or say. "I told you I'm sorry, Egwene. I really am glad you had fun dancing. Really."

"Tell me they're alive," she mumbled into his chest.

"What?"

She pushed back to arm's length, her hands on his arms, and looked up at him in the darkness. "Rand and Mat. The others. Tell me they are alive."

He took a deep breath and looked around uncertainly. "They are alive," he said finally.

"Good." She scrubbed at her cheeks with quick fingers. "That is what I wanted to hear. Good night, Perrin. Sleep well." Standing on tiptoe, she brushed a kiss across his cheek and hurried past him before he could speak.

He turned to watch her. Ila rose to meet her, and the two women went into the wagon talking quietly. *Rand might understand it,* he thought, *but I don't.*

In the distant night the wolves howled the first thin sliver of the new moon toward the horizon, and he shivered. Tomorrow would be time enough to worry about the wolves again. He was wrong. They were waiting to greet him in his dreams.

CHAPTER
26

Whitebridge

The last unsteady note of what had been barely recognizable as "The Wind That Shakes the Willow" faded mercifully away, and Mat lowered Thom's gold-and-silver-chased flute. Rand took his hands from his ears. A sailor coiling a line on the deck nearby heaved a loud sigh of relief. For a moment the only sounds were the water slapping against the hull, the rhythmic creak of the oars, and now and again the hum of rigging strummed by the wind. The wind blew dead on to the *Spray*'s bow, and the useless sails were furled.

"I suppose I should thank you," Thom Merrilin muttered finally, "for teaching me how true the old saying is. Teach him how you will, a pig will never play the flute." The sailor burst out laughing, and Mat raised the flute as if to throw it at him. Deftly, Thom snagged the instrument from Mat's fist and fitted it into its hard leather case. "I thought all you shepherds whiled away the time with the flock playing the pipes or the flute. That will show me to trust what I don't know firsthand."

"Rand's the shepherd," Mat grumbled. "He plays the pipes, not me."

"Yes, well, he does have a little aptitude. Perhaps we had better
work on juggling, boy. At least you show some talent for that."

"Thom," Rand said, "I don't know why you're trying so hard." He
glanced at the sailor and lowered his voice. "After all, we aren't really
trying to become gleemen. It's only something to hide behind until we
find Moiraine and the others."

Thom tugged at an end of his mustache and seemed to be studying
the smooth, dark brown leather of the flute case on his knees. "What
if you don't find them, boy? There's nothing to say they're even still
alive."

"They're alive," Rand said firmly. He turned to Mat for support,
but Mat's eyebrows were pinched down on his nose, and his mouth
was a thin line, and his eyes were fixed on the deck. "Well, speak up,"
Rand told him. "You can't be that mad over not being able to play
the flute. I can't either, not very well. You never wanted to play the
flute before."

Mat looked up, still frowning. "What if they are dead?" he said
softly. "We have to accept facts, right?"

At that moment the lookout in the bow sang out, "Whitebridge!
Whitebridge ahead!"

For a long minute, unwilling to believe that Mat could say something
like that so casually, Rand held his friend's gaze amid the scramble of
sailors preparing to put in. Mat glowered at him with his head pulled
down between his shoulders. There was so much Rand wanted to say,
but he could not manage to get it all into words. They had to believe
the others were alive. They had to. *Why?* nagged a voice in the back
of his head. *So it will all turn out like one of Thom's stories? The heroes
find the treasure and defeat the villain and live happily ever after? Some
of his stories don't end that way. Sometimes even heroes die. Are you
a hero, Rand al'Thor? Are you a hero, sheepherder?*

Abruptly Mat flushed and pulled his eyes away. Freed from his
thoughts, Rand jumped up to move through the hurly-burly to the rail.
Mat came after him slowly, not even making an effort to dodge the
sailors who ran across his path.

Men dashed about the boat, bare feet thumping the deck, hauling
on ropes, tying off some lines and untying others. Some brought up
big oilskin bags stuffed almost to bursting with wool, while others readied cables as thick as Rand's wrist. Despite their haste, they moved
with the assurance of men who had done it all a thousand times before,
but Captain Domon stumped up and down the deck shouting orders
and cursing those who did not move fast enough to suit him.

Rand's attention was all for what lay ahead, coming plainly into sight as they rounded a slight bend of the Arinelle. He had heard of it, in song and story and peddlers' tales, but now he would actually see the legend.

The White Bridge arched high over the wide waters, twice as high as the *Spray*'s mast and more, and from end to end it gleamed milky white in the sunlight, gathering the light until it seemed to glow. Spidery piers of the same stuff plunged into the strong currents, appearing too frail to support the weight and width of the bridge. It looked all of one piece, as if it had been carved from a single stone or molded by a giant's hand, broad and tall, leaping the river with an airy grace that almost made the eye forget its size. All in all it dwarfed the town that sprawled about its foot on the east bank, though Whitebridge was larger by far than Emond's Field, with houses of stone and brick as tall as those in Taren Ferry and wooden docks like thin fingers sticking out into the river. Small boats dotted the Arinelle thickly, fishermen hauling their nets. And over it all the White Bridge towered and shone.

"It looks like glass," Rand said to no one in particular.

Captain Domon paused behind him and tucked his thumbs behind his broad belt. "Nay, lad. Whatever it be, it no be glass. Never so hard the rains come, it no be slippery, and the best chisel and the strongest arm no make a mark on it."

"A remnant from the Age of Legends," Thom said. "I have always thought it must be."

The captain gave a dour grunt. "Mayhap. But still useful despite. Could be someone else built it. Does no *have* to be Aes Sedai work, Fortune prick me. It no has to be so old as all that. Put your back into it, you bloody fool!" He hurried off down the deck.

Rand stared even more wonderingly. *From the Age of Legends.* Made by Aes Sedai, then. That was why Captain Domon felt the way he did, for all his talk about the wonder and strangeness of the world. Aes Sedai work. One thing to hear about it, another to see it, and touch it. *You know that, don't you?* For an instant it seemed to Rand that a shadow rippled through the milk-white structure. He pulled his eyes away, to the docks coming nearer, but the bridge still loomed in the corner of his vision.

"We made it, Thom," he said, then forced a laugh. "And no mutiny."

The gleeman only harrumphed and blew out his mustaches, but two sailors readying a cable nearby gave Rand a sharp glance, then bent

quickly back to their work. He stopped laughing and tried not to look
at the two for the rest of the approach to Whitebridge.

The *Spray* curved smoothly in beside the first dock, thick timbers
sitting on heavy, tar-coated pilings, and stopped with a backing of oars
that swirled the water to froth around the blades. As the oars were
drawn in, sailors tossed cables to men on the dock, who fastened them
off with a flourish, while other crewmen slung the bags of wool over
the side to protect the hull from the dock pilings.

Before the boat was even pulled snug against the dock, carriages
appeared at the end of the dock, tall and lacquered shiny black, each
one with a name painted on the door in large letters, gold or scarlet.
The carriages' passengers hurried up the gangplank as soon as it
dropped in place, smooth-faced men in long velvet coats and silk-lined
cloaks and cloth slippers, each followed by a plainly dressed servant
carrying his iron-bound moneybox.

They approached Captain Domon with painted smiles that slipped
when he abruptly roared in their faces. "You!" He thrust a thick finger
past them, stopping Floran Gelb in his tracks at the length of the boat.
The bruise on Gelb's forehead from Rand's boot had faded away, but
he still fingered the spot from time to time as if to remind himself.
"You've slept on watch for the last time on my vessel! Or on any
vessel, if I have my way of it. Choose your own side—the dock or the
river—but off my vessel *now!*"

Gelb hunched his shoulders, and his eyes glittered hate at Rand and
his friends, at Rand especially, a poisonous glare. The wiry man
looked around the deck for support, but there was little hope in that
look. One by one, every man in the crew straightened from what he
was doing and stared back coldly. Gelb wilted visibly, but then his
glare returned, twice as strong as it had been. With a muttered curse
he darted below to the crew's quarters. Domon sent two men after
him to see he did no mischief and dismissed him with a grunt. When
the captain turned back to them, the merchants took up their smiles
and bows as if they had never been interrupted.

At a word from Thom, Mat and Rand began gathering their things
together. There was not much aside from the clothes on their backs,
not for any of them. Rand had his blanketroll and saddlebags, and his
father's sword. He held the sword for a minute, and homesickness
rolled over him so strongly that his eyes stung. He wondered if he
would ever see Tam again. Or home? Home. *Going to spend the rest
of your life running, running and afraid of your own dreams.* With a
shuddering sigh he slipped the belt around his waist over his coat.

Gelb came back on deck, followed by his twin shadows. He looked straight ahead, but Rand could still feel hatred coming off him in waves. Back rigid and face dark, Gelb walked stiff-legged down the gangplank and pushed roughly into the thin crowd on the dock. In a minute he was gone from sight, vanished beyond the merchants' carriages.

There were not a great many people on the dock, and those were a plainly dressed mix of workmen, fishermen mending nets, and a few townspeople who had come out to see the first boat of the year to come downriver from Saldaea. None of the girls was Egwene and no one looked the least bit like Moiraine, or Lan, or anyone else Rand was hoping to see.

"Maybe they didn't come down to the dock," he said.

"Maybe," Thom replied curtly. He settled his instrument cases on his back with care. "You two keep an eye out for Gelb. He will make trouble if he can. We want to pass through Whitebridge so softly that nobody remembers we were here five minutes after we're gone."

Their cloaks flapped in the wind as they walked to the gangplank. Mat carried his bow crossed in front on his chest. Even after all their days on the boat, it still got a few looks from the crewmen; their bows were short affairs.

Captain Domon left the merchants to intercept Thom at the gangplank.

"You be leaving me now, gleeman? Can I no talk you into continuing on? I be going all the way down to Illian, where folk have a proper regard for gleemen. There be no finer place in the world for your art. I'd get you there in good time for the Feast of Sefan. The competitions, you know. A hundred gold marks for the best telling of *The Great Hunt of the Horn*."

"A great prize, Captain," Thom replied with an elaborate bow and a flourish of his cloak that set the patches to fluttering, "and great competitions, which rightly draw gleemen from the whole world over. But," he added dryly, "I fear we could not afford the fare at the rates you charge."

"Aye, well, as to that. . . ." The captain produced a leather purse from his coat pocket and tossed it to Thom. It clinked when Thom caught it. "Your fares back, and a bit more besides. The damage was no so bad as I thought, and you've worked your way and more with your tales and your harp. I could maybe manage as much again if you stay aboard to the Sea of Storms. And I would set you ashore in Illian. A good gleeman can make his fortune there, even aside from the competitions."

Thom hesitated, weighing the purse on his palm, but Rand spoke up. "We're meeting friends here, Captain, and going on to Caemlyn together. We'll have to see Illian another time."

Thom's mouth twisted wryly, then he blew out his long mustaches and tucked the purse into his pocket. "Perhaps if the people we are to meet are not here, Captain."

"Aye," Domon said sourly. "You think on it. Too bad I can no keep Gelb aboard to take the others' anger, but I do what I say I will do. I suppose I must ease up now, even if it means taking three times as long to reach Illian as I should. Well, mayhap those Trollocs *were* after you three."

Rand blinked but kept silent, but Mat was not so cautious.

"Why do you think they weren't?" he demanded. "They were after the same treasure we were hunting."

"Mayhap," the captain grunted, sounding unconvinced. He combed thick fingers through his beard, then pointed at the pocket where Thom had put the purse. "Twice that if you come back to keep the men's minds off how hard I work them. Think on it. I sail with the first light on the morrow." He turned on his heel and strode back to the merchants, arms spreading wide as he began an apology for keeping them waiting.

Thom still hesitated, but Rand hustled him down the gangplank without giving him a chance to argue, and the gleeman let himself be herded. A murmur passed through the people on the dock as they saw Thom's patch-covered cloak, and some called out to discover where he would be performing. *So much for not being noticed,* Rand thought, dismayed. By sundown it would be all over Whitebridge that there was a gleeman in town. He hurried Thom along, though, and Thom, wrapped in sulky silence, did not even try to slow down enough to preen under the attention.

The carriage drivers looked down at Thom with interest from their high perches, but apparently the dignity of their positions forbade shouting. With no idea of where to go exactly, Rand turned up the street that ran along the river and under the bridge.

"We need to find Moiraine and the others," he said. "And fast. We should have thought of changing Thom's cloak."

Thom suddenly shook himself and stopped dead. "An innkeeper will be able to tell us if they're here, or if they've passed through. The right innkeeper. Innkeepers have all the news and gossip. If they aren't here. . . ." He looked back and forth from Rand to Mat. "We have to talk, we three." Cloak swirling around his ankles, he set off into the town, away from the river. Rand and Mat had to step quickly to keep up.

The broad, milk-white arch that gave the town its name dominated Whitebridge as much close up as it did from afar, but once Rand was in the streets he realized that the town was every bit as big as Baerlon, though not so crowded with people. A few carts moved in the streets, pulled by horse or ox or donkey or man, but no carriages. Those most likely all belonged to the merchants and were clustered down at the dock.

Shops of every description lined the streets, and many of the tradesmen worked in front of their establishments, under the signs swinging in the wind. They passed a man mending pots, and a tailor holding folds of cloth up to the light for a customer. A shoemaker, sitting in his doorway, tapped his hammer on the heel of a boot. Hawkers cried their services at sharpening knives and scissors, or tried to interest the passersby in their skimpy trays of fruit or vegetables, but none was getting much interest. Shops selling food had the same pitiful displays of produce Rand remembered from Baerlon. Even the fishmongers displayed only small piles of small fish, for all the boats on the river. Times were not really hard yet, but everyone could see what was coming if the weather did not change soon, and those faces that were not fixed into worried frowns seemed to stare at something unseen, something unpleasant.

Where the White Bridge came down in the center of the town was a big square, paved with stones worn by generations of feet and wagon wheels. Inns surrounded the square, and shops, and tall, red brick houses with signs out front bearing the same names Rand had seen on the carriages at the dock. It was into one of those inns, seemingly chosen at random, that Thom ducked. The sign over the door, swinging in the wind, had a striding man with a bundle on his back on one side and the same man with his head on a pillow on the other, and proclaimed The Wayfarers' Rest.

The common room stood empty except for the fat innkeeper drawing ale from a barrel and two men in rough workman's clothes staring glumly into their mugs at a table in the back. Only the innkeeper looked up when they came in. A shoulder-high wall split the room in two from front to back, with tables and a blazing fireplace on each side. Rand wondered idly if all innkeepers were fat and losing their hair.

Rubbing his hands together briskly, Thom commented to the innkeeper on the late cold and ordered hot spiced wine, then added quietly, "Is there somewhere my friends and I could talk without being disturbed?"

The innkeeper nodded to the low wall. "The other side that's as best I've got unless you want to take a room. For when sailors come up from the river. Seems like half the crews got grudges against the other half. I won't have my place broke up by fights, so I keep them apart." He had been eyeing Thom's cloak the whole while, and now he cocked his head to one side, a sly look in his eyes. "You staying? Haven't had a gleeman here in some time. Folks would pay real good for something as would take their minds off things. I'd even take some off on your room and meals."

Unnoticed, Rand thought glumly.

"You are too generous," Thom said with a smooth bow. "Perhaps I will take up your offer. But for now, a little privacy."

"I'll bring your wine. Good money here for a gleeman."

The tables on the far side of the wall were all empty, but Thom chose one right in the middle of the space. "So no one can listen without us knowing," he explained. "Did you hear that fellow? He'll take some off. Why, I'd double his custom just by sitting here. Any honest innkeeper gives a gleeman room and board and a good bit besides."

The bare table was none too clean, and the floor had not been swept in days if not weeks. Rand looked around and grimaced. Master al'Vere would not have let his inn get that dirty if he had had to climb out of a sickbed to see to it. "We're only after information. Remember?"

"Why here?" Mat demanded. "We passed other inns that looked cleaner."

"Straight on from the bridge," Thom said, "is the road to Caemlyn. Anyone passing through Whitebridge comes through this square, unless they're going by river, and we know your friends aren't doing that. If there is no word of them here, it doesn't exist. Let me do the talking. This has to be done carefully."

Just then the innkeeper appeared, three battered pewter mugs gripped in one fist by the handles. The fat man flicked at the table with a towel, set the mugs down, and took Thom's money. "If you stay, you won't have to pay for your drinks. Good wine, here."

Thom's smile touched only his mouth. "I will think on it, innkeeper. What news is there? We have been away from hearing things."

"Big news, that's what. Big news."

The innkeeper draped the towel over his shoulder and pulled up a chair. He crossed his arms on the table, took root with a long sigh, saying what a comfort it was to get off his feet. His name was Bartim, and he went on about his feet in detail, about corns and bunions and how much time he spent standing and what he soaked them in, until Thom mentioned the news again, and then he shifted over with hardly a pause.

The news was just as big as he said it was. Logain, the false Dragon, had been captured after a big battle near Lugard while he was trying to move his army from Ghealdan to Tear. The Prophecies, they understood? Thom nodded, and Bartim went on. The roads in the south were packed with people, the lucky ones with what they could carry on their backs. Thousands fleeing in all directions.

"None"—Bartim chuckled wryly—"supported Logain, of course. Oh, no, you won't find many to admit to that, not now. Just refugees trying to find a safe place during the troubles."

Aes Sedai had been involved in taking Logain, of course. Bartim spat on the floor when he said that, and again when he said they were taking the false Dragon north to Tar Valon. Bartim was a decent man, he said, a respectable man, and Aes Sedai could all go back to the Blight where they came from and take Tar Valon with them, as far as he was concerned. He would get no closer to an Aes Sedai than a thousand miles, if he had his way. Of course, they were stopping at every village and town on the way north to display Logain, so he had heard. To show people that the false Dragon had been taken and the world was safe again. He would have liked to see that, even if it did mean getting close to Aes Sedai. He was halfway tempted to go to Caemlyn.

"They'll be taking him there to show to Queen Morgase." The innkeeper touched his forehead respectfully. "I've never seen the Queen. Man ought to see his own Queen, don't you think?"

Logain could do "things," and the way Bartim's eyes shifted and his tongue darted across his lips made it clear what he meant. He had seen the last false Dragon, two years ago, when he was paraded through the countryside, but that was just some fellow who thought he could make himself a king. There had been no need for Aes Sedai, that time. Soldiers had had him chained up on a wagon. A sullen-looking fellow who moaned in the middle of the wagonbed, covering his head with his arms whenever people threw stones or poked him with sticks. There had been a lot of that, and the soldiers had done nothing to stop it, as long as they did not kill the fellow. Best to let the people see he was nothing special after all. He could not do "things." This Logain would be something to see, though. Something for Bartim to tell his grandchildren about. If only the inn would let him get away.

Rand listened with an interest that did not have to be faked. When Padan Fain had brought word to Emond's Field of a false Dragon, a man actually wielding the Power, it had been the biggest news to come into the Two Rivers in years. What had happened since had pushed it to the back of his mind, but it was still the sort of thing people would be talking about for years, and telling their grandchildren about, too. Bartim would probably tell his that he had seen Logain whether he did or not. Nobody would ever think what happened to some village folk from the Two Rivers was worth talking about, not unless they were Two Rivers people themselves.

"That," Thom said, "would be something to make a story of, a story they'd tell for a thousand years. I wish I had been there." He sounded as if it was the simple truth, and Rand thought it really was. "I might try to see him anyway. You didn't say what route they were taking. Perhaps there are some other travelers around? They might have heard the route."

Bartim waved a grubby hand dismissively. "North, that's all anybody knows around here. You want to see him, go to Caemlyn. That's all I know, and if there's anything to know in Whitebridge, I know it."

"No doubt you do," Thom said smoothly. "I expect a lot of strangers passing through stop here. Your sign caught my eye from the foot of the White Bridge."

"Not just from the west, I'll have you know. Two days ago there was a fellow in here, an Illianer, with a proclamation all done up with seals and ribbons. Read it right out there in the square. Said he's taking it all the way to the Mountains of Mist, maybe even to the Aryth Ocean, if the passes are open. Said they've sent men to read it in every land in the world." The innkeeper shook his head. "The Mountains of Mist. I hear they're covered with fog all the year round, and there's things in the fog will strip the flesh off your bones before you can run." Mat snickered, earning a sharp look from Bartim.

Thom leaned forward intently. "What did the proclamation say?"

"Why, the hunt for the Horn, of course," Bartim exclaimed. "Didn't I say that? The Illianers are calling on everybody as will swear their lives to the hunt to gather in Illian. Can you imagine that? Swearing your life to a legend? I suppose they'll find some fools. There's always fools around. This fellow claimed the end of the world is coming. The last battle with the Dark One." He chuckled, but it had a hollow sound, a man laughing to convince himself something really was worth laughing at. "Guess they think the Horn of Valere has to be found before it happens. Now what do you think of that?" He chewed a knuckle pensively for a minute. "Course, I don't know as I could argue with them after this winter. The winter, and this fellow Logain, and those other two before, as well. Why all these fellows the last few years claiming to be the Dragon? And the winter. Must mean something. What do you think?"

Thom did not seem to hear him. In a soft voice the gleeman began to recite to himself.

> "In the last, lorn fight
> 'gainst the fall of long night,
> the mountains stand guard,
> and the dead shall be ward,
> for the grave is no bar to my call."

"That's it." Bartim grinned as if he could already see the crowds handing him their money while they listened to Thom. "That's it. *The Great Hunt of the Horn.* You tell that one, and they'll be hanging from the rafters in here. Everybody's heard about the proclamation."

Thom still seemed to be a thousand miles away, so Rand said, "We're looking for some friends who were coming this way. From the west. Have there been many strangers passing through in the last week or two?"

"Some," Bartim said slowly. "There's always some, from east and west both." He looked at each of them in turn, suddenly wary. "What do they look like, these friends of yours?"

Rand opened his mouth, but Thom, abruptly back from wherever he had been, gave him a sharp, silencing look. With an exasperated sigh the gleeman turned to the innkeeper. "Two men and three women," he said reluctantly. "They may be together, or maybe not." He gave thumbnail sketches, painting each one in just a few words, enough for anyone who had seen them to recognize without giving away anything about who they were.

Bartim rubbed one hand over his head, disarranging his thinning hair, and stood up slowly. "Forget about performing here, gleeman. In fact, I'd appreciate it if you drank your wine and left. Leave Whitebridge, if you're smart."

"Someone else has been asking after them?" Thom took a drink, as if the answer were the least important thing in the world, and raised an eyebrow at the innkeeper. "Who would that be?"

Bartim scrubbed his hand through his hair again and shifted his feet on the point of walking away, then nodded to himself. "About a week ago, as near as I can say, a weaselly fellow came over the bridge. Crazy, everybody thought. Always talking to himself, never stopped moving even when he was standing still. Asked about the same people . . . some of them. He asked like it was important, then acted like he didn't care what the answer was. Half the time he was saying as he had to wait here for them, and the other half as he had to go on, he was in a hurry. One minute he was whining and begging, the next making demands like a king. Near got himself a thrashing a time or two, crazy or not. The Watch almost took him in custody for his own safety. He went off toward Caemlyn that same day, talking to himself and crying. Crazy, like I said."

Rand looked at Thom and Mat questioningly, and they both shook their heads. If this weaselly fellow was looking for them, he was still nobody they recognized.

"Are you sure it was the same people he wanted?" Rand asked.

"Some of them. The fighting man, and the woman in silk. But it wasn't them as he cared about. It was three country boys." His eyes slid across Rand and Mat and away again so fast that Rand was not sure if he had really seen the look or imagined it. "He was desperate to find them. But crazy, like I said."

Rand shivered, and wondered who the crazy man could be, and why he was looking for them. *A Darkfriend? Would Ba'alzamon use a madman?*

"He was crazy, but the other one. . . ." Bartim's eyes shifted uneasily, and his tongue ran over his lips as if he could not find enough spit to moisten them. "Next day . . . next day the other one came for the first time." He fell silent.

"The other one?" Thom prompted finally.

Bartim looked around, although their side of the divided room was still empty except for them. He even raised up on his toes and looked over the low wall. When he finally spoke, it was in a whispered rush.

"All in black he is. Keeps the hood of his cloak pulled up so you can't see his face, but you can feel him looking at you, feel it like an icicle shoved into your spine. He . . . he spoke to me." He flinched and stopped to chew at his lip before going on. "Sounded like a snake crawling through dead leaves. Fair turned my stomach to ice. Every time as he comes back, he asks the same questions. Same questions the crazy man asked. Nobody ever sees him coming—he's just there all of a sudden, day or night, freezing you where you stand. People are starting to look over their shoulders. Worst of it is, the gatetenders claim as he's never passed through any of the gates, coming or going."

Rand worked at keeping his face blank; he clenched his jaw until his teeth ached. Mat scowled, and Thom studied his wine. The word none of them wanted to say hung in the air between them. Myrddraal.

"I think I'd remember if I ever met anyone like that," Thom said after a minute.

Bartim's head bobbed furiously. "Burn me, but you would. Light's truth, you would. He . . . he wants the same lot as the crazy man, only he says as there's a girl with them. And"—he glanced sideways at Thom—"and a white-haired gleeman."

Thom's eyebrows shot up in what Rand was sure was unfeigned surprise. "A white-haired gleeman? Well, I'm hardly the only gleeman in the world with a little age on him. I assure you, I don't know this fellow, and he can have no reason to be looking for me."

"That's as may be," Bartim said glumly. "He didn't say it in so many words, but I got the impression as he would be very displeased with anyone as tried to help these people, or tried to hide them from him. Anyway, I'll tell you what I told him. I haven't seen any of them, nor heard tell of them, and that's the truth. Not any of them," he finished pointedly. Abruptly he slapped Thom's money down on the table. "Just finish your wine and go. All right? All right?" And he trundled away as fast as he could, looking over his shoulder.

"A Fade," Mat breathed when the innkeeper was gone. "I should have known they'd be looking for us here."

"And he'll be back," Thom said, leaning across the table and lowering his voice. "I say we sneak back to the boat and take Captain Domon up on his offer. The hunt will center on the road to Caemlyn while we're on our way to Illian, a thousand miles from where the Myrddraal expect us."

"No," Rand said firmly. "We wait for Moiraine and the others in Whitebridge, or we go on to Caemlyn. One or the other, Thom. That's what we decided."

"That's crazed, boy. Things have changed. You listen to me. No matter what this innkeeper says, when a Myrddraal stares at him, he'll tell all about us down to what we had to drink and how much dust we had on our boots." Rand shivered, remembering the Fade's eyeless stare. "As for Caemlyn. . . . You think the Halfmen don't know you want to get to Tar Valon? It's a good time to be on a boat headed south."

"No, Thom." Rand had to force the words out, thinking of being a thousand miles from where the Fades were looking, but he took a deep breath and managed to firm his voice. "No."

"Think, boy. Illian! There isn't a grander city on the face of the earth. And the Great Hunt of the Horn! There hasn't been a Hunt of the Horn in near four hundred years. A whole new cycle of stories waiting to be made. Just think. You never dreamed of anything like it. By the time the Myrddraal figure out where you've gone to, you'll be old and gray and so tired of watching your grandchildren you won't care if they do find you."

Rand's face took on a stubborn set. "How many times do I have to say no? They'll find us wherever we go. There'd be Fades waiting in Illian, too. And how do we escape the dreams? I want to know what's happening to me, Thom, and why. I'm going to Tar Valon. With Moiraine if I can; without her if I have to. Alone, if I have to. I need to know."

"But Illian, boy! And a safe way out, downriver while they're looking for you in another direction. Blood and ashes, a dream can't hurt you."

Rand kept silent. *A dream can't hurt? Do dream thorns draw real blood?* He almost wished he had told Thom about that dream, too. *Do you dare tell anybody? Ba'alzamon is in your dreams, but what's between dreaming and waking, now? Who do you dare to tell that the Dark One is touching you?*

Thom seemed to understand. The gleeman's face softened. "Even *those* dreams, lad. They are still just dreams, aren't they? For the Light's sake, Mat, talk to him. I know you don't want to go to Tar Valon, at least."

Mat's face reddened, half embarrassment and half anger. He avoided looking at Rand and scowled at Thom instead. "Why are you going to all this fuss and bother? You want to go back to the boat? Go back to the boat. We'll take care of ourselves."

The gleeman's thin shoulders shook with silent laughter, but his voice was anger tight. "You think you know enough about Myrddraal to escape by yourself, do you? You're ready to walk into Tar Valon alone and hand yourself over to the Amyrlin Seat? Can you even tell one Ajah from another? The Light burn me, boy, if you think you can even get to Tar Valon alone, you tell me to go."

"Go," Mat growled, sliding a hand under his cloak. Rand realized with a shock that he was gripping the dagger from Shadar Logoth, maybe even ready to use it.

Raucous laughter broke out on the other side of the low wall dividing the room, and a scornful voice spoke up loudly.

"Trollocs? Put on a gleeman's cloak, man! You're drunk! Trollocs! Borderland fables!"

The words doused anger like a pot of cold water. Even Mat half turned to the wall, eyes widening.

Rand stood just enough to see over the wall, then ducked back down again with a sinking feeling in his stomach. Floran Gelb sat on the other side of the wall, at the table in the back with the two men who had been there when they came in. They were laughing at him, but they were listening. Bartim was wiping a table that badly needed it, not looking at Gelb and the two men, but he was listening, too, scrubbing one spot over and over with his towel and leaning toward them until he seemed almost ready to fall over.

"Gelb," Rand whispered as he dropped back into his chair, and the others tensed. Thom swiftly studied their side of the room.

On the other side of the wall the second man's voice chimed in. "No, no, there used to be Trollocs. But they killed them all in the Trolloc Wars."

"Borderland fables!" the first man repeated.

"It's true, I tell you," Gelb protested loudly. "I've been in the Borderlands. I've seen Trollocs, and these were Trollocs as sure as I'm sitting here. Those three claimed the Trollocs were chasing them, but I know better. That's why I wouldn't stay on the *Spray*. I've had my suspicions about Bayle Domon for some time, but those three are Darkfriends for sure. I tell you. . . ." Laughter and coarse jokes drowned out the rest of what Gelb had to say.

How long, Rand wondered, before the innkeeper heard a description of "those three"? If he had not already. If he did not just leap to the three strangers he had already seen. The only door from their half of the common room would take them right past Gelb's table.

"Maybe the boat isn't such a bad idea," Mat muttered, but Thom shook his head.

"Not anymore." The gleeman spoke softly and fast. He pulled out the leather purse Captain Domon had given him and hastily divided the money into three piles. "That story will be all through the town in an hour, whether anybody believes it or not, and the Halfman could hear any time. Domon isn't sailing until tomorrow morning. At best he'll have Trollocs chasing him all the way to Illian. Well, he's half expecting it for some reason, but that won't do us any good. There's nothing for it but to run, and run hard."

Mat quickly stuffed the coins Thom shoved in front of him into his pocket. Rand picked his pile up more slowly. The coin Moiraine had given him was not among them. Domon had given an equal weight of silver, but Rand, for some reason he could not fathom, wished he had the Aes Sedai's coin instead. Stuffing the money in his pocket, he looked a question at the gleeman.

"In case we're separated," Thom explained. "We probably won't be, but if it does happen . . . well, you two will make out all right by yourselves. You're good lads. Just keep clear of Aes Sedai, for your lives."

"I thought you were staying with us," Rand said.

"I am, boy. I am. But they're getting close, now, and the Light only knows. Well, no matter. It isn't likely anything will happen." Thom paused, looking at Mat. "I hope you no longer mind me staying with you," he said dryly.

Mat shrugged. He eyed each of them, then shrugged again. "I'm just on edge. I can't seem to get rid of it. Every time we stop for a breath, they're there, hunting us. I feel like somebody's staring at the back of my head all the time. What are we going to do?"

The laughter erupted on the other side of the wall, broken again by Gelb, trying loudly to convince the two men that he was telling the truth. How much longer, Rand wondered. Sooner or later Bartim had to put together Gelb's three and the three of them.

Thom eased his chair and rose, but kept his height crouched. No one looking casually toward the wall from the other side could see him. He motioned for them to follow, whispering, "Be very quiet."

The windows on either side of the fireplace on their side of the wall looked out into an alleyway. Thom studied one of the windows carefully before drawing it up just enough for them to squeeze through. It barely made a sound, nothing that could have been heard three feet away over the laughing argument on the other side of the low wall.

Once in the alley, Mat started for the street right away, but Thom caught his arm. "Not so fast," the gleeman told him. "Not till we know what we're doing." Thom lowered the window again as much as he could from outside, and turned to study the alley.

Rand followed Thom's eyes. Except for half a dozen rain barrels against the inn and the next building, a tailor shop, the alley was empty, the hard-packed dirt dry and dusty.

"Why are you doing this?" Mat demanded again. "You'd be safer if you left us. Why are you staying with us?"

Thom stared at him for a long moment. "I had a nephew, Owyn," he said wearily, shrugging out of his cloak. He made a pile with his blanket-roll as he talked, carefully setting his cased instruments on top. "My brother's only son, my only living kin. He got in trouble with the Aes Sedai, but I was too busy with . . . other things. I don't know what I could have done, but when I finally tried, it was too late. Owyn died a few years later. You could say Aes Sedai killed him." He straightened up, not looking at them. His voice was still level, but Rand glimpsed tears in his eyes as he turned his head away. "If I can keep you two free of Tar Valon, maybe I can stop thinking about Owyn. Wait here." Still avoiding their eyes, he hurried to the mouth of the alley, slowing before he reached it. After one quick look around, he strolled casually into the street and out of sight.

Mat half rose to follow, then settled back. "He won't leave these," he said, touching the leather instrument cases. "You believe that story?"

Rand squatted patiently beside the rain barrels. "What's the matter with you, Mat? You aren't like this. I haven't heard you laugh in days."

"I don't like being hunted like a rabbit," Mat snapped. He sighed, letting his head fall back against the brick wall of the inn. Even like that he seemed tense. His eyes shifted warily. "Sorry. It's the running, and all these strangers, and . . . and just everything. It makes me jumpy. I look at somebody, and I can't help wondering if he's going to tell the Fades about us, or cheat us, or rob us, or. . . . Light, Rand, doesn't it make you nervous?"

Rand laughed, a quick bark in the back of his throat. "I'm too scared to be nervous."

"What do you think the Aes Sedai did to his nephew?"

"I don't know," Rand said uneasily. There was only one kind of trouble that he knew of for a man to get into with Aes Sedai. "Not like us, I guess."

"No. Not like us."

For a time they leaned against the wall, not talking. Rand was not sure how long they waited. A few minutes, probably, but it felt like an hour, waiting for Thom to come back, waiting for Bartim and Gelb to open the window and denounce them for Darkfriends. Then a man turned in at the mouth of the alley, a tall man with the hood of his cloak pulled up to hide his face, a cloak black as night against the light of the street.

Rand scrambled to his feet, one hand wrapped around the hilt of Tam's sword so hard that his knuckles hurt. His mouth went dry, and no amount of swallowing helped. Mat rose to a crouch with one hand under his cloak.

The man came closer, and Rand's throat grew tighter with every step. Abruptly the man stopped and tossed back his cowl. Rand's knees almost gave way. It was Thom.

"Well, if you don't recognize me"—the gleeman grinned—"I guess it's a good enough disguise for the gates."

Thom pushed past them and began transferring things from his patch-covered cloak to his new one so nimbly that Rand could not make out any of them. The new cloak was dark brown, Rand saw now. He drew a deep, ragged breath; his throat still felt as if it were clutched in a fist. Brown, not black. Mat still had his hand under his cloak, and he stared at Thom's back as if he were thinking of using the hidden dagger.

Thom glanced up at them, then gave them a sharper look. "This is no time to get skittish." Deftly he began folding his old cloak into a bundle around his instrument cases, inside out so the patches were hidden. "We'll walk out of here one at a time, just close enough to keep each other in sight. Shouldn't be remembered especially, that way. Can't you slouch?" he added to Rand. "That height of yours is as bad as a banner." He slung the bundle across his back and stood, drawing his hood back up. He looked nothing like a white-haired gleeman. He was just another traveler, a man too poor to afford a horse, much less a carriage. "Let's go. We've wasted too much time already."

Rand agreed fervently, but even so he hesitated before stepping out of the alley into the square. None of the sparse scattering of people gave them a second look—most did not look at them at all—but his shoulders knotted, waiting for the cry of Darkfriend that could turn ordinary people into a mob bent on murder. He ran his eyes across the open area, over people moving about on their daily business, and when he brought them back a Myrddraal was halfway across the square.

Where the Fade had come from, he could not begin to guess, but it strode toward the three of them with a slow deadliness, a predator with the prey under its gaze. People shied away from the black-cloaked shape, avoided looking at it. The square began to empty out as people decided they were needed elsewhere.

The black cowl froze Rand where he stood. He tried to summon up the void, but it was like fumbling after smoke. The Fade's hidden gaze knifed to his bones and turned his marrow to icicles.

"Don't look at its face," Thom muttered. His voice shook and cracked, and it sounded as if he were forcing the words out. "The Light burn you, don't look at its face!"

Rand tore his eyes away—he almost groaned; it felt like tearing a leech off of his face—but even staring at the stones of the square he could still see the Myrddraal coming, a cat playing with mice, amused at their feeble efforts to escape, until finally the jaws snapped shut. The Fade had halved the distance. "Are we just going to stand here?" he mumbled. "We have to run . . . get away." But he could not make his feet move.

Mat had the ruby-hilted dagger out at last, in a trembling hand. His lips were drawn back from his teeth, a snarl and a rictus of fear.

"Think. . . ." Thom stopped to swallow, and went on hoarsely. "Think you can outrun it, do you, boy?" He began to mutter to himself; the only word Rand could make out was "Owyn." Abruptly Thom growled, "I never should have gotten mixed up with you boys. Should never have." He shrugged the bundled gleeman's cloak off of his back and thrust it into Rand's arms. "Take care of that. When I say run, you run and don't stop until you get to Caemlyn. The Queen's Blessing. An inn. Remember that, in case. . . . Just remember it."

"I don't understand," Rand said. The Myrddraal was not twenty paces away, now. His feet felt like lead weights.

"Just remember it!" Thom snarled. "The Queen's Blessing. Now. RUN!"

He gave them a push, one hand on the shoulder of each of them, to get them started, and Rand stumbled away in a lurching run with Mat at his side.

"RUN!" Thom sprang into motion, too, with a long, wordless roar. Not after them, but toward the Myrddraal. His hands flourished as if he were performing at his best, and daggers appeared. Rand stopped, but Mat pulled him along.

The Fade was just as startled. Its leisurely pace faltered in midstride. Its hand swept toward the hilt of the black sword hanging at its waist, but the gleeman's long legs covered the distance quickly. Thom crashed into the Myrddraal before the black blade was half drawn, and both went down in a thrashing heap. The few people still in the square fled.

"RUN!" The air in the square flashed an eye-searing blue, and Thom began to scream, but even in the middle of the scream he managed a word. *"RUN!"*

Rand obeyed. The gleeman's screams pursued him.

Clutching Thom's bundle to his chest, he ran as hard as he could. Panic spread from the square out through the town as Rand and Mat fled on the crest of a wave of fear. Shopkeepers abandoned their goods as the boys passed. Shutters banged down over storefronts, and frightened faces appeared in the windows of houses, then vanished. People who had not been close enough to see ran through the streets wildly, paying no heed. They bumped into one another, and those who were knocked down scrambled to their feet or were trampled. Whitebridge roiled like a kicked anthill.

As he and Mat pounded toward the gates, Rand abruptly remembered what Thom had said about his height. Without slowing down, he crouched as best he could without looking as if he was crouching. But the gates themselves, thick wood bound with black iron straps, stood open. The two gatetenders, in steel caps and mail tunics worn over cheap-looking red coats with white collars, fingered their halberds and stared uneasily into the town. One of them glanced at Rand and Mat, but they were not the only ones running out of the gates. A steady stream boiled through, panting men clutching wives, weeping women carrying babes and dragging crying children, pale-faced craftsmen still in their aprons, still heedlessly gripping their tools.

There would be no one who could tell which way they had gone, Rand thought as he ran, dazed. *Thom. Oh, Light save me, Thom.*

Mat staggered beside him, caught his balance, and they ran until the last of the fleeing people had fallen away, ran until the town and the White Bridge were far out of sight behind them.

Finally Rand fell to his knees in the dust, pulling air raggedly into his raw throat with great gulps. The road behind stretched empty until it was lost to sight among bare trees. Mat plucked at him.

"Come on. Come on." Mat panted the words. Sweat and dust streaked his face, and he looked ready to collapse. "We have to keep going."

"Thom," Rand said. He tightened his arms around the bundle of Thom's cloak; the instrument cases were hard lumps inside. "Thom."

"He's dead. You saw. You heard. Light, Rand, he's dead!"

"You think Egwene and Moiraine and the rest are dead, too. If they're dead, why are the Myrddraal still hunting them? Answer me that?"

Mat dropped to his knees in the dust beside him. "All right. Maybe they are alive. But Thom— You saw! Blood and ashes, Rand, the same thing can happen to us."

Rand nodded slowly. The road behind them was still empty. He had been halfway expecting—hoping, at least—to see Thom appear, striding along, blowing out his mustaches to tell them how much trouble they were. The Queen's Blessing in Caemlyn. He struggled to his feet and slung Thom's bundle on his back alongside his blanketroll. Mat stared up at him, narrow-eyed and wary.

"Let's go," Rand said, and started down the road toward Caemlyn. He heard Mat muttering, and after a moment he caught up to Rand.

They trudged along the dusty road, heads down and not talking. The wind spawned dustdevils that whirled across their path. Sometimes Rand looked back, but the road behind was always empty.

CHAPTER
27

Shelter From the Storm

Perrin fretted over the days spent with the Tuatha'an, traveling south and east in a leisurely fashion. The Traveling People saw no need to hurry; they never did. The colorful wagons did not roll out of a morning until the sun was well above the horizon, and they stopped as early as midafternoon if they came across a congenial spot. The dogs trotted easily alongside the wagons, and often the children did, too. They had no difficulty in keeping up. Any suggestion that they might go further, or more quickly, was met with laughter, or perhaps, "Ah, but would you make the poor horses work so hard?"

He was surprised that Elyas did not share his feelings. Elyas would not ride on the wagons—he preferred to walk, sometimes loping along at the head of the column—but he never suggested leaving, or pressing on ahead.

The strange bearded man in his strange skin clothes was so different from the gentle Tuatha'an that he stood out wherever he went among the wagons. Even from across the camp there was no mistaking Elyas for one of the People, and not just because of clothes. Elyas moved with the lazy grace of a wolf, only emphasized by his skins and his fur hat, radiating danger as naturally as a fire radiated heat, and the contrast with the Traveling People was sharp. Young and old, the People were joyful on their feet. There was no danger in their grace, only delight. Their children darted about filled with the pure zest of moving, of course, but among the Tuatha'an, graybeards and grandmothers, too, still stepped lightly, their walk a stately dance no less exuberant for its dignity. All the People seemed on the point of dancing, even when standing still, even during the rare times when there was no music in the camp. Fiddles and flutes, dulcimers and zithers and drums spun harmony and counterpoint around the wagons at almost any hour, in camp or on the move. Joyous songs, merry songs, laughing songs, sad songs; if someone was awake in the camp there was usually music.

Elyas met friendly nods and smiles at every wagon he passed, and a cheerful word at any fire where he paused. This must be the face the People always showed to outsiders—open, smiling faces. But Perrin had learned that hidden beneath the surface was the wariness of a half-tame deer. Something deep lay behind the smiles directed at the Emond's Fielders, something that wondered if they were safe, something that faded only slightly over the days. With Elyas the wariness was strong, like deep summer heat shimmering in the air, and it did not fade. When he was not looking they watched him openly as if unsure what he was going to do. When he walked across the camp, feet ready for dancing seemed ready for flight, as well.

Elyas was certainly no more comfortable with their Way of the Leaf than they were with him. His mouth wore a permanent twist when he was around the Tuatha'an. It was not quite condescension and certainly not contempt, but looked as though he would rather be elsewhere than where he was, almost anywhere else. Yet whenever Perrin brought up leaving, Elyas made soothing noises about resting, just for a few days.

"You had hard days before you met me," Elyas said, the third or fourth time he asked, "and you'll have harder still ahead, with Trollocs and Halfmen after you, and Aes Sedai for friends." He grinned around a mouthful of Ila's dried-apple pie. Perrin still found his yellow-eyed gaze disconcerting, even when he was smiling. Perhaps even more when he was smiling; smiles seldom touched those hunter's eyes. Elyas lounged beside Raen's fire, as usual refusing to sit on the logs drawn up for the purpose. "Don't be in such a bloody hurry to put yourself in Aes Sedai hands."

"What if the Fades find us? What's to keep them from it if we just sit here, waiting? Three wolves can't hold them off, and the Traveling People won't be any help. They won't even defend themselves. The Trollocs will butcher them, and it will be our fault. Anyway, we have to leave them sooner or later. It might as well be sooner."

"Something tells me to wait. Just a few days."

"Something!"

"Relax, lad. Take life as it comes. Run when you have to, fight when you must, rest when you can."

"What are you talking about, something?"

"Have some of this pie. Ila doesn't like me, but she surely feeds me well when I visit. Always good food in the People's camps."

"What 'something'?" Perrin demanded. "If you know something you aren't telling the rest of us. . . ."

Elyas frowned at the piece of pie in his hand, then set it down and dusted his hands together. "Something," he said finally, with a shrug of his shoulders as if he did not understand it completely himself. "Something tells me it's important to wait. A few more days. I don't get feelings like this often, but when I do, I've learned to trust them. They've saved my life in the past. This time it's different, somehow, but it's important. That's clear. You want to run on, then run on. Not me."

That was all he would say, no matter how many times Perrin asked. He lay about, talking with Raen, eating, napping with his hat over his eyes, and refused to discuss leaving. Something told him to wait. Something told him it was important. He would know when it was time to go. Have some pie, lad. Don't lather yourself. Try some of this stew. Relax.

Perrin could not make himself relax. At night he wandered among the rainbow wagons worrying, as much because no one else seemed to see anything to worry about as for any other reason. The Tuatha'an sang and danced, cooked and ate around their campfires—fruits and nuts, berries and vegetables; they ate no meat—and went about a myriad domestic chores as if they had not a care in the world. The children ran and played everywhere, hide-and-seek among the wagons, climbing in the trees around the camp, laughing and rolling on the ground with the dogs. Not a care in the world, for anyone.

Watching them, he itched to get away. *Go, before we bring the hunters down on them. They took us in, and we repay their kindness by endangering them. At least they have reason to be lighthearted. Nothing is hunting them. But the rest of us. . . .*

It was hard to get a word with Egwene. Either she was talking with Ila, their heads together in a way that said no men were welcome, or she was dancing with Aram, swinging round and round to the flutes and fiddles and drums, to tunes the Tuatha'an had gathered from all over the world, or to the sharp, trilling songs of the Traveling People themselves, sharp whether they were quick or slow. They knew many songs, some he recognized from home, though often under different names than they were called in the Two Rivers. "Three Girls in the Meadow," for instance, the Tinkers named "Pretty Maids Dancing," and they said "The Wind From the North" was called "Hard Rain Falling" in some lands and "Berin's Retreat" in others. When he asked, not thinking, for "The Tinker Has My Pots," they fell all over themselves laughing. They knew it, but as "Toss the Feathers."

He could understand wanting to dance to the People's songs. Back in Emond's Field no one considered him more than an adequate dancer, but these songs tugged at his feet, and he thought he had never danced so long, or so hard, or so well in his life. Hypnotic, they made his blood pound in rhythm to the drums.

It was the second evening when for the first time Perrin saw women dance to some of the slow songs. The fires burned low, and the night hung close around the wagons, and fingers tapped a slow rhythm on the drums. First one drum, then another, until every drum in the camp kept the same low, insistent beat. There was silence except for the drums. A girl in a red dress swayed into the light, loosening her shawl. Strings of beads hung in her hair, and she had kicked off her shoes. A flute began the melody, wailing softly, and the girl danced. Outstretched arms spread her shawl behind her; her hips undulated as her bare feet shuffled to the beat of the drums. The girl's dark eyes fastened on Perrin, and her smile was as slow as her dance. She turned in small circles, smiling over her shoulder at him.

He swallowed hard. The heat in his face was not from the fire. A second girl joined the first, the fringe on their shawls shaking in time to the drums and the slow rotation of their hips. They smiled at him, and he cleared his throat hoarsely. He was afraid to look around; his face was as red as a beet, and anyone who was not watching the dancers was probably laughing at him. He was sure of it.

As casually as he could manage, he slid off the log as if he were just getting comfortable, but he carefully ended up looking away from the fire, away from the dancers. There was nothing like that in Emond's Field. Dancing with the girls on the Green on a feastday did not even come close. For once he wished that the wind would pick up, to cool him off.

The girls danced into his field of view again, only now they were three. One gave him a sly wink. His eyes darted frantically. *Light,* he thought. *What do I do now? What would Rand do? He knows about girls.*

The dancing girls laughed softly; beads clicked as they tossed their long hair on their shoulders, and he thought his face would burn up. Then a slightly older woman joined the girls, to show them how it was done. With a groan, he gave up altogether and shut his eyes. Even behind his eyelids their laughter taunted and tickled. Even behind his eyelids he could still see them. Sweat beaded on his forehead, and he wished for the wind.

According to Raen the girls did not dance that dance often, and the women rarely did, and according to Elyas it was thanks to Perrin's blushes that they did so every night thereafter.

"I have to thank you," Elyas told him, his tone sober and solemn. "It's different with you young fellows, but at my age it takes more than a fire to warm my bones." Perrin scowled. There was something about Elyas's back as he walked away that said even if nothing showed, he was laughing inside.

Perrin soon learned better than to look away from the dancing women and girls, though the winks and smiles still made him wish he could. One would have been all right, maybe—but five or six, with everyone watching. . . . He never did entirely conquer his blushes.

Then Egwene began learning the dance. Two of the girls who had danced that first night taught her, clapping the rhythm while she repeated the shuffling steps with a borrowed shawl swaying behind her. Perrin started to say something, then decided it was wiser not to crack his teeth. When the girls added the hip movements Egwene started laughing, and the three girls fell giggling into one another's arms. But Egwene persevered, with her eyes glistening and bright spots of color in her cheeks.

Aram watched her dancing with a hot, hungry gaze. The handsome young Tuatha'an had given her a string of blue beads that she wore all the time. Worried frowns now replaced the smiles Ila had worn when she first noticed her grandson's interest in Egwene. Perrin resolved to keep a close eye on young Master Aram.

Once he managed to get Egwene alone, beside a wagon painted in green and yellow. "Enjoying yourself, aren't you?" he said.

"Why shouldn't I?" She fingered the blue beads around her neck, smiling at them. "We don't all have to work at being miserable, the way you do. Don't we deserve a little chance to enjoy ourselves?"

Aram stood not far off—he never got far from Egwene—with his arms folded across his chest, a little smile on his face, half smugness and half challenge. Perrin lowered his voice. "I thought you wanted to get to Tar Valon. You won't learn to be an Aes Sedai here."

Egwene tossed her head. "And I thought you didn't like me wanting to become an Aes Sedai," she said, too sweetly.

"Blood and ashes, do you believe we're safe here? Are these people safe with us here? A Fade could find us anytime."

Her hand trembled on the beads. She lowered it and took a deep breath. "Whatever is going to happen will happen whether we leave today or next week. That's what I believe now. Enjoy yourself, Perrin. It might be the last chance we have."

She brushed his cheek sadly with her fingers. Then Aram held out his hand to her, and she darted to him, already laughing again. As they ran away to where fiddles sang, Aram flashed a triumphant grin over his shoulder at Perrin as if to say, she is not yours, but she will be mine.

They were all falling too much under the spell of the People, Perrin thought. *Elyas is right. They don't have to try to convert you to the Way of the Leaf. It seeps into you.*

Ila had taken one look at him huddling out of the wind, then produced a thick wool cloak out of her wagon; a dark green cloak, he was pleased to see, after all the reds and yellows. As he swung it round his shoulders, thinking what a wonder it was that the cloak was big enough for him, Ila said primly, "It could fit better." She glanced at the axe at his belt, and when she looked up at him her eyes were sad above her smile. "It could fit much better."

All the Tinkers did that. Their smiles never slipped, there was never any hesitation in their invitations to join them for a drink or to listen to the music, but their eyes always touched the axe, and he could feel what they thought. A tool of violence. There is never any excuse for violence to another human being. The Way of the Leaf.

Sometimes he wanted to shout at them. There were Trollocs in the world, and Fades. There were those who would cut down every leaf. The Dark One was out there, and the Way of the Leaf would burn in Ba'alzamon's eyes. Stubbornly he continued to wear the axe. He took to keeping his cloak thrown back, even when it was windy, so the half-moon blade was never hidden. Now and again Elyas looked quizzically at the weapon hanging heavy at his side and grinned at him, those yellow eyes seeming to read his mind. That almost made him cover the axe. Almost.

If the Tuatha'an camp was a source of constant irritation, at least his dreams were normal there. Sometimes he woke up sweating from a dream of Trollocs and Fades storming into the camp, rainbow-colored wagons turning to bonfires from hurled torches, people falling in pools of blood, men and women and children who ran and screamed and died but made no effort to defend themselves against slashing scythe-like swords. Night after night he bolted upright in the dark, panting and reaching for his axe before he realized the wagons were not in flames, that no bloody-muzzled shapes snarled over torn and twisted bodies littering the ground. But those were ordinary nightmares, and oddly comforting in their way. If there was ever a place for the Dark One to be in his dreams, it was in those, but he was not. No Ba'alzamon. Just ordinary nightmares.

He was aware of the wolves, though, when he was awake. They kept their distance from the camps, and from the caravan on the move, but he always knew where they were. He could feel their contempt for the dogs guarding the Tuatha'an. Noisy beasts who had forgotten what their jaws were for, had forgotten the taste of warm blood; they might frighten humans, but they would slink away on their bellies if the pack ever came. Each day his awareness was sharper, more clear.

Dapple grew more impatient with every sunset. That Elyas wanted to do this thing of taking the humans south made it worth doing, but if it must be done, then let it be done. Let this slow travel end. Wolves were meant to roam, and she did not like being away from the pack so long. Impatience burned in Wind, too. Hunting was worse than poor here, and he despised living on field mice, something for cubs to stalk while learning to hunt, fit food for the old, no longer able to pull down a deer or hamstring a wild ox. Sometimes Wind thought that Burn had been right; leave human troubles to humans. But he was wary of such thoughts when Dapple was around, and even more so around Hopper. Hopper was a scarred and grizzled fighter, impassive with the knowledge of years, with guile that more than made up for anything of which age might have robbed him. For humans he cared nothing, but Dapple wished this thing done, and Hopper would wait as she waited and run as she ran. Wolf or man, bull or bear, whatever challenged Dapple would find Hopper's jaws waiting to send him to the long sleep. That was the whole of life for Hopper, and that kept Wind cautious, and Dapple seemed to ignore the thoughts of both.

All of it was clear in Perrin's mind. Fervently he wished for Caem-lyn, for Moiraine and Tar Valon. Even if there were no answers, there could be an end to it. Elyas looked at him, and he was sure the yellow-eyed man knew. *Please, let there be an end.*

The dream began more pleasantly than most he had of late. He was at Alsbet Luhhan's kitchen table, sharpening his axe with a stone. Mistress Luhhan never allowed forge work, or anything that smacked of it, to be brought into the house. Master Luhhan even had to take her knives outside to sharpen them. But she tended her cooking and never said a word about the axe. She did not even say anything when a wolf entered from deeper in the house and curled up between Perrin and the door to the yard. Perrin went on sharpening; it would be time to use it, soon.

Abruptly the wolf rose, rumbling deep in its throat, the thick ruff of fur on its neck rising. Ba'alzamon stepped into the kitchen from the yard. Mistress Luhhan went on with her cooking.

Perrin scrambled to his feet, raising the axe, but Ba'alzamon ignored the weapon, concentrating on the wolf, instead. Flames danced where his eyes should be. "Is this what you have to protect you? Well, I have faced this before. Many times before."

He crooked a finger, and the wolf howled as fire burst out of its eyes and ears and mouth, out of its skin. The stench of burning meat and hair filled the kitchen. Alsbet Luhhan lifted the lid on a pot and stirred with a wooden spoon.

Perrin dropped the axe and jumped forward, trying to beat out the flames with his hands. The wolf crumpled to black ash between his palms. Staring at the shapeless pile of char on Mistress Luhhan's clean-swept floor, he backed away. He wished he could wipe the greasy soot from his hands, but the thought of scrubbing it off on his clothes turned his stomach. He snatched up the axe, gripping the haft until his knuckles cracked.

"Leave me alone!" he shouted. Mistress Luhhan tapped the spoon on the rim of the pot and replaced the lid, humming to herself.

"You cannot run from me," Ba'alzamon said. "You cannot hide from me. If you are the one, you are mine." The heat from the fires of his face forced Perrin across the kitchen until his back came up against the wall. Mistress Luhhan opened the oven to check her bread. "The Eye of the World will consume you," Ba'alzamon said. "I mark you mine!" He flung out his clenched hand as if throwing something; when his fingers opened, a raven streaked at Perrin's face.

Perrin screamed as the black beak pierced his left eye . . .

. . . and sat up, clutching his face, surrounded by the sleeping wagons of the Traveling People. Slowly he lowered his hands. There was no pain, no blood. But he could remember it, remember the stabbing agony.

He shuddered, and suddenly Elyas was squatting beside him in the predawn, one hand outstretched as if to shake him awake. Beyond the trees where the wagons lay, the wolves howled, one sharp cry from three throats. He shared their sensations. *Fire. Pain. Fire. Hate. Hate! Kill!*

"Yes," Elyas said softly. "It is time. Get up, boy. It's time for us to go."

Perrin scrambled out of his blankets. While he was still bundling his blanketroll, Raen came out of his wagon, rubbing sleep from his eyes. The Seeker glanced at the sky and froze halfway down the steps, his hands still raised to his face. Only his eyes moved as he studied the sky intently, though Perrin could not understand what he was looking at. A few clouds hung in the east, undersides streaked with pink from the sun yet to rise, but there was nothing else to see. Raen seemed to listen, as well, and smell the air, but there was no sound except the wind in the trees and no smell but the faint smoky remnant of last night's campfires.

Elyas returned with his own scanty belongings, and Raen came the rest of the way down. "We must change the direction we travel, my old friend." The Seeker looked uneasily at the sky again. "We go another way this day. Will you be coming with us?" Elyas shook his head, and Raen nodded as if he had known all along. "Well, take care, my old friend. There is something about today. . . ." He started to look up once more, but pulled his eyes back down before they rose above the wagon tops. "I think the wagons will go east. Perhaps all the way to the Spine of the World. Perhaps we'll find a *stedding,* and stay there awhile."

"Trouble never enters the *stedding,*" Elyas agreed. "But the Ogier are none too open to strangers."

"Everyone is open to the Traveling People," Raen said, and grinned. "Besides, even Ogier have pots and things to mend. Come, let us have some breakfast, and we'll talk about it."

"No time," Elyas said. "We move on today, too. As soon as possible. It's a day for moving, it seems."

Raen tried to convince him to at least stay long enough for food, and when Ila appeared from the wagon with Egwene, she added her arguments, though not as strenuously as her husband. She said all of the right words, but her politeness was stiff, and it was plain she would be glad to see Elyas's back, if not Egwene's.

Egwene did not notice the regretful, sidelong looks Ila gave her. She asked what was going on, and Perrin prepared himself for her to say she wanted to stay with the Tuatha'an, but when Elyas explained she only nodded thoughtfully and hurried back into the wagon to gather her things.

Finally Raen threw up his hands. "All right. I don't know that I have ever let a visitor leave this camp without a farewell feast, but. . . ." Uncertainly, his eyes raised toward the sky again. "Well, we need an early start ourselves, I think. Perhaps we will eat as we journey. But at least let everyone say goodbye."

Elyas started to protest, but Raen was already hurrying from wagon to wagon, pounding on the doors where there was no one awake. By the time a Tinker came, leading Bela, the whole camp had turned out in their finest and brightest, a mass of color that made Raen and Ila's red-and-yellow wagon seem almost plain. The big dogs strolled through the crowd with their tongues lolling out of their mouths, looking for someone to scratch their ears, while Perrin and the others endured handshake after handshake and hug after hug. The girls who had danced every night would not be content with shaking hands, and their hugs made Perrin suddenly wish he was not leaving after all—until he remembered how many others were watching, and then his face almost matched the Seeker's wagon.

Aram drew Egwene a little aside. Perrin could not hear what he had to say to her over the noise of goodbyes, but she kept shaking her head, slowly at first, then more firmly as he began to gesture pleadingly. His face shifted from pleading to arguing, but she continued to shake her head stubbornly until Ila rescued her with a few sharp words to her grandson. Scowling, Aram pushed away through the crowd, abandoning the rest of the farewell. Ila watched him go, hesitating on the point of calling him back. *She's relieved, too,* Perrin thought. *Relieved he doesn't want to go with us—with Egwene.*

When he had shaken every hand in the camp at least once and hugged every girl at least twice, the crowd moved back, opening a little space around Raen and Ila, and the three visitors.

"You came in peace," Raen intoned, bowing formally, hands on his chest. "Depart now in peace. Always will our fires welcome you, in peace. The Way of the Leaf is peace."

"Peace be on you always," Elyas replied, "and on all the People." He hesitated, then added, "I will find the song, or another will find the song, but the song will be sung, this year or in a year to come. As it once was, so shall it be again, world without end."

Raen blinked in surprise, and Ila looked completely flabbergasted, but all the other Tuatha'an murmured in reply, "World without end.

World and time without end." Raen and his wife hurriedly said the same after everyone else.

Then it really was time to go. A few last farewells, a few last admonitions to take care, a few last smiles and winks, and they were making their way out of the camp. Raen accompanied them as far as the edge of the trees, a pair of the dogs cavorting by his side.

"Truly, my old friend, you must take great care. This day. . . . There is wickedness loose in the world, I fear, and whatever you pretend, you are not so wicked that it will not gobble you up."

"Peace be on you," Elyas said.

"And on you," Raen said sadly.

When Raen was gone, Elyas scowled at finding the other two looking at him. "So I don't believe in their fool song," he growled. "No need to make them feel bad by messing up their ceremony, was there? I told you they set a store by ceremony sometimes."

"Of course," Egwene said gently. "No need at all." Elyas turned away muttering to himself.

Dapple, Wind, and Hopper came to greet Elyas, not frolicking as the dogs had done, but a dignified meeting of equals. Perrin caught what passed between them. *Fire eyes. Pain. Heartfang. Death. Heartfang.* Perrin knew what they meant. The Dark One. They were telling about his dream. Their dream.

He shivered as the wolves ranged out ahead, scouting the way. It was Egwene's turn to ride Bela, and he walked beside her. Elyas led, as usual, a steady, ground-eating pace.

Perrin did not want to think about his dream. He had thought that the wolves made them safe. *Not complete. Accept. Full heart. Full mind. You still struggle. Only complete when you accept.*

He forced the wolves out of his head, and blinked in surprise. He had not known he could do that. He determined not to let them back in again. *Even in dreams?* He was not sure if the thought was his or theirs.

Egwene still wore the string of blue beads Aram had given her, and a little sprig of something with tiny, bright red leaves in her hair, another gift from the young Tuatha'an. That Aram had tried to talk her into staying with the Traveling People, Perrin was sure. He was glad she had not given in, but he wished she did not finger the beads so fondly.

Finally he said, "What did you spend so much time talking about with Ila? If you weren't dancing with that long-legged fellow, you were talking to her like it was some kind of secret."

"Ila was giving me advice on being a woman," Egwene replied absently. He began laughing, and she gave him a hooded, dangerous look that he failed to see.

"Advice! Nobody tells us how to be men. We just are."

"That," Egwene said, "is probably why you make such a bad job of it." Up ahead, Elyas cackled loudly.

CHAPTER
28

Footprints in Air

Nynaeve stared in wonder at what lay ahead down the river, the White Bridge gleaming in the sun with a milky glow. Another legend, she thought, glancing at the Warder and the Aes Sedai, riding just ahead of her. *Another legend, and they don't even seem to notice.* She resolved not to stare where they could see. *They'll laugh if they see me gaping like a country bumpkin.* The three rode on silently toward the fabled White Bridge.

Since that morning after Shadar Logoth, when she had found Moiraine and Lan on the bank of the Arinelle, there had been little in the way of real conversation between her and the Aes Sedai. There had been talk, of course, but nothing of substance as Nynaeve saw it. Moiraine's attempts to talk her into going to Tar Valon, for instance. Tar Valon. She would go there, if need be, and take their training, but not for the reasons the Aes Sedai thought. If Moiraine had brought harm to Egwene and the boys. . . .

Sometimes, against her will, Nynaeve had found herself thinking of what a Wisdom could do with the One Power, of what she could do.

Whenever she realized what was in her head, though, a flash of anger burned it out. The Power was a filthy thing. She would have nothing to do with it. Unless she had to.

The cursed woman only wanted to talk about taking her to Tar Valon for training. Moiraine would not tell her anything! It was not as if she wanted to know so much.

"How do you mean to find them?" she remembered demanding.

"As I have told you," Moiraine replied without bothering to look back at her, "I will know when I am close to the two who have lost their coins." It was not the first time Nynaeve had asked, but the Aes Sedai's voice was like a still pond that refused to ripple no matter how many stones Nynaeve threw; it made the Wisdom's blood boil every time she was exposed to it. Moiraine went on as if she could not feel Nynaeve's eyes on her back; Nynaeve knew she must be able to, she was staring so hard. "The longer it takes, the closer I must come, but I will know. As for the one who still has his token, so long as he has it in his possession I can follow him across half the world, if need be."

"And then? What do you plan when you've found them, Aes Sedai?" She did not for a minute believe the Aes Sedai would be so intent on finding them if she did not have plans.

"Tar Valon, Wisdom."

"Tar Valon, Tar Valon. That's all you ever say, and I am becoming—"

"Part of the training you will receive in Tar Valon, Wisdom, will teach you to control your temper. You can do nothing with the One Power when emotion rules your mind." Nynaeve opened her mouth, but the Aes Sedai went right on. "Lan, I must speak with you a moment."

The two put their heads together, and Nynaeve was left with a sullen glower that she hated every time she realized it was on her face. It came too often as the Aes Sedai deftly turned her questions off onto another subject, slid easily by her conversational traps, or ignored her shouts until they ended in silence. The scowl made her feel like a girl who had been caught acting the fool by someone in the Women's Circle. That was a feeling Nynaeve was not used to, and the calm smile on Moiraine's face only made it worse.

If only there was some way to get rid of the woman. Lan would be better by himself—a Warder should be able to handle what was needed, she told herself hastily, feeling a sudden flush; no other reason—but one meant the other.

And yet, Lan made her even more furious than Moiraine. She could not understand how he managed to get under her skin so easily. He rarely said anything—sometimes not a dozen words in a day—and he never took part in any of the . . . discussions with Moiraine. He was often apart from the two women, scouting the land, but even when he was there he kept a little to one side, watching them as if watching a duel. Nynaeve wished he would stop. If it was a duel, she had not managed to score once, and Moiraine did not even seem to realize she was in a fight. Nynaeve could have done without his cool blue eyes, without even a silent audience.

That had been the way of their journey, for the most part. Quiet, except when her temper got the best of her, and sometimes when she shouted the sound of her voice seemed to crash in the silence like breaking glass. The land itself was quiet, as if the world were pausing to catch its breath. The wind moaned in the trees, but all else was still. The wind seemed distant, too, even when it was cutting through the cloak on her back.

At first the stillness was restful after everything that had happened. It seemed as if she had not known a moment of quiet since before Winternight. By the end of the first day alone with the Aes Sedai and the Warder, though, she was looking over her shoulder and fidgeting in her saddle as if she had an itch in the middle of her back where she could not reach. The silence seemed like crystal doomed to shatter, and waiting for the first crack put her teeth on edge.

It weighed on Moiraine and Lan, too, as outwardly unperturbable as they were. She soon realized that, beneath their calm surfaces, hour by hour they wound tighter and tighter, like clocksprings being forced to the breaking point. Moiraine seemed to listen to things that were not there, and what she heard put a crease in her forehead. Lan watched the forest and the river as if the leafless trees and wide, slow water carried the signs of traps and ambushes waiting ahead.

Part of her was glad that she was not the only one who apprehended that poised-on-the-brink feel to the world, but if it affected them, it was real, and another part of her wanted nothing so much as for it to be just her imagination. Something of it tickled the corners of her mind, as when she listened to the wind, but now she knew that that had to do with the One Power, and she could not bring herself to embrace those ripples at the edge of thought.

"It is nothing," Lan said quietly when she asked. He did not look at her while he spoke; his eyes never ceased their scanning. Then, contradicting what he had just said, he added, "You should go back to your Two Rivers when we reach Whitebridge, and the Caemlyn

Road. It's too dangerous here. Nothing will try to stop you going back, though." It was the longest speech he made all that day.

"She is part of the Pattern, Lan," Moiraine said chidingly. Her gaze was elsewhere, too. "It is the Dark One, Nynaeve. The storm has left us . . . for a time, at least." She raised one hand as though feeling the air, then scrubbed it on her dress unconsciously, as if she had touched filth. "He is still watching, however"—she sighed—"and his gaze is stronger. Not on us, but on the world. How much longer before he is strong enough to. . . ."

Nynaeve hunched her shoulders; suddenly she could almost feel someone staring at her back. It was one explanation she would just as soon the Aes Sedai had not given her.

Lan scouted their path down the river, but where before he had chosen the way, now Moiraine did so, as surely as if she followed some unseen track, footprints in air, the scent of memory. Lan only checked the route she intended, to see that it was safe. Nynaeve had the feeling that even if he said it was not, Moiraine would insist on it anyway. And he would go, she was sure. Straight down the river to. . . .

With a start, Nynaeve pulled out of her thoughts. They were at the foot of the White Bridge. The pale arch shone in the sunlight, a milky spiderweb too delicate to stand, sweeping across the Arinelle. The weight of a man would bring it crashing down, much less that of a horse. Surely it would collapse under its own weight any minute.

Lan and Moiraine rode unconcernedly ahead, up the gleaming white approach and onto the bridge, hooves ringing, not like steel on glass, but like steel on steel. The surface of the bridge certainly looked as slick as glass, wet glass, but it gave the horses a firm, sure footing.

Nynaeve made herself follow, but from the first step she half waited for the entire structure to shatter under them. *If lace were made of glass,* she thought, *it would look like this.*

It was not until they were almost all the way across that she noticed the tarry smell of char thickening the air. In a moment she saw.

Around the square at the foot of the White Bridge piles of blackened timbers, still leaking smoky threads, replaced half a dozen buildings. Men in poorly fitting red uniforms and tarnished armor patrolled the streets, but they marched quickly, as if afraid of finding anything, and they looked over their shoulders as they went. Townspeople—the few who were out—almost ran, shoulders hunched, as though something were chasing them.

Lan looked grim, even for him, and people walked wide of the three of them, even the soldiers. The Warder sniffed the air and grimaced, growling under his breath. It was no wonder to Nynaeve, with the stink of burn·so strong.

"The Wheel weaves as the Wheel wills," Moiraine mumbled. "No eye can see the Pattern until it is woven."

In the next moment she was down off Aldieb and speaking to towns-folk. She did not ask questions; she gave sympathy, and to Nynaeve's surprise it appeared genuine. People who shied away from Lan, ready to hurry from any stranger, stopped to speak with Moiraine. They appeared startled themselves at what they were doing, but they opened up, after a fashion, under Moiraine's clear gaze and soothing voice. The Aes Sedai's eyes seemed to share the people's hurt, to empathize with their confusion, and tongues loosened.

They still lied, though. Most of them. Some denied there had been any trouble at all. Nothing at all. Moiraine mentioned the burned buildings all around the square. Everything was fine, they insisted, staring past what they did not want to see.

One fat fellow spoke with a hollow heartiness, but his cheek twitched at every noise behind him. With a grin that kept slipping, he claimed an overturned lamp had started a fire that spread with the wind before anything could be done. One glance showed Nynaeve that no burned structure stood alongside another.

There were almost as many different stories as there were people. Several women lowered their voices conspiratorially. The truth of the matter was there was a man somewhere in the town meddling with the One Power. It was time to have the Aes Sedai in; past time, was the way they saw it, no matter what the men said about Tar Valon. Let the Red Ajah settle matters.

One man claimed it had been an attack by bandits, and another said a riot by Darkfriends. "Those ones going to see the false Dragon, you know," he confided darkly. "They're all over the place. Darkfriends, every one."

Still others spoke of some kind of trouble—they were vague about exactly what kind—that had come downriver on a boat.

"We showed them," a narrow-faced man muttered, scrubbing his hands together nervously. "Let them keep that kind of thing in the Borderlands, where it belongs. We went down to the docks and—" He cut off so abruptly his teeth clicked. Without another word he scurried off, peering back over his shoulder at them as if he thought they might chase him down.

The boat had gotten away—that much was clear, eventually, from others—cutting its moorings and fleeing downriver only the day before while a mob poured onto the docks. Nynaeve wondered if Egwene and the boys had been on board. One woman said that a gleeman had been on the boat. If that had been Thom Merrilin. . . .

She tried her opinion on Moiraine, that some of the Emond's Fielders might have fled on the boat. The Aes Sedai listened patiently, nodding, until she was done.

"Perhaps," Moiraine said then, but she sounded doubtful.

An inn still stood in the square, the common room divided in two by a shoulder-high wall. Moiraine paused as she stepped into the inn, feeling the air with her hand. She smiled at whatever it was she felt, but she would say nothing of it, then.

Their meal was consumed in silence, silence not only at their table, but throughout the common room. The handful of people eating there concentrated on their own plates and their own thoughts. The innkeeper, dusting tables with a corner of his apron, muttered to himself continually, but always too low to be heard. Nynaeve thought it would not be pleasant sleeping there; even the air was heavy with fear.

About the time they pushed their plates away, wiped clean with the last scraps of bread, one of the red-uniformed soldiers appeared in the doorway. He seemed resplendent to Nynaeve, in his peaked helmet and burnished breastplate, until he took a pose just inside the door, with a hand resting on the hilt of his sword and a stern look on his face, and used a finger to ease his too-tight collar. It made her think of Cenn Buie trying to act the way a Village Councilor should.

Lan spared him one glance and snorted. "Militia. Useless."

The soldier looked over the room, letting his eyes come to rest on them. He hesitated, then took a deep breath before stomping over to demand, all in a rush, who they were, what their business was in Whitebridge, and how long they intended to stay.

"We are leaving as soon as I finish my ale," Lan said. He took another slow swallow before looking up at the solider. "The Light illumine good Queen Morgase."

The red-uniformed man opened his mouth, then took a good look at Lan's eyes and stepped back. He caught himself immediately, with a glance at Moiraine and her. She thought for a moment that he was going to do something foolish to keep from looking the coward in front of two women. In her experience, men were often idiots that way. But too much had happened in Whitebridge; too much uncertainty had escaped from the cellars of men's minds. The militiaman looked back at Lan and reconsidered once more. The Warder's hard-planed face was expressionless, but there were those cold blue eyes. So cold.

The militiaman settled on a brisk nod. "See that you do. Too many strangers around these days for the good of the Queen's peace." Turning on his heel he stomped out again, practicing his stern look on the way. None of the locals in the inn seemed to notice.

"Where are we going?" Nynaeve demanded of the Warder. The mood in the room was such that she kept her voice low, but she made sure it was firm, too. "After the boat?"

Lan looked at Moiraine, who shook her head slightly and said, "First I must find the one I can be sure of finding, and at present he is somewhere to the north of us. I do not think the other two went with the boat in any case." A small, satisfied smile touched her lips. "They were in this room, perhaps a day ago, no more than two. Afraid, but they left alive. The trace would not have lasted without that strong emotion."

"Which two?" Nynaeve leaned over the table intently. "Do you know?" The Aes Sedai shook her head, the slightest of motions, and Nynaeve settled back. "If they're only a day or two ahead, why don't we go after them first?"

"I know they were here," Moiraine said in that insufferably calm voice, "but beyond that I cannot say if they went east or north or south. I trust they are smart enough to have gone east, toward Caemlyn, but I do not know, and lacking their tokens, I will not know where they are until I am perhaps within half a mile. In two days they could have gone twenty miles, or forty, in any direction, if fear urged them, and they were certainly afraid when they left here."

"But—"

"Wisdom, however fearful they were, in whatever direction they ran, eventually they will remember Caemlyn, and it is there I will find them. But I will help the one I can find now, first."

Nynaeve opened her mouth again, but Lan cut her off in a soft voice. "They had reason to be afraid." He looked around, then lowered his voice. "There was a Halfman here." He grimaced, the way he had in the square. "I can still smell him everywhere."

Moiraine sighed. "I will keep hope until I know it is gone. I refuse to believe the Dark One can win so easily. I will find all three of them alive and well. I must believe it."

"I want to find the boys, too," Nynaeve said, "but what about Egwene? You never even mention her, and you ignore me when I ask. I thought you were going to take her off to"—she glanced at the other tables, and lowered her voice—"to Tar Valon."

The Aes Sedai studied the tabletop for a moment before raising her eyes to Nynaeve's, and when she did, Nynaeve started back from a flash of anger that almost seemed to make Moiraine's eyes glow. Then her back stiffened, her own anger rising, but before she could say a word, the Aes Sedai spoke coldly.

"I hope to find Egwene alive and well, too. I do not easily give up young women with that much ability once I have found them. But it will be as the Wheel weaves."

Nynaeve felt a cold ball in the pit of her stomach. *Am I one of those young women you won't give up? We'll see about that, Aes Sedai. The Light burn you, we'll see about that!*

The meal was finished in silence, and it was a silent three who rode through the gates and down the Caemlyn Road. Moiraine's eyes searched the horizon to the northeast. Behind them, the smoke-stained town of Whitebridge cowered.

CHAPTER
29

Eyes Without Pity

E lyas pushed for speed across the brown grass flatland as if trying to make up for the time spent with the Traveling People,
setting a pace southward that had even Bela grateful to stop
when twilight deepened. Despite his desire for haste, though, he took
precautions he had not taken before. At night they had a fire only if
there was dead wood already on the ground. He would not let them
break so much as a twig off of a standing tree. The fires he made were
small, and always hidden in a pit carefully dug where he had cut away
a plug of sod. As soon as their meal was prepared, he buried the coals
and replaced the plug. Before they set out again in the gray false dawn,
he went over the campsite inch by inch to make sure there was no sign
that anyone had ever been there. He even righted overturned rocks
and straightened bent-down weeds. He did it quickly, never taking
more than a few minutes, but they did not leave until he was satisfied.

Perrin did not think the precautions were much good against
dreams, but when he began to think of what they might be good
against, he wished it were only the dreams. The first time, Egwene

asked anxiously if the Trollocs were back, but Elyas only shook his head and urged them on. Perrin said nothing. He knew there were no Trollocs close; the wolves scented only grass and trees and small animals. It was not fear of Trollocs that drove Elyas, but that something else of which even Elyas was not sure. The wolves knew nothing of what it was, but they sensed Elyas's urgent wariness, and they began to scout as if danger ran at their heels or waited in ambush over the next rise.

The land became long, rolling crests, too low to be called hills, rising across their path. A carpet of tough grass, still winter sere and dotted With rank weeds, spread before them, rippled by an east wind that had nothing to cut it for a hundred miles. The groves of trees grew more scattered. The sun rose reluctantly, without warmth.

Among the squat ridges Elyas followed the contours of the land as much as possible, and he avoided topping the rises whenever possible. He seldom talked, and when he did. . . .

"You know how long this is taking, going around every bloody little hill like this? Blood and ashes! I'll be till summer getting you off my hands. No, we can't just go in a straight line! How many times do I have to tell you? You have any idea, even the faintest, how a man stands out on a ridgeline in country like this? Burn me, but we're going back and forth as much as forward. Wiggling like a snake. I could move faster with my feet tied. Well, you going to stare at me, or you going to walk?"

Perrin exchanged glances with Egwene. She stuck her tongue out at Elyas's back. Neither of them said anything. The one time Egwene had protested that Elyas was the one who wanted to go around the hills and he should not blame them, it got her a lecture on how sound carried, delivered in a growl that could have been heard a mile off. He gave the lecture over his shoulder, and he never even slowed to give it.

Whether he was talking or not, Elyas's eyes searched all around them, sometimes staring as if there were something to see except the same coarse grass that was under their feet. If he did see anything, Perrin could not, and neither could the wolves. Elyas's forehead grew extra furrows, but he would not explain, not why they had to hurry, not what he was afraid was hunting them.

Sometimes a longer ridge than usual lay across their path, stretching miles and miles to east and west. Even Elyas had to agree that going around those would take them too far out of their way. He did not let them simply cross over, though. Leaving them at the base of the slope, he would creep up to the crest on his belly, peering over as cautiously as though the wolves had not scouted there ten minutes before. Waiting at the bottom of the ridge, minutes passed like hours, and the not knowing pressed on them. Egwene chewed her lip and unconsciously clicked the beads Aram had given her through her fingers. Perrin waited doggedly. His stomach twisted up in a sick knot, but he managed to keep his face calm, managed to keep the turmoil hidden inside.

The wolves will warn if there's danger. It would be wonderful if they went away, if they just vanished, but right now . . . right now, they'll give warning. What is he looking for? What?

After a long search with only his eyes above the rise, Elyas always motioned them to come ahead. Every time the way ahead was clear—until the next time they found a ridge they could not go around. At the third such ridge, Perrin's stomach lurched. Sour fumes rose in his throat, and he knew if he had to wait even five minutes he would vomit. "I. . . ." He swallowed. "I'm coming, too."

"Keep low," was all Elyas said.

As soon as he spoke Egwene jumped down from Bela.

The fur-clad man pushed his round hat forward and peered at her from under the edge. "You expecting to make that mare crawl?" he said dryly.

Her mouth worked, but no sound came out. Finally she shrugged, and Elyas turned away without another word and began climbing the easy slope. Perrin hurried after him.

Well short of the crest Elyas made a downward motion and a moment later flattened himself on the ground, wriggling forward the last few yards. Perrin flopped on his belly.

At the top, Elyas took off his hat before raising his head ever so slowly. Peering through a clump of thorny weeds, Perrin saw only the same rolling plain that lay behind them. The downslope was bare, though a clump of trees a hundred paces across grew in the hollow, perhaps half a mile south from the ridge. The wolves had already been through it, smelling no trace of Trollocs or Myrddraal.

East and west the land was the same as far as Perrin could see, rolling grassland and wide-scattered thickets. Nothing moved. The wolves were more than a mile ahead, out of sight; at that distance he could barely feel them. They had seen nothing when they covered this ground. *What is he looking for? There's nothing there.*

"We're wasting time," he said, starting to stand, and a flock of ravens burst out of the trees below, fifty, a hundred black birds, spiraling into the sky. He froze in a crouch as they milled over the trees. *The*

Dark One's Eyes. Did they see me? Sweat trickled down his face.

As if one thought had suddenly sparked in a hundred tiny minds, every raven broke sharply in the same direction. South. The flock disappeared over the next rise, already descending. To the east another thicket disgorged more ravens. The black mass wheeled twice and headed south.

Shaking, he lowered himself to the ground slowly. He tried to speak, but his mouth was too dry. After a minute he managed to work up some spit. "Was that what you were afraid of? Why didn't you say something? Why didn't the wolves see them?"

"Wolves don't look up in trees much," Elyas growled. "And no, I wasn't looking for this. I told you, I didn't know what. . . ." Far to the west a black cloud rose over yet another grove and winged southward. They were too far off to make out individual birds. "It isn't a big hunt, thank the Light. They don't know. Even after. . . ." He turned to stare back the way they had come.

Perrin swallowed. Even after the dream, Elyas had meant. "Not big?" he said. "Back home you won't see that many ravens in a whole year."

Elyas shook his head. "In the Borderlands I've seen sweeps with a thousand ravens to the flock. Not too often—there's a bounty on ravens there—but it has happened." He was still looking north. "Hush, now."

Perrin felt it, then; the effort of reaching out to the distant wolves. Elyas wanted Dapple and her companions to quit scouting ahead, to hurry back and check their backtrail. His already gaunt face tightened and thinned under the strain. The wolves were so far away Perrin could not even feel them. *Hurry. Watch the sky. Hurry.*

Faintly Perrin caught the reply from far to the south. *We come.* An image flashed in his mind—wolves running, muzzles pointing into the wind of their haste, running as if wildfire raced behind, running—flashed and was gone in an instant.

Elyas slumped and drew a deep breath. Frowning, he peered over the ridge, then back to the north, and muttered under his breath.

"You think there are more ravens behind us?" Perrin asked.

"Could be," Elyas said vaguely. "They do it that way, sometimes. I know a place, if we can reach it by dark. We have to keep moving until full dark anyway, even if we don't get there, but we can't go as fast as I would like. Can't afford to get too close to the ravens ahead of us. But if they're behind us, too. . . ."

"Why dark?" Perrin said. "What place? Somewhere safe from the ravens?"

"Safe from ravens," Elyas said, "but too many people know. . . . Ravens roost for the night. We don't have to worry about them finding us in the dark. The Light send ravens are all we have to worry about then." With one more look over the crest, he rose and waved to Egwene to bring Bela up. "But dark is a long way off. We have to get moving." He started down the far slope in a shambling run, each stride barely catching him on the edge of falling. "Move, burn you!"

Perrin moved, half running, half sliding, after him.

Egwene topped the rise behind them, kicking Bela to a trot. A grin of relief bloomed on her face when she saw them. "What's going on?" she called, urging the shaggy mare to catch up. "When you disappeared like that, I thought. . . . What happened?"

Perrin saved his breath for running until she reached them. He explained about the ravens and Elyas's safe place, but it was a disjointed story. After a strangled, "Ravens!" she kept interrupting with questions for which, as often as not, he had no answers. Between them, he did not finish until they reached the next ridge.

Ordinarily—if anything about the journey could be called ordinary—they would have gone around this one rather than over, but Elyas insisted on scouting anyway.

"You want to just saunter right into the middle of them, boy?" was his sour comment.

Egwene stared at the crest of the ridge, licking her lips, as if she wanted to go with Elyas this time and wanted to stay where she was, too. Elyas was the only one who showed no hesitation.

Perrin wondered if the ravens ever doubled back. It would be a fine thing to reach the crest at the same time as a flock of ravens.

At the top he inched his head up until he could just see, and heaved a sigh of relief when all he saw was a copse of trees a little to the west. There were no ravens to be seen. Abruptly a fox burst out of the trees, running hard. Ravens poured from the branches after it. The beat of their wings almost drowned out a desperate whining from the fox. A black whirlwind dove and swirled around it. The fox's jaws snapped at them, but they darted in, and darted away untouched, black beaks glistening wetly. The fox turned back toward the trees, seeking the safety of its den. It ran awkwardly now, head low, fur dark and bloody, and the ravens flapped around it, more and more of them at once, the fluttering mass thickening until it hid the fox completely. As suddenly as they had descended the ravens rose, wheeled, and vanished over the next rise to the south. A misshapen lump of torn fur marked what had been the fox.

Perrin swallowed hard. *Light! They could do that to us. A hundred ravens. They could—*

"Move," Elyas growled, jumping up. He waved to Egwene to come on, and without waiting set off at a trot toward the trees. "Move, burn you!" he called over his shoulder. "Move!"

Egwene galloped Bela over the rise and caught them before they reached the bottom of the slope. There was no time for explanations, but her eyes picked out the fox right away. Her face went as white as snow.

Elyas reached the trees and turned there, at the edge of the copse, waving vigorously for them to hurry. Perrin tried to run faster and stumbled. Arms windmilling, he barely caught himself short of going flat on his face. *Blood and ashes! I'm running as fast as I can!*

A lone raven winged out of the copse. It tilted toward them, screamed, and spun toward the south. Knowing he was already too late, Perrin fumbled his sling from around his waist. He was still trying to get a stone from his pocket to the sling when the raven abruptly folded up in mid-air and plummeted to the ground. His mouth dropped open, and then he saw the sling hanging from Egwene's hand. She grinned at him unsteadily.

"Don't stand there counting your toes!" Elyas called.

With a start Perrin hurried into the trees, then jumped out of the way to avoid being trampled by Egwene and Bela.

Far to the west, almost out of sight, what seemed like a dark mist rose into the air. Perrin felt the wolves passing in that direction, heading north. He felt them notice ravens, to the left and right of them, without slowing. The dark mist swirled northward as if pursuing the wolves, then abruptly broke off and flashed to the south.

"Do you think they saw us?" Egwene asked. "We were already in the trees, weren't we? They couldn't see us at that distance. Could they? Not that far off."

"We saw them at that distance," Elyas said dryly. Perrin shifted uneasily, and Egwene drew a frightened breath. "If they had seen us," Elyas growled, "they'd have been down on us like they were on that fox. Think, if you want to stay alive. Fear will kill you if you don't control it." His penetrating stare held on each of them for a moment. Finally he nodded. "They're gone, now, and we should be, too. Keep those slings handy. Might be useful again."

As they moved out of the copse, Elyas angled them westward from the line of march they had been following. Perrin's breath snagged in his throat; it was as if they were chasing after the last ravens they had seen. Elyas kept on tirelessly, and there was nothing for them to do but follow. After all, Elyas knew a safe place. Somewhere. So he said.

They ran to the next hill, waited till the ravens moved on, then ran again, waited, ran. The steady progress they had been keeping had been tiring enough, but all except Elyas quickly began to flag under this jerky pace. Perrin's chest heaved, and he gulped air when he had a few minutes to lie on a hilltop, leaving the search to Elyas. Bela stood head down, nostrils flaring, at every stop. Fear lashed them on, and Perrin did not know if it was controlled or not. He only wished the wolves would tell them what was behind them, if anything was, whatever it was.

Ahead were more ravens than Perrin ever hoped to see again. To the left and right the black birds billowed up, and to the south. A dozen times they reached the hiding place of a grove or the scant shelter of a slope only moments before ravens swept into the sky. Once, with the sun beginning to slide from its midday height, they stood in the open, frozen as still as statues, half a mile from the nearest cover, while a hundred of the Dark One's feathered spies flashed by a bare mile to the east. Sweat rolled down Perrin's face despite the wind, until the last black shape dwindled to a dot and vanished. He lost count of the stragglers they brought down with their slings.

He saw more than enough evidence lying in the path the ravens had covered to justify his fear. He had stared with a queasy fascination at a rabbit that had been torn to pieces. The eyeless head stood upright, with the other bits—legs, entrails—scattered in a rough circle around it. Birds, too, stabbed to shapeless masses of feathers. And two more foxes.

He remembered something Lan had said. All the Dark One's creatures delight in killing. The Dark One's power is death. And if the ravens found them? Pitiless eyes shining like black beads. Stabbing beaks swirling around them. Needle-sharp beaks drawing blood. A hundred of them. *Or can they call more of their kind? Maybe all of them in the hunt?* A sickening image built up in his mind. A pile of ravens as big as a hill, seething like maggots, fighting over a few bloody shreds.

Suddenly the image was swept away by others, each one clear for an instant, then spinning and fading into another. The wolves had found ravens to the north. Screaming birds dove and whirled and dove again, beaks drawing blood with every swoop. Snarling wolves dodged and leaped, twisting in the air, jaws snapping. Again and again Perrin tasted feathers and the foul taste of fluttering ravens crushed alive, felt the pain of oozing gashes all over his body, knew with a despair that never touched on giving up that all his effort was not enough. Suddenly the ravens broke away, wheeling overhead for one last shriek of rage at the wolves. Wolves did not die as easily as foxes, and they had a mission. A flap of black wings, and they were gone, a few black feathers drifting down on their dead. Wind licked at a puncture on his left foreleg. There was something wrong with one of Hopper's eyes. Ignoring her own hurts, Dapple gathered them and they settled into a painful lope in the direction the ravens had gone. Blood matted their fur. *We come. Danger comes before us.*

Moving in a stumbling trot, Perrin exchanged a glance with Elyas. The man's yellow eyes were expressionless, but he knew. He said nothing, just watched Perrin and waited, all the while maintaining that effortless lope.

Waiting for me. Waiting for me to admit I feel the wolves.

"Ravens," Perrin panted reluctantly. "Behind us."

"He was right," Egwene breathed. "You can talk to them."

Perrin's feet felt like lumps of iron on the ends of wooden posts, but he tried to make them move faster. If he could outrun their eyes, outrun the ravens, outrun the wolves, but above all Egwene's eyes, that knew him now for what he was. *What are you? Tainted, the Light blind me! Cursed!*

His throat burned as it never had from breathing the smoke and heat of Master Luhhan's forge. He staggered and hung on to Egwene's stirrup until she climbed down and all but pushed him into the saddle despite his protests that he could keep going. It was not long, though, before she was clutching the stirrup as she ran, holding up her skirts with her other hand, and only a little while after that until he dismounted, his knees still wobbling. He had to pick her up to make her take his place, but she was too tired to fight him.

Elyas would not slow down. He urged them, and taunted them, and kept them so close behind the searching ravens to the south that Perrin thought all it would take would be for one bird to look back. "Keep moving, burn you! Think you'll do any better than that fox did, if they catch us? The one with its insides piled on its head?" Egwene swayed out of the saddle and vomited noisily. "I knew you'd remember. Just keep going a little more. That's all. Just a little more. Burn you, I thought farm youngsters had endurance. Work all day and dance all night. Sleep all day and sleep all night, looks like to me. Move your bloody feet!"

They began coming down off the hills as soon as the last raven vanished over the next one, then while the last trailers still flapped above the hilltop. *One bird looking back.* To east and west the ravens searched while they hurried across the open spaces between. *One bird is all it will take.*

The ravens behind were coming fast. Dapple and the other wolves worked their way around them and were coming on without stopping to lick their wounds, but they had learned all the lessons they needed about watching the sky. *How close? How long?* The wolves had no notions of time the way men did, no reasons to divide a day into hours. The seasons were time enough for them, and the light and the dark. No need for more. Finally Perrin worked out an image of where the sun would stand in the sky when the ravens overran them from behind. He glanced over his shoulder at the setting sun, and licked his lips with a dry tongue. In an hour the ravens would be on them, maybe less. An hour, and it was a good two hours to sunset, at least two to full dark.

We'll die with the setting sun, he thought, staggering as he ran. Slaughtered like the fox. He fingered his axe, then moved to his sling. That would be more use. Not enough, though. Not against a hundred ravens, a hundred darting targets, a hundred stabbing beaks.

"It's your turn to ride, Perrin," Egwene said tiredly.

"In a bit," he panted. "I'm good for miles, yet." She nodded, and stayed in the saddle. *She is tired. Tell her? Or let her think we still have a chance to escape? An hour of hope, even if it is desperate, or an hour of despair?*

Elyas was watching him again, saying nothing. He must know, but he did not speak. Perrin looked at Egwene again and blinked away hot tears. He touched his axe and wondered if he had the courage. In the last minutes, when the ravens descended on them, when all hope was gone, would he have the courage to spare her the death the fox had died? *Light make me strong!*

The ravens ahead of them suddenly seemed to vanish. Perrin could still make out dark, misty clouds, far to the east and west, but ahead . . . nothing. *Where did they go? Light, if we've overrun them. . . .*

Abruptly a chill ran through him, one cold, clean tingle as if he had jumped into the Winespring Water in midwinter. It rippled through him and seemed to carry away some of his fatigue, a little of the ache in his legs and the burning of his lungs. It left behind . . . something. He could not say what, only he felt different. He stumbled to a halt and looked around, afraid.

Elyas watched him, watched them all, with a gleam behind his eyes.

He knew what it was, Perrin was sure of it, but he only watched them.

Egwene reined in Bela and looked around uncertainly, half wondering and half fearful. "It's . . . strange," she whispered. "I feel as if I lost something." Even the mare had her head up expectantly, nostrils flaring as if they detected a faint odor of new-mown hay.

"What . . . what was that?" Perrin asked.

Elyas cackled suddenly. He bent over, shoulders shaking, to rest his hands on his knees. "Safety, that's what. We made it, you bloody fools. No raven will cross that line . . . not one that carries the Dark One's eyes, anyways. A Trolloc would have to be driven across, and there'd need to be something fierce pushing the Myrddraal to make him do the driving. No Aes Sedai, either. The One Power won't work here; they can't touch the True Source. Can't even feel the Source, like it vanished. Makes them itch inside, that does. Gives them the shakes like a seven-day drunk. It's safety."

At first, to Perrin's eyes, the land was unchanged from the rolling hills and ridges they had crossed the whole day. Then he noticed green shoots among the grass; not many, and they were struggling, but more than he had seen anywhere else. There were fewer weeds in the grass, too. He could not imagine what it was, but there was . . . something about this place. And something in what Elyas said tickled his memory.

"What is it?" Egwene asked. "I feel. . . . What is this place? I don't think I like it."

"A *stedding*," Elyas roared. "You never listen to stories? Of course, there hasn't been an Ogier here in three thousand odd years, not since the Breaking of the World, but it's the *stedding* makes the Ogier, not the Ogier make the *stedding*."

"Just a legend," Perrin stammered. In the stories, the *stedding* were always havens, places to hide, whether it was from Aes Sedai or from creatures of the Father of Lies.

Elyas straightened; if not exactly fresh, he gave no sign that he had spent most of a day running. "Come on. We'd better get deeper into this legend. The ravens can't follow, but they can still see us this close to the edge, and there could be enough of them to watch the whole border of it. Let them keep hunting right on by it."

Perrin wanted to stay right there, now that he was stopped; his legs trembled and told him to lie down for a week. Whatever refreshment he had felt had been momentary; all the weariness and aches were back. He forced himself to take one step, then another. It did not get easier, but he kept at it. Egwene flapped the reins to get Bela moving again. Elyas settled into an effortless lope, only slowing to a walk when it became apparent the others could not keep up. A fast walk.

"Why don't—we stay here?" Perrin panted. He was breathing through his mouth, and he forced the words out between deep, wracking breaths. "If it's really—a *stedding*. We'd be safe. No Trollocs. No Aes Sedai. Why don't we—just stay here—until it's all over?" *Maybe the wolves won't come here, either.*

"How long will that be?" Elyas looked over his shoulder with one eyebrow raised. "What would you eat? Grass, like the horse? Besides, there's others know about this place, and nothing keeps men out, not even the worst of them. And there is only one place where there's still water to be found." Frowning uneasily, he turned in a complete circle, scanning the land. When he was done, he shook his head and muttered to himself. Perrin felt him calling to the wolves. *Hurry. Hurry.* "We take our chances on a choice of evils, and the ravens are sure. Come on. It's only another mile or two."

Perrin would have groaned if he had been willing to spare the breath.

Huge boulders began to dot the low hills, irregular lumps of gray, lichen-coated stone half buried in the ground, some as big as a house. Brambles webbed them, and low brush half hid most. Here and there amid the desiccated brown of brambles and brush a lone green shoot announced that this was a special place. Whatever wounded the land beyond its borders hurt it, too, but here the wound did not go quite as deep.

Eventually they straggled over one more rise, and at the base of this hill lay a pool of water. Any of them could have waded across it in two strides, but it was clear and clean enough to show the sandy bottom like a sheet of glass. Even Elyas hurried eagerly down the slope.

Perrin threw himself full length on the ground when he reached the pool and plunged his head in. An instant later he was spluttering from the cold of water that had welled up from the depths of the earth. He shook his head, his long hair spraying a rain of drops. Egwene grinned and splashed back at him. Perrin's eyes grew sober. She frowned and opened her mouth, but he stuck his face back in the water. *No questions. Not now. No explanations. Not ever.* But a small voice taunted him. *But you would have done it, wouldn't you?*

Eventually Elyas called them away from the pool. "Anybody wants to eat, I want some help."

Egwene worked cheerfully, laughing and joking as they prepared their scanty meal. There was nothing left but cheese and dried meat;

there had been no chance to hunt. At least there was still tea. Perrin did his share, but silently. He felt Egwene's eyes on him, saw growing worry on her face, but he avoided meeting her eyes as much as he could. Her laughter faded, and the jokes came further apart, each one more strained than the last. Elyas watched, saying nothing. A somber mood descended, and they began their meal in silence. The sun grew red in the west, and their shadows stretched out long and thin.

Not quite an hour till dark. If not for the stedding, *all of you would be dead now. Would you have saved her? Would you have cut her down like so many bushes? Bushes don't bleed, do they? Or scream, and look in your eyes and ask, why?*

Perrin drew in on himself more. He could feel something laughing at him, deep in the back of his mind. Something cruel. Not the Dark One. He almost wished it was. Not the Dark One; himself.

For once Elyas had broken his rule about fires. There were no trees, but he had snapped dead branches from the brush and built his fire against a huge chunk of rock sticking out of the hillside. From the layers of soot staining the stone, Perrin thought the site must have been used by generation after generation of travelers.

What showed above ground of the big rock was rounded somewhat, with a sharp break on one side where moss, old and brown, covered the ragged surface. The grooves and hollows eroded in the rounded part looked odd to Perrin, but he was too absorbed in gloom to wonder about it. Egwene, though, studied it as she ate.

"That," she said finally, "looks like an eye." Perrin blinked; it *did* look like an eye, under all that soot.

"It is," Elyas said. He sat with his back to the fire and the rock, studying the land around them while he chewed a strip of dried meat almost as tough as leather. "Artur Hawkwing's eye. The eye of the High King himself. This is what his power and glory came to, in the end." He said it absently. Even his chewing was absentminded; his eyes and his attention were on the hills.

"Artur Hawkwing!" Egwene exclaimed. "You're joking with me. It isn't an eye at all. Why would somebody carve Artur Hawkwing's eye on a rock out here?"

Elyas glanced over his shoulder at her, muttering, "What do they teach you village whelps?" He snorted and straightened back to his watching, but he went on talking. "Artur Paendrag Tanreall, Artur Hawkwing, the High King, united all the lands from the Great Blight to the Sea of Storms, from the Aryth Ocean to the Aiel Waste, and even some beyond the Waste. He even sent armies the other side of the Aryth Ocean. The stories say he ruled the whole world, but what he really did rule was enough for any man outside of a story. And he brought peace and justice to the land."

"All stood equal before the law," Egwene said, "and no man raised his hand against another."

"So you've heard the stories, at least." Elyas chuckled, a dry sound. "Artur Hawkwing brought peace and justice, but he did it with fire and sword. A child could ride alone with a bag of gold from the Aryth Ocean to the Spine of the World and never have a moment's fear, but the High King's justice was as hard as that rock there for anyone who challenged his power, even if it was just by being who they were, or by people thinking they were a challenge. The common folk had peace, and justice, and full bellies, but he laid a twenty-year siege to Tar Valon and put a price of a thousand gold crowns on the head of every Aes Sedai."

"I thought you didn't like Aes Sedai," Egwene said.

Elyas gave a wry smile. "Doesn't matter what I like, girl. Artur Hawkwing was a proud fool. An Aes Sedai healer could have saved him when he took sick—or was poisoned, as some say—but every Aes Sedai still alive was penned up behind the Shining Walls, using all their Power to hold off an army that lit up the night with their campfires. He wouldn't have let one near him, anyway. He hated Aes Sedai as much as he hated the Dark One."

Egwene's mouth tightened, but when she spoke, all she said was, "What does all that have to do with whether that's Artur Hawkwing's eye?"

"Just this, girl. With peace except for what was going on across the ocean, with the people cheering him wherever he went—they really loved him, you see; he was a harsh man, but never with the common folk—well, with all of that, he decided it was time to build himself a capital. A new city, not connected in any man's mind with any old cause or faction or rivalry. Here, he'd build it, at the very center of the land bordered by the seas and the Waste and the Blight. Here, where no Aes Sedai would ever come willing or could use the Power if they did. A capital from which, one day, the whole world would receive peace and justice. When they heard the proclamation, the common people subscribed enough money to build a monument to him. Most of them looked on him as only a step below the Creator. A short step. It took five years to carve and build. A statue of Hawkwing, himself, a hundred times bigger than the man. They raised it right here, and the city was to rise around it."

"There was never any city here," Egwene scoffed. "There would have to be something left if there was. Something."

Elyas nodded, still keeping his watch. "Indeed there was not. Artur Hawkwing died the very day the statue was finished, and his sons and the rest of his blood fought over who would sit on Hawkwing's throne. The statue stood alone in the midst of these hills. The sons and the nephews and the cousins died, and the last of the Hawkwing's blood vanished from the earth—except maybe for some of those who went over the Aryth Ocean. There were those who would have erased even the memory of him, if they could. Books were burned just because they mentioned his name. In the end there was nothing left of him but the stories, and most of them wrong. That's what his glory came to.

"The fighting didn't stop, of course, just because the Hawkwing and his kin were dead. There was still a throne to be won, and every lord and lady who could muster fighting men wanted it. It was the beginning of the War of the Hundred Years. Lasted a hundred and twenty-three, really, and most of the history of that time is lost in the smoke of burning towns. Many got a part of the land, but none got the whole, and sometime during those years the statue was pulled down. Maybe they couldn't stand measuring themselves against it any longer."

"First you sound as if you despise him," Egwene said, "and now you sound as if you admire him." She shook her head.

Elyas turned to look at her, a flat, unblinking stare. "Get some more tea now, if you want any. I want the fire out before dark."

Perrin could make out the eye clearly now, despite the failing light. It was bigger than a man's head, and the shadows falling across it made it seem like a raven's eye, hard and black and without pity. He wished they were sleeping somewhere else.

CHAPTER
30

Children of Shadow

E gwene sat by the fire, staring up at the fragment of statue, but
Perrin went down by the pool to be alone. Day was fading,
and the night wind was already rising out of the east, ruffling
the surface of the water. He took the axe from the loop on his belt
and turned it over in his hands. The ashwood haft was as long as his
arm, and smooth and cool to the touch. He hated it. He was ashamed
of how proud he had been of the axe back in Emond's Field. Before
he knew what he might be willing to do with it.

"You hate her that much?" Elyas said behind him.

Startled, he jumped and half raised the axe before he saw who it
was. "Can . . . ? Can you read my mind, too? Like the wolves?"

Elyas cocked his head to one side and eyed him quizzically. "A blind
man could read your face, boy. Well, speak up. Do you hate the girl?
Despise her? That's it. You were ready to kill her because you despise
her, always dragging her feet, holding you back with her womanish
ways."

"Egwene never dragged her feet in her life," he protested. "She

always does her share. I don't despise her, I love her." He glared at
Elyas, daring him to laugh. "Not like that. I mean, she isn't like a
sister, but she and Rand. . . . Blood and ashes! If the ravens caught
us. . . . If. . . . I don't know."

"Yes, you do. If she had to choose her way of dying, which do you
think she'd pick? One clean blow of your axe, or the way the animals
we saw today died? I know which I'd take."

"I don't have any right to choose for her. You won't tell her, will
you? About. . . ." His hands tightened on the axe haft; the muscles in
his arms corded, heavy muscles for his age, built by long hours swinging the hammer at Master Luhhan's forge. For an instant he thought
the thick wooden shaft would snap. "I hate this bloody thing," he
growled. "I don't know what I'm doing with it, strutting around like
some kind of fool. I couldn't have done it, you know. When it was all
pretend and maybe, I could swagger, and play as if I. . . ." He sighed,
his voice fading. "It's different, now. I don't ever want to use it again."

"You'll use it."

Perrin raised the axe to throw it in the pool, but Elyas caught his
wrist.

"You'll use it, boy, and as long as you hate using it, you will use it
more wisely than most men would. Wait. If ever you don't hate it any
longer, then will be the time to throw it as far as you can and run the
other way."

Perrin hefted the axe in his hands, still tempted to leave it in the
pool. *Easy for him to say wait. What if I wait and then* can't *throw it
away?*

He opened his mouth to ask Elyas, but no words came out. A sending from the wolves, so urgent that his eyes glazed over. For an instant
he forgot what he had been going to say, forgot he had been going to
say anything, forgot even how to speak, how to breathe. Elyas's face
sagged, too, and his eyes seemed to peer inward and far away. Then
it was gone, as quickly as it had come. It had only lasted a heartbeat,
but that was enough.

Perrin shook himself and filled his lungs deeply. Elyas did not pause;
as soon as the veil lifted from his eyes, he sped toward the fire without
any hesitation. Perrin ran wordlessly behind him.

"Douse the fire!" Elyas called hoarsely to Egwene. He gestured urgently, and he seemed to be trying to shout in a whisper. "Get it out!"

She rose to her feet, staring at him uncertainly, then stepped closer
to the fire, but slowly, clearly not understanding what was happening.

Elyas pushed roughly past her and snatched up the tea kettle, cursing when it burned him. Juggling the hot pot, he upended it over the fire just the same. A step behind him, Perrin arrived in time to start kicking dirt over the hissing coals as the last of the tea splashed into the fire, hissing and rising in tendrils of steam. He did not stop until the last vestige of the fire was buried.

Elyas tossed the kettle to Perrin, who immediately let it fall with a choked-off yell. Perrin blew on his hands, frowning at Elyas, but the fur-clad man was too busy giving their campsite a hasty look to pay any attention.

"No chance to hide that somebody's been here," Elyas said. "We'll just have to hurry and hope. Maybe they won't bother. Blood and ashes, but I was sure it was the ravens."

Hurriedly Perrin tossed the saddle on Bela, propping the axe against his thigh while he bent to tighten the girth.

"What is it?" Egwene asked. Her voice shook. "Trollocs? A Fade?"

"Go east or west," Elyas told Perrin. "Find a place to hide, and I'll join you as soon as I can. If they see a wolf. . . ." He darted away, crouching almost as if he intended to go to all fours, and vanished into the lengthening shadows of evening.

Egwene hastily gathered her few belongings, but she still demanded an explanation from Perrin. Her voice was insistent and growing more frightened by the minute as he kept silent. He was frightened, too, but fear made them move faster. He waited until they were headed toward the setting sun. Trotting ahead of Bela and holding the axe across his chest in both hands, he told what he knew over his shoulder in snatches while hunting for a place to go to ground and wait for Elyas.

"There are a lot of men coming, on horses. They came up behind the wolves, but the men didn't see them. They're heading toward the pool. Probably they don't have anything to do with us; it's the only water for miles. But Dapple says. . . ." He glanced over his shoulder. The evening sun painted odd shadows on her face, shadows that hid her expression. *What is she thinking? Is she looking at you as if she doesn't know you anymore? Does she know you?* "Dapple says they smell wrong. It's . . . sort of the way a rabid dog smells wrong." The pool was lost to sight behind them. He could still pick out boulders—fragments of Artur Hawkwing's statue—in the deepening twilight, but not to tell which was the stone where the fire had been. "We'll stay away from them, find a place to wait for Elyas."

"Why should they bother us?" she demanded. "We're supposed to be safe here. It's supposed to be safe. Light, there has to be some place safe."

Perrin began looking harder for somewhere to hide. They could not be very far from the pool, but the twilight was thickening. Soon it would be too dark to travel. Faint light still bathed the crests. From the hollows between, where there was barely enough to see, it seemed bright by contrast. Off to the left a dark shape stood sharp against the sky, a large, flat stone slanting out of a hillside, cloaking the slope beneath in darkness.

"This way," he said.

He trotted toward the hill, glancing over his shoulder for any sign of the men who were coming. There was nothing—yet. More than once he had to stop and wait while the others stumbled after him. Egwene was crouched over Bela's neck, and the mare was picking her way carefully over the uneven ground. Perrin thought they both must be more tired than he had believed. *This had better be a good hiding place. I don't think we can hunt for another.*

At the base of the hill he studied the massive, flat rock outlined against the sky, jutting out the slope almost at the crest. There was an odd familiarity to the way the top of the huge slab seemed to form irregular steps, three up and one down. He climbed the short distance and felt across the stone, walking along it. Despite the weathering of centuries he could still feel four joined columns. He glanced up at the step-like top of the stone, towering over his head like a huge lean-to. Fingers. *We'll shelter in Artur Hawkwing's hand. Maybe some of his justice is left here.*

He motioned for Egwene to join him. She did not move, so he slid back down to the base of the hill and told her what he had found.

Egwene peered up the hill with her head pushed forward. "How can you see anything?" she asked.

Perrin opened his mouth, then shut it. He licked his lips as he looked around, for the first time really aware of what he was seeing. The sun was down. All the way down, now, and clouds hid the full moon, but it still seemed like the deep purple fringes of twilight to him. "I felt the rock," he said finally. "That's what it has to be. They won't be able to pick us out against the shadow of it even if they come this far." He took Bela's bridle to lead her to the shelter of the hand. He could feel Egwene's eyes on his back.

As he was helping her down from the saddle, the night broke out in shouts back toward the pool. She laid a hand on Perrin's arm, and he heard her unspoken question.

"The men saw Wind," he said reluctantly. It was difficult to pick out the meaning of the wolves' thoughts. Something about fire. "They have torches." He pressed her down at the base of the fingers and crouched beside her. "They're breaking up into parties to search. So many of them, and the wolves are all hurt." He tried to make his voice heartier. "But Dapple and the others should be able to keep out of their way, even injured, and they don't expect us. People don't see what they don't expect. They'll give up soon enough and make camp." Elyas was with the wolves, and would not leave them while they were hunted. *So many riders. So persistent. Why so persistent?*

He saw Egwene nod, but in the dark she did not realize it. "We'll be all right, Perrin."

Light, he thought wonderingly, she's *trying to comfort* me.

The shouts went on and on. Small knots of torches moved in the distance, flickering points of light in the darkness.

"Perrin," Egwene said softly, "will you dance with me at Sunday? If we're home by then?"

His shoulders shook. He made no sound, and he did not know if he was laughing or crying. "I will. I promise." Against his will his hands tightened on the axe, reminding him that he still held it. His voice dropped to a whisper. "I promise," he said again, and hoped.

Groups of torch-carrying men now rode through the hills, bunches of ten or twelve. Perrin could not tell how many groups there were. Sometimes three or four were in sight at once, quartering back and forth. They continued to shout to one another, and sometimes there were screams in the night, the screams of horses, the screams of men.

He saw it all from more than one vantage. He crouched on the hillside with Egwene, watching the torches move through the darkness like fireflies, and in his mind he ran in the night with Dapple, and Wind, and Hopper. The wolves had been too hurt by the ravens to run far or fast, so they intended to drive the men out of the darkness, drive them to the shelter of their fires. Men always sought the safety of fires in the end, when wolves roamed the night. Some of the mounted men led strings of horses without riders; they whinnied and reared with wide, rolling eyes when the gray shapes darted among them, screaming and pulling their lead ropes from the hands of the men who held them, scattering in all directions as fast as they could run. Horses with men on their backs screamed, too, when gray shadows flashed out of the dark with hamstringing fangs, and sometimes their riders screamed as well, just before jaws tore out their throats. Elyas was out there, also, more dimly sensed, stalking the night with his long knife, a two-legged wolf with one sharp steel tooth. The shouts became curses more often than not, but the searchers refused to give up.

Abruptly Perrin realized that the men with torches were following a pattern. Each time some of the parties came in view, one of them, at least, was closer to the hillside where he and Egwene were hiding. Elyas had said to hide, but. . . . *What if we run? Maybe we could hide in the dark, if we keep moving. Maybe. It has to be dark enough for that.*

He turned to Egwene, but as he did the decision was taken away from him. Bunched torches, a dozen of them, came around the base of the hill, wavering with the trot of the horses. Lanceheads gleamed in the torchlight. He froze, holding his breath, hands tightening on his axe haft.

The horsemen rode past the hill, but one of the men shouted, and the torches swung back. He thought desperately, seeking for a way to go. But as soon as they moved they would be seen, if they had not already been, and once they were marked they would have no chance, not even with the darkness to help.

The horsemen drew up at the foot of the hill, each man holding a torch in one hand and a long lance in the other, guiding his horse by the pressure of his knees. By the light of the torches Perrin could see the white cloaks of the Children of the Light. They held the torches high and leaned forward in their saddles, peering up at the deep shadows under Artur Hawkwing's fingers.

"There *is* something up there," one of them said. His voice was too loud, as if he was afraid of what lay outside the light of his torch. "I told you somebody could hide in that. Isn't that a horse?"

Egwene laid a hand on Perrin's arm; her eyes were big in the dark. Her silent question plain despite the shadow hiding her features. What to do? Elyas and the wolves still hunted through the night. The horses below shifted their feet nervously. *If we run now, they'll chase us down.*

One of the Whitecloaks stepped his horse forward and shouted up the hill. "If you can understand human speech, come down and surrender. You'll not be harmed if you walk in the Light. If you don't surrender, you will all be killed. You have one minute." The lances lowered, long steel heads bright with torchlight.

"Perrin," Egwene whispered, "we can't outrun them. If we don't give up, they'll kill us. Perrin?"

Elyas and the wolves were still free. Another distant, bubbling scream marked a Whitecloak who had hunted Dapple too closely. *If we run. . . .* Egwene was looking at him, waiting for him to tell her what to do. *If we run. . . .* He shook his head wearily and stood up like a man in a trance, stumbling down the hill toward the Children of the Light. He heard Egwene sigh and follow him, her feet dragging reluctantly. *Why are the Whitecloaks so persistent, as if they hate wolves with a passion? Why do they smell wrong?* He almost thought he could smell the wrongness himself, when the wind gusted from the riders.

"Drop that axe," the leader barked.

Perrin stumbled toward him, wrinkling his nose to get rid of the smell he thought he smelt.

"Drop it, bumpkin!" The leader's lance shifted toward Perrin's chest.

For a moment he stared at the lancehead, enough sharp steel to go completely through him, and abruptly he shouted, "No!" It was not at the horseman he shouted.

Out of the night Hopper came, and Perrin was one with the wolf. Hopper, the cub who had watched the eagles soar, and wanted so badly to fly through the sky as the eagles did. The cub who hopped and jumped and leaped until he could leap higher than any other wolf, and who never lost the cub's yearning to soar through the sky. Out of the night Hopper came and left the ground in a leap, soaring like the eagles. The Whitecloaks had only a moment to begin cursing before Hopper's jaws closed on the throat of the man with his lance leveled at Perrin. The big wolf's momentum carried them both off the other side of the horse. Perrin felt the throat crushing, tasted the blood.

Hopper landed lightly, already apart from the man he had killed. Blood matted his fur, his own blood and that of others. A gash down his face crossed the empty socket where his left eye had been. His good eye met Perrin's two for just an instant. *Run, brother!* He whirled to leap again, to soar one last time, and a lance pinned him to the earth. A second length of steel thrust through his ribs, driving into the ground under him. Kicking, he snapped at the shafts that held him. *To soar.*

Pain filled Perrin, and he screamed, a wordless scream that had something of a wolf's cry in it. Without thinking he leaped forward, still screaming. All thought was gone. The horsemen had bunched too much to be able to use their lances, and the axe was a feather in his hands, one huge wolf's tooth of steel. Something crashed into his head, and as he fell, he did not know if it was Hopper or himself who died.

". . . soar like the eagles."

Mumbling, Perrin opened his eyes woozily. His head hurt, and he could not remember why. Blinking against the light, he looked around. Egwene was kneeling and watching him where he lay. They were in a square tent as big as a medium-sized room in a farmhouse, with a ground cloth for a floor. Oil lamps on tall stands, one in each corner, gave a bright light.

"Thank the Light, Perrin," she breathed. "I was afraid they had killed you."

Instead of answering, he stared at the gray-haired man seated in the lone chair in the tent. A dark-eyed, grandfatherly face looked back at him, a face at odds in his mind with the white-and-gold tabard the man wore, and the burnished armor strapped over his pure-white undercoat. It seemed a kindly face, bluff and dignified, and something about it fit the elegant austerity of the tent's furnishings. A table and a folding bed, a washstand with a plain white basin and pitcher, a single wooden chest inlaid in simple geometric patterns. Where there was wood, it was polished to a soft glow, and the metal gleamed, but not too brightly, and nothing was showy. Everything in the tent had the look of craftsmanship, but only someone who had watched the work of craftsmen—like Master Luhhan, or Master Aydaer, the cabinetmaker—would see it.

Frowning, the man stirred two small piles of objects on the table with a blunt finger. Perrin recognized the contents of his pockets in one of those piles, and his belt knife. The silver coin Moiraine had given him toppled out, and the man pushed it back thoughtfully. Pursing his lips, he left the piles and lifted Perrin's axe from the table, hefting it. His attention came back to the Emond's Fielders.

Perrin tried to get up. Sharp pain stabbing along his arms and legs turned the movement into a flop. For the first time he realized that he was tied, hand and foot. His eyes went to Egwene. She shrugged ruefully, and twisted so that he could see her back. Half a dozen lashings wrapped her wrists and ankles, the cords making ridges in her flesh. A length of rope ran between the bonds around ankles and wrists, short enough to stop her from straightening to more than a crouch if she got to her feet.

Perrin stared. That they were tied was shock enough, but they wore enough ropes to hold horses. *What do they think we are?*

The gray-haired man watched them, curious and thoughtful, like Master al'Vere puzzling out a problem. He held the axe as if he had forgotten it.

The tent flap shifted aside, and a tall man stepped into the tent. His face was long and gaunt, with eyes so deeply set they seemed to look out from caves. There was no excess flesh on him, no fat at all; his skin was pulled tight over the muscle and bone beneath.

Perrin had a glimpse of night outside, and campfires, and two white-cloaked guards at the entrance of the tent, then the flap fell back into place. As soon as the newcomer was into the tent, he stopped, standing as rigid as an iron rod, staring straight ahead of him at the far wall of the tent. His plate-and-mail armor gleamed like silver against his snowy cloak and undercoat.

"My Lord Captain." His voice was as hard as his posture, and grating, but somehow flat, without expression.

The gray-haired man made a casual gesture. "Be at your ease, Child Byar. You have tallied our costs for this . . . encounter?"

The tall man moved his feet apart, but other than that Perrin did not see anything ease about his stance. "Nine men dead, my Lord Captain, and twenty-three injured, seven seriously. All can ride, though. Thirty horses had to be put down. They were hamstrung!" He emphasized that in his emotionless voice, as if what had happened to the horses were worse than the deaths and injuries to men. "Many of the remounts are scattered. We may find some at daybreak, my Lord Captain, but with wolves to send them on their way, it will take days to gather them all. The men who were supposed to be watching them have been assigned to night guard until we reach Caemlyn."

"We do not have days, Child Byar," the gray-haired man said mildly. "We ride at dawn. Nothing can change that. We must be in Caemlyn in time, yes?"

"As you command, my Lord Captain."

The gray-haired man glanced at Perrin and Egwene, then away again. "And what have we to show for it, aside from these two younglings?"

Byar drew a deep breath and hesitated. "I have had the wolf that was with this lot skinned, my Lord Captain. The hide should make a fine rug for my Lord Captain's tent."

Hopper! Not even realizing what he was doing, Perrin growled and struggled against his bonds. The ropes dug into his skin—his wrists became slippery with blood—but they did not give.

For the first time Byar looked at the prisoners. Egwene started back from him. His face was as expressionless as his voice, but a cruel light burned in his sunken eyes, as surely as flames burned in Ba'alzamon's. Byar hated them as if they were enemies of long years instead of people never seen before tonight.

Perrin stared back defiantly. His mouth curled into a tight smile at the thought of his teeth meeting in the man's throat.

Abruptly his smile faded, and he shook himself. *My teeth? I'm a man, not a wolf! Light, there has to be an end to this!* But he still met Byar's glare, hate for hate.

"I do not care about wolf-hide rugs, Child Byar." The rebuke in the Lord Captain's voice was gentle, but Byar's back snapped rigid again, his eyes locking to the wall of the tent. "You were reporting on what we achieved this night, no? If we achieved anything."

"I would estimate the pack that attacked us at fifty beasts or more, my Lord Captain. Of that, we killed at least twenty, perhaps thirty. I did not consider it worth the risk of losing more horses to have the carcasses brought in tonight. In the morning I will have them gathered and burned, those that aren't dragged off in the dark. Besides these two, there were at least a dozen other men. I believe we disposed of four or five, but it is unlikely we will find any bodies, given the Dark-friends' propensity for carrying away their dead to hide their losses. This seems to have been a coordinated ambush, but that raises the question of. . . ."

Perrin's throat tightened as the gaunt man went on. Elyas? Cautiously, reluctantly, he felt for Elyas, for the wolves . . . and found nothing. It was as if he had never been able to feel a wolf's mind. *Either they're dead, or they've abandoned you.* He wanted to laugh, a bitter laugh. At last he had what he had been wishing for, but the price was high.

The gray-haired man did laugh, just then, a rich, wry chuckle that made a red spot bloom on each of Byar's cheeks. "So, Child Byar, it is your considered estimate that we were attacked in a planned ambush by upwards of fifty wolves and better than half a score of Darkfriends? Yes? Perhaps when you've seen a few more actions. . . ."

"But, my Lord Captain Bornhald. . . ."

"I would say six or eight wolves, Child Byar, and perhaps no other humans than these two. You have the true zeal, but no experience outside the cities. It is a different thing, bringing the Light, when streets and houses are far distant. Wolves have a way of seeming more than they are, in the night—and men, also. Six or eight at most, I think." Byar's flush deepened slowly. "I also suspect they were here for the same reason we are: the only easy water for at least a day in any direction. A much simpler explanation than spies or traitors within the Children, and the simplest explanation is usually the truest. You will learn, with experience."

Byar's face went deathly white as the grandfatherly man spoke; by contrast, the two spots in his hollow cheeks deepened from red to purple. He cut his eyes toward the two prisoners for an instant.

He hates us even more, now, Perrin thought, *for hearing this. But why did he hate us in the first place?*

"What do you think of this?" the Lord Captain said, holding up Perrin's axe.

Byar looked a question at his commander and waited for an answering nod before he broke his rigid stance to take the weapon. He hefted the axe and gave a surprised grunt, then whirled it in a tight arc above his head that barely missed the top of the tent. He handled it as surely as if he had been born with an axe in his hands. A look of grudging admiration flickered across his face, but by the time he lowered the axe he was expressionless once more.

"Excellently balanced, my Lord Captain. Plainly made, but by a very good weaponsmith, perhaps even a master." His eyes burned darkly at the prisoners. "Not a villager's weapon, my Lord Captain. Nor a farmer's."

"No." The gray-haired man turned toward Perrin and Egwene with a weary, slightly chiding smile, a kindly grandfather who knew his grandchildren had been up to some mischief. "My name is Geofram Bornhald," he told them. "You are Perrin, I understand. But you, young woman, what is your name?"

Perrin glowered at him, but Egwene shook her head. "Don't be silly, Perrin. I'm Egwene."

"Just Perrin, and just Egwene," Bornhald murmured. "But I suppose if you truly are Darkfriends, you wish to hide your identities as much as possible."

Perrin heaved himself up to his knees; he could rise no further because of the way he was bound. "We aren't Darkfriends," he protested angrily.

The words were not completely out of his mouth before Byar reached him. The man moved like a snake. He saw the handle of his own axe swinging toward him and tried to duck, but the thick haft caught him over the ear. Only the fact that he was moving away from the blow kept his skull from being split. Even so, lights flashed in his eyes. Breath left him as he struck the ground. His head rung, and blood ran down his cheek.

"You have no right," Egwene began, and screamed as the axe handle whipped toward her. She threw herself aside, and the blow whistled through empty air as she tumbled to the ground cloth.

"You will keep a civil tongue," Byar said, "when speaking to an Anointed of the Light, or you will have no tongue." The worst of it was his voice still had no emotion at all. Cutting out their tongues would give him no pleasure and no regret; it was just something he would do.

"Go easy, Child Byar." Bornhald looked at the captives again. "I expect you do not know much about the Anointed, or about Lords Captain of the Children of the Light, do you? No, I thought not. Well, for Child Byar's sake, at least, try not to argue or shout, yes? I want no more than that you should walk in the Light, and letting anger get the better of you won't help any of us."

Perrin looked up at the gaunt-faced man standing over them. *For Child Byar's sake?* He noticed that the Lord Captain did not tell Byar to leave them alone. Byar met his eyes and smiled; the smile touched only his mouth, but the skin of his face drew tighter, until it looked like a skull. Perrin shivered.

"I have heard of this thing of men running with wolves," Bornhald said musingly, "though I have not seen it before. Men supposedly talking with wolves, and with other creatures of the Dark One. A filthy business. It makes me fear the Last Battle is indeed coming soon."

"Wolves aren't—" Perrin cut off as Byar's boot drew back. Taking a deep breath, he went on in a milder tone. Byar lowered his foot with a disappointed grimace. "Wolves aren't creatures of the Dark One. They hate the Dark One. At least, they hate Trollocs, and Fades." He was surprised to see the gaunt-faced man nod as if to himself.

Bornhald raised an eyebrow. "Who told you that?"

"A Warder," Egwene said. She scrunched away from Byar's heated eyes. "He said wolves hate Trollocs, and Trollocs are afraid of wolves." Perrin was glad she had not mentioned Elyas.

"A Warder," the gray-haired man sighed. "A creature of the Tar Valon witches. What else would that sort tell you, when he is a Darkfriend himself, and a servant of Darkfriends? Do you not know Trollocs have wolves' muzzles and teeth, and wolves' fur?"

Perrin blinked, trying to clear his head. His brain still felt like jellied pain, but there was something wrong here. He could not get his thoughts straight enough to puzzle it out.

"Not all of them," Egwene muttered. Perrin gave Byar a wary look, but the gaunt man only watched her. "Some of them have horns, like rams or goats, or hawks' beaks, or . . . or . . . all sorts of things."

Bornhald shook his head sadly. "I give you every chance, and you dig yourself deeper with every word." He held up one finger. "You run with wolves, creatures of the Dark One." A second finger. "You admit to being acquainted with a Warder, another creature of the Dark

One. I doubt he would have told you what he did if it was only in passing." A third finger. "You, boy, carry a Tar Valon mark in your pocket. Most men outside Tar Valon get rid of those as fast as they can. Unless they serve the Tar Valon witches." A fourth. "You carry a fighting man's weapon while you dress like a farmboy. A skulker, then." The thumb rose. "You know Trollocs, and Myrddraal. This far south, only a few scholars and those who have traveled in the Borderlands believe they are anything but stories. Perhaps you have been to the Borderlands? If so, tell me where? I have traveled a good deal in the Borderlands; I know them well. No? Ah, well, then." He looked at his spread hand, then dropped it hard on the table. The grandfatherly expression said the grandchildren had been up to some very serious mischief indeed. "Why do you not tell me the truth of how you came to be running in the night with wolves?"

Egwene opened her mouth, but Perrin saw the stubborn set of her jaw and knew right away she was going to tell one of the stories they had worked out. That would not do. Not now, not here. His head ached, and he wished he had time to think it out, but there was no time. Who could tell where this Bornhald had traveled, with what lands and cities he was familiar? If he caught them in a lie, there would be no going back to the truth. Bornhald would be convinced they were Darkfriends, then.

"We're from the Two Rivers," he said quickly.

Egwene stared at him openly before she caught herself, but he pressed on with the truth—or a version of it. The two of them had left the Two Rivers to see Caemlyn. On the way they had heard of the ruins of a great city, but when they found Shadar Logoth, there were Trollocs there. The two of them managed to escape across the River Arinelle, but by that time they were completely lost. Then they fell in with a man who offered to guide them to Caemlyn. He had said his name was none of their business, and he hardly seemed friendly, but they needed a guide. The first either of them had seen of wolves had been after the Children of the Light appeared. All they had been trying to do was hide so they would not get eaten by wolves or killed by the men on horses.

". . . If we'd known you were Children of the Light," he finished, "we'd have gone to you for help."

Byar snorted with disbelief. Perrin did not care overmuch; if the Lord Captain was convinced, Byar could not harm them. It was plain that Byar would stop breathing if Lord Captain Bornhald told him to.

"There is no Warder in that," the gray-haired man said after a moment.

Perrin's invention failed him; he knew he should have taken time to think it out. Egwene leaped into the breach. "We met him in Baerlon. The city was crowded with men who had come down from the mines after the winter, and we were put at the same table in an inn. We only talked to him for the length of a meal."

Perrin breathed again. *Thank you, Egwene.*

"Give them back their belongings, Child Byar. Not the weapons, of course." When Byar looked at him in surprise, Bornhald added, "Or are you one of those who have taken to looting the unenlightened, Child Byar? It is a bad business, that, yes? No man can be a thief and walk in the Light." Byar seemed to struggle with disbelief at the suggestion.

"Then you're letting us go?" Egwene sounded surprised. Perrin lifted his head to stare at the Lord Captain.

"Of course not, child," Bornhald said sadly. "You may be telling the truth about being from the Two Rivers, since you know about Baerlon, and the mines. But Shadar Logoth . . . ? That is a name very, very few know, most of them Darkfriends, and anyone who knows enough to know the name, knows enough not to go there. I suggest you think of a better story on the journey to Amador. You will have time, since we must pause in Caemlyn. Preferably the truth, child. There is freedom in truth and the Light."

Byar forgot some of his diffidence toward the gray-haired man. He spun from the prisoners, and there was an outraged snap to his words. "You can't! It is not allowed!" Bornhald raised one eyebrow quizzically, and Byar pulled himself up short, swallowing. "Forgive me, my Lord Captain. I forgot myself, and I humbly beg pardon and submit myself for penance, but as my Lord Captain himself has pointed out, we must reach Caemlyn in time, and with most of our remounts gone, we will be hard pressed enough without carrying prisoners along."

"And what would you suggest?" Bornhald asked calmly.

"The penalty for Darkfriends is death." The flat voice made it all the more jarring. He might have been suggesting stepping on a bug. "There is no truce with the Shadow. There is no mercy for Darkfriends."

"Zeal is to be applauded, Child Byar, but, as I must often tell my son, Dain, overzealousness can be a grievous fault. Remember that the Tenets also say, 'No man is so lost that he cannot be brought to the Light.' These two are young. They cannot yet be deep in the Shadow. They can yet be led to the Light, if they will only allow the Shadow to be lifted from their eyes. We must give them that chance."

For a moment Perrin almost felt affection for the grandfatherly man who stood between them and Byar. Then Bornhald turned his grandfather's smile on Egwene.

"If you refuse to come to the Light by the time we reach Amador, I will be forced to turn you over to the Questioners, and beside them Byar's zeal is but a candle beside the sun." The gray-haired man sounded like a man who regretted what he must do, but who had no intention of ever doing anything but his duty as he saw it. "Repent, renounce the Dark One, come to the Light, confess your sins and tell what you know of this vileness with wolves, and you will be spared that. You will walk free, in the Light." His gaze centered on Perrin, and he sighed sadly. Ice filled Perrin's spine. "But you, just Perrin from the Two Rivers. You killed two of the Children." He touched the axe that Byar still held. "For you, I fear, a gibbet waits in Amador."

CHAPTER 31

Play for Your Supper

Rand narrowed his eyes, watching the dust-tail that rose ahead, three or four bends of the road away. Mat was already headed toward the wild hedgerow alongside the roadway. Its evergreen leaves and densely intermeshed branches would hide them as well as a stone wall, if they could find a way through to the other side. The other side of the road was marked by the sparse brown skeletons of head-high bushes, and beyond was an open field for half a mile to the woods. It might have been part of a farm not too long abandoned, but it offered no quick hiding place. He tried to judge the speed of the dust-tail, and the wind.

A sudden gust swirled road dust up around him, obscuring everything. He blinked and adjusted the plain, dark scarf across his nose and mouth. None too clean now, it made his face itch, but it kept him from inhaling dust with every breath. A farmer had given it to him, a long-faced man with grooves in his cheeks from worry.

"I don't know what you're running from," he had said with an anxious frown, "and I don't want to. You understand? My family."

Abruptly the farmer had dug two long scarves out of his coat pocket and pushed the tangle of wool at them. "It's not much, but here. Belong to my boys. They have others. You don't know me, understand? It's hard times."

Rand treasured the scarf. The list of kindnesses he had made in his mind in the days since Whitebridge was a short one, and he did not believe it would get much longer.

Mat, all but his eyes hidden by the scarf wrapped around his head, hunted swiftly along the tall hedgerow, pulling at the leafy branches. Rand touched the heron-marked hilt at his belt, but let his hand fall away. Once already, cutting a hole through a hedge had almost given them away. The dust-tail was moving toward them, and staying together too long. Not the wind. At least it was not raining. Rain settled the dust. No matter how hard it fell, it never turned the hard-packed road to mud, but when it rained there was no dust. Dust was the only warning they had before whoever it was came close enough to hear. Sometimes that was too late.

"Here," Mat called softly. He seemed to step right through the hedge.

Rand hurried to the spot. Someone had cut a hole there, once. It was partly grown over, and from three feet away it looked as solid as the rest, but close up there was only a thin screen of branches. As he pushed through, he heard horses coming. Not the wind.

He crouched behind the barely covered opening, clutching the hilt of his sword as the horsemen rode by. Five . . . six . . . seven of them. Plainly dressed men, but swords and spears said they were not villagers. Some wore leather tunics with metal studs, and two had round steel caps. Merchants' guards, perhaps, between hirings. Perhaps.

One of them casually swung his eyes toward the hedge as he went by the opening, and Rand bared an inch of his sword. Mat snarled silently like a cornered badger, squinting above his scarf. His hand was under his coat; he always clutched the dagger from Shadar Logoth when there was danger. Rand was no longer sure if it was to protect himself or to protect the ruby-hilted dagger. Of late Mat seemed to forget he had a bow, sometimes.

The riders passed at a slow trot, going somewhere with a purpose but not too great a haste. Dust sifted through the hedge.

Rand waited until the clop of the hooves faded before he stuck his head cautiously back through the hole. The dust-tail was well down the road, going the way they had come. Eastward the sky was clear. He climbed out onto the roadway, watching the column of dust move west.

"Not after us," he said, halfway between a statement and a question.

Mat scrambled out after him, looking warily in both directions. "Maybe," he said. "Maybe."

Rand had no idea which way he meant it, but he nodded. Maybe. It had not begun like this, their journey down the Caemlyn Road.

For a long time after leaving Whitebridge, Rand would suddenly find himself staring back down the road behind them. Sometimes he would see someone who made his breath catch, a tall, skinny man hurrying up the road, or a lanky, white-haired fellow up beside the driver on a wagon, but it was always a pack-peddler, or farmers making their way to market, never Thom Merrilin. Hope faded as the days passed.

There was considerable traffic on the road, wagons and carts, people on horses and people afoot. They came singly and in groups, a train of merchants' wagons or a dozen horsemen together. They did not jam the road, and often there was nothing in sight except the all but leafless trees lining the hard-packed roadbed, but there were certainly more people traveling than Rand had ever seen in the Two Rivers.

Most traveled in the same direction that they did, eastward toward Caemlyn. Sometimes they got a ride in a farmer's wagon for a little distance, a mile, or five, but more often they walked. Men on horseback they avoided; when they spotted even one rider in the distance they scrambled off the road and hid until he was past. None ever wore a black cloak, and Rand did not really think a Fade would let them see him coming, but there was no point in taking chances. In the beginning it was just the Halfmen they feared.

The first village after Whitebridge looked so much like Emond's Field that Rand's steps dragged when he saw it. Thatched roofs with high peaks, and goodwives in their aprons gossiping over the fences between their houses, and children playing on a village green. The women's hair hung unbraided around their shoulders, and other small things were different, too, but the whole together was like home. Cows cropped on the green, and geese waddled self-importantly across the road. The children tumbled, laughing, in the dust where the grass was gone altogether. They did not even look around when Rand and Mat went by. That was another thing that was different. Strangers were no oddity there; two more did not draw so much as a second glance. Village dogs only raised their heads to sniff as he and Mat passed; none stirred themselves.

It was coming on evening as they went through the village, and he felt a pang of homesickness as lights appeared in the windows. *No matter what it looks like,* a small voice whispered in his mind, *it isn't really home. Even if you go into one of those houses Tam won't be there. If he was, could you look him in the face? You know, now, don't you? Except for little things like where you come from and who you are. No fever-dreams.* He hunched his shoulders against taunting laughter inside his head. *You might as well stop,* the voice snickered. *One place is as good as another when you aren't from anywhere, and the Dark One has you marked.*

Mat tugged at his sleeve, but he pulled loose and stared at the houses. He did not want to stop, but he did want to look and remember. *So much like home, but you'll never see that again, will you?*

Mat yanked at him again. His face was taut, the skin around his mouth and eyes white. "Come on," Mat muttered. "Come on." He looked at the village as if he suspected something of hiding there. "Come on. We can't stop yet."

Rand turned in a complete circle, taking in the whole village, and sighed. They were not very far from Whitebridge. If the Myrddraal could get past Whitebridge's wall without being seen, it would have no trouble at all searching this small village. He let himself be drawn on into the countryside beyond, until the thatch-roofed houses were left behind.

Night fell before they found a spot by moonlight, under some bushes still bearing their dead leaves. They filled their bellies with cold water from a shallow rivulet not far away and curled up on the ground, wrapped in their cloaks, without a fire. A fire could be seen; better to be cold.

Uneasy with his memories, Rand woke often, and every time he could hear Mat muttering and tossing in his sleep. He did not dream, that he could remember, but he did not sleep well. *You'll never see home again.*

That was not the only night they spent with just their cloaks to protect them from the wind, and sometimes the rain, cold and soaking. It was not the only meal they made from nothing but cold water. Between them they had enough coins for a few meals at an inn, but a bed for the night would take too much. Things cost more outside the Two Rivers, more this side of the Arinelle than in Baerlon. What money they had left had to be saved for an emergency.

One afternoon Rand mentioned the dagger with the ruby in its hilt, while they were trudging down the road with bellies too empty to rumble, and the sun low and weak, and nothing in view for the coming night but more bushes. Dark clouds built up overhead for rain during the night. He hoped they were lucky; maybe no more than an icy drizzle.

He went on a few steps before he realized that Mat had stopped. He stopped, too, wriggling his toes in his boots. At least his feet felt warm. He eased the straps across his shoulders. His blanketroll and Thom's bundled cloak were not heavy, but even a few pounds weighed heavy after miles on an empty stomach. "What's the matter, Mat?" he said.

"Why are you so anxious to sell it?" Mat demanded angrily. "I found it, after all. You ever think I might like to keep it? For a while, anyway. If you want to sell something, sell that bloody sword!"

Rand rubbed his hand along the heron-marked hilt. "My father gave this sword to me. It was his. I wouldn't ask you to sell something your father gave you. Blood and ashes, Mat, do you like going hungry? Anyway, even if I could find somebody to buy it, how much would a sword bring? What would a farmer want with a sword? That ruby would fetch enough to take us all the way to Caemlyn in a carriage. Maybe all the way to Tar Valon. And we'd eat every meal in an inn, and sleep every night in a bed. Maybe you like the idea of walking halfway across the world and sleeping on the ground?" He glared at Mat, and his friend glared back.

They stood like that in the middle of the road until Mat suddenly gave an uncomfortable shrug, and dropped his eyes to the road. "Who would I sell it to, Rand? A farmer would have to pay in chickens; we couldn't buy a carriage with chickens. And if I even showed it in any village we've been through, they'd probably think we stole it. The Light knows what would happen then."

After a minute Rand nodded reluctantly. "You're right. I know it. I'm sorry; I didn't mean to snap at you. It's only that I'm hungry and my feet hurt."

"Mine, too." They started down the road again, walking even more wearily than before. The wind gusted up, blowing dust in their faces. "Mine, too." Mat coughed.

Farms did provide some meals and a few nights out of the cold. A haystack was nearly as warm as a room with a fire, at least compared to lying under the bushes, and a haystack, even one without a tarp over it, kept all but the heaviest rain off, if you dug yourself in deeply enough. Sometimes Mat tried his hand at stealing eggs, and once he attempted to milk a cow left unattended, staked out on a long rope to crop in a field. Most farms had dogs, though, and farm dogs were watchful. A two-mile run with baying hounds at their heels was too high a price for two or three eggs as Rand saw it, especially when the dogs sometimes took hours to go away and let them down out of the tree where they had taken shelter. The hours were what he regretted.

He did not really like doing it, but Rand preferred to approach a farmhouse openly in broad daylight. Now and again they had the dogs set on them anyway, without a word being said, for the rumors and the times made everyone who lived apart from other people nervous about strangers, but often an hour or so chopping wood or hauling water would earn a meal and a bed, even if the bed was a pile of straw in the barn. But an hour or two doing chores was an hour or two of daylight when they were standing still, an hour or two for the Myrddraal to catch up. Sometimes he wondered how many miles a Fade could cover in an hour. He begrudged every minute of it—though admittedly not so much when he was wolfing down a goodwife's hot soup. And when they had no food, knowing they had spent every possible minute moving toward Caemlyn did not do much to soothe an empty belly. Rand could not make up his mind if it was worse to lose time or go hungry, but Mat went beyond worrying about his belly or pursuit.

"What do we know about them, anyway?" Mat demanded one afternoon while they were mucking out stalls on a small farm.

"Light, Mat, what do they know about us?" Rand sneezed. They were working stripped to the waist, and sweat and straw covered them both liberally, and motes of straw-dust hung in the air. "What I know is they'll give us some roast lamb and a real bed to sleep in."

Mat dug his hayfork into the straw and manure and gave a sidelong frown at the farmer, coming from the back of the barn with a bucket in one hand and his milking stool in the other. A stooped old man with skin like leather and thin, gray hair, the farmer slowed when he saw Mat looking at him, then looked away quickly and hurried on out of the barn, slopping milk over the rim of the bucket in his haste.

"He's up to something, I tell you," Mat said. "See the way he wouldn't meet my eye? Why are they so friendly to a couple of wanderers they never laid eyes on before? Tell me that."

"His wife says we remind her of their grandsons. Will you stop worrying about them? What we have to worry about is behind us. I hope."

"He's up to something," Mat muttered.

When they finished, they washed up at the trough in front of the barn, their shadows stretching long with the sinking sun. Rand toweled off with his shirt as they walked to the farmhouse. The farmer met them at the door; he leaned on a quarterstaff in a too-casual manner. Behind him his wife clutched her apron and peered past his shoulder, chewing her lip. Rand sighed; he did not think he and Mat reminded them of their grandsons any longer.

"Our sons are coming to visit tonight," the old man said. "All four of them. I forgot. They're all four coming. Big lads. Strong. Be here any time, now. I'm afraid we don't have the bed we promised you."

His wife thrust a small bundle wrapped in a napkin past him. "Here. It's bread, and cheese, and pickles, and lamb. Enough for two meals, maybe. Here." Her wrinkled face asked them to please take it and go.

Rand took the bundle. "Thank you. I understand. Come on, Mat."

Mat followed him, grumbling while he pulled his shirt over his head. Rand thought it best to cover as many miles as they could before stopping to eat. The old farmer had a dog.

It could have been worse, he thought. Three days earlier, while they were still working, they'd had the dogs set on them. The dogs, and the farmer, and his two sons waving cudgels chased them out to the Caemlyn Road and half a mile down it before giving up. They had barely had time to snatch up their belongings and run. The farmer had carried a bow with a broad-head arrow nocked.

"Don't come back, hear!" he had shouted after them. "I don't know what you're up to, but don't let me see your shifty eyes again!"

Mat had started to turn back, fumbling at his quiver, but Rand pulled him on. "Are you crazy?" Mat gave him a sullen look, but at least he kept running.

Rand sometimes wondered if it was worthwhile stopping at farms. The further they went, the more suspicious of strangers Mat became, and the less he was able to hide it. Or bothered to. The meals got skimpier for the same work, and sometimes not even the barn was offered as a place to sleep. But then a solution to all their problems came to Rand, or so it seemed, and it came at Grinwell's farm.

Master Grinwell and his wife had nine children, the eldest a daughter not more than a year younger than Rand and Mat. Master Grinwell was a sturdy man, and with his children he probably had no need of any more help, but he looked them up and down, taking in their travel-stained clothes and dusty boots, and allowed as how he could always find work for more hands. Mistress Grinwell said that if they were going to eat at her table, they would not do it in those filthy things. She was about to do laundry, and some of her husband's old clothes would fit them well enough for working. She smiled when she said it, and for a minute she looked to Rand just like Mistress al'Vere, though her hair was yellow; he had never seen hair that color before. Even Mat seemed to lose some of his tension when her smile touched him. The eldest daughter was another matter.

Dark-haired, big-eyed, and pretty, Else grinned impudently at them whenever her parents were not looking. While they worked, moving barrels and sacks of grain in the barn, she hung over a stall door, humming to herself and chewing the end of one long pigtail, watching them. Rand she watched especially. He tried to ignore her, but after a few minutes he put on the shirt Master Grinwell had loaned him. It was tight across the shoulders and too short, but it was better than nothing. Else laughed out loud when he tugged it on. He began to think that this time it would not be Mat's fault when they were chased off.

Perrin would know how to handle this, he thought. *He'd make some offhand comment, and pretty soon she'd be laughing at his jokes instead of mooning around where her father can see.* Only he could not think of any offhand comment, or any jokes, either. Whenever he looked in her direction, she smiled at him in a way that would have her father loosing the dogs on them if he saw. Once she told him she liked tall men. All the boys on the farms around there were short. Mat gave a nasty snicker. Wishing he could think of a joke, Rand tried to concentrate on his hayfork.

The younger children, at least, were a blessing in Rand's eyes. Mat's wariness always eased a little when there were children around. After supper they all settled in front of the fireplace, with Master Grinwell in his favorite chair thumbing his pipe full of tabac and Mistress Grinwell fussing with her sewing box and the shirts she had washed for him and Mat. Mat dug out Thom's colored balls and began to juggle. He never did that unless there were children. The children laughed when he pretended to be dropping the balls, snatching them at the last minute, and they clapped for fountains and figure-eights and a six-ball circle that he really did almost drop. But they took it in good part, Master Grinwell and his wife applauding as hard as their children. When Mat was done, bowing around the room with as many flourishes as Thom might have made, Rand took Thom's flute from its case.

He could never handle the instrument without a pang of sadness. Touching its gold-and-silver scrollwork was like touching Thom's memory. He never handled the harp except to see that it was safe and dry—Thom had always said the harp was beyond a farmboy's clumsy hands—but whenever a farmer allowed them to stay, he always played one tune on the flute after supper. It was just a little something extra to pay the farmer, and maybe a way of keeping Thom's memory fresh.

With a laughing mood already set by Mat's juggling, he played "Three Girls in the Meadow." Master and Mistress Grinwell clapped along, and the smaller children danced around the floor, even the smallest boy, who could barely walk, stomping his feet in time. He knew he would win no prizes at Bel Tine, but after Thom's teaching he would not be embarrassed to enter.

Else was sitting cross-legged in front of the fire, and as he lowered the flute after the last note, she leaned forward with a long sigh and smiled at him. "You play so beautifully. I never heard anything so beautiful."

Mistress Grinwell suddenly paused in her sewing and raised an eyebrow at her daughter, then gave Rand a long, appraising look.

He had picked up the leather case to put the flute away, but under her stare he dropped the case and almost the flute, too. If she accused him of trifling with her daughter. . . . In desperation he put the flute back to his lips and played another song, then another, and another. Mistress Grinwell kept watching him. He played "The Wind That Shakes the Willow," and "Coming Home From Tarwin's Gap," and "Mistress Aynora's Rooster," and "The Old Black Bear." He played every song he could think of, but she never took her eyes off him. She never said anything, either, but she watched, and weighed.

It was late when Master Grinwell finally stood up, chuckling and rubbing his hands together. "Well, this has been rare fun, but it's way past our bedtime. You traveling lads make your own hours, but morning comes early on a farm. I'll tell you lads, I have paid good money at an inn for no better entertainment than I've had this night. For worse."

"I think they should have a reward, father," Mistress Grinwell said as she picked up her youngest boy, who had long since fallen asleep in front of the fire. "The barn is no fit place to sleep. They can sleep in Else's room tonight, and she will sleep with me."

Else grimaced. She was careful to keep her head down, but Rand saw it. He thought her mother did, too.

Master Grinwell nodded. "Yes, yes, much better than the barn. If you don't mind sleeping two to a bed, that is." Rand flushed; Mistress Grinwell was still looking at him. "I do wish I could hear more of that flute. And your juggling, too. I like that. You know, there's a little task you could help with tomorrow, and—"

"They'll be wanting an early start, father," Mistress Grinwell cut in. "Arien is the next village the way they're going, and if they intend to try their luck at the inn there, they'll have to walk all day to get there before dark."

"Yes, mistress," Rand said, "we will. And thank you."

She gave him a tight-lipped smile as if she knew very well that his thanks were for more than her advice, or even supper and a warm bed.

The whole next day Mat twitted him about Else as they made their way down the road. He kept trying to change the subject, and what the Grinwells had suggested about performing at inns was the easiest thing to mind. In the morning, with Else pouting as he left, and Mistress Grinwell watching with a sharp-eyed look of good-riddance and soonest-mended, it was just something to keep Mat from talking. By the time they did reach the next village, it was something else again.

With dusk descending, they entered the only inn in Arien, and Rand spoke to the innkeeper. He played "Ferry O'er the River"—which the plump innkeeper called "Darling Sara"—and part of "The Road to Dun Aren," and Mat did a little juggling, and the upshot was that they slept in a bed that night and ate roasted potatoes and hot beef. It was the smallest room in the inn, to be sure, up under the eaves in the back, and the meal came in the middle of a long night of playing and juggling, but it was still a bed beneath a roof. Even better, to Rand, every daylight hour had been spent traveling. And the inn's patrons did not seem to care if Mat stared at them suspiciously. Some of them even looked askance at one another. The times made suspicion of strangers a commonplace, and there were always strangers at an inn.

Rand slept better than he had since leaving Whitebridge, despite sharing a bed with Mat and his nocturnal muttering. In the morning the innkeeper tried to talk them into staying another day or two, but when he could not, he called over a bleary-eyed farmer who had drunk too much to drive his cart home the night before. An hour later they were five miles further east, sprawling on their backs on the straw in the back of Eazil Forney's cart.

That became the way of their traveling. With a little luck, and maybe a ride or two, they could almost always reach the next village by dark. If there was more than one inn in a village, the innkeepers would bid for them once they heard Rand's flute and saw Mat juggle. Together they still did not come close to a gleeman, but they were more than most villages saw in a year. Two or three inns in a town meant a better room, with two beds, and more generous portions of a better cut of meat, and sometimes even a few coppers in their pockets when they left besides. In the mornings there was almost always someone to offer a ride, another farmer who had stayed too late and drunk too much, or a merchant who had liked their entertainment enough not to mind if they hopped up on the back of one of his wagons. Rand began to think their problems were over till they reached Caemlyn. But then they came to Four Kings.

CHAPTER
32

Four Kings in Shadow

The village was bigger than most, but still a scruffy town to bear a name like Four Kings. As usual, the Caemlyn Road ran straight through the center of the town, but another heavily traveled highway came in from the south, too. Most villages were markets and gathering places for the farmers of the area, but there were few farmers to be seen here. Four Kings survived as a stopover for merchants' wagon trains on their way to Caemlyn and to the mining towns in the Mountains of Mist beyond Baerlon, as well as the villages between. The southern road carried Lugard's trade with the mines in the west; Lugarder merchants going to Caemlyn had a more direct route. The surrounding country held few farms, barely enough to feed themselves and the town, and everything in the village centered on the merchants and their wagons, the men who drove them and the laborers who loaded the goods.

Plots of bare earth, ground to dust, lay scattered through Four Kings, filled with wagons parked wheel to wheel and abandoned except for a few bored guards. Stables and horse-lots lined the streets, all of which were wide enough to allow wagons to pass and deeply rutted from too many wheels. There was no village green, and the children played in the ruts, dodging wagons and the curses of wagon drivers. Village women, their heads covered with scarves, kept their eyes down and walked quickly, sometimes followed by wagoneers' comments that made Rand blush; even Mat gave a start at some of them. No woman stood gossiping over the fence with a neighbor. Drab wooden houses stood cheek by jowl, with only narrow alleys between and white-wash—where anyone had bothered to whitewash the weathered boards—faded as if it had not been freshened in years. Heavy shutters on the houses had not been open in so long that the hinges were solid lumps of rust. Noise hung over everything, clanging from blacksmiths, shouts from the wagon drivers, raucous laughter from the town's inns.

Rand swung down from the back of a merchant's canvas-topped wagon as they came abreast of a garishly painted inn, all greens and yellows that caught the eye from afar among the leaden houses. The line of wagons kept moving. None of the drivers even seemed to notice that he and Mat had gone; dusk was falling, and they all had their eyes on unhitching the horses and reaching the inns. Rand stumbled in a rut, then leaped quickly to avoid a heavy-laden wagon clattering the other way. The driver shouted a curse at him as the wagon rolled by. A village woman stepped around him and hurried on without ever meeting his eye.

"I don't know about this place," he said. He thought he could hear music mixed in the din, but he could not tell from where it was coming. From the inn, maybe, but it was hard to be sure. "I don't like it. Maybe we'd better go on this time."

Mat gave him a scornful look, then rolled his eyes at the sky. Dark clouds thickened overhead. "And sleep under a hedge tonight? In that? I'm used to a bed again." He cocked his head to listen, then grunted. "Maybe one of these places doesn't have musicians. Anyway, I'll bet they don't have a juggler." He slung his bow across his shoulders and started for the bright yellow door, studying everything through narrowed eyes. Rand followed doubtfully.

There were musicians inside, their zither and drum almost drowned in coarse laughter and drunken shouting. Rand did not bother to find the landlord. The next two inns had musicians as well, and the same deafening cacophony. Roughly dressed men filled the tables and stumbled across the floor, waving mugs and trying to fondle serving maids who dodged with fixed, long-suffering smiles. The buildings shook with the racket, and the smell was sour, a stench of old wine and unwashed bodies. Of the merchants, in their silk and velvet and lace, there was no sign; private dining rooms abovestairs protected their ears and noses. He and Mat only put their heads in the doors before leaving. He was beginning to think they would have no choice but to move on.

The fourth inn, The Dancing Cartman, stood silent.

It was as gaudy as the other inns, yellow trimmed in bright red and bilious, eye-wrenching green, though here the paint was cracked and peeling. Rand and Mat stepped inside.

Only half a dozen men sat at the tables that filled the common room, hunched over their mugs, each one glumly alone with his thoughts. Business was definitely not good, but it had been better once. Exactly as many serving maids as there were patrons busied themselves around the room. There was plenty for them to do—dirt crusted the floor and cobwebs filled the corners of the ceiling—but most were not doing anything really useful, only moving so they would not be seen standing still.

A bony man with long, stringy hair to his shoulders turned to scowl at them as they came through the door. The first slow peal of thunder rumbled across Four Kings. "What do you want?" He was rubbing his hands on a greasy apron that hung to his ankles. Rand wondered if more grime was coming off on the apron or on the man's hands. He was the first skinny innkeeper Rand had seen. "Well? Speak up, buy a drink, or get out! Do I look like a raree show?"

Flushing, Rand launched into the spiel he had perfected at inns before this. "I play the flute, and my friend juggles, and you'll not see two better in a year. For a good room and a good meal, we'll fill this common room of yours." He remembered the filled common rooms he had already seen that evening, especially the man who had vomited right in front of him at the last one. He had had to step lively to keep his boots untouched. He faltered, but caught himself and went on. "We'll fill your inn with men who will repay the little we cost twenty times over with the food and drink they buy. Why should—"

"I've got a man plays the dulcimer," the innkeeper said sourly.

"You have a drunk, Saml Hake," one of the serving maids said. She was passing him with a tray and two mugs, and she paused to give Rand and Mat a plump smile. "Most times, he can't see well enough to find the common room," she confided in a loud whisper. "Haven't even seen him in two days."

Without taking his eyes off Rand and Mat, Hake casually backhanded her across the face. She gave a surprised grunt and fell heavily to the unwashed floor; one of the mugs broke, and the spilled wine washed rivulets in the dirt. "You're docked for the wine and breakage. Get 'em fresh drinks. And hurry. Men don't pay to wait while you laze around." His tone was as offhand as the blow. None of the patrons looked up from their wine, and the other serving maids kept their eyes averted.

The plump woman rubbed her cheek and stared pure murder at Hake, but she gathered the empty mug and the broken pieces on her tray and went off without a word.

Hake sucked his teeth thoughtfully, eyeing Rand and Mat. His gaze clung to the heron-mark sword before he pulled it away. "Tell you what," he said finally. "You can have a couple of pallets in an empty storeroom in the back. Rooms are too expensive to give away. You eat when everybody's gone. There ought to be something left."

Rand wished there was an inn in Four Kings they had not yet tried. Since leaving Whitebridge he had met coolness, indifference, and outright hostility, but nothing that gave him the sense of unease that this man and this village did. He told himself it was just the dirt and squalor and noise, but the misgivings did not go away. Mat was watching Hake as if he suspected some trap, but he gave no sign of wanting to give up The Dancing Cartman for a bed under a hedge. Thunder rattled the windows. Rand sighed.

"The pallets will do if they're clean, and if there are enough clean blankets. But we eat two hours after full dark, no later, and the best you have. Here. We'll show you what we can do." He reached for the flute case, but Hake shook his head.

"Don't matter. This lot'll be satisfied with any kind of screeching so long as it sounds something like music." His eyes touched Rand's sword again; his thin smile touched nothing but his lips. "Eat when you want, but if you don't bring the crowd in, out you go in the street." He nodded over his shoulder at two hard-faced men sitting against the wall. They were not drinking, and their arms were thick enough for legs. When Hake nodded at them, their eyes shifted to Rand and Mat, flat and expressionless.

Rand put one hand on his sword hilt, hoping the twisting in his stomach did not show on his face. "As long as we get what's agreed on," he said in a level tone.

Hake blinked, and for a moment he seemed uneasy himself. Abruptly he nodded. "What I said, isn't it? Well, get started. You won't bring anybody in just standing there." He stalked off, scowling and shouting at the serving maids as if there were fifty customers they were neglecting.

There was a small, raised platform at the far end of the room, near the door to the back. Rand lifted a bench up on it, and settled his cloak, blanketroll, and Thom's bundled cloak behind the bench with the sword lying atop them.

He wondered if he had been wise to keep wearing the sword openly. Swords were common enough, but the heron-mark attracted attention and speculation. Not from everybody, but any notice at all made him uncomfortable. He could be leaving a clear trail for the Myrddraal—if Fades needed that kind of trail. They did not seem to. In any case, he was reluctant to stop wearing it. Tam had given it to him. His father. As long as he wore the sword, there was still some connection between Tam and him, a thread that gave him the right to still call Tam father. *Too late now,* he thought. He was not sure what he meant, but he was sure it was true. *Too late.*

At the first note of "Cock o' the North" the half-dozen patrons in the common room lifted their heads out of their wine. Even the two bouncers sat forward a little. They all applauded when he finished, including the two toughs, and once more when Mat sent a shower of colored balls spinning through his hands. Outside, the sky muttered again. The rain was holding off, but the pressure of it was palpable; the longer it waited, the harder it would fall.

Word spread, and by the time it was dark outside the inn was packed full with men laughing and talking so loud that Rand could barely hear what he was playing. Only the thunder overpowered the noise in the common room. Lightning flashed in the windows, and in the momentary lulls he could faintly hear rain drumming on the roof. Men who came in now dripped trails across the floor.

Whenever he paused, voices shouted the names of tunes through the din. A good many names he did not recognize, though when he got someone to hum a bit of it, he often found he did know the song. It had been that way other places, before. "Jolly Jaim" was "Rhea's Fling" here, and had been "Colors of the Sun" at an earlier stop. Some names stayed the same; others changed with ten miles' distance, and he had learned new songs, too. "The Drunken Peddler" was a new one, though sometimes it was called "Tinker in the Kitchen." "Two Kings Came Hunting" was "Two Horses Running" and several other names besides. He played the ones he knew, and men pounded the tables for more.

Others called for Mat to juggle again. Sometimes fights broke out between those wanting music and those who fancied juggling. Once a knife flashed, and a woman screamed, and a man reeled back from a table with blood streaming down his face, but Jak and Strom, the two bouncers, closed in swiftly and with complete impartiality threw everyone involved into the street with lumps on their heads. That was their tactic with any trouble. The talk and the laughing went on as if nothing had occurred. Nobody even looked around except those the bouncers jostled on their way to the door.

The patrons were free with their hands, too, when one of the serving maids let herself grow unwary. More than once Jak or Strom had to rescue one of the women, though they were none too quick about it. The way Hake carried on, screaming and shaking the woman involved, he always considered it her fault, and the teary eyes and stammered apologies said she was willing to accept his opinion. The women jumped whenever Hake frowned, even if he was looking somewhere else. Rand wondered why any of them put up with it.

Hake smiled when he looked at Rand and Mat. After a while Rand realized Hake was not smiling at them; the smiles came when his eyes slid behind them, to where the heron-mark sword lay. Once, when Rand set the gold-and-silver-chased flute down beside his stool, the flute got a smile, too.

The next time he changed places with Mat at the front of the dais, he leaned over to speak in Mat's ear. Even that close he had to speak loudly, but with all the noise he doubted if anyone else could hear. "Hake's going to try to rob us."

Mat nodded as if it was nothing he had not expected. "We'll have to bar our door tonight."

"Bar our door? Jak and Strom could break down a door with their fists. Let's get out of here."

"Wait till after we eat, at least. I'm hungry. They can't do anything here," Mat added. The packed common room shouted impatiently for them to get on with it. Hake was glaring at them. "Anyway, you want to sleep outside tonight?" An especially strong crack of lightning drowned out everything else, and for an instant the light through the windows was stronger than the lamps.

"I just want to get out without my head being broken," Rand said, but Mat was already slouching back to take his rest on the stool. Rand sighed and launched into "The Road to Dun Aren." A lot of them seemed to like that one; he had already played it four times, and they still shouted for it.

The trouble was that Mat was right, as far as he went. He was hungry, too. And he could not see how Hake could give them any trouble while the common room was full, and getting fuller. For every man who left or was thrown out by Jak and Strom, two came in from the street. They shouted for the juggling or for a particular tune, but mostly they were interested in drinking and fondling the serving maids. One man was different, though.

He stood out in every way among the crowd in The Dancing Cartman. Merchants apparently had no use for the run-down inn; there were not even any private dining rooms for them, as far as he could make out. The patrons were all rough-dressed, with the tough skin of men who labored in the sun and wind. This man was sleekly fleshy, with a soft look to his hands, and a velvet coat, and a dark green velvet cloak lined with blue silk was slung around his shoulders. All of his clothes had an expensive cut to them. His shoes—soft velvet slippers, not boots—were not made for the rutted streets of Four Kings, or for any streets at all, for that matter.

He came in well after dark, shaking the rain off his cloak as he looked around, a twist of distaste on his mouth. He scanned the room once, already turning to go, then suddenly gave a start at nothing Rand could see and sat down at a table Jak and Strom had just emptied. A serving maid stopped at his table, then brought him a mug of wine which he pushed to one side and never touched again. She seemed in a hurry to leave his table both times, though he did not try to touch her or even look at her. Whatever it was about him that made her uneasy, others who came close to him noticed it, too. For all of his soft look, whenever some callus-handed wagon driver decided to share his table, one glance was all it took to send the man looking elsewhere. He sat as if there were no one else in the room but him—and Rand and Mat. Them he watched over steepled hands that glittered with a ring on each finger. He watched them with a smile of satisfied recognition.

Rand murmured to Mat as they were changing places again, and Mat nodded. "I saw him," he muttered. "Who *is* he? I keep thinking I know him."

The same thought had occurred to Rand, tickling the back of his memory, but he could not bring it forward. Yet he was sure that face was one he had never seen before.

When they had been performing for two hours, as near as Rand could estimate, he slipped the flute into its case and he and Mat gathered up their belongings. As they were stepping down from the low platform, Hake came bustling up, anger twisting his narrow face.

"It's time to eat," Rand said to forestall him, "and we don't want our things stolen. You want to tell the cook?" Hake hesitated, still angry, trying unsuccessfully to keep his eyes off what Rand held in his arms. Casually Rand shifted his bundles so he could rest one hand on the sword. "Or you can *try* throwing us out." He made the emphasis deliberately, then added, "There's a lot of night left for us to play, yet. We have to keep our strength up if we're going to perform well enough to keep this crowd spending money. How long do you think this room will stay full if we fall over from hunger?"

Hake's eyes twitched over the room full of men putting money in his pocket, then he turned and stuck his head through the door to the rear of the inn. "Feed 'em!" he shouted. Rounding on Rand and Mat, he snarled, "Don't be all night about it. I expect you up there till the last man's gone."

Some of the patrons were shouting for the musician and the juggler, and Hake turned to soothe them. The man in the velvet cloak was one of the anxious ones. Rand motioned Mat to follow him.

A stout door separated the kitchen from the front of the inn, and, except when it opened to let a serving maid through, the rain pounding the roof was louder in the kitchen than the shouts from the common room. It was a big room, hot and steamy from stoves and ovens, with a huge table covered with half-prepared food and dishes ready to be served. Some of the serving maids sat clustered on a bench near the rear door, rubbing their feet and chattering away all at once with the fat cook, who talked back at the same time and waved a big spoon to emphasize her points. They all glanced up as Rand and Mat came in, but it did not slow their conversation or stop their foot rubbing.

"We ought to get out of here while we have the chance," Rand said softly, but Mat shook his head, his eyes fixed on the two plates the cook was filling with beef and potatoes and peas. She hardly looked at the two of them, keeping up her talk with the other women while she pushed things aside on the table with her elbows and set the plates down, adding forks.

"After we eat is time enough." Mat slid onto a bench and began using his fork as if it were a shovel.

Rand sighed, but he was right behind Mat. He had had only a butt-end of bread to eat since the night before. His belly felt as empty as a beggar's purse, and the cooking smells that filled the kitchen did not help. He quickly had his mouth full, though Mat was getting his plate refilled by the cook before he had finished half of his.

He did not mean to eavesdrop on the women's talk, but some of the words reached out and grabbed him.

"Sounds crazy to me."

"Crazy or not, it's what I hear. He went to half the inns in town before he came here. Just walked in, looked around, and walked out without saying one word, even at the Royal Inn. Like it wasn't raining at all."

"Maybe he thought here was the most comfortable." That brought gales of laughter.

"What I hear is he didn't even get to Four Kings till after nightfall, and his horses blowing like they'd been pushed hard."

"Where'd he come from, to get caught out after dark? Nobody but a fool or a madman travels anywhere and plans it that badly."

"Well, maybe he's a fool, but he's a rich one. I hear he even has another carriage for his servants and baggage. There's money there, mark my words. Did you see that cloak of his? I wouldn't mind having that my ownself."

"He's a little plump for my taste, but I always say a man can't be too fat if enough gold comes with it." They all doubled over giggling, and the cook threw back her head and roared with laughter.

Rand dropped his fork on his plate. A thought he did not like bubbled in his head. "I'll be back in a minute," he said. Mat barely nodded, stuffing a piece of potato into his mouth.

Rand picked up his sword belt along with his cloak as he stood, and buckled it around his waist on the way to the back door. No one paid him any mind.

The rain was bucketing down. He swung his cloak around his shoulders and pulled the hood over his head, holding the cloak closed as he trotted across the stableyard. A curtain of water hid everything except when lightning flashed, but he found what he was hunting. The horses had been taken into the stable, but the two black-lacquered carriages glistened wetly outside. Thunder grumbled, and a bolt of lightning streaked above the inn. In the brief burst of light he made out a name in gold script on the coach doors. Howal Gode.

Unmindful of the rain beating at him, he stood staring at the name he could no longer see. He remembered where he had last seen black-lacquered coaches with their owners' names on the door, and sleek, overfed men in silk-lined velvet cloaks and velvet slippers. White-bridge. A Whitebridge merchant could have a perfectly legitimate reason to be on his way to Caemlyn. *A reason that sends him to half the inns in town before he chooses the one where you are? A reason that makes him look at you as if he's found what he's searching for?*

Rand shivered, and suddenly he was aware of rain trickling down his back. His cloak was tightly woven, but it had never been meant to stand up to this kind of downpour. He hurried back to the inn, splashing through deepening puddles. Jak blocked the door as he started through.

"Well, well, well. Out here alone in the dark. Dark's dangerous, boy."

Rain slicked Rand's hair down across his forehead. The stableyard was empty except for them. He wondered if Hake had decided he wanted the sword and the flute badly enough to forgo keeping the crowd in the common room.

Brushing water out of his eyes with one hand, he put the other on his sword. Even wet, the nobby leather made a sure grip for his fingers. "Has Hake decided all those men will stay just for his ale, instead of going where there's entertainment, too? If he has, we'll call the meal even for what we've done so far and be on our way."

Dry in the doorway, the big man looked out at the rain and snorted. "In this?" His eyes slid down to Rand's hand on the sword. "You know, me and Strom got a bet. He figures you stole that from your old grandmother. Me, I figure your grandmother'd kick you round the pigpen and hang you out to dry." He grinned. His teeth were crooked and yellow, and the grin made him look even meaner. "Night's long yet, boy."

Rand brushed past him, and Jak let him by with an ugly chuckle.

Inside, he tossed off his cloak and dropped on the bench at the table he had left only minutes before. Mat was done with his second plate and working on a third, eating more slowly now, but intently, as if he planned to finish every bite if it killed him. Jak took up a place by the door to the stableyard, leaning against the wall and watching them. Even the cook seemed to feel no urge to talk with him there.

"He's from Whitebridge," Rand said softly. There was no need to say who "he" was. Mat's head swiveled toward him, a piece of beef on the end of the fork suspended halfway to his mouth. Conscious of Jak watching, Rand stirred the food on his plate. He could not have gotten a mouthful down if he had been starving, but he tried to pretend an interest in the peas as he told Mat about the carriages, and what the women had said, in case Mat had not been listening.

Obviously he had not been. Mat blinked in surprise and whistled between his teeth, then frowned at the meat on his fork and grunted as he tossed the fork onto his plate. Rand wished he would make at least an effort to be circumspect.

"After us," Mat said when he finished. The creases in Mat's forehead deepened. "A Darkfriend?"

"Maybe. I don't know." Rand glanced at Jak and the big man stretched elaborately, shrugging shoulders as big as any blacksmith's. "Do you think we can get past him?"

"Not without him making enough noise to bring Hake and the other one. I knew we should never have stopped here."

Rand gaped, but before he could say anything Hake pushed through the door from the common room. Strom bulked large over his shoulder. Jak stepped in front of the back door. "You going to eat all night?" Hake barked. "I didn't feed you so you could lie around out here."

Rand looked at his friend. Later, Mat mouthed, and they gathered their things under the watchful eyes of Hake, Strom, and Jak.

In the common room, cries for juggling and the names of tunes burst through the clamor as soon as Rand and Mat appeared. The man in the velvet cloak—Howal Gode—still appeared to ignore everyone around him, but he was nonetheless seated on the edge of his chair. At the sight of them he leaned back, the satisfied smile returning to his lips.

Rand took the first turn at the front of the dais, playing "Drawing Water From the Well" with only half his mind on it. No one seemed to notice the few wrong notes. He tried to think of how they were going to get away, and tried to avoid looking at Gode, too. If he was after them, there was no point in letting him know they knew it. As for getting away. . . .

He had never realized before what a good trap an inn made. Hake, Jak, and Strom did not even have to keep a close eye on them; the crowd would let them know if he or Mat left the dais. As long as the common room was full of people, Hake could not send Jak and Strom after them, but as long as the common room was full of people they could not get away without Hake knowing. And Gode was watching their every move, too. It was so funny he would have laughed if he had not been on the point of throwing up. They would just have to be wary and wait their chance.

When he changed places with Mat, Rand groaned to himself. Mat glared at Hake, at Strom, at Jak, without a care to whether they noticed or wondered why. When he was not actually handling the balls, his hand rested under his coat. Rand hissed at him, but he paid no attention. If Hake saw that ruby, he might not wait until they were alone. If the men in the common room saw it, half of them might join in with Hake.

Worst of all, Mat stared at the Whitebridge merchant—the Darkfriend?—twice as hard as at anyone else, and Gode noticed. There was no way he could avoid noticing. But it did not disturb his aplomb in the least. His smile deepened, if anything, and he nodded to Mat as if to an old acquaintance, then looked at Rand and raised a questioning eyebrow. Rand did not want to know what the question was. He tried to avoid looking at the man, but he knew it was too late for that. *Too late. Too late again.*

Only one thing seemed to shake the velvet-cloaked man's equilibrium. Rand's sword. He had left it on. Two or three men staggered up to ask if he thought his playing was so bad that he needed protection, but none of them had noticed the heron on the hilt. Gode noticed. His pale hands clenched, and he frowned at the sword for a long time before his smile came back. When it did, it was not as sure as before.

One good thing, at least, Rand thought. *If he believes I can live up to the heron-mark, maybe he'll leave us alone. Then all we have to worry about is Hake and his bullies.* It was hardly a comforting thought, and, sword or no sword, Gode kept watching. And smiling.

To Rand the night seemed to last a year. All those eyes looking at him: Hake and Jak and Strom like vultures watching a sheep caught in a bog, Gode waiting like something even worse. He began to think that everybody in the room was watching with some hidden motive. Sour wine fumes and the stench of dirty, sweating bodies made his head swim, and the din of voices beat at him till his eyes blurred and even the sound of his own flute scratched at his ears. The crash of the thunder seemed to be inside his skull. Weariness hung on him like an iron weight.

Eventually the need to be up with the dawn began to pull men reluctantly out into the dark. A farmer had only himself to answer to, but merchants were notoriously unfeeling about hangovers when they were paying drivers' wages. In the small hours the common room slowly emptied as even those who had rooms abovestairs staggered off to find their beds.

Gode was the last patron. When Rand reached for the leather flute case, yawning, Gode stood up and slung his cloak over his arm. The serving maids were cleaning up, muttering among themselves about the mess of spilled wine and broken crockery. Hake was locking the front door with a big key. Gode cornered Hake for a moment, and Hake called one of the women to show him to a room. The velvet-cloaked man gave Mat and Rand a knowing smile before he disappeared upstairs.

Hake was looking at Rand and Mat. Jak and Strom stood at his shoulders.

Rand hastily finished hanging his things from his shoulders, holding them all awkwardly behind him with his left hand so he could reach his sword. He made no move toward it, but he wanted to know it was ready. He suppressed a yawn; how tired he was was something they should not know.

Mat shouldered his bow and his few other belongings awkwardly, but he put his hand under his coat as he watched Hake and his toughs approach.

Hake was carrying an oil lamp, and to Rand's surprise he gave a little bow and gestured to a side door with it. "Your pallets are this way." Only a slight twist of his lips spoiled his act.

Mat thrust his chin out at Jak and Strom. "You need those two to show us our beds?"

"I'm a man of property," Hake said, smoothing the front of his soiled apron, "and men of property can't be too careful." A crash of thunder rattled the windows, and he glanced significantly at the ceiling, then gave them a toothy grin. "You want to see your beds or not?"

Rand wondered what would happen if he said they wanted to leave. *If you really did know more about using a sword than the few exercises Lan showed you.* . . . "Lead the way," he said, trying to make his voice hard. "I don't like having anybody behind me."

Strom snickered, but Hake nodded placidly and turned toward the side door, and the two big men swaggered after him. Taking a deep breath, Rand gave a wishful glance at the door to the kitchen. If Hake had already locked the back door, running now would only begin what he was hoping to avoid. He followed the innkeeper glumly.

At the side door he hesitated, and Mat crowded into his back. The reason for Hake's lamp was apparent. The door let into a hall as black as pitch. Only the lamp Hake carried, silhouetting Jak and Strom, gave him the courage to keep on. If they turned, he would know it. *And do what?* The floor creaked under his boots.

The hall ended in a rough, unpainted door. He had not seen if there were any other doors along the way. Hake and his bullies went through, and he followed quickly, before they could have a chance to set a trap, but Hake merely lifted the lamp high and gestured at the room.

"Here it is."

An old storeroom, he had called it, and by the look of it not used in some time. Weathered barrels and broken crates filled half the floor.

Steady drips fell from more than one place on the ceiling, and a broken pane in the filthy window let the rain blow in freely. Unidentifiable odds and ends littered the shelves, and thick dust covered almost everything. The presence of the promised pallets was a surprise.

The sword makes him nervous. He won't try anything until we're sound asleep. Rand had no intention of sleeping under Hake's roof. As soon as the innkeeper left, he intended to be out the window. "It'll do," he said. He kept his eyes on Hake, wary for a signal to the two grinning men at the innkeeper's side. It was an effort not to wet his lips. "Leave the lamp."

Hake grunted, but pushed the lamp onto a shelf. He hesitated, looking at them, and Rand was sure he was about to give the word for Jak and Strom to jump them, but his eyes went to Rand's sword with a calculating frown, and he jerked his head at the two big men. Surprise flashed across their broad faces, but they followed him out of the room without a backward glance.

Rand waited for the *creak-creak-creak* of their footsteps to fade away, then counted to fifty before sticking his head into the hall. The blackness was broken only by a rectangle of light that seemed as distant as the moon: the door to the common room. As he pulled his head in, something big moved in the darkness near the far door. Jak or Strom, standing guard.

A quick examination of the door told him all he needed to know, little of it good. The boards were thick and stout, but there was no lock, and no bar on the inside. It did open into the room, though.

"I thought they were going for us," Mat said. "What are they waiting for?" He had the dagger out, gripped in a white-knuckled fist. Lamplight flickered on the blade. His bow and quiver lay forgotten on the floor.

"For us to go to sleep." Rand started rummaging through the barrels and crates. "Help me find something to block the door."

"Why? You don't really intend to sleep here, do you? Let's get out the window and gone. I'd rather be wet than dead."

"One of them is at the end of the hall. We make any noise, and they'll be down on us before we can blink. I think Hake would rather face us awake than risk letting us get away."

Muttering, Mat joined his search, but there was nothing useful in any of the litter on the floor. The barrels were empty, the crates splintered, and the whole lot of them piled in front of the door would not stop anyone from opening it. Then something familiar on a shelf caught Rand's eye. Two splitting wedges, covered with rust and dust. He took them down with a grin.

Hastily he shoved them under the door and, when the next roll of thunder rattled the inn, drove them in with two quick kicks of his heel. The thunder faded, and he held his breath, listening. All he heard was the rain pounding on the roof. No floorboards creaking under running feet.

"The window," he said.

It had not been opened in years, from the dirt crusted around it. They strained together, pushing up with all their might. Rand's knees wobbled before the sash budged; it groaned with each reluctant inch. When the opening was wide enough for them to slip through, he crouched, then stopped.

"Blood and ashes!" Mat growled. "No wonder Hake wasn't worried about us slipping out."

Iron bars in an iron frame glistened wetly in the light from the lamp. Rand pushed at them; they were as solid as a boulder.

"I saw something," Mat said. He pawed hurriedly through the litter on the shelves and came back with a rusty crowbar. He rammed the end of it under the iron frame on one side, and Rand winced.

"Remember the noise, Mat."

Mat grimaced and muttered under his breath, but he waited. Rand put his hands on the crowbar and tried to find good footing in the growing puddle of water under the window. Thunder rolled and they heaved. With a tortured squeal of nails that made the hairs lift on Rand's neck, the frame shifted—a quarter of an inch, if that. Timing themselves to peals of thunder and lightning cracks, they heaved on the crowbar again and again. Nothing. A quarter of an inch. Nothing. A hairsbreadth. Nothing. Nothing.

Suddenly Rand's feet slipped in the water, and they crashed to the floor. The crowbar clattered against the bars like a gong. He lay in a puddle holding his breath and listening. Silence but for the rain.

Mat nursed bruised knuckles and glared at him. "We'll never get out at this rate." The iron frame was pushed out from the window not quite far enough to get two fingers under it. Dozens of thick nails crossed the narrow opening.

"We just have to keep trying," Rand said, getting up. But as he set the crowbar under the edge of the frame, the door creaked as someone tried to open it. The splitting wedges held it shut. He exchanged a worried look with Mat. Mat pulled the dagger out again. The door gave another screak.

Rand took a deep breath and tried to make his voice steady. "Go away, Hake. We're trying to sleep."

"I fear you mistake me." The voice was so sleek and full of itself that it named its owner. Howal Gode. "Master Hake and his . . . minions will not trouble us. They sleep soundly, and in the morning they will only be able to wonder where you vanished to. Let me in, my young friends. We must talk."

"We don't have anything to talk to you about," Mat said. "Go away and let us sleep."

Gode's chuckle was nasty. "Of course we have things to talk about. You know that as well as I. I saw it in your eyes. I know what you are, perhaps better than you do. I can feel it coming from you in waves. Already you halfway belong to my master. Stop running and accept it. Things will be so much easier for you. If the Tar Valon hags find you, you'll wish you could cut your own throat before they are done, but you won't be able to. Only my master can protect you from them."

Rand swallowed hard. "We don't know what you're talking about. Leave us alone." The floorboards in the hall squeaked. Gode was not alone. How many men could he have brought in two carriages?

"Stop being foolish, my young friends. You know. You know very well. The Great Lord of the Dark has marked you for his own. It is written that when he awakes, the new Dreadlords will be there to praise him. You must be two of them, else I would not have been sent to find you. Think of it. Life everlasting, and power beyond dreams." His voice was thick with hunger for that power himself.

Rand glanced back at the window just as lightning split the sky, and he almost groaned. The brief flash of light showed men outside, men ignoring the rain that drenched them as they stood watching the window.

"I tire of this," Gode announced. "You will submit to my master—to your master—or you will be made to submit. That would not be pleasant for you. The Great Lord of the Dark rules death, and he can give life in death or death in life as he chooses. Open this door. One way or another, your running is at an end. Open it, I say!"

He must have said something else, too, for suddenly a heavy body thudded against the door. It shivered, and the wedges slid a fraction of an inch with a grate of rust rubbing off on wood. Again and again the door trembled as bodies hurled themselves at it. Sometimes the wedges held; sometimes they slid another tiny bit, and bit by tiny bit the door crept inexorably inward.

"Submit," Gode demanded from the hall, "or spend eternity wishing that you had!"

"If we don't have any choice—" Mat licked his lips under Rand's stare. His eyes darted like the eyes of a badger in a trap; his face was pale, and he panted as he spoke. "We could say yes, and then get away later. Blood and ashes, Rand, there's no way out!"

The words seemed to drift to Rand through wool stuffed in his ears. *No way out.* Thunder muttered overhead, and was drowned in a slash of lightning. *Have to find a way out.* Gode called to them, demanding, appealing; the door slid another inch toward being open. *A way out!*

Light filled the room, flooding vision; the air roared and burned. Rand felt himself picked up and dashed against the wall. He slid down in a heap, ears ringing and every hair on his body trying to stand on end. Dazed, he staggered to his feet. His knees wobbled, and he put a hand against the wall to steady himself. He looked around in amazement.

The lamp, lying on its side on the edge of one of the few shelves still clinging to the walls, still burned and gave light. All the barrels and crates, some blackened and smoldering, lay toppled where they had been hurled. The window, bars and all, and most of the wall, too, had vanished, leaving a splintered hole. The roof sagged, and tendrils of smoke fought the rain around the jagged edges of the opening. The door hung off its hinges, jammed in the doorframe at an angle slanting into the hall.

With a feeling of woozy unreality he stood the lamp up. It seemed the most important thing in the world was making sure it did not break.

A pile of crates suddenly heaved apart, and Mat stood up in the middle of it. He weaved on his feet, blinking and fumbling at himself as if wondering if everything was still attached. He peered toward Rand. "Rand? Is that you? You're alive. I thought we were both—" He broke off, biting his lip and shaking. It took Rand a moment to realize he was laughing, and on the edge of hysteria.

"What happened, Mat? Mat? Mat! What happened?"

One last shiver wracked Mat, and then he was still. "Lightning, Rand. I was looking right at the window when it hit the bars. Lightning. I can't see worth—" He broke off, squinting at the aslant door, and his voice went sharp. "Where's Gode?"

Nothing moved in the dark corridor beyond the door. Of Gode and his companions there was neither sign nor sound, though anything could have lain in the blackness. Rand found himself hoping they were dead, but he would not have put his head into the hall to find out for sure if he had been offered a crown. Nothing moved out in the night beyond where the wall had been, either, but others were up and about. Confused shouts came from abovestairs in the inn, and the pounding of running feet.

"Let's go while we can," Rand said.

Hastily helping separate their belongings from the rubble, he grabbed Mat's arm and half pulled, half guided his friend through the gaping hole into the night. Mat clutched his arm, stumbling beside him with his head pushed forward in an effort to see.

As the first rain hit Rand's face, lightning forked above the inn, and he came to a convulsive stop. Gode's men were still there, lying with their feet toward the opening. Pelted by the rain, their open eyes stared at the sky.

"What is it?" Mat asked. "Blood and ashes! I can hardly see my own bloody hand!"

"Nothing," Rand said. *Luck. The Light's own. . . . Is it?* Shivering, he carefully guided Mat around the bodies. "Just the lightning."

There was no light save the lightning, and he stumbled in the ruts as they ran staggering away from the inn. With Mat almost hanging on him, every stumble almost pulled them both down, but tottering, panting, they ran.

Once he looked back. Once, before the rain thickened to a deafening curtain that blotted The Dancing Cartman from sight. Lightning silhouetted the figure of a man at the back of the inn, a man shaking his fist at them, or at the sky. Gode or Hake, he did not know, but either one was as bad as the other. The rain came in a deluge, isolating them in a wall of water. He hurried through the night, listening through the roar of the storm for the sound of pursuit.

CHAPTER
33

The Dark Waits

Under a leaden sky the high-wheeled cart bumped east along the Caemlyn Road. Rand pulled himself out of the straw in back to look over the side. It was easier than it had been an hour earlier. His arms felt as if they might stretch instead of drawing him up, and for a minute his head wanted to keep on going and float away, but it was easier. He hooked his elbows over the low slats and watched the land roll past. The sun, still hidden by dull clouds, yet stood high overhead, but the cart was clattering into another village of vine-covered, red brick houses. Towns had been getting closer together since Four Kings.

Some of the people waved or called a greeting to Hyam Kinch, the farmer whose cart it was. Master Kinch, leathery-faced and taciturn, shouted back a few words each time, around the pipe in his teeth. The clenched teeth made what he said all but unintelligible, but it sounded jovial and seemed to satisfy; they went back to what they were doing without another glance at the cart. No one appeared to pay any mind to the farmer's two passengers.

The village inn moved through Rand's field of vision. It was white-washed, with a gray slate roof. People bustled in and out, nodding casually and waving to one another. Some of them stopped to speak. They knew one another. Villagers, mostly, by their clothes—boots and trousers and coats not much different from what he wore himself, though with an inordinate fondness for colorful stripes. The women wore deep bonnets that hid their faces and white aprons with stripes. Maybe they were all townsmen and local farmfolk. *Does that make any difference?*

He dropped back on the straw, watching the village dwindle between his feet. Fenced fields and trimmed hedges lined the road, and small farmhouses with smoke rising from red brick chimneys. The only woods near the road were coppices, well tended for firewood, tame as a farmyard. But the branches stood leafless against the sky, as stark as in the wild woods to the west.

A line of wagons heading the other way rumbled down the center of the road, crowding the cart over onto the verge. Master Kinch shifted his pipe to the corner of his mouth and spat between his teeth. With one eye on his off-side wheel, to make sure it did not tangle in the hedge, he kept the cart moving. His mouth tightened as he glanced at the merchants' train.

None of the wagon drivers cracking their long whips in the air above eight-horse teams, none of the hard-faced guards slouching in their saddles alongside the wagons, looked at the cart. Rand watched them go, his chest tight. His hand was under his cloak, gripping his sword hilt, until the last wagon lurched by.

As that final wagon rattled away toward the village they had just left, Mat turned on the seat beside the farmer and leaned back until he found Rand's eyes. The scarf that did duty for dust, when need be, shaded his own eyes, folded over thickly and tied low around his forehead. Even so he squinted in the gray daylight. "You see anything back there?" he asked quietly. "What about the wagons?"

Rand shook his head, and Mat nodded. He had seen nothing either.

Master Kinch glanced at them out of the corner of his eye, then shifted his pipe again, and flapped the reins. That was all, but he had noticed. The horse picked up the pace a step.

"Your eyes still hurt?" Rand asked.

Mat touched the scarf around his head. "No. Not much. Not unless I look almost right at the sun, anyway. What about you? Are you feeling any better?"

"Some." He really was feeling better, he realized. It was a wonder to get over being sick so fast. More than that, it was a gift of the Light. *It has to be the Light. It has to be.*

Suddenly a body of horsemen was passing the cart, heading west like the merchants' wagons. Long white collars hung down over their mail and plate, and their cloaks and undercoats were red, like the gate-tenders' uniforms in Whitebridge, but better made and better fitting. Each man's conical helmet shone like silver. They sat their horses with straight backs. Thin red streamers fluttered beneath the heads of their lances, every lance held at the same angle.

Some of them glanced into the cart as they passed in two columns. A cage of steel bars masked each face. Rand was glad his cloak covered his sword. A few nodded to Master Kinch, not as if they knew him, but in a neutral greeting. Master Kinch nodded back in much the same way, but despite his unchanging expression there was a hint of approval in his nod.

Their horses were at a walk, but with the speed of the cart added, they went by quickly. With a part of his mind Rand counted them. Ten . . . twenty . . . thirty . . . thirty-two. He raised his head to watch the columns move on down the Caemlyn Road.

"Who were they?" Mat asked, half wondering, half suspicious.

"Queen's Guards," Master Kinch said around his pipe. He kept his eyes on the road ahead. "Won't go much further than Breen's Spring, 'less they're called for. Not like the old days." He sucked on his pipe, then added, "I suppose, these days, there's parts of the Realm don't see the Guards in a year or more. Not like the old days."

"What are they doing?" Rand asked.

The farmer gave him a look. "Keeping the Queen's peace and upholding the Queen's law." He nodded to himself as if he liked the sound of that, and added, "Searching out malefactors and seeing them before a magistrate. Mmmph!" He let out a long streamer of smoke. "You two must be from pretty far off not to recognize the Queen's Guard. Where you from?"

"Far off," Mat said at the same instant that Rand said, "The Two Rivers." He wished he could take it back as soon as he said it. He still was not thinking clearly. Trying to hide, and mentioning a name a Fade would hear like a bell.

Master Kinch glanced at Mat out of the corner of his eye, and puffed his pipe in silence for a while. "That's far off, all right," he said finally. "Almost to the border of the Realm. But things must be worse than I thought if there's places in the Realm where people don't even *recognize* the Queen's Guards. Not like the old days at all."

Rand wondered what Master al'Vere would say if someone told him
the Two Rivers was part of some Queen's Realm. The Queen of
Andor, he supposed. Perhaps the Mayor did know—he knew a lot of
things that surprised Rand—and maybe others did, too, but he had
never heard anyone mention it. The Two Rivers was the Two Rivers.
Each village handled its own problems, and if some difficulty involved
more than one village the Mayors, and maybe the Village Councils,
solved it between them.

Master Kinch pulled on the reins, drawing the cart to a halt. "Far
as I go." A narrow cart path led off to the north; several farmhouses
were visible in that direction across open fields, plowed but still bare
of crops. "Two days will see you in Caemlyn. Least, it would if your
friend had his legs under him."

Mat hopped down and retrieved his bow and other things, then
helped Rand climb off the tail of the cart. Rand's bundles weighed on
him, and his legs wobbled, but he shrugged off his friend's hand and
tried a few steps on his own. He still felt unsteady, but his legs held
him up. They even seemed to grow stronger as he used them.

The farmer did not start his horse up again right away. He studied
them for a minute, sucking on his pipe. "You can rest up a day or two
at my place, if you want. Won't miss anything in that time, I suppose.
Whatever sickness you're getting over, young fellow . . . well, the old
woman and me, we already had about every sickness you can think of
before you were born, and nursed our younglings through 'em, too. I
expect you're past the catching stage, anyway."

Mat's eyes narrowed, and Rand caught himself frowning. *Not everyone is part of it. It can't be everybody.*

"Thank you," he said, "but I'm all right. Really. How far to the
next village?"

"Carysford? You can reach it before dark, walking." Master Kinch
took his pipe from between his teeth and pursed his lips thoughtfully
before going on. "First off, I reckoned you for runaway 'prentices, but
now I expect it's something more serious you're running from. Don't
know what. Don't care. I'm a good enough judge to say you're not
Darkfriends, and not likely to rob or hurt anybody. Not like some on
the road these days. I got in trouble a time or two myself when I was
your age. You need a place to keep out of sight a few days, my farm
is five miles that way"—he jerked his head toward the cart
track—"and don't nobody ever come out there. Whatever's chasing
you, won't likely find you there." He cleared his throat as if embarrassed by speaking so many words together.

"How would you know what Darkfriends look like?" Mat demanded. He backed away from the cart, and his hand went under his coat. "What do you know about Darkfriends?"

Master Kinch's face tightened. "Suit yourselves," he said, and clucked to his horse. The cart rolled off down the narrow path, and he never looked back.

Mat looked at Rand, and his scowl faded. "Sorry, Rand. You need a place to rest. Maybe if we go after him. . . ." He shrugged. "I just can't get over the feeling that everybody's after us. Light, I wish I knew why they were. I wish it was over. I wish. . . ." He trailed off miserably.

"There are still some good people," Rand said. Mat started toward the cart path, jaw clenched as if it were the last thing he wanted to do, but Rand stopped him. "We can't afford to stop just to rest, Mat. Besides, I don't think there is anywhere to hide."

Mat nodded, his relief evident. He tried to take some of Rand's burdens, the saddlebags and Thom's cloak wrapped around the cased harp, but Rand held onto them. His legs really did feel stronger. *Whatever's chasing us?* he thought as they started off down the road. *Not chasing. Waiting.*

The rain had continued through the night they staggered away from The Dancing Cartman, hammering at them as hard as the thunder out of a black sky split by lightning. Their clothes became sodden in minutes; in an hour Rand's skin felt sodden, too, but they had left Four Kings behind them. Mat was all but blind in the dark, squinting painfully at the sharp flashes that made trees stand out starkly for an instant. Rand led him by the hand, but Mat still felt out each step uncertainly. Worry creased Rand's forehead. If Mat did not regain his sight, they would be slowed to a crawl. They would never get away.

Mat seemed to sense his thought. Despite the hood of his cloak, the rain had plastered Mat's hair across his face. "Rand," he said, "you won't leave me, will you? If I can't keep up?" His voice quavered.

"I won't leave you." Rand tightened his grip on his friend's hand. "I won't leave you no matter what." *Light help us!* Thunder crashed overhead, and Mat stumbled, almost falling, almost pulling him down, too. "We have to stop, Mat. If we keep going, you'll break a leg."

"Gode." Lightning split the dark right above them as Mat spoke, and the thunder crack pounded every other sound into the ground, but in the flash Rand could make out the name on Mat's lips.

"He's dead." *He has to be. Light, let him be dead.*

He led Mat to some bushes the lightning flash had showed him. They had leaves enough to give a little shelter from the driving rain. Not as much as a good tree might, but he did not want to risk another lightning strike. They might not be so lucky, next time.

Huddled together beneath the bushes, they tried to arrange their cloaks to make a little tent over the branches. It was far too late to think of staying dry, but just stopping the incessant pelting of the raindrops would be something. They crouched against each other to share what little body warmth was left to them. Dripping wet as they were, and more drips coming through the cloaks, they shivered themselves into sleep.

Rand knew right away it was a dream. He was back in Four Kings, but the town was empty except for him. The wagons were there, but no people, no horses, no dogs. Nothing alive. He knew someone was waiting for him, though.

As he walked down the rutted street, the buildings seemed to blur as they slid behind him. When he turned his head, they were all there, solid, but the indistinctness remained at the corners of his vision. It was as if only what he saw really existed, and then just while he was seeing. He was sure if he turned quickly enough he would see. . . . He was not sure what, but it made him uneasy, thinking about it.

The Dancing Cartman appeared in front of him. Somehow its garish paint seemed gray and lifeless. He went in. Gode was there, at a table.

He only recognized the man from his clothes, his silk and dark velvets. Gode's skin was red, burned and cracked and oozing. His face was almost a skull, his lips shriveled to bare teeth and gums. As Gode turned his head, some of his hair cracked off, powdering to soot when it hit his shoulder. His lidless eyes stared at Rand.

"So you are dead," Rand said. He was surprised that he was not afraid. Perhaps it was knowing that it was a dream this time.

"Yes," said Ba'alzamon's voice, "but he did find you for me. That deserves some reward, don't you think?"

Rand turned, and discovered he could be afraid, even knowing it was a dream. Ba'alzamon's clothes were the color of dried blood, and rage and hate and triumph battled on his face.

"You see, youngling, you cannot hide from me forever. One way or another I find you. What protects you also makes you vulnerable. One time you hide, the next you light a signal fire. Come to me, youngling." He held out his hand to Rand. "If my hounds must pull you down, they may not be gentle. They are jealous of what you will be, once you have knelt at my feet. It is your destiny. You belong to me."

Gode's burned tongue made an angry, eager garble of sound.

Rand tried to wet his lips, but he had no spit in his mouth. "No," he managed, and then the words came more easily. "I belong to myself. Not you. Not ever. Myself. If your Darkfriends kill me, you'll never have me."

The fires in Ba'alzamon's face heated the room till the air swam. "Alive or dead, youngling, you are mine. The grave belongs to me. Easier dead, but better alive. Better for you, youngling. The living have more power in most things." Gode made a gabbling sound again. "Yes, my good hound. Here is your reward."

Rand looked at Gode just in time to see the man's body crumble to dust. For an instant the burned face held a look of sublime joy that turned to horror in the final moment, as if he had seen something waiting he did not expect. Gode's empty velvet garments settled on the chair and the floor among the ash.

When he turned back, Ba'alzamon's outstretched hand had become a fist. "You are mine, youngling, alive or dead. The Eye of the World will never serve you. I mark you as mine." His fist opened, and a ball of flame shot out. It struck Rand in the face, exploding, searing.

Rand lurched awake in the dark, water dripping through the cloaks onto his face. His hand trembled as he touched his cheeks. The skin felt tender, as if sunburned.

Suddenly he realized Mat was twisting and moaning in his sleep. He shook him, and Mat came awake with a whimper.

"My eyes! Oh, Light, my eyes! He took my eyes!"

Rand held him close, cradling him against his chest as if he were a baby. "You're all right, Mat. You're all right. He can't hurt us. We won't let him." He could feel Mat shaking, sobbing into his coat. "He can't hurt us," he whispered, and wished he believed it. *What protects you makes you vulnerable. I am going mad.*

Just before first light the downpour dwindled, the last drizzle fading as dawn came. The clouds remained, threatening until well into the morning. The wind came up, then, driving the clouds off to the south, baring a warmthless sun and slicing through their dripping wet clothes. They had not slept again, but groggily they donned their cloaks and set off eastward, Rand leading Mat by the hand. After a while Mat even felt well enough to complain about what the rain had done to his bowstring. Rand would not let him stop to exchange it for a dry string from his pocket, though; not yet.

They came on another village shortly after midday. Rand shivered harder at the sight of snug brick houses and smoke rising from chim-

neys, but he kept clear, leading Mat through the woods and fields to
the south. A lone farmer working with a spading fork in a muddy field
was the only person he saw, and he took care that the man did not
see them, crouching through the trees. The farmer's attention was all
on his work, but Rand kept one eye on him till he was lost to sight.
If any of Gode's men were alive, perhaps they would believe he and
Mat had taken the southern road out of Four Kings when they could
not find anyone who had seen them in this village. They came back to
the road out of sight of the town, and walked their clothes, if not dry,
at least to just damp.

An hour beyond the town a farmer gave them a ride in his half-
empty haywain. Rand had been taken by surprise while lost in worry
about Mat. Mat shielded his eyes from the sun with his hand, weak as
the afternoon light was, squinting through slitted lids even so, and he
muttered continually about how bright the sun was. When Rand heard
the rumble of the haywain, it was too late already. The sodden road
deadened sound, and the wagon with its two-horse hitch was only fifty
yards behind them, the driver already peering at them.

To Rand's surprise he drew up and offered them a lift. Rand hesitated, but it was too late to avoid being seen, and refusing a ride might
fix them in the man's mind. He helped Mat up to the seat beside the
farmer, then climbed up behind him.

Alpert Mull was a stolid man, with a square face and square hands,
both worn and grooved from hard work and worry, and he wanted
someone to talk to. His cows had gone dry, his chickens had stopped
laying, and there was no pasture worth the name. For the first time in
memory he had had to buy hay, and half a wagon was all "old Bain"
would let him have. He wondered whether there was any chance of
getting hay on his own land this year, or any kind of crop.

"The Queen should do something, the Light illumine her," he muttered, knuckling his forehead respectfully but absentmindedly.

He hardly looked at Rand or Mat, but when he let them down by
the narrow, rail-lined track that led off to his farm, he hesitated, then
said, almost as if to himself, "I don't know what you're running from,
and I don't want to. I have a wife and children. You understand? My
family. It's hard times for helping strangers."

Mat tried to stick his hand under his coat, but Rand had his wrist
and he held on. He stood in the road, looking at the man without
speaking.

"If I was a good man," Mull said, "I'd offer a couple of lads soaked
to the skin a place to dry out and get warm in front of my fire. But

it's hard times, and strangers. . . . I don't know what you're running from, and I don't want to. You understand? My family." Suddenly he pulled two long, woolen scarves, dark and thick, out of his coat pocket. "It's not much, but here. Belong to my boys. They have others. You don't know me, understand? It's hard times."

"We never even saw you," Rand agreed as he took the scarves. "You *are* a good man. The best we've met in days."

The farmer looked surprised, then grateful. Gathering his reins, he turned his horses down the narrow lane. Before he completed the turn Rand was leading Mat on down the Caemlyn Road.

The wind stiffened as dusk closed in. Mat began to ask querulously when they were going to stop, but Rand kept moving, pulling Mat behind him, searching for more shelter than a spot under a hedge. With their clothes still clammy and the wind getting colder by the minute, he was not sure they could survive another night in the open. Night fell without him spotting anything useful. The wind grew icy, beating his cloak. Then, through the darkness ahead, he saw lights. A village.

His hand slid into his pocket, feeling the coins there. More than enough for a meal and a room for the two of them. A room out of the cold night. If they stayed in the open, in the wind and cold in damp clothes, anyone who found them would likely as not find only two corpses. They just had to keep from attracting any more notice than they could help. No playing the flute, and with his eyes, Mat certainly could not juggle. He grasped Mat's hand again and set out toward the beckoning lights.

"When are we going to stop?" Mat asked again. The way he peered ahead, with his head stuck forward, Rand was not sure if Mat could see him, much less the village lights.

"When we're somewhere warm," he replied.

Pools of light from house windows lit the streets of the town, and people walked them unconcerned with what might be out in the dark. The only inn was a sprawling building, all on one floor, with the look of having had rooms added in bunches over the years without any particular plan. The front door opened to let someone out, and a wave of laughter rolled out after him.

Rand froze in the street, the drunken laughter at The Dancing Cartman echoing in his head. He watched the man go down the street with a none-too-steady stride, then took a deep breath and pushed the door open. He took care that his cloak covered his sword. Laughter swept over him.

Lamps hanging from the high ceiling made the room bright, and right away he could see and feel the difference from Saml Hake's inn. There was no drunkenness here, for one thing. The room was filled with people who looked to be farmers and townsmen, if not entirely sober, not too far from it. The laughter was real, if a bit forced around the edges. People laughing to forget their troubles, but with true mirth in it, too. The common room itself was neat and clean, and warm from a fire roaring in a big fireplace at the far end. The serving maids' smiles were as warm as the fire, and when they laughed Rand could tell it was because they wanted to.

The innkeeper was as clean as his inn, with a gleaming white apron around his bulk. Rand was glad to see he was a stout man; he doubted if he would ever again trust a skinny innkeeper. His name was Rulan Allwine—a good omen, Rand thought, with so much of the sound of Emond's Field to it—and he eyed them up and down, then politely mentioned paying in advance.

"Not suggesting you're the sort, understand, but there's some on the road these days aren't too particular about paying up come morning. Seems to be a lot of young folks headed for Caemlyn."

Rand was not offended, not as damp and bedraggled as he was. When Master Allwine mentioned the price, though, his eyes widened, and Mat made a sound as if he had choked on something.

The innkeeper's jowls swung as he shook his head regretfully, but he seemed to be used to it. "Times are hard," he said in a resigned voice. "There isn't much, and what there is costs five times what it used to. It'll be more next month, I'll lay oath on it."

Rand dug his money out and looked at Mat. Mat's mouth tightened stubbornly. "You want to sleep under a hedge?" Rand asked. Mat sighed and reluctantly emptied his pocket. When the reckoning was paid, Rand grimaced at the little that remained to divide with Mat.

But ten minutes later they were eating stew at a table in a corner near the fireplace, pushing it onto their spoons with chunks of bread. The portions were not as large as Rand could have wished, but they were hot, and filling. Warmth from the hearth seeped into him slowly. He pretended to keep his eyes on his plate, but he watched the door intently. Those who came in or went out all looked like farmers, but it was not enough to quiet his fear.

Mat ate slowly, savoring each bite, though he muttered about the light from the lamps. After a time he dug out the scarf Alpert Mull had given him and wound it around his forehead, pulling it down until his eyes were almost hidden. That got them some looks Rand wished they could have avoided. He cleaned his plate hurriedly, urging Mat to do the same, then asked Master Allwine for their room.

The innkeeper seemed surprised that they were retiring so early, but he made no comment. He got a candle and showed them through a jumble of corridors to a small room, with two narrow beds, back in a far corner of the inn. When he left, Rand dropped his bundles beside his bed, tossed his cloak over a chair, and fell on the coverlet fully dressed. All of his clothes were still damp and uncomfortable, but if they had to run, he wanted to be ready. He left the sword belt on, too, and slept with his hand on the hilt.

A rooster crowing jerked him awake in the morning. He lay there, watching dawn lighten the window, and wondered if he dared sleep a little longer. Sleep during daylight, when they could be moving. A yawn made his jaws crack.

"Hey," Mat exclaimed, "I can see!" He sat up on his bed, squinting around the room. "Some, anyway. Your face is still a little blurry, but I can tell who you are. I knew I'd be all right. By tonight I'll see better than you do. Again."

Rand sprang out of bed, scratching as he scooped up his cloak. His clothes were wrinkled from drying on him while he slept, and they itched. "We're wasting daylight," he said. Mat scrambled up as fast as he had; he was scratching, too.

Rand did feel good. They were a day away from Four Kings, and none of Gode's men had showed up. A day closer to Caemlyn, where Moiraine would be waiting for them. She would. No more worrying about Darkfriends once they were back with the Aes Sedai and the Warder. It was strange to be looking forward so much to being with an Aes Sedai. *Light, when I see Moiraine again, I'll kiss her!* He laughed at the thought. He felt good enough to invest some of their dwindling stock of coins in breakfast—a big loaf of bread and a pitcher of milk, cold from the springhouse.

They were eating in the back of the common room when a young man came in, a village youth by the look of him, with a cocky spring to his walk and twirling a cloth cap, with a feather in it, on one finger. The only other person in the room was an old man sweeping out; he never looked up from his broom. The young man's eyes swept jauntily around the room, but when they lit on Rand and Mat, the cap fell off his finger. He stared at them for a full minute before snatching the cap from the floor, then stared some more, running his fingers through his thick head of dark curls. Finally he came over to their table, his feet dragging.

He was older than Rand, but he stood looking down at them diffidently. "Mind if I sit down?" he asked, and immediately swallowed hard as if he might have said the wrong thing.

Rand thought he might be hoping to share their breakfast, though he looked able to buy his own. His blue-striped shirt was embroidered around the collar, and his dark blue cloak all around the hem. His leather boots had never been near any work that scuffed them, that Rand could see. He nodded to a chair.

Mat stared at the fellow as he drew the chair to the table. Rand could not tell if he was glaring or just trying to see clearly. In any case, Mat's frown had an effect. The young man froze halfway to sitting, and did not lower himself all the way until Rand nodded again.

"What's your name?" Rand asked.

"My name? My name. Ah . . . call me Paitr." His eyes shifted nervously. "Ah . . . this is not my idea, you understand. I have to do it. I didn't want to, but they made me. You have to understand that. I don't—"

Rand was beginning to tense when Mat growled, "Darkfriend."

Paitr gave a jerk and half lifted out of his chair, staring wildly around the room as if there were fifty people to overhear. The old man's head was still bent over the broom, his attention on the floor. Paitr sat back down and looked from Rand to Mat and back uncertainly. Sweat beaded on his upper lip. It was accusation enough to make anyone sweat, but he said not a word against it.

Rand shook his head slowly. After Gode, he knew that Darkfriends did not necessarily have the Dragon's Fang on their foreheads, but except for his clothes this Paitr could have fit right in Emond's Field. Nothing about him hinted at murder and worse. Nobody would have remarked him twice. At least Gode had been . . . different.

"Leave us alone," Rand said. "And tell your friends to leave us alone. We want nothing from them, and they'll get nothing from us."

"If you don't," Mat added fiercely, "I'll name you for what you are. See what your village friends think of that."

Rand hoped he did not really mean it. That could cause as much trouble for the two of them as it did for Paitr.

Paitr seemed to take the threat seriously. His face grew pale. "I . . . I heard what happened at Four Kings. Some of it, anyway. Word travels. We have ways of hearing things. But there's nobody here to trap you. I'm alone, and . . . and I just want to talk."

"About what?" Mat asked at the same time that Rand said, "We're not interested." They looked at each other, and Mat shrugged. "We're not interested," he said.

Rand gulped the last of the milk and stuffed the heel of his half of
the bread into his pocket. With their money almost gone, it might be
their next meal.

How to leave the inn? If Paitr discovered that Mat was almost blind,
he would tell others . . . other Darkfriends. Once Rand had seen a
wolf separate a crippled sheep from the flock; there were other wolves
around, and he could neither leave the flock nor get a clear shot with
his bow. As soon as the sheep was alone, bleating with terror, hobbling
frantically on three legs, the one wolf chasing it became ten as if by
magic. The memory of it turned his stomach. They could not stay
there, either. Even if Paitr was telling the truth about being alone,
how long would he stay that way?

"Time to go, Mat," he said, and held his breath. As Mat started to
stand, he pulled Paitr's eyes to himself by leaning forward and saying, "Leave us alone, Darkfriend. I won't tell you again.
Leave—us—alone."

Paitr swallowed hard and pressed back in his chair; there was no
blood left in his face at all. It made Rand think of a Myrddraal.

By the time he looked back at Mat, Mat was on his feet, his awk-
wardness unseen. Rand hastily hung his own saddlebags and other
bundles around him, trying to keep his cloak over the sword as he did.
Maybe Paitr already knew about it; maybe Gode had told Ba'alzamon,
and Ba'alzamon had told Paitr; but he did not think so. He thought
Paitr had only the vaguest idea of what had happened in Four Kings.
That was why he was so frightened.

The comparatively bright outline of the door helped Mat make a
beeline for it, if not quickly, then not slow enough to seem unnatural,
either. Rand followed closely, praying for him not to stumble. He was
thankful Mat had a clear, straight path, with no tables or chairs in the
way.

Behind him Paitr suddenly leaped to his feet. "Wait," he said desperately. "You have to wait."

"Leave us alone," Rand said without looking back. They were almost to the door, and Mat had not put a foot wrong yet.

"Just listen to me," Paitr said, and put his hand on Rand's shoulder
to stop him.

Images spun in his head. The Trolloc, Narg, leaping at him in his
own home. The Myrddraal threatening at the Stag and Lion in Baerlon. Halfmen everywhere, Fades chasing them to Shadar Logoth, coming for them in Whitebridge. Darkfriends everywhere. He whirled, his
hand balling up. "I said, leave us alone!" His fist took Paitr flush on
the nose.

The Darkfriend fell on his bottom and sat there on the floor staring at Rand. Blood trickled from his nose. "You won't get away," he spat angrily. "No matter how strong you are, the Great Lord of the Dark is stronger. The Shadow will swallow you!"

There was a gasp from further into the common room, and the clatter of a broom handle hitting the floor. The old man with the broom had finally heard. He stood staring wide-eyed at Paitr. The blood drained from his wrinkled face and his mouth worked, but no sound came out. Paitr stared back for an instant, then gave a wild curse and sprang to his feet, darting out of the inn and down the street as if starving wolves were at his heels. The old man shifted his attention to Rand and Mat, looking not a whit less frightened.

Rand hustled Mat out of the inn and out of the village as fast as he could, listening all the while for a hue and cry that never came but was no less loud in his ears for that.

"Blood and ashes," Mat growled, "they're always there, always right on our heels. We'll never get away."

"No they're not," Rand said. "If Ba'alzamon knew we were here, do you think he'd have left it to that fellow? There'd have been another Gode, and twenty or thirty bullyboys. They're still hunting, but they won't know until Paitr tells them, and maybe he really is alone. He might have to go all the way to Four Kings, for all we know."

"But he said—"

"I don't care." He was unsure which "he" Mat meant, but it changed nothing. "We're not going to lie down and let them take us."

They got six rides, short ones, during the day. A farmer told them that a crazy old man at the inn in Market Sheran was claiming there were Darkfriends in the village. The farmer could hardly talk for laughing; he kept wiping tears off his cheeks. Darkfriends in Market Sheran! It was the best story he had heard since Ackley Farren got drunk and spent the night on the inn roof.

Another man, a round-faced wagonwright with tools hanging from the sides of his cart and two wagon wheels in the back, told a different story. Twenty Darkfriends had held a gathering in Market Sheran. Men with twisted bodies, and the women worse, all dirty and in rags. They could make your knees grow weak and your stomach heave just by looking at you, and when they laughed, the filthy cackles rang in your ears for hours and your head felt as if it were splitting open. He had seen them himself, just at a distance, far enough off to be safe. If the Queen would not do something, then somebody ought to ask the Children of the Light for help. Somebody should do something.

It was a relief when the wagonwright let them down.

With the sun low behind them they walked into a small village, much like Market Sheran. The Caemlyn Road split the town neatly in two, but on both sides of the wide road stood rows of small brick houses with thatched roofs. Webs of vine covered the bricks, though only a few leaves hung on them. The village had one inn, a small place no bigger than the Winespring Inn, with a sign on a bracket out front, creaking back and forth in the wind. The Queen's Man.

Strange, to think of the Winespring Inn as small. Rand could remember when he thought it was about as big as a building could be. Anything bigger would be a palace. But he had seen a few things, now, and suddenly he realized that nothing would look the same to him when he got back home. *If you ever do.*

He hesitated in front of the inn, but even if prices at The Queen's Man were not as high as in Market Sheran, they could not afford a meal or a room, either one.

Mat saw where he was looking and patted the pocket where he kept Thom's colored balls. "I can see well enough, as long as I don't try to get too fancy." His eyes had been getting better, though he still wore the scarf around his forehead, and had squinted whenever he looked at the sky during the day. When Rand said nothing, Mat went on. "There can't be Darkfriends at every inn between here and Caemlyn. Besides, I don't want to sleep under a bush if I can sleep in a bed." He made no move toward the inn, though, just stood waiting for Rand.

After a moment Rand nodded. He felt as tired as he had at any time since leaving home. Just thinking of a night in the open made his bones ache. *It's all catching up. All the running, all the looking over your shoulder.*

"They can't be everywhere," he agreed.

With the first step he took into the common room, he wondered if he had made a mistake. It was a clean place, but crowded. Every table was filled, and some men leaned against the walls because there was nowhere for them to sit. From the way the serving maids scurried between the tables with harried looks—and the landlord, too—it was a larger crowd than they were used to. Too many for this small village. It was easy to pick out the people who did not belong there. They were dressed no differently from the rest, but they kept their eyes on their food and drink. The locals watched the strangers as much as anything else.

A drone of conversation hung in the air, enough that the innkeeper took them into the kitchen when Rand made him understand that they needed to talk to him. The noise was almost as bad there, with the cook and his helpers banging pots and darting about.

The innkeeper mopped his face with a large handkerchief. "I suppose you're on your way to Caemlyn to see the false Dragon like every other fool in the Realm. Well, it's six to a room and two or three to a bed, and if that doesn't suit, I've nothing for you."

Rand gave his spiel with a feeling of queasiness. With so many people on the road, every other one could be a Darkfriend, and there was no way to pick them out from the rest. Mat demonstrated his juggling—he kept it to three balls, and was careful even then—and Rand took out Thom's flute. After only a dozen notes of "The Old Black Bear," the innkeeper nodded impatiently.

"You'll do. I need something to take those idiots' minds off this Logain. There's been three fights already over whether or not he's really the Dragon. Stow your things in the corner, and I'll go clear a space for you. If there's any room to. Fools. The world's full of fools who don't know enough to stay where they belong. That's what's causing all the trouble. People who won't stay where they belong." Mopping his face again, he hurried out of the kitchen, muttering under his breath.

The cook and his helpers ignored Rand and Mat. Mat kept adjusting the scarf around his head, pushing it up, then blinking at the light and tugging it back down again. Rand wondered if he could see well enough to do anything more complicated than juggle three balls. As for himself. . . .

The queasiness in his stomach grew thicker. He dropped on a low stool, holding his head in his hands. The kitchen felt cold. He shivered. Steam filled the air; stoves and ovens crackled with heat. His shivers became stronger, his teeth chattering. He wrapped his arms around himself, but it did no good. His bones felt as if they were freezing.

Dimly he was aware of Mat asking him something, shaking his shoulder, and of someone cursing and running out of the room. Then the innkeeper was there, with the cook frowning at his side, and Mat was arguing loudly with them both. He could not make out any of what they said; the words were a buzz in his ears, and he could not seem to think at all.

Suddenly Mat took his arm, pulling him to his feet. All of their things—saddlebags, blanketrolls, Thom's bundled cloak and instrument cases—hung from Mat's shoulders with his bow. The innkeeper was watching them, wiping his face anxiously. Weaving, more than half supported by Mat, Rand let his friend steer him toward the back door.

"S-s-sorry, M-m-mat," he managed. He could not stop his teeth from chattering. "M-m-must have . . . b-been t-the . . . rain. O-one m-more . . . night out . . . w-won't h-hurt . . . I guess." Twilight darkened the sky, spotted by a handful of stars.

"Not a bit of it," Mat said. He was trying to sound cheerful, but Rand could hear the hidden worry. "He was scared the other folk would find out there was somebody sick in his inn. I told him if he kicked us out, I'd take you into the common room. That'd empty half his rooms in ten minutes. For all his talk about fools, he doesn't want that."

"Then w-where?"

"Here," Mat said, pulling open the stable door with a loud creak of hinges.

It was darker inside than out, and the air smelled of hay and grain and horses, with a strong undersmell of manure. When Mat lowered him to the straw-covered floor, he folded over with his chest on his knees, still hugging himself and shaking from head to toe. All of his strength seemed to go for the shaking. He heard Mat stumble and curse and stumble again, then a clatter of metal. Suddenly light blossomed. Mat held up a battered old lantern.

If the inn was full, so was its stable. Every stall had a horse, some raising their heads and blinking at the light. Mat eyed the ladder to the hayloft, then looked at Rand, crouched on the floor, and shook his head.

"Never get you up there," Mat muttered. Hanging the lantern on a nail, he scrambled up the ladder and began tossing down armloads of hay. Hurriedly climbing back down, he made a bed at the back of the stable and got Rand onto it. Mat covered him with both their cloaks, but Rand pushed them off almost immediately.

"Hot," he murmured. Vaguely he knew that he had been cold only a moment before, but now he felt as if he were in an oven. He tugged at his collar, tossing his head. "Hot." He felt Mat's hand on his forehead.

"I'll be right back," Mat said, and disappeared.

He twisted fitfully on the hay, how long he was not sure, until Mat returned with a heaped plate in one hand, a pitcher in the other, and two white cups dangling from fingers by their handles.

"There's no Wisdom here," he said, dropping to his knees beside Rand. He filled one of the cups and held it to Rand's mouth. Rand gulped the water down as if he had had nothing to drink in days; that was how he felt. "They don't even know what a Wisdom is. What they do have is somebody called Mother Brune, but she's off somewhere birthing a baby, and nobody knows when she'll be back. I did get some bread, and cheese, and sausage. Good Master Inlow will give us anything as long as we stay out of sight of his guests. Here, try some."

Rand turned his head away from the food. The sight of it, the thought of it, made his stomach heave. After a minute Mat sighed and settled down to eat himself. Rand kept his eyes averted, and tried not to listen.

The chills came once more, and then the fever, to be replaced by the chills, and the fever again. Mat covered him when he shook, and fed him water when he complained of thirst. The night deepened, and the stable shifted in the flickering lantern light. Shadows took shape and moved on their own. Then he saw Ba'alzamon striding down the stable, eyes burning, a Myrddraal at either side with faces hidden in the depths of their black cowls.

Fingers scrabbling for his sword hilt, he tried to get to his feet, yelling, "Mat! Mat, they're here! Light, they're here!"

Mat jerked awake where he sat cross-legged against the wall. "What? Darkfriends? Where?"

Wavering on his knees, Rand pointed frantically down the stable . . . and gaped. Shadows stirred, and a horse stamped in its sleep. Nothing more. He fell back on the straw.

"There's nobody but us," Mat said. "Here, let me take that." He reached for Rand's sword belt, but Rand tightened his grip on the hilt.

"No. No. I have to keep it. He's my father. You understand? He's m-my f-father!" The shivering swept over him once more, but he clung to the sword as if to a lifeline. "M-my f-father!" Mat gave up trying to take it and pulled the cloaks back over him.

There were other visitations in the night, while Mat dozed. Rand was never sure if they were really there or not. Sometimes he looked at Mat, with his head on his chest, wondering if he would see them, too, if he woke.

Egwene stepped out of the shadows, her hair in a long, dark braid as it had been in Emond's Field, her face pained and mournful. "Why did you leave us?" she asked. "We're dead because you left us."

Rand shook his head weakly on the hay. "No, Egwene. I didn't want to leave you. Please."

"We're all dead," she said sadly, "and death is the kingdom of the Dark One. The Dark One has us, because you abandoned us."

"No. I had no choice, Egwene. Please. Egwene, don't go. Come back, Egwene!"

But she turned into the shadows, and was shadow.

Moiraine's expression was serene, but her face was bloodless and pale. Her cloak might as well have been a shroud, and her voice was a lash. "That is right, Rand al'Thor. You have no choice. You must go to Tar Valon, or the Dark One will take you for his own. Eternity chained in the Shadow. Only Aes Sedai can save you, now. Only Aes Sedai."

Thom grinned at him sardonically. The gleeman's clothes hung in charred rags that made him see the flashes of light as Thom wrestled with the Fade to give them time to run. The flesh under the rags was blackened and burned. "Trust Aes Sedai, boy, and you'll wish you were dead. Remember, the price of Aes Sedai help is always smaller than you can believe, always greater than you can imagine. And what Ajah will find you first, eh? Red? Maybe Black. Best to run, boy. Run."

Lan's stare was as hard as granite, and blood covered his face. "Strange to see a heron-mark blade in the hands of a sheepherder. Are you worthy of it? You had better be. You're alone, now. Nothing to hold to behind you, and nothing before, and anyone can be a Darkfriend." He smiled a wolf's smile, and blood poured out of his mouth. "Anyone."

Perrin came, accusing, pleading for help. Mistress al'Vere, weeping for her daughter, and Bayle Domon, cursing him for bringing Fades down on his vessel, and Master Fitch, wringing his hands over the ashes of his inn, and Min, screaming in a Trolloc's clutches, people he knew, people he had only met. But the worst was Tam. Tam stood over him, frowning and shaking his head, and said not a word.

"You have to tell me," Rand begged him. "Who am I? Tell me, please. Who am I? *Who am I?*" he shouted.

"Easy, Rand."

For a moment he thought it was Tam answering, but then he saw that Tam was gone. Mat bent over him, holding a cup of water to his lips.

"Just rest easy. You're Rand al'Thor, that's who you are, with the ugliest face and the thickest head in the Two Rivers. Hey, you're sweating! The fever's broken."

"Rand al'Thor?" Rand whispered. Mat nodded, and there was something so comforting in it that Rand drifted off to sleep without even touching the water.

It was a sleep untroubled by dreams—at least by any he remembered—but light enough that his eyes drifted open whenever Mat checked on him. Once he wondered if Mat was getting any sleep at all, but he fell back asleep himself before the thought got very far.

The squeal of the door hinges roused him fully, but for a moment he only lay there in the hay wishing he was still asleep. Asleep he would not be aware of his body. His muscles ached like wrung-out rags, and had about as much strength. Weakly he tried to raise his head; he made it on the second try.

Mat sat in his accustomed place against the wall, within arm's reach of Rand. His chin rested on his chest, which rose and fell in the easy rhythm of deep sleep. The scarf had slipped down over his eyes.

Rand looked toward the door.

A woman stood there holding it open with one hand. For a moment she was only a dark shape in a dress, outlined by the faint light of early morning, then she stepped inside, letting the door swing shut behind her. In the lantern light he could see her more clearly. She was about the same age as Nynaeve, he thought, but she was no village woman. The pale green silk of her dress shimmered as she moved. Her cloak was a rich, soft gray, and a frothy net of lace caught up her hair. She fingered a heavy gold necklace as she looked thoughtfully at Mat and him.

"Mat," Rand said, then louder, "Mat!"

Mat snorted and almost fell over as he came awake. Scrubbing sleep from his eyes, he stared at the woman.

"I came to look at my horse," she said, gesturing vaguely at the stalls. She never took her eyes away from the two of them, though. "Are you ill?"

"He's all right," Mat said stiffly. "He just caught a chill in the rain, that's all."

"Perhaps I should look at him," she said. "I have some knowledge. . . ."

Rand wondered if she were Aes Sedai. Even more than her clothes, her self-assured manner, the way she held her head as if on the point of giving a command, did not belong here. *And if she is Aes Sedai, of what Ajah?*

"I'm fine, now," he told her. "Really, there's no need."

But she came down the length of the stable, holding her skirt up and placing her gray slippers gingerly. With a grimace for the straw, she knelt beside him and felt his forehead.

"No fever," she said, studying him with a frown. She was pretty, in a sharp-featured fashion, but there was no warmth in her face. It was not cold, either; it just seemed to lack any feeling whatsoever. "You *were* sick, though. Yes. Yes. And still weak as a day-old kitten. I think. . . ." She reached under her cloak, and suddenly things were happening too fast for Rand to do more than give a strangled shout.

Her hand flashed from under her cloak; something glittered as she lunged across Rand toward Mat. Mat toppled sideways in a flurry of motion, and there was a solid *tchunk* of metal driven into wood. It all took just an instant, and then everything was still.

Mat lay half on his back, one hand gripping her wrist just above the dagger she had driven into the wall where his chest had been, his other hand holding the blade from Shadar Logoth to her throat.

Moving nothing but her eyes, she tried to look down at the dagger Mat held. Eyes widening, she drew a ragged breath and tried to pull back from it, but he kept the edge against her skin. After that, she was as still as a stone.

Licking his lips, Rand stared at the tableau above him. Even if he had not been so weak, he did not believe he could have moved. Then his eyes fell on her dagger, and his mouth went dry. The wood around the blade was blackening; thin tendrils of smoke rose from the char.

"Mat! Mat, her dagger!"

Mat flicked a glance at the dagger, then back to the woman, but she had not moved. She was licking *her* lips nervously. Roughly Mat pried her hand off the hilt and gave her a push; she toppled back, sprawling away from them and catching herself with her hands behind her, still watching the blade in his hand. "Don't move," he said. "I'll use this if you move. Believe me, I will." She nodded slowly; her eyes never left Mat's dagger. "Watch her, Rand."

Rand was not sure what he was supposed to do if she tried anything—shout, maybe; he certainly could not run after her if she tried to flee—but she sat there without twitching while Mat yanked her dagger free of the wall. The black spot stopped growing, though a faint wisp of smoke still trailed up from it.

Mat looked around for somewhere to put the dagger, then thrust it toward Rand. He took it gingerly, as if it were a live adder. It looked ordinary, if ornate, with a pale ivory hilt and a narrow, gleaming blade no longer than the palm of his hand. Just a dagger. Only he had seen what it could do. The hilt was not even warm, but his hand began to sweat. He hoped he did not drop it in the hay.

The woman did not move from her sprawl as she watched Mat slowly turn toward her. She watched him as if wondering what he would do next, but Rand saw the sudden tightening of Mat's eyes, the tightening of his hand on the dagger. "Mat, no!"

"She tried to kill me, Rand. She'd have killed you, too. She's a Darkfriend." Mat spat the word.

"But we're not," Rand said. The woman gasped as if she had just realized what Mat had intended. "We are not, Mat."

For a moment Mat remained frozen, the blade in his fist catching the lantern light. Then he nodded. "Move over there," he told the woman, gesturing with the dagger toward the door to the tack room.

She got to her feet slowly, pausing to brush the straw from her dress. Even when she started in the direction Mat indicated, she moved as if there were no reason to hurry. But Rand noticed that she kept a wary eye on the ruby-hi'ted dagger in Mat's hand. "You really should stop struggling," she said. "It would be for the best, in the end. You will see."

"The best?" Mat said wryly, rubbing his chest where her blade would have gone if he had not moved. "Get over there."

She gave a casual shrug as she obeyed. "A mistake. There has been considerable . . . confusion since what happened with that egotistical fool Gode. Not to mention whoever the idiot was who started the panic in Market Sheran. No one is sure what happened there, or how. That makes it more dangerous for you, don't you see? You will have honored places if you come to the Great Lord of your own free will, but as long as you run, there will be pursuit, and who can tell what will happen then?"

Rand felt a chill. *My hounds are jealous, and may not be gentle.*

"So you're having trouble with a couple of farmboys." Mat's laugh was grim. "Maybe you Darkfriends aren't as dangerous as I've always heard." He flung open the door of the tack room and stepped back.

She paused just through the doorway, looking at him over her shoulder. Her gaze was ice, and her voice colder still. "You will find out how dangerous we are. When the Myrddraal gets here—"

Whatever else she had to say was cut off as Mat slammed the door and pulled the bar down into its brackets. When he turned, his eyes were worried. "Fade," he said in a tight voice, tucking the dagger back under his coat. "Coming here, she says. How are your legs?"

"I can't dance," Rand muttered, "but if you'll help me get on my feet, I can walk." He looked at the blade in his hand and shuddered. "Blood and ashes, I'll run."

Hurriedly hanging himself about with their possessions, Mat pulled Rand to his feet. Rand's legs wobbled, and he had to lean on his friend to stay upright, but he tried not to slow Mat down. He held the woman's dagger well away from himself. Outside the door was a

bucket of water. He tossed the dagger into it as they passed. The blade
entered the water with a hiss; steam rose from the surface. Grimacing,
he tried to take faster steps.

With light come, there were plenty of people in the streets, even so
early. They were about their own business, though, and no one had
any attention to spare for two young men walking out of the village,
not with so many strangers about. Just the same, Rand stiffened every
muscle, trying to stand straight. With each step he wondered if any of
the folk hurrying by were Darkfriends. *Are any of them waiting for the
woman with the dagger? For the Fade?*

A mile outside the village his strength gave out. One minute he was
panting along, hanging on Mat; the next they were both on the ground.
Mat tugged him over to the side of the road.

"We have to keep going," Mat said. He scrubbed his hand through
his hair, then tugged the scarf down above his eyes. "Sooner or later,
somebody will let her out, and they'll be after us again."

"I know," Rand panted. "I know. Give me a hand."

Mat pulled him up again, but he wavered there, knowing it was no
good. The first time he tried to take a step, he would be flat on his
face again.

Holding him upright, Mat waited impatiently for a horse-cart, approaching from the village, to pass them. Mat gave a grunt of surprise
when the cart slowed to a stop before them. A leathery-faced man
looked down from the driver's seat.

"Something wrong with him?" the man asked around his pipe.

"He's just tired," Mat said.

Rand could see that was not going to do, not leaning on Mat the
way he was. He let go of Mat and took a step away from him. His
legs quivered, but he willed himself to stay erect. "I haven't slept in
two days," he said. "Ate something that made me sick. I'm better,
now, but I haven't slept."

The man blew a streamer of smoke from the corner of his mouth.
"Going to Caemlyn, are you? Was your age, I expect I might be off
to see this false Dragon myself."

"Yes." Mat nodded. "That's right. We're going to see the false
Dragon."

"Well, climb on up, then. Your friend in the back. If he's sick again,
best it's on the straw, not up here. Name's Hyam Kinch."

CHAPTER

34

The Last Village

I t was after dark when they reached Carysford, longer than Rand
had thought it would take from what Master Kinch said when he
let them down. He wondered if his whole sense of time was getting skewed. Only three nights since Howal Gode and Four Kings, two
since Paitr had surprised them in Market Sheran. Just a bare day since
the nameless Darkfriend woman tried to kill them in the stable of The
Queen's Man, but even that seemed a year ago, or a lifetime.

Whatever was happening to time, Carysford appeared normal
enough, on the surface, at least. Neat, vine-covered brick houses and
narrow lanes, except for the Caemlyn Road itself, quiet and outwardly
peaceful. *But what's underneath?* he wondered. Market Sheran had
been peaceful to look at, and so had the village where the woman. . . .
He had never learned the name of that one, and he did not want to
think about it.

Light spilled from the windows of the houses into streets all but
empty of people. That suited Rand. Slinking from corner to corner,
he avoided the few people abroad. Mat stuck to his shoulder, freezing

when the crunch of gravel announced the approach of a villager, dodging from shadow to shadow when the dim shape had gone past.

The River Cary was a bare thirty paces wide there, and the black water moved sluggishly, but the ford had long since been bridged over. Centuries of rain and wind had worn the stone abutments until they seemed almost like natural formations. Years of freight wagons and merchant trains had ground at the thick wooden planks, too. Loose boards rattled under their boots, sounding as loud as drums. Until long after they were through the village and into the countryside beyond, Rand waited for a voice to demand to know who they were. Or worse, knowing who they were.

The countryside had been filling up the further they went, becoming more and more settled. There were always the lights of farmhouses in sight. Hedges and rail fences lined the road and the fields beyond. Always the fields were there, and never a stretch of woods close to the road. It seemed as if they were always on the outskirts of a village, even when they were hours from the nearest town. Neat and peaceful. And with never an indication that Darkfriends or worse might be lurking.

Abruptly Mat sat down in the road. He had pushed the scarf up on top of his head, now that the only light came from the moon. "Two paces to the span," he muttered. "A thousand spans to the mile, four miles to the league. . . . I'm not walking another ten paces unless there's a place to sleep at the end of it. Something to eat wouldn't be amiss, either. You haven't been hiding anything in your pockets, have you? An apple, maybe? I won't hold it against you if you have. You could at least look."

Rand peered down the road both ways. They were the only things moving in the night. He glanced at Mat, who had pulled off one boot and was rubbing his foot. Or they had been. His own feet hurt, too. A tremor ran up his legs as if to tell him he had not yet regained as much strength as he thought.

Dark mounds stood in a field just ahead of them. Haystacks, diminished by winter feeding, but still haystacks.

He nudged Mat with his toe. "We'll sleep there."

"Haystacks again." Mat sighed, but he tugged on his boot and got up.

The wind was rising, the night chill growing deeper. They climbed over the smooth poles of the fence and quickly were burrowing into the hay. The tarp that kept the rain off the hay cut the wind, too.

Rand twisted around in the hollow he had made until he found a comfortable position. Hay still managed to poke at him through his clothes, but he had learned to put up with that. He tried counting the haystacks he had slept in since Whitebridge. Heroes in the stories never had to sleep in haystacks, or under hedges. But it was not easy to pretend, anymore, that he was a hero in a story, even for a little while. With a sigh, he pulled his collar up in the hopes of keeping hay from getting down his back.

"Rand?" Mat said softly. "Rand, do you think we'll make it?"

"Tar Valon? It's a long way yet, but—"

"Caemlyn. Do you think we'll make it to Caemlyn?"

Rand raised his head, but it was dark in their burrow; the only thing that told him where Mat was was his voice. "Master Kinch said two days. Day after tomorrow, the next day, we'll get there."

"If there aren't a hundred Darkfriends waiting for us down the road, or a Fade or two." There was silence for a moment, then Mat said, "I think we're the last ones left, Rand." He sounded frightened. "Whatever it's all about, it's just us two, now. Just us."

Rand shook his head. He knew Mat could not see in the darkness, but it was more for himself than Mat, anyway. "Go to sleep, Mat," he said tiredly. But he lay awake a long time himself, before sleep came. *Just us*.

A cock's crow woke him, and he scrambled out into the false dawn, brushing hay off his clothes. Despite his precautions some had worked its way down his back; the straws clung between his shoulder blades, itching. He took off his coat and pulled his shirt out of his breeches to get to it. It was while he had one hand down the back of his neck and the other twisted up behind him that he became aware of the people.

The sun was not yet truly up, but already a steady trickle moved down the road in ones and twos, trudging toward Caemlyn, some with packs or bundles on their backs, others with nothing but a walking staff, if that. Most were young men, but here and there was a girl, or someone older. One and all they had the travel-stained look of having walked a long way. Some had their eyes on their feet and a weary slump to their shoulders, early as it was; others had their gaze fixed on something out of sight ahead, something toward the dawn.

Mat rolled out of the haystack, scratching vigorously. He only paused long enough to wrap the scarf around his head; it shaded his eyes a little less this morning. "You think we might get something to eat today?"

Rand's stomach rumbled in sympathy. "We can think about that when we're on the road," he said. Hastily arranging his clothes, he dug his share of their bundles out of the haystack.

By the time they reached the fence, Mat had noticed the people, too. He frowned, stopping in the field while Rand climbed over. A young man, not much older than they, glanced at them as he passed. His clothes were dusty, and so was the blanketroll strapped across his back.

"Where are you bound?" Mat called.

"Why, Caemlyn, for to see the Dragon," the fellow shouted back without stopping. He raised an eyebrow at the blankets and saddlebags hanging from their shoulders, and added, "Just like you." With a laugh he went on, his eyes already seeking eagerly ahead.

Mat asked the same question several times during the day, and the only people who did not give much the same answer were local folk. If those answered at all, it was by spitting and turning away in disgust. They turned away, but they kept a watchful eye, too. They looked at all the travelers the same way, out of the corners of their eyes. Their faces said strangers might get up to anything if not watched.

People who lived in the area were not only wary of the strangers, they seemed more than a little put out. Just enough people were on the road, scattered out just enough, that when farmers' carts and wagons appeared with the sun peeking over the horizon, even their usually slow pace was halved. None of them was in any mood to give a ride. A sour grimace, and maybe a curse for the work they were missing, were more likely.

The merchants' wagons rolled by with little hindrance beyond shaken fists, whether they were going toward Caemlyn or away from it. When the first merchants' train appeared, early on in the morning, coming at a stiff trot with the sun barely above the horizon behind the wagons, Rand stepped out of the road. They gave no sign of slowing for anything, and he saw other folk scrambling out of the way. He moved all the way over onto the verge, but kept walking.

A flicker of motion as the first wagon rumbled close was all the warning he had. He went sprawling on the ground as the wagon driver's whip cracked in the air where his head had been. From where he lay he met the driver's eyes as the wagon rolled by. Hard eyes above a mouth in a tight grimace. Not a care that he might have drawn blood, or taken an eye.

"Light blind you!" Mat shouted after the wagon. "You can't—" A mounted guard caught him on the shoulder with the butt of his spear, knocking him down atop Rand.

"Out of the way, you dirty Darkfriend!" the guard growled without slowing.

After that, they kept their distance from the wagons. There were certainly enough of them. The rattle and clatter of one hardly faded before another could be heard coming. Guards and drivers, they all stared at the travelers heading for Caemlyn as if seeing dirt walk.

Once Rand misjudged a driver's whip, just by the length of the tip. Clapping his hand to the shallow gash over his eyebrow, he swallowed hard to keep from vomiting at how close it had come to his eye. The driver smirked at him. With his other hand he grabbed Mat, to stop him nocking an arrow.

"Let it go," he said. He jerked his head at the guards riding alongside the wagons. Some of them were laughing; others gave Mat's bow a hard eye. "If we're lucky, they'd just beat us with their spears. If we're lucky."

Mat grunted sourly, but he let Rand pull him on down the road.

Twice squadrons of the Queen's Guards came trotting down the road, streamers on their lances fluttering in the wind. Some of the farmers hailed them, wanting something done about the strangers, and the Guards always paused patiently to listen. Near midday Rand stopped to listen to one such conversation.

Behind the bars of his helmet, the Guard captain's mouth was a tight line. "If one of them steals something, or trespasses on your land," he growled at the lanky farmer frowning beside his stirrup, "I'll haul him before a magistrate, but they break no Queen's Law by walking on the Queen's Highway."

"But they're all over the place," the farmer protested. "Who knows who they are, or what they are. All this talk about the Dragon. . . ."

"Light, man! You only have a handful here. Caemlyn's walls are bulging with them, and more coming every day." The captain's scowl deepened as he caught sight of Rand and Mat, standing in the road nearby. He gestured down the road with a steel-backed gauntlet. "Get on with you, or I'll have you in for blocking traffic."

His voice was no rougher with them than with the farmer, but they moved on. The captain's eyes followed them for a time; Rand could feel them on his back. He suspected the Guards had little patience left with the wanderers, and no sympathy for a hungry thief. He decided to stop Mat if he suggested stealing eggs again.

Still, there was a good side to all the wagons and people on the road, especially all the young men heading for Caemlyn. For any Darkfriends hunting them, it would be like trying to pick out two particular pigeons in a flock. If the Myrddraal on Winternight had not known exactly who it was after, maybe its fellow would do no better here.

His stomach rumbled frequently, reminding him that they had next to no money left, certainly not enough for a meal at the prices charged this close to Caemlyn. He realized once he had a hand on the flute case, and firmly pushed it around to his back. Gode had known all about the flute, and the juggling. There was no telling how much Ba'alzamon had learned from him before the end—if what Rand had seen had *been* the end—or how much had been passed to other Darkfriends.

He looked regretfully at a farm they were passing. A man patrolled the fences with a pair of dogs, growling and tugging at their leashes. The man looked as if he wanted nothing more than an excuse to let them loose. Not every farm had the dogs out, but no one was offering jobs to travelers.

Before the sun went down, he and Mat walked through two more villages. The village folk stood in knots, talking among themselves and watching the steady stream pass by. Their faces were no friendlier than the faces of the farmers, or the wagon drivers, or the Queen's Guards. All these strangers going to see the false Dragon. Fools who did not know enough to stay where they belonged. Maybe followers of the false Dragon. Maybe even Darkfriends. If there was any difference between the two.

With evening coming, the stream began to thin at the second town. The few who had money disappeared into the inn, though there seemed to be some argument about letting them inside; others began hunting for handy hedges or fields with no dogs. By dusk he and Mat had the Caemlyn Road to themselves. Mat began talking about finding another haystack, but Rand insisted on keeping on.

"As long as we can see the road," he said. "The further we go before stopping, the further ahead we are." *If they are chasing you. Why should they chase now, when they've been waiting for you to come to them so far?*

It was argument enough for Mat. With frequent glances over his shoulder, he quickened his step. Rand had to hurry to keep up.

The night thickened, relieved only a bit by scant moonlight. Mat's burst of energy faded, and his complaints started up again. Aching knots formed in Rand's calves. He told himself he had walked further in a hard day working on the farm with Tam, but repeat it as often as he would, he could not make himself believe it. Gritting his teeth, he ignored the aches and pains and would not stop.

With Mat complaining and him concentrating on the next step, they were almost on the village before he saw the lights. He tottered to a stop, suddenly aware of a burning that ran from his feet right up his legs. He thought he had a blister on his right foot.

At the sight of the village lights, Mat sagged to his knees with a groan. "Can we stop now?" he panted. "Or do you want to find an inn and hang out a sign for the Darkfriends? Or a Fade."

"The other side of the town," Rand answered, staring at the lights. From this distance, in the dark, it could have been Emond's Field. *What's waiting there?* "Another mile, that's all."

"All! I'm not walking another span!"

Rand's legs felt like fire, but he made himself take a step, and then another. It did not get any easier, but he kept on, one step at a time. Before he had gone ten paces he heard Mat staggering after him, muttering under his breath. He thought it was just as well he could not make out what Mat was saying.

It was late enough for the streets of the village to be empty, though most houses had a light in at least one window. The inn in the middle of town was brightly lit, surrounded by a golden pool that pushed back the darkness. Music and laughter, dimmed by thick walls, drifted from the building. The sign over the door creaked in the wind. At the near end of the inn, a cart and horse stood in the Caemlyn Road with a man checking the harness. Two men stood at the far end of the building, on the very edge of the light.

Rand stopped in the shadows beside a house that stood dark. He was too tired to hunt through the lanes for a way around. A minute resting could not hurt. Just a minute. Just until the men went away. Mat slumped against the wall with a grateful sigh, leaning back as if he meant to go to sleep right there.

Something about the two men at the rim of the shadows made Rand uneasy. He could not put a finger on anything, at first, but he realized the man at the cart felt the same way about them. He reached the end of the strap he was checking, adjusted the bit in the horse's mouth, then went back and started over from the beginning again. He kept his head down the whole while, his eyes on what he was doing and away from the other men. It could have been that he simply was not aware of them, though they were less than fifty feet off, except for the stiff way he moved and the way he sometimes turned awkwardly in what he was doing so he would not be looking toward them.

One of the men in the shadows was only a black shape, but the other stood more into the light, with his back to Rand. Even so it was plain he was not overjoyed at the conversation he was having. He wrung his hands and kept his eyes on the ground, jerking his head in a nod now and then at something the other had said. Rand could not hear anything, but he got the impression that the man in the shadows was doing all the talking; the nervous man just listened, and nodded, and wrung his hands anxiously.

Eventually the one who was wrapped in darkness turned away, and the nervous fellow started back into the light. Despite the chill he was mopping his face with the long apron he wore, as if he were drenched in sweat.

Skin prickling, Rand watched the shape moving off in the night. He did not know why, but his uneasiness seemed to follow that one, a vague tingling in the back of his neck and the hair stirring on his arms as if he had suddenly realized something was sneaking up on him. With a quick shake of his head, he rubbed his arms briskly. *Getting as foolish as Mat, aren't you?*

At that moment the form slipped by the edge of the light from a window—just on the brink of it—and Rand's skin crawled. The inn's sign went *scree-scree-scree* in the wind, but the dark cloak never stirred.

"Fade," he whispered, and Mat jerked to his feet as if he had shouted.

"What—?"

He clamped a hand over Mat's mouth. "Softly." The dark shape was lost in the darkness. *Where?* "It's gone, now. I think. I hope." He took his hand away; the only sound Mat made was a long, indrawn breath.

The nervous man was almost to the inn door. He stopped and smoothed down his apron, visibly composing himself before he went inside.

"Strange friends you've got, Raimun Holdwin," the man by the cart said suddenly. It was an old man's voice, but strong. The speaker straightened, shaking his head. "Strange friends in the dark for an innkeeper."

The nervous man jumped when the other spoke, looking around as if he had not seen the cart and the other man until right then. He drew a deep breath and gathered himself, then asked sharply, "And what do you mean by that, Almen Bunt?"

"Just what I said, Holdwin. Strange friends. He's not from around here, is he? Lot of odd folk coming through the last few weeks. Awful lot of odd folk."

"You're a fine one to talk." Holdwin cocked an eye at the man by the cart. "I know a lot of men, even men from Caemlyn. Not like you, cooped up alone out on that farm of yours." He paused, then went on as if he thought he had to explain further. "He's from Four Kings. Looking for a couple of thieves. Young men. They stole a heron-mark sword from him."

Rand's breath had caught at the mention of Four Kings; at the mention of the sword he glanced at Mat. His friend had his back pressed hard against the wall and was staring into the darkness with eyes so wide they seemed to be all whites. Rand wanted to stare into the night, too—the Halfman could be anywhere—but his eyes went back to the two men in front of the inn.

"A heron-mark sword!" Bunt exclaimed. "No wonder he wants it back."

Holdwin nodded. "Yes, and them, too. My friend's a rich man, a . . . a merchant, and they've been stirring up trouble with the men who work for him. Telling wild stories and getting people upset. They're Darkfriends, and followers of Logain, too."

"Darkfriends *and* followers of the false Dragon? And telling wild stories, too? Getting up to a lot for young fellows. You did say they were young?" There was a sudden note of amusement in Bunt's voice, but the innkeeper did not seem to notice.

"Yes. Not yet twenty. There's a reward—a hundred crowns in gold—for the two of them." Holdwin hesitated, then added, "They've sly tongues, these two. The Light knows what kind of tales they'll tell, trying to turn people against one another. And dangerous, too, even if they don't look it. Vicious. Best you stay clear if you think you see them. Two young men, one with a sword, and both looking over their shoulders. If they're the right ones, my . . . my friend will pick them up once they're located."

"You sound almost as if you know them to look at."

"I'll know them when I see them," Holdwin said confidently. "Just don't try to take them yourself. No need for anyone to get hurt. Come tell me if you see them. My . . . friend will deal with them. A hundred crowns for the two, but he wants the pair."

"A hundred crowns for the two," Bunt mused. "How much for this sword he wants so bad?"

Abruptly Holdwin appeared to realize the other man was making fun of him. "I don't know why I'm telling you," he snapped. "You're still fixed on that fool plan of yours, I see."

"Not such a fool plan," Bunt replied placidly. "There might not be another false Dragon to see before I die—Light send it so!—and I'm too old to eat some merchant's dust all the way to Caemlyn. I'll have the road to myself, and I'll be in Caemlyn bright and early tomorrow."

"To yourself?" The innkeeper's voice had a nasty quiver. "You can never tell what might be out in the night, Almen Bunt. All alone on the road, in the dark. Even if somebody hears you scream, there's no one will unbar a door to help. Not these days, Bunt. Not your nearest neighbor."

None of that seemed to ruffle the old farmer at all; he answered as calmly as before. "If the Queen's Guards can't keep the road safe this close to Caemlyn, then we're none of us safe even in our own beds. If you ask me, one thing the Guards could do to make sure the roads are safe would be clap that friend of yours in irons. Sneaking around in the dark, afraid to let anybody get a look at him. Can't tell me he's not up to no good."

"Afraid!" Holdwin exclaimed. "You old fool, if you knew—" His teeth clicked shut abruptly, and he gave himself a shake. "I don't know why I'm wasting time on you. Get off with you! Stop cluttering up the front of my place of business." The door of the inn boomed shut behind him.

Muttering to himself, Bunt took hold of the edge of the cart seat and set his foot on the wheelhub.

Rand hesitated only a moment. Mat caught his arm as he started forward.

"Are you crazy, Rand? He'll recognize us for sure!"

"You'd rather stay here? With a Fade around? How far do you think we'll get on foot before it finds us?" He tried not to think of how far they would get in a cart if it found them. He shook free of Mat and trotted up the road. He carefully held his cloak shut so the sword was hidden; the wind and the cold were excuse enough for that.

"I couldn't help overhearing you're going to Caemlyn," he said.

Bunt gave a start, jerking a quarterstaff out of the cart. His leathery face was a mass of wrinkles and half his teeth were gone, but his gnarled hands held the staff steady. After a minute he lowered one end of the staff to the ground and leaned on it. "So you two are going to Caemlyn. To see the Dragon, eh?"

Rand had not realized that Mat had followed him. Mat was keeping well back, though, out of the light, watching the inn and the old farmer with as much suspicion as he was the night.

"The false Dragon," Rand said with emphasis.

Bunt nodded. "Of course. Of course." He threw a sideways look at the inn, then abruptly shoved his staff back under the cart seat. "Well, if you want a ride, get in. I've wasted enough time." He was already climbing to the seat.

Rand clambered over the back as the farmer flicked the reins. Mat ran to catch up as the cart started off. Rand caught his arms and pulled him aboard.

The village faded quickly into the night at the pace Bunt set. Rand lay back on the bare boards, fighting the lulling creak of the wheels. Mat stifled his yawns with a fist, warily staring into the countryside. Darkness weighed heavily on the fields and farms, dotted with the lights of farmhouses. The lights seemed distant, seemed to struggle vainly against the night. An owl called, a mourner's cry, and the wind moaned like lost souls in the Shadow.

It could be out there anywhere, Rand thought.

Bunt seemed to feel the oppression of the night, too, for he suddenly spoke up. "You two ever been to Caemlyn before?" He gave a little chuckle. "Don't suppose you have. Well, wait till you see it. The greatest city in the world. Oh, I've heard all about Illian and Ebou Dar and Tear and all—there's always some fool thinks a thing is bigger and better just because it's off somewheres over the horizon—but for my money, Caemlyn is the grandest there is. Couldn't be grander. No, it couldn't. Unless maybe Queen Morgase, the Light illumine her, got rid of that witch from Tar Valon."

Rand was lying back with his head pillowed on his blanketroll atop the bundle of Thom's cloak, watching the night drift by, letting the farmer's words wash by him. A human voice kept the darkness at bay and muted the mournful wind. He twisted around to look up at the dark mass of Bunt's back. "You mean an Aes Sedai?"

"What else would I mean? Sitting there in the Palace like a spider. I'm a good Queen's man—never say I'm not—but it just isn't right. I'm not one of those saying Elaida's got too much influence over the Queen. Not me. And as for the fools who claim Elaida's really the queen in all but name. . . ." He spat into the night. "That for them. Morgase is no puppet to dance for any Tar Valon witch."

Another Aes Sedai. If . . . when Moiraine got to Caemlyn, she might well go to a sister Aes Sedai. If the worst happened, this Elaida might help them reach Tar Valon. He looked at Mat, and just as if he had spoken aloud Mat shook his head. He could not see Mat's face, but he knew it was fixed in denial.

Bunt went right on talking, flicking the reins whenever his horse slowed but otherwise letting his hands rest on his knees. "I'm a good

Queen's man, like I said, but even fools say something worthwhile now and again. Even a blind pig finds an acorn sometimes. There's got to be some changes. This weather, the crops failing, cows drying up, calves and lambs born dead, or with two heads. Bloody ravens don't even wait for things to die. People are scared. They want somebody to blame. Dragon's Fang turning up on people's doors. Things creeping about in the night. Barns getting burned. Fellows around like that friend of Holdwin, scaring people. The Queen's got to do something before it's too late. You see that, don't you?"

Rand made a noncommittal sound. It sounded as if they had been even luckier than he had thought to find this old man and his cart. They might not have gotten further than that last village if they had waited for daylight. Things creeping about in the night. He lifted up to look over the side of the cart at the darkness. Shadows and shapes seemed to writhe in the black. He dropped back before his imagination convinced him there was something there.

Bunt took it for agreement. "Right. I'm a good Queen's man, and I'll stand against any who try to harm her, but I'm right. You take the Lady Elayne and the Lord Gawyn, now. There's a change wouldn't harm anything, and might do some good. Sure, I know we've always done it that way in Andor. Send the Daughter-Heir off to Tar Valon to study with the Aes Sedai, and the eldest son off to study with the Warders. I believe in tradition, I do, but look what it got us last time. Luc dead in the Blight before he was ever anointed First Prince of the Sword, and Tigraine vanished—run off or dead—when it came time for her to take the throne. Still troubling us, that.

"There's some saying she's still alive, you know, that Morgase isn't the rightful Queen. Bloody fools. I remember what happened. Remember like it was yesterday. No Daughter-Heir to take the throne when the old Queen died, and every House in Andor scheming and fighting for the right. And Taringail Damodred. You wouldn't have thought he'd lost his wife, him hot to figure which House would win so he could marry again and become Prince Consort after all. Well, he managed it, though why Morgase chose . . . ah, no man knows the mind of a woman, and a queen is twice a woman, wed to a man, wed to the land. He got what he wanted, anyway, if not the way he wanted it.

"Brought Cairhien into the plotting before he was done, and you know how that ended. The Tree chopped down, and black-veiled Aiel coming over the Dragonwall. Well, he got himself decently killed after he'd fathered Elayne and Gawyn, so there's an end to it, I suppose.

But why send them to Tar Valon? It's time men didn't think of the throne of Andor and Aes Sedai in the same thought anymore. If they've got to go some place else to learn what they need, well, Illian's got libraries as good as Tar Valon, and they'll teach the Lady Elayne as much about ruling and scheming as ever the witches could. Nobody knows more about scheming than an Illianer. And if the Guards can't teach the Lord Gawyn enough about soldiering, well, they've soldiers in Illian, too. And in Shienar, and Tear, for that matter. I'm a good Queen's man, but I say let's stop all this truck with Tar Valon. Three thousand years is long enough. Too long. Queen Morgase can lead us and put things right without help from the White Tower. I tell you, there's a woman makes a man proud to kneel for her blessing. Why, once. . . ."

Rand fought the sleep his body cried out for, but the rhythmic creak and sway of the cart lulled him and he floated off on the drone of Bunt's voice. He dreamed of Tam. At first they were at the big oak table in the farmhouse, drinking tea while Tam told him about Prince Consorts, and Daughter-Heirs, and the Dragonwall, and black-veiled Aielmen. The heron-mark sword lay on the table between them, but neither of them looked at it. Suddenly he was in the Westwood, pulling the makeshift litter through the moon-bright night. When he looked over his shoulder, it was Thom on the litter, not his father, sitting cross-legged and juggling in the moonlight.

"The Queen is wed to the land," Thom said as brightly colored balls danced in a circle, "but the Dragon . . . the Dragon is one with the land, and the land is one with the Dragon."

Further back Rand saw a Fade coming, black cloak undisturbed by the wind, horse ghosting silently through the trees. Two severed heads hung at the Myrddraal's saddlebow, dripping blood that ran in darker streams down its mount's coal-black shoulder. Lan and Moiraine, faces distorted in grimaces of pain. The Fade pulled on a fistful of tethers as it rode. Each tether ran back to the bound wrists of one of those who ran behind the soundless hooves, their faces blank with despair. Mat and Perrin. And Egwene.

"Not her!" Rand shouted. "The Light blast you, it's me you want, not her!"

The Halfman gestured, and flames consumed Egwene, flesh crisping to ash, bone blacking and crumbling.

"The Dragon is one with the land," Thom said, still juggling unconcernedly, "and the land is one with the Dragon."

Rand screamed . . . and opened his eyes.

The cart creaked along the Caemlyn Road, filled with night and the sweetness of long-vanished hay and the faint smell of horse. A shape blacker than the night rested on his chest, and eyes blacker than death looked into his.

"You are mine," the raven said, and the sharp beak stabbed into his eye. He screamed as it plucked his eyeball out of his head.

With a throat-ripping shriek, he sat up, clapping both hands to his face.

Early morning daylight bathed the cart. Dazed, he stared at his hands. No blood. No pain. The rest of the dream was already fading, but that. . . . Gingerly he felt his face and shuddered.

"At least. . . ." Mat yawned, cracking his jaws. "At least you got some sleep." There was little sympathy in his bleary eyes. He was huddled under his cloak, with his blanketroll doubled up beneath his head. "He talked all bloody night."

"You all the way awake?" Bunt said from the driver's seat. "Gave me a start, you did, yelling like that. Well, we're there." He swept a hand out in front of them in a grand gesture. "Caemlyn, the grandest city in the world."

CHAPTER
35

Caemlyn

Rand twisted up to kneel behind the driver's seat. He could not help laughing with relief. "We made it, Mat! I told you we'd. . . ."

Words died in his mouth as his eyes fell on Caemlyn. After Baerlon, even more after the ruins of Shadar Logoth, he had thought he knew what a great city would look like, but this . . . this was more than he would have believed.

Outside the great wall, buildings clustered as if every town he had passed through had been gathered and set down there, side-by-side and all pushed together. Inns thrust their upper stories above the tile roofs of houses, and squat warehouses, broad and windowless, shouldered against them all. Red brick and gray stone and plastered white, jumbled and mixed together, they spread as far as the eye could see. Baerlon could have vanished into it without being noticed, and Whitebridge swallowed up twenty times over with hardly a ripple.

And the wall itself. The sheer, fifty-foot height of pale gray stone, streaked with silver and white, swept out in a great circle, curving to north and south till he wondered how far it must run. All along its length towers rose, round and standing high above the wall's own height, red-and-white banners whipping in the wind atop each one. From inside the wall other towers peeked out, slender towers even taller than those at the walls, and domes gleaming white and gold in the sun. A thousand stories had painted cities in his mind, the great cities of kings and queens, of thrones and powers and legends, and Caemlyn fit into those mind-deep pictures as water fits into a jug.

The cart creaked down the wide road toward the city, toward tower-flanked gates. The wagons of a merchants' train rolled out of those gates, under a vaulting archway in the stone that could have let a giant through, or ten giants abreast. Unwalled markets lined the road on both sides, roof tiles glistening red and purple, with stalls and pens in the spaces between. Calves bawled, cattle lowed, geese honked, chickens clucked, goats bleated, sheep baaed, and people bargained at the top of their lungs. A wall of noise funneled them toward the gates of Caemlyn.

"What did I tell you?" Bunt had to raise his voice to near a shout in order to be heard. "The grandest city in the world. Built by Ogier, you know. Least, the Inner City and the Palace were. It's that old, Caemlyn is. Caemlyn, where good Queen Morgase, the Light illumine her, makes the law and holds the peace for Andor. The greatest city on earth."

Rand was ready to agree. His mouth hung open, and he wanted to put his hands over his ears to shut out the din. People crowded the road, as thick as folk in Emond's Field crowded the Green at Bel Tine. He remembered thinking there were too many people in Baerlon to be believed, and almost laughed. He looked at Mat and grinned. Mat did have his hands over his ears, and his shoulders were hunched up as if he wanted to cover them with those, too.

"How are we going to hide in this?" he demanded loudly when he saw Rand looking. "How can we tell who to trust with so many? So bloody many. Light, the noise!"

Rand looked at Bunt before answering. The farmer was caught up in staring at the city; with the noise, he might not have heard anyway. Still, Rand put his mouth close to Mat's ear. "How can they find us among so many? Can't you see it, you wool-headed idiot? We're safe, if you ever learn to watch your bloody tongue!" He flung out a hand to take in everything, the markets, the city walls still ahead. "Look at it, Mat! Anything could happen here. Anything! We might even find Moiraine waiting for us, and Egwene, and all the rest."

"If they're alive. If you ask me, they're as dead as the gleeman."

The grin faded from Rand's face, and he turned to watch the gates come nearer. Anything could happen in a city like Caemlyn. He held that thought stubbornly.

The horse could not move any faster, flap the reins as Bunt would; the closer to the gates they came, the thicker the crowd grew, jostling together shoulder to shoulder, pressing against the carts and wagons heading in. Rand was glad to see a good many were dusty young men afoot with little in the way of belongings. Whatever their ages, a lot of the crowd pushing toward the gates had a travel-worn look, rickety carts and tired horses, clothes wrinkled from many nights of sleeping rough, dragging steps and weary eyes. But weary or not, those eyes were fixed on the gates as if getting inside the walls would strip away all their fatigue.

Half a dozen of the Queen's Guards stood at the gates, their clean red-and-white tabards and burnished plate-and-mail a sharp contrast to most of the people streaming under the stone arch. Backs rigid and heads straight, they eyed the incomers with disdainful wariness. It was plain they would just as soon have turned away most of those coming in. Aside from keeping a way clear for traffic leaving the city, though, and having a hard word with those who tried to push too fast, they did not hinder anyone.

"Keep your places. Don't push. Don't push, the Light blind you! There's room for everybody, the Light help us. Keep your places."

Bunt's cart rolled past the gates with the slow tide of the throng, into Caemlyn.

The city rose on low hills, like steps climbing to a center. Another wall encircled that center, shining pure white and running over the hills. Inside that were even more towers and domes, white and gold and purple, their elevation atop the hills making them seem to look down on the rest of Caemlyn. Rand thought that must be the Inner City of which Bunt had spoken.

The Caemlyn Road itself changed as soon as it was inside the city, becoming a wide boulevard, split down the middle by broad strips of grass and trees. The grass was brown and the tree branches bare, but people hurried by as if they saw nothing unusual, laughing, talking, arguing, doing all the things that people do. Just as if they had no idea that there had been no spring yet this year and might be none. They did not see, Rand realized, could not or would not. Their eyes slid away from leafless branches, and they walked across the dead and dying grass without once looking down. What they did not see, they could ignore; what they did not see was not really there.

Gaping at the city and the people, Rand was taken by surprise when the cart turned down a side street, narrower than the boulevard, but still twice as wide as any street in Emond's Field. Bunt drew the horse to a halt and turned to look back at them hesitantly. The traffic was a bit lighter here; the crowd split around the cart without breaking stride.

"What you're hiding under your cloak, is it really what Holdwin says?"

Rand was in the act of tossing his saddlebags over his shoulder. He did not even twitch. "What do you mean?" His voice was steady, too. His stomach was a sour knot, but his voice was steady.

Mat stifled a yawn with one hand, but he shoved the other under his coat—clutching the dagger from Shadar Logoth, Rand knew—and his eyes had a hard, hunted look under the scarf around his head. Bunt avoided looking at Mat, as if he knew there was a weapon in that hidden hand.

"Don't mean nothing, I suppose. Look, now, if you heard I was coming to Caemlyn, you were there long enough to hear the rest. Was I after a reward, I'd have made some excuse to go in the Goose and Crown, speak to Holdwin. Only I don't much like Holdwin, and I don't like that friend of his, not at all. Seems like he wants you two more than he wants . . . anything else."

"I don't know what he wants," Rand said. "We've never seen him before." It might even be the truth; he could not tell one Fade from another.

"Uh-huh. Well, like I say, I don't know nothing, and I guess I don't want to. There's enough trouble around for everybody without I go looking for more."

Mat was slow in gathering his things, and Rand was already in the street before he started climbing down. Rand waited impatiently. Mat turned stiffly from the cart, hugging bow and quiver and blanketroll to his chest, muttering under his breath. Heavy shadows darkened the undersides of his eyes.

Rand's stomach rumbled, and he grimaced. Hunger combined with a sour twisting in his gut made him afraid he was going to vomit. Mat was staring at him now, expectantly. *Which way to go? What to do now?*

Bunt leaned over and beckoned him closer. He went, hoping for advice about Caemlyn.

"I'd hide that. . . ." The old farmer paused and looked around warily. People pushed by on both sides of the cart, but except for a few passing curses about blocking the way, no one paid them any attention. "Stop wearing it," he said, "hide it, sell it. Give it away. That's my advice. Thing like that's going to draw attention, and I guess you don't want any of that."

Abruptly he straightened, clucking to his horse, and drove slowly on down the crowded street without another word or a backward glance. A wagon loaded with barrels rumbled toward them. Rand jumped out of the way, staggered, and when he looked again Bunt and his cart were lost to sight.

"What do we do now?" Mat demanded. He licked his lips, staring wide-eyed at all the people pushing by and the buildings towering as much as six stories above the street. "We're in Caemlyn, but what do we do?" He had uncovered his ears, but his hands twitched as if he wanted to put them back. A hum lay on the city, the low, steady drone of hundreds of shops working, thousands of people talking. To Rand it was like being inside a giant beehive, constantly buzzing. "Even if they are here, Rand, how could we find them in all of this?"

"Moiraine will find us," Rand said slowly. The immensity of the city was a weight on his shoulders; he wanted to get away, to hide from all the people and noise. The void eluded him despite Tam's teachings; his eyes drew the city into it. He concentrated instead on what was right around him, ignoring everything that lay beyond. Just looking at that one street, it almost seemed like Baerlon. Baerlon, the last place they had all thought they were safe. *Nobody's safe anymore. Maybe they* are *all dead. What do you do then?*

"They're alive! Egwene's alive!" he said fiercely. Several passersby looked at him oddly.

"Maybe," Mat said. "Maybe. What if Moiraine doesn't find us? What if nobody does but the . . . the. . . ." He shuddered, unable to say it.

"We'll think about that when it happens," he told Mat firmly. "If it happens." The worst meant seeking out Elaida, the Aes Sedai in the Palace. He would go on to Tar Valon, first. He did not know if Mat remembered what Thom had said about the Red Ajah—and the Black—but he surely did. His stomach twisted again. "Thom said to find an inn called The Queen's Blessing. We'll go there first."

"How? We can't afford one meal between the two of us."

"At least it's a place to start. Thom thought we could find help there."

"I can't. . . . Rand, they're everywhere." Mat dropped his eyes to the paving stones and seemed to shrink in on himself, trying to pull away from the people that were all around them. "Wherever we go, they're right behind us, or they're waiting for us. They'll be at The Queen's Blessing, too. I can't. . . . I. . . . Nothing's going to stop a Fade."

Rand grabbed Mat's collar in a fist that he was trying hard to keep from trembling. He needed Mat. Maybe the others were alive—*Light, please!*—but right then and there, it was just Mat and him. The thought of going on alone. . . . He swallowed hard, tasting bile.

He looked around quickly. No one seemed to have heard Mat mention the Fade; the crowd pressed past lost in its own worries. He put his face close to Mat's. "We've made it this far, haven't we?" he asked in a hoarse whisper. "They haven't caught us yet. We can make it all the way, if we just don't quit. I won't just quit and wait for them like a sheep for slaughter. I won't! Well? Are you going to stand here till you starve to death? Or until they come pick you up in a sack?"

He let go of Mat and turned away. His fingernails dug into his palms, but his hands still trembled. Suddenly Mat was walking alongside him, his eyes still down, and Rand let out a long breath.

"I'm sorry, Rand," Mat mumbled.

"Forget it," Rand said.

Mat barely looked up enough to keep from walking into people while the words poured out in a lifeless voice. "I can't stop thinking I'll never see home again. I want to go home. Laugh if you want; I don't care. What I wouldn't give to have my mother blessing me out for something right now. It's like weights on my brain; hot weights. Strangers all around, and no way to tell who to trust, if I can trust anybody. Light, the Two Rivers is so far away it might as well be on the other side of the world. We're alone, and we'll never get home. We're going to die, Rand."

"Not yet, we won't," Rand retorted. "Everybody dies. The Wheel turns. I'm not going to curl up and wait for it to happen, though."

"You sound like Master al'Vere," Mat grumbled, but his voice had a little spirit in it.

"Good," Rand said. "Good." *Light, let the others be all right. Please don't let us be alone.*

He began asking directions to The Queen's Blessing. The responses varied widely, a curse for all those who did not stay where they belonged or a shrug and a blank look being the most common. Some stalked on by with no more than a glance, if that.

A broad-faced man, nearly as big as Perrin, cocked his head and

said, "The Queen's Blessing, eh? You country boys Queen's men?"
He wore a white cockade on his wide-brimmed hat, and a white armband on his long coat. "Well, you've come too late."

He went off roaring with laughter, leaving Rand and Mat to stare
at one another in puzzlement. Rand shrugged; there were plenty of
odd folk in Caemlyn, people like he had never seen before.

Some of them stood out in the crowd, skins too dark or too pale,
coats of strange cut or bright colors, hats with pointed peaks or long
feathers. There were women with veils across their faces, women in
stiff dresses as wide as the wearer was tall, women in dresses that left
more skin bare than any tavernmaid he had seen. Occasionally a carriage, all vivid paint and gilt, squeezed through the thronged streets
behind a four- or six-horse team with plumes on their harness. Sedan
chairs were everywhere, the polemen pushing along with never a care
for who they shoved aside.

Rand saw one fight start that way, a brawling heap of men swinging
their fists while a pale-skinned man in a red-striped coat climbed out
of the sedan chair lying on its side. Two roughly dressed men, who
seemed to have been just passing by up till then, jumped on him before he was clear. The crowd that had stopped to watch began to turn
ugly, muttering and shaking fists. Rand pulled at Mat's sleeve and hurried on. Mat needed no second urging. The roar of a small riot followed them down the street.

Several times men approached the two of them instead of the other
way around. Their dusty clothes marked them as newcomers, and
seemed to act like a magnet on some types. Furtive fellows who offered relics of Logain for sale with darting eyes and feet set to run.
Rand calculated he was offered enough scraps of the false Dragon's
cloak and fragments of his sword to make two swords and half a dozen
cloaks. Mat's face brightened with interest, the first time at least, but
Rand gave them all a curt no, and they took it with a bob of the head
and a quick, "Light illumine the Queen, good master," and vanished.
Most of the shops had plates and cups painted with fanciful scenes
purporting to show the false Dragon being displayed before the Queen
in chains. And there were Whitecloaks in the streets. Each walked in
an open space that moved with him, just as in Baerlon.

Staying unnoticed was something Rand thought about a great deal.
He kept his cloak over his sword, but that would not be good enough
for very long. Sooner or later someone would wonder what he was
hiding. He would not—could not—take Bunt's advice to stop wearing
it, not his link to Tam. To his father.

Many others among the throng wore swords, but none with the heron-mark to pull the eye. All the Caemlyn men, though, and some of the strangers, had their swords wound in strips of cloth, sheath and hilt, red bound with white cord, or white bound with red. A hundred heron-marks could be hidden under those wrappings and no one would see. Besides, following local fashion would make them seem to fit in more.

A good many shops were fronted with tables displaying the cloth and cord, and Rand stopped at one. The red cloth was cheaper than the white, though he could see no difference apart from the color, so he bought that and the white cord to go with it, despite Mat's complaints about how little money they had left. The tight-lipped shopkeeper eyed them up and down with a twist to his mouth while he took Rand's coppers, and cursed them when Rand asked for a place inside to wrap his sword.

"We didn't come to see Logain," Rand said patiently. "We just came to see Caemlyn." He remembered Bunt, and added, "The grandest city in the world." The shopkeeper's grimace remained in place. "The Light illumine good Queen Morgase," Rand said hopefully.

"You make any trouble," the man said sourly, "and there's a hundred men in sound of my voice will take care of you even if the Guards won't." He paused to spit, just missing Rand's foot. "Get on about your filthy business."

Rand nodded as if the man had bid him a cheerful farewell, and pulled Mat away. Mat kept looking back over his shoulder toward the shop, growling to himself, until Rand tugged him into an empty alleyway. With their backs to the street no passerby could see what they were doing. Rand pulled off the sword belt and set to wrapping the sheath and hilt.

"I'll bet he charged you double for that bloody cloth," Mat said. "Triple."

It was not as easy as it looked, fastening the strips of cloth and the cord so the whole thing would not fall off.

"They'll all be trying to cheat us, Rand. They think we've come to see the false Dragon, like everybody else. We'll be lucky if somebody doesn't hit us on the head while we sleep. This is no place to be. There are too many people. Let's leave for Tar Valon now. Or south, to Illian. I wouldn't mind seeing them gather for the Hunt of the Horn. If we can't go home, let's just go."

"I'm staying," Rand said. "If they're not here already, they'll come here sooner or later, looking for us."

He was not sure if he had the wrappings done the way everyone else did, but the herons on scabbard and hilt were hidden and he thought it was secure. As he went back out on the street, he was sure that he had one less thing to worry about causing trouble. Mat trailed along beside him as reluctantly as if he were being pulled on a leash.

Bit by bit Rand did get the directions he wanted. At first they were vague, on the order of "somewhere in that direction" and "over that way." The nearer they came, though, the clearer the instructions, until at last they stood before a broad stone building with a sign over the door creaking in the wind. A man kneeling before a woman with red-gold hair and a crown, one of her hands resting on his bowed head. The Queen's Blessing.

"Are you sure about this?" Mat asked.

"Of course," Rand said. He took a deep breath and pushed open the door.

The common room was large and paneled with dark wood, and fires on two hearths warmed it. A serving maid was sweeping the floor, though it was clean, and another was polishing candlesticks in the corner. Each smiled at the two newcomers before going back to her work.

Only a few tables had people at them, but a dozen men was a crowd for so early in the day, and if none looked exactly happy to see him and Mat, at least they looked clean and sober. The smells of roasting beef and baking bread drifted from the kitchen, making Rand's mouth water.

The innkeeper was fat, he was pleased to see, a pink-faced man in a starched white apron, with graying hair combed back over a bald spot that it did not quite cover. His sharp eye took them in from head to toe, dusty clothes and bundles and worn boots, but he had a ready, pleasant smile, too. Basel Gill was his name.

"Master Gill," Rand said, "a friend of ours told us to come here. Thom Merrilin. He—" The innkeeper's smile slipped. Rand looked at Mat, but he was too busy sniffing the aromas coming from the kitchen to notice anything else. "Is something wrong? You do know him?"

"I know him," Gill said curtly. He seemed more interested in the flute case at Rand's side now, than in anything else. "Come with me." He jerked his head toward the back. Rand gave Mat a jerk to get him started, then followed, wondering what was going on.

In the kitchen, Master Gill paused to speak to the cook, a round woman with her hair in a bun at the back of her head who almost matched the innkeeper pound for pound. She kept stirring her pots while Master Gill talked. The smells were so good—two days' hunger made a fine sauce for anything, but this smelled as good as Mistress al'Vere's kitchen—that Rand's stomach growled. Mat was leaning toward the pots, nose first. Rand nudged him; Mat hastily wiped his chin where he had begun drooling.

Then the innkeeper was hurrying them out the back door. In the stableyard he looked around to make sure no one was close, then rounded on them. On Rand. "What's in the case, lad?"

"Thom's flute," Rand said slowly. He opened the case, as if showing the gold-and-silver-chased flute would help. Mat's hand crept under his coat.

Master Gill did not take his eyes off Rand. "Aye, I recognize it. I saw him play it often enough, and there's not likely two like that outside a royal court." The pleasant smiles were gone, and his sharp eyes were suddenly as sharp as a knife. "How did you come by it? Thom would part with his arm as soon as that flute."

"He gave it to me." Rand took Thom's bundled cloak from his back and set it on the ground, unfolding enough to show the colored patches, as well as the end of the harp case. "Thom's dead, Master Gill. If he was your friend, I'm sorry. He was mine, too."

"Dead, you say. How?"

"A . . . a man tried to kill us. Thom pushed this at me and told us to run." The patches fluttered in the wind like butterflies. Rand's throat caught; he folded the cloak carefully back up again. "We'd have been killed if it hadn't been for him. We were on our way to Caemlyn together. He told us to come here, to your inn."

"I'll believe he's dead," the innkeeper said slowly, "when I see his corpse." He nudged the bundled cloak with his toe and cleared his throat roughly. "Nay, nay, I believe you saw whatever it was you saw; I just don't believe he's dead. He's a harder man to kill than you might believe, is old Thom Merrilin."

Rand put a hand on Mat's shoulder. "It's all right, Mat. He's a friend."

Master Gill glanced at Mat, and sighed. "I suppose I am at that."

Mat straightened up slowly, folding his arms over his chest. He was still watching the innkeeper warily, though, and a muscle in his cheek twitched.

"Coming to Caemlyn, you say?" The innkeeper shook his head. "This is the last place on earth I'd expect Thom to come, excepting maybe it was Tar Valon." He waited for a stableman to pass, leading a horse, and even then he lowered his voice. "You've trouble with the Aes Sedai, I take it."

"Yes," Mat grumbled at the same time that Rand said, "What makes you think that?"

Master Gill chuckled dryly. "I know the man, that's what. He'd jump into that kind of trouble, especially to help a couple of lads about the age of you. . . ." The reminiscence in his eyes flickered out, and he stood up straight with a chary look. "Now . . . ah . . . I'm not making any accusations, mind, but . . . ah . . . I take it neither of you can . . . ah . . . what I'm getting at is . . . ah . . . what exactly is the nature of your trouble with Tar Valon, if you don't mind my asking?"

Rand's skin prickled as he realized what the man was suggesting. The One Power. "No, no, nothing like that. I swear. There was even an Aes Sedai helping us. Moiraine was. . . ." He bit his tongue, but the innkeeper's expression never changed.

"Glad to hear it. Not that I've all that much love for Aes Sedai, but better them than . . . that other thing." He shook his head slowly. "Too much talk of that kind of thing, with Logain being brought here. No offense meant, you understand, but . . . well, I had to know, didn't I?"

"No offense," Rand said. Mat's murmur could have been anything, but the innkeeper appeared to take it for the same as Rand had said.

"You two look the right sort, and I do believe you were–are—friends of Thom, but it's hard times and stony days. I don't suppose you can pay? No, I didn't think so. There's not enough of anything, and what there is costs the earth, so I'll give you beds—not the best, but warm and dry—and something to eat, and I cannot promise more, however much I'd like."

"Thank you," Rand said with a quizzical glance at Mat. "It's more than I expected." What was the right sort, and why *should* he promise more?

"Well, Thom's a good friend. An old friend. Hot-headed and liable to say the worst possible thing to the one person he shouldn't, but a good friend all the same. If he doesn't show up . . . well, we'll figure something out then. Best you don't talk any more talk about Aes Sedai helping you. I'm a good Queen's man, but there are too many in Caemlyn right now who'd take it wrong, and I don't mean just the Whitecloaks."

Mat snorted. "For all I care, the ravens can take every Aes Sedai straight to Shayol Ghul!"

"Watch your tongue," Master Gill snapped. "I said I don't love them; I didn't say I'm a fool thinks they're behind everything that's wrong. The Queen supports Elaida, and the Guards stand for the

Queen. The Light send things don't go so bad that changes. Anyway, lately some Guards have forgotten themselves enough to be a little rough with folks they overhear speaking against Aes Sedai. Not on duty, thank the Light, but it's happened, just the same. I don't need off-duty Guards breaking up my common room to teach you a lesson, and I don't need Whitecloaks egging somebody on to paint the Dragon's Fang on my door, so if you want any help out of me, you just keep thoughts about Aes Sedai to yourself, good or bad." He paused thoughtfully, then added, "Maybe it's best you don't mention Thom's name, either, where anyone but me can hear. Some of the Guards have long memories, and so does the Queen. No need taking chances."

"Thom had trouble with the Queen?" Rand said incredulously, and the innkeeper laughed.

"So he didn't tell you everything. Don't know why he should. On the other hand, I don't know why you shouldn't know, either. Not like it's a secret, exactly. Do you think every gleeman thinks as much of himself as Thom does? Well, come to think of it, I guess they do, but it always seemed to me Thom had an extra helping of thinking a lot of himself. He wasn't always a gleeman, you know, wandering from village to village and sleeping under a hedge as often as not. There was a time Thom Merrilin was Court-bard right here in Caemlyn, and known in every royal court from Tear to Maradon."

"Thom?" Mat said.

Rand nodded slowly. He could picture Thom at a Queen's court, with his stately manner and grand gestures.

"That he was," Master Gill said. "It was not long after Taringail Damodred died that the . . . trouble about his nephew cropped up. There were some said Thom was, shall we say, closer to the Queen than was proper. But Morgase was a young widow, and Thom was in his prime, then, and the Queen can do as she wishes is the way I look at it. Only she's always had a temper, has our good Morgase, and he took off without a word when he learned what kind of trouble his nephew was in. The Queen didn't much like that. Didn't like him meddling in Aes Sedai matters, either. Can't say I think it was right, either, nephew or no. Anyway, when he came back, he said some words, all right. Words you don't say to a Queen. Words you don't say to any woman with Morgase's spirit. Elaida was set against him because of his trying to mix in the business with his nephew, and between the Queen's temper and Elaida's animosity, Thom left Caemlyn half a step ahead of a trip to prison, if not the headsman's axe. As far as I know, the writ still stands."

"If it was a long time ago," Rand said, "maybe nobody re-members."

Master Gill shook his head. "Gareth Bryne is Captain-General of the Queen's Guards. He personally commanded the Guardsmen Mor-gase sent to bring Thom back in chains, and I misdoubt he'll ever forget returning empty-handed to find Thom had already been back to the Palace and left again. And the Queen never forgets *anything*. You ever know a woman who did? My, but Morgase was in a taking. I'll swear the whole city walked soft and whispered for a month. Plenty of other Guardsmen old enough to remember, too. No, best you keep Thom as close a secret as you keep that Aes Sedai of yours. Come, I'll get you something to eat. You look as if your bellies are gnawing at your backbones."

CHAPTER
36

Web of the Pattern

Master Gill took them to a corner table in the common room and had one of the serving maids bring them food. Rand shook his head when he saw the plates, with a few thin slices of gravy-covered beef, a spoonful of mustard greens, and two potatoes on each. It was a rueful, resigned headshake, though, not angry. Not enough of anything, the innkeeper had said. Picking up his knife and fork, Rand wondered what would happen when there was nothing left. It made his half-covered plate seem like a feast. It made him shiver.

Master Gill had chosen a table well away from anyone else, and he sat with his back to the corner, where he could watch the room. Nobody could get close enough to overhear what they said without him seeing. When the maid left, he said softly, "Now, why don't you tell me about this trouble of yours? If I'm going to help, I'd best know what I'm getting into."

Rand looked at Mat, but Mat was frowning at his plate as if he were mad at the potato he was cutting. Rand took a deep breath. "I don't really understand it myself," he began.

He kept the story simple, and he kept Trollocs and Fades out of it. When somebody offered help, it would not do to tell them it was all about fables. But he did not think it was fair to understate the danger, either, not fair to pull someone in when they had no idea what they were getting into. Some men were after him and Mat, and a couple of friends of theirs, too. They appeared where they were least expected, these men, and they were deadly dangerous and set on killing him and his friends, or worse. Moiraine said some of them were Darkfriends. Thom did not trust Moiraine completely, but he stayed on with them, he said, because of his nephew. They had been separated during an attack while trying to reach Whitebridge, and then, in Whitebridge, Thom died saving them from another attack. And there had been other tries. He knew there were holes in it, but it was the best he could do on short notice without telling more than was safe.

"We just kept on till we reached Caemlyn," he explained. "That was the plan, originally. Caemlyn, and then Tar Valon." He shifted uncomfortably on the edge of his chair. After keeping everything secret for so long, it felt odd to be telling somebody even as much as he was. "If we stay on that route, the others will be able to find us, sooner or later."

"If they're alive," Mat muttered at his plate.

Rand did not even glance at Mat. Something compelled him to add, "It could bring you trouble, helping us."

Master Gill waved it off with a plump hand. "Can't say as I want trouble, but it wouldn't be the first I've seen. No bloody Darkfriend will make me turn my back on Thom's friends. This friend of yours from up north, now—if she comes to Caemlyn, I'll hear. There are people keep their eyes on comings and goings like that around here, and word spreads."

Rand hesitated, then asked, "What about Elaida?"

The innkeeper hesitated, too, and finally shook his head. "I don't think so. Maybe if you didn't have a connection to Thom. She'd winkle it out, and then where would you be? No telling. Maybe in a cell. Maybe worse. They say she has a way of feeling things, what's happened, what's going to happen. They say she can cut right through to what a man wants to hide. I don't know, but I wouldn't risk it. If it wasn't for Thom, you could go to the Guards. They'd take care of any Darkfriends quick enough. But even if you could keep Thom quiet from the Guards, word would reach Elaida as soon as you mentioned Darkfriends, and then you're back where we started."

"No Guards," Rand agreed. Mat nodded vigorously while stuffing a fork into his mouth and got gravy on his chin.

"Trouble is, you're caught up in the fringes of politics, lad, even if it's none of your doing, and politics is a foggy mire full of snakes."

"What about—" Rand began, but the innkeeper grimaced suddenly, his chair creaking under his bulk as he sat up straight.

The cook was standing in the doorway to the kitchen, wiping her hands with her apron. When she saw the innkeeper looking she motioned for him to come, then vanished back into the kitchen.

"Might as well be married to her." Master Gill sighed. "Finds things that need fixing before I know there's anything wrong. If it's not the drains stopped up, or the downspouts clogged, it's rats. I keep a clean place, you understand, but with so many people in the city, rats are everywhere. Crowd people together and you get rats, and Caemlyn has a plague of them all of a sudden. You wouldn't believe what a good cat, a prime ratter, fetches these days. Your room is in the attic. I'll tell the girls which; any of them can show you to it. And don't worry about Darkfriends. I can't say much good about the Whitecloaks, but between them and the Guards, that sort won't dare show their filthy faces in Caemlyn." His chair squeaked again as he pushed it back and stood. "I hope it isn't the drains again."

Rand went back to his food, but he saw that Mat had stopped eating. "I thought you were hungry," he said. Mat kept staring at his plate, pushing one piece of potato in a circle with his fork. "You have to eat, Mat. We need to keep up our strength if we're going to reach Tar Valon."

Mat let out a low, bitter laugh. "Tar Valon! All this time it's been Caemlyn. Moiraine would be waiting for us in Caemlyn. We'd find Perrin and Egwene in Caemlyn. Everything would be all right if we only got to Caemlyn. Well, here we are, and nothing's right. No Moiraine, no Perrin, no anybody. Now it's everything will be all right if we only get to Tar Valon."

"We're alive," Rand said, more sharply than he had intended. He took a deep breath and tried to moderate his tone. "We are alive. That much is all right. And I intend to stay alive. I intend to find out why we're so important. I won't give up."

"All these people, and any of them could be Darkfriends. Master Gill promised to help us awfully quick. What kind of man just shrugs off Aes Sedai and Darkfriends? It isn't natural. Any decent person would tell us to get out, or . . . or . . . or something."

"Eat," Rand said gently, and watched until Mat began chewing a piece of beef.

He left his own hands resting beside his plate for a minute, pressing them against the table to keep them from shaking. He was scared. Not about Master Gill, of course, but there was enough without that. Those tall city walls would not stop a Fade. Maybe he should tell the innkeeper about that. But even if Gill believed, would he be as willing to help if he thought a Fade might show up at The Queen's Blessing? And the rats. Maybe rats did thrive where there were a lot of people, but he remembered the dream that was not a dream in Baerlon, and a small spine snapping. *Sometimes the Dark One uses carrion eaters as his eyes,* Lan had said. *Ravens, crows, rats. . . .*

He ate, but when he was done he could not remember tasting a single bite.

A serving maid, the one who had been polishing candlesticks when they came in, showed them up to the attic room. A dormer window pierced the slanting outer wall, with a bed on either side of it and pegs beside the door for hanging their belongings. The dark-eyed girl had a tendency to twist her skirt and giggle whenever she looked at Rand. She was pretty, but he knew if he said anything to her he would just make a fool of himself. She made him wish he had Perrin's way with girls; he was glad when she left.

He expected some comment from Mat, but as soon as she was gone, Mat threw himself on one of the beds, still in his cloak and boots, and turned his face to the wall.

Rand hung his things up, watching Mat's back. He thought Mat had his hand under his coat, clutching that dagger again.

"You just going to lie up here hiding?" he said finally.

"I'm tired," Mat mumbled.

"We have questions to ask Master Gill, yet. He might even be able to tell us how to find Egwene, and Perrin. They could be in Caemlyn already if they managed to hang onto their horses."

"They're dead," Mat said to the wall.

Rand hesitated, then gave up. He closed the door softly behind him, hoping Mat really would sleep.

Downstairs, however, Master Gill was nowhere to be found, though the sharp look in the cook's eye said she was looking for him, too. For a while Rand sat in the common room, but he found himself eyeing every patron who came in, every stranger who could be anyone—or anything—especially in the moment when he was first silhouetted as a cloaked black shape in the doorway. A Fade in the room would be like a fox in a chicken coop.

A Guardsman entered from the street. The red-uniformed man stopped just inside the door, running a cool eye over those in the room

who were obviously from outside the city. Rand studied the tabletop
when the Guardsman's eyes fell on him; when he looked up again, the
man was gone.

The dark-eyed maid was passing with her arms full of towels. "They
do that sometimes," she said in a confiding tone as she went by. "Just
to see there's no trouble. They look after good Queen's folk, they do.
Nothing for you to worry about." She giggled.

Rand shook his head. Nothing for him to worry about. It was not
as if the Guardsman would have come over and demanded to know if
he knew Thom Merrilin. He was getting as bad as Mat. He scraped
back his chair.

Another maid was checking the oil in the lamps along the wall.

"Is there another room where I could sit?" he asked her. He did
not want to go back upstairs and shut himself up with Mat's sullen
withdrawal. "Maybe a private dining room that's not being used?"

"There's the library." She pointed to a door. "Through there, to
your right, at the end of the hall. Might be empty, this hour."

"Thank you. If you see Master Gill, would you tell him Rand
al'Thor needs to talk to him if he can spare a minute?"

"I'll tell him," she said, then grinned. "Cook wants to talk to him,
too."

The innkeeper was probably hiding, he thought as he turned away
from her.

When he stepped into the room to which she had directed him, he
stopped and stared. The shelves must have held three or four hundred
books, more than he had ever seen in one place before. Clothbound,
leatherbound with gilded spines. Only a few had wooden covers. His
eyes gobbled up the titles, picking out old favorites. *The Travels of
Jain Farstrider. The Essays of Willim of Maneches.* His breath caught
at the sight of a leatherbound copy of *Voyages Among the Sea Folk.*
Tam had always wanted to read that.

Picturing Tam, turning the book over in his hands with a smile, getting the feel of it before settling down before the fireplace with his
pipe to read, his own hand tightened on his sword hilt with a sense of
loss and emptiness that dampened all his pleasure in the books.

A throat cleared behind him, and he suddenly realized he was not
alone. Ready to apologize for his rudeness, he turned. He was used to
being taller than almost everyone he met, but this time his eyes traveled up and up and up, and his mouth fell open. Then he came to the
head almost reaching the ten-foot ceiling. A nose as broad as the face,
so wide it was more a snout than a nose. Eyebrows that hung down

like tails, framing pale eyes as big as teacups. Ears that poked up to tufted points through a shaggy, black mane. *Trolloc!* He let out a yell and tried to back up and draw his sword. His feet got tangled, and he sat down hard, instead.

"I wish you humans wouldn't do that," rumbled a voice as deep as a drum. The tufted ears twitched violently, and the voice became sad. "So few of you remember us. It's our own fault, I suppose. Not many of us have gone out among men since the Shadow fell on the Ways. That's . . . oh, six generations, now. Right after the Trolloc Wars, it was." The shaggy head shook and let out a sigh that would have done credit to a bull. "Too long, too long, and so few to travel and see, it might as well have been none."

Rand sat there for a minute with his mouth hanging open, staring up at the apparition in wide-toed, knee-high boots and a dark blue coat that buttoned from the neck to the waist, then flared out to his boot tops like a kilt over baggy trousers. In one hand was a book, seeming tiny by comparison, with a finger broad enough for three marking the place.

"I thought you were—" he began, then caught himself. "What are—?" That was not any better. Getting to his feet, he gingerly offered his hand. "My name is Rand al'Thor."

A hand as big as a ham engulfed his; it was accompanied by a formal bow. "Loial, son of Arent son of Halan. Your name sings in my ears, Rand al'Thor."

That sounded like a ritual greeting to Rand. He returned the bow. "Your name sings in my ears, Loial, son of Arent . . . ah . . . son of Halan."

It was all a little unreal. He still did not know *what* Loial was. The grip of Loial's huge fingers was surprisingly gentle, but he was still relieved to get his hand back in one piece.

"You humans are very excitable," Loial said in that bass rumble. "I had heard all the stories, and read the books, of course, but I didn't realize. My first day in Caemlyn, I could not believe the uproar. Children cried, and women screamed, and a mob chased me all the way across the city, waving clubs and knives and torches, and shouting, 'Trolloc!' I'm afraid I was almost beginning to get a little upset. There's no telling what would have happened if a party of the Queen's Guards hadn't come along."

"A lucky thing," Rand said faintly.

"Yes, but even the Guardsmen seemed almost as afraid of me as the others. Four days in Caemlyn now, and I haven't been able to put my nose outside this inn. Good Master Gill even asked me not to use the common room." His ears twitched. "Not that he hasn't been very hospitable, you understand. But there was a bit of trouble that first night. All the humans seemed to want to leave at once. Such screaming and shouting, everyone trying to get through the door at the same time. Some of them could have been hurt."

Rand stared in fascination at those twitching ears.

"I'll tell you, it was not for this I left the *stedding*."

"You're an Ogier!" Rand exclaimed. "Wait. Six generations? You said the Trolloc Wars! How old are you?" He knew it was rude as soon as he said it, but Loial became defensive rather than offended.

"Ninety years," the Ogier said stiffly. "In only ten more I'll be able to address the Stump. I think the Elders should have let me speak, since they were deciding whether I could leave or not. But then they always worry about anyone of any age going Outside. You humans are so hasty, so erratic." He blinked and gave a short bow. "Please forgive me. I shouldn't have said that. But you do fight all the time, even when there's no need to."

"That's all right," Rand said. He was still trying to take in Loial's age. Older than old Cenn Buie, and still not old enough to. . . . He sat down in one of the high-backed chairs. Loial took another, made to hold two; he filled it. Sitting, he was as tall as most men standing. "At least they did let you go."

Loial looked at the floor, wrinkling his nose and rubbing at it with one thick finger. "Well, as to that, now. You see, the Stump had not been meeting very long, not even a year, but I could tell from what I heard that by the time they reached a decision I would be old enough to go without their permission. I am afraid they'll say I put a long handle on my axe, but I just . . . left. The Elders always said I was too hot-headed, and I fear I've proven them right. I wonder if they have realized I'm gone, yet? But I had to go."

Rand bit his lip to keep from laughing. If Loial was a hot-headed Ogier, he could imagine what most Ogier were like. Had not been meeting very long, not even a year? Master al'Vere would just shake his head in wonder; a Village Council meeting that lasted half a day would have everybody jumping up and down, even Haral Luhhan. A wave of homesickness swept over him, making it hard to breathe for memories of Tam, and Egwene, and the Winespring Inn, and Bel Tine on the Green in happier days. He forced them away.

"If you don't mind my asking," he said, clearing his throat, "why did you want to go . . . ah, Outside, so much? I wish I'd never left my home, myself."

"Why, to see," Loial said as if it were the most obvious thing in the world. "I read the books, all the travelers' accounts, and it began to burn in me that I had to see, not just read." His pale eyes brightened, and his ears stiffened. "I studied every scrap I could find about traveling, about the Ways, and customs in human lands, and the cities we built for you humans after the Breaking of the World. And the more I read, the more I knew that I had to go Outside, go to those places we had been, and see the groves for myself."

Rand blinked. "Groves?"

"Yes, the groves. The trees. Only a few of the Great Trees, of course, towering to the sky to keep memories of the *stedding* fresh." His chair groaned as he shifted forward, gesturing with his hands, one of which still held the book. His eyes were brighter than ever, and his ears almost quivered. "Mostly they used the trees of the land and the place. You cannot make the land go against itself. Not for long; the land will rebel. You must shape the vision to the land, not the land to the vision. In every grove was planted every tree that would grow and thrive in that place, each balanced against the next, each placed to complement the others, for the best growing, of course, but also so that the balance would sing in the eye and the heart. Ah, the books spoke of groves to make Elders weep and laugh at the same time, groves to remain green in memory forever."

"What about the cities?" Rand asked. Loial gave him a puzzled look. "The cities. The cities the Ogier built. Here, for instance. Caemlyn. Ogier built Caemlyn, didn't you? The stories say so."

"Working with stone. . . ." His shoulders gave a massive shrug. "That was just something learned in the years after the Breaking, during the Exile, when we were still trying to find the *stedding* again. It is a fine thing, I suppose, but not the true thing. Try as you will—and I have read that the Ogier who built those cities truly did try—you cannot make stone live. A few still do work with stone, but only because you humans damage the buildings so often with your wars. There were a handful of Ogier in . . . ah . . . Cairhien, it's called now . . . when I passed through. They were from another *stedding,* luckily, so they didn't know about me, but they were still suspicious that I was Outside alone so young. I suppose it's just as well there was no reason for me to linger there. In any case, you see, working with stone is just something that was thrust on us by the weaving of the Pattern; the groves came from the heart."

Rand shook his head. Half the stories he had grown up with had just been stood on their heads. "I didn't know Ogier believed in the Pattern, Loial."

"Of course, we believe. The Wheel of Time weaves the Pattern of the Ages, and lives are the threads it weaves. No one can tell how the thread of his own life will be woven into the Pattern, or how the thread of a people will be woven. It gave us the Breaking of the World, and the Exile, and Stone, and the Longing, and eventually it gave us back the *stedding* before we all died. Sometimes I think the reason you humans are the way you are is because your threads are so short. They must jump around in the weaving. Oh, there, I've done it again. The Elders say you humans don't like to be reminded of how short a time you live. I hope I didn't hurt your feelings."

Rand laughed and shook his head. "Not at all. I suppose it'd be fun to live as long as you do, but I never really thought about it. I guess if I live as long as old Cenn Buie, that'll be long enough for anybody."

"He is a very old man?"

Rand just nodded. He was not about to explain that old Cenn Buie was not quite as old as Loial.

"Well," Loial said, "perhaps you humans do have short lives, but you do so much with them, always jumping around, always so hasty. And you have the whole world to do it in. We Ogier are bound to our *stedding*."

"You're Outside."

"For a time, Rand. But I must go back, eventually. This world is yours, yours and your kind's. The *stedding* are mine. There's too much hurly-burly Outside. And so much is changed from what I read about."

"Well, things do change over the years. Some, anyway."

"Some? Half the cities I read about aren't even there any longer, and most of the rest are known by different names. You take Cairhien. The city's proper name is Al'cair'rahienallen, Hill of the Golden Dawn. They don't even remember, for all of the sunrise on their banners. And the grove there. I doubt if it has been tended since the Trolloc Wars. It's just another forest, now, where they cut firewood. The Great Trees are all gone, and no one remembers them. And here? Caemlyn is still Caemlyn, but they let the city grow right over the grove. We're not a quarter of a mile from the center of it right where we sit—from where the center of it should be. Not a tree of it left. I've been to Tear and Illian, too. Different names, and no memories. There's only pasture for their horses where the grove was at Tear, and at Illian the grove is the King's park, where he hunts his deer, and none allowed inside without his permission. It has all changed, Rand. I fear very much that I will find the same everywhere I go. All the groves gone, all the memories gone, all the dreams dead."

"You can't give up, Loial. You can't ever give up. If you give up, you might as well be dead." Rand sank back in his chair as far as he could go, his face turning red. He expected the Ogier to laugh at him, but Loial nodded gravely instead.

"Yes, that's the way of your kind, isn't it?" The Ogier's voice changed, as if he were quoting something. "Till shade is gone, till water is gone, into the Shadow with teeth bared, screaming defiance with the last breath, to spit in Sightblinder's eye on the Last Day." Loial cocked his shaggy head expectantly, but Rand had no idea what it was he expected.

A minute went by with Loial waiting, then another, and his long eyebrows began to draw down in puzzlement. But he still waited, the silence growing uncomfortable for Rand.

"The Great Trees," Rand said finally, just for something to break that silence. "Are they like *Avendesora*?"

Loial sat up sharply; his chair squealed and cracked so loudly Rand thought it was going to come apart. "You know better than that. You, of all people."

"Me? How would I know?"

"Are you playing a joke on me? Sometimes you Aielmen think the oddest things are funny."

"What? I'm not an Aielman! I'm from the Two Rivers. I never even saw an Aielman!"

Loial shook his head, and the tufts on his ears drooped outward. "You see? Everything is changed, and half of what I know is useless. I hope I did not offend you. I'm sure your Two Rivers is a very fine place, wherever it is."

"Somebody told me," Rand said, "that it was once called Manetheren. I'd never heard it, but maybe you. . . ."

The Ogier's ears had perked up happily. "Ah! Yes. Manetheren." The tufts went down again. "There was a very fine grove there. Your pain sings in my heart, Rand al'Thor. We could not come in time."

Loial bowed where he sat, and Rand bowed back. He suspected Loial would be hurt if he did not, would think he was rude at the least. He wondered if Loial thought he had the same sort of memories the Ogier seemed to. The corners of Loial's mouth and eyes were certainly turned down as if he were sharing the pain of Rand's loss, just as if the destruction of Manetheren were not something that happened two thousand years ago, near enough, something that Rand only knew about because of Moiraine's story.

After a time Loial sighed. "The Wheel turns," he said, "and no one knows its turning. But you have come almost as far from your home as I have. A very considerable distance, as things are now. When the Ways were freely open, of course—but that is long past. Tell me, what brings you so far? Is there something you want to see, too?"

Rand opened his mouth to say that they had come to see the false Dragon—and he could not say it. Perhaps it was because Loial acted as if he were no older than Rand, ninety years old or no ninety years old. Maybe for an Ogier ninety years was not any older than he was. It had been a long time since he had been able to really talk to anyone about what was happening. Always the fear that they might be Darkfriends, or think he was. Mat was so drawn in on himself, feeding his fears on his own suspicions, that he was no good for talking. Rand found himself telling Loial about Winternight. Not a vague story about Darkfriends; the truth about Trollocs breaking in the door, and a Fade on the Quarry Road.

Part of him was horrified at what he was doing, but it was almost as if he were two people, one trying to hold his tongue while the other only felt the relief at being able to tell it all finally. The result was that he stumbled and stuttered and jumped around in the story. Shadar Logoth and losing his friends in the night, not knowing if they were alive or dead. The Fade in Whitebridge, and Thom dying so they could escape. The Fade in Baerlon. Darkfriends later, Howal Gode, and the boy who was afraid of them, and the woman who tried to kill Mat. The Halfman outside the Goose and Crown.

When he started babbling about dreams, even the part of him that wanted to talk felt the hackles rising on the back of his neck. He bit his tongue clamping his teeth shut. Breathing heavily through his nose, he watched the Ogier warily, hoping he thought he had meant nightmares. The Light knew it all sounded like a nightmare, or enough to give anyone nightmares. Maybe Loial would just think he was going mad. Maybe. . . .

"*Ta'veren,*" Loial said.

Rand blinked. "What?"

"*Ta'veren.*" Loial rubbed behind a pointed ear with one blunt finger and gave a little shrug. "Elder Haman always said I never listened, but sometimes I did. Sometimes, I listened. You know how the Pattern is woven, of course?"

"I never really thought about it," he said slowly. "It just is."

"Um, yes, well. Not exactly. You see, the Wheel of Time weaves the Pattern of the Ages, and the threads it uses are lives. It is not fixed, the Pattern, not always. If a man tries to change the direction of his life and the Pattern has room for it, the Wheel just weaves on and takes it in. There is always room for small changes, but sometimes the Pattern simply won't accept a big change, no matter how hard you try. You understand?"

Rand nodded. "I could live on the farm or in Emond's Field, and that would be a small change. If I wanted to be a king, though. . . ." He laughed, and Loial gave a grin that almost split his face in two. His teeth were white, and as broad as chisels.

"Yes, that's it. But sometimes the change chooses you, or the Wheel chooses it for you. And sometimes the Wheel bends a life-thread, or several threads, in such a way that all the surrounding threads are forced to swirl around it, and those force other threads, and those still others, and on and on. That first bending to make the Web, that is *ta'veren*, and there is nothing you can do to change it, not until the Pattern itself changes. The Web—*ta'maral'ailen*, it's called—can last for weeks, or for years. It can take in a town, or even the whole Pattern. Artur Hawkwing was *ta'veren*. So was Lews Therin Kinslayer, for that matter, I suppose." He let out a booming chuckle. "Elder Haman would be proud of me. He always droned on, and the books about traveling were much more interesting, but I did listen sometimes."

"That's all very well," Rand said, "but I don't see what it has to do with me. I'm a shepherd, not another Artur Hawkwing. And neither is Mat, or Perrin. It's just . . . ridiculous."

"I didn't say you were, but I could almost feel the Pattern swirl just listening to you tell your tale, and I have no Talent there. You are *ta'veren*, all right. You, and maybe your friends, too." The Ogier paused, rubbing the bridge of his broad nose thoughtfully. Finally he nodded to himself as if he had reached a decision. "I wish to travel with you, Rand."

For a minute Rand stared, wondering if he had heard correctly. "With me?" he exclaimed when he could speak. "Didn't you hear what I said about . . . ?" He eyed the door suddenly. It was shut tight, and thick enough that anyone trying to listen on the other side would hear only a murmur, even with his ear pressed against the wooden panels. Just the same he went on in a lower voice. "About who's chasing me? Anyway, I thought you wanted to go see your trees."

"There is a very fine grove at Tar Valon, and I have been told the Aes Sedai keep it well tended. Besides, it is not just the groves I want to see. Perhaps you are not another Artur Hawkwing, but for a time, at least, part of the world will shape itself around you, perhaps is even now shaping itself around you. Even Elder Haman would want to see that."

Rand hesitated. It would be good to have someone else along. The way Mat was behaving, being with him was almost like being alone. The Ogier was a comforting presence. Maybe he was young as Ogier reckoned age, but he seemed as unflappable as a rock, just like Tam. And Loial had been all of those places, and knew about others. He looked at the Ogier, sitting there with his broad face a picture of patience. Sitting there, and taller sitting than most men standing. *How do you hide somebody almost ten feet tall?* He sighed and shook his head.

"I don't think that is a good idea, Loial. Even if Moiraine finds us here, we'll be in danger all the way to Tar Valon. If she does not. . . ." *If she doesn't, then she's dead and so is everyone else. Oh, Egwene.* He gave himself a shake. Egwene was not dead, and Moiraine would find them.

Loial looked at him sympathetically and touched his shoulder. "I am sure your friends are well, Rand."

Rand nodded his thanks. His throat was too tight to speak.

"Will you at least talk with me sometimes?" Loial sighed, a bass rumble. "And perhaps play a game of stones? I have not had anyone to talk to in days, except good Master Gill, and he is busy most of the time. The cook seems to run him unmercifully. Perhaps she really owns the inn?"

"Of course, I will." His voice was hoarse. He cleared his throat and tried to grin. "And if we meet in Tar Valon, you can show me the grove there." *They have to be all right. Light send they're all right.*

CHAPTER 37

The Long Chase

Nynaeve gripped the reins of the three horses and peered into the night as if she could somehow pierce the darkness and find the Aes Sedai and the Warder. Skeletal trees surrounded her, stark and black in the dim moonlight. The trees and the night made an effective screen for whatever Moiraine and Lan were doing, not that either of them had paused to let her know what that was. A low "Keep the horses quiet," from Lan, and they were gone, leaving her standing like a stableboy. She glanced at the horses and sighed with exasperation.

Mandarb blended into the night almost as well as his master's cloak. The only reason the battle-trained stallion was letting her get this close was because Lan had handed her the reins himself. He seemed calm enough now, but she remembered all too well the lips drawing back silently when she reached for his bridle without waiting for Lan's approval. The silence had made the bared teeth seem that much more dangerous. With a last wary look at the stallion, she turned to peer in the direction the other two had gone, idly stroking her own horse. She gave a startled jump when Aldieb pushed a pale muzzle under her hand, but after a minute she gave the white mare a pat, too.

"No need to take it out on you, I suppose," she whispered, "just because your mistress is a cold-faced—" She strained at the darkness again. *What were they doing?*

After leaving Whitebridge they had ridden through villages that seemed unreal in their normality, ordinary market villages that seemed to Nynaeve unconnected to a world that had Fades and Trollocs and Aes Sedai. They had followed the Caemlyn Road, until at last Moiraine sat forward in Aldieb's saddle, peering eastward as if she could see the whole length of the great highway, all the many miles to Caemlyn, and see, too, what waited there.

Eventually the Aes Sedai let out a long breath and settled back. "The Wheel weaves as the Wheel wills," she murmured, "but I cannot believe it weaves an end to hope. I must first take care of that of which I can be certain. It will be as the Wheel weaves." And she turned her mare north, off the road into the forest. One of the boys was in that direction with the coin Moiraine had given him. Lan followed.

Nynaeve gave a long last look at the Caemlyn Road. Few people shared the roadway with them there, a couple of high-wheeled carts and one empty wagon in the distance, a handful of folk afoot with their belongings on their backs or piled on pushcarts. Some of those were willing to admit they were on their way to Caemlyn to see the false Dragon, but most denied it vehemently, especially those who had come through Whitebridge. At Whitebridge she had begun to believe Moiraine. Somewhat. More, at any rate. And there was no comfort in that.

The Warder and the Aes Sedai were almost out of sight through the trees before she started after them. She hurried to catch up. Lan looked back at her frequently, and waved for her to come on, but he kept at Moiraine's shoulder, and the Aes Sedai had her eyes fixed ahead.

One evening after they left the road, the invisible trail failed. Moiraine, the unflappable Moiraine, suddenly stood up beside the small fire where the tea kettle was boiling, her eyes widening. "It is gone," she whispered at the night.

"He is . . . ?" Nynaeve could not finish the question. *Light, I don't even know which one it is!*

"He did not die," the Aes Sedai said slowly, "but he no longer has the token." She sat down, her voice level and her hands steady as she took the kettle off the flames and tossed in a handful of tea. "In the morning we will keep on as we've been going. When I get close enough, I can find him without the coin."

As the fire burned down to coals, Lan rolled himself in his cloak and went to sleep. Nynaeve could not sleep. She watched the Aes Sedai. Moiraine had her eyes closed, but she sat upright, and Nynaeve knew she was awake.

Long after the last glow had faded from the coals, Moiraine opened her eyes and looked at her. She could feel the Aes Sedai's smile even in the dark. "He has regained the coin, Wisdom. All will be well." She lay down on her blankets with a sigh and almost at once was breathing deep in slumber.

Nynaeve had a hard time joining her, tired as she was. Her mind conjured up the worst no matter how she tried to stop it. *All will be well.* After Whitebridge, she could no longer make herself believe that so easily.

Abruptly Nynaeve was jerked from memory back to the night; there really was a hand on her arm. Stifling the cry that rose in her throat, she fumbled for the knife at her belt, her hand closing on the hilt before she realized that the hand was Lan's.

The Warder's hood was thrown back, but his chameleon-like cloak blended so well with the night that the dim blur of his face seemed to hang suspended in the night. The hand on her arm appeared to come out of thin air.

She drew a shuddering breath. She expected him to comment on how easily he had come on her unaware, but instead he turned to dig into his saddlebags. "You are needed," he said, and knelt to fasten hobbles on the horses.

As soon as the horses were secured, he straightened, grasped her hand, and headed off into the night again. His dark hair fit into the night almost as well as his cloak, and he made even less noise than she did. Grudgingly she had to admit that she could never have followed him through the darkness without his grip as a guide. She was not certain she could pull loose if he did not want to release her, anyway; he had very strong hands.

As they came up on a small rise, barely enough to be called a hill, he sank to one knee, pulling her down beside him. It took her a moment to see that Moiraine was there, too. Unmoving, the Aes Sedai could have passed for a shadow in her dark cloak. Lan gestured down the hillside to a large clearing in the trees.

Nynaeve frowned in the dim moonlight, then suddenly smiled in understanding. Those pale blurs were tents in regular rows, a darkened encampment.

"Whitecloaks," Lan whispered, "two hundred of them, maybe more. There's good water down there. And the lad we're after."

"In the camp?" She felt, more than saw, Lan nod.

"In the middle of it. Moiraine can point right to him. I went close enough to see he's under guard."

"A prisoner?" Nynaeve said. "Why?"

"I don't know. The Children should not be interested in a village boy, not unless there was something to make them suspicious. The Light knows it doesn't take much to make Whitecloaks suspicious, but it still worries me."

"How are you going to free him?" It was not until he glanced at her that she realized how much assurance there had been in her that he could march into the middle of two hundred men and come back with the boy. *Well, he* is *a warder.* Some *of the stories must be true.*

She wondered if he was laughing at her, but his voice was flat and businesslike. "I can bring him out, but he'll likely be in no shape for stealth. If we're seen, we may find two hundred Whitecloaks on our heels, and us riding double. Unless they are too busy to chase us. Are you willing to take a chance?"

"To help an Emond's Fielder? Of course! What kind of chance?"

He pointed into the darkness again, beyond the tents. This time she could make out nothing but shadows. "Their horse-lines. If the picket-ropes are cut, not all the way through, but enough so they'll break when Moiraine creates a diversion, the Whitecloaks will be too busy chasing their own horses to come after us. There are two guards on that side of the camp, beyond the picket-lines, but if you are half as good as I think you are, they'll never see you."

She swallowed hard. Stalking rabbits was one thing; guards, though, with spears and swords. . . . *So he thinks I'm good, does he?* "I'll do it."

Lan nodded again, as if he had expected no less. "One other thing. There are wolves about, tonight. I saw two, and if I saw that many, there are probably more." He paused, and though his voice did not change she had the feeling he was puzzled. "It was almost as if they wanted me to see them. Anyway, they shouldn't bother you. Wolves usually stay away from people."

"I wouldn't have known that," she said sweetly. "I only grew up around shepherds." He grunted, and she smiled into the darkness.

"We'll do it now, then," he said.

Her smile faded as she peered down at the camp full of armed men. Two hundred men with spears and swords and. . . . Before she could reconsider, she eased her knife in its sheath and started to slip away. Moiraine caught her arm in a grip almost as strong as Lan's.

"Take care," the Aes Sedai said softly. "Once you cut the ropes, return as quickly as you can. You are a part of the Pattern, too, and I would not risk you, any more than any of the others, if the whole world was not at risk in these days."

Nynaeve rubbed her arm surreptitiously when Moiraine released it. She was not about to let the Aes Sedai know the grip had hurt. But Moiraine turned back to watching the camp below as soon as she let go. And the Warder was gone, Nynaeve realized with a start. She had not heard him leave. *Light blind the bloody man!* Quickly she tied her skirts up to give her legs freedom, and hurried into the night.

After that first rush, with fallen branches cracking under her feet, she slowed down, glad there was no one there to see her blush. The idea was to be quiet, and she was not in any kind of competition with the Warder. *Oh, no?*

She shook off the thought and concentrated on making her way through the dark woods. It was not hard in and of itself; the faint light of the waning moon was more than enough for anyone who had been taught by her father, and the ground had a slow, easy roll. But the trees, bare and stark against the night sky, constantly reminded her that this was no childhood game, and the keening wind sounded all too much like Trolloc horns. Now that she was alone in the darkness, she remembered that the wolves that usually ran away from people had been behaving differently in the Two Rivers this winter.

Relief flooded through her like warmth when she finally caught the smell of horses. Almost holding her breath, she got down on her stomach and crawled upwind, toward the smell.

She was nearly on the guards before she saw them, marching toward her out of the night, white cloaks flapping in the wind and almost shining in the moonlight. They might as well have carried torches; torchlight could not have made them much more visible. She froze, trying to make herself a part of the ground. Nearly in front of her, not ten paces away, they marched to a halt with a stomp of feet, facing each other, spears shouldered. Just beyond them she could make out shadows that had to be the horses. The stable smell, horse and manure, was strong.

"All is well with the night," one white-cloaked shape announced. "The Light illumine us, and protect us from the Shadow."

"All is well with the night," the other replied. "The Light illumine us, and protect us from the Shadow."

With that they turned and marched off into the darkness again.

Nynaeve waited, counting to herself while they made their circuit twice. Each time they took exactly the same count, and each time they rigidly repeated the same formula, not a word more or less. Neither so much as glanced to one side; they stared straight ahead as they marched up, then marched away. She wondered if they would have noticed her even if she had been standing up.

Before the night swallowed the pale swirls of their cloaks a third time, she was already on her feet, running in a crouch toward the horses. As she came close, she slowed so as not to startle the animals. The Whitecloak guards might not see what was not shoved under their noses, but they would certainly investigate if the horses suddenly began whickering.

The horses along the picket-lines—there was more than one row—were barely realized masses in the darkness, heads down. Occasionally one snorted or stamped a foot in its sleep. In the dim moonlight she was nearly on the endpost of the picket-line before she saw it. She reached for the picket-line, and froze when the nearest horse raised its head and looked at her. Its single lead-rein was tied in a big loop around the thumb-thick line that ended at the post. *One whinny.* Her heart tried to pound its way out of her chest, sounding loud enough to bring the guards.

Never taking her eyes off the horse, she sliced at the picket-rope, feeling in front of her blade to see how far she had cut. The horse tossed its head, and her breath went cold. *Just one whinny.*

Only a few thin strands of hemp remained whole under her fingers. Slowly she headed toward the next line, watching the horse until she could no longer see if it was looking at her or not, then drew a ragged breath. If they were all like that, she did not think she would last.

At the next picket-rope, though, and the next, and the next, the horses remained asleep, even when she cut her thumb and bit off a yelp. Sucking the cut, she looked warily back the way she had come. Upwind as she was, she could no longer hear the guards make their exchange, but they might have heard her if they were in the right place. If they were coming to see what the noise had been, the wind would keep her from hearing them until they were right on top of her. *Time to go. With four horses out of five running loose, they won't be chasing anyone.*

But she did not move. She could imagine Lan's eyes when he heard what she had done. There would be no accusation in them; her reasoning was sound, and he would not expect any more of her. She was a

Wisdom, not a bloody great invincible Warder who could make himself all but invisible. Jaw set, she moved to the last picket-line. The first horse on it was Bela.

There was no mistaking that squat, shaggy shape; for there to be another horse like that, here and now, was too big a coincidence. Suddenly she was so glad that she had not left off this last line that she was shaking. Her arms and legs trembled so that she was afraid to touch the picket-rope, but her mind was as clear as the Winespring Water. Whichever of the boys was in the camp, Egwene was there, too. And if they left riding double, some of the Children would catch them no matter how well the horses were scattered, and some of them would die. She was as certain as if she were listening to the wind. That stuck a spike of fear into her belly, fear of *how* she was certain. This had nothing to do with weather or crops or sickness. *Why did Moiraine tell me I can use the Power? Why couldn't she leave me alone?*

Strangely, the fear stilled her trembling. With hands as steady as if she were grinding herbs in her own house she slit the picket-rope as she had the others. Thrusting the dagger back into its sheath, she untied Bela's lead-rein. The shaggy mare woke with a start, tossing her head, but Nynaeve stroked her nose and spoke comforting words softly in her ear. Bela gave a low snort and seemed content.

Other horses along that line were awake, too, and looking at her. Remembering Mandarb, she reached hesitantly to the next lead-rein, but that horse gave no objection to a strange hand. Indeed, it seemed to want some of the muzzle-stroking that Bela had received. She gripped Bela's rein tightly and wrapped the other around her other wrist, all the while watching the camp nervously. The pale tents were only thirty yards off, and she could see men moving among them. If they noticed the horses stirring and came to see what caused it. . . .

Desperately she wished for Moiraine not to wait on her return. Whatever the Aes Sedai was going to do, let her do it now. *Light, make her do it now, before.* . . .

Abruptly lightning shattered the night overhead, for a moment obliterating darkness. Thunder smote her ears, so hard she thought her knees would buckle, as a jagged trident stabbed the ground just beyond the horses, splashing dirt and rocks like a fountain. The crash of riven earth fought the thunderstroke. The horses went mad, screaming and rearing; the picket-ropes snapped like thread where she had cut them. Another lightning bolt sliced down before the image of the first faded.

Nynaeve was too busy to exult. At the first clash Bela jerked one way while the other horse reared away in the opposite direction. She thought her arms were being pulled out of their sockets. For an endless minute she hung suspended between the horses, her feet off the ground, her scream flattened by the second crash. Again the lightning struck, and again, and again, in one continuous, raging roar from the heavens. Balked in the way they wanted to go, the horses surged back, letting her drop. She wanted to crouch on the ground and soothe her tortured shoulders, but there was no time. Bela and the other horse buffeted her, eyes rolling wildly till only whites showed, threatening to knock her down and trample her. Somehow she made her arms lift, clutched her hands in Bela's mane, pulled herself onto the heaving mare's back. The other rein was still around her wrist, pulled tight into the flesh.

Her jaw dropped as a long, gray shadow snarled past, seeming to ignore her and the horses with her, but teeth snapping at the crazed animals now darting in every direction. A second shadow of death followed close behind. Nynaeve wanted to scream again, but nothing came out. *Wolves! Light help us! What is Moiraine doing?*

The heels she dug into Bela's sides were not needed. The mare ran, and the other was more than happy to follow. Anywhere, so long as they could run, so long as they could escape the fire from the sky that killed the night.

CHAPTER
38

Rescue

Perrin shifted as best he could with his wrists bound behind him and finally gave up with a sigh. Every rock he avoided brought him two more. Awkwardly he tried to work his cloak back over him. The night was cold, and the ground seemed to draw all the heat out of him, as it had every night since the Whitecloaks took them. The Children did not think prisoners needed blankets, or shelter. Especially not dangerous Darkfriends.

Egwene lay huddled against his back for warmth, sleeping the deep sleep of exhaustion. She never even murmured at his shifting. The sun was long hours below the horizon, and he ached from head to foot after a day walking behind a horse with a halter around his neck, but sleep would not come for him.

The column did not move that fast. With most of their remounts lost to the wolves in the *stedding*, the Whitecloaks could not push on as hard as they wanted; the delay was another thing they held against the Emond's Fielders. The sinuous double line did move steadily, though—Lord Bornhald meant to reach Caemlyn in time for whatever

it was—and always in the back of Perrin's mind was the fear that if he
fell the Whitecloak holding his leash would not stop, no matter Lord
Captain Bornhald's orders to keep them alive for the Questioners in
Amador. He knew he could not save himself if that happened; the
only times they freed his hands were when he was fed and for visits to
the latrine pit. The halter made every step momentous, every rock
underfoot potentially fatal. He walked with muscles tense, scanning
the ground with anxious eyes. Whenever he glanced at Egwene, she
was doing the same. When she met his eyes, her face was tight and
frightened. Neither of them dared take their eyes off the ground long
enough for more than a glance.

Usually he collapsed like a wrung-out rag as soon as the Whitecloaks
let him stop, but tonight his mind was racing. His skin crawled with
dread that had been building for days. If he closed his eyes, he would
see only the things Byar promised for them once they reached
Amador.

He was sure Egwene still did not believe what Byar told them in
that flat voice. If she did, she would not be able to sleep no matter
how tired she was. In the beginning he had not believed Byar either.
He still did not want to; people just did not do things like that to other
people. But Byar did not really threaten; as if he were talking about
getting a drink of water he talked about hot irons and pincers, about
knives slicing away skin and needles piercing. He did not appear to be
trying to frighten them. There was never even a touch of gloating in
his eyes. He just did not care if they were frightened or not, if they
were tortured or not, if they were alive or not. That was what brought
cold sweat to Perrin's face once it got through to him. That was what
finally convinced him Byar was telling the simple truth.

The two guards' cloaks gleamed grayly in the faint moonlight. He
could not make out their faces, but he knew they were watching. As
if they could try something, tied hand and foot the way they were.
From when there had still been light enough to see, he remembered
the disgust in their eyes and the pinched looks on their faces, as though
they had been set to guard filth-soaked monsters, stinking and repel-
lent to look at. All the Whitecloaks looked at them that way. It never
changed. *Light, how do I make them believe we aren't Darkfriends
when they're already convinced we are?* His stomach twisted sicken-
ingly. In the end, he would probably confess to anything just to make
the Questioners stop.

Someone was coming, a Whitecloak carrying a lantern. The man
stopped to speak with the guards, who answered respectfully. Perrin

could not hear what was said, but he recognized the tall, gaunt shape.

He squinted as the lantern was held close to his face. Byar had Perrin's axe in his other hand; he had appropriated the weapon as his own. At least, Perrin never saw him without it.

"Wake up," Byar said emotionlessly, as if he thought Perrin slept with his head raised. He accompanied the words with a heavy kick in the ribs.

Perrin gave a grunt through gritted teeth. His sides were a mass of bruises already from Byar's boots.

"I said, wake up." The foot went back again, and Perrin spoke quickly.

"I'm awake." You had to acknowledge what Byar said, or he found ways to get your attention.

Byar set the lantern on the ground and bent to check his bonds. The man jerked roughly at his wrist, twisting his arms in their sockets. Finding those knots still as tight as he had left them, Byar pulled at his ankle rope, scraping him across the rocky ground. The man looked too skeletal to have any strength, but Perrin might as well have been a child. It was a nightly routine.

As Byar straightened, Perrin saw that Egwene was still asleep. "Wake up!" he shouted. "Egwene! Wake up!"

"Wha . . . ? What?" Egwene's voice was frightened and still thick with sleep. She lifted her head, blinking in the lantern light.

Byar gave no sign of disappointment at not being able to kick her awake; he never did. He just jerked at her ropes the same way he had Perrin's, ignoring her groans. Causing pain was another of those things that seemed not to affect him one way or another; Perrin was the only one he really went out of his way to hurt. Even if Perrin could not remember it, Byar remembered that he had killed two of the Children.

"Why should Darkfriends sleep," Byar said dispassionately, "when decent men must stay awake to guard them?"

"For the hundredth time," Egwene said wearily, "we aren't Darkfriends."

Perrin tensed. Sometimes such a denial brought a lecture delivered in a grating near monotone, on confession and repentance, leading into a description of the Questioners' methods of obtaining them. Sometimes it brought the lecture and a kick. To his surprise, this time Byar ignored it.

Instead the man squatted in front of him, all angles and sunken hollows, with the axe across his knees. The golden sun on his cloak's left breast, and the two golden stars beneath it, glittered in the lantern light. Taking off his helmet, he set it beside the lantern. For a change there was something besides disdain or hatred on his face, something intent and unreadable. He rested his arms on the axehandle and studied Perrin silently. Perrin tried not to shift under that hollow-eyed stare.

"You are slowing us down, Darkfriend, you and your wolves. The Council of the Anointed has heard reports of such things, and they want to know more, so you must be taken to Amador and given to the Questioners, but you are slowing us down. I had hoped we could move fast enough, even without the remounts, but I was wrong." He fell silent, frowning at them.

Perrin waited; Byar would tell him when he was ready.

"The Lord Captain is caught in the cleft of a dilemma," Byar said finally. "Because of the wolves he must take you to the Council, but he must reach Caemlyn, too. We have no spare horses to carry you, but if we continue to let you walk, we will not reach Caemlyn by the appointed time. The Lord Captain sees his duties with a single-minded vision, and he intends to see you before the Council."

Egwene made a sound. Byar was staring at Perrin, and he stared back, almost afraid to blink. "I don't understand," he said slowly.

"There is nothing to understand," Byar replied. "Nothing but idle speculation. If you escaped, we would not have time to track you down. We don't have an hour to spare if we are to reach Caemlyn in time. If you frayed your ropes on a sharp rock, say, and vanished into the night, the Lord Captain's problem would be solved." Never taking his gaze from Perrin, he reached under his cloak and tossed something on the ground.

Automatically Perrin's eyes followed it. When he realized what it was, he gasped. A rock. A split rock with a sharp edge.

"Just idle speculation," Byar said. "Your guards tonight also speculate."

Perrin's mouth was suddenly dry. *Think it through! Light help me, think it through and don't make any mistakes!*

Could it be true? Could the Whitecloaks' need to get to Caemlyn quickly be important enough for this? Letting suspected Darkfriends escape? There was no use trying that way; he did not know enough. Byar was the only Whitecloak who would talk to them, aside from Lord Captain Bornhald, and neither was exactly free with information. Another way. If Byar wanted them to escape, why not simply cut their bonds? If Byar wanted them to escape? Byar, who was convinced to his marrow that they were Darkfriends. Byar, who hated Darkfriends worse than he did the Dark One himself. Byar, who looked for any excuse to cause him pain because he had killed two Whitecloaks. *Byar* wanted them to escape?

If he had thought his mind was racing before, now it sped like an avalanche. Despite the cold, sweat ran down his face in rivulets. He glanced at the guards. They were only shadows of pale gray, but it seemed to him that they were poised, waiting. If he and Egwene were killed trying to escape, and their ropes had been cut on a rock that could have been lying there by chance. . . . The Lord Captain's dilemma would be solved, all right. And Byar would have them dead, the way he wanted them.

The gaunt man picked up his helmet from beside the lantern and started to stand.

"Wait," Perrin said hoarsely. His thoughts tumbled over and over as he searched in vain for some way out. "Wait, I want to talk. I—" *Help comes!*

The thought blossomed in his mind, a clear burst of light in the midst of chaos, so startling that for a moment he forgot everything else, even where he was. Dapple was alive. *Elyas,* he thought at the wolf, demanding without words to know if the man was alive. An image came back. Elyas, lying on a bed of evergreen branches beside a small fire in a cave, tending a wound in his side. It all took only an instant. He gaped at Byar, and his face broke into a foolish grin. Elyas was alive. Dapple was alive. Help was coming.

Byar paused, risen only to a crouch, looking at him. "Some thought has come to you, Perrin of the Two Rivers, and I would know what it is."

For a moment Perrin thought he meant the thought from Dapple. Panic fled across his face, followed by relief. Byar could not possibly know.

Byar watched his changes of expression, and for the first time the Whitecloak's eyes went to the rock he had tossed on the ground.

He was reconsidering, Perrin realized. If he changed his mind about the rock, would he dare risk leaving them alive to talk? Ropes could be frayed after the people wearing them were dead, even if it made for risk of discovery. He looked into Byar's eyes—the shadowed hollows of the man's eye sockets made them appear to stare at him from dark caves—and he saw death decided.

Byar opened his mouth, and as Perrin waited for sentence to be pronounced, things began to happen too fast for thought.

Suddenly one of the guards vanished. One minute there were two dim shapes, the next the night swallowed one of them. The second guard turned, the beginning of a cry on his lips, but before the first syllable was uttered there was a solid *tchunk* and he toppled over like a felled tree.

Byar spun, swift as a striking viper, the axe whirling in his hands so fast that it hummed. Perrin's eyes bulged as the night seemed to flow into the lantern light. His mouth opened to yell, but his throat locked tight with fear. For an instant he even forgot that Byar wanted to kill them. The Whitecloak was another human being, and the night had come alive to take them all.

Then the darkness invading the light became Lan, cloak swirling through shades of gray and black as he moved. The axe in Byar's hands lashed out like lightning . . . and Lan seemed to lean casually aside, letting the blade pass so close he must have felt the wind of it. Byar's eyes widened as the force of his blow carried him off balance, as the Warder struck with hands and feet in rapid succession, so quick that Perrin was not sure what he had just seen. What he was sure of was Byar collapsing like a puppet. Before the falling Whitecloak had finished settling to the ground, the Warder was on his knees extinguishing the lantern.

In the sudden return to darkness, Perrin stared blindly. Lan seemed to have vanished again.

"Is it really . . . ?" Egwene gave a stifled sob. "We thought you were dead. We thought you were all dead."

"Not yet." The Warder's deep whisper was tinged with amusement.

Hands touched Perrin, found his bonds. A knife sliced through the ropes with barely a tug, and he was free. Aching muscles protested as he sat up. Rubbing his wrists, he peered at the graying mound that marked Byar. "Did you . . . ? Is he . . . ?"

"No," Lan's voice answered quietly from the darkness. "I do not kill unless I mean to. But he won't bother anyone for a while. Stop asking questions and get a pair of their cloaks. We do not have much time."

Perrin crawled to where Byar lay. It took an effort to touch the man, and when he felt the Whitecloak's chest rising and falling he almost jerked his hands away. His skin crawled as he made himself unfasten the white cloak and pull it off. Despite what Lan said, he could imagine the skull-faced man suddenly rearing up. Hastily he fumbled around till he found his axe, then crawled to another guard. It seemed strange, at first, that he felt no reluctance to touch this un- conscious man, but the reason came to him. All the Whitecloaks hated him, but that was a human emotion. Byar felt nothing beyond that he should die; there was no hate in it, no emotion at all.

Gathering the two cloaks in his arms, he turned—and panic grabbed him. In the darkness he suddenly had no sense of direction, of how to find his way back to Lan and the others. His feet rooted to the ground, afraid to move. Even Byar was hidden by the night without his white cloak. There was nothing by which to orient himself. Any way he went might be out into the camp.

"Here."

He stumbled toward Lan's whisper until hands stopped him. Egwene was a dim shadow, and Lan's face was a blur; the rest of the Warder seemed not to be there at all. He could feel their eyes on him, and he wondered if he should explain.

"Put on the cloaks," Lan said softly. "Quickly. Bundle your own. And make no sound. You aren't safe yet."

Hurriedly Perrin passed one of the cloaks to Egwene, relieved at being saved from having to tell of his fear. He made his own cloak into a bundle to carry, and swung the white cloak around his shoulders in its place. He felt a prickle as it settled around his shoulders, a stab of worry between his shoulder blades. Was it Byar's cloak he had ended up with? He almost thought he could smell the gaunt man on it.

Lan directed them to hold hands, and Perrin gripped his axe in one hand and Egwene's hand with the other, wishing the Warder would get on with their escape so he could stop his imagination from running wild. But they just stood there, surrounded by the tents of the Children, two shapes in white cloaks and one that was sensed but not seen.

"Soon," Lan whispered. "Very soon."

Lightning broke the night above the camp, so close that Perrin felt the hair on his arms, his head, lifting as the bolt charged the air. Just beyond the tents the earth erupted from the blow, the explosion on the ground merging with that in the sky. Before the light faded Lan was leading them forward.

At their first step another strike sliced open the blackness. Lightning came like hail, so that the night flickered as if the darkness were coming in momentary flashes. Thunder drummed wildly, one roar rumbling into the next, one continuous, rippling peal. Fear-stricken horses screamed, their whinnies drowned except for moments when the thunder faded. Men tumbled out of their tents, some in their white cloaks, some only half clothed, some dashing to and fro, some standing as if stunned.

Through the middle of it Lan pulled them at a trot, Perrin bringing up the rear. Whitecloaks looked at them, wild-eyed, as they passed. A few shouted at them, the shouts lost in the pounding from the heavens, but with their white cloaks gathered around them no one tried to stop them. Through the tents, out of the camp and into the night, and no one raised a hand against them.

The ground turned uneven under Perrin's feet, and brush slapped at him as he let himself be drawn along. The lightning flickered fitfully and was gone. Echoes of thunder rolled across the sky before they, too, faded away. Perrin looked over his shoulder. A handful of fires burned back there, among the tents. Some of the lightning must have struck home, or perhaps men had knocked over lamps in their panic. Men still shouted, voices tiny in the night, trying to restore order, to find out what had happened. The land began to slope upwards, and tents and fires and shouting were left behind.

Suddenly he almost trod on Egwene's heels as Lan stopped. Ahead in the moonlight stood three horses.

A shadow stirred, and Moiraine's voice came, weighted with irritation. "Nynaeve has not returned. I fear that young woman has done something foolish." Lan spun on his heel as if to return the way they had come, but a single whip-crack word from Moiraine halted him. "No!" He stood looking at her sideways, only his face and hands truly visible, and they but dimly shadowed blurs. She went on in a gentler tone; gentler but no less firm. "Some things are more important than others. You know that." The Warder did not move, and her voice hardened again. "Remember your oaths, al'Lan Mandragoran, Lord of the Seven Towers! What of the oath of a Diademed Battle Lord of the Malkieri?"

Perrin blinked. Lan was all of that? Egwene was murmuring, but he could not take his eyes off the tableau in front of him, Lan standing like a wolf from Dapple's pack, a wolf at bay before the diminutive Aes Sedai and vainly seeking escape from doom.

The frozen scene was broken by a crash of breaking branches in the woods. In two long strides Lan was between Moiraine and the sound, the pale moonlight rippling along his sword. To the crackle and snap of underbrush a pair of horses burst from the trees, one with a rider.

"Bela!" Egwene exclaimed at the same time that Nynaeve said from the shaggy mare's back, "I almost didn't find you again. Egwene! Thank the Light you're alive!"

She slid down off Bela, but as she started toward the Emond's Fielders Lan caught her arm and she stopped short, staring up at him.

"We must go, Lan," Moiraine said, once more sounding unruffled, and the Warder released his grip.

Nynaeve rubbed her arm as she hurried to hug Egwene, but Perrin thought he heard her give a low laugh, too. It puzzled him because he did not think it had anything to do with her happiness at seeing them again.

"Where are Rand and Mat?" he asked.

"Elsewhere," Moiraine replied, and Nynaeve muttered something in a sharp tone that made Egwene gasp. Perrin blinked; he had caught the edge of a wagoneer's oath, and a coarse one. "The Light send they are well," the Aes Sedai went on as if she had not noticed.

"We will none of us be well," Lan said, "if the Whitecloaks find us. Change your cloaks, and get mounted."

Perrin scrambled up onto the horse Nynaeve had brought behind Bela. The lack of a saddle did not hamper him; he did not ride often at home, but when he did it was more likely bareback than not. He still carried the white cloak, now rolled up and tied to his belt. The Warder said they must leave no more traces for the Children to find than they could help. He still thought he could smell Byar on it.

As they started out, the Warder leading on his tall black stallion, Perrin felt Dapple's touch on his mind once more. *One day again.* More a feeling than words, it sighed with the promise of a meeting foreordained, with anticipation of what was to come, with resignation to what was to come, all streaked in layers. He tried to ask when and why, fumbling in haste and sudden fear. The trace of the wolves grew fainter, fading. His frantic questions brought only the same heavy-laden answer. *One day again.* It hung haunting in his mind long after awareness of the wolves winked out.

Lan pressed southward slowly but steadily. The night-draped wilderness, all rolling ground and underbrush hidden until it was underfoot, shadowed trees thick against the sky, allowed no great speed in any case. Twice the Warder left them, riding back toward the slivered moon, he and Mandarb becoming one with the night behind. Both times he returned to report no sign of pursuit.

Egwene stayed close beside Nynaeve. Soft-spoken scraps of excited talk floated back to Perrin. Those two were as buoyed up as if they had found home again. He hung back at the tail of their little column. Sometimes the Wisdom turned in her saddle to look back at him, and each time he gave her a wave, as if to say that he was all right, and stayed where he was. He had a lot to think about, though he could not get any of it straight in his head. *What was to come. What was to come?*

Perrin thought it could not be much short of dawn when Moiraine finally called a halt. Lan found a gully where he could build a fire hidden within a hollow in one of the banks.

Finally they were allowed to rid themselves of the white cloaks, burying them in a hole dug near the fire. As he was about to toss in the cloak he had used, the embroidered golden sun on the breast caught his eye, and the two golden stars beneath. He dropped the cloak as if it stung and walked away, scrubbing his hands on his coat, to sit alone.

"Now," Egwene said, once Lan was shoveling dirt into the hole, "will somebody tell me where Rand and Mat are?"

"I believe they are in Caemlyn," Moiraine said carefully, "or on their way there." Nynaeve gave a loud, disparaging grunt, but the Aes Sedai went on as if she had not been interrupted. "If they are not, I will yet find them. That I promise."

They made a quiet meal on bread and cheese and hot tea. Even Egwene's enthusiasm succumbed to weariness. The Wisdom produced an ointment from her bag for the weals the ropes had left on Egwene's wrists, and a different one for her other bruises. When she came to where Perrin sat on the edge of the firelight, he did not look up.

She stood looking at him silently for a time, then squatted with her bag beside her, saying briskly, "Take your coat and shirt off, Perrin. They tell me one of the Whitecloaks took a dislike to you."

He complied slowly, still half lost in Dapple's message, until Nynaeve gasped. Startled, he stared at her, then at his own bare chest. It was a mass of color, the newer, purple blotches overlaying older ones faded into shades of brown and yellow. Only thick slabs of muscle earned by hours at Master Luhhan's forge had saved him from broken ribs. With his mind filled by the wolves, he had managed to forget the pain, but he was reminded of it now, and it came back gladly. Involuntarily he took a deep breath, and clamped his lips on a groan.

"How could he have disliked you so much?" Nynaeve asked wonderingly.

I killed two men. Aloud, he said, "I don't know."

She rummaged in her bag, and he flinched when she began spreading a greasy ointment over his bruises. "Ground ivy, five-finger, and sunburst root," she said.

It was hot and cold at the same time, making him shiver while he broke into a sweat, but he did not protest. He had had experience of Nynaeve's ointments and poultices before. As her fingers gently rubbed the mixture in, the heat and cold vanished, taking the pain with them. The purple splotches faded to brown, and the brown and yellow paled, some disappearing altogether. Experimentally, he took a deep breath; there was barely a twinge.

"You look surprised," Nynaeve said. She looked a little surprised herself, and strangely frightened. "Next time, you can go to *her*."

"Not surprised," he said soothingly, "just glad." Sometimes Nynaeve's ointments worked fast and sometimes slow, but they always worked. "What . . . what happened to Rand and Mat?"

Nynaeve began stuffing her vials and pots back into her bag, jamming each one in as if she were thrusting it through a barrier. "*She* says they're all right. *She* says we'll find them. In Caemlyn, *she* says. *She* says it's too important for us not to, whatever *that* means. *She* says a great many things."

Perrin grinned in spite of himself. Whatever else had changed, the Wisdom was still herself, and she and the Aes Sedai were still far from fast friends.

Abruptly Nynaeve stiffened, staring at his face. Dropping her bag, she pressed the backs of her hands to his cheeks and forehead. He tried to pull back, but she caught his head in both hands and thumbed back his eyelids, peering into his eyes and muttering to herself. Despite her small size she held his face easily; it was never easy to get away from Nynaeve when she did not want you to.

"I don't understand," she said finally, releasing him and settling back to sit on her heels. "If it was yelloweye fever, you wouldn't be able to stand. But you don't have any fever, and the whites of your eyes aren't yellowed, just the irises."

"Yellow?" Moiraine said, and Perrin and Nynaeve both jumped where they sat. The Aes Sedai's approach had been utterly silent. Egwene was asleep by the fire, wrapped in her cloaks, Perrin saw. His own eyelids wanted to slide closed.

"It isn't anything," he said, but Moiraine put a hand under his chin and turned his face up so she could peer into his eyes the way Nynaeve had. He jerked away, prickling. The two women were handling him as if he were a child. "I said it isn't anything."

"There was no foretelling this." Moiraine spoke as if to herself. Her eyes seemed to look at something beyond him. "Something ordained to be woven, or a change in the Pattern? If a change, by what hand? The Wheel weaves as the Wheel wills. It must be that."

"Do you know what it is?" Nynaeve asked reluctantly, then hesitated. "Can you do something for him? Your Healing?" The request for aid, the admission that she could do nothing, came out of her as if dragged.

Perrin glared at both the women. "If you're going to talk about me, talk to me. I'm sitting right here." Neither looked at him.

"Healing?" Moiraine smiled. "Healing can do nothing about this. It is not an illness, and it will not. . . ." She hesitated briefly. She did glance at Perrin, then, a quick look that regretted many things. The look did not include him, though, and he muttered sourly as she turned back to Nynaeve. "I was going to say it will not harm him, but who can say what the end will be? At least I can say it will not harm him directly."

Nynaeve stood, dusting off her knees, and confronted the Aes Sedai eye to eye. "That's not good enough. If there's something wrong with—"

"What is, is. What is woven already is past changing." Moiraine turned away abruptly. "We must sleep while we can and leave at first light. If the Dark One's hand grows too strong. . . . We must reach Caemlyn quickly."

Angrily, Nynaeve snatched up her bag and stalked off before Perrin could speak. He started to growl an oath, but a thought hit him like a blow and he sat there gaping silently. Moiraine knew. The Aes Sedai knew about the wolves. And she thought it could be the Dark One's doing. A shiver ran through him. Hastily he shrugged back into his shirt, tucking it in awkwardly, and pulled his coat and cloak back on. The clothing did not help very much; he felt chilled right down to his bones, his marrow like frozen jelly.

Lan dropped to the ground cross-legged, tossing back his cloak. Perrin was glad of that. It was unpleasant, looking at the Warder and having his eyes slide past.

For a long moment they simply stared at one another. The hard planes of the Warder's face were unreadable, but in his eyes Perrin thought he saw . . . something. Sympathy? Curiosity? Both?

"You know?" he said, and Lan nodded.

"I know some, not all. Did it just come to you, or did you meet a guide, an intermediary?"

"There was a man," Perrin said slowly. *He knows, but does he think the same as Moiraine?* "He said his name was Elyas. Elyas Machera." Lan drew a deep breath, and Perrin looked at him sharply. "You know him?"

"I knew him. He taught me much, about the Blight, and about this." Lan touched his sword hilt. "He was a Warder, before . . . before what happened. The Red Ajah. . . ." He glanced to where Moiraine was, lying before the fire.

It was the first time Perrin could remember any uncertainty in the Warder. At Shadar Logoth Lan had been sure and strong, and when he was facing Fades and Trollocs. He was not afraid now—Perrin was convinced of that—but he was wary, as if he might say too much. As if what he said could be dangerous.

"I've heard of the Red Ajah," he told Lan.

"And most of what you've heard is wrong, no doubt. You must understand, there are . . . factions within Tar Valon. Some would fight the Dark One one way, some another. The goal is the same, but the differences . . . the differences can mean lives changed, or ended. The lives of men or nations. He is well, Elyas?"

"I think so. The Whitecloaks said they killed him, but Dapple—" Perrin glanced at the Warder uncomfortably. "I don't know." Lan seemed to accept that he did not, reluctantly, and it emboldened him to go on. "This communicating with the wolves. Moiraine seems to think it's something the . . . something the Dark One did. It isn't, is it?" He would not believe Elyas was a Darkfriend.

But Lan hesitated, and sweat started on Perrin's face, chill beads made colder by the night. They were sliding down his cheeks by the time the Warder spoke.

"Not in itself, no. Some believe it is, but they are wrong; it was old and lost long before the Dark One was found. But what of the chance involved, blacksmith? Sometimes the Pattern has a randomness to it—to our eyes, at least—but what chance that you should meet a man who could guide you in this thing, and you one who could follow the guiding? The Pattern is forming a Great Web, what some call the Lace of Ages, and you lads are central to it. I don't think there is much chance left in your lives, now. Have you been chosen out, then? And if so, by the Light, or by the Shadow?"

"The Dark One can't touch us unless we name him." Immediately Perrin thought of the dreams of Ba'alzamon, the dreams that were more than dreams. He scrubbed the sweat off his face. "He can't."

"Rock-hard stubborn," the Warder mused. "Maybe stubborn enough to save yourself, in the end. Remember the times we live in, blacksmith. Remember what Moiraine Sedai told you. In these times many things are dissolving, and breaking apart. Old barriers weaken, old walls crumble. The barriers between what is and what was, between what is and what will be." His voice turned grim. "The walls of the Dark One's prison. This may be the end of an Age. We may see a new Age born before we die. Or perhaps it is the end of Ages, the end of time itself. The end of the world." Suddenly he grinned, but his grin was as dark as a scowl; his eyes sparkled merrily, laughing at the foot of the gallows. "But that's not for us to worry about, eh, blacksmith? We'll fight the Shadow as long as we have breath, and if it overruns us, we'll go under biting and clawing. You Two Rivers folk are too stubborn to surrender. Don't you worry whether the Dark One has stirred in your life. You are back among friends, now. Remember, the Wheel weaves as the Wheel wills, and even the Dark One cannot change that, not with Moiraine to watch over you. But we had better find your friends soon."

"What do you mean?"

"They have no Aes Sedai touching the True Source to protect them. Blacksmith, perhaps the walls have weakened enough for the Dark One himself to touch events. Not with a free hand, or we'd be done already, but maybe tiny shiftings in the threads. A chance turning of one corner instead of another, a chance meeting, a chance word, or what seems like chance, and they could be so far under the Shadow not even Moiraine could bring them back."

"We have to find them," Perrin said, and the Warder gave a grunt of a laugh.

"What have I been saying? Get some sleep, blacksmith." Lan's cloak swung back around him as he stood. In the faint light from fire and moon he seemed almost part of the shadows beyond. "We have a hard few days to Caemlyn. Just you pray we find them there."

"But Moiraine . . . she can find them anywhere, can't she? She says she can."

"But can she find them in time? If the Dark One is strong enough to take a hand himself, time is running out. You pray we find them in Caemlyn, blacksmith, or we may all be lost."

CHAPTER
39

Weaving of the Web

Rand looked down on the crowds from the high window of his room in The Queen's Blessing. They ran shouting along the street, all streaming in the same direction, waving pennants and banners, the white lion standing guard on a thousand fields of red. Caemlyners and outlanders, they ran together, and for a change no one appeared to want to bash anyone else's head. Today, maybe, there was only one faction.

He turned from the window grinning. Next to the day when Egwene and Perrin walked in, alive and laughing over what they had seen, this was the day he had been waiting for most.

"Are you coming?" he asked again.

Mat glowered from where he lay curled up in a ball on his bed. "Take that Trolloc you're so friendly with."

"Blood and ashes, Mat, he's not a Trolloc. You're just being stubborn stupid. How many times do you want to have this argument? Light, it's not as if you'd never heard of Ogier before."

"I never heard they looked like Trollocs." Mat pushed his face into his pillow and curled himself tighter.

"Stubborn stupid," Rand muttered. "How long are you going to hide up here? I'm not going to keep bringing you your meals up all those stairs forever. You could do with a bath, too." Mat shrugged around on the bed as if he were trying to burrow deeper into it. Rand sighed, then went to the door. "Last chance to go together, Mat. I'm leaving now." He closed the door slowly, hoping that Mat would change his mind, but his friend did not stir. The door clicked shut.

In the hallway, he leaned against the doorframe. Master Gill said there was an old woman two streets over, Mother Grubb, who sold herbs and poultices, besides birthing babies, tending the sick, and telling fortunes. She sounded a little like a Wisdom. Nynaeve was who Mat needed, or maybe Moiraine, but Mother Grubb was who he had. Bringing her to The Queen's Blessing might bring the wrong kind of attention as well, though, if she would even come. For her as well as for Mat and him.

Herbalists and hedge-doctors were lying low in Caemlyn right now; there was talk against anyone who did any kind of healing, or fortune-telling. Every night the Dragon's Fang was scrawled on doors with a free hand, sometimes even in the daylight, and people might forget who had cured their fevers and poulticed their toothaches when the cry of Darkfriend went up. That was the temper in the city.

It was not as if Mat were really sick. He ate everything Rand carried up from the kitchen—he would take nothing from anyone else's hand, though—and never complained about aches or fever. He just refused to leave the room. But Rand had been sure today would bring him out.

He settled his cloak on his shoulders and hitched his sword belt around so the sword, and the red cloth wrapped around it, was covered more.

At the foot of the stairs he met Master Gill just starting up. "There's someone been asking after you in the city," the innkeeper said around his pipe. Rand felt a surge of hope. "Asking after you and those friends of yours, by name. You younglings, anyway. Seems to want you three lads most."

Anxiety replaced hope. "Who?" Rand asked. He still could not help glancing up and down the hall. Except for they two, it was empty, from the exit into the alley to the common room door.

"Don't know his name. Just heard about him. I hear most things in Caemlyn, eventually. Beggar." The innkeeper grunted. "Half mad, I hear. Even so, he could take the Queen's Bounty at the Palace, even with things as hard as they are. On High Days, the Queen gives it out with her own hands, and there's never anyone turned away for any reason. No one needs to beg in Caemlyn. Even a man under warrant can't be arrested while he's taking the Queen's Bounty."

"A Darkfriend?" Rand said reluctantly. *If the Darkfriends know our names.* . . .

"You've got Darkfriends on the brain, young fellow. They're around, certainly, but just because the Whitecloaks have everybody stirred up is no reason for you to think the city's full of them. Do you know what rumor those idiots have started now? 'Strange shapes.' Can you believe it? Strange shapes creeping around outside the city in the night." The innkeeper chuckled till his belly shook.

Rand did not feel like laughing. Hyam Kinch had talked about strange shapes, and there had surely enough been a Fade back there. "What kind of shapes?"

"What kind? I don't know what kind. Strange shapes. Trollocs, probably. The Shadowman. Lews Therin Kinslayer himself, come back fifty feet high. What kind of shapes do you *think* people will imagine now the idea's in their heads? It's none of our worry." Master Gill eyed him for a moment. "Going out, are you? Well, I can't say I care for it, myself, even today, but there's hardly anybody left here but me. Not your friend?"

"Mat's not feeling very well. Maybe later."

"Well, be that as it may. You watch yourself, now. Even today good Queen's men will be outnumbered out there, Light burn the day I ever thought to see it so. Best you leave by the alleyway. There's two of those blood-be-damned traitors sitting across the street watching my front door. They know where I stand, by the Light!"

Rand stuck his head out and looked both ways before slipping into the alley. A bulky man Master Gill had hired stood at the head of the alley, leaning on a spear and watching the people run past with an apparent lack of interest. It was only apparent, Rand knew. The fellow—his name was Lamgwin—saw everything through those heavy-lidded eyes, and for all his bullish bulk he could move like a cat. He also thought Queen Morgase was the Light made flesh, or near enough. There were a dozen like him scattered around The Queen's Blessing.

Lamgwin's ear twitched when Rand reached the mouth of the alley, but he never took his disinterest off the street. Rand knew the man had heard him coming.

"Watch your back today, man." Lamgwin's voice sounded like gravel in a pan. "When the trouble starts, you'll be a handy one to have here, not somewhere with a knife in your back."

Rand glanced at the blocky man, but his surprise was muted. He always tried to keep the sword out of sight, but this was not the first time one of Master Gill's men had assumed he would know his way in a fight. Lamgwin did not look back at him. The man's job was guarding the inn, and he did it.

Pushing his sword back a little further under his cloak, Rand joined the flow of people. He saw the two men the innkeeper had mentioned, standing on upturned barrels across the street from the inn so they could see over the crowd. He did not think they noticed him coming out of the alley. They made no secret of their allegiance. Not only were their swords wrapped in white tied with red, they wore white armbands and white cockades on their hats.

He had not been in Caemlyn long before learning that red wrappings on a sword, or a red armband or cockade, meant support for Queen Morgase. White said the Queen and her involvement with Aes Sedai and Tar Valon were to blame for everything that had gone wrong. For the weather, and the failed crops. Maybe even for the false Dragon.

He did not want to get involved in Caemlyn politics. Only, it was too late, now. It was not just that he had already chosen—by accident, but there it was. Matters in the city had gone beyond letting anyone stay neutral. Even outlanders wore cockades and armbands, or wrapped their swords, and more wore the white than the red. Maybe some of them did not think that way, but they were far from home and that was the way sentiment was running in Caemlyn. Men who supported the Queen went about in groups for their own protection, when they went out at all.

Today, though, it was different. On the surface, at least. Today, Caemlyn celebrated a victory of the Light over the Shadow. Today the false Dragon was being brought into the city, to be displayed before the Queen before he was taken north to Tar Valon.

No one talked about that part of it. No one but the Aes Sedai could deal with a man who could actually wield the One Power, of course, but no one wanted to talk about it. The Light had defeated the Shadow, and soldiers from Andor had been in the forefront of the battle. For today, that was all that was important. For today, everything else could be forgotten.

Or could it, Rand wondered. The crowd ran, singing and waving banners, laughing, but men displaying the red kept together in knots of ten or twenty, and there were no women or children with them. He thought there were at least ten men showing white for every one proclaiming allegiance to the Queen. Not for the first time, he wished white cloth had been the cheaper. *But would Master Gill have helped if you'd been showing the white?*

The crowd was so thick that jostling was inevitable. Even Whitecloaks did not enjoy their little open spaces in the throng today. As Rand let the crowd carry him toward the Inner City, he realized that not all animosities were being reined in. He saw one of the Children of the Light, one of three, bumped so hard he almost fell. The Whitecloak barely caught himself and started an angry oath at the man who had bumped him when another man staggered him with a deliberate, aimed shoulder. Before matters could go any further the Whitecloak's companions pulled him over to the side of the street to where they could shelter in a doorway. The three seemed caught between their normal glaring stare and disbelief. The crowd streamed on by as if none had noticed, and perhaps none had.

No one would have dared do such a thing two days earlier. More, Rand realized, the men who had done the bumping wore white cockades on their hats. It was widely believed the Whitecloaks supported those who opposed the Queen and her Aes Sedai advisor, but that made no difference. Men were doing things of which they had never before thought. Jostling a Whitecloak, today. Tomorrow, perhaps pulling down a Queen? Suddenly he wished there were a few more men close to him showing red; jostled by white cockades and armbands, he abruptly felt very alone.

The Whitecloaks noticed him looking at them and stared back as if meeting a challenge. He let a singing swirl in the crowd sweep him out of their sight, and joined in their song.

> "Forward the Lion,
> forward the Lion,
> the White Lion takes the field.
> Roar defiance at the Shadow.
> Forward the Lion,
> forward, Andor triumphant."

The route that would bring the false Dragon into Caemlyn was well known. Those streets themselves were kept clear by solid lines of the Queen's Guards and red-cloaked pikemen, but people packed the edges of them shoulder to shoulder, even the windows and the rooftops. Rand worked his way into the Inner City, trying to get closer to the Palace. He had some thought of actually seeing Logain displayed before the Queen. To see the false Dragon and a Queen, both . . .

that was something he had never dreamed of back home.

The Inner City was built on hills, and much of what the Ogier had made still remained. Where streets in the New City mostly ran every which way in a crazy-quilt, here they followed the curves of the hills as if they were a natural part of the earth. Sweeping rises and dips presented new and surprising vistas at every turn. Parks seen from different angles, even from above, where their walks and monuments made patterns pleasing to the eye though barely touched with green. Towers suddenly revealed, tile-covered walls glittering in the sunlight with a hundred changing colors. Sudden rises where the gaze was thrown out across the entire city to the rolling plains and forests beyond. All in all, it would have been something to see if not for the crowd that hurried him along before he had a chance to really take it in. And all those curving streets made it impossible to see very far ahead.

Abruptly he was swept around a bend, and there was the Palace. The streets, even following the natural contours of the land, had been laid out to spiral in on this—this gleeman's tale of pale spires and golden domes and intricate stonework traceries, with the banner of Andor waving from every prominence, a centerpiece for which all the other vistas had been designed. It seemed more sculpted by an artist than simply built like ordinary buildings.

That glimpse showed him he would get no nearer. No one was being allowed close to the Palace. Queen's Guards made scarlet ranks ten deep flanking the Palace gates. Along the tops of the white walls, on high balconies and towers, more Guards stood rigidly straight, bows precisely slanted across breastplated chests. They, too, looked like something out of a gleeman's tale, a guard of honor, but Rand did not believe that was why they were there. The clamoring crowd lining the streets was almost solid with white-wrapped swords, white armbands, and white cockades. Only here and there was the white wall broken by a knot of red. The red-uniformed guards seemed a thin barrier against all that white.

Giving up on making his way closer to the Palace, he sought a place where he could use his height to advantage. He did not have to be in the front row to see everything. The crowd shifted constantly, people shoving to get nearer the front, people hurrying off to what they thought was a better vantage point. In one of those shifts he found himself only three people from the open street, and all in front of him were shorter than he, including the pikemen. Almost everyone was. People crowded against him from both sides, sweating from the press of so many bodies. Those behind him muttered about not being able to see, and tried to wriggle past. He stood his ground, making an impervious wall with those to either side. He was content. When the false Dragon passed by, he would be close enough to see the man's face clearly.

Across the street and down toward the gates to the New City, a ripple passed through the tight-packed crowd; around the curve, an eddy of people was drawing back to let something go by. It was not like the clear space that followed Whitecloaks on any day but today. These people jerked themselves back with startled glances that became grimaces of distaste. Pressing themselves out of the way, they turned their faces from whatever it was, but watched out of the corners of their eyes until it was past.

Other eyes around him noted the disturbance, too. Keyed for the coming of the Dragon but with nothing to do now but wait, the crowd found anything at all worthy of comment. He heard speculation ranging from an Aes Sedai to Logain himself, and a few coarser suggestions that brought rough laughter from the men and disdainful sniffs from the women.

The ripple meandered through the crowd, drawing closer to the edge of the street as it came. No one seemed to hesitate in letting it go where it wanted, even if that meant losing a good spot for viewing as the crowd flowed back in on itself behind the passing. Finally, directly across from Rand, the crowd bulged into the street, pushing aside red-cloaked pikemen who struggled to shove them back, and broke open. The stooped shape that shuffled hesitantly out into the open looked more like a pile of filthy rags than a man. Rand heard murmurs of disgust around him.

The ragged man paused on the far edge of the street. His cowl, torn and stiff with dirt, swung back and forth as if searching for something, or listening. Abruptly he gave a wordless cry and flung out a dirty claw of a hand, pointing straight at Rand. Immediately he began to scuttle across the street like a bug.

The beggar. Whatever ill chance had led the man to find him like this, Rand was suddenly sure that, Darkfriend or not, he did not want to meet him face-to-face. He could feel the beggar's eyes, like greasy water on his skin. Especially he did not want the man close to him here, surrounded by people balanced on the brink of violence. The same voices that had laughed before now cursed him as he pushed his way back, away from the street.

He hurried, knowing the densely packed mass through which he had to shove and wriggle would give way before the filthy man. Struggling to force a path through the crowd, he staggered and almost fell when he abruptly broke free. Flailing his arms to keep his balance he turned the stagger into a run. People pointed at him; he was the only one not pressing the other way, and running at that. Shouts followed him. His cloak flapped behind him, exposing his red-clad sword. When he realized that, he ran faster. A lone supporter of the Queen, running, could well spark a white-cockaded mob to pursuit, even today. He ran, letting his long legs eat paving stones. Not until the shouts were left far behind did he allow himself to collapse against a wall, panting.

He did not know where he was, except that he was still within the Inner City. He could not remember how many twists and turns he had taken along those curving streets. Poised to run again, he looked back the way he had come. Only one person moved on the street, a woman walking placidly along with her shopping basket. Almost everyone in the city was gathered for a glimpse of the false Dragon. *He can't have followed me. I must have left him behind.*

The beggar would not give up; he was sure of it, though he could not say why. That ragged shape would be working its way through the crowds at that very minute, searching, and if Rand returned to see Logain he ran the risk of a meeting. For a moment he considered going back to The Queen's Blessing, but he was sure he would never get another chance to see a Queen, and he hoped he would never have another to see a false Dragon. There seemed to be something cowardly in letting a bent beggar, even a Darkfriend, chase him into hiding.

He looked around, considering. The way the Inner City was laid out, buildings were kept low, if there were buildings at all, so that someone standing at a particular spot would have nothing to interrupt the planned view. There had to be places from where he could see the procession pass with the false Dragon. Even if he could not see the Queen, he could see Logain. Suddenly determined, he set off.

In the next hour he found several such places, every last one already packed cheek-to-cheek with people avoiding the crush along the procession route. They were a solid front of white cockades and armbands. No red at all. Thinking what the sight of his sword might do in a crowd like that, he slipped away carefully, and quickly.

Shouting floated up from the New City, cries and the blaring of trumpets, the martial beat of drums. Logain and his escort were already in Caemlyn, already on their way to the Palace.

Dispirited, he wandered the all but empty streets, still halfheartedly hoping to find some way to see Logain. His eyes fell on the slope, bare of buildings, rising above the street where he was walking. In a normal spring the slope would be an expanse of flowers and grass, but now it was brown all the way to the high wall along its crest, a wall over which the tops of trees were visible.

This part of the street had not been designed for any grand view, but just ahead, over the rooftops, he could see some of the Palace spires, topped by White Lion banners fluttering in the wind. He was not sure exactly where the curve of the street ran after it rounded the hill beyond his sight, but he suddenly had a thought about that hilltop wall.

The drums and trumpets were drawing nearer, the shouting growing louder. Anxiously he scrambled up the slope. It was not meant to be climbed, but he dug his boots into the dead sod and pulled himself up using leafless shrubs as handholds. Panting as much with desire as effort, he scrambled the last yards to the wall. It reared above him, easily twice his height and more. The air thundered with the drumbeat, rang with trumpet blasts.

The face of the wall had been left much in the natural state of the stone, the huge blocks fitted together so well that the joins were nearly invisible, the roughness making it seem almost a natural cliff. Rand grinned. The cliffs just beyond the Sand Hills were higher, and even Perrin had climbed those. His hands sought rocky knobs, his booted feet found ridges. The drums raced him as he climbed. He refused to let them win. He would reach the top before they reached the Palace. In his haste, the stone tore his hands and scraped his knees through his breeches, but he flung his arms over the top and heaved himself up with a sense of victory.

Hastily he twisted himself around to a seat on the flat, narrow top of the wall. The leafy branches of a towering tree stuck out over his head, but he had no thought for that. He looked across tiled rooftops, but from the wall his line of sight was clear. He leaned out, just a little, and could see the Palace gate, and the Queen's Guards drawn up there, and the expectant crowd. Expectant. Their shouts drowned out by the thunder of drums and trumpets, but waiting still. He grinned. *I won.*

Even as he settled in place, the first part of the procession rounded the final curve before the Palace. Twenty ranks of trumpeters came first, splitting the air with peal after triumphant peal, a fanfare of victory. Behind them, as many drummers thundered. Then came the banners of Caemlyn, white lions on red, borne by mounted men, followed by the soldiers of Caemlyn, rank on rank on rank of horsemen, armor gleaming, lances proudly held, crimson pennants fluttering. Treble rows of pikemen and archers flanked them, and came on and on after the horsemen began passing between the waiting Guards and through the Palace gates.

The last of the foot soldiers rounded the curve, and behind them was a massive wagon. Sixteen horses pulled it in hitches of four. In the center of its flat bed was a large cage of iron bars, and on each corner of the wagonbed sat two women, watching the cage as intently as if the procession and the crowd did not exist. Aes Sedai, he was certain. Between the wagon and the footmen, and to either side, rode a dozen Warders, their cloaks swirling and tangling the eye. If the Aes Sedai ignored the crowd, the Warders scanned it as if there were no other guards but they.

With all of that, it was the man in the cage who caught and held Rand's eyes. He was not close enough to see Logain's face, as he had wanted to, but suddenly he thought he was as close as he cared for. The false Dragon was a tall man, with long, dark hair curling around his broad shoulders. He held himself upright against the sway of the wagon with one hand on the bars over his head. His clothes seemed ordinary, a cloak and coat and breeches that would not have caused comment in any farming village. But the way he wore them. The way he held himself. Logain was a king in every inch of him. The cage might as well not have been there. He held himself erect, head high, and looked over the crowd as if they had come to do him honor. And wherever his gaze swept, there the people fell silent, staring back in awe. When Logain's eyes left them, they screamed with redoubled fury as if to make up for their silence, but it made no difference in the way the man stood, or in the silence that passed along with him. As the wagon rolled through the Palace gates, he turned to look back at the assembled masses. They howled at him, beyond words, a wave of sheer animal hate and fear, and Logain threw back his head and laughed as the Palace swallowed him.

Other contingents followed behind the wagons, with banners representing more who had fought and defeated the false Dragon. The Golden Bees of Illian, the three White Crescents of Tear, the Rising Sun of Cairhien, others, many others, of nations and of cities, and of great men with their own trumpets, their own drums to thunder their grandeur. It was anticlimactic after Logain.

Rand leaned out a bit further to try to catch one last sight of the caged man. *He* was *defeated, wasn't he? Light, he wouldn't be in a bloody cage if he wasn't defeated.*

Overbalanced, he slipped and grabbed at the top of the wall, pulled himself back to a somewhat safer seat. With Logain gone, he became aware of the burning in his hands, where the stone had scraped his palms and fingers. Yet he could not shake free of the images. The cage and the Aes Sedai. Logain, undefeated. No matter the cage, that had not been a defeated man. He shivered and rubbed his stinging hands on his thighs.

"Why were the Aes Sedai watching him?" he wondered aloud.

"They're keeping him from touching the True Source, silly."

He jerked to look up, toward the girl's voice, and suddenly his precarious seat was gone. He had only time to realize that he was toppling backward, falling, when something struck his head and a laughing Logain chased him into spinning darkness.

CHAPTER
40

The Web Tightens

I t seemed to Rand that he was sitting at table with Logain and
Moiraine. The Aes Sedai and the false Dragon sat watching him
silently, as if neither knew the other was there. Abruptly he realized the walls of the room were becoming indistinct, fading off into
gray. A sense of urgency built in him. Everything was going, blurring
away. When he looked back to the table, Moiraine and Logain had
vanished, and Ba'alzamon sat there instead. Rand's whole body vi-
brated with urgency; it hummed inside his head, louder and louder.
The hum became the pounding of blood in his ears.

With a jerk he sat up, and immediately groaned and clutched his
head, swaying. His whole skull hurt; his left hand found sticky dampness in his hair. He was sitting on the ground, on green grass. That
troubled him, vaguely, but his head spun and everything he looked at
lurched, and all he could think of was lying down until it stopped.

The wall! The girl's voice!

Steadying himself with one hand flat on the grass, he looked around
slowly. He had to do it slowly; when he tried to turn his head quickly

everything started whirling again. He was in a garden, or a park; a slate-paved walk meandered by through flowering bushes not six feet away, with a white stone bench beside it and a leafy arbor over the bench for shade. He *had* fallen inside the wall. *And the girl?*

He found the tree, close behind his back, and found her, too—climbing down out of it. She reached the ground and turned to face him, and he blinked and groaned again. A deep blue velvet cloak lined with pale fur rested on her shoulders, its hood hanging down behind to her waist with a cluster of silver bells at the peak. They jingled when she moved. A silver filigree circlet held her long, red-gold curls, and delicate silver rings hung at her ears, while a necklace of heavy silver links and dark green stones he thought were emeralds lay around her throat. Her pale blue dress was smudged with bark stains from her tree climbing, but it was still silk, and embroidered with painstakingly intricate designs, the skirt slashed with inserts the color of rich cream. A wide belt of woven silver encircled her waist, and velvet slippers peeked from under the hem of her dress.

He had only ever seen two women dressed in this fashion, Moiraine and the Darkfriend who had tried to kill Mat and him. He could not begin to imagine who would choose to climb trees in clothes like that, but he was sure she had to be someone important. The way she was looking at him redoubled the impression. She did not seem in the least troubled at having a stranger tumble into her garden. There was a self-possession about her that made him think of Nynaeve, or Moiraine.

He was so enmeshed in worrying whether or not he had gotten himself into trouble, whether or not she was someone who could and would call the Queen's Guards even on a day when they had other things to occupy them, that it took him a few moments to see past the elaborate clothes and lofty attitude to the girl herself. She was perhaps two or three years younger than he, tall for a girl, and beautiful, her face a perfect oval framed by that mass of sunburst curls, her lips full and red, her eyes bluer than he could believe. She was completely different from Egwene in height and face and body, but every bit as beautiful. He felt a twinge of guilt, but told himself that denying what his eyes saw would not bring Egwene safely to Caemlyn one whit faster.

A scrabbling sound came from up in the tree and bits of bark fell, followed by a boy dropping lightly to the ground behind her. He was a head taller than she and a little older, but his face and hair marked him as her close kin. His coat and cloak were red and white and gold, embroidered and brocaded, and for a male even more ornate than hers. That increased Rand's anxiety. Only on a feastday would any ordinary man dress in anything like that, and never with that much grandeur. This was no public park. Perhaps the Guards were too busy to bother with trespassers.

The boy studied Rand over the girl's shoulder, fingering the dagger at his waist. It seemed more a nervous habit than any thought that he might use it. Not completely, though. The boy had the same self-possession as the girl, and they both looked at him as if he were a puzzle to be solved. He had the odd feeling that the girl, at least, was cataloguing everything about him from the condition of his boots to the state of his cloak.

"We will never hear the end of this, Elayne, if mother finds out," the boy said suddenly. "She told us to stay in our rooms, but you just had to get a look at Logain, didn't you? Now look what it has got us."

"Be quiet, Gawyn." She was clearly the younger of the two, but she spoke as though she took it for granted that he would obey. The boy's face struggled as if he had more to say, but to Rand's surprise he held his peace. "Are you all right?" she said suddenly.

It took Rand a minute to realize she was speaking to him. When he did, he tried to struggle to his feet. "I'm fine. I just—" He tottered, and his legs gave way. He sat back down hard. His head swum. "I'll just climb back over the wall," he muttered. He attempted to stand again, but she put a hand on his shoulder, pressing him down. He was so dizzy the slight pressure was enough to hold him in place.

"You *are* hurt." Gracefully she knelt beside him. Her fingers gently parted the blood-matted hair on the left side of his head. "You must have struck a branch coming down. You will be lucky if you didn't break anything more than your scalp. I don't think I ever saw anyone as skillful at climbing as you, but you don't do so well falling."

"You'll get blood on your hands," he said, drawing back.

Firmly she pulled his head back to where she could get at it. "Hold still." She did not speak sharply, but again there was that note in her voice as if she expected to be obeyed. "It does not look *too* bad, thank the Light." From pockets on the inside of her cloak she began taking out an array of tiny vials and twisted packets of paper, finishing with a handful of wadded bandage.

He stared at the collection in amazement. It was the sort of thing he would have expected a Wisdom to carry, not someone dressed as she was. She had gotten blood on her fingers, he saw, but it did not seem to bother her.

"Give me your water flask, Gawyn," she said. "I need to wash this."

The boy she called Gawyn unfastened a leather bottle from his belt and handed it to her, then squatted easily at Rand's feet with his arms folded on his knees. Elayne went about what she was doing in a very workmanlike manner. He did not flinch at the sting of cold water when she washed the cut in his scalp, but she held the top of his head with one hand as if she expected him to try to pull away again and would have none of it. The ointment she smoothed on after, from one of her small vials, soothed almost as much as one of Nynaeve's preparations would have.

Gawyn smiled at him as she worked, a calming smile, as if he, too, expected Rand to jerk away and maybe even run. "She's always finding stray cats and birds with broken wings. You are the first human being she has had to work on." He hesitated, then added, "Do not be offended. I am not calling you a stray." It was not an apology, just a statement of fact.

"No offense taken," Rand said stiffly. But the pair were acting as if he were a skittish horse.

"She does know what she is doing," Gawyn said. "She has had the best teachers. So do not fear, you are in good hands."

Elayne pressed some of the bandaging against his temple and pulled a silk scarf from her belt, blue and cream and gold. For any girl in Emond's Field it would have been a treasured feastday cloth. Elayne deftly began winding it around his head to hold the wad of bandage in place.

"You can't use that," he protested.

She went on winding. "I told you to hold still," she said calmly.

Rand looked at Gawyn. "Does she always expect everybody to do what she tells them?"

A flash of surprise crossed the young man's face, and his mouth tightened with amusement. "Most of the time she does. And most of the time they do."

"Hold this," Elayne said. "Put your hand there while I tie—" She exclaimed at the sight of his hands. "You did not do that falling. Climbing where you should not have been climbing is more like it." Quickly finishing her knot, she turned his hands palms upward in front of him, muttering to herself about how little water was left. The washing made the lacerations burn, but her touch was surprisingly delicate. "Hold still, this time."

The vial of ointment was produced again. She spread it thinly along the scrapes, all of her attention apparently on rubbing it in without hurting him. A coolness spread through his hands, as if she were rubbing the torn places away.

"Most of the time they do exactly what she says," Gawyn went on with an affectionate grin at the top of her head. "Most people. Not Mother, of course. Or Elaida. And not Lini. Lini was her nurse. You can't give orders to someone who switched you for stealing figs when you were little. And even not so little." Elayne raised her head long enough to give him a dangerous look. He cleared his throat and carefully blanked his expression before hurrying on. "And Gareth, of course. No one gives orders to Gareth."

"Not even Mother," Elayne said, bending her head back over Rand's hands. "She makes suggestions, and he always does what she suggests, but I've never heard her give him a command." She shook her head.

"I don't know why that always surprises you," Gawyn answered her. "Even you don't try telling Gareth what to do. He's served three Queens and been Captain-General, and First Prince Regent, for two. I daresay there are some think he's more a symbol of the Throne of Andor than the Queen is."

"Mother should go ahead and marry him," she said absently. Her attention was on Rand's hands. "She wants to; she can't hide it from me. And it would solve so many problems."

Gawyn shook his head. "One of them must bend first. Mother cannot, and Gareth will not."

"If she commanded him. . . ."

"He would obey. I think. But she won't. You know she won't."

Abruptly they turned to stare at Rand. He had the feeling they had forgotten he was there. "Who . . . ?" He had to stop to wet his lips. "Who is your mother?"

Elayne's eyes widened in surprise, but Gawyn spoke in an ordinary tone that made his words all the more jarring. "Morgase, by the Grace of the Light, Queen of Andor, Protector of the Realm, Defender of the People, High Seat of the House Trakand."

"The Queen," Rand muttered, shock spreading through him in waves of numbness. For a minute he thought his head was going to begin spinning again. *Don't attract any attention. Just fall into the Queen's garden and let the Daughter-Heir tend your cuts like a hedge-doctor.* He wanted to laugh, and knew it for the fringes of panic.

Drawing a deep breath, he scrambled hastily to his feet. He held himself tightly in rein against the urge to run, but the need to get away filled him, to get away before anyone else discovered him there.

Elayne and Gawyn watched him calmly, and when he leaped up they rose gracefully, not hurried in the least. He put up a hand to pull the scarf from his head, and Elayne seized his elbow. "Stop that. You will start the bleeding again." Her voice was still calm, still sure that he would do as he was told.

"I have to go," Rand said. "I'll just climb back over the wall and—"

"You really didn't know." For the first time she seemed as startled as he was. "Do you mean you climbed up on that wall to see Logain without even knowing where you were? You could have gotten a much better view down in the streets."

"I . . . I don't like crowds," he mumbled. He sketched a bow to each of them. "If you'll pardon me, ah . . . my Lady." In the stories, royal courts were full of people all calling one another Lord and Lady and Royal Highness and Majesty, but if he had ever heard the correct form of address for the Daughter-Heir, he could not think clearly enough to remember. He could not think clearly about anything beyond the need to be far away. "If you will pardon me, I'll just leave now. Ah . . . thank you for the. . . ." He touched the scarf around his head. "Thank you."

"Without even telling us your name?" Gawyn said. "A poor payment for Elayne's care. I've been wondering about you. You sound like an Andorman, though not a Caemlyner, certainly, but you look like. . . . Well, you know our names. Courtesy would suggest you give us yours."

Looking longingly at the wall, Rand gave his right name before he thought what he was doing, and even added, "From Emond's Field, in the Two Rivers."

"From the west," Gawyn murmured. "Very far to the west."

Rand looked around at him sharply. There had been a note of surprise in the young man's voice, and Rand caught some of it still on his face when he turned. Gawyn replaced it with a pleasant smile so quickly, though, that he almost doubted what he had seen.

"Tabac and wool," Gawyn said. "I have to know the principal products of every part of the Realm. Of every land, for that matter. Part of my training. Principal products and crafts, and what the people are like. Their customs, their strengths and weaknesses. It's said Two Rivers people are stubborn. They can be led, if they think you are worthy, but the harder you try to push them, the harder they dig in. Elayne ought to choose her husband from there. It'll take a man with a will like stone to keep from being trampled by her."

Rand stared at him. Elayne was staring, too. Gawyn looked as much under control as ever, but he was babbling. *Why?*

"What's this?"

All three of them jumped at the sudden voice, and spun to face it.

The young man who stood there was the handsomest man Rand had ever seen, almost too handsome for masculinity. He was tall and slender, but his movements spoke of whipcord strength and a sure confidence. Dark of hair and eye, he wore his clothes, only a little less elaborate in red and white than Gawyn's, as if they were of no importance. One hand rested on his sword hilt, and his eyes were steady on Rand.

"Stand away from him, Elayne," the man said. "You, too, Gawyn."

Elayne stepped in front of Rand, between him and the newcomer, head high and as confident as ever. "He is a loyal subject of our mother, and a good Queen's man. And he is under my protection, Galad."

Rand tried to remember what he had heard from Master Kinch, and since from Master Gill. Galadedrid Damodred was Elayne's half-brother, Elayne's and Gawyn's, if he remembered correctly; the three shared the same father. Master Kinch might not have liked Taringail Damodred too well—neither did anyone else that he had heard—but the son was well thought of by wearers of the red and the white alike, if talk in the city was any guide.

"I am aware of your fondness for strays, Elayne," the slender man said reasonably, "but the fellow is armed, and he hardly looks reputable. In these days, we cannot be too careful. If he's a loyal Queen's man, what is he doing here where he does not belong? It is easy enough to change the wrappings on a sword, Elayne."

"He is here as my guest, Galad, and I vouch for him. Or have you appointed yourself my nurse, to decide whom I may talk to, and when?"

Her voice was rich with scorn, but Galad seemed unmoved. "You know I make no claims for control over your actions, Elayne, but this . . . guest of yours is not proper, and you know that as well as I. Gawyn, help me convince her. Our mother would—"

"Enough!" Elayne snapped. "You are right that you have no say over my actions, nor have you any right to judge them. You may leave me. Now!"

Galad gave Gawyn a rueful look; at one and the same time it seemed to ask for help while saying that Elayne was too headstrong to be helped. Elayne's face darkened, but just as she opened her mouth again, he bowed, in all formality yet with the grace of a cat, took a step back, then turned and strode down the paved path, his long legs carrying him quickly out of sight beyond the arbor.

"I hate him," Elayne breathed. "He is vile and full of envy."

"There you go too far, Elayne," Gawyn said. "Galad does not know the meaning of envy. Twice he has saved my life, with none to know if he held his hand. If he had not, he would be your First Prince of the Sword in my place."

"Never, Gawyn. I would choose anyone before Galad. Anyone. The lowest stableboy." Suddenly she smiled and gave her brother a mock-stern look. "You say I am fond of giving orders. Well, I command you to let nothing happen to you. I command you to be my First Prince of the Sword when I take the throne—the Light send that day is far off!—and to lead the armies of Andor with the sort of honor Galad cannot dream of."

"As you command, my Lady." Gawyn laughed, his bow a parody of Galad's.

Elayne gave Rand a thoughtful frown. "Now we must get you out of here quickly."

"Galad always does the right thing," Gawyn explained, "even when he should not. In this case, finding a stranger in the gardens, the right thing is to notify the Palace guards. Which I suspect he is on his way to do right this minute."

"Then it's time I was back over the wall," Rand said. *A fine day for going unnoticed! I might as well carry a sign!* He turned to the wall, but Elayne caught his arm.

"Not after the trouble I went to with your hands. You'll only make fresh scrapes and then let some back-alley crone put the Light knows what on them. There is a small gate on the other side of the garden. It's overgrown, and no one but me even remembers it's there."

Suddenly Rand heard boots pounding toward them over the slate paving stones.

"Too late," Gawyn muttered. "He must have started running as soon as he was out of eyeshot."

Elayne growled an oath, and Rand's eyebrows shot up. He had heard that one from the stablemen at The Queen's Blessing and had been shocked then. The next moment she was in cool self-possession once more.

Gawyn and Elayne appeared content to remain where they were, but he could not make himself stay for the Queen's Guards with such equanimity. He started once more for the wall, knowing he would be no more than halfway up before the guards arrived, but unable to stand still.

Before he had taken three steps red-uniformed men burst into sight,

breastplates catching the sun as they dashed up the path. Others came
like breaking waves of scarlet and polished steel, seemingly from every
direction. Some held drawn swords; others only waited to set their
boots before raising bows and nocking feathered shafts. Behind the
barred face-guards every eye was grim, and every broadhead arrow
was pointed unwaveringly at him.

Elayne and Gawyn leaped as one, putting themselves between him
and the arrows, their arms spread to cover him. He stood very still
and kept his hands in plain sight, away from his sword.

While the thud of boots and the creak of bowstrings still hung in the
air, one of the soldiers, with the golden knot of an officer on his shoulder, shouted, "My Lady, my Lord, down, quickly!"

Despite her outstretched arms Elayne drew herself up regally. "You
dare to bring bare steel into my presence, Tallanvor? Gareth Bryne
will have you mucking stables with the meanest trooper for this, if you
are lucky!"

The soldiers exchanged puzzled glances, and some of the bowmen
uneasily half lowered their bows. Only then did Elayne let her arms
down, as if she had only held them up because she wished to. Gawyn
hesitated, then followed her example. Rand could count the bows that
had not been lowered. The muscles of his stomach tensed as though
they could stop a broadhead shaft at twenty paces.

The man with the officer's knot seemed the most perplexed of all.
"My Lady, forgive me, but Lord Galadedrid reported a dirty peasant
skulking in the gardens, armed and endangering my Lady Elayne and
my Lord Gawyn." His eyes went to Rand, and his voice firmed. "If
my Lady and my Lord will please to step aside, I will take the villain
into custody. There is too much riff-raff in the city these days."

"I doubt very much if Galad reported anything of the kind," Elayne
said. "Galad does not lie."

"Sometimes I wish he would," Gawyn said softly, for Rand's ear.
"Just once. It might make living with him easier."

"This man is my guest," Elayne continued, "and here under my
protection. You may withdraw, Tallanvor."

"I regret that will not be possible, My Lady. As My Lady knows,
the Queen, your lady mother, has given orders regarding anyone on
Palace grounds without Her Majesty's permission, and word has been
sent to Her Majesty of this intruder." There was more than a hint of
satisfaction in Tallanvor's voice. Rand suspected the officer had had to
accept other commands from Elayne that he did not think proper; this
time the man was not about to, not when he had a perfect excuse.

Elayne stared back at Tallanvor; for once she seemed at a loss.

Rand looked a question at Gawyn, and Gawyn understood. "Prison," he murmured. Rand's face went white, and the young man added quickly, "Only for a few days, and you will not be harmed. You'll be questioned by Gareth Bryne, the Captain-General, personally, but you will be set free once it's clear you meant no harm." He paused, hidden thoughts in his eyes. "I hope you were telling the truth, Rand al'Thor from the Two Rivers."

"You will conduct all three of us to my mother," Elayne announced suddenly. A grin bloomed on Gawyn's face.

Behind the steel bars across his face, Tallanvor appeared taken aback. "My Lady, I—"

"Or else conduct all three of us to a cell," Elayne said. "We will remain together. Or will you give orders for hands to be laid upon my person?" Her smile was victorious, and the way Tallanvor looked around as if he expected to find help in the trees said he, too, thought she had won.

Won what? How?

"Mother is viewing Logain," Gawyn said softly, as if he had read Rand's thoughts, "and even if she was not busy, Tallanvor would not dare troop into her presence with Elayne and me, as if *we* were under guard. Mother has a bit of a temper, sometimes."

Rand remembered what Master Gill had said about Queen Morgase. *A bit of a temper?*

Another red-uniformed soldier came running down the path, skidding to a halt to salute with an arm across his chest. He spoke softly to Tallanvor, and his words brought satisfaction back to Tallanvor's face.

"The Queen, your lady mother," Tallanvor announced, "commands me to bring the intruder to her immediately. It is also the Queen's command that my Lady Elayne and my Lord Gawyn attend her. Also immediately."

Gawyn winced, and Elayne swallowed hard. Her face composed, she still began industriously brushing at the stains on her dress. Aside from dislodging a few pieces of bark, her effort did little good.

"If my Lady pleases?" Tallanvor said smugly. "My Lord?"

The soldiers formed around them in a hollow box that started along the slate path with Tallanvor leading. Gawyn and Elayne walked on either side of Rand, both appearing lost in unpleasant thoughts. The soldiers had sheathed their swords and returned arrows to quivers, but they were no less on guard than when they had had weapons in hand.

They watched Rand as if they expected him at any moment to snatch his sword and try to cut his way to freedom.

Try anything? I won't try anything. *Unnoticed! Hah!*

Watching the soldiers watching him, he suddenly became aware of the garden. He had regained his balance completely since the fall. One thing had happened after another, each new shock coming before the last had a chance to fade, and his surroundings had been a blur, except for the wall and his devout wish to be back on the other side of it. Now he *saw* the green grass that had only tickled the back of his mind before. *Green!* A hundred shades of green. Trees and bushes green and thriving, thick with leaves and fruit. Lush vines covering arbors over the path. Flowers everywhere. So many flowers, spraying the garden with color. Some he knew—bright golden sunburst and tiny pink tallowend, crimson starblaze and purple Emond's Glory, roses in every color from purest white to deep, deep red—but others were strange, so fanciful in shape and hue he wondered if they could be real.

"It's green," he whispered. "Green." The soldiers muttered to themselves; Tallanvor gave them a sharp look over his shoulder and they fell silent.

"Elaida's work," Gawyn said absently.

"It is not right," Elayne said. "She asked if I wanted to pick out the one farm she could do the same for, while all around it the crops still failed, but it still isn't right for us to have flowers when there are people who do not have enough to eat." She drew a deep breath, and refilled her self-possession. "Remember yourself," she told Rand briskly. "Speak up clearly when you are spoken to, and keep silent otherwise. And follow my lead. All will be well."

Rand wished he could share her confidence. It would have helped if Gawyn had seemed to have it as well. As Tallanvor led them into the Palace, he looked back at the garden, at all the green streaked with blossoms, colors wrought for a Queen by an Aes Sedai's hand. He was in deep water, and there was no bank in sight.

Palace servants filled the halls, in red liveries with collars and cuffs of white, the White Lion on the left breast of their tunics, scurrying about intent on tasks that were not readily apparent. When the soldiers trooped by with Elayne and Gawyn, and Rand, in their midst, they stopped dead in their tracks to stare openmouthed.

Through the middle of all the consternation a gray-striped tomcat wandered unconcernedly down the hall, weaving between the goggling servants. Suddenly the cat struck Rand as odd. He had been in Baerlon long enough to know that even the meanest shop had cats lurking in every corner. Since entering the Palace, the tom was the only cat he had seen.

"You don't have rats?" he said in disbelief. *Every* place had rats.

"Elaida doesn't like rats," Gawyn muttered vaguely. He was frowning worriedly down the hall, apparently already seeing the coming meeting with the Queen. "We never have rats."

"Both of you be quiet." Elayne's voice was sharp, but as absent as her brother's. "I am trying to think."

Rand watched the cat over his shoulder until the guards took him round a corner, hiding the tom from sight. A lot of cats would have made him feel better; it would have been nice if there was one thing normal about the Palace, even if it was rats.

The path Tallanvor took turned so many times that Rand lost his sense of direction. Finally the young officer stopped before tall double doors of dark wood with a rich glow, not so grand as some they had passed, but still carved all over with rows of lions, finely wrought in detail. A liveried servant stood to either side.

"At least it isn't the Grand Hall." Gawyn laughed unsteadily. "I never heard that Mother commanded anyone's head cut off from here." He sounded as if he thought she might set a precedent.

Tallanvor reached for Rand's sword, but Elayne moved to cut him off. "He is my guest, and by custom and law, guests of the royal family may go armed even in Mother's presence. Or will you deny my word that he is my guest?"

Tallanvor hesitated, locking eyes with her, then nodded. "Very well, my Lady." She smiled at Rand as Tallanvor stepped back, but it lasted only a moment. "First rank to accompany me," Tallanvor commanded. "Announce the Lady Elayne and the Lord Gawyn to Her Majesty," he told the doorkeepers. "Also Guardsman-Lieutenant Tallanvor, at Her Majesty's command, with the intruder under guard."

Elayne scowled at Tallanvor, but the doors were already swinging open. A sonorous voice sounded, announcing those who came.

Grandly Elayne swept through the doors, spoiling her regal entrance only a little by motioning for Rand to keep close behind her. Gawyn squared his shoulders and strode in flanking her, one measured pace to her rear. Rand followed, uncertainly keeping level with Gawyn on her other side. Tallanvor stayed close to Rand, and ten soldiers came with him. The doors closed silently behind them.

Suddenly Elayne dropped into a deep curtsy, simultaneously bowing from the waist, and stayed there, holding her skirt wide. Rand gave a start, then hastily emulated Gawyn and the other men, shifting awkwardly until he had it right. Down on his right knee, head bowed, bending forward to press the knuckles of his right hand against the marble tiles, his left hand resting on the end of his sword hilt. Gawyn, without a sword, put his hand on his dagger the same way.

Rand was just congratulating himself on getting it right when he noticed Tallanvor, his head still bent, glaring sideways at him from behind his face-guard. *Was I supposed to do something else?* He was suddenly angry that Tallanvor expected him to know what to do when no one had told him. And angry over being afraid of the guards. He had done nothing to be fearful for. He knew his fear was not Tallanvor's fault, but he was angry at him anyway.

Everyone held their positions, frozen as if waiting for the spring thaw. He did not know what they were waiting for, but he took the opportunity to study the place to which he had been brought. He kept his head down, just turning it enough to see. Tallanvor's scowl deepened, but he ignored it.

The square chamber was about the size of the common room at The Queen's Blessing, its walls presenting hunting scenes carved in relief in stone of the purest white. The tapestries between the carvings were gentle images of bright flowers and brilliantly plumaged hummingbirds, except for the two at the far end of the room, where the White Lion of Andor stood taller than a man on scarlet fields. Those two hangings flanked a dais, and on the dais a carved and gilded throne where sat the Queen.

A bluff, blocky man stood bareheaded by the Queen's right hand in the red of the Queen's Guards, with four golden knots on the shoulder of his cloak and wide golden bands breaking the white of his cuffs. His temples were heavy with gray, but he looked as strong and immovable as a rock. That had to be the Captain-General, Gareth Bryne. Behind the throne and to the other side a woman in deep green silk sat on a low stool, knitting something out of dark, almost black, wool. At first the knitting made Rand think she was old, but at second glance he could not put an age to her at all. Young, old, he did not know. Her attention seemed to be entirely on her needles and yarn, just as if there were not a Queen within arm's reach of her. She was a handsome woman, outwardly placid, yet there was something terrible in her concentration. There was no sound in the room except for the click of her needles.

He tried to look at everything, yet his eyes kept going back to the woman with the gleaming wreath of finely wrought roses on her brow, the Rose Crown of Andor. A long red stole, the Lion of Andor marching along its length, hung over her silken dress of red and white pleats, and when she touched the Captain-General's arm with her left hand, a ring in the shape of the Great Serpent, eating its own tail, glittered. Yet it was not the grandeur of clothes or jewelry or even crown that drew Rand's eyes again and again: it was the woman who wore them.

Morgase had her daughter's beauty, matured and ripened. Her face and figure, her presence, filled the room like a light that dimmed the other two with her. If she had been a widow in Emond's Field, she would have had a line of suitors outside her door even if she was the worst cook and most slovenly housekeeper in the Two Rivers. He saw her studying him and ducked his head, afraid she might be able to tell his thoughts from his face. *Light, thinking about the Queen like she was a village woman! You fool!*

"You may rise," Morgase said in a rich, warm voice that held Elayne's assurance of obedience a hundred times over.

Rand stood with the rest.

"Mother—" Elayne began, but Morgase cut her off.

"You have been climbing trees, it seems, daughter." Elayne plucked a stray fragment of bark from her dress and, finding there was no place to put it, held it clenched in her hand. "In fact," Morgase went on calmly, "it would seem that despite my orders to the contrary you have contrived to take your look at this Logain. Gawyn, I have thought better of you. You must learn not only to obey your sister, but at the same time to be counterweight for her against disaster." The Queen's eyes swung to the blocky man beside her, then quickly away again. Bryne remained impassive, as if he had not noticed, but Rand thought those eyes noticed everything. "That, Gawyn, is as much the duty of the First Prince as is leading the armies of Andor. Perhaps if your training is intensified, you will find less time for letting your sister lead you into trouble. I will ask the Captain-General to see that you do not lack for things to do on the journey north."

Gawyn shifted his feet as if about to protest, then bowed his head instead. "As you command, mother."

Elayne grimaced. "Mother, Gawyn cannot keep me out of trouble if he is not with me. It was for that reason alone he left his rooms. Mother, surely there could be no harm in just looking at Logain. Almost everyone in the city was closer to him than we."

"Everyone in the city is not the Daughter-Heir." Sharpness underlay the Queen's voice. "I have seen this fellow Logain from close, and he is dangerous, child. Caged, with Aes Sedai to guard him every minute, he is still as dangerous as a wolf. I wish he had never been brought near Caemlyn."

"He will be dealt with in Tar Valon." The woman on the stool did not take her eyes from her knitting as she spoke. "What is important is that the people see that the Light has once again vanquished the Dark. And that they see you are part of that victory, Morgase."

Morgase waved a dismissive hand. "I would still rather he had never come near Caemlyn. Elayne, I know your mind."

"Mother," Elayne protested, "I do mean to obey you. Truly I do."

"You do?" Morgase asked in mock surprise, then chuckled. "Yes, you do try to be a dutiful daughter. But you constantly test how far you may go. Well, I did the same with my mother. That spirit will stand you in good stead when you ascend to the throne, but you are not Queen yet, child. You have disobeyed me and had your look at Logain. Be satisfied with that. On the journey north you will not be allowed within one hundred paces of him, neither you nor Gawyn. If I did not know just how hard your lessons will be in Tar Valon, I would send Lini along to see that you obey. She, at least, seems able to make you do as you must."

Elayne bowed her head sullenly.

The woman behind the throne seemed occupied with counting her stitches. "In one week," she said suddenly, "you will be wanting to come home to your mother. In a month you will be wanting to run away with the Traveling People. But my sisters will keep you away from the unbeliever. That sort of thing is not for you, not yet." Abruptly she turned on the stool to look intently at Elayne, all her placidity gone as if it had never been. "You have it in you to be the greatest Queen that Andor has ever seen, that any land has seen in more than a thousand years. It is for that we will shape you, if you have the strength for it."

Rand stared at her. She had to be Elaida, the Aes Sedai. Suddenly he was glad he had not come to her for help, no matter what her Ajah. A sternness far beyond Moiraine's radiated from her. He had sometimes thought of Moiraine as steel covered with velvet; with Elaida the velvet was only an illusion.

"Enough, Elaida," Morgase said, frowning uneasily. "She has heard that more than enough. The Wheel weaves as the Wheel wills." For a moment she was silent, looking at her daughter. "Now there is the problem of this young man"—she gestured to Rand without taking her eyes off Elayne's face—"and how and why he came here, and why you claimed guest-right for him to your brother."

"May I speak, mother?" When Morgase nodded her assent, Elayne told of events simply, from the time she first saw Rand climbing up the slope to the wall. He expected her to finish by proclaiming the innocence of what he had done, but instead she said, "Mother, often you tell me I must know our people, from the highest to the lowest, but whenever I meet any of them it is with a dozen attendants. How can I come to know anything real or true under such circumstances? In speaking with this young man I have already learned more about the people of the Two Rivers, what kind of people they are, than I ever could from books. It says something that he has come so far and has put on the red, when so many incomers wear the white from fear. Mother, I beg you not to misuse a loyal subject, and one who has taught me much about the people you rule."

"A loyal subject from the Two Rivers." Morgase sighed. "My child, you should pay more heed to those books. The Two Rivers has not seen a tax collector in six generations, nor the Queen's Guards in seven. I daresay they seldom even think to remember they are part of the Realm." Rand shrugged uncomfortably, recalling his surprise when he was told the Two Rivers was part of the Realm of Andor. The Queen saw him, and smiled ruefully at her daughter. "You see, child?"

Elaida had put down her knitting, Rand realized, and was studying him. She rose from her stool and slowly came down from the dais to stand before him. "From the Two Rivers?" she said. She reached a hand toward his head; he pulled away from her touch, and she let her hand drop. "With that red in his hair, and gray eyes? Two Rivers people are dark of hair and eye, and they seldom have such height." Her hand darted out to push back his coat sleeve, exposing lighter skin the sun had not reached so often. "Or such skin."

It was an effort not to clench his fists. "I was born in Emond's Field," he said stiffly. "My mother was an outlander; that's where my eyes come from. My father is Tam al'Thor, a shepherd and farmer, as I am."

Elaida nodded slowly, never taking her eyes from his face. He met her gaze with a levelness that belied the sour feeling in his stomach. He saw her note the steadiness of his look. Still meeting him eye to eye, she moved her hand slowly toward him again. He resolved not to flinch this time.

It was his sword she touched, not him, her hand closing around the hilt at the very top. Her fingers tightened and her eyes opened wide with surprise. "A shepherd from the Two Rivers," she said softly, a whisper meant to be heard by all, "with a heron-mark sword."

Those last few words acted on the chamber as if she had announced the Dark One. Leather and metal creaked behind Rand, boots scuffling on the marble tiles. From the corner of his eye he could see Tallanvor and another of the guardsmen backing away from him to gain room, hands on their swords, prepared to draw and, from their faces, prepared to die. In two quick strides Gareth Bryne was at the front of the dais, between Rand and the Queen. Even Gawyn put himself in front of Elayne, a worried look on his face and a hand on his dagger. Elayne herself looked at him as if she were seeing him for the first time. Morgase did not change expression, but her hands tightened on the gilded arms of her throne.

Only Elaida showed less reaction than the Queen. The Aes Sedai gave no sign that she had said anything out of the ordinary. She took her hand from the sword, causing the soldiers to tense even more. Her eyes stayed on his, unruffled and calculating.

"Surely," Morgase said, her voice level, "he is too young to have earned a heron-mark blade. He cannot be any older than Gawyn."

"It belongs with him," Gareth Bryne said.

The Queen looked at him in surprise. "How can that be?"

"I do not know, Morgase," Bryne said slowly. "He *is* too young, yet still it belongs with him, and he with it. Look at his eyes. Look how he stands, how the sword fits him, and he it. He is too young, but the sword is his."

When the Captain-General fell silent, Elaida said, "How did you come by this blade, Rand al'Thor from the Two Rivers?" She said it as if she doubted his name as much as she did where he was from.

"My father gave it to me," Rand said. "It was his. He thought I'd need a sword, out in the world."

"Yet *another* shepherd from the Two Rivers with a heron-mark blade." Elaida's smile made his mouth go dry. "When did you arrive in Caemlyn?"

He had had enough of telling this woman the truth. She made him as afraid as any Darkfriend had. It was time to start hiding again. "Today," he said. "This morning."

"Just in time," she murmured. "Where are you staying? Don't say you have not found a room somewhere. You look a little tattered, but you have had a chance to freshen. Where?"

"The Crown and Lion." He remembered passing The Crown and Lion while looking for The Queen's Blessing. It was on the other side of the New City from Master Gill's inn. "I have a bed there. In the attic." He had the feeling that she knew he was lying, but she only nodded.

"What chance this?" she said. "Today the unbeliever is brought into Caemlyn. In two days he will be taken north to Tar Valon, and with him goes the Daughter-Heir for her training. And at just this juncture a young man appears in the Palace gardens, claiming to be a loyal subject from the Two Rivers . . ."

"I *am* from the Two Rivers." They were all looking at him, but all ignored him. All but Tallanvor and the guards; those eyes never blinked.

". . . with a story calculated to entice Elayne and bearing a heron-mark blade. He does not wear an armband or a cockade to proclaim his allegiance, but wrappings that carefully conceal the heron from inquisitive eyes. What chance this, Morgase?"

The Queen motioned the Captain-General to stand aside, and when he did she studied Rand with a troubled look. It was to Elaida that she spoke, though. "What are you naming him? Darkfriend? One of Logain's followers?"

"The Dark One stirs in Shayol Ghul," the Aes Sedai replied. "The Shadow lies across the Pattern, and the future is balanced on the point of a pin. This one is dangerous."

Suddenly Elayne moved, throwing herself onto her knees before the throne. "Mother, I beg you not to harm him. He would have left immediately had I not stopped him. He wanted to go. It was I who made him stay. I cannot believe he is a Darkfriend."

Morgase made a soothing gesture toward her daughter, but her eyes remained on Rand. "Is this a Foretelling, Elaida? Are you reading the Pattern? You say it comes on you when you least expect it and goes as suddenly as it comes. If this is a Foretelling, Elaida, I command you to speak the truth clearly, without your usual habit of wrapping it in so much mystery that no one can tell if you have said yes or no. Speak. What do you see?"

"This I Foretell," Elaida replied, "and swear under the Light that I can say no clearer. From this day Andor marches toward pain and division. The Shadow has yet to darken to its blackest, and I cannot see if the Light will come after. Where the world has wept one tear, it will weep thousands. This I Foretell."

A pall of silence clung to the room, broken only by Morgase expelling her breath as if it were her last.

Elaida continued to stare into Rand's eyes. She spoke again, barely moving her lips, so softly that he could barely hear her less than an arm's length away. "This, too, I Foretell. Pain and division come to the whole world, and this man stands at the heart of it. I obey the Queen," she whispered, "and speak it clearly."

Rand felt as if his feet had become rooted in the marble floor. The cold and stiffness of the stone crept up his legs and sent a shiver up his spine. No one else could have heard. But she was still looking at him, and he had heard.

"I'm a shepherd," he said for the entire room. "From the Two Rivers. A shepherd."

"The Wheel weaves as the Wheel wills," Elaida said aloud, and he could not tell if there was a touch of mockery in her tone or not.

"Lord Gareth," Morgase said, "I need the advice of my Captain-General."

The blocky man shook his head. "Elaida Sedai says the lad is dangerous, My Queen, and if she could tell more I would say summon the headsman. But all she says is what any of us can see with our own eyes. There's not a farmer in the countryside won't say things will get worse, without any Foretelling. Myself, I believe the boy is here through mere happenstance, though an ill one for him. To be safe, My Queen, I say clap him in a cell till the Lady Elayne and the Lord Gawyn are well on their way, then let him go. Unless, Aes Sedai, you have more to Foretell concerning him?"

"I have said all that I have read in the Pattern, Captain-General," Elaida said. She flashed a hard smile at Rand, a smile that barely bent her lips, mocking his inability to say that she was not telling the truth. "A few weeks imprisoned will not harm him, and it may give me a chance to learn more." Hunger filled her eyes, deepening his chill. "Perhaps another Foretelling will come."

For a time Morgase considered, chin on her fist and elbow on the arm of her throne. Rand would have shifted under her frowning gaze if he could have moved at all, but Elaida's eyes froze him solid. Finally the Queen spoke.

"Suspicion is smothering Caemlyn, perhaps all of Andor. Fear and black suspicion. Women denounce their neighbors for Darkfriends. Men scrawl the Dragon's Fang on the doors of people they have known for years. I will not become part of it."

"Morgase—" Elaida began, but the Queen cut her off.

"I will not become part of it. When I took the throne I swore to uphold justice for the high and the low, and I will uphold it even if I am the last in Andor to remember justice. Rand al'Thor, do you swear under the Light that your father, a shepherd in the Two Rivers, gave you this heron-mark blade?"

Rand worked his mouth to get enough moisture to speak. "I do." Abruptly remembering to whom he was speaking he hastily added,

"My Queen." Lord Gareth raised a heavy eyebrow, but Morgase did not seem to mind.

"And you climbed the garden wall simply to gain a look at the false Dragon?"

"Yes, my Queen."

"Do you mean harm to the throne of Andor, or to my daughter, or my son?" Her tone said the last two would gain him even shorter shrift than the first.

"I mean no harm to anyone, my Queen. To you and yours least of all."

"I will give you justice then, Rand al'Thor," she said. "First, because I have the advantage of Elaida and Gareth in having heard Two Rivers speech when I was young. You have not the look, but if a dim memory can serve me you have the Two Rivers on your tongue. Second, no one with your hair and eyes would claim that he is a Two Rivers shepherd unless it was true. And that your father gave you a heron-mark blade is too preposterous to be a lie. And third, the voice that whispers to me that the best lie is often one too ridiculous to be taken for a lie . . . that voice is not proof. I will uphold the laws I have made. I give you your freedom, Rand al'Thor, but I suggest you take a care where you trespass in the future. If you are found on the Palace grounds again, it will not go so easily with you."

"Thank you, my Queen," he said hoarsely. He could feel Elaida's displeasure like a heat on his face.

"Tallanvor," Morgase said, "escort this . . . escort my daughter's guest from the Palace, and show him every courtesy. The rest of you go as well. No, Elaida, you stay. And if you will too, please, Lord Gareth. I must decide what to do about these Whitecloaks in the city."

Tallanvor and the guardsmen sheathed their swords reluctantly, ready to draw again in an instant. Still Rand was glad to let the soldiers form a hollow box around him and to follow Tallanvor. Elaida was only half attending what the Queen was saying; he could feel her eyes on his back. *What would have happened if Morgase had not kept the Aes Sedai with her?* The thought made him wish the soldiers would walk faster.

To his surprise, Elayne and Gawyn exchanged a few words outside the door, then fell in beside him. Tallanvor was surprised, too. The young officer looked from them back to the doors, closing now.

"My mother," Elayne said, "ordered him to be escorted from the Palace, Tallanvor. With every courtesy. What are you waiting for?"

Tallanvor scowled at the doors, behind which the Queen was conferring with her advisors. "Nothing, my Lady," he said sourly, and need-lessly ordered the escort forward.

The wonders of the Palace slid by Rand unseen. He was befuddled, snatches of thought spinning by too fast to grasp. *You have not the look. This man stands at the heart of it.*

The escort stopped. He blinked, startled to find himself in the great court at the front of the Palace, standing at the tall, gilded gates, gleaming in the sun. Those gates would not be opened for a single man, certainly not for a trespasser, even if the Daughter-Heir did claim guest-right for him. Wordlessly Tallanvor unbarred a sally-port, a small door set within one gate.

"It is the custom," Elayne said, "to escort guests as far as the gates, but not to watch them go. It is the pleasure of a guest's company that should be remembered, not the sadness of parting."

"Thank you, my Lady," Rand said. He touched the scarf bandaging his head. "For everything. Custom in the Two Rivers is for a guest to bring a small gift. I'm afraid I have nothing. Although," he added dryly, "apparently I did teach you something of the Two Rivers folk."

"If I had told Mother I think you are handsome, she certainly would have had you locked in a cell." Elayne favored him with a dazzling smile. "Fare you well, Rand al'Thor."

Gaping, he watched her go, a younger version of Morgase's beauty and majesty.

"Do not try to bandy words with her." Gawyn laughed. "She will win every time."

Rand nodded absently. *Handsome? Light, the Daughter-Heir to the throne of Andor!* He gave himself a shake to clear his head.

Gawyn seemed to be waiting for something. Rand looked at him for a moment.

"My Lord, when I told you I was from the Two Rivers you were surprised. And everybody else, your mother, Lord Gareth, Elaida Sedai"—a shiver ran down his back—"none of them. . . ." He could not finish it; he was not even sure why he started. *I am Tam al'Thor's son, even if I was not born in the Two Rivers.*

Gawyn nodded as if it was for this he had been waiting. Still he hesitated. Rand opened his mouth to take back the unspoken question, and Gawyn said, "Wrap a *shoufa* around your head, Rand, and you would be the image of an Aielman. Odd, since Mother seems to think you *sound* like a Two Rivers man, at least. I wish we could have come to know one another, Rand al'Thor. Fare you well."

An Aielman.

Rand stood watching Gawyn's retreating back until an impatient cough from Tallanvor reminded him where he was. He ducked through the sally-port, barely clearing his heels before Tallanvor slammed it behind him. The bars inside were jammed into place loudly.

The oval plaza in front of the Palace was empty, now. All the soldiers gone, all the crowds, trumpets, and drums vanished in silence. Nothing left but a scattering of litter blowing across the pavement and a few people hurrying about their business now that the excitement was done. He could not make out if they showed the red or the white. *Aielman.*

With a start he realized he was standing right in front of the Palace gates, right where Elaida could find him easily once she finished with the Queen. Pulling his cloak close, he broke into a trot, across the plaza and into the streets of the Inner City. He looked back frequently to see if anyone was following him, but the sweeping curves kept him from seeing very far. He could remember Elaida's eyes all too well, though, and imagined them watching. By the time he reached the gates to the New City, he was running.

CHAPTER
41

Old Friends and New Threats

B ack at The Queen's Blessing, Rand threw himself against the
front doorframe, panting. He had run all the way, not caring
if anyone saw that he wore the red, or even if they took his
running as an excuse to chase him. He did not think even a Fade could
have caught him.

Lamgwin was sitting on a bench by the door, a brindle cat in his
arms, when he came running up. The man stood to look for trouble
the way Rand had come, still calmly scratching behind the cat's ears.
Seeing nothing, he sat back down again, careful not to disturb the
animal. "Fools tried to steal some of the cats a while back," he said.
He examined his knuckles before going back to his scratching. "Good
money in cats these days."

The two men showing the white were still across the way, Rand saw,
one with a black eye and a swollen jaw. That one wore a sour scowl
and rubbed his sword hilt with a sullen eagerness as he watched the
inn.

"Where's Master Gill?" Rand asked.

"Library," Lamgwin replied. The cat began purring, and he grinned. "Nothing bothers a cat for long, not even somebody trying to stick him in a sack."

Rand hurried inside, through the common room, now with its usual complement of men wearing the red and talking over their ale. About the false Dragon, and whether the Whitecloaks would make trouble when he was taken north. No one cared what happened to Logain, but they all knew the Daughter-Heir and Lord Gawyn would be traveling in the party, and no man there would countenance any risk to them.

He found Master Gill in the library, playing stones with Loial. A plump tabby sat on the table, feet tucked under her, watching their hands move over the cross-hatched board.

The Ogier placed another stone with a touch oddly delicate for his thick fingers. Shaking his head, Master Gill took the excuse of Rand's appearance to turn from the table. Loial almost always won at stones. "I was beginning to worry where you were, lad. Thought you might have had trouble with some of those white-flashing traitors, or run into that beggar or something."

For a minute Rand stood there with his mouth open. He had forgotten all about that bundle-of-rags of a man. "I saw him," he said finally, "but that's nothing. I saw the Queen, too, and Elaida; that's where the trouble is."

Master Gill snorted a laugh. "The Queen, eh? You don't say. We had Gareth Bryne out in the common room an hour or so ago, arm-wrestling the Lord Captain-Commander of the Children, but the Queen, now . . . that's something."

"Blood and ashes," Rand growled, "everybody thinks I'm lying today." He tossed his cloak across the back of a chair and threw himself onto another. He was too wound up to sit back. He perched on the front edge, mopping his face with a handkerchief. "I saw the beggar, and he saw me, and I thought. . . . That's not important. I climbed up on a wall around a garden, where I could see the plaza in front of the Palace, where they took Logain in. And I fell off, on the inside."

"I almost believe you aren't making fun," the innkeeper said slowly.

"Ta'veren," Loial murmured.

"Oh, it happened," Rand said. "Light help me, it did."

Master Gill's skepticism melted slowly as he went on, turning to quiet alarm. The innkeeper leaned more and more forward until he was perched on the edge of his chair the same as Rand was. Loial listened impassively, except that every so often he rubbed his broad nose and the tufts on his ears gave a little twitch.

Rand told everything that had happened, everything except what Elaida had whispered to him. And what Gawyn had said at the Palace gate. One he did not want to think about; the other had nothing to do with anything. *I'm Tam al'Thor's son, even if I wasn't born in the Two Rivers. I am! I'm Two Rivers blood, and Tam is my father.*

Abruptly he realized he had stopped talking, caught up in his thoughts, and they were looking at him. For one panicky moment he wondered if he had said too much.

"Well," Master Gill said, "there's no more waiting for your friends for you. You will have to leave the city, and fast. Two days at the most. Can you get Mat on his feet in that time, or should I send for Mother Grubb?"

Rand gave him a perplexed look. "Two days?"

"Elaida is Queen Morgase's advisor, right next to Captain-General Gareth Bryne himself. Maybe ahead of him. If she sets the Queen's Guards looking for you—Lord Gareth won't stop her unless she interferes with their other duties—well, the Guards can search every inn in Caemlyn in two days. And that's saying some ill chance doesn't bring them here the first day, or the first hour. Maybe there's a little time if they start over at the Crown and Lion, but none for dawdling."

Rand nodded slowly. "If I can't get Mat out of that bed, you send for Mother Grubb. I have a little money left. Maybe enough."

"I'll take care of Mother Grubb," the innkeeper said gruffly. "And I suppose I can lend you a couple of horses. You try walking to Tar Valon and you'll wear through what's left of your boots halfway there."

"You're a good friend," Rand said. "It seems like we've brought you nothing but trouble, but you're still willing to help. A good friend."

Master Gill seemed embarrassed. He shrugged his shoulders and cleared his throat and looked down. That brought his eyes to the stones board, and he jerked them away again. Loial was definitely winning. "Aye, well, Thom's always been a good friend to me. If he's willing to go out of his way for you, I can do a little bit, too."

"I would like to go with you when you leave, Rand," Loial said suddenly.

"I thought that was settled, Loial." He hesitated—Master Gill still did not know the whole of the danger—then added, "You know what waits for Mat and me, what's chasing us."

"Darkfriends," the Ogier replied in a placid rumble, "and Aes Sedai, and the Light knows what else. Or the Dark One. You are going to Tar Valon, and there is a very fine grove there, which I have heard the Aes Sedai tend well. In any case, there is more to see in the world than the groves. You truly are *ta'veren,* Rand. The Pattern weaves itself around you, and you stand in the heart of it."

This man stands at the heart of it. Rand felt a chill. "I don't stand at the heart of anything," he said harshly.

Master Gill blinked, and even Loial seemed taken aback at his anger. The innkeeper and the Ogier looked at each other, and then at the floor. Rand forced his expression smooth, drawing deep breaths. For a wonder he found the void that had eluded him so often of late, and calmness. They did not deserve his anger.

"You can come, Loial," he said. "I don't know why you would want to, but I'd be grateful for the company. You . . . you know how Mat is."

"I know," Loial said. "I still cannot go into the streets without raising a mob shouting 'Trolloc' after me. But Mat, at least, only uses words. He has not tried to kill me."

"Of course not," Rand said. "Not Mat." *He wouldn't go that far. Not Mat.*

A tap came at the door, and one of the serving maids, Gilda, stuck her head into the room. Her mouth was tight, and her eyes worried. "Master Gill, come quickly, please. There's Whitecloaks in the common room."

Master Gill leaped up with an oath, sending the cat jumping from the table to stalk out of the room, tail stiff and offended. "I'll come. Run tell them I'm coming, then stay out of their way. You hear me, girl? Keep away from them." Gilda bobbed her head and vanished. "You had best stay here," he told Loial.

The Ogier snorted, a sound like sheets ripping. "I have no desire for any more meetings with the Children of the Light."

Master Gill's eye fell on the stones board and his mood seemed to lighten. "It looks as if we'll have to start the game over later."

"No need for that." Loial stretched an arm to the shelves and took down a book; his hands dwarfed the clothbound volume. "We can take up from where the board lies. It is your turn."

Master Gill grimaced. "If it isn't one thing, it's another," he muttered as he hurried from the room.

Rand followed him, but slowly. He had no more desire than Loial to become involved with the Children. *This man stands at the heart of it.* He stopped at the door to the common room, where he could see what went on, but far enough back that he hoped he would not be noticed.

Dead silence filled the room. Five Whitecloaks stood in the middle of the floor, studiously being ignored by the folk at the tables. One of them had the silver lightning-flash of an under-officer beneath the sunburst on his cloak. Lamgwin was lounging against the wall by the front door, intently cleaning his fingernails with a splinter. Four more of the guards Master Gill had hired were spaced across the wall with him, all industriously paying no attention at all to the Whitecloaks. If the Children of the Light noticed anything, they gave no sign. Only the under-officer showed any emotion at all, impatiently tapping his steel-backed gauntlets against his palm as he waited for the innkeeper.

Master Gill crossed the room to him quickly, a cautiously neutral look on his face. "The Light illumine you," he said with a careful bow, not too deep, but not slight enough to actually be insulting, either, "and our good Queen Morgase. How may I help—"

"I've no time for your drivel, innkeeper," the under-officer snapped. "I've been to twenty inns already today, each a worse pigsty than the last, and I'll see twenty more before the sun sets. I'm looking for Darkfriends, a boy from the Two Rivers—"

Master Gill's face grew darker with every word. He puffed up as if he would explode, and finally he did, cutting the Whitecloak off in turn. "There are no Darkfriends in my establishment! Every man here is a good Queen's man!"

"Yes, and we all know where Morgase stands," the under-officer twisted the Queen's name into a sneer, "and her Tar Valon witch, don't we?"

The scrape of chair legs was loud. Suddenly every man in the room was on his feet. They stood still as statues, but every one staring grimly at the Whitecloaks. The under-officer did not appear to notice, but the four behind him looked around uneasily.

"It will go easier with you, innkeeper," the under-officer said, "if you cooperate. The temper of the times goes hard with those who shelter Darkfriends. I wouldn't think an inn with the Dragon's Fang on its door would get much custom. Might have trouble with fire, with that on your door."

"You get out of here now," Master Gill said quietly, "or I'll send for the Queen's Guards to cart what's left of you to the middens."

Lamgwin's sword rasped out of its sheath, and the coarse scrape of steel on leather was repeated throughout the room as swords and daggers filled hands. Serving maids scurried for the doors.

The under-officer looked around in scornful disbelief. "The Dragon's Fang—"

"Won't help you five," Master Gill finished for him. He held up a clenched fist and raised his forefinger. "One."

"You must be mad, innkeeper, threatening the Children of the Light."

"Whitecloaks hold no writ in Caemlyn. Two."

"Can you really believe this will end here?"

"Three."

"We'll be back," the under-officer snapped, and then he was hastily turning his men around, trying to pretend he was leaving in good order and in his own time. He was hampered in this by the eagerness his men showed for the door, not running, but not making secret that they wanted to be outside.

Lamgwin stood across the door with his sword, only giving way in response to Master Gill's frantic waves. When the Whitecloaks were gone, the innkeeper dropped heavily onto a chair. He rubbed a hand across his forehead, then stared at it as if surprised that it was not covered with sweat. All over the room men seated themselves again, laughing over what they had done. Some went over to clap Master Gill on the shoulder.

When he saw Rand, the innkeeper tottered off the chair and over to him. "Who would have thought I had it in me to be a hero?" he said wonderingly. "The Light illumine me." Abruptly he gave himself a shake, and his voice regained almost its normal tone. "You'll have to stay out of sight until I can get you out of the city." With a careful look back into the common room, he pushed Rand deeper into the hall. "That lot will be back, or else a few spies wearing red for the day. After that little show I put on, I doubt they'll care whether you're here or not, but they'll act as though you are."

"That's crazy," Rand protested. At the innkeeper's gesture he lowered his voice. "The Whitecloaks don't have any reason to be after me."

"I don't know about reasons, lad, but they're after you and Mat for certain sure. What *have* you been up to? Elaida *and* the Whitecloaks."

Rand raised his hands in protest, then let them fall. It made no sense, but he had heard the Whitecloak. "What about you? The Whitecloaks will make trouble for you even when they don't find us."

"No worries about that, lad. The Queen's Guards still uphold the law, even if they do let traitors strut around showing white. As for the night . . . well, Lamgwin and his friends might not get much sleep, but I could almost pity anybody who tries to put a mark on my door."

Gilda appeared beside them, dropping a curtsy to Master Gill. "Sir, there's . . . there's a lady. In the kitchens." She sounded scandalized at the combination. "She's asking for Master Rand, sir, and Master Mat, by name."

Rand exchanged a puzzled look with the innkeeper.

"Lad," Master Gill said, "if you've actually managed to bring the Lady Elayne down from the Palace to my inn, we'll all end up facing the headsman." Gilda squeaked at the mention of the Daughter-Heir and gave Rand a round-eyed stare. "Off with you, girl," the innkeeper said sharply. "And keep quiet about what you've heard. It's nobody's business." Gilda bobbed again and darted down the hallway, flashing glances over her shoulder at Rand as she went. "In five minutes"—Master Gill sighed—"she will be telling the other women you're a prince in disguise. By nightfall it will be all over the New City."

"Master Gill," Rand said, "I never mentioned Mat to Elayne. It can't be—" Suddenly a huge smile lit up his face, and he ran for the kitchens.

"Wait!" the innkeeper called behind him. "Wait until you know. Wait, you fool!"

Rand threw open the door to the kitchens, and there they were. Moiraine rested her serene eyes on him, unsurprised. Nynaeve and Egwene ran laughing to throw their arms around him, with Perrin crowding in behind them, all three patting his shoulders as if they had to be convinced that he was really there. In the doorway leading to the stableyard Lan lounged with one boot up on the doorframe, dividing his attention between the kitchen and the yard outside.

Rand tried to hug the two women and shake Perrin's hand, all at the same time, and it was a tangle of arms and laughter complicated by Nynaeve trying to feel his face for fever. They looked somewhat the worse for wear—bruises on Perrin's face, and he had a way of keeping his eyes downcast that he had never had before—but they were alive, and together again. His throat was so tight he could barely talk. "I was afraid I'd never see you again," he managed finally. "I was afraid you were all. . . ."

"I knew you were alive," Egwene said against his chest. "I always knew it. Always."

"I did not," Nynaeve said. Her voice was sharp for just that moment, but it softened in the next, and she smiled up at him. "You look well, Rand. Not overfed by any means, but well, thank the Light."

"Well," Master Gill said behind him, "I guess you know these people after all. Those friends you were looking for?"

Rand nodded. "Yes, my friends." He made introductions all around; it still felt odd to be giving Lan and Moiraine their right names. They both eyed him sharply when he did.

The innkeeper greeted everyone with an open smile, but he was properly impressed at meeting a Warder, and especially at Moiraine. At her he gaped openly—it was one thing knowing an Aes Sedai had been helping the boys, quite something else having her appear in the kitchen—then bowed deeply. "You are welcome to The Queen's Blessing, Aes Sedai, as my guest. Though I suppose you will be staying at the Palace with Elaida Sedai, and the Aes Sedai who came with the false Dragon." Bowing again, he gave Rand a quick, worried look. It was all very well to say he did not speak ill of Aes Sedai, but that was not the same as saying he wanted one sleeping under his roof.

Rand nodded encouragingly, trying to tell him silently that it was all right. Moiraine was not like Elaida, with a threat hidden behind every glance, under every word. *Are you sure? Even now, are you sure?*

"I believe I will stay here," Moiraine said, "for the short time I remain in Caemlyn. And you must allow me to pay."

A calico cat sauntered in from the hallway to strop the innkeeper's ankles. No sooner had the calico begun than a fuzzy gray sprang from under the table, arching its back and hissing. The calico crouched with a threatening growl, and the gray streaked past Lan into the stableyard.

Master Gill began apologizing for the cats at the same time he protested that Moiraine would honor him by being his guest, and was she sure she would not prefer the Palace, which he would quite understand, but he hoped she would accept his best room as a gift. It made a jumble to which Moiraine seemed to pay no attention at all. Instead she bent down to scratch the orange-and-white cat; it promptly left Master Gill's ankles for hers.

"I've seen four other cats here, so far," she said. "You have a problem with mice? Rats?"

"Rats, Moiraine Sedai." The innkeeper sighed. "A terrible problem. Not that I don't keep a clean place, you understand. It's all the people. The whole city is full of people and rats. But my cats take care of it. You'll not be troubled, I promise."

Rand exchanged a fleeting look with Perrin, who put his eyes down again right away. There was something odd about Perrin's eyes. And he was so silent; Perrin was almost always slow to speak, but now he was saying nothing at all. "It could be all the people," he said.

"With your permission, Master Gill," Moiraine said, as if she took it for granted. "It is a simple matter to keep rats away from this street. With luck, the rats will not even realize they are being kept away."

Master Gill frowned at that last, but he bowed, accepting her offer. "If you are sure you don't want to stay at the Palace, Aes Sedai."

"Where is Mat?" Nynaeve said suddenly. "*She* said he was here, too."

"Upstairs," Rand said. "He's . . . not feeling well."

Nynaeve's head came up. "He's sick? I'll leave the rats to *her,* and I'll attend to him. Take me to him now, Rand."

"All of you go up," Moiraine said. "I will join you in a few minutes. We are crowding Master Gill's kitchen, and it would be best if we could all be somewhere quiet for a time." There was an undercurrent in her voice. *Stay out of sight. The hiding is not done yet.*

"Come on," Rand said. "We'll go up the back way."

The Emond's Field folk crowded after him to the back staircase, leaving the Aes Sedai and the Warder in the kitchen with Master Gill. He could not get over being back together. It was nearly as if he were home again. He could not stop grinning.

The same relief, almost joyous, seemed to be affecting the others. They chuckled to themselves, and kept reaching out to grip his arm. Perrin's voice seemed subdued, and he still kept his head down, but he began to talk as they climbed.

"Moiraine said she could find you and Mat, and she did. When we rode into the city, the rest of us couldn't stop staring—well, all except Lan, of course—all the people, the buildings, everything." His thick curls swung as he shook his head in disbelief. "It's all so big. And so many people. Some of them kept staring at us, too, shouting 'Red or white?' like it made some kind of sense."

Egwene touched Rand's sword, fingering the red wrappings. "What does it mean?"

"Nothing," he said. "Nothing important. We're leaving for Tar Valon, remember?"

Egwene gave him a look, but she removed her hand from the sword and took up where Perrin had left off. "Moiraine didn't look at anything any more than Lan did. She led us back and forth through all those streets so many times, like a dog hunting a scent, that I thought you couldn't be here. Then, all of a sudden, she took off down a street, and the next thing I knew we were handing the horses to the stablemen and marching into the kitchen. She never even asked if you were here. Just told a woman who was mixing batter to go tell Rand al'Thor and Mat Cauthon that someone wanted to see them. And there you were"—she grinned—"like a ball popping into the gleeman's hand out of nowhere."

"Where is the gleeman?" Perrin asked. "Is he with you?"

Rand's stomach lurched and the good feeling of having friends around him dimmed. "Thom's dead. I think he's dead. There was a Fade. . . ." He could not say any more. Nynaeve shook her head, muttering under her breath.

The silence thickened around them, stifling the little chuckles, flattening the joy, until they reached the head of the stairs.

"Mat's not sick, exactly," he said then. "It's. . . . You'll see." He flung open the door to the room he shared with Mat. "Look who's here, Mat."

Mat was still curled up in a ball on the bed, just as Rand had left him. He raised his head to stare at them. "How do you know they're really who they look like?" he said hoarsely. His face was flushed, the skin tight and slick with sweat. "How do I know you're who you look like?"

"Not sick?" Nynaeve gave Rand a disdainful look as she pushed past him, already unslinging her bag from her shoulder.

"Everybody changes," Mat rasped. "How can I be sure? Perrin? Is that you? You've changed, haven't you?" His laugh sounded more like a cough. "Oh, yes, you've changed."

To Rand's surprise Perrin dropped onto the edge of the other bed with his head in hands, staring at the floor. Mat's hacking laughter seemed to pierce him.

Nynaeve knelt beside Mat's bed and put a hand to his face, pushing up his headcloth. He jerked back from her with a scornful look. His eyes were bright and glazed. "You're burning," she said, "but you should not be sweating with this much fever." She could not keep the worry out of her voice. "Rand, you and Perrin fetch some clean cloths and as much cool water as you can carry. I'll bring your temperature down first, Mat, and—"

"Pretty Nynaeve," Mat spat. "A Wisdom isn't supposed to think of herself as a woman, is she? Not a pretty woman. But you do, don't you? Now. You can't make yourself forget that you're a pretty woman, now, and it frightens you. Everybody changes." Nynaeve's face paled as he spoke—whether with anger or something else, Rand could not tell. Mat gave a sly laugh, and his feverish eyes slid to Egwene. "Pretty Egwene," he croaked. "Pretty as Nynaeve. And you share other things now, don't you? Other dreams. What do you dream about now?" Egwene took a step back from the bed.

"We are safe from the Dark One's eyes for the time being," Moiraine announced as she walked into the room with Lan at her heels. Her
eyes fell on Mat as she stepped through the doorway, and she hissed
as if she had touched a hot stove. "Get away from him!"

Nynaeve did not move except for turning to stare at the Aes Sedai
in surprise. In two quick steps Moiraine seized the Wisdom by the
shoulders, hauling her across the floor like a sack of grain. Nynaeve
struggled and protested, but Moiraine did not release her until she was
well away from the bed. The Wisdom continued her protests as she
got to her feet, angrily straightening her clothes, but Moiraine ignored
her completely. The Aes Sedai watched Mat to the exclusion of everything else, eyeing him the way she would a viper.

"All of you stay away from him," she said. "And be quiet."

Mat stared back as intently as she. He bared his teeth in a silent,
snarling rictus, and pulled himself into an ever tighter knot, but he
never took his eyes from hers. Slowly she put one hand on him, lightly,
on a knee drawn up to his chest. A convulsion shook him at her touch,
a shudder of revulsion spasming through his entire body, and abruptly
he pulled one hand out, slashing at her face with the ruby-hilted
dagger.

One minute Lan was in the doorway, the next he was at the bedside,
as if he had not bothered with the intervening space. His hand caught
Mat's wrist, stopping the slash as if it had struck stone. Still Mat held
himself in that tight ball. Only the hand with the dagger tried to move,
straining against the Warder's implacable grip. Mat's eyes never left
Moiraine, and they burned with hate.

Moiraine also did not move. She did not flinch from the blade only
inches from her face, as she had not when he first struck. "How did
he come by this?" she asked in a steel voice. "I asked if Mordeth had
given you anything. I asked, and I warned you, and you said he had
not."

"He didn't," Rand said. "He. . . . Mat took it from the treasure
room." Moiraine looked at him, her eyes seeming to burn as much as
Mat's. He almost stepped back before she turned away again, back to
the bed. "I didn't know until after we were separated. I didn't know."

"You did not know." Moiraine studied Mat. He still lay with his
knees pulled up to his chest, still snarled soundlessly at her, and his
hand yet fought Lan to reach her with the dagger. "It is a wonder you
got this far, carrying this. I felt the evil of it when I laid eyes on him,
the touch of Mashadar, but a Fade could sense it for miles. Even
though he would not know exactly where, he would know it was near,

and Mashadar would draw his spirit while his bones remembered that this same evil swallowed an army—Dreadlords, Fades, Trollocs, and all. Some Darkfriends could probably feel it, too. Those who have truly given away their souls. There could not help but be those who would wonder at suddenly feeling this, as if the very air around them itched. They would be compelled to seek it. It should have drawn them to it as a magnet draws iron filings."

"There were Darkfriends," Rand said, "more than once, but we got away from them. And a Fade, the night before we reached Caemlyn, but he never saw us." He cleared his throat. "There are rumors of strange things in the night outside the city. It could be Trollocs."

"Oh, it's Trollocs, sheepherder," Lan said wryly. "And where Trollocs are, there are Fades." Tendons stood out on the back of his hand from the effort of holding Mat's wrist, but there was no strain in his voice. "They've tried to hide their passage, but I have seen sign for two days. And heard farmers and villagers mutter about things in the night. The Myrddraal managed to strike into the Two Rivers unseen, somehow, but every day they come closer to those who can send soldiers to hunt them down. Even so, they won't stop now, sheepherder."

"But we're in Caemlyn," Egwene said. "They can't get to us as long as—"

"They can't?" the Warder cut her off. "The Fades are building their numbers in the countryside. That's plain enough from the sign, if you know what to look for. Already there are more Trollocs than they need just to watch all the ways out of the city, a dozen fists, at least. There can only be one reason; when the Fades have enough numbers, they will come into the city after you. That act may send half the armies of the south marching to the Borderlands, but the evidence is that they're willing to take that risk. You three have escaped them too long. It looks as if you've brought a new Trolloc War to Caemlyn, sheepherder."

Egwene gave a gasping sob, and Perrin shook his head as though to deny it. Rand felt a sickness in his stomach at the thought of Trollocs in the streets of Caemlyn. All those people at one another's throats, never realizing the real threat waiting to come over the walls. What would they do when they suddenly found Trollocs and Fades in their midst, killing them? He could see the towers burning, flames breaking through the domes, Trollocs pillaging through the curving streets and vistas of the Inner City. The Palace itself in flames. Elayne, and Gawyn, and Morgase . . . dead.

"Not yet," Moiraine said absently. She was still intent on Mat. "If we can find a way out of Caemlyn, the Halfmen will have no more interest here. If. So many if's."

"Better we were all dead," Perrin said suddenly, and Rand jumped at the echo of his own thoughts. Perrin still sat staring at the floor—glaring at it now—and his voice was bitter. "Everywhere we go, we bring pain and suffering on our backs. It would be better for everyone if we were dead."

Nynaeve rounded on him, her face half fury and half worried fear, but Moiraine forestalled her.

"What do you think to gain, for yourself or anyone else, by dying?" the Aes Sedai asked. Her voice was level, yet sharp. "If the Lord of the Grave has gained as much freedom to touch the Pattern as I fear, he can reach you dead more easily than alive, now. Dead, you can help no one, not the people who have helped you, not your friends and family back in the Two Rivers. The Shadow is falling over the world, and none of you can stop it dead."

Perrin raised his head to look at her, and Rand gave a start. The irises of his friend's eyes were more yellow than brown. With his shaggy hair and the intensity of his gaze, there was something about him. . . . Rand could not grasp it enough to make it out.

Perrin spoke with a soft flatness that gave his words more weight than if he had shouted. "We can't stop it alive, either, now can we?"

"I will have time to argue with you later," Moiraine said, "but your friend needs me now." She stepped aside so they could all see Mat clearly. His eyes still on her with a rage-filled stare, he had not moved or changed his position on the bed. Sweat stood out on his face, and his lips were bloodless in an unchanging snarl. All of his strength seemed to be pouring into the effort to reach Moiraine with the dagger Lan held motionless. "Or had you forgotten?"

Perrin gave an embarrassed shrug and spread his hands wordlessly.

"What's wrong with him?" Egwene asked, and Nynaeve added, "Is it catching? I can still treat him. I don't seem to catch sick, no matter what it is."

"Oh, it is catching," Moiraine said, "and your . . . protection would not save you." She pointed to the ruby-hilted dagger, careful not to let her finger touch it. The blade trembled as Mat strained to reach her with it. "This is from Shadar Logoth. There is not a pebble of that city that is not tainted and dangerous to bring outside the walls, and this is far more than a pebble. The evil that killed Shadar Logoth is in it, and in Mat, too, now. Suspicion and hatred so strong that even those closest are seen as enemies, rooted so deep in the bone that eventually the only thought left is to kill. By carrying the dagger beyond the walls of Shadar Logoth he freed it, this seed of it, from what bound it to that place. It will have waxed and waned in him, what he is in the heart of him fighting what the contagion of Mashadar sought to make him, but now the battle inside him is almost done, and he almost defeated. Soon, if it does not kill him first, he will spread that evil like a plague wherever he goes. Just as one scratch from that blade is enough to infect and destroy, so, soon, a few minutes with Mat will be just as deadly."

Nynaeve's face had gone white. "Can you do anything?" she whispered.

"I hope so." Moiraine sighed. "For the sake of the world, I hope I am not too late." Her hand delved into the pouch at her belt and came out with the silk-shrouded *angreal*. "Leave me. Stay together, and find somewhere you will not be seen, but leave me. I will do what I can for him."

CHAPTER 42

Remembrance of Dreams

It was a subdued group that Rand led back down the stairs. None of them wanted to talk to him now, or to one another. He did not feel much like talking, either.

The sun was far enough across the sky to dim the back stairwell, but the lamps had not yet been lit. Sunlight and shadow striped the stairs. Perrin's face was as closed as the others, but where worry creased everyone else's brow, his was smooth. Rand thought the look Perrin wore was resignation. He wondered why, and wanted to ask, but whenever Perrin walked through a deeper patch of shadow, his eyes seemed to gather in what little light there was, glowing softly like polished amber.

Rand shivered and tried to concentrate on his surroundings, on the walnut paneled walls and the oak stair railing, on sturdy, everyday things. He wiped his hands on his coat several times, but each time sweat sprang out on his palms anew. *It'll all be all right, now. We're together again, and. . . . Light, Mat.*

He took them to the library by the back way that went by the kitchens, avoiding the common room. Not many travelers used the library; most of those who could read stayed at more elegant inns in the Inner City. Master Gill kept it more for his own enjoyment than for the handful of patrons who wanted a book now and then. Rand did not want to think why Moiraine wanted them to keep out of sight, but he kept remembering the Whitecloak under-officer saying he would be back, and Elaida's eyes when she asked where he was staying. Those were reasons enough, whatever Moiraine wanted.

He took five steps into the library before he realized that everyone else had stopped, crowded together in the doorway, openmouthed and goggling. A brisk blaze crackled in the fireplace, and Loial was sprawled on the long couch, reading, a small black cat with white feet curled and half asleep on his stomach. When they entered he closed the book with a huge finger marking his place and gently set the cat on the floor, then stood to bow formally.

Rand was so used to the Ogier that it took him a minute to realize that Loial was the object of the others' stares. "These are the friends I was waiting for, Loial," he said. "This is Nynaeve, the Wisdom of my village. And Perrin. And this is Egwene."

"Ah, yes," Loial boomed, "Egwene. Rand has spoken of you a great deal. Yes. I am Loial."

"He's an Ogier," Rand explained, and watched their amazement change in kind. Even after Trollocs and Fades in the flesh, it was still astonishing to meet a legend walking and breathing. Remembering his own first reaction to Loial, he grinned ruefully. They were doing better than he had.

Loial took their gaping in his stride. Rand supposed he hardly noticed it compared with a mob shouting "Trolloc." "And the Aes Sedai, Rand?" Loial asked.

"Upstairs with Mat."

The Ogier raised one bushy eyebrow thoughtfully. "Then he *is* ill. I suggest we all be seated. She will be joining us? Yes. Then there's nothing to do but wait."

The act of sitting seemed to loosen some catch inside the Emond's Field folk, as if being in a well-stuffed chair with a fire in the fireplace and a cat now curled up on the hearth made them feel at home. As soon as they were settled they excitedly began asking the Ogier questions. To Rand's surprise, Perrin was the first to speak.

"The *stedding*, Loial. Are they really havens, the way the stories say?" His voice was intent, as if he had a particular reason for asking.

Loial was glad to tell about the *stedding*, and how he came to be at

The Queen's Blessing, and what he had seen in his travels. Rand soon leaned back, only partly listening. He had heard it all before, in detail. Loial liked to talk, and talk at length when he had the slightest chance, though he usually seemed to think a story needed two or three hundred years of background to make it understood. His sense of time was very strange; to him three hundred years seemed a reasonable length of time for a story or explanation to cover. He always talked about leaving the *stedding* as if it were just a few months before, but it had finally come out that he had been gone more than three years.

Rand's thoughts drifted to Mat. *A dagger. A bloody knife, and it might kill him just from carrying it. Light, I don't want any more adventure. If she can heal him, we should all go . . . not home. Can't go home. Somewhere. We'll all go somewhere they've never heard of Aes Sedai or the Dark One. Somewhere.*

The door opened, and for a moment Rand thought he was still imagining. Mat stood there, blinking, with his coat buttoned up and the dark scarf wrapped low around his forehead. Then Rand saw Moiraine, with her hand on Mat's shoulder, and Lan behind them. The Aes Sedai was watching Mat carefully, as one watches someone only lately out of a sickbed. As always, Lan was watching everything while appearing to watch nothing.

Mat looked as if he had never been sick a day. His first, hesitant smile included everyone, though it slipped into an openmouthed stare at the sight of Loial, as if he were seeing the Ogier for the first time. With a shrug and a shake, he turned his attention back to his friends. "I . . . ah . . . that is. . . ." He took a deep breath. "It . . . ah . . . it seems I've been acting . . . ah . . . sort of oddly. I don't remember much of it, really." He gave Moiraine an uneasy look. She smiled back confidently, and he went on. "Everything is hazy after Whitebridge. Thom, and the. . . ." He shivered and hurried on. "The further from Whitebridge, the hazier it gets. I don't really remember arriving in Caemlyn at all." He eyed Loial askance. "Not really. Moiraine Sedai says I . . . upstairs, I . . . ah. . . ." He grinned, and suddenly he truly was the old Mat. "You can't hold a man to blame for what he does when he's crazy, can you?"

"You always were crazy," Perrin said, and for a moment he, too, sounded as of old.

"No," Nynaeve said. Tears made her eyes bright, but she was smiling. "None of us blames you."

Rand and Egwene began talking at once then, telling Mat how happy they were to see him well and how well he looked, with a few laughing comments thrown in about hoping that he was done with tricks now that one so ugly had been played on him. Mat met banter with banter as he found a chair with all of his old swagger. As he sat down, still grinning, he absentmindedly touched his coat as if to make sure that something tucked behind his belt was still there, and Rand's breath caught.

"Yes," Moiraine said quietly, "he still has the dagger." The laughter and talk was still going on among the rest of the Emond's Field folk, but she had noticed his sudden intake of breath and had seen what had caused it. She moved closer to his chair, where she did not have to raise her voice for him to hear clearly. "I cannot take it away from him without killing him. The binding has lasted too long, and grown too strong. That must be unknotted in Tar Valon; it is beyond me, or any lone Aes Sedai, even with an *angreal.*"

"But he doesn't look sick anymore." He had a thought and looked up at her. "As long as he has the dagger, the Fades will know where we are. Darkfriends, too, some of them. You said so."

"I have contained that, after a fashion. If they come close enough to sense it now, they will be on top of us anyway. I cleansed the taint from him, Rand, and did what I could to slow its return, but return it will, in time, unless he receives help in Tar Valon."

"A good thing that's where we're going, isn't it?" He thought maybe it was the resignation in his voice, and the hope for something else, that made her give him a sharp look before turning away.

Loial was on his feet, bowing to her. "I am Loial, son of Arent son of Halan, Aes Sedai. The *stedding* offers sanctuary to the Servants of the Light."

"Thank you, Loial, son of Arent," Moiraine answered dryly, "but I would not be too free with that greeting if I were you. There are perhaps twenty Aes Sedai in Caemlyn at this moment, and every one but I of the Red Ajah." Loial nodded sagely, as if he understood. Rand could only shake his head in confusion; he would be Light-blinded if *he* knew what she meant. "It is strange to find you here," the Aes Sedai went on. "Few Ogier leave the *stedding* in recent years."

"The old stories caught me, Aes Sedai. The old books filled my unworthy head with pictures. I want to see the groves. And the cities we built, too. There do not seem to be many of either still standing, but if buildings are a poor substitute for trees, they are still worth seeing. The Elders think I'm odd, wanting to travel. I always have, and they always have. None of them believe there is anything worth seeing outside the *stedding*. Perhaps when I return and tell them what

I've seen, they will change their minds. I hope so. In time."

"Perhaps they will," Moiraine said smoothly. "Now, Loial, you must forgive me for being abrupt. It is a failing of humankind, I know. My companions and I have urgent need to plan our journey. If you could excuse us?"

It was Loial's turn to look confused. Rand came to his rescue. "He's coming with us. I promised him he could."

Moiraine stood looking at the Ogier as if she had not heard, but finally she nodded. "The Wheel weaves as the Wheel wills," she murmured. "Lan, see that we are not taken unaware." The Warder vanished from the room, silently but for the click of the door shutting behind him.

Lan's disappearance acted like a signal; all talk was cut off. Moiraine moved to the fireplace, and when she turned back to the room every eye was on her. Slight of build as she was, her presence dominated. "We cannot remain long in Caemlyn, nor are we safe here in The Queen's Blessing. The Dark One's eyes are already in the city. They have not found what they are searching for, or they would not still be looking. That we have to our advantage. I have set wards to keep them away, and by the time the Dark One realizes that there is a part of the city the rats no longer enter, we will be gone. Any ward that will turn a man aside, though, would be as good as a beacon fire for the Myrddraal, and there are Children of the Light in Caemlyn, also, looking for Perrin and Egwene." Rand made a sound, and Moiraine raised an eyebrow at him.

"I thought they were looking for Mat and me," he said.

The explanation made both the Aes Sedai's eyebrows lift. "Why would you think the Whitecloaks were looking for you?"

"I heard one say they were looking for someone from the Two Rivers. Darkfriends, he said. What else was I supposed to think? With everything that's been happening, I'm lucky I can think at all."

"It has been confusing, I know, Rand," Loial put in, "but you can think more clearly than that. The Children hate Aes Sedai. Elaida would not—"

"Elaida?" Moiraine cut in sharply. "What has Elaida Sedai to do with this?"

She was looking at Rand so hard that he wanted to lean back. "She wanted to throw me in prison," he said slowly. "All I wanted was a look at Logain, but she wouldn't believe I was in the Palace gardens with Elayne and Gawyn just by chance." They were all staring at him as if he had suddenly sprouted a third eye, all except Loial. "Queen

Morgase let me go. She said there was no proof I meant any harm and she was going to uphold the law no matter what Elaida suspected." He shook his head, the memory of Morgase in all her radiance making him forget for a minute that anyone was looking at him. "Can you imagine me meeting a Queen? She's beautiful, like the queens in stories. So is Elayne. And Gawyn . . . you'd like Gawyn, Perrin. Perrin? Mat?" They were still staring. "Blood and ashes, I just climbed up on the wall for a look at the false Dragon. I didn't do anything wrong."

"That's what I always say," Mat said blandly, though he was suddenly grinning hard, and Egwene asked in a decidedly neutral voice, "Who's Elayne?"

Moiraine muttered something crossly.

"A Queen," Perrin said, shaking his head. "You really have had adventures. All we met were Tinkers and some Whitecloaks." He avoided looking at Moiraine so obviously that Rand saw the avoidance plain. Perrin touched the bruises on his face. "On the whole, singing with the Tinkers was more fun than the Whitecloaks."

"The Traveling People live for their songs," Loial said. "For all songs, for that matter. For the search for them, at least. I met some Tuatha'an a few years back, and they wanted to learn the songs we sing to trees. Actually, the trees won't listen to very many anymore, and so not many Ogier learn the songs. I have a scrap of that Talent, so Elder Arent insisted I learn. I taught the Tuatha'an what they could learn, but the trees never listen to humans. For the Traveling People they were only songs, and just as well received for that, since none was the song they seek. That's what they call the leader of each band, the Seeker. They come to Stedding Shangtai, sometimes. Few humans do."

"If you please, Loial," Moiraine said, but he cleared his throat suddenly and went on in a quick rumble as if afraid she might stop him.

"I've just remembered something, Aes Sedai, something I have always wanted to ask an Aes Sedai if ever I met one, since you know many things and have great libraries in Tar Valon, and now I have, of course, and . . . may I?"

"If you make it brief," she said curtly.

"Brief," he said as though wondering what it meant. "Yes. Well. Brief. There was a man came to Stedding Shangtai a little time back. This was not unusual in itself, at the time, since a great many refugees had come to the Spine of the World fleeing what you humans call the Aiel War." Rand grinned. A little time back; twenty years, near enough. "He was at the point of death, though there was no wound

or mark on him. The Elders thought it might be something Aes Sedai
had done"—Loial gave Moiraine an apologetic look—"since as soon
as he was within the *stedding* he quickly got well. A few months. One
night he left without a word to anyone, simply sneaked away when the
moon was down." He looked at Moiraine's face and cleared his throat
again. "Yes. Brief. Before he left, he told a curious tale which he said
he meant to carry to Tar Valon. He said the Dark One intended to
blind the Eye of the World, and slay the Great Serpent, kill time itself.
The Elders said he was as sound in his mind as in his body, but that
was what he said. What I have wanted to ask is, can the Dark One do
such a thing? Kill time itself? And the Eye of the World? Can he blind
the eye of the Great Serpent? What does it mean?"

Rand expected almost anything from Moiraine except what he saw.
Instead of giving Loial an answer, or telling him she had no time for
it now, she stood there staring right through the Ogier, frowning in
thought.

"That's what the Tinkers told us," Perrin said.

"Yes," Egwene said, "the Aiel story."

Moiraine turned her head slowly. No other part of her moved.
"What story?"

It was an expressionless look she gave them, but it made Perrin take
a deep breath, though when he spoke he was as deliberate as ever.
"Some Tinkers crossing the Waste—they said they could do that unharmed—found Aiel dying after a battle with Trollocs. Before the last
Aiel died, she—they were all women, apparently—told the Tinkers
what Loial just said. The Dark One—they called him Sightblinder—intends to blind the Eye of the World. This was only three years ago,
not twenty. Does it mean something?"

"Perhaps everything," Moiraine said. Her face was still, but Rand
had the feeling her mind raced behind those dark eyes.

"Ba'alzamon," Perrin said suddenly. The name cut off all sound in
the room. No one appeared to breathe. Perrin looked at Rand, then
at Mat, his eyes strangely calm and more yellow than ever. "At the
time I wondered where I'd heard that name before . . . the Eye of the
World. Now I remember. Don't you?"

"I don't want to remember anything," Mat said stiffly.

"We have to tell her," Perrin continued. "It's important now. We
can't keep it secret any longer. You see it, don't you, Rand?"

"Tell me what?" Moiraine's voice was harsh, and she seemed to be
bracing for a blow. Her gaze had settled on Rand.

He did not want to answer. He did not want to remember any more than Mat, but he did remember—and he knew Perrin was right. "I've. . . ." He looked at his friends. Mat nodded reluctantly, Perrin decisively, but at least they had done it. He did not have to face her alone. "We have had . . . dreams." He rubbed the spot on his finger where the thorn had stuck him once, remembering the blood when he woke. Queasily remembering the sunburned feel of his face another time. "Except maybe they weren't dreams, exactly. Ba'alzamon was in them." He knew why Perrin had used that name; it was easier than saying the Dark One had been in your dreams, inside your head. "He said . . . he said all sorts of things, but once he said the Eye of the World would never serve me." For a minute his mouth was as dry as dust.

"He told me the same thing," Perrin said, and Mat sighed heavily, then nodded. Rand found he had spit in his mouth again. "You aren't angry with us?" Perrin asked, sounding surprised, and Rand realized that Moiraine did not seem angry. She was studying them, but her eyes were clear and calm, if intent.

"More with myself than you. But I did ask you to tell me if you had strange dreams. In the beginning, I asked." Though her voice remained level, a flash of anger crossed her eyes, and was gone in an instant. "Had I known after the first such, I might have been able to. . . . There has not been a Dreamwalker in Tar Valon for nearly a thousand years, but I could have tried. Now it is too late. Each time the Dark One touches you, he makes the next touching easier for him. Perhaps my presence can still shield you somewhat, but even then. . . . Remember the stories of the Forsaken binding men to them? Strong men, men who had fought the Dark One from the start. Those stories are true, and none of the Forsaken had a tenth of the strength of their master, not Aginor or Lanfear, not Balthamel or Demandred, not even Ishamael, the Betrayer of Hope himself."

Nynaeve and Egwene were looking at him, Rand saw, him and Mat and Perrin all three. The women's faces were a blood-drained blend of fear and horror. *Are they afraid for us, or afraid of us?*

"What can we do?" he asked. "There has to be something."

"Staying close by me," Moiraine replied, "will help. Some. The protection from touching the True Source extends around me a little, remember. But you cannot always remain close to me. You can defend yourself, if you have the strength for it, but you must find the strength and will within yourself. I cannot give it to you."

"I think I've already found my protection," Perrin said, sounding resigned rather than happy.

"Yes," Moiraine said, "I suppose you have." She looked at him until he dropped his eyes, and even then she stood considering. Finally she turned to the others. "There are limits to the Dark One's power inside you. Yield even for an instant and he will have a string tied to your heart, a string you may never be able to cut. Surrender, and you will be his. Deny him, and his power fails. It is not easy when he touches your dreams, but it can be done. He can still send Halfmen against you, and Trollocs, and Draghkar, and other things, but he cannot make you his unless you let him."

"Fades are bad enough," Perrin said.

"I don't want him inside my head again," Mat growled. "Isn't there any way to keep him out?"

Moiraine shook her head. "Loial has nothing to fear, nor Egwene, nor Nynaeve. Out of the mass of humanity, the Dark One can touch an individual only by chance, unless that person seeks it. But for a time, at least, you three are central to the Pattern. A Web of Destiny is being woven, and every thread leads straight to you. What else did the Dark One say to you?"

"I don't remember it all that well," Perrin said. "There was something about one of us being chosen, something like that. I remember him laughing," he finished bleakly, "about who we were chosen by. He said I—we could serve him or die. And then we'd still serve him."

"He said the Amyrlin Seat would try to use us," Mat added, his voice fading as he remembered to whom he was speaking. He swallowed and went on. "He said just like Tar Valon used—he had some names. Davian, I think. I can't remember very well, either."

"Raolin Darksbane," Perrin said.

"Yes," Rand said, frowning. He had tried to forget everything about those dreams. It was unpleasant bringing them back. "Yurian Stonebow was another, and Guaire Amalasan." He stopped suddenly, hoping Moiraine had not noticed how suddenly. "I don't recognize any of them."

But he had recognized one, now that he dredged them from the depths of memory. The name he had barely stopped himself from saying. Logain. The false Dragon. *Light! Thom said they were dangerous names. Is that what Ba'alzamon meant? Moiraine wants to use one of us as a false Dragon? Aes Sedai hunt down false Dragons, they don't use them. Do they? Light help me, do they?*

Moiraine was looking at him, but he could not read her face. "Do you know them?" he asked her. "Do they mean anything?"

"The Father of Lies is a good name for the Dark One," Moiraine replied. "It was always his way to seed the worm of doubt wherever he could. It eats at men's minds like a canker. When you believe the Father of Lies, it is the first step toward surrender. Remember, if you surrender to the Dark One, he will make you his."

An Aes Sedai never lies, but the truth she speaks may not be the truth you think you hear. That was what Tam had said, and she had not really answered his question. He kept his face expressionless and held his hands still on his knees, trying not to scrub the sweat off them on his breeches.

Egwene was crying softly. Nynaeve had her arms around her, but she looked as if she wanted to cry, too. Rand almost wished he could.

"They are *all ta'veren,*" Loial said abruptly. He seemed brightened by the prospect, looking forward to watching from close by as the Pattern wove itself around them. Rand looked at him incredulously, and the Ogier gave an abashed shrug, but it was not enough to dim his eagerness.

"So they are," Moiraine said. "*Three* of them, when I expected one. A great many things have happened that I did not expect. This news concerning the Eye of the World changes much." She paused, frowning. "For a time the Pattern does seem to be swirling around all three of you, just as Loial says, and the swirl will grow greater before it becomes less. Sometimes being *ta'veren* means the Pattern is forced to bend to you, and sometimes it means the Pattern forces you to the needed path. The Web can still be woven many ways, and some of those designs would be disastrous. For you, for the world.

"We cannot remain in Caemlyn, but by any road, Myrddraal and Trollocs will be on us before we have gone ten miles. And just at this point we hear of a threat to the Eye of the World, not from one source, but three, each seeming independent of the others. The Pattern is forcing our path. The Pattern still weaves itself around you three, but what hand now sets the warp, and what hand controls the shuttle? Has the Dark One's prison weakened enough for him to exert that much control?"

"There's no need for that kind of talk!" Nynaeve said sharply. "You'll only frighten them."

"But not you?" Moiraine asked. "It frightens me. Well, perhaps you are right. Fear cannot be allowed to affect our course. Whether this is a trap or a timely warning, we must do what we must, and that is to reach the Eye of the World quickly. The Green Man must know of this threat."

Rand gave a start. *The Green Man?* The others stared, too, all but Loial, whose broad face looked worried.

"I cannot even risk stopping in Tar Valon for help," Moiraine continued. "Time traps us. Even if we could ride out of the city unhindered, it would take many weeks to reach the Blight, and I fear we no longer have weeks."

"The Blight!" Rand heard himself echoed in a chorus, but Moiraine ignored them all.

"The Pattern presents a crisis, and at the same time a way to surmount it. If I did not know it was impossible, I could almost believe the Creator is taking a hand. There is a way." She smiled as if at a private joke, and turned to Loial. "There was an Ogier grove here at Caemlyn, and a Waygate. The New City now spreads out over where the grove once stood, so the Waygate must be inside the walls. I know not many Ogier learn the Ways now, but one who has a Talent and learns the old Songs of Growing must be drawn to such knowledge, even if he believes it will never be used. Do you know the Ways, Loial?"

The Ogier shifted his feet uneasily. "I do, Aes Sedai, but—"

"Can you find the path to Fal Dara along the Ways?"

"I've never heard of Fal Dara," Loial said, sounding relieved.

"In the days of the Trolloc Wars it was known as Mafal Dadaranell. Do you know *that* name?"

"I know it," Loial said reluctantly, "but—"

"Then you can find the path for us," Moiraine said. "A curious turn, indeed. When we can neither stay nor leave by any ordinary means, I learn of a threat to the Eye, and in the same place there is one who can take us there in days. Whether it is the Creator, or fate, or even the Dark One, the Pattern has chosen our path for us."

"No!" Loial said, an emphatic rumble like thunder. Everyone turned to look at him and he blinked under the attention, but there was nothing hesitant about his words. "If we enter the Ways, we will all die—or be swallowed by the Shadow."

CHAPTER
43

Decisions and Apparitions

The Aes Sedai appeared to know what Loial meant, but she said nothing. Loial peered at the floor, rubbing under his nose with a thick finger, as if he was abashed by his outburst. No one wanted to speak.

"Why?" Rand asked at last. "Why would we die? What *are* the Ways?"

Loial glanced at Moiraine. She turned away to take a chair in front of the fireplace. The little cat stretched, its claws scratching on the hearthstone, and languidly walked over to butt its head against her ankles. She rubbed behind its ears with one finger. The cat's purring was a strange counterpoint to the Aes Sedai's level voice. "It is your knowledge, Loial. The Ways are the only path to safety for us, the only path to forestalling the Dark One, if only for a time, but the telling is yours."

The Ogier did not appear comforted by her speech. He shifted awkwardly on his chair before beginning. "During the Time of Madness, while the world was still being broken, the earth was in upheaval, and humankind was being scattered like dust on the wind. We Ogier were scattered, too, driven from the *stedding*, into the Exile and the Long Wandering, when the Longing was graven on our hearts." He gave Moiraine another sidelong look. His long eyebrows drew down into two points. "I will try to be brief, but this is not a thing that can be told too briefly. It is of the others I must speak, now, those few Ogier who held in their *stedding* while around them the world was tearing apart. And of the Aes Sedai"—he avoided looking at Moiraine, now—"the male Aes Sedai who were dying even as they destroyed the world in their madness. It was to those Aes Sedai—those who had so far managed to avoid the madness—that the *stedding* first made the offer of sanctuary. Many accepted, for in the *stedding* they were protected from the taint of the Dark One that was killing their kind. But they were cut off from the True Source. It was not just that they could not wield the One Power, or touch the Source; they could no longer even sense that the Source existed. In the end, none could accept that isolation, and one by one they left the *stedding*, hoping that by that time the taint was gone. It never was."

"Some in Tar Valon," Moiraine said quietly, "claim that Ogier sanctuary prolonged the Breaking and made it worse. Others say that if all of those men had been allowed to go mad at once, there would have been nothing left of the world. I am of the Blue Ajah, Loial; unlike the Red Ajah, we hold to the second view. Sanctuary helped to save what could be saved. Continue, please."

Loial nodded gratefully. Relieved of a concern, Rand realized.

"As I was saying," the Ogier went on, "the Aes Sedai, the male Sedai, left. But before they went, they gave a gift to the Ogier in thanks for our sanctuary. The Ways. Enter a Waygate, walk for a day, and you may depart through another Waygate a hundred miles from where you started. Or five hundred. Time and distance are strange in the Ways. Different paths, different bridges, lead to different places, and how long it takes to get there depends on which path you take. It was a marvelous gift, made more so by the times, for the Ways are not part of the world we see around us, nor perhaps of any world outside themselves. Not only did the Ogier so gifted not have to travel through the world, where even after the Breaking men fought like animals to live, in order to reach another *stedding*, but within the Ways there was no Breaking. The land between two *stedding* might split open into deep canyons or rise in mountain ranges, but in the Way between them there was no change.

"When the last Aes Sedai left the *stedding*, they gave to the Elders a key, a talisman, that could be used for growing more. They are a living thing in some fashion, the Ways and the Waygates. I do not understand it; no Ogier ever has, and even the Aes Sedai have forgotten, I am told. Over the years the Exile ended for us. As those Ogier who had been gifted by the Aes Sedai found a *stedding* where Ogier had returned from the Long Wandering, they grew a Way to it. With the stonework we learned during the Exile, we built cities for men, and planted the groves to comfort the Ogier who did the building, so the Longing would not overcome them. To those groves Ways were grown. There was a grove, and a Waygate, at Mafal Dadaranell, but that city was razed during the Trolloc Wars, no stone left standing on another, and the grove was chopped down and burned for Trolloc fires." He left no doubt which had been the greater crime.

"Waygates are all but impossible to destroy," Moiraine said, "and humankind not much less so. There are people at Fal Dara still, though not the great city the Ogier built, and the Waygate yet stands."

"How did they make them?" Egwene asked. Her puzzled look took in Moiraine and Loial both. "The Aes Sedai, the men. If they couldn't use the One Power in a *stedding*, how could they make the Ways? Or did they use the Power at all? Their part of the True Source was tainted. Is tainted. I don't know much about what Aes Sedai can do, yet. Maybe it's a silly question."

Loial explained. "Each *stedding* has a Waygate on its border, but outside. Your question is not silly. You've found the seed of why we do not dare travel the Ways. No Ogier has used the Ways in my lifetime, and before. By edict of the Elders, all the Elders of all the *stedding,* none may, human or Ogier.

"The Ways were made by men wielding Power fouled by the Dark One. About a thousand years ago, during what you humans call the War of the Hundred Years, the Ways began to change. So slowly in the beginning that none really noticed, they grew dank and dim. Then darkness fell along the bridges. Some who went in were never seen again. Travelers spoke of being watched from the dark. The numbers who vanished grew, and some who came out had gone mad, raving about *Machin Shin,* the Black Wind. Aes Sedai Healers could aid some, but even with Aes Sedai help they were never the same. And they never remembered anything of what had occurred. Yet it was as if the darkness had sunken into their bones. They never laughed again, and they feared the sound of the wind."

For a moment there was silence but for the cat purring beside Moiraine's chair, and the snap and crackle of the fire, popping out sparks.

Then Nynaeve burst out angrily, "And you expect us to follow you into that? You must be mad!"

"Which would you choose instead?" Moiraine asked quietly. "The Whitecloaks within Caemlyn, or the Trollocs without? Remember that my presence in itself gives some protection from the Dark One's works."

Nynaeve settled back with an exasperated sigh.

"You still have not explained to me," Loial said, "why I should break the edict of the Elders. And I have no desire to enter the Ways. Muddy as they often are, the roads men make have served me well enough since I left Stedding Shangtai."

"Humankind and Ogier, everything that lives, we are at war with the Dark One," Moiraine said. "The greater part of the world does not even know it yet, and most of the few who do fight skirmishes and believe they are battles. While the world refuses to believe, the Dark One may be at the brink of victory. There is enough power in the Eye of the World to undo his prison. If the Dark One has found some way to bend the Eye of the World to his use. . . ."

Rand wished the lamps in the room were lit. Evening was creeping over Caemlyn, and the fire in the fireplace did not give enough light. He wanted no shadows in the room.

"What can we do?" Mat burst out. "Why are we so important? Why do we have to go to the Blight? The Blight!"

Moiraine did not raise her voice, but it filled the room, compelling. Her chair by the fire suddenly seemed like a throne. Suddenly even Morgase would have paled in her presence. "One thing we can do. We can try. What seems like chance is often the Pattern. Three threads have come together here, each giving a warning: the Eye. It cannot be chance; it is the Pattern. You three did not choose; you were chosen by the Pattern. And you are here, where the danger is known. You can step aside, and perhaps doom the world. Running, hiding, will not save you from the weaving of the Pattern. Or you can try. You can go to the Eye of the World, three ta'veren, three centerpoints of the Web, placed where the danger lies. Let the Pattern be woven around you there, and you may save the world from the Shadow. The choice is yours. I cannot make you go."

"I'll go," Rand said, trying to sound resolute. However hard he sought the void, images kept flashing through his head. Tam, and the farmhouse, and the flock in the pasture. It had been a good life; he had never really wanted anything more. There was comfort—a small comfort—hearing Perrin and Mat add their agreement to his. They sounded as dry-mouthed as he.

"I suppose there isn't any choice for Egwene or me, either," Nynaeve said.

Moiraine nodded. "You are part of the Pattern, too, both of you, in some fashion. Perhaps not *ta'veren*—perhaps—but strong even so. I have known it since Baerlon. And no doubt by this time the Fades know it, too. And Ba'alzamon. Yet you have as much choice as the young men. You could remain here, proceed to Tar Valon once the rest of us have gone."

"Stay behind!" Egwene exclaimed. "Let the rest of you go off into danger while we hide under the covers? I won't do it!" She caught the Aes Sedai's eye and drew back a little, but not all of her defiance vanished. "I won't do it," she muttered stubbornly.

"I suppose that means both of us will accompany you." Nynaeve sounded resigned, but her eyes flashed when she added, "You still need my herbs, Aes Sedai, unless you've suddenly gained some ability I don't know about." Her voice held a challenge Rand did not understand, but Moiraine merely nodded and turned to the Ogier.

"Well, Loial, son of Arent son of Halan?"

Loial opened his mouth twice, his tufted ears twitching, before he spoke. "Yes, well. The Green Man. The Eye of the World. They're mentioned in the books, of course, but I don't think any Ogier has actually seen them in, oh, quite a long time. I suppose. . . . But must it be the Ways?" Moiraine nodded, and his long eyebrows sagged till the ends brushed his cheeks. "Very well, then. I suppose I must guide you. Elder Haman would say it's no less than I deserve for being so hasty all the time."

"Our choices are made, then," Moiraine said. "And now that they are made, we must decide what to do about them, and how."

Long into the night they planned. Moiraine did most of it, with Loial's advice concerning the Ways, but she listened to questions and suggestions from everyone. Once dark fell Lan joined them, adding his comments in that iron-cored drawl. Nynaeve made a list of what supplies they needed, dipping her pen in the inkwell with a steady hand despite the way she kept muttering under her breath.

Rand wished he could be as matter-of-fact as the Wisdom. He could not stop pacing up and down, as if he had energy to burn or burst from it. He knew his decision was made, knew it was the only one he could make with the knowledge he had, but that did not make him like it. The Blight. Shayol Ghul was somewhere in the Blight, beyond the Blasted Lands.

He could see the same worry in Mat's eyes, the same fear he knew was in his own. Mat sat with his hands clasped, knuckles white. If he let go, Rand thought, he would be clutching the dagger from Shadar Logoth instead.

There was no worry on Perrin's face at all, but what was there was worse: a mask of weary resignation. Perrin looked as though he had fought something until he could fight it no longer and was waiting for it to finish him. Yet sometimes. . . .

"We do what we must, Rand," he said. "The Blight. . . ." For an instant those yellow eyes lit with eagerness, flashing in the fixed tiredness of his face, as if they had a life of their own apart from the big blacksmith's apprentice. "There's good hunting along the Blight," he whispered. Then he shuddered, as if he had just heard what he had said, and once more his face was resigned.

And Egwene. Rand drew her apart at one point, over by the fireplace where those planning around the table could not hear. "Egwene, I. . . ." Her eyes, like big dark pools drawing him in, made him stop and swallow. "It's me the Dark One's after, Egwene. Me, and Mat, and Perrin. I don't care what Moiraine Sedai says. In the morning you and Nynaeve could start for home, or Tar Valon, or anywhere you want to go, and nobody will try to stop you. Not the Trollocs, not the Fades, not anybody. As long as you aren't with us. Go home, Egwene. Or go to Tar Valon. But go."

He waited for her to tell him she had as much right to go where she wanted as he did, that he had no right to tell her what to do. To his surprise, she smiled and touched his cheek.

"Thank you, Rand," she said softly. He blinked, and closed his mouth as she went on. "You know I can't, though. Moiraine Sedai told us what Min saw, in Baerlon. You should have told me who Min was. I thought. . . . Well, Min says I am part of this, too. And Nynaeve. Maybe I'm not *ta'veren*," she stumbled over the word, "but the Pattern sends me to the Eye of the World, too, it seems. Whatever involves you, involves me."

"But, Egwene—"

"Who is Elayne?"

For a minute he stared at her, then told the simple truth. "She's the Daughter-Heir to the throne of Andor."

Her eyes seemed to catch fire. "If you can't be serious for more than a minute, Rand al'Thor, I do not want to talk to you."

Incredulous, he watched her stiff back return to the table, where she leaned on her elbows next to Moiraine to listen to what the Warder was saying. *I need to talk to Perrin,* he thought. *He knows how to deal with women.*

Master Gill entered several times, first to light the lamps, then to bring food with his own hands, and later to report on what was happening outside. Whitecloaks were watching the inn from down the street in both directions. There had been a riot at the gates to the Inner City, with the Queen's Guards arresting white cockades and red alike. Someone had tried to scratch the Dragon's Fang on the front door and been sent on his way by Lamgwin's boot.

If the innkeeper found it odd that Loial was with them, he gave no sign of it. He answered the few questions Moiraine put to him without trying to discover what they were planning, and each time he came he knocked at the door and waited till Lan opened it for him, just as if it were not his inn and his library. On his last visit, Moiraine gave him the sheet of parchment covered in Nynaeve's neat hand.

"It won't be easy this time of night," he said, shaking his head as he perused the list, "but I'll arrange it all."

Moiraine added a small wash-leather bag that clinked as she handed it to him by the drawstrings. "Good. And see that we are wakened before daybreak. The watchers will be at their least alert, then."

"We'll leave them watching an empty box, Aes Sedai." Master Gill grinned.

Rand was yawning by the time he shuffled out of the room with the rest in search of baths and beds. As he scrubbed himself, with a coarse cloth in one hand and a big yellow cake of soap in the other, his eyes drifted to the stool beside Mat's tub. The golden-sheathed tip of the dagger from Shadar Logoth peeked from under the edge of Mat's neatly folded coat. Lan glanced at it from time to time, too. Rand wondered if it was really as safe to have around as Moiraine claimed.

"Do you think my da'll ever believe it?" Mat laughed, scrubbing his back with a long-handled brush. "Me, saving the world? My sisters won't know whether to laugh or cry."

He sounded like the old Mat. Rand wished he could forget the dagger.

It was pitch-black when he and Mat finally got up to their room under the eaves, the stars obscured by clouds. For the first time in a long while Mat undressed before getting into bed, but he casually tucked the dagger under his pillow, too. Rand blew out the candle and crawled into his own bed. He could feel the wrongness from the other bed, not from Mat, but from beneath his pillow. He was still worrying about it when sleep came.

From the first he knew it was a dream, one of those dreams that was not entirely dream. He stood staring at the wooden door, its surface dark and cracked and rough with splinters. The air was cold and dank, thick with the smell of decay. In the distance water dripped, the splashes hollow echoes down stone corridors.

Deny it. Deny him, and his power fails.

He closed his eyes and concentrated on The Queen's Blessing, on his bed, on himself asleep in his bed. When he opened his eyes the door was still there. The echoing splashes came on his heartbeat, as if his pulse counted time for them. He sought the flame and the void, as Tam had taught him, and found inner calm, but nothing outside of him changed. Slowly he opened the door and went in.

Everything was as he remembered it in the room that seemed burned out of the living rock. Tall, arched windows led onto an un-railed balcony, and beyond it the layered clouds streamed like a river in flood. The black metal lamps, their flames too bright to look at, gleamed, black yet somehow as bright as silver. The fire roared but gave no heat in the fearsome fireplace, each stone still vaguely like a face in torment.

All was the same, but one thing was different. On the polished table-top stood three small figures, the rough, featureless shapes of men, as if the sculptor had been hasty with his clay. Beside one stood a wolf, its clear detail emphasized by the crudeness of the man-shape, and another clutched a tiny dagger, a point of red on the hilt glittering in the light. The last held a sword. The hair stirring on the back of his neck, he moved close enough to see the heron in exquisite detail on that small blade.

His head jerked up in panic, and he stared directly into the lone mirror. His reflection was still a blur, but not so misty as before. He could almost make out his own features. If he imagined he was squinting, he could nearly tell who it was.

"You've hidden from me too long."

He whirled from the table, breath rasping his throat. A moment before he had been alone, but now Ba'alzamon stood before the windows. When he spoke caverns of flame replaced his eyes and mouth.

"Too long, but not much longer."

"I deny you," Rand said hoarsely. "I deny that you hold any power over me. I deny that you are."

Ba'alzamon laughed, a rich sound rolling from fire. "Do you think it is that easy? But then, you always did. Each time we have stood like this, you have thought you could defy me."

"What do you mean, each time? I deny you!"

"You always do. In the beginning. This contest between us has taken place countless times before. Each time your face is different, and your name, but each time it is you."

"I deny you." It was a desperate whisper.

"Each time you throw your puny strength against me, and each time, in the end, you know which of us is the master. Age after Age, you kneel to me, or die wishing you still had strength to kneel. Poor fool, you can never win against me."

"Liar!" he shouted. "Father of Lies. Father of Fools if you can't do better than that. Men found you in the last Age, in the Age of Legends, and bound you back where you belong."

Ba'alzamon laughed again, peal after mocking peal, until Rand wanted to cover his ears to shut it out. He forced his hands to stay at his sides. Void or no, they were trembling when the laughter finally stopped.

"You worm, you know nothing at all. As ignorant as a beetle under a rock, and as easily crushed. This struggle has gone on since the moment of creation. Always men think it a new war, but it is just the same war discovered anew. Only now change blows on the winds of time. Change. This time there will be no drifting back. Those proud Aes Sedai who think to stand you up against me. I will dress them in chains and send them running naked to do my bidding, or stuff their souls into the Pit of Doom to scream for eternity. All but those who already serve me. They will stand but a step beneath me. You can choose to stand with them, with the world groveling at your feet. I offer it one more time, one last time. You can stand above them, above every power and dominion but mine. There have been times when you made that choice, times when you lived long enough to know your power."

Deny him! Rand grabbed hold to what he could deny. "No Aes Sedai serve you. Another lie!"

"Is that what they told you? Two thousand years ago I took my Trollocs across the world, and even among Aes Sedai I found those who knew despair, who knew the world could not stand before Shai'tan. For two thousand years the Black Ajah has dwelt among the others, unseen in the shadows. Perhaps even those who claim to help you."

Rand shook his head, trying to shake away the doubts that came welling up in him, all the doubts he had had about Moiraine, about what the Aes Sedai wanted with him, about what she planned for him. "What do you want from me?" he cried. *Deny him! Light help me deny him!*

"Kneel!" Ba'alzamon pointed to the floor at his feet. "Kneel, and acknowledge me your master! In the end, you will. You will be my creature, or you will die."

The last word echoed through the room, reverberating back on itself, doubling and redoubling, till Rand threw up his arms as if to shield his head from a blow. Staggering back until he thumped into the table, he shouted, trying to drown the sound in his ears. "Noooooooooooo!"

As he cried out, he spun, sweeping the figures to the floor. Something stabbed his hand, but he ignored it, stomping the clay to shapeless smears underfoot. But when his shout failed, the echo was still there, and growing stronger:

die-die-die-die-die-DIE-DIE-DIE-DIE-DIE-DIE-DIE-DIE-DIE-DIE-DIE-DIE

The sound pulled on him like a whirlpool, drawing him in, ripping the void in his mind to shreds. The light dimmed, and his vision narrowed down to a tunnel with Ba'alzamon standing tall in the last spot of brightness at the end, dwindling until it was the size of his hand, a fingernail, nothing. Around and around the echo whirled him, down into blackness and death.

The thump as he hit the floor woke him, still struggling to swim up out of that darkness. The room was dark, but not so dark as that. Frantically he tried to center on the flame, to shovel fear into it, but the calm of the void eluded him. Tremors ran down his arms and legs, but he held the image of the single flame until the blood stopped pounding in his ears.

Mat was tossing and twisting on his bed, groaning in his sleep. ". . . deny you, deny you, deny you. . . ." It faded off into unintelligible moans.

Rand reached out to shake him awake, and at the first touch Mat sat up with a strangled grunt. For a minute Mat stared around wildly, then drew a long, shuddering breath and dropped his head into his hands. Abruptly he twisted around, digging under his pillow, then sank back clutching the ruby-hilted dagger in both hands on his chest. He turned his head to look at Rand, his face hidden in shadow. "He's back, Rand."

"I know."

Mat nodded. "There were these three figures. . . ."

"I saw them, too."

"He knows who I am, Rand. I picked up the one with the dagger, and he said, 'So that's who you are.' And when I looked again, the figure had my face. My face, Rand! It looked like flesh. It felt like flesh. Light help me, I could feel my own hand gripping me, like I was the figure."

Rand was silent for a moment. "You have to keep denying him, Mat."

"I did, and he laughed. He kept talking about some eternal war, and saying we'd met like that a thousand times before, and. . . . Light, Rand, the Dark One knows me."

"He said the same thing to me. I don't think he does," he added slowly. "I don't think he knows which of us. . . ." *Which of us what?*

As he levered himself up, pain stabbed his hand. Making his way to the table, he managed to get the candle lit after three tries, then spread his hand open in the light. Driven into his palm was a thick splinter of dark wood, smooth and polished on one side. He stared at it, not breathing. Abruptly he was panting, plucking at the splinter, fumbling with haste.

"What's the matter?" Mat asked.

"Nothing."

Finally he had it, and a sharp yank pulled it free. With a grunt of disgust he dropped it, but the grunt froze in his throat. As soon as the splinter left his fingers, it vanished.

The wound was still there in his hand, though, bleeding. There was water in the stoneware pitcher. He filled the basin, his hands shaking so that he splashed water onto the table. Hurriedly he washed his hands, kneading his palm till his thumb brought more blood, then washed them again. The thought of the smallest sliver remaining in his flesh terrified him.

"Light," Mat said, "he made me feel dirty, too." But he still lay where he was, holding the dagger in both hands.

"Yes," Rand said. "Dirty." He fumbled a towel from the stack beside the basin. There was a knock at the door, and he jumped. It came again. "Yes?" he said.

Moiraine put her head into the room. "You are awake already. Good. Dress quickly and come down. We must be away before first light."

"Now?" Mat groaned. "We haven't had an hour's sleep yet."

"An hour?" she said. "You have had four. Now hurry, we do not have much time."

Rand shared a confused look with Mat. He could remember every second of the dream clearly. It had begun as soon as he closed his eyes, and lasted only minutes.

Something in that exchange must have communicated itself to Moiraine. She gave them a penetrating look and came all the way in. "What has happened? The dreams?"

"He knows who I am," Mat said. "The Dark One knows my face."

Rand held up his hand wordlessly, palm toward her. Even in the shadowed light from the one candle the blood was plain.

The Aes Sedai stepped forward and grasped his upheld hand, her thumb across his palm covering the wound. Cold pierced him to the bone, so chill that his fingers cramped and he had to fight to keep them open. When she took her fingers away, the chill went, too.

He turned his hand, then, stunned, scrubbed the thin smear of blood away. The wound was gone. Slowly he raised his eyes to meet those of the Aes Sedai.

"Hurry," she said softly. "Time grows very short."

He knew she was not speaking of the time for their leaving anymore.

CHAPTER
44

The Dark Along the Ways

In the darkness just before dawn Rand followed Moiraine down to the back hall, where Master Gill and the others were waiting, Nynaeve and Egwene as anxiously as Loial, Perrin almost as calm as the Warder. Mat stayed on Rand's heels as if he were afraid to be even a little alone now, even as much as a few feet away. The cook and her helpers straightened, staring as the party passed silently into the kitchen, already brightly lit and hot with preparations for breakfast. It was not usual for patrons of the inn to be up and out at that hour. At Master Gill's soothing words, the cook gave a loud sniff and slapped her dough down hard. They were all back to tending griddles and kneading dough before Rand reached the stableyard door.

Outside, the night was still pitch-black. To Rand, everyone else was only a darker shadow at best. He followed the innkeeper and Lan blindly, blind in truth, hoping Master Gill's knowledge of his own stableyard and the Warder's instincts would get them across it without someone breaking a leg. Loial stumbled more than once.

"I don't see why we can't have just one light," the Ogier grumbled.

"We don't go running about in the dark in the *stedding*. I'm an Ogier, not a cat." Rand had a sudden image of Loial's tufted ears twitching irritably.

The stable loomed up suddenly out of the night, a threatening mass until the stable door creaked open, spilling a narrow stream of light into the yard. The innkeeper only opened it wide enough for them to go in one at a time, and hastily pulled it to behind Perrin, almost clipping his heels. Rand blinked in the sudden light inside.

The stablemen were not surprised by their appearance, as the cook had been. Their horses were saddled and waiting. Mandarb stood arrogantly, ignoring everyone but Lan, but Aldieb stretched her nose out to nuzzle Moiraine's hand. There was a packhorse, bulky with wicker panniers, and a huge animal with hairy fetlocks, taller even than the Warder's stallion, for Loial. It looked big enough to pull a loaded haywain by itself, but compared with the Ogier it seemed a pony.

Loial eyed the big horse and muttered doubtfully, "My own feet have always been good enough."

Master Gill motioned to Rand. The innkeeper was lending him a bay almost the color of his own hair, tall and deep of chest, but with none of the fire in his step that Cloud had had, Rand was glad to see. Master Gill said his name was Red.

Egwene went straight to Bela, and Nynaeve to her long-legged mare.

Mat brought his dun-colored horse over by Rand. "Perrin's making me nervous," he muttered. Rand looked at him sharply. "Well, he's acting strange. Don't you see it, too? I swear it's not my imagination, or . . . or. . . ."

Rand nodded. *Not the dagger taking hold of him again, thank the Light.* "He is, Mat, but just be easy. Moiraine knows about . . . whatever it is. Perrin's fine." He wished he could believe it, but it seemed to satisfy Mat, a little at least.

"Of course," Mat said hastily, still watching Perrin out of the corner of his eye. "I never said he wasn't."

Master Gill conferred with the head groom. That leathery-skinned man, with a face like one of the horses, knuckled his forehead and hurried to the back of the stable. The innkeeper turned to Moiraine with a satisfied smile on his round face. "Ramey says the way is clear, Aes Sedai."

The rear wall of the stable appeared solid and stout, lined with heavy racks of tools. Ramey and another stableman cleared away the hayforks, rakes, and shovels, then reached behind the racks to manipulate hidden latches. Abruptly a section of the wall swung inward on hinges so well concealed that Rand was not sure he could find them even with the disguised door standing open. Light from the stable illuminated a brick wall only a few feet away.

"It's only a narrow run between buildings," the innkeeper said, "but nobody outside this stable knows there's a way into it from here. Whitecloaks or white cockades, there'll not be any watchers to see where you come out."

The Aes Sedai nodded. "Remember, good innkeeper, if you fear any trouble from this, write to Sheriam Sedai, of the Blue Ajah, in Tar Valon, and she will help. I fear my sisters and I have a good deal to put right already for those who have helped me."

Master Gill laughed; not the laugh of a worried man. "Why, Aes Sedai, you've already given me the only inn in all of Caemlyn without any rats. What more could I ask for? I can double my custom on that alone." His grin faded into seriousness. "Whatever you're up to, the Queen holds with Tar Valon, and I hold with the Queen, so I wish you well. The Light illumine you, Aes Sedai. The Light illumine you all."

"The Light illumine you, also, Master Gill," Moiraine replied with a bow of her head. "But if the Light is to shine on any of us, we must be quick." Briskly she turned to Loial. "Are you ready?"

With a wary look at its teeth, the Ogier took the reins of the big horse. Trying to keep that mouth the length of the reins from his hand, he led the animal to the opening at the back of the stable. Ramey hopped from one foot to the other, impatient to close it again. For a moment Loial paused with his head cocked as if feeling a breeze on his cheek. "This way," he said, and turned down the narrow alley.

Moiraine followed right behind Loial's horse, then Rand, and Mat. Rand had the first turn leading the packhorse. Nynaeve and Egwene made the middle of the column, with Perrin behind them, and Lan bringing up the rear. The hidden door swung hastily shut as soon as Mandarb stepped into the dirt alleyway. The *snick-snick* of latches locking, shutting them off, sounded unnaturally loud to Rand.

The run, as Master Gill had called it, was very narrow indeed, and even darker than the stableyard, if that was possible. Tall, blank walls of brick or wood lined both sides, with only a narrow strip of black sky overhead. The big, woven baskets slung on the packhorse scraped the buildings on both sides. The panniers bulged with supplies for the journey, most of it clay jars filled with oil. A bundle of poles was lashed lengthwise down the horse's back, and each had a lantern swinging at the end of it. In the Ways, Loial said, it was darker than the darkest night.

The partially-filled lanterns sloshed with the motion of the horse, and clinked against each other with a tinny sound. It was not a very loud noise, but in the hour before dawn Caemlyn was quiet. Silent. The dull metallic clinks sounded as if they could be heard a mile away.

When the run let out into a street, Loial chose his direction without a pause. He seemed to know exactly where he was going, now, as if the route he needed to follow was becoming clearer. Rand did not understand how the Ogier could find the Waygate, and Loial had not been able to explain very well. He just knew, he said; he could feel it. Loial claimed it was like trying to explain how to breathe.

As they hurried up the street Rand looked back toward the corner where The Queen's Blessing lay. According to Lamgwin, there were still half a dozen Whitecloaks not far down from that corner. Their interest was all on the inn, but a noise would surely bring them. No one was out at this hour for a reputable reason. The horseshoes seemed to ring on the paving stones like bells; the lanterns clattered as if the packhorse were shaking them deliberately. Not until they had rounded another corner did he stop looking over his shoulder. He heard relieved sighs from the other Emond's Fielders as they came round it, too.

Loial appeared to be following the most direct path to the Waygate, wherever it took them. Sometimes they trotted down broad avenues, empty save for an occasional dog skulking in the dark. Sometimes they hurried along alleys as narrow as the stable run, where things squished under an unwary step. Nynaeve complained softly about the resulting smells, but no one slowed down.

The darkness began to lessen, fading toward a dark gray. Faint glimmers of dawn pearled the sky above the eastern rooftops. A few people appeared on the streets, bundled up against the early cold, heads down while they yet dreamed of their beds. Most paid no mind to anyone else. Only a handful even glanced at the line of people and horses with Loial at its head, and only one of those truly saw them.

That one man flicked his eyes at them, just like the others, already sinking back into his own thoughts when suddenly he stumbled and almost fell, turning himself back around to stare. There was only light enough to see shapes, but that was too much. Seen at a distance by himself, the Ogier could have passed for a tall man leading an ordinary horse, or for an ordinary man leading an under-sized horse. With the others in a line behind him to give perspective, Loial looked exactly as big as he was, half again as tall as any man should be. The man took one look and, with a strangled cry, set off running, his cloak flapping behind him.

There would be more people in the streets soon—very soon. Rand eyed a woman hurrying past on the other side of the street, seeing nothing but the pavement in front of her feet. More people to notice soon. The eastern sky grew lighter.

"There," Loial announced at last. "It is under there." It was a shop he pointed to, still closed for the night. The tables out front were bare, the awnings over them rolled up tight, the door stoutly shuttered. The windows above, where the shopkeeper lived, were still dark.

"Under?" Mat exclaimed incredulously. "How in the Light can we—?"

Moiraine raised a hand that cut him off, and motioned for them to follow her into the alley beside the shop. Horses and people together, they crowded the opening between the two buildings. Shaded by the walls, it was darker there than on the street, near to full night again.

"There must be a cellar door," Moiraine muttered. "Ah, yes."

Abruptly light blossomed. A coolly glowing ball the size of a man's fist hung suspended over the Aes Sedai's palm, moving as she moved her hand. Rand thought that it was a measure of what they had been through that everyone seemed to take it as a matter of course. She put it close to the doors she had found, slanted almost flat to the ground, with a hasp held by thick bolts and an iron lock bigger than Rand's hand and thick with old rust.

Loial gave the lock a tug. "I can pull it off, hasp and all, but it will make enough noise to wake the whole neighborhood."

"Let us not damage the goodman's property if we can avoid it." Moiraine studied the lock intently for a moment. Suddenly she gave the rusty iron a tap with her staff, and the lock fell open neatly.

Hastily Loial undid the lock and swung the doors up, propping them back. Moiraine went down the ramp thus revealed, lighting her way with the glowing ball. Aldieb stepped delicately behind her.

"Light the lanterns and come down," she called softly. "There is plenty of room. Hurry. It will be light out soon."

Rand hurriedly untied the poled lanterns off the packhorse, but even before the first was lit he realized he could see Mat's features. People would be filling the streets in minutes, and the shopkeeper would be coming down to open up for business, all wondering why the alleyway was crammed full of horses. Mat muttered something nervously about taking horses indoors, but Rand was glad to lead his down the ramp. Mat followed, grumbling but no less quickly.

Rand's lantern swung on the end of its pole, bumping the ceiling if he was not careful, and neither Red nor the packhorse liked the ramp. Then he was down and getting out of Mat's way. Moiraine let her floating light die, but as the rest joined them, the added lanterns lit the open space.

The cellar was as long and as wide as the building above, much of the space taken up by brick columns, flaring up from narrow bases to five times as big at the ceiling. The place seemed made up from a series of arches. There was plenty of room, but Rand still felt crowded. Loial's head brushed the ceiling. As the rusted lock had foretold, the cellar had not been used in a long time. The floor was bare except for a few broken barrels filled with odds and ends, and a thick layer of dust. Motes, stirred up by so many feet, sparkled in the lantern light.

Lan was last in, and as soon as he had Mandarb down the ramp he climbed back to pull the doors shut.

"Blood and ashes," Mat growled, "why would they build one of these gates in a place like this?"

"It was not always like this," Loial said. His rumbling voice echoed in the cavernous space. "Not always. No!" The Ogier was angry, Rand realized with a shock. "Once trees stood here. Every kind of tree that would grow in this place, every kind of tree that Ogier could coax to grow here. The Great Trees, a hundred spans high. Shade of branch, and cool breezes to catch the smell of leaf and flower and hold the memory of the peace of the *stedding*. All that, murdered for this!" His fist thumped a column.

The column seemed to shake under that blow. Rand was certain he heard bricks crack. Waterfalls of dry mortar slid down the column.

"What is already woven cannot be undone," Moiraine said gently. "It will not make the trees grow again for you to bring the building down on our heads." Loial's drooping eyebrows made him look more abashed than a human face could have managed. "With your help, Loial, perhaps we can keep the groves that still stand from falling under the Shadow. You have brought us to what we seek."

As she moved to one of the walls, Rand realized that that wall was different from the others. They were ordinary brick; this was intricately worked stone, fanciful swirls of leaves and vines, pale even under its coat of dust. The brick and mortar were old, but something about the stone said it had stood there long, long before the brick was fired. Later builders, themselves centuries gone, had incorporated what already stood, and still later men had made it part of a cellar.

One part of the carved stone wall, right in the center, was more elaborate than the rest. As well done as the rest was, it appeared a crude copy in comparison. Worked in hard stone, those leaves seemed soft, caught in one frozen moment as a gentle summer breeze stirred them. For all of that, they had the feel of age, as much greater than the rest of the stone as the rest was older than the brick. That old and more. Loial looked at them as if he would rather be anywhere else but there, even out in the streets with another mob.

"*Avendesora*," Moiraine murmured, resting her hand on a trefoil leaf in the stonework. Rand scanned the carving; that was the only leaf of its kind he could find. "The leaf of the Tree of Life is the key," the Aes Sedai said, and the leaf came away in her hand.

Rand blinked; from behind him he heard gasps. That leaf had seemed no less a part of the wall than any other. Just as simply, the Aes Sedai set it against the pattern a handspan lower. The three-pointed leaf fit there as if the space had been intended for it, and once more it was a part of the whole. As soon as it was in place the entire nature of the central stonework changed.

He was sure now that he could see the leaves ruffled by some unfelt breeze; he almost thought they were verdant under the dust, a tapestry of thick spring greenery there in the lantern-lit cellar. Almost imperceptibly at first, a split opened up in the middle of the ancient carving, widening as the two halves slowly swung into the cellar until they stood straight out. The backs of the gates were worked as the fronts, the same profusion of vines and leaves, almost alive. Behind, where should have been dirt or the cellar of the next building, a dull, reflective shimmering faintly caught their images.

"I have heard," Loial said, half mourning, half fearful, "that once the Waygates shone like mirrors. Once, who entered the Ways walked through the sun and the sky. Once."

"We have no time for waiting," Moiraine said.

Lan went past her, leading Mandarb, poled lantern in hand. His shadowy reflection approached him, leading a shadowy horse. Man and reflection seemed to step into each other at the shimmering surface, and both were gone. For a moment the black stallion balked, an apparently continuous rein connecting him to the dim shape of his own image. The rein tightened, and the warhorse, too, vanished.

For a minute everyone in the cellar stood staring at the Waygate.

"Hurry," Moiraine urged. "I must be the last through. We cannot leave this open for anyone to find by chance. Hurry."

With a heavy sigh Loial strode into the shimmer. Tossing its head, his big horse tried to hold back from the surface and was hauled through. They were gone as completely as the Warder and Mandarb.

Hesitantly, Rand poked his lantern at the Waygate. The lantern sank into its reflection, the two merging until both were gone. He made himself keep on walking forward, watching the pole disappear into itself inch by inch, and then he was stepping into himself, entering the gate. His mouth fell open. Something icy slid along his skin, as if he were passing through a wall of cold water. Time stretched out; the cold enveloped one hair at a time, shivered over his clothes thread by thread.

Abruptly the chill burst like a bubble, and he paused to catch his breath. He was inside the Ways. Just ahead Lan and Loial waited patiently by their horses. All around them was blackness that seemed to stretch on forever. Their lanterns made a small pool of light around them, too small, as if something pressed back the light, or ate it.

Of a sudden anxious, he jerked at his reins. Red and the packhorse came leaping through, nearly knocking him down. Stumbling, he caught himself and hurried to the Warder and the Ogier, pulling the nervous horses behind him. The animals whickered softly. Even Mandarb appeared to take some comfort from the presence of other horses.

"Go easy when you pass through a Waygate, Rand," Loial cautioned. "Things are . . . different inside the Ways than out. Look."

He looked back the way the Ogier pointed, thinking to see the same dull shimmer. Instead he could see into the cellar, as if through a large piece of smoked glass set in the blackness. Disturbingly the darkness around the window into the cellar gave a sense of depth, as though the opening stood alone with nothing around or behind it but the dark. He said as much with a shaky laugh, but Loial took him seriously.

"You could walk all the way around it, and you would not see a thing from the other side. I would not advise it, though. The books aren't very clear about what lies behind the Waygates. I think you could become lost there, and never find your way out."

Rand shook his head and tried to concentrate on the Waygate itself rather than what lay behind it, but that was just as disturbing in its own fashion. If there had been anything to look at in the darkness besides the Waygate, he would have looked at it. In the cellar, through the smoky dimness, Moiraine and the others were plain enough, but they moved as if in a dream. Every blink of an eye seemed a deliberate, exaggerated gesture. Mat was making his way to the Waygate as though walking through clear jelly, his legs seeming to swim forward.

"The Wheel turns faster in the Ways," Loial explained. He looked at the darkness surrounding them, and his head sunk in between his shoulders. "None alive know more than fragments. I fear what I don't know about the Ways, Rand."

"The Dark One," Lan said, "cannot be defeated without chancing risks. But we are alive at this moment, and before us is the hope of remaining alive. Do not surrender before you are beaten, Ogier."

"You would not speak so confidently if you had ever been in the Ways." The normal distant thunder of Loial's voice was muted. He stared at the blackness as if he saw things there. "I never have before, either, but I've seen Ogier who have been through a Waygate and come out again. You would not speak so if you had."

Mat stepped through the gate and regained normal speed. For an instant he stared at the seemingly endless darkness, then came running to join them, his lantern bobbing on its pole, his horse leaping behind him, almost sending him sprawling. One by one the others passed through, Perrin and Egwene and Nynaeve, each pausing in shocked silence before hurrying to join the rest. Each lantern enlarged the pool of light, but not as much as it should have. It was as if the dark became denser the more light there was, thickening as it fought against being diminished.

That was not a line of reasoning Rand wanted to follow. It was bad enough just being there without giving the darkness a will of its own. Everyone seemed to feel the oppressiveness, though. There were no wry comments from Mat here, and Egwene looked as if she wished she could rethink her decision to come. They all silently watched the Waygate, that last window into the world they knew.

Finally only Moiraine was left in the cellar, dimly lit by the lantern she had taken. The Aes Sedai still moved in that dreamlike way. Her hand crept as it found the leaf of *Avendesora*. It was located lower in the stonework on this side, Rand saw, just where she had placed it on the other. Plucking it free, she put it back in the original position. He wondered suddenly if the leaf on the other side had moved back, too.

The Aes Sedai came through, leading Aldieb, as the stone gates slowly, slowly began closing behind her. She came to join them, the light of her lantern leaving the gates before they were shut. Blackness swallowed the narrowing view of the cellar. In the constrained light of their lanterns, blackness surrounded them totally.

Suddenly it seemed as if the lanterns were the only light left in the world. Rand realized that he was jammed shoulder-to-shoulder in between Perrin and Egwene. Egwene gave him a wide-eyed look and pressed closer, and Perrin made no move to give him room. There was something comforting about touching another human being when the whole world had just been swallowed up by dark. Even the horses seemed to feel the Ways pushing them into a tighter and tighter knot.

Outwardly unconcerned, Moiraine and Lan swung into their saddles, and the Aes Sedai leaned forward, arms resting on her carved staff across the high pommel of her saddle. "We must be on our way, Loial."

Loial gave a start, and nodded vigorously. "Yes. Yes, Aes Sedai, you are right. Not a minute longer than need be." He pointed to a broad strip of white running under their feet, and Rand stepped away from it hastily. All the Two Rivers folk did. Rand thought the floor had been smooth once, but the smoothness was pitted now, as if the stone had the pox. The white line was broken in several places. "This leads from the Waygate to the first Guiding. From there. . . ." Loial looked around anxiously, then scrambled onto his horse with none of the reluctance he had shown earlier. The horse wore the biggest saddle the head groom had been able to find, but Loial filled it from pommel to cantle. His feet hung down on either side almost to the animal's knees. "Not a minute longer than need be," he muttered. Reluctantly the others mounted.

Moiraine and Lan rode on either side of the Ogier, following the white line through the dark. Everyone else crowded in behind as close as they could get, the lanterns bobbing over their heads. The lanterns should have given enough light to fill a house, but ten feet away from them it stopped. The blackness stopped it as if it had struck a wall. The creak of saddles and click of horseshoes on stone seemed to travel only to the edge of light.

Rand's hand kept drifting to his sword. It was not that he thought there was anything out there against which he could use the sword to defend himself; it did not seem as if there was anywhere for something to be. The bubble of light around them could as well have been a cave surrounded by stone, completely surrounded, with no way out. The horses might have been walking a treadmill for the change around them. He gripped the hilt as if the pressure of his hand there could press away the stone he felt weighing down on him. Touching the sword, he could remember Tam's teaching. For a little while he could find the calm of the void. But the weight always returned, compressing the void until it was only a cavern inside his mind, and he had to start over again, touching Tam's sword to remember.

It was a relief when something did change, even if it was only a tall slab of stone, standing on end, that appeared out of the dark before them, the broad white line stopping at its base. Sinuous curves of metal inlaid the wide surface, graceful lines that vaguely reminded Rand of vines and leaves. Discolored pocks marked stone and metal alike.

"The Guiding," Loial said, and leaned out of his saddle to frown at the cursive metal inlays.

"Ogier script," Moiraine said, "but so broken I can barely make out what it says."

"I hardly can, either," Loial said, "but enough to know we go this way." He turned his horse aside from the Guiding.

The edges of their light caught other stoneworks, what appeared to be stone-walled bridges arcing off into the darkness, and gently sloping ramps, without railings of any kind, leading up and down. Between the bridges and the ramps ran a chest-high balustrade, however, as though falling was a danger there at any rate. Plain white stone made the balustrade, in simple curves and rounds fitted together in complex patterns. Something about all of it seemed almost familiar to Rand, but he knew it had to be his imagination groping for anything familiar where everything was strange.

At the foot of one of the bridges Loial paused to read the single line on the narrow column stone there. Nodding, he rode up onto the bridge. "This is the first bridge of our path," he said over his shoulder.

Rand wondered what held the bridge up. The horses' hooves made a gritty sound, as if bits of stone flaked off at every step. Everything he could see was covered with shallow holes, some tiny pinpricks, others shallow, rough-edged craters a stride across, as if there had been a rain of acid, or the stone was rotting. The guardwall showed cracks and holes, too. In places it was gone altogether for as much as a span. For all he knew the bridge could be solid stone all the way to the center of the earth, but what he saw made him hope it would stand long enough for them to reach the other end. *Wherever that is.*

The bridge did end, eventually, in a place that looked no different from its beginning. All Rand could see was what their little pool of light touched, but he had the impression that it was a large space, like a flat-topped hill, with bridges and ramps leaving all around it. An Island, Loial called it. There was another script-covered Guiding—Rand placed it in the middle of the Island, with no way of knowing if he was right or not. Loial read, then took them up one of the ramps, curving up and up.

After an interminable climb, curving continuously, the ramp let off onto another Island just like the one where it had begun. Rand tried to imagine the curve of the ramp and gave up. *This Island can't be right on top of the other one. It can't be.*

Loial consulted yet another slab filled with Ogier script, found another signpost column, led them onto another bridge. Rand no longer had any idea in what direction they were traveling.

In their huddle of light in the dark, one bridge was exactly like another, except that some had breaks in the guardwalls and some did not. Only the degree of damage to the Guidings gave any difference to the Islands. Rand lost track of time; he was not even sure how many bridges they had crossed or how many ramps they had traveled. The Warder must have had a clock in his head, though. Just when Rand felt the first stir of hunger, Lan announced quietly that it was midday and dismounted to parcel out bread and cheese and dried meat from the packhorse. Perrin was leading the animal by that time. They were on an Island, and Loial was busily deciphering the directions on the Guiding.

Mat started to climb down from his saddle, but Moiraine said, "Time is too valuable in the Ways to waste. For us, much too valuable. We will stop when it is time to sleep." Lan was already back on Mandarb.

Rand's appetite slipped at the thought of sleeping in the Ways. It was always night there, but not the kind of night for sleeping. He ate while he rode, though, like everyone else. It was an awkward affair, trying to juggle his food, the lantern pole, and his reins, but for all of his imagined lack of appetite he licked the last crumbs of bread and cheese off his hands when he was done, and thought fondly of more. He even began to think the Ways were not so bad, not nearly as bad as Loial made out. They might have the heavy feel of the hour before a storm, but nothing changed. Nothing happened. The Ways were almost boring.

Then the silence was broken by a startled grunt from Loial. Rand stood in his stirrups to peer past the Ogier, and swallowed hard at what he saw. They were in the middle of a bridge, and only a few feet ahead of Loial the bridge ended in a jagged gap.

CHAPTER
45

What Follows in Shadow

The light of their lanterns stretched just far enough to touch the other side, thrusting out of the dark like a giant's broken teeth. Loial's horse stamped a hoof nervously, and a loose stone fell away into the dead black below. If there was any sound of it striking bottom, Rand never heard it.

He edged Red closer to the gap. As far down as he could thrust his lantern on its pole, there was nothing. Blackness below as blackness above, shearing off the light. If there was a bottom, it could be a thousand feet down. Or never. But on the other side, he could see what was under the bridge, holding it up. Nothing. Less than a span in thickness, and absolutely nothing underneath.

Abruptly the stone under his feet seemed as thin as paper, and the endless drop over the edge pulled at him. The lantern and pole seemed suddenly heavy enough to pull him right out of the saddle. Head spinning, he backed the bay away from the abyss as cautiously as he had approached.

"Is it to this you've brought us, Aes Sedai?" Nynaeve said. "All this just to find out we have to go back to Caemlyn after all?"

"We do not have to go back," Moiraine said. "Not all the way to Caemlyn. There are many paths along the Ways to any place. We need only go back far enough for Loial to find another path that will lead to Fal Dara. Loial? Loial!"

The Ogier pulled himself away from staring at the gap with a visible effort. "What? Oh. Yes, Aes Sedai. I can find another path. I had. . . ." His eyes drifted back to the chasm, and his ears twitched. "I had not dreamed the decay had gone so far. If the bridges themselves are breaking, it may be that I cannot find the path you want. It may be that I cannot find a path back, either. The bridges could be falling behind us even now."

"There has to be a way," Perrin said, his voice flat. His eyes seemed to gather the light, to glow golden. *A wolf at bay,* Rand thought, startled. *That's what he looks like.*

"It will be as the Wheel weaves," Moiraine said, "but I do not believe the decay is as fast as you fear. Look at the stone, Loial. Even I can tell that this is an old break."

"Yes," Loial said slowly. "Yes, Aes Sedai. I can see it. There is no rain or wind here, but that stone has been in the air for ten years, at least." He nodded with a relieved grin, so happy with the discovery that for a moment he seemed to forget his fear. Then he looked around and shrugged uncomfortably. "I could find other paths more easily than Mafal Dadaranell. Tar Valon, for instance? Or Stedding Shangtai. It's only three bridges to Stedding Shangtai from the last Island. I suppose the Elders want to talk to me by this time."

"Fal Dara, Loial," Moiraine said firmly. "The Eye of the World lies beyond Fal Dara, and we must reach the Eye."

"Fal Dara," the Ogier agreed reluctantly.

Back at the Island Loial pored over the script-covered slab intently, drooping eyebrows drawn down as he muttered half to himself. Soon he was talking completely to himself, for he dropped into the Ogier language. That inflected tongue sounded like deep-voiced birds singing. It seemed odd to Rand that a people so big had such a musical language.

Finally the Ogier nodded. As he led them to the chosen bridge, he turned to peer forlornly at the signpost beside another. "Three crossings to Stedding Shangtai." He sighed. But he took them on past without stopping and turned onto the third bridge beyond. He looked back regretfully as they started across, though the bridge to his home was hidden in the dark.

Rand took the bay up beside the Ogier. "When this is over, Loial, you show me your *stedding,* and I'll show you Emond's Field. No Ways, though. We'll walk, or ride, if it takes all summer."

"You believe it will ever be over, Rand?"

He frowned at the Ogier. "You said it would take two days to reach Fal Dara."

"Not the Ways, Rand. All the rest." Loial looked over his shoulder at the Aes Sedai, talking softly with Lan as they rode side-by-side. "What makes you believe it will ever be over?"

The bridges and ramps led up and down and across. Sometimes a white line ran off into the dark from the Guiding, just like the line they had followed from the Waygate in Caemlyn. Rand saw that he was not the only one who eyed those lines curiously, and a little wistfully. Nynaeve, Perrin, Mat, and even Egwene left the lines reluctantly. There was a Waygate at the other end of each of them, a gate back into the world, where there was sky and sun and wind. Even the wind would have been welcome. Leave them they did, under the Aes Sedai's sharp eye. But Rand was not the only one to look back even after dark swallowed Island and Guiding and line.

Rand was yawning by the time Moiraine announced that they would stop for the night on one of the Islands. Mat looked at the blackness all around them and snickered loudly, but he got down as quickly as anyone else. Lan and the boys unsaddled and hobbled the horses while Nynaeve and Egwene set up a small oil stove to make tea. Looking like the base of a lantern, it was what Lan said Warders used in the Blight, where the wood could be dangerous to burn. The Warder produced tripod legs from the baskets they took off the packhorse, so the lantern poles could be set in a circle around their campsite.

Loial examined the Guiding for a moment, then dropped down cross-legged and rubbed a hand across the dusty, pockmarked stone. "Once things grew on the Islands," he said sadly. "All the books tell of it. There was green grass to sleep on, soft as any feather bed. Fruit trees to spice the food you'd brought with an apple or a pear or a bellfruit, sweet and crisp and juicy whatever the time of year outside."

"Nothing to hunt," Perrin growled, then looked surprised that he had spoken.

Egwene handed Loial a cup of tea. He held it without drinking, staring at it as if he could find the fruit trees in its depths.

"Aren't you going to set wards?" Nynaeve asked Moiraine. "Surely there must be worse than rats in this. Even if I haven't seen anything, I can still feel."

The Aes Sedai rubbed her fingers against her palms distastefully. "You feel the taint, the corruption of the Power that made the Ways. I will not use the One Power in the Ways unless I must. The taint is so strong that whatever I tried to do would surely be corrupted."

That made everyone as silent as Loial. Lan settled down to his meal methodically, as if he were stoking a fire, the food less important than fueling his body. Moiraine ate well, too, and as tidily as if they were not squatting on bare stone quite literally in the middle of nowhere, but Rand only picked at his food. The tiny flame of the oil stove gave just enough heat to boil water, but he crouched toward it as if he could soak up warmth. His shoulders brushed Mat and Perrin. They all made a tight circle around the stove. Mat held his bread and meat and cheese forgotten in his hands, and Perrin set his tin plate down after only a few bites. The mood became more and more glum, and everyone looked down, avoiding the dark around them.

Moiraine studied them as she ate. Finally she put her plate aside and patted her lips with a napkin. "I can tell you one cheerful thing. I do not think Thom Merrilin is dead."

Rand looked at her sharply. "But . . . the Fade. . . ."

"Mat told me what happened in Whitebridge," the Aes Sedai said. "People there mentioned a gleeman, but they said nothing of him dying. They would have, I think, if a gleeman had been killed. Whitebridge is not so big as for a gleeman to be a small thing. And Thom is a part of the Pattern that weaves itself around you three. Too important a part, I believe, to be cut off yet."

Too important? Rand thought. *How could Moiraine know . . . ?* "Min? She saw something about Thom?"

"She saw a great deal," Moiraine said wryly. "About all of you. I wish I could understand half of what she saw, but even she does not. Old barriers fail. But whether what Min does is old or new, she sees true. Your fates are bound together. Thom Merrilin's, too."

Nynaeve gave a dismissive sniff and poured herself another cup of tea.

"I don't see how she saw anything about any of us," Mat said with a grin. "As I remember it, she spent most of her time looking at Rand."

Egwene raised an eyebrow. "Oh? You didn't tell me that, Moiraine Sedai."

Rand glanced at her. She was not looking at him, but her tone had been too carefully neutral. "I talked to her once," he said. "She dresses like a boy, and her hair is as short as mine."

"You talked to her. Once." Egwene nodded slowly. Still not looking at him, she raised her cup to her lips.

"Min was just somebody who worked at the inn in Baerlon," Perrin said. "Not like Aram."

Egwene choked on her tea. "Too hot," she muttered.

"Who's Aram?" Rand asked. Perrin smiled, much like Mat's smile in the old days when he was up to mischief, and hid behind his cup.

"One of the Traveling People," Egwene said casually, but red spots bloomed in her cheeks.

"One of the Traveling People," Perrin said blandly. "He dances. Like a bird. Wasn't that what you said, Egwene? It was like flying with a bird?"

Egwene set her cup down deliberately. "I don't know if anyone else is tired, but I'm going to sleep."

As she rolled herself up in her blankets, Perrin reached over to nudge Rand in the ribs and winked. Rand found himself grinning back. *Burn me, if I didn't come out best for a change. I wish I knew as much about women as Perrin.*

"Maybe, Rand," Mat said slyly, "you ought to tell Egwene about Farmer Grinwell's daughter, Else." Egwene lifted her head to stare first at Mat, then at him.

He hastily got up to fetch his own blankets. "Sleep sounds good to me right now."

All the Emond's Field people began seeking their blankets then, and Loial, too. Moiraine sat sipping her tea. And Lan. The Warder did not look as if he ever intended to sleep, or needed to.

Even rolled up for sleep, no one wanted to get very far from the others. They made a small circle of blanket-covered mounds right around the stove, almost touching one another.

"Rand," Mat whispered, "*was* there anything between you and Min? I barely got a look at her. She *was* pretty, but she must be nearly as old as Nynaeve."

"What about this Else?" Perrin added from the other side of him. "She pretty?"

"Blood and ashes," he mumbled, "can't I even talk to a girl? You two are as bad as Egwene."

"As the Wisdom would say," Mat chided mockingly, "watch your tongue. Well, if you won't talk about it, I'm going to get some sleep."

"Good," Rand grumbled. "That's the first decent thing you've said."

Sleep was not easily come by, though. The stone was hard, however Rand lay, and he could feel the pits through his blanket. There was no way to imagine he was anywhere but in the Ways, made by the men who had broken the world, tainted by the Dark One. He kept picturing the broken bridge, and the nothing under it.

When he turned one way he found Mat looking at him; looking through him, really. Mocking was forgotten when the dark around them was remembered. He rolled the other way, and Perrin had his eyes open, too. Perrin's face was less afraid than Mat's, but he had his hands on his chest, tapping his thumbs together worriedly.

Moiraine made a circuit of them, kneeling by each person's head and bending down to speak softly. Rand could not hear what she said to Perrin, but it made his thumbs stop. When she bent over Rand, her face almost touching his, she said in a low, comforting voice, "Even here, your destiny protects you. Not even the Dark One can change the Pattern completely. You are safe from him, so long as I am close. Your dreams are safe. For a time, yet, they are safe."

As she passed from him to Mat, he wondered if she thought it was that simple, that she could tell him he was safe and he would believe it. But somehow he did feel safe—safer, at least. Thinking that, he drifted into sleep and did not dream.

Lan woke them. Rand wondered if the Warder had slept; he did not look tired, not even as tired as those who had laid some hours on the hard stone. Moiraine allowed enough time to make tea, but only one cup apiece. They ate breakfast in the saddle, Loial and the Warder leading. It was the same meal as the others, bread and meat and cheese. Rand thought it would be easy to get tired of bread and meat and cheese.

Not long after the last crumb was licked off a finger, Lan said quietly, "Someone is following us. Or something." They were in the middle of a bridge, both ends of it hidden.

Mat jerked an arrow from his quiver and, before anyone could stop him, loosed it in the dark behind them.

"I knew I shouldn't have done this," Loial muttered. "Never deal with an Aes Sedai except in a *stedding*."

Lan pushed the bow down before Mat could nock another. "Stop that, you village idiot. There's no way to tell who it is."

"That's the only place they're safe," the Ogier went on.

"What else would be in a place like this besides something evil?" Mat demanded.

"That's what the Elders say, and I should have listened to them."

"We are, for one," the Warder said dryly.

"Maybe it's another traveler," Egwene said hopefully. "An Ogier, perhaps."

"Ogier have more sense than to use the Ways," Loial growled. "All but Loial, who has no sense at all. Elder Haman always said it, and it's true."

"What do you feel, Lan?" Moiraine asked. "Is it something that serves the Dark One?"

The Warder shook his head slowly. "I don't know," he said as if that surprised him. "I cannot tell. Perhaps it's the Ways, and the taint. It all feels wrong. But whoever it is, or whatever, he's not trying to catch us. He almost caught up at the last Island and scampered back across the bridge so as not to. If I fall behind, I might surprise him though, and see who, or what, he is."

"If you fall behind, Warder," Loial said firmly, "you'll spend the rest of your life in the Ways. Even if you can read Ogier, I have never heard or read of a human who could find his path off the first Island lacking an Ogier guide. *Can* you read Ogier?"

Lan shook his head again, and Moiraine said, "So long as he does not trouble us, we will not trouble him. We have no time. No time."

As they rode off the bridge onto the next Island, Loial said, "If I remember the last Guiding correctly, there is a path from here that leads toward Tar Valon. Half a day's journey at most. Not quite as long as it will take us to reach Mafal Dadaranell. I'm sure that—"

He cut off as the light of their lanterns reached the Guiding. Near the top of the slab, deeply chiseled lines, sharp and angular, made wounds in the stone. Suddenly Lan's alertness was no longer hidden. He remained easily erect in his saddle, but Rand had the sudden impression that the Warder could feel everything around him, even feel the rest of them breathing. Lan began circling his stallion around the Guiding, spiraling outward. He rode as if he were ready to be attacked, or to attack himself.

"This explains much," Moiraine said softly, "and it makes me afraid. So much. I should have guessed. The taint, the decay. I should have guessed."

"Guessed what?" Nynaeve demanded just as Loial asked, "What is it? Who did this? I've never seen or heard of anything like it."

The Aes Sedai faced them calmly. "Trollocs." She ignored their frightened gasps. "Or Fades. Those are Trolloc runes. The Trollocs have discovered how to enter the Ways. That must be how they got to the Two Rivers undiscovered; through the Waygate at Manetheren. There is at least one Waygate in the Blight." She glanced toward Lan before continuing; the Warder was far enough away that only the faint light of his lantern could be seen. "Manetheren was destroyed, but almost nothing can destroy a Waygate. That is how the Fades could gather a small army around Caemlyn without raising an alarm in every nation between the Blight and Andor." Pausing, she touched her lips thoughtfully. "But they cannot know all the paths yet, else they would have been pouring into Caemlyn through the gate we used. Yes."

Rand shivered. Walking through the Waygate to find Trollocs waiting in the dark, hundreds of them, perhaps thousands, twisted giants with half-animal faces snarling as they leaped forward in the blackness to kill. Or worse.

"They don't use the Ways easily," Lan called. His lantern was no more than twenty spans off, but the light of it was only a dim, fuzzy ball that seemed very distant to those around the Guiding. Moiraine led the way to him. Rand wished his stomach were empty when he saw what the Warder had found.

At the foot of one of the bridges the frozen shapes of Trollocs reared, caught flailing about them with hooked axes and scythe-like swords. Gray and pitted like the stone, the huge bodies were half sunken in the swollen, bubbled surface. Some of the bubbles had burst, revealing more snouted faces, forever snarling with fear. Rand heard someone retching behind him, and swallowed hard to keep from joining whoever it was. Even for Trollocs it had been a horrible way to die.

A few feet beyond the Trollocs the bridge ended. The signpost lay shattered into a thousand shards.

Loial got down from his horse gingerly, eyeing the Trollocs, as if he thought they might come back to life. He examined the remains of the signpost hurriedly, picking out the metal script that had been inlaid in the stone, then scrambled back into his saddle. "This was the first bridge of the path from here to Tar Valon," he said.

Mat was scrubbing the back of his hand across his mouth, with his head turned away from the Trollocs. Egwene hid her face in her hands. Rand moved his horse close to Bela and touched her shoulder. She twisted around and clutched him, shuddering. He wanted to shudder, too; her holding him was the only thing that kept him from it.

"As well we are not going to Tar Valon yet," Moiraine said.

Nynaeve rounded on the Aes Sedai. "How can you take it so calmly? The same could happen to us!"

"Perhaps," Moiraine said serenely, and Nynaeve ground her teeth so hard Rand could hear them grate. "It is more likely, though," Moiraine went on, unruffled, "that the men, the Aes Sedai, who made the Ways protected them, building in traps for creatures of the Dark

One. It is something they must have feared then, before the Halfmen and Trollocs had been driven into the Blight. In any case, we cannot tarry here, and whatever way we choose, back or ahead, is as likely to have a trap as any other. Loial, do you know the next bridge?"

"Yes. Yes, they did not ruin that part of the Guiding, thank the Light." For the first time Loial seemed as eager to go on as Moiraine did. He had his big horse moving before he finished speaking.

Egwene clung to Rand's arm for two more bridges. He regretted it when she finally let go with a murmured apology and a forced laugh, and not just because it had felt good having her hold onto him that way. It was easier to be brave, he discovered, when someone needed your protection.

Moiraine might not have believed a trap could be set for them, but for all the haste she spoke of, she made them travel more slowly than before, pausing before letting them onto any bridge, or off one onto an Island. She would step Aldieb forward, feeling the air in front of her with an outstretched hand, and not even Loial, or Lan, was allowed to go ahead until she gave permission.

Rand had to trust her judgment about traps, but he peered into the darkness around them as if he could actually see anything more than ten feet away, and strained his ears listening. If Trollocs could use the Ways, then whatever was following them could be another creature of the Dark One. Or more than one. Lan had said he could not tell in the Ways. But as they crossed bridge after bridge, ate a midday meal riding, and crossed still more bridges, all he could hear were their own saddles creaking, and the horses' hooves, and sometimes one of the others coughing, or muttering to himself. Later there was a distant wind, too, off in the black somewhere. He could not say in which direction. At first he thought it was his imagination, but with time he became sure.

It'll be good to feel the wind again, even if it's cold.

Suddenly he blinked. "Loial, didn't you say there isn't any wind in the Ways?"

Loial pulled his horse up just short of the next Island and cocked his head to listen. Slowly his face paled, and he licked his lips. *"Machin Shin,"* he whispered hoarsely. "The Black Wind. The Light illumine and protect us. It's the Black Wind."

"How many more bridges?" Moiraine asked sharply. "Loial, how many more bridges?"

"Two. I think, two."

"Quickly, then," she said, trotting Aldieb onto the Island. "Find it quickly!"

Loial talked to himself, or to anyone who was listening, while he read the Guiding. "They came out mad, screaming about *Machin Shin.* Light help us! Even those Aes Sedai could heal, they. . . ." He scanned the stone hastily, and galloped toward the chosen bridge with a shouted, "This way!"

This time Moiraine did not wait to check. She urged them on to a gallop, the bridge trembling beneath the horses, lanterns swinging wildly overhead. Loial ran his eyes over the next Guiding and wheeled his big mount around like a racer almost before it had stopped. The sound of the wind became louder. Rand could hear it even over the pounding of hooves on stone. Behind them, and gusting closer.

They did not bother with the last Guiding. As soon as the light of the lanterns caught the white line running from it, they swung in that direction, still galloping. The Island vanished behind, and there was only the pitted, gray stone underfoot and the white line. Rand was breathing so hard he was no longer sure if he could hear the wind.

Out of the darkness the gates appeared, vine-carved and standing alone in the black like a tiny piece of wall in the night. Moiraine leaned out of her saddle, reaching toward the carvings, and suddenly pulled back. "The *Avendesora* leaf is not here!" she said. "The key is gone!"

"Light!" Mat shouted. "Bloody Light!" Loial threw back his head and gave a mournful cry, like a howl of dying.

Egwene touched Rand's arm. Her lips trembled, but she only looked at him. He put his hand on top of hers, hoping he did not look more frightened than she did. He felt it. Back toward the Guiding, the wind howled. He almost thought he could hear voices in it, voices screaming vileness that, even half understood, brought bile up in his throat.

Moiraine raised her staff and flame lanced from the end of it. It was not the pure, white flame that Rand remembered from Emond's Field, and the battle before Shadar Logoth. Sickly yellow streaked through the fire, and slow-drifting flecks of black, like soot. A thin, acrid smoke drifted from the flame, setting Loial coughing and the horses dancing nervously, but Moiraine thrust it at the gates. The smoke rasped Rand's throat and burned his nose.

Stone melted like butter, leaf and vine withering in the flame and vanishing. The Aes Sedai moved the fire as fast as she could, but cutting an opening big enough for everyone to get through was no quick task. To Rand, it seemed as if the line of melted stone crept along its arc at a snail's pace. His cloak stirred, as if caught by the edge of a breeze, and his heart froze.

"I can feel it," Mat said, his voice quavering. "Light, I can bloody feel it!"

The flame winked out, and Moiraine lowered her staff. "Done," she said. "Half done."

A thin line ran across the stone carving. Rand thought he could see light—dim, but still light—through the crack. But despite the cutting, the two big, curved wedges of stone still stood there, half an arc out of each door. The opening would be big enough for everyone to ride through, though Loial might have to lie flat on his horse's back. Once the two wedges of stone were gone, it would be big enough. He wondered how much each weighed. A thousand pounds? More? *Maybe if we all get down and push. Maybe we can push one of them over before the wind gets here.* A gust tugged at his cloak. He tried not to listen to what the voices cried.

As Moiraine stepped back, Mandarb leaped forward, straight toward the gates, Lan crouched in the saddle. At the last instant the warhorse twisted to catch the stone with his shoulder, just as he had been taught to catch other horses in battle. With a crash the stone toppled outward, and the Warder and his horse were carried by their momentum through the smoky shimmer of a Waygate. The light that came through was midmorning light, pale and thin, but it seemed to Rand as if the noonday summer sun blazed in his face.

On the far side of the gate Lan and Mandarb slowed to a crawl, stumbling in slow motion as the Warder reined back around toward the gate. Rand did not wait. Pushing Bela's head toward the opening, he slapped the shaggy mare hard on the croup. Egwene had just enough time to throw a startled look over her shoulder at him before Bela carried her out of the Ways.

"All of you, out!" Moiraine directed. "Quickly! Go!"

As she spoke, the Aes Sedai thrust her staff out at arm's length, pointed back toward the Guiding. Something leaped from the end of the staff, like liquid light rendered to a syrup of fire, a blazing spear of white and red and yellow, streaking into the black, exploding, coruscating like shattered diamonds. The wind shrieked in agony; it screamed in rage. The thousand murmurs that hid in the wind roared like thunder, roars of madness, half-heard voices cackling and howling promises that twisted Rand's stomach as much by the pleasure in them as by what he almost understood them to say.

He booted Red forward, crowding into the opening, squeezing after the others, all forcing through the smoky glistening at once. The icy chill ran through him again, the peculiar sensation of being slowly lowered facedown into a winter pond, the cold water crawling across his skin by infinitesimal increments. Just as before it seemed to go on forever, while his mind raced, wondering if the wind could catch them while they were held like that.

As suddenly as a pricked bubble the chill vanished, and he was outside. His horse, for one abrupt instant moving twice as fast as he had been, stumbled and almost pitched him over his head. He threw both arms around the bay's neck and hung on for dear life. While he got back into the saddle, Red shook himself, then trotted over to join the others as calmly as if nothing at all odd had happened. It was cold, not the chill of the Waygate, but welcome, natural winter-cold that slowly, steadily burrowed into flesh.

He pulled his cloak around him, his eyes on the dull glimmer of the Waygate. Beside him Lan leaned forward in his saddle, one hand on his sword; man and horse were tensed, as if on the point of charging back through if Moiraine did not appear.

The Waygate stood in a jumble of stones at the base of a hill, hidden by bushes except where the falling pieces had broken down the bare, brown branches. Alongside the carvings on the remains of the gates, the brush looked more lifeless than the stone.

Slowly the murky surface bulged like some strange, long bubble rising to the surface of a pond. Moiraine's back broke through the bubble. Inchmeal, the Aes Sedai and her dim reflection backed out of each other. She still held her staff out in front of her, and she kept it there as she drew Aldieb out of the Waygate after her, the white mare dancing with fear, eyes rolling. Still watching the Waygate, Moiraine backed away.

The Waygate darkened. The hazy shimmer became murkier, sinking through gray to charcoal, then to black as deep as the heart of the Ways. As if from a great distance the wind howled at them, hidden voices filled with an unquenchable thirst for living things, filled with a hunger for pain, filled with frustration.

The voices seemed to whisper in Rand's ears, right at the brink of understanding, and within it. *Flesh so fine, so fine to tear, to gash the skin; skin to strip, to plait, so nice to plait the strips, so nice, so red the drops that fall; blood so red, so red, so sweet; sweet screams, pretty screams, singing screams, scream your song, sing your screams. . . .*

The whispers drifted, the blackness lessened, faded, and the Waygate was again a murky shimmer seen through an arch of carved stone.

Rand let out a long, shuddering breath. He was not the only one; he heard other relieved exhalations. Egwene had Bela alongside Nynaeve's horse, and the two women had their arms around each other, their heads on each other's shoulders. Even Lan seemed relieved, though the hard planes of his face showed nothing; it was more in the way he sat Mandarb, a loosening of the shoulders as he looked at Moiraine, a tilt of the head.

"It could not pass," Moiraine said. "I thought it could not; I hoped it could not. Faugh!" She tossed her staff on the ground and scrubbed her hand on her cloak. Char, thick and black, marked the staff for over half its length. "The taint corrupts everything in that place."

"What was that?" Nynaeve demanded. "What was it?"

Loial appeared confused. "Why, *Machin Shin,* of course. The Black Wind that steals souls."

"But *what* is it?" Nynaeve persisted. "Even with a Trolloc, you can look at it, touch it if you have a strong stomach. But that. . . ." She gave a convulsive shiver.

"Something left from the Time of Madness, perhaps," Moiraine replied. "Or even from the War of the Shadow, the War of Power. Something hiding in the Ways so long it can no longer get out. No one, not even among the Ogier, knows how far the Ways run, or how deep. It could even be something of the Ways themselves. As Loial said, the Ways are living things, and all living things have parasites. Perhaps even a creature of the corruption itself, something born of the decay. Something that hates life and light."

"Stop!" Egwene cried. "I don't want to hear any more. I could hear *it,* saying. . . ." She cut off, shivering.

"There is worse to be faced yet," Moiraine said softly. Rand did not think she meant it to be heard.

The Aes Sedai climbed into her saddle wearily and settled there with a grateful sigh. "This is dangerous," she said, looking at the broken gates. Her charred staff received only a glance. "The thing cannot get out, but anyone could wander in. Agelmar must send men to wall it up, once we reach Fal Dara." She pointed to the north, to towers in the misty distance above the barren treetops.

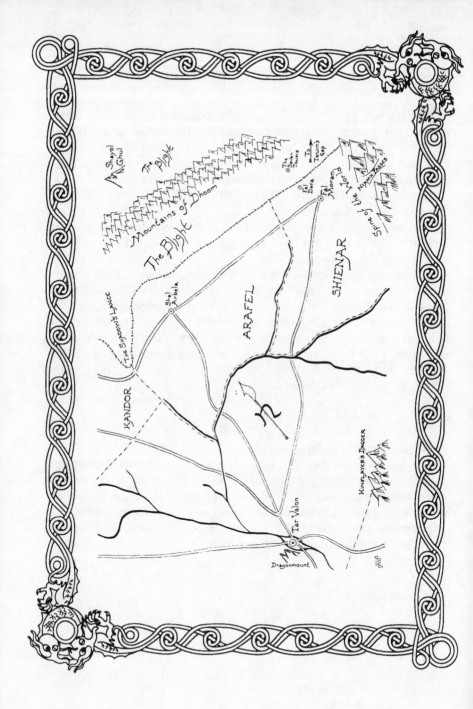

CHAPTER
46

Fal Dara

T he country around the Waygate was rolling, forested hills, but aside from the gates themselves there was no sign of any Ogier grove. Most of the trees were gray skeletons clawing at the sky. Fewer evergreens than Rand was used to dotted the forest, and of them, dead, brown needles and leaves covered many. Loial made no comment beyond a sad shaking of his head.

"As dead as the Blasted Lands," Nynaeve said, frowning. Egwene pulled her cloak around her and shivered.

"At least we're out," Perrin said, and Mat added, "Out where?"

"Shienar," Lan told them. "We're in the Borderlands." In his hard voice was a note that said home, almost.

Rand gathered his cloak against the cold. The Borderlands. Then the Blight was close by. The Blight. The Eye of the World. And what they had come to do.

"We are close to Fal Dara," Moiraine said. "Only a few miles." Across the treetops, towers rose to the north and east of them, dark against the morning sky. Between the hills and the woods, the towers often vanished as they rode, only to reappear again when they topped a particularly tall rise.

Rand noticed trees split open as if struck by lightning.

"The cold," Lan answered when he asked. "Sometimes the winter is so cold here the sap freezes, and trees burst. There are nights when you can hear them cracking like fireworks, and the air is so sharp you think that might shatter, too. There are more than usual, this winter past."

Rand shook his head. Trees *bursting*? And that was during an ordinary winter. What must this winter have been like? Surely like nothing he could imagine.

"Who says winter's past?" Mat said, his teeth chattering.

"Why this, a fine spring, sheepherder," Lan said. "A fine spring to be alive. But if you want warm, well, it will be warm in the Blight."

Softly Mat muttered, "Blood and ashes. Blood and bloody ashes!" Rand barely heard him, but it sounded heartfelt.

They began to pass farms, but though it was the hour for midday meals to be cooking, no smoke rose from the high stone chimneys. The fields were empty of men and livestock both, though sometimes a plow or a wagon stood abandoned as if the owner meant to be back any minute.

At one farm close by the road a lone chicken scratched in the yard. One barn door swung freely with the wind; the other had broken off the bottom hinge and hung at an angle. The tall house, odd to Rand's Two Rivers eyes, with its sharp-peaked roof of big wooden shingles running almost to the ground, was still and silent. No dog came out to bark at them. A scythe lay in the middle of the barnyard; buckets were overturned in a heap beside the well.

Moiraine frowned at the farmhouse as they rode by. She lifted Aldieb's reins, and the white mare quickened her pace.

The Emond's Fielders were clustered with Loial a little behind the Aes Sedai and the Warder.

Rand shook his head. He could not imagine anything growing there ever. But then he could not really imagine the Ways, either. Even now that he was past them, he could not.

"I don't think she expected this," Nynaeve said quietly, with a gesture that took in all the empty farms they had seen.

"Where did they all go?" Egwene said. "Why? They can't have been gone very long."

"What makes you say that?" Mat asked. "From the look of that barn door, they could have been gone all winter." Nynaeve and Egwene both looked at him as if he were slow-witted.

"The curtains in the windows," Egwene said patiently. "They look too light for winter curtains, even here. As cold as it is here, no woman would have had those up more than a week or two, maybe less." The Wisdom nodded.

"Curtains." Perrin chuckled. He immediately wiped the smile off his face when the two women raised their eyebrows at him. "Oh, I agree with you. There wasn't enough rust on that scythe for any more than a week in the open. You should have seen that, Mat. Even if you missed the curtains."

Rand glanced sideways at Perrin, trying not to stare. His eyes were sharper than Perrin's—or had been, when they used to hunt rabbits together—but he had not been able to see that scythe-blade well enough to make out any rust.

"I really don't care where they went," Mat grumbled. "I just want to find someplace with a fire. Soon."

"But why did they go?" Rand said under his breath. The Blight was not far off here. The Blight, where all the Fades and Trollocs were, those not down in Andor chasing them. The Blight, where they were going.

He raised his voice enough to be heard by those close to him. "Nynaeve, maybe you and Egwene don't have to go to the Eye with us." The two women looked at him as if he were speaking gibberish, but with the Blight so close he had to make one last try. "Maybe it's enough for you to be close. Moiraine didn't say you have to go. Or you, Loial. You could stay at Fal Dara. Until we come back. Or you could start for Tar Valon. Maybe there'll be a merchant train, or I'll bet Moiraine would even hire a coach. We will meet in Tar Valon, when it's all over."

"Ta'veren." Loial's sigh was a rumble like thunder on the horizon. "You swirl lives around you, Rand al'Thor, you and your friends. Your fate chooses ours." The Ogier shrugged, and suddenly a broad grin split his face. "Besides, it will be something to meet the Green Man. Elder Haman always talks about his meeting with the Green Man, and so does my father, and most of the Elders."

"So many?" Perrin said. "The stories say the Green Man is hard to find, and no one can find him twice."

"Not twice, no," Loial agreed. "But then, I have never met him, and neither have you. He doesn't seem to avoid Ogier quite the way he does you humans. He knows so much about trees. Even the Tree Songs."

Rand said, "The point I was trying to make is—"

The Wisdom cut him off. "*She* says Egwene and I are part of the Pattern, too. All woven in with you three. If she is to be believed, there's something about the way that piece of the Pattern is woven that might stop the Dark One. And I am afraid I do believe her; too much has happened not to. But if Egwene and I go away, what might we change about the Pattern?"

"I was only trying to—"

Again Nynaeve interrupted, sharply. "I know what you were trying to do." She looked at him until he shifted uneasily in his saddle, then her face softened. "I know what you were trying to do, Rand. I have little liking for any Aes Sedai, and this one least of all, I think. I have less for going into the Blight, but least of all is the liking I have for the Father of Lies. If you boys . . . you men, can do what has to be done when you'd rather do almost anything else, why do you think I will do less? Or Egwene?" She did not appear to expect an answer. Gathering her reins, she frowned toward the Aes Sedai up ahead. "I wonder if we're going to reach this Fal Dara place soon, or does she mean us to spend the night out in this?"

As she trotted toward Moiraine, Mat said, "She called us men. It seems like only yesterday she was saying we shouldn't be off leading strings, and now she calls us men."

"You still shouldn't be off your mother's apron strings," Egwene said, but Rand did not think her heart was in it. She moved Bela close to his bay, and lowered her voice so none of the others could hear although Mat, at least, tried. "I only danced with Aram, Rand," she said softly, not looking at him. "You wouldn't hold it against me, dancing with somebody I will never see again, would you?"

"No," he told her. *What had made her bring it up now?* "Of course not." But suddenly he remembered something Min had said in Baerlon, what seemed a hundred years ago. *She's not for you, nor you for her; at least, not in the way you both want.*

The town of Fal Dara was built on hills higher than the surrounding country. It was nowhere near as big as Caemlyn, but the wall around it was as high as Caemlyn's. For a full mile outside that wall in every direction the ground was clear of anything taller than grass, and that cut low. Nothing could come close without being seen from one of the many tall towers topped by wooden hoardings. Where the walls of Caemlyn had a beauty about them, the builders of Fal Dara seemed not to have cared if anyone found their wall beautiful. The gray stone was grimly implacable, proclaiming that it existed for one purpose alone: to hold. Pennants atop the hoardings whipped in the wind, making the stooping Black Hawk of Shienar seem to fly all along the walls.

Lan tossed back the hood of his cloak and, despite the cold, motioned for the others to do the same. Moiraine had already lowered hers. "It's the law in Shienar," the Warder said. "In all the Borderlands. No one may hide his face inside a town's walls."

"Are they all that good-looking?" Mat laughed.

"A Halfman can't hide with his face exposed," the Warder said in a flat voice.

Rand's grin slid off his face. Hastily Mat pushed back his hood.

The gates stood open, tall and covered with dark iron, but a dozen armored men stood guard in golden yellow surcoats bearing the Black Hawk. The hilts of long swords on their backs peeked over their shoulders, and broadsword or mace or axe hung at every waist. Their horses were tethered nearby, made grotesque by the steel bardings covering chests and necks and heads, with lances to stirrup, all ready to ride at an instant. The guards made no move to stop Lan and Moiraine and the others. Indeed, they waved and called out happily.

"Dai Shan!" one cried, shaking steel-gauntleted fists over his head as they rode past. "Dai Shan!"

A number of others shouted, "Glory to the Builders!" and, *"Kiserai ti Wansho!"* Loial looked surprised, then a broad smile split his face and he waved to the guards.

One man ran alongside Lan's horse a little way, unhampered by the armor he wore. "Will the Golden Crane fly again, Dai Shan?"

"Peace, Ragan," was all the Warder said, and the man fell away. He returned the guards' waves, but his face was suddenly even more grim.

As they rode through stone-paved streets crowded with people and wagons, Rand frowned worriedly. Fal Dara was bulging at the seams, but the people were neither the eager crowds of Caemlyn, enjoying the grandeur of the city even as they squabbled, nor the milling throngs of Baerlon. Packed cheek by jowl, these folk watched their party ride by with leaden eyes and faces blanked of emotion. Carts and wagons jammed every alleyway and half the streets, piled high with jumbled household furnishings, and carved chests packed so tight that clothes spilled. On top sat the children. Adults kept the younglings up where they could be seen and did not let them stray even to play. The children were even more silent than their elders, their eyes bigger, more haunting in their stares. The nooks and crannies between the wagons were filled with shaggy cattle and black-spotted pigs in makeshift pens. Crates of chickens and ducks and geese fitfully made up for the silence of the people. He knew now where all the farmers had gone.

Lan led the way to the fortress in the middle of the town, a massive
stone pile atop the highest hill. A dry moat, deep and wide, its bottom
a forest of sharp steel spikes, razor-edged and as tall as a man, surrounded the towered walls of the keep. A place for a last defense, if
the rest of the town fell. From one of the gate towers an armored man
called down, "Welcome, Dai Shan." Another shouted to the inside of
the fortress, "The Golden Crane! The Golden Crane!"

Their hooves drummed on the heavy timbers of the lowered draw-
bridge as they crossed the moat and rode under the sharp points of
the stout portcullis. Once through the gates, Lan swung down out of
his saddle to lead Mandarb, signaling the others to dismount.

The first courtyard was a huge square paved with big stone blocks
and surrounded by towers and battlements as fierce as those on the
outside of the walls. As big as it was, the courtyard appeared just as
crowded as the streets, and as much in turmoil, though there was an
order to the crowding here. Everywhere were armored men and armored horses. At half a dozen smithies around the court, hammers
clanged, and big bellows, tugged by two leather-aproned men apiece,
made the forge-fires roar. A steady stream of boys ran with new-made
horseshoes for the farriers. Fletchers sat making arrows, and every
time a basket was filled it was whisked away and replaced with an
empty one.

Liveried grooms appeared on the run, eager and smiling in black-
and-gold. Rand hastily untied his belongings from behind the saddle
and gave the bay up to one of the grooms as a man in plate-and-mail
and leather bowed formally. He wore a bright yellow cloak edged in
red over his armor, with the Black Hawk on the breast, and a yellow
surcoat bearing a gray owl. He wore no helmet and was bareheaded,
truly, for his hair had all been shaved except for a topknot tied with
a leather cord. "It has been long, Moiraine Aes Sedai. It is good to see
you, Dai Shan. Very good." He bowed again, to Loial, and murmured,
"Glory to the Builders. *Kiserai ti Wansho.*"

"I am unworthy," Loial replied formally, "and the work small.
Tsingu ma choba."

"You honor us, Builder," the man said. *"Kiserai ti Wansho."* He
turned back to Lan. "Word was sent to Lord Agelmar, Dai Shan, as
soon as you were seen coming. He is waiting for you. This way,
please."

As they followed him into the fortress, along drafty stone corridors
hung with colorful tapestries and long silk screens of hunting scenes

and battles, he continued. "I am glad the call reached you, Dai Shan. Will you raise the Golden Crane banner once more?" The halls were stark except for the wall hangings, and even they used the fewest figures made with the fewest lines necessary to convey meaning, though in bright colors.

"Are things really as bad as they appear, Ingtar?" Lan asked quietly. Rand wondered if his own ears were twitching like Loial's.

The man's topknot swayed as he shook his head, but he hesitated before putting on a grin. "Things are never as bad as they appear, Dai Shan. A little worse than usual this year, that is all. The raids continued through the winter, even in the hardest of it. But the raiding was no worse than anywhere else along the Border. They still come in the night, but what else can be expected in the spring, if this can be called spring. Scouts return from the Blight—those who do come back—with news of Trolloc camps. Always fresh news of more camps. But we will meet them at Tarwin's Gap, Dai Shan, and turn them back as we always have."

"Of course," Lan said, but he did not sound certain.

Ingtar's grin slipped, but came back immediately. Silently he showed them into Lord Agelmar's study, then claimed the press of his duties and left.

It was a room as purpose-made as all the rest of the fortress, with arrowslits in the outer wall and a heavy bar for the thick door, which had its own arrowpiercings and was bound by iron straps. Only one tapestry hung here. It covered an entire wall and showed men, armored like the men of Fal Dara, fighting Myrddraal and Trollocs in a mountain pass.

A table, one chest, and a few chairs were the only furnishings except for two racks on the wall, and they caught Rand's eye as much as the tapestry. One held a two-handed sword, taller than a man, a more ordinary broadsword, and below them a studded mace and a long, kite-shaped shield bearing three foxes. From the other hung a suit of armor, complete and arranged as one would wear it. Crested helmet with its barred face-guard over a double-mail camail. Mail hauberk, split for riding, and leather undercoat, polished from wear. Breastplate, steel gauntlets, knee and elbow cops, and half-plate for shoulders and arms and legs. Even here in the heart of the Keep, weapons and armor seemed ready to be donned at any moment. Like the furniture, they were simply and severely decorated with gold.

Agelmar himself rose at their entrance and came around the table, littered with maps and sheafs of paper and pens standing in inkpots.

He seemed at first glance too peaceful for the room in his blue velvet coat with its tall, wide collar, and soft leather boots, but a second look showed Rand differently. Like all the fighting men he had seen, Agelmar's head was shaved except for a topknot, and that pure white. His face was as hard as Lan's, the only lines creases at the corners of his eyes, and those eyes like brown stone, though they bore a smile now.

"Peace, but it is good to see you, Dai Shan," the Lord of Fal Dara said. "And you, Moiraine Aes Sedai, perhaps even more. Your presence warms me, Aes Sedai."

"Ninte calichniye no domashita, Agelmar Dai Shan," Moiraine replied formally, but with a note in her voice that said they were old friends. "Your welcome warms me, Lord Agelmar."

"Kodome calichniye ga ni Aes Sedai hei. Here is always a welcome for Aes Sedai." He turned to Loial. "You are far from the *stedding,* Ogier, but you honor Fal Dara. Always glory to the Builders. *Kiserai ti Wansho hei."*

"I am unworthy," Loial said, bowing. "It is you who do me honor." He glanced at the stark stone walls and seemed to struggle with himself. Rand was glad the Ogier managed to refrain from adding further comment.

Servants in black-and-gold appeared on silent, soft-slippered feet. Some brought folded cloths, damp and hot, on silver trays for wiping the dust from faces and hands. Others bore mulled wine and silver bowls of dried plums and apricots. Lord Agelmar gave orders for rooms to be prepared, and baths.

"A long journey from Tar Valon," he said. "You must be tired."

"A short journey the path we came," Lan told him, "but more tiring than the long way."

Agelmar looked puzzled when the Warder said no more, but he merely said, "A few days' rest will put you all in fine fettle."

"I ask one night's shelter, Lord Agelmar," Moiraine said, "for ourselves and our horses. And fresh supplies in the morning, if you can spare them. We must leave you early, I am afraid."

Agelmar frowned. "But I thought. . . . Moiraine Sedai, I have no right to ask it of you, but you would be worth a thousand lances in Tarwin's Gap. And you, Dai Shan. A thousand men *will* come when they hear the Golden Crane flies once more."

"The Seven Towers are broken," Lan said harshly, "and Malkier is dead; the few of her people left, scattered across the face of the earth. I am a Warder, Agelmar, sworn to the Flame of Tar Valon, and I am bound into the Blight."

"Of course, Dai Sh— Lan. Of course. But surely a few days' delay, a few weeks at most, will make no difference. You are needed. You, and Moiraine Sedai."

Moiraine took a silver goblet from one of the servants. "Ingtar seems to believe you will defeat this threat as you have defeated many others across the years."

"Aes Sedai," Agelmar said wryly, "if Ingtar had to ride alone to Tarwin's Gap, he would ride the whole way proclaiming that the Trollocs would be turned back once more. He has almost pride enough to believe he *could* do it alone."

"He is not as confident as you think, this time, Agelmar." The Warder held a cup, but he did not drink. "How bad is it?"

Agelmar hesitated, pulling a map from the tangle on the table. He stared unseeing at the map for a moment, then tossed it back. "When we ride to the Gap," he said quietly, "the people will be sent south to Fal Moran. Perhaps the capital can hold. Peace, it must. Something must hold."

"That bad?" Lan said, and Agelmar nodded wearily.

Rand exchanged worried looks with Mat and Perrin. It was easy to believe the Trollocs gathering in the Blight were after him, after them. Agelmar went on grimly.

"Kandor, Arafel, Saldaea—the Trollocs raided them all straight through the winter. Nothing like that has happened since the Trolloc Wars; the raids have never been so fierce, or so large, or pressed home so hard. Every king and council is sure a great thrust is coming out of the Blight, and every one of the Borderlands believes it is coming at them. None of their scouts, and none of the Warders, report Trolloc massing above their borders, as we have here, but they believe, and each is afraid to send fighting men elsewhere. People whisper that the world is ending, that the Dark One is loose again. Shienar will ride to Tarwin's Gap alone, and we will be outnumbered at least ten to one. At least. It may be the last Ingathering of the Lances.

"Lan—no!—Dai Shan, for you *are* a Diademed Battle Lord of Malkier whatever you say. Dai Shan, the Golden Crane banner in the van would put heart into men who know they are riding north to die. The word will spread like wildfire, and though their kings have told them to hold where they are, lances will come from Arafel and Kandor, and even from Saldaea. Though they cannot come in time to stand with us in the Gap, they may save Shienar."

Lan peered into his wine. His face did not change, but wine slopped over his hand; the silver goblet crumpled in his grip. A servant took the ruined cup and wiped the Warder's hand with a cloth; a second put a fresh goblet in his hand while the other was whisked away. Lan did not seem to notice. "I cannot!" he whispered hoarsely. When he raised his head his blue eyes burned with a fierce light, but his voice was calm again, and flat. "I am a Warder, Agelmar." His sharp gaze slid across Rand and Mat and Perrin to Moiraine. "At first light I ride to the Blight."

Agelmar sighed heavily. "Moiraine Sedai, will you not come, at least? An Aes Sedai could make the difference."

"I cannot, Lord Agelmar." Moiraine seemed troubled. "There is indeed a battle to be fought, and it is not chance that the Trollocs gather above Shienar, but our battle, the true battle with the Dark One, will take place in the Blight, at the Eye of the World. You must fight your battle, and we ours."

"You cannot be saying he is loose!" Rocklike Agelmar sounded shaken, and Moiraine quickly shook her head.

"Not yet. If we win at the Eye of the World, perhaps not ever again."

"Can you even find the Eye, Aes Sedai? If holding the Dark One depends on that, we might as well be dead. Many have tried and failed."

"I can find it, Lord Agelmar. Hope is not lost yet."

Agelmar studied her, and then the others. He appeared puzzled by Nynaeve and Egwene; their farmclothes contrasted sharply with Moiraine's silk dress, though all were travel-stained. "They are Aes Sedai, too?" he asked doubtfully. When Moiraine shook her head, he seemed even more confused. His gaze ran over the young men from Emond's Field, settling on Rand, brushing the red-wrapped sword at his waist. "A strange guard you take with you, Aes Sedai. Only one fighting man." He glanced at Perrin, and at the axe hanging from his belt. "Perhaps two. But both barely more than lads. Let me send men with you. A hundred lances more or less will make no difference in the Gap, but you will need more than one Warder and three youths. And two women will not help, unless they are Aiel in disguise. The Blight is worse than usual this year. It—stirs."

"A hundred lances would be too many," Lan said, "and a thousand not enough. The larger the party we take into the Blight, the more chance we will attract attention. We must reach the Eye without fighting, if we can. You know the outcome is all but foretold when Trollocs force battle inside the Blight."

Agelmar nodded grimly, but he refused to give up. "Fewer, then.

Even ten good men would give you a better chance of escorting Moiraine Sedai and the other two women to the Green Man than will just these young fellows."

Rand abruptly realized the Lord of Fal Dara assumed it was Nynaeve and Egwene who with Moiraine would fight against the Dark One. It was natural. That sort of struggle meant using the One Power, and that meant women. *That sort of struggle means using the Power.* He tucked his thumbs behind his sword belt and gripped the buckle hard to keep his hands from shaking.

"No men," Moiraine said. Agelmar opened his mouth again, and she went on before he could speak. "It is the nature of the Eye, and the nature of the Green Man. How many from Fal Dara have ever found the Green Man and the Eye?"

"Ever?" Agelmar shrugged. "Since the War of the Hundred Years, you could count them on the fingers of one hand. No more than one in five years from all the Borderlands together."

"No one finds the Eye of the World," Moiraine said, "unless the Green Man wants them to find it. Need is the key, and intention. I know where to go—I have been there before." Rand's head whipped around in surprise; his was not the only one among the Emond's Fielders, but the Aes Sedai did not seem to notice. "But one among us seeking glory, seeking to add his name to those four, and we may never find it though I take us straight to the spot I remember."

"You have seen the Green Man, Moiraine Sedai?" The Lord of Fal Dara sounded impressed, but in the next breath he frowned. "But if you have already met him once. . . ."

"Need is the key," Moiraine said softly, "and there can be no greater need than mine. Than ours. And I have something those other seekers have not."

Her eyes barely stirred from Agelmar's face, but Rand was sure they had drifted toward Loial, just for an instant before the Aes Sedai pulled them back. Rand met the Ogier's eyes, and Loial shrugged.

"Ta'veren," the Ogier said softly.

Agelmar threw up his hands. "It will be as you say, Aes Sedai. Peace, if the real battle is to be at the Eye of the World, I am tempted to take the Black Hawk banner after you instead of to the Gap. I could cut a path for you—"

"That would be disaster, Lord Agelmar. Both at Tarwin's Gap and at the Eye. You have your battle, and we ours."

"Peace! As you say, Aes Sedai."

Having reached a decision, however much he disliked it, the shaven-

headed Lord of Fal Dara seemed to put it out of his mind. He invited
them to table with him, all the while making conversation about hawks
and horses and dogs, but with never a mention of Trollocs, or Tarwin's
Gap, or the Eye of the World.

The chamber where they ate was as stark and plain as Lord
Agelmar's study had been, with little more furnishing it than the table
and chairs themselves, and they were severe in line and form. Beautiful, but severe. A big fireplace warmed the room, but not so much
that a man called out hurriedly would be stunned by the cold outside.
Liveried servants brought soup and bread and cheese, and the talk was
of books and music until Lord Agelmar realized the Emond's Field
folk were not talking. Like a good host he asked gently probing questions designed to bring them out of their quiet.

Rand soon found himself competing to tell about Emond's Field and
the Two Rivers. It was an effort not to say too much. He hoped the
others were guarding their tongues, Mat especially. Nynaeve alone
held herself back, eating and drinking silently.

"There's a song in the Two Rivers," Mat said. "'Coming Home
From Tarwin's Gap.'" He finished hesitantly, as if suddenly realizing
that he was bringing up what they had been avoiding, but Agelmar
handled it smoothly.

"Little wonder. Few lands have not sent men to hold back the Blight
over the years."

Rand looked at Mat and Perrin. Mat silently formed the word
Manetheren.

Agelmar whispered to one of the servants, and while others cleared
the table that man vanished and returned with a canister, and clay
pipes for Lan, Loial, and Lord Agelmar. "Two Rivers tabac," the
Lord of Fal Dara said as they filled their pipes. "Hard to come by,
here, but worth the cost."

When Loial and the two older men were puffing contentedly,
Agelmar glanced at the Ogier. "You seem troubled, Builder. Not beset
by the Longing, I hope. How long have you been away from the
stedding?"

"It is not the Longing; I have not been gone such a time as that."
Loial shrugged, and the blue-gray streamer rising from his pipe made
a spiral above the table as he gestured. "I expected—hoped—that the
grove would still be here. Some remnant of Mafal Dadaranell, at
least."

"Kiserai ti Wansho," Agelmar murmured. "The Trolloc Wars left
nothing but memories, Loial, son of Arent, and people to build on

them. They could not duplicate the Builders' work, any more than could I. Those intricate curves and patterns your people create are beyond human eyes and hands to make. Perhaps we wished to avoid a poor imitation that would only have been an ever-present reminder to us of what we had lost. There is a different beauty in simplicity, in a single line placed just so, a single flower among the rocks. The harshness of the stone makes the flower more precious. We try not to dwell too much on what is gone. The strongest heart will break under that strain."

"The rose petal floats on water," Lan recited softly. "The kingfisher flashes above the pond. Life and beauty swirl in the midst of death."

"Yes," Agelmar said. "Yes. That one has always symbolized the whole of it to me, too." The two men bowed their heads to one another.

Poetry out of Lan? The man was like an onion; every time Rand thought he knew something about the Warder, he discovered another layer underneath.

Loial nodded slowly. "Perhaps I also dwell too much on what is gone. And yet, the groves were beautiful." But he was looking at the stark room as if seeing it anew, and suddenly finding things worth seeing.

Ingtar appeared and bowed to Lord Agelmar. "Your pardon, Lord, but you wanted to know of anything out of the ordinary, however small."

"Yes, what is it?"

"A small thing, Lord. A stranger tried to enter the town. Not of Shienar. By his accent, a Lugarder. Sometimes, at least. When the South Gate guards attempted to question him, he ran away. He was seen to enter the forest, but only a short time later he was found scaling the wall."

"A small thing!" Agelmar's chair scraped across the floor as he stood. "Peace! The tower watch is so negligent a man can reach the walls unseen, and you call it a small thing?"

"He is a madman, Lord." Awe touched Ingtar's voice. "The Light shields madmen. Perhaps the Light cloaked the tower watch's eyes and allowed him to reach the walls. Surely one poor madman can do no harm."

"Has he been brought to the keep yet? Good. Bring him to me here. Now." Ingtar bowed and left, and Agelmar turned to Moiraine. "Your pardon, Aes Sedai, but I must see to this. Perhaps he is only a pitiful wretch with his mind blinded by the Light, but. . . . Two days gone,

five of our own people were found in the night trying to saw through
the hinges of a horsegate. Small, but enough to let Trollocs in." He
grimaced. "Darkfriends, I suppose, though I hate to think it of any
Shienaran. They were torn to pieces by the people before the guards
could take them, so I'll never know. If Shienarans can be Darkfriends,
I must be especially careful of outlanders in these days. If you wish to
withdraw, I will have you shown to your rooms."

"Darkfriends know neither border nor blood," Moiraine said. "They
are found in every land, and are *of* none. I, too, am interested in
seeing this man. The Pattern is forming a Web, Lord Agelmar, but the
final shape of the Web is not yet set. It may yet entangle the world,
or unravel and set the Wheel to a new weaving. At this point, even
small things can change the shape of the Web. At this point I am wary
of small things out of the ordinary."

Agelmar glanced at Nynaeve and Egwene. "As you wish, Aes
Sedai."

Ingtar returned, with two guards carrying long bills, and escorting a
man who looked like a ragbag turned inside out. Grime layered his
face and matted his scraggly, uncut hair and beard. He hunched into
the room, sunken eyes darting this way and that. A rancid smell wafted
ahead of him.

Rand sat forward intently, trying to see through all the dirt.

"You've no cause to be holding me like this," the filthy man whined.
"I'm only a poor destitute, abandoned by the Light and seeking a
place, like everyone else, to shelter from the Shadow."

"The Borderlands are a strange place to seek—" Agelmar began,
when Mat cut him off.

"The peddler!"

"Padan Fain," Perrin agreed, nodding.

"The beggar," Rand said, suddenly hoarse. He sat back at the sudden hatred that flared in Fain's eyes. "He's the man who was asking
about us in Caemlyn. He has to be."

"So this concerns you after all, Moiraine Sedai," Agelmar said
slowly.

Moiraine nodded. "I greatly fear that it does."

"I didn't want to." Fain began to cry. Fat tears cut runnels in the
dirt on his cheeks, but they were unable to reach the bottom layer.
"He made me! Him and his burning eyes." Rand flinched. Mat had
his hand under his coat, no doubt clutching the dagger from Shadar
Logoth again. "He made me his hound! His hound, to hunt and follow
with never a bit of rest. Only his hound, even after he threw me
away."

"It does concern us all," Moiraine said grimly. "Is there a place where I can talk with him alone, Lord Agelmar?" Her mouth tightened with distaste. "And wash him first. I may need to touch him." Agelmar nodded and spoke softly to Ingtar, who bowed and disappeared through the door.

"I will not be compelled!" The voice was Fain's, but he was no longer crying, and an arrogant snap had replaced the whine. He stood upright, not crouching at all. Throwing back his head, he shouted at the ceiling. "Never again! I—will—not!" He faced Agelmar as if the men flanking him were his own bodyguard and the Lord of Fal Dara his equal rather than his captor. His tone became sleek and oily. "There is a misunderstanding here, Great Lord. I am sometimes taken by spells, but that will pass soon. Yes, soon I will be rid of them." Contemptuously he flicked his fingers against the rags he wore. "Do not be misled by these, Great Lord. I have had to disguise myself against those who have tried to stop me, and my journey has been long and hard. But at last I have reached lands where men still know the dangers of Ba'alzamon, where men still fight the Dark One."

Rand stared, goggling. It *was* Fain's voice, but the words did not sound like the peddler at all.

"So you've come here because we fight Trollocs," Agelmar said. "And you are so important that someone wants to stop you. These people say you are a peddler called Padan Fain, and that you are following them."

Fain hesitated. He glanced at Moiraine and hurriedly pulled his eyes away from the Aes Sedai. His gaze ran across the Emond's Fielders, then jerked back to Agelmar. Rand felt the hate in that look, and the fear. When Fain spoke again, though, his voice was unruffled. "Padan Fain is simply one of the many disguises I have been forced to wear over the years. Friends of the Dark pursue me, for I have learned how to defeat the Shadow. I can show you how to defeat him, Great Lord."

"We do as well as men can," Agelmar said dryly. "The Wheel weaves as the Wheel wills, but we have fought the Dark One almost since the Breaking of the World without peddlers to teach us how."

"Great Lord, your might is unquestioned, but can it stand against the Dark One forever? Do you not often find yourself pressed to hold? Forgive my temerity, Great Lord; he will crush you in the end, as you are. I know; believe me, I do. But I can show you how to scour the Shadow from the land, Great Lord." His tone became even more unctuous, though still haughty. "If you but try what I advise, you will see, Great Lord. You will cleanse the land. You, Great Lord, can do it, if you direct your might in the right direction. Avoid letting Tar Valon entangle you in its snares, and you can save the world. Great Lord, you will be the man remembered through history for bringing final victory to the Light." The guards held their places, but their hands shifted on the long shafts of the bills as if they thought they might have to use them.

"He thinks a great deal of himself for a peddler," Agelmar said to Lan over his shoulder. "I think Ingtar is right. He is mad."

Fain's eyes tightened angrily, but his voice remained smooth. "Great Lord, I know my words must appear grandiose, but if you will only—" He cut off abruptly, stepping back, as Moiraine rose and started slowly around the table. Only the guards' lowered bills kept Fain from backing right out of the room.

Stopping behind Mat's chair, Moiraine put a hand on his shoulder and bent to whisper in his ear. Whatever she said, the tension went out of his face, and he took his hand from under his coat. The Aes Sedai went on until she stood beside Agelmar, confronting Fain. As she came to a halt, the peddler sank into a crouch once more.

"I hate him," he whimpered. "I want to be free of him. I want to walk in the Light again." His shoulders began to shake, and tears streamed down his face even more heavily than before. "He made me do it."

"I am afraid he is more than a peddler, Lord Agelmar," Moiraine said. "Less than human, worse than vile, more dangerous than you can imagine. He can be bathed after I have spoken with him. I dare not waste a minute. Come, Lan."

CHAPTER

47

More Tales of the Wheel

A n itchy restlessness had Rand pacing beside the dining table. Twelve strides. The table was exactly twelve strides long no matter how many times he stepped it off. Irritably he made himself stop keeping tally. *Stupid thing to be doing. I don't care how long the bloody table is.* A few minutes later he discovered that he was counting the number of trips he made up the table and back. *What is he saying to Moiraine and Lan? Does he know why the Dark One is after us? Does he know which of us the Dark One wants?*

He glanced at his friends. Perrin had crumbled a piece of bread and was idly pushing the crumbs around on the table with one finger. His yellow eyes stared unblinking at the crumbs, but they seemed to see something far off. Mat slouched in his chair, eyes half closed and the beginnings of a grin on his face. It was a nervous grin, not amusement. Outwardly he looked like the old Mat, but from time to time he unconsciously touched the Shadar Logoth dagger through his coat. *What is Fain telling her? What does he know?*

Loial, at least, did not look worried. The Ogier was studying the walls. First he had stood in the middle of the room and stared, turning slowly in a circle; now he was almost pressing his broad nose against the stone while he gently traced a particular join with fingers thicker than most men's thumbs. Sometimes he closed his eyes, as if the feeling was more important than seeing. His ears gave an occasional twitch, and he muttered to himself in Ogier, appearing to have forgotten anyone else was in the room with him.

Lord Agelmar stood talking quietly with Nynaeve and Egwene in front of the long fireplace at the end of the room. He was a good host, adept at making people forget their troubles; several of his stories had Egwene in giggles. Once even Nynaeve threw back her head and roared with laughter. Rand gave a start at the unexpected sound, and jumped again when Mat's chair crashed to the floor.

"Blood and ashes!" Mat growled, ignoring the way Nynaeve's mouth tightened at his language. "What's taking her so long?" He righted his chair and sat back down without looking at anyone. His hand strayed to his coat.

The Lord of Fal Dara looked at Mat disapprovingly—his gaze took in Rand and Perrin without any improvement—then turned back to the women. Rand's pacing had taken him close to them.

"My Lord," Egwene was saying, as glibly as if she had been using titles all of her life, "I thought he was a Warder, but you call him Dai Shan, and talk about a Golden Crane banner, and so did those other men. Sometimes you sound almost as if he's a king. I remember once Moiraine called him the last Lord of the Seven Towers. Who is he?"

Nynaeve began studying her cup intently, but it was obvious to Rand that abruptly she was listening even more closely than was Egwene. Rand stopped and tried to overhear without seeming to eavesdrop.

"Lord of the Seven Towers," Agelmar said with a frown. "An ancient title, Lady Egwene. Not even the High Lords of Tear have older, though the Queen of Andor comes close." He heaved a sigh, and shook his head. "He will not speak of it, yet the story is well known along the Border. He is a king, or should have been, al'Lan Mandragoran, Lord of the Seven Towers, Lord of the Lakes, crownless King of the Malkieri." His shaven head lifted high, and there was a light in his eye as if he felt a father's pride. His voice grew stronger, filled with the force of his feeling. The whole room could hear without straining. "We of Shienar call ourselves Bordermen, but fewer than fifty years ago, Shienar was not truly of the Borderlands. North of us, and of Arafel, was Malkier. The lances of Shienar rode north, but it was Malkier that held back the Blight. Malkier, Peace favor her memory, and the Light illumine her name."

"Lan is from Malkier," the Wisdom said softly, looking up. She seemed troubled.

It was not a question, but Agelmar nodded. "Yes, Lady Nynaeve, he is the son of al'Akir Mandragoran, last crowned King of the Malkieri. How did he become as he is? The beginning, perhaps, was Lain. On a dare, Lain Mandragoran, the King's brother, led his lances through the Blight to the Blasted Lands, perhaps to Shayol Ghul itself. Lain's wife, Breyan, made that dare for the envy that burned her heart that al'Akir had been raised to the throne instead of Lain. The King and Lain were as close as brothers could be, as close as twins even after the royal 'al' was added to Akir's name, but jealousy wracked Breyan. Lain was acclaimed for his deeds, and rightfully so, but not even he could outshine al'Akir. He was, man and king, such as comes once in a hundred years, if that. Peace favor him, and el'Leanna.

"Lain died in the Blasted Lands with most of those who followed him, men Malkier could ill afford to lose, and Breyan blamed the King, saying that Shayol Ghul itself would have fallen if al'Akir had led the rest of the Malkieri north with her husband. For revenge, she plotted with Cowin Gemallan, called Cowin Fairheart, to seize the throne for her son, Isam. Now Fairheart was a hero almost as well loved as al'Akir himself, and one of the Great Lords, but when the Great Lords had cast the rods for king, only two separated him from Akir, and he never forgot that two men laying a different color on the Crowning Stone would have set him on the throne instead. Between them, Cowin and Breyan moved soldiers back from the Blight to seize the Seven Towers, stripping the Borderforts to bare garrisons.

"But Cowin's jealousy ran deeper." Disgust tinged Agelmar's voice. "Fairheart the hero, whose exploits in the Blight were sung throughout the Borderlands, was a Darkfriend. With the Borderforts weakened, Trollocs poured into Malkier like a flood. King al'Akir and Lain together might have rallied the land; they had done so before. But Lain's doom in the Blasted Lands had shaken the people, and the Trolloc invasion broke men's spirit and their will to resist. Too many men. Overwhelming numbers pushed the Malkieri back into the heartland.

"Breyan fled with her infant son Isam, and was run down by Trollocs as she rode south with him. No one knows their fate of a certainty, but it can be guessed. I can find pity only for the boy. When Cowin Fairheart's treachery was revealed and he was taken by young Jain Charin—already called Jain Farstrider—when Fairheart was brought to the Seven Towers in chains, the Great Lords called for his head on a pike. But because he had been second only to al'Akir and Lain in the hearts of the people, the King faced him in single combat and slew him. Al'Akir wept when he killed Cowin. Some say he wept for a friend who had given himself to the Shadow, and some say for Malkier." The Lord of Fal Dara shook his head sadly.

"The first peal of the doom of the Seven Towers had been struck. There was no time to gather aid from Shienar or Arafel, and no hope that Malkier could stand alone, with five thousand of her lances dead in the Blasted Lands, her Borderforts overrun.

"Al'Akir and his Queen, el'Leanna, had Lan brought to them in his cradle. Into his infant hands they placed the sword of Malkieri kings, the sword he wears today. A weapon made by Aes Sedai during the War of Power, the War of the Shadow that brought down the Age of Legends. They anointed his head with oil, naming him Dai Shan, a Diademed Battle Lord, and consecrated him as the next King of the Malkieri, and in his name they swore the ancient oath of Malkieri kings and queens." Agelmar's face hardened, and he spoke the words as if he, too, had sworn that oath, or one much similar. "To stand against the Shadow so long as iron is hard and stone abides. To defend the Malkieri while one drop of blood remains. To avenge what cannot be defended." The words rang in the chamber.

"El'Leanna placed a locket around her son's neck, for remembrance, and the infant, wrapped in swaddling clothes by the Queen's own hand, was given over to twenty chosen from the King's Bodyguard, the best swordsmen, the most deadly fighters. Their command: to carry the child to Fal Moran.

"Then did al'Akir and el'Leanna lead the Malkieri out to face the Shadow one last time. There they died, at Herot's Crossing, and the Malkieri died, and the Seven Towers were broken. Shienar, and Arafel, and Kandor, met the Halfmen and the Trollocs at the Stair of Jehaan and threw them back, but not as far as they had been. Most of Malkier remained in Trolloc hands, and year by year, mile by mile, the Blight has swallowed it." Agelmar drew a heavyhearted breath. When he went on, there was a sad pride in his eyes and voice.

"Only five of the Bodyguards reached Fal Moran alive, every man wounded, but they had the child unharmed. From the cradle they taught him all they knew. He learned weapons as other children learn toys, and the Blight as other children their mother's garden. The oath sworn over his cradle is graven in his mind. There is nothing left to defend, but he can avenge. He denies his titles, yet in the Borderlands he is called the Uncrowned, and if ever he raised the Golden Crane of Malkier, an army would come to follow. But he will not lead men to their deaths. In the Blight he courts death as a suitor courts a maiden, but he will not lead others to it.

"If you must enter the Blight, and with only a few, there is no man better to take you there, nor to bring you safely out again. He is the best of the Warders, and that means the best of the best. You might as well leave these boys here, to gain a little seasoning, and put your entire trust in Lan. The Blight is no place for untried boys."

Mat opened his mouth, and shut it again at a look from Rand. *I wish he'd learn to keep it shut.*

Nynaeve had listened just as wide-eyed as Egwene, but now she was staring into her cup again, her face pale. Egwene put a hand on her arm and gave her a sympathetic look.

Moiraine appeared in the doorway, Lan at her heels. Nynaeve turned her back on them.

"What did he say?" Rand demanded. Mat rose, and Perrin, too.

"Country oaf," Agelmar muttered, then raised his voice to a normal tone. "Did you learn anything, Aes Sedai, or is he simply a madman?"

"He is mad," Moiraine said, "or close to it, but there is nothing simple about Padan Fain." One of the black-and-gold-liveried servants bowed his way in with a blue washbasin and pitcher, a bar of yellow soap, and a small towel on a silver tray; he looked anxiously at Agelmar. Moiraine directed him to put them on the table. "Your pardon for commanding your servants, Lord Agelmar," she said. "I took the liberty of asking for this."

Agelmar nodded to the servant, who put the tray on the table and left hurriedly. "My servants are yours to command, Aes Sedai."

The water Moiraine poured into the basin steamed as if only just off the boil. She pushed up her sleeves and began vigorously washing her hands without regard for the heat of the water. "I said he was worse than vile, but I did not come close. I do not believe I have ever met someone so abject and debased, yet at the same time so foul. I feel soiled from touching him, and I do not mean for the filth on his skin. Soiled in here." She touched her breast. "The degradation of his soul almost makes me doubt he has one. There is something worse to him than a Darkfriend."

"He looked so pitiful," Egwene murmured. "I remember him arriving in Emond's Field each spring, always laughing and full of news from outside. Surely there's some hope for him? 'No man can stand in the Shadow so long that he cannot find the Light again,'" she quoted.

The Aes Sedai toweled her hands briskly. "I have always believed it so," she said. "Perhaps Padan Fain can be redeemed. But he has been a Darkfriend more than forty years, and what he has done for that, in blood and pain and death, would freeze your heart to hear. Among the least of these—though not small to you, I suspect—he brought the Trollocs to Emond's Field."

"Yes," Rand said softly. He heard Egwene gasp. *I should have guessed. Burn me, I should have, as soon as I recognized him.*

"Did he bring any here?" Mat asked. He looked at the stone walls around them and shivered. Rand thought he was remembering the Myddraal more than Trollocs; walls had not stopped the Fade at Baerlon, or at Whitebridge.

"If he did"—Agelmar laughed—"they'll break their teeth on the walls of Fal Dara. Many others have before." He was speaking to everyone, but obviously addressing his words to Egwene and Nynaeve, from the glances he gave them. "And do not worry yourself about Halfmen, either." Mat's face reddened. "Every street and alley in Fal Dara is lit by night. And no man may hide his face inside the walls."

"Why would Master Fain do that?" Egwene asked.

"Three years ago. . . ." With a heavy sigh Moiraine sat down, folding up as if what she had done with Fain had drained her. "Three years, this summer. As far back as that. The Light surely favors us, else the Father of Lies would have triumphed while I still sat planning in Tar Valon. Three years, Fain has been hunting you for the Dark One."

"That's crazy!" Rand said. "He's come into the Two Rivers every spring as regular as a clock. Three years? We've been right there in front of him, and he never looked at any of us twice before last year." The Aes Sedai pointed a finger at him, fixing him.

"Fain told me everything, Rand. Or almost everything. I believe he managed to hold back something, something important, despite all I could do, but he said enough. Three years ago, a Halfman came for him in a town in Murandy. Fain was terrified, of course, but it is considered a very great honor among Darkfriends to be so summoned. Fain believed he had been chosen for great things, and he had, though not in the manner he believed. He was brought north to the Blight, to the Blasted Lands. To Shayol Ghul. Where he met a man with eyes of fire, who named himself Ba'alzamon."

Mat shifted uneasily, and Rand swallowed hard. It had to have been that way, of course, but that did not make it any easier to accept. Only Perrin looked at the Aes Sedai as if nothing could surprise him any longer.

"The Light protect us," Agelmar said fervently.

"Fain did not like what was done to him at Shayol Ghul," Moiraine continued calmly. "While we talked, he screamed often of fire and burning. It almost killed him, bringing it all out from where he had it hidden. Even with my Healing he is a shattered ruin. It will take much to make him whole again. I will make the effort, though, if for no other reason than to learn what more he still hides. He had been chosen because of where he did his peddling. No," she said quickly when they stirred, "not the Two Rivers only, not then. The Father of Lies knew roughly where to find what he sought, but not much better than we in Tar Valon.

"Fain said he has been made the Dark One's hound, and in a way he is right. The Father of Lies set Fain to hunt, first changing him so he could carry out that hunt. It is the things done to bring about those changes that Fain fears to remember; he hates his master for them as much as he fears him. So Fain was sent sniffing and hunting through all the villages around Baerlon, and all the way to the Mountains of Mist, and down to the Taren and across into the Two Rivers."

"Three springs ago?" Perrin said slowly. "I remember that spring. Fain came later than usual, but what was strange was that he lingered on. A whole week he remained, idle and gnashing his teeth about laying out money for a room at the Winespring Inn. Fain likes his money."

"I remember, now," Mat said. "Everybody was wondering was he sick, or had he fallen for a local woman? Not that any of them would marry a peddler, of course. As well marry one of the Traveling People." Egwene raised an eyebrow at him, and he shut his mouth.

"After that, Fain was taken to Shayol Ghul again, and his mind was—distilled." Rand's stomach turned over at the tone in the Aes Sedai's voice; it told more of what she meant than the grimace that flashed across her face. "What he had . . . sensed . . . was concentrated and fed back. When he entered the Two Rivers the next year, he was able to choose his targets out more clearly. Indeed, more clearly even than the Dark One had expected. Fain knew for a certainty that the one he sought was one of three in Emond's Field."

Perrin grunted, and Mat began cursing in a soft monotone that even Nynaeve's glare did not stop. Agelmar looked at them curiously. Rand felt only the faintest chill, and wondered at it. Three years the Dark One had been hunting him . . . hunting them. He was sure it should have made his teeth chatter.

Moiraine did not allow Mat to interrupt her. She raised her voice enough to be heard over him. "When Fain returned to Lugard, Ba'alzamon came to him in a dream. Fain abased himself and performed rites that would strike you deaf to hear the half of them, binding himself even more tightly to the Dark One. What is done in dreams can be more dangerous than what is done awake." Rand stirred at the sharp, warning look, but she did not pause. "He was promised great rewards, power over kingdoms after Ba'alzamon's victory, and told that when he returned to Emond's Field he was to mark the three he had found. A Halfman would be there, waiting for him with Trollocs. We know now how the Trollocs came to the Two Rivers. There must have been an Ogier grove and a Waygate at Manetheren."

"The most beautiful of all," Loial said, "except for Tar Valon." He had been listening as intently as everyone else. "Manetheren is remembered fondly by the Ogier." Agelmar formed the name silently, his eyebrows raised in wonder. Manetheren.

"Lord Agelmar," Moiraine said, "I will tell you how to find the Waygate of Mafal Dadaranell. It must be walled up and a guard set, and none allowed near. The Halfmen have not learned all of the Ways yet, but that Waygate is to the south and only hours from Fal Dara."

The Lord of Fal Dara gave himself a shake, as if he were coming out of a trance. "South? Peace! We don't need that, the Light shine on us. It shall be done."

"Did Fain follow us through the Ways?" Perrin asked. "He must have done."

Moiraine nodded. "Fain would follow you three into the grave, because he must. When the Myrddraal failed at Emond's Field, it brought Fain with the Trollocs on our trail. The Fade would not let Fain ride with him; although he thought he should have the best horse in the Two Rivers and ride at the head of the band, the Myrddraal forced him to run with the Trollocs, and the Trollocs to carry him when his feet gave out. They talked so that he could understand, arguing about the best way to cook him when his usefulness was done. Fain claims he turned against the Dark One before they reached the Taren. But sometimes his greed for his promised rewards seeps into the open.

"When we had escaped across the Taren the Myrddraal took the Trollocs back to the closest Waygate, in the Mountains of Mist, and sent Fain across alone. He thought he was free then, but before he reached Baerlon another Fade found him, and that one was not so kind. It made him sleep doubled up on himself in a Trolloc kettle at night, to remind him of the price of failure. That one used him as far as Shadar Logoth. By then Fain was willing to give the Myrddraal his mother if it would free him, but the Dark One never willingly loosens a hold he has gained.

"What I did there, sending an illusion of our tracks and smell off toward the mountains, fooled the Myrddraal, but not Fain. The Half-men did not believe him; afterward, they dragged him behind them on a leash. Only when we seemed to keep always just ahead, no matter how hard they pressed, did some begin to credit him. Those were the four who returned to Shadar Logoth. Fain claims it was Ba'alzamon himself who drove the Myrddraal."

Agelmar shook his head contemptuously. "The Dark One? Pah! The man's lying or mad. If Heartsbane were loose, we'd all of us be dead by now, or worse."

"Fain spoke the truth as he saw it," Moiraine said. "He could not lie to me, though he hid much. His words. 'Ba'alzamon appeared like a flickering candle flame, vanishing and reappearing, never in the same place twice. His eyes seared the Myrddraal, and the fires of his mouth scourged us.'"

"*Something,*" Lan said, "drove four Fades to where they feared to go—a place they fear almost as much as they fear the wrath of the Dark One."

Agelmar grunted as if he had been kicked; he looked sick.

"It was evil against evil in the ruins of Shadar Logoth," Moiraine continued, "foul fighting vile. When Fain spoke of it, his teeth chattered and he whimpered. Many Trollocs were slain, consumed by Mashadar and other things, including the Trolloc that held Fain's leash. He fled the city as if it were the Pit of Doom, at Shayol Ghul."

"Fain believed he was free at last. He intended to run until Ba'alzamon could never find him again, to the ends of the earth if necessary. Imagine his horror when he discovered that the compulsion to hunt did not lessen. Instead, it grew stronger and sharper with every day that passed. He could not eat, except what he could scavenge while he hunted you—beetles and lizards snatched while he ran, half-rotten refuse dug from midden heaps in the dark of night—nor could he stop until exhaustion collapsed him like an empty sack. And as soon as he had strength to stand again, he was driven on. By the time he reached Caemlyn he could *feel* his quarry even when it was a mile away. Here, in the cells below, he would sometimes look up without realizing what he was doing. He was looking in the direction of this room."

Rand had a sudden itch between his shoulder blades; it was as if he could feel Fain's eyes on him then, through the intervening stone. The Aes Sedai noticed his uneasy shrug, but she went on implacably.

"If Fain was half mad by the time he reached Caemlyn, he sank even further when he realized that only two of those he sought were there. He was compelled to find *all* of you, but he could do no other than follow the two who were there, either. He spoke of screaming when the Waygate opened in Caemlyn. The knowledge of how to do it was in his mind; he does not know how it came there; his hands moved of their own accord, burning with the fires of Ba'alzamon when he tried to stop them. The owner of the shop, who came to investigate the noise, Fain murdered. Not because he had to, but out of envy that the man could walk freely out of the cellar while his feet carried him inexorably into the Ways."

"Then Fain was the one you sensed following us," Egwene said. Lan nodded. "How did he escape the . . . the Black Wind?" Her voice shook; she stopped to swallow. "It was right behind us at the Waygate."

"He escaped, and he did not," Moiraine said. "The Black Wind caught him—and he claimed to understand the voices. Some greeted him as like to them; others feared him. No sooner did the Wind envelop Fain than it fled."

"The Light preserve us." Loial's whisper rumbled like a giant bumblebee.

"Pray that it does," Moiraine said. "There is much yet hidden about Padan Fain, much I must learn. The evil goes deeper in him, and stronger, than in any man I have yet seen. It may be that the Dark One, in doing what he did to Fain, impressed some part of himself on the man, perhaps even, unknowing, some part of his intent. When I mentioned the Eye of the World, Fain clamped his jaws shut, but I felt something knowing behind the silence. If only I had the time now. But we cannot wait."

"If this man knows something," Agelmar said, "I can get it out of him." His face held no mercy for Darkfriends; his voice promised no pity for Fain. "If you can learn even a part of what you will face in the Blight, it's worth an extra day. Battles have been lost for not knowing what the enemy intends."

Moiraine sighed and shook her head ruefully. "My lord, if we did not need at least one good night's sleep before facing the Blight, I would ride within the hour, though it meant the risk of meeting a Trolloc raid in the dark. Consider what I did learn from Fain. Three years ago the Dark One had to have Fain brought to Shayol Ghul to touch him, despite the fact that Fain is a Darkfriend dedicated to his marrow. One year ago, the Dark One could command Fain, the Darkfriend, through his dreams. This year, Ba'alzamon walks in the dreams of those who live in the Light, and actually appears, if with difficulty, at Shadar Logoth. Not in his own body, of course, but even a projection of the Dark One's mind, even a projection that flickers and cannot hold, is more deathly dangerous to the world than all the Trolloc hordes combined. The seals on Shayol Ghul are weakening desperately, Lord Agelmar. There is no time."

Agelmar bowed his head in acquiescence, but when he raised it again there was still a stubborn set to his mouth. "Aes Sedai, I can accept that when I lead the lances to Tarwin's Gap we will be no more than a diversion, or a skirmish on the outskirts of the real battle. Duty takes men where it will as surely as does the Pattern, and neither promises that what we do will have greatness. But our skirmish will be useless, even should we win, if you lose the battle. If you say your party must be small, I say well and good, but I beg you to make every effort to see that you *can* win. Leave these young men here, Aes Sedai. I swear to you that I can find three experienced men with no thought of glory in their heads to replace them, good swordsmen who are almost as handy in the Blight as Lan. Let me ride to the Gap knowing that I have done what I can to help you be victorious."

"I must take them and no others, Lord Agelmar," Moiraine said gently. "They are the ones who will fight the battle at the Eye of the World."

Agelmar's jaw dropped, and he stared at Rand and Mat and Perrin. Suddenly the Lord of Fal Dara took a step back, his hand groping unconsciously for the sword he never wore inside the fortress. "They aren't. . . . You are not Red Ajah, Moiraine Sedai, but surely not even you would. . . ." Sudden sweat glistened on his shaven head.

"They are *ta'veren*," Moiraine said soothingly. "The Pattern weaves itself around them. Already the Dark One has tried to kill each of them more than once. Three *ta'veren* in one place are enough to change the life around them as surely as a whirlpool changes the path of a straw. When the place is the Eye of the World, the Pattern might weave even the Father of Lies into itself, and make him harmless again."

Agelmar stopped trying to find his sword, but he still looked at Rand and the others doubtfully. "Moiraine Sedai, if you say they are, then they are, but I cannot see it. Farmboys. Are you certain, Aes Sedai?"

"The old blood," Moiraine said, "split out like a river breaking into a thousand times a thousand streams, but sometimes streams join together to make a river again. The old blood of Manetheren is strong and pure in almost all these young men. Can you doubt the strength of Manetheren's blood, Lord Agelmar?"

Rand glanced sideways at the Aes Sedai. *Almost all.* He risked a look at Nynaeve; she had turned back to watch as well as listen, though she still avoided looking at Lan. He caught the Wisdom's eye. She shook her head; she had not told the Aes Sedai that he was not Two Rivers born. *What does Moiraine know?*

"Manetheren," Agelmar said slowly, nodding. "I would not doubt that blood." Then, more quickly, "The Wheel brings strange times. Farmboys carry the honor of Manetheren into the Blight, yet if any blood can strike a fell blow at the Dark One, it would be the blood of Manetheren. It shall be done as you wish, Aes Sedai."

"Then let us go to our rooms," Moiraine said. "We must leave with the sun, for time grows short. The young men must sleep close to me. Time is too short before the battle to allow the Dark One another strike at them. Too short."

Rand felt her eyes on him, studying him and his friends, weighing their strength, and he shivered. Too short.

CHAPTER
48

The Blight

The wind whipped Lan's cloak, sometimes making him hard to see even in the sunlight, and Ingtar and the hundred lances Lord Agelmar had sent to escort them to the Border, in case they met a Trolloc raid, made a brave display in double column with their armor and their red pennants and their steel-clad horses led by Ingtar's Gray Owl banner. They were easily as grand as a hundred of the Queen's Guards, but it was the towers just in sight ahead of them that Rand studied. He had had all morning to watch the Shienaran lances.

Each tower stood tall and solid atop a hill, half a mile from its neighbor. East and west others rose, and more beyond those. A broad, walled ramp spiraled around each stone shaft, winding all the way around by the time it reached the heavy gates halfway to the crenellated top. A sortie from the garrison would be protected by the wall until it reached the ground, but enemies striving to reach the gate would climb under a hail of arrows and stones and hot oil from the big kettles poised on the outward flaring ramparts above. A large steel mirror, carefully turned down, away from the sun, now, glittered atop each tower below the high iron cup where signal fires could be lit when the sun did not shine. The signal would be flashed, to towers further from the Border, and by those to still others, and so relayed to the heartland fortresses, from where the lances would ride to turn back the raid. Were times normal, they would.

From the two nearest tower tops men watched them approach. Just a few men on each, peering curiously through the crenels. In the best of times the towers were only manned enough for self-defense, depending more on stone walls than strong arms to survive, but every man who could be spared, and more, was riding to Tarwin's Gap. The fall of the towers would not matter if the lances failed to hold the Gap.

Rand shivered as they rode between the towers. It was almost as if he had ridden through a wall of colder air. This was the Border. The land beyond looked no different from Shienar, but out there, somewhere beyond the leafless trees, was the Blight.

Ingtar lifted a steel fist to halt the lances short of a plain stone post in sight of the towers. A borderpost, marking the boundary between Shienar and what once was Malkier. "Your pardon, Moiraine Aes Sedai. Pardon, Dai Shan. Pardon, Builder. Lord Agelmar commanded me to go no further." He sounded unhappy about it, disgruntled at life in general.

"That is as we planned, Lord Agelmar and I," Moiraine said.

Ingtar grunted sourly. "Pardon, Aes Sedai," he apologized, not sounding as if he meant it. "To escort you here means we may not reach the Gap before the fighting is done. I am robbed of the chance to stand with the rest, and at the same time I am commanded not to ride one step beyond the borderpost, as if I had never before been in the Blight. And My Lord Agelmar will not tell me why." Behind the bars of his face-guard, his eyes turned the last word into a question to the Aes Sedai. He scorned to look at Rand and the others; he had learned they would accompany Lan into the Blight.

"He can have my place," Mat muttered to Rand. Lan gave them both a sharp look. Mat dropped his eyes, his face turning red.

"Each of us has his part in the Pattern, Ingtar," Moiraine said firmly. "From here we must thread ours alone."

Ingtar's bow was stiffer than his armor made it. "As you wish it, Aes Sedai. I must leave you, now, and ride hard in order to reach Tarwin's Gap. At least I will be . . . *allowed* . . . to face Trollocs there."

"Are you truly that eager?" Nynaeve asked. "To fight Trollocs?"

Ingtar gave her a puzzled look, then glanced at Lan as if the Warder might explain. "That is what I do, Lady," he said slowly. "That is why I am." He raised a gauntleted hand to Lan, open palm toward the warder. *"Suravye ninto manshima taishite, Dai Shan.* Peace favor your sword." Pulling his horse around, Ingtar rode east with his bannerman and his hundred lances. They went at a walk, but a steady pace, as fast as armored horses could manage with a far distance yet to go.

"What a strange thing to say," Egwene said. "Why do they use it like that? Peace."

"When you have never known a thing except to dream," Lan replied, heeling Mandarb forward, "it becomes more than a talisman."

As Rand followed the Warder past the stone borderpost, he turned in his saddle to look back, watching Ingtar and the lances disappear behind barren trees, and the borderpost vanish, and last of all the towers on their hilltops, looking over the trees. All too soon they were alone, riding north under the leafless canopy of the forest. Rand sank into watchful silence, and for once even Mat had nothing to say.

That morning the gates of Fal Dara had opened with the dawn. Lord Agelmar, armored and helmeted now like his soldiers, rode with the Black Hawk banner and the Three Foxes from the East Gate toward the sun, still only a red sliver above the trees. Like a steel snake undulating to mounted kettle-drums, the column wound its way out of the town four abreast, Agelmar at its head hidden in the forest before its tail left Fal Dara keep. There were no cheers in the streets to speed them on their way, only their own drums and their pennants' cracking in the wind, but their eyes looked toward the rising sun with purpose. Eastward they would join other steel serpents, from Fal Moran, behind King Easar himself with his sons at his side, and from Ankor Dail, that held the Eastern Marches and guarded the Spine of the World; from Mos Shirare and Fal Sion and Camron Caan, and all the other fortresses in Shienar, great and small. Joined into a greater serpent, they would turn north to Tarwin's Gap.

Another exodus had begun at the same time, using the King's Gate that led out on the way to Fal Moran. Carts and wagons, people mounted and people afoot, driving their livestock, carrying children on their backs, faces as long as the morning shadows. Reluctance to leave their homes, perhaps forever, slowed their feet, yet fear of what was coming spurred them, so that they went in bursts, feet dragging, then breaking into a run for a dozen paces only to fall back, once more, to shuffling through the dust. A few paused outside the town to watch the soldiers' armored line winding into the forest. Hope blossomed in some eyes, and prayers were muttered, prayers for the soldiers, prayers for themselves, before they turned south again, trudging.

The smallest column went out of the Malkier Gate. Left behind were a few who would remain, soldiers and a sprinkling of older men, their wives dead and their grown children making the slow way south. A last handful so that whatever happened in Tarwin's Gap, Fal Dara would not fall undefended. Ingtar's Gray Owl led the way, but it was Moiraine who took them north. The most important column of all, and the most desperate.

For at least an hour after they passed the borderpost there was no change in land or forest. The Warder kept them at a hard pace, as fast a walk as the horses could maintain, but Rand kept wondering when they would reach the Blight. The hills became a little higher, but the trees, and the creepers, and the underbrush were no different than what he had seen in Shienar, gray and all but leafless. He began to feel warmer, warm enough to sling his cloak across the pommel of his saddle.

"This is the best weather we've seen all year," Egwene said, shrugging out of her own cloak.

Nynaeve shook her head, frowning as if listening to the wind. "It feels wrong."

Rand nodded. He could feel it, too, though he could not say what it was exactly he was feeling. The wrongness went beyond the first warmth he could remember out of doors this year; it was more than the simple fact that it should not be so warm this far north. It must be the Blight, but the land was the same.

The sun climbed high, a red ball that could not give so much warmth despite the cloudless sky. A little while later he unbuttoned his coat. Sweat trickled down his face.

He was not the only one. Mat took his coat off, openly displaying the gold-and-ruby dagger, and wiped his face with the end of his scarf. Blinking, he rewound the scarf into a narrow band low over his eyes. Nynaeve and Egwene fanned themselves; they rode slumped as if they were wilting. Loial undid his high-collared tunic all the way down, and his shirt as well; the Ogier had a narrow strip of hair up the middle of his chest, as thick as fur. He muttered apologies all around.

"You must forgive me. Stedding Shangtai is in the mountains, and cool." His broad nostrils flared, drawing in air that was becoming warmer by the minute. "I don't like this heat, and damp."

It *was* damp, Rand realized. It felt like the Mire in the depths of summer, back in the Two Rivers. In that boggy swamp every breath came as if through a wool blanket soaked in hot water. There was no soggy ground here—only a few ponds and streams, trickles to someone used to the Waterwood—but the air was like that in the Mire. Only Perrin, still in his coat, was breathing easily. Perrin and the Warder.

There were a few leaves now, on trees that were not evergreen. Rand reached out to touch a branch, and stopped with his hand short of the leaves. Sickly yellow mottled the red of the new growth, and black flecks like disease.

"I told you not to touch anything." The Warder's voice was flat. He still wore his shifting cloak, as if heat made no more impression on him than cold; it almost made his angular face seem to float unsupported above Mandarb's back. "Flowers can kill in the Blight, and leaves maim. There's a little thing called a Stick that likes to hide where the leaves are thickest, looking like its name, waiting for something to touch it. When something does, it bites. Not poison. The juice begins to digest the Stick's prey for it. The only thing that can save you is to cut off the arm or leg that was bitten. But a Stick won't bite unless you touch it. Other things in the Blight will."

Rand jerked his hand back, leaves untouched, and wiped it on his pants leg.

"Then we're in the Blight?" Perrin said. Strangely, he did not sound frightened.

"Just the fringe," Lan said grimly. His stallion kept moving forward, and he spoke over his shoulder. "The real Blight still lies ahead. There are things in the Blight that hunt by sound, and some may have wandered this far south. Sometimes they cross the Mountains of Dhoom. Much worse than Sticks. Keep quiet and keep up, if you want to stay alive." He continued to set a hard pace, not waiting for an answer.

Mile by mile the corruption of the Blight became more apparent. Leaves covered the trees in ever greater profusion, but stained and spotted with yellow and black, with livid red streaks like blood poisoning. Every leaf and creeper seemed bloated, ready to burst at a touch. Flowers hung on trees and weeds in a parody of spring, sickly pale and pulpy, waxen things that appeared to be rotting while Rand watched. When he breathed through his nose, the sweet stench of decay, heavy and thick, sickened him; when he tried breathing through his mouth, he almost gagged. The air tasted like a mouthful of spoiled meat. The horses' hooves made a soft squishing as rotten-ripe things broke open under them.

Mat leaned out of his saddle and spewed until his stomach was empty. Rand sought the void, but calmness was little help against the

burning bile that kept creeping up his throat. Empty or not, Mat
heaved again a mile later, bringing up nothing, and yet again after
that. Egwene looked as if she wanted to be sick, too, swallowing constantly, and Nynaeve's face was a white mask of determination, her
jaw set and her eyes fixed on Moiraine's back. The Wisdom would not
admit to feeling ill unless the Aes Sedai did, first, but Rand did not
think she would have to wait long. Moiraine's eyes were tight, and her
lips pale.

Despite the heat and damp, Loial wrapped a scarf around his nose
and mouth. When he met Rand's gaze, the Ogier's outrage and disgust
were plain in his eyes. "I had heard—" he began, his voice muffled
by the wool, then stopped to clear his throat with a grimace. "Faugh!
It tastes like. . . . Faugh! I had heard and read about the Blight, but
nothing could describe. . . ." His gesture somehow took in the smell
as well as the eye-sickening growth. "That even the Dark One should
do this to trees! Faugh!"

The Warder was not affected, of course, at least not that Rand could
see, but to his surprise neither was Perrin. Or rather, not in the way
the rest of them were. The big youth glared at the obscene forest
through which they rode as he might have at an enemy, or the banner
of an enemy. He caressed the axe at his belt as if unaware of what he
was doing, and muttered to himself, half growling in a way that made
the hair on Rand's neck stir. Even in full sunlight his eyes glowed,
golden and fierce.

The heat did not abate as the bloody sun fell toward the horizon.
In the distance to the north, mountains rose, higher than the Mountains of Mist, black against the sky. Sometimes an icy wind from the
sharp peaks gusted far enough to reach them. The torrid humidity
leached away most of the mountain chill, but what remained was
winter-cold compared to the swelter it replaced, if just for a moment.
The sweat on Rand's face seemed to flash into beads of ice; as the wind
died, the beads melted again, running angry lines down his cheeks, and
the thick heat returned harder than before by comparison. For the
instant the wind surrounded them, it swept away the fetor, yet he
would have done without that, too, if he could have. The cold was the
chill of the grave, and it carried the dusty must of an old tomb newly
opened.

"We cannot reach the mountains by nightfall," Lan said, "and it is
dangerous to move at night, even for a Warder alone."

"There is a place not far off," Moiraine said. "It will be a good
omen for us to camp there."

The Warder gave her a flat look, then nodded reluctantly. "Yes. We must camp somewhere. It might as well be there."

"The Eye of the World was beyond the high passes when I found it," Moiraine said. "Better to cross the Mountains of Dhoom in full daylight, at noon, when the Dark One's powers in this world are weakest."

"You talk as if the Eye isn't always in the same place." Egwene spoke to the Aes Sedai, but it was Loial who answered.

"No two among the Ogier have found it in exactly the same place. The Green Man seems to be found where he is needed. But it has always been beyond the high passes. They are treacherous, the high passes, and haunted by creatures of the Dark One."

"We must reach the passes before we need worry about them," Lan said. "Tomorrow we will be truly into the Blight."

Rand looked at the forest around him, every leaf and flower diseased, every creeper decaying as it grew, and he could not repress a shudder. *If this isn't truly the Blight, what is?*

Lan turned them westward, at an angle to the sinking sun. The Warder maintained the pace he had set before, but there was reluctance in the set of his shoulders.

The sun was a sullen red ball just touching the treetops when they crested a hill and the Warder drew rein. Beyond them to the west lay a network of lakes, the waters glittering darkly in the slanting sunlight, like beads of random size on a necklace of many strings. In the distance, circled by the lakes, stood jagged-topped hills, thick in the creeping shadows of evening. For one brief instant the sun's rays caught the shattered tops, and Rand's breath stilled. Not hills. The broken remnants of seven towers. He was not sure if anyone else had seen it; the sight was gone as quickly as it came. The Warder was dismounting, his face as lacking in emotion as a stone.

"Couldn't we camp down by the lakes?" Nynaeve asked, patting her face with her kerchief. "It must be cooler down by the water."

"Light," Mat said, "I'd just like to stick my head in one of them. I might never take it out."

Just then something roiled the waters of the nearest lake, the dark water phosphorescing as a huge body rolled beneath the surface. Length on man-thick length sent ripples spreading, rolling on and on until at last a tail rose, waving a point like a wasp's stinger for an instant in the twilight, at least five spans into the air. All along that length fat tentacles writhed like monstrous worms, as many as a centipede's legs. It slid slowly beneath the surface and was gone, only the fading ripples to say it had ever been.

Rand closed his mouth and exchanged a look with Perrin. Perrin's yellow eyes were as disbelieving as he knew his own must be. Nothing that big could live in a lake that size. *Those couldn't have been* hands *on those tentacles. They couldn't have been.*

"On second thought," Mat said faintly, "I like it right here just fine."

"I will set guarding wards around this hill," Moiraine said. She had already dismounted from Aldieb. "A true barrier would draw the attention we do not want like flies to honey, but if any creation of the Dark One or anything that serves the Shadow comes within a mile of us, I will know."

"I'd be happier with the barrier," Mat said as his boots touched the ground, "just as long as it kept that, that . . . thing on the other side."

"Oh, do be quiet, Mat," Egwene said curtly, at the same time as Nynaeve spoke. "And have them waiting for us when we leave in the morning? You *are* a fool, Matrim Cauthon." Mat glowered at the two women as they climbed down, but he kept his mouth shut.

As he took Bela's reins, Rand shared a grin with Perrin. For a moment it was almost like being home, having Mat saying what he should not at the worst possible time. Then the smile faded from Perrin's face; in the twilight his eyes *did* glow, as if they had a yellow light behind them. Rand's grin slipped away, too. *It isn't like home at all.*

Rand and Mat and Perrin helped Lan unsaddle and hobble the horses while the others began setting up the camp. Loial muttered to himself as he set up the Warder's tiny stove, but his thick fingers moved deftly. Egwene was humming as she filled the tea kettle from a bulging waterbag. Rand no longer wondered why the Warder had insisted on bringing so many full waterskins.

Setting the bay's saddle in line with the others, he unfastened his saddlebags and blanketroll from the cantle, turned, and stopped with a tingle of fear. The Ogier and the women were gone. So was the stove and all the wicker panniers from the packhorse. The hilltop was empty except for evening shadows.

With a numb hand he fumbled for his sword, dimly hearing Mat curse. Perrin had his axe out, his shaggy head swiveling to find the danger.

"Sheepherders," Lan muttered. Unconcernedly the Warder strode across the hilltop, and at his third step, he vanished.

Rand exchanged wide-eyed looks with Mat and Perrin, and then they were all darting for where the Warder had disappeared. Abruptly Rand skidded to a halt, taking another step when Mat ran into his back. Egwene looked up from setting the kettle atop the tiny stove. Nynaeve was closing the mantle on a second lit lantern. They were all there, Moiraine sitting cross-legged, Lan lounging on an elbow, Loial taking a book out of his pack.

Cautiously Rand looked behind him. The hillside was there as it had been, the shadowed trees, the lakes beyond sinking into darkness. He was afraid to step back, afraid they would all disappear again and perhaps this time he would not be able to find them. Edging carefully around him, Perrin let out a long breath.

Moiraine noticed the three of them standing there, gaping. Perrin looked abashed, and slipped his axe back into the heavy belt loop as if he thought no one might notice. A smile touched her lips. "It is a simple thing," she said, "a bending, so any eye looking at us sees around us, instead. We cannot have the eyes that will be out there seeing our lights tonight, and the Blight is no place to be in the dark."

"Moiraine Sedai says I might be able to do it." Egwene's eyes were bright. "She says I can handle enough of the One Power right now."

"Not without training, child," Moiraine cautioned. "The simplest matter concerning the One Power can be dangerous to the untrained, and to those around them." Perrin snorted, and Egwene looked so uncomfortable that Rand wondered if she had already been trying her abilities.

Nynaeve set down the lantern. Together with the tiny flame of the stove, the pair of lanterns gave a generous light. "When you go to Tar Valon, Egwene," she said carefully, "perhaps I'll go with you." The look she gave Moiraine was strangely defensive. "It will do her good to see a familiar face among strangers. She'll need someone to advise her besides Aes Sedai."

"Perhaps that would be for the best, Wisdom," Moiraine said simply.

Egwene laughed and clapped her hands. "Oh, that *will* be wonderful. And you, Rand. You'll come, too, won't you?" He paused in the act of sitting across the stove from her, then slowly lowered himself. He thought her eyes had never been bigger, or brighter, or more like pools that he could lose himself in. Spots of color appeared in her cheeks, and she gave a smaller laugh. "Perrin, Mat, you two will come, won't you? We'll all be together." Mat gave a grunt that could have signified anything, and Perrin only shrugged, but she took it for assent. "You see, Rand. We'll all be together."

Light, but a man could drown in those eyes and be happy doing it. Embarrassed, he cleared his throat. "Do they have sheep in Tar Valon? That's all I know, herding sheep and growing tabac."

"I believe," Moiraine said, "that I can find something for you to do in Tar Valon. For all of you. Not herding sheep, perhaps, but something you will find interesting."

"There," Egwene said as if it were settled. "I know. I will make you my Warder, when I'm an Aes Sedai. You would like being a Warder, wouldn't you? My Warder?" She sounded sure, but he saw the question in her eyes. She wanted an answer, needed it.

"I'd like being your Warder," he said. *She's not for you, nor you for her. Why did Min have to tell me that?*

Darkness came down heavily, and everyone was tired. Loial was the first to roll over and ready himself for sleep, but others followed soon after. No one used their blankets, except for a pillow. Moiraine had put something in the oil of the lamps that dispelled the stench of the Blight from the hilltop, but nothing diminished the heat. The moon gave a wavering, watery light, but the sun might have been at its zenith for all the cool the night had.

Rand found sleep impossible, even with the Aes Sedai stretched out not a span away to shield his dreams. It was the thick air that kept him awake. Loial's soft snores were a rumble that made Perrin's seem nonexistent, but they did not stop weariness from claiming the others. The Warder was still awake, seated not far from him with his sword across his knees, watching the night. To Rand's surprise, so was Nynaeve.

The Wisdom looked at Lan silently for a long time, then poured a cup of tea and brought it to him. When he reached out with a murmur of thanks, she did not let go right away. "I should have known you would be a king," she said quietly. Her eyes were steady on the Warder's face, but her voice trembled slightly.

Lan looked back at her just as intently. It seemed to Rand that the Warder's face actually softened. "I am not a king, Nynaeve. Just a man. A man without as much to his name as even the meanest farmer's croft."

Nynaeve's voice steadied. "Some women don't ask for land, or gold. Just the man."

"And the man who would ask her to accept so little would not be worthy of her. You are a remarkable woman, as beautiful as the sunrise, as fierce as a warrior. You are a lioness, Wisdom."

"A Wisdom seldom weds." She paused to take a deep breath, as if steeling herself. "But if I go to Tar Valon, it may be that I will be something other than a Wisdom."

"Aes Sedai marry as seldom as Wisdoms. Few men can live with so much power in a wife, dimming them by her radiance whether she wishes to or not."

"Some men are strong enough. I know one such." If there could have been any doubt, her look left none as to whom she meant.

"All I have is a sword, and a war I cannot win, but can never stop fighting."

"I've told you I care nothing for that. Light, you've made me say more than is proper already. Will you shame me to the point of asking you?"

"I will never shame you." The gentle tone, like a caress, sounded odd to Rand's ears in the Warder's voice, but it made Nynaeve's eyes brighten. "I will hate the man you choose because he is not me, and love him if he makes you smile. No woman deserves the sure knowledge of widow's black as her brideprice, you least of all." He set the untouched cup on the ground and rose. "I must check the horses."

Nynaeve remained there, kneeling, after he had gone.

Sleep or no, Rand closed his eyes. He did not think the Wisdom would like it if he watched her cry.

CHAPTER
49

The Dark One Stirs

Dawn woke Rand with a start, the sullen sun pricking his eyelids as it peeked reluctantly over the treetops of the Blight. Even so early, heat covered the spoiled lands in a heavy blanket. He lay on his back with his head pillowed on his blanketroll, staring at the sky. It was still blue, the sky. Even here, that, at least, was untouched.

He was surprised to realize that he had slept. For a minute the dim memory of a conversation overheard seemed like part of some dream. Then he saw Nynaeve's red-rimmed eyes; she had not slept, obviously. Lan's face was harder than ever, as if he had resumed a mask and did not intend to let it slip again.

Egwene went over and crouched beside the Wisdom, her face concerned. He could not make out what they said. Egwene spoke, and Nynaeve shook her head. Egwene said something else, and the Wisdom waved her away dismissively. Instead of going, Egwene bent her head closer, and for a few minutes the two women talked even more softly, with Nynaeve still shaking her head. The Wisdom ended it with a laugh, hugging Egwene and, by her expression, making soothing talk. When Egwene stood, though, she glared at the Warder. Lan did not seem to notice; he did not look in Nynaeve's direction at all.

Shaking his head, Rand gathered his things, and gave his hands and face and teeth a hasty wash with the little water Lan allowed for such things. He wondered if women had a way of reading men's minds. It was an unsettling thought. *All women are Aes Sedai.* Telling himself he was letting the Blight get to him, he rinsed out his mouth and hurried to get the bay saddled.

It was more than a little disconcerting, having the campsite disappear before he reached the horses, but by the time his saddle girth was tight everything on the hill winked back into view. Everyone was hurrying.

The seven towers stood plain in the morning light, distant broken stumps, like huge, rough hills that merely hinted at grandeur gone. The hundred lakes were a smooth, unruffled blue. Nothing broke the surface this morning. When he looked at the lakes and the ruined towers, he could almost ignore the sickly things growing around the hill. Lan did not seem to be avoiding looking at the towers, any more than he seemed to be avoiding Nynaeve, but somehow he never did as he concentrated on getting them ready to go.

After the wicker panniers were fastened on the packhorse, after every scrap and smudge and track were gone and everyone else was mounted, the Aes Sedai stood in the middle of the hilltop with her eyes closed, not even seeming to breathe. Nothing happened that Rand could see, except that Nynaeve and Egwene shivered despite the heat and rubbed their arms briskly. Egwene's hands suddenly froze on her arms, and she opened her mouth, staring at the Wisdom. Before she could speak, Nynaeve also ceased her rubbing and gave her a sharp look. The two women looked at one another, then Egwene nodded and grinned, and after a moment Nynaeve did, too, though her smile was only halfhearted.

Rand scrubbed his fingers through his hair, already more damp with sweat than with the water he had splashed in his face. He was sure there was something in the silent exchange that he should understand, but that feather-light brush across his mind vanished before he could grasp it.

"What are we waiting for?" Mat demanded, the low band of his scarf across his forehead. He had his bow across the pommel of his saddle with an arrow nocked, and his quiver pulled around on his belt for an easy reach.

Moiraine opened her eyes and started down the hill. "For me to remove the last vestige of what I did here last night. The residues would have dissipated on their own in a day, but I will not take any risk I can avoid now. We are too close, and the Shadow is too strong here. Lan?"

The Warder only waited for her to settle in Aldieb's saddle before he led them north, toward the Mountains of Dhoom, looming in the near distance. Even under the sunrise the peaks rose black and lifeless, like jagged teeth. In a wall they stretched, east and west as far as the eye could see.

"Will we reach the Eye today, Moiraine Sedai?" Egwene asked.

The Aes Sedai gave Loial a sidelong look. "I hope that we will. When I found it before, it was just the other side of the mountains, at the foot of the high passes."

"He says it moves," Mat said, nodding at Loial. "What if it isn't where you expect?"

"Then we will continue to hunt until we do find it. The Green Man senses need, and there can be no need greater than ours. Our need is the hope of the world."

As the mountains drew closer, so did the true Blight. Where a leaf had been spotted black and mottled yellow before, now foliage fell wetly while he watched, breaking apart from the weight of its own corruption. The trees themselves were tortured, crippled things, twisted branches clawing at the sky as if begging mercy from some power that refused to hear. Ooze slid like pus from bark cracked and split. As if nothing truly solid was left to them, the trees seemed to tremble from the passage of the horses over the ground.

"Look as if they want to grab us," Mat said nervously. Nynaeve gave him an exasperated, scornful look, and he added fiercely, "Well, they do look it."

"And some of them do want it," the Aes Sedai said. Her eyes over her shoulder were harder than Lan's for an instant. "But they want no part of what I am, and my presence protects you."

Mat laughed uneasily, as if he thought it a joke on her part.

Rand was not so sure. This *was* the Blight, after all. *But trees don't move. Why would a tree grab a man, even if it could? We're imagining things, and she's just trying to keep us alert.*

Abruptly he stared off to his left, into the forest. That tree, not twenty paces away, *had* trembled, and it was none of his imagination. He could not say what kind it was, or had been, so gnarled and tormented was its shape. As he watched, the tree suddenly whipped back and forth again, then bent down, flailing at the ground. Something screamed, shrill and piercing. The tree sprang back straight; its limbs entwined around a dark mass that writhed and spat and screamed.

He swallowed hard and tried to edge Red away, but trees stood on every side, and trembled. The bay rolled his eyes, whites showing all the way around. Rand found himself in a solid knot of horseflesh as everyone else tried to do the same as he.

"Keep moving," Lan commanded, drawing his sword. The Warder wore steel-backed gauntlets now, and his gray-green scale tunic. "Stay with Moiraine Sedai." He pulled Mandarb around, not toward the tree and its prey, but in the other direction. With his color-shifting cloak, he was swallowed by the Blight before the black stallion was out of sight.

"Close," Moiraine urged. She did not slow her white mare, but she motioned the others to huddle nearer to her. "Stay as close as you can."

A roar sprang up from the direction the Warder had gone. It beat at the air, and the trees quivered from it, and when it faded away, it seemed to echo still. Again the roar came, filled with rage and death.

"Lan," Nynaeve said. "He—"

The awful sound cut her off, but there was a new note in it. Fear. Abruptly it was gone.

"Lan can look after himself," Moiraine said. "Ride, Wisdom."

From out of the trees the Warder appeared, holding his sword well clear of himself and his mount. Black blood stained the blade, and steam rose from it. Carefully, Lan wiped the blade clean with a cloth he took from his saddlebags, examining the steel to make sure he had gotten every spot. When he dropped the cloth, it fell apart before it reached the ground, even the fragments dissolving.

Silently a massive body leaped out of the trees at them. The Warder spun Mandarb, but even as the warhorse reared, ready to strike with steel-shod hooves, Mat's arrow flashed, piercing the one eye in a head that seemed mostly mouth and teeth. Kicking and screaming, the thing fell, one bound short of them. Rand stared as they hurried past. Stiff hair like long bristles covered it, and it had too many legs, joining a body as big as a bear at odd angles. Some of them at least, those coming out of its back, had to be useless for walking, but the finger-long claws at their ends tore the earth in its death agony.

"Good shooting, sheepherder." Lan's eyes had already forgotten what was dying behind them, and were searching the forest.

Moiraine shook her head. "It should not have been willing to come so close to one who touches the True Source."

"Agelmar said the Blight stirs," Lan said. "Perhaps the Blight also knows a Web is forming in the Pattern."

"Hurry." Moiraine dug her heels into Aldieb's flanks. "We must get over the high passes quickly."

But even as she spoke the Blight rose against them. Trees whipped in, reaching for them, not caring if Moiraine touched the True Source or not.

Rand's sword was in his hand; he did not remember unsheathing it. He struck out again and again, the heron-mark blade slicing through corrupted limbs. Hungry branches jerked back severed, writhing stumps—he almost thought he heard them scream—but always more came, wriggling like snakes, attempting to snare his arms, his waist, his neck. Teeth bared in a rictus snarl, he sought the void, and found it in the stony, stubborn soil of the Two Rivers. "Manetheren!" He screamed back at the trees till his throat ached. The heron-mark steel flashed in the strengthless sunlight. "Manetheren! Manetheren!"

Standing in his stirrups, Mat sent arrow after arrow flashing into the forest, striking at deformed shapes that snarled and gnashed uncounted teeth on the shafts that killed them, bit at the clawed forms fighting to get over them, to reach the mounted figures. Mat, too, was lost to the present. *"Carai an Caldazar!"* he shouted as he drew fletchings to cheek and loosed. *"Carai an Ellisande! Al Ellisande! Mordero daghain pas duente cuebiyar! Al Ellisande!"*

Perrin also stood in his stirrups, silent and grim. He had taken the lead, and his axe hewed a path through forest and foul flesh alike, whichever came before him. Flailing trees and howling things shied from the stocky axeman, shying as much from the fierce golden eyes as from the whistling axe. He forced his horse forward, step by determined step.

Fireballs streaked from Moiraine's hands, and where they struck, a writhing tree became a torch, a toothed shape shrieked and beat with human hands, rent its own flaming flesh with fierce claws until it died.

Again and again the Warder took Mandarb into the trees, his blade and gauntlets dripping with blood that bubbled and steamed. When he came back now, more often than not there were gashes in his armor, bleeding gashes in his flesh, and his warhorse stumbled and bled, too. Each time the Aes Sedai paused to lay her hands on the wounds, and when she took them away, only the blood was left on unmarked flesh.

"I light signal fires for the Halfmen," she said bitterly. "Press on. Press on!" They made their way one slow pace at a time.

If the trees had not struck into the mass of attacking flesh as much as at the humans, if the creatures, no two alike, had not fought the trees and one another as much as to reach them, Rand was sure they would have been overwhelmed. He was not certain it would not happen still. Then a fluting cry arose behind them. Distant and thin, it cut through the snarling from the denizens of the Blight around them.

In an instant the snarling ceased, as if it had been sliced off with a knife. The attacking shapes froze; the trees went still. As suddenly as the things with legs had appeared, they melted away, vanishing into the twisted forest.

The reedy shrill came again, like a cracked shepherd's pipes, and was answered in kind by a chorus. Half a dozen, singing among themselves, far behind.

"Worms," Lan said grimly, bringing a moan from Loial. "They've given us a respite, if we have time to use it." His eyes were measuring the distance yet to the mountains. "Few things in the Blight will face a Worm, can it be avoided." He dug his heels into Mandarb's flanks. "Ride!" The whole party plunged after him, through a Blight that suddenly seemed truly dead, except for the piping behind.

"They were scared off by worms?" Mat said incredulously. He was bouncing in his saddle, trying to sling his bow across his back.

"A Worm"—there was a sharp difference in the way the Warder said it from the way Mat had—"can kill a Fade, if the Fade hasn't the Dark One's own luck with it. We have an entire pack on our trail. Ride! Ride!" The dark peaks were closer now. An hour, Rand estimated, at the pace the Warder was setting.

"Won't the Worms follow us into the mountains?" Egwene asked breathlessly, and Lan gave a sharp laugh.

"They won't. Worms are afraid of what lives in the high passes." Loial moaned again.

Rand wished the Ogier would stop doing that. He was well aware that Loial knew more about the Blight than any of them except Lan, even if it was from reading books in the safety of a *stedding*. *But why does he have to keep reminding me that there's worse yet than we've seen?*

The Blight flowed past, weeds and grasses splashing rotten under galloping hooves. Trees of the kinds that had earlier attacked did not so much as twitch even when they rode directly under the twisted branches. The Mountains of Dhoom filled the sky ahead, black and bleak, and almost near enough to touch, it seemed. The piping came both sharp and clear, and there were squishing sounds behind them, louder than the things crushed under hooves. Too loud, as if half-

decayed trees were being crushed by huge bodies slithering over them.
Too near. Rand looked over his shoulder. Back there treetops whipped
and went down like grass. The land began sloping upward, toward the
mountains, tilting enough so that he knew they were climbing.

"We are not going to make it," Lan announced. He did not slow
Mandarb's gallop, but his sword was suddenly in his hand again.
"Watch yourself in the high passes, Moiraine, and you'll get through."

"No, Lan!" Nynaeve called.

"Be quiet, girl! Lan, even you cannot stop a Wormpack. I will not
have it. I will need you for the Eye."

"Arrows," Mat called breathlessly.

"The Worms wouldn't even feel them," the Warder shouted. "They
must be cut to pieces. Don't feel much but hunger. Sometimes fear."

Clinging to his saddle with a deathgrip, Rand shrugged, trying to
loosen the tightness in his shoulders. His whole chest felt tight, until
he could hardly breathe, and his skin stung in hot pinpricks. The Blight
had turned to foothills. He could see the route they must climb once
they reached the mountains, the twisting path and the high pass beyond, like an axe blow cleaving into the black stone. *Light, what's up
ahead that can scare what's behind? Light help me, I've never been so
afraid. I don't want to go any further. No further!* Seeking the flame
and the void, he railed at himself. *Fool! You frightened, cowardly fool!
You can't stay here, and you can't go back. Are you going to leave
Egwene to face it alone?* The void eluded him, forming, then shivering
into a thousand points of light, re-forming and shattering again, each
point burning into his bones until he quivered with the pain and
thought he must burst open. *Light help me, I can't go on. Light help
me!*

He was gathering the bay's reins to turn back, to face the Worms or
anything rather than what lay ahead, when the nature of the land
changed. Between one slope of a hill and the next, between crest and
peak, the Blight was gone.

Green leaves covered peacefully spreading branches. Wildflowers
made a carpet of bright patches in grasses stirred by a sweet spring
breeze. Butterflies fluttered from blossom to blossom, with buzzing
bees, and birds trilled their songs.

Gaping, he galloped on, until he suddenly realized that Moiraine
and Lan and Loial had stopped, the others, too. Slowly he drew rein,
his face frozen in astonishment. Egwene's eyes were about to come
out of her head, and Nynaeve's jaw had dropped.

"We have reached safety," Moiraine said. "This is the Green Man's place, and the Eye of the World is here. Nothing of the Blight can enter here."

"I thought it was on the other side of the mountains," Rand mumbled. He could still see the peaks filling the northern horizon, and the high passes. "You said it was always beyond the passes."

"This place," said a deep voice from the trees, "is always where it is. All that changes is where those who need it are."

A figure stepped out of the foliage, a man-shape as much bigger than Loial as the Ogier was bigger than Rand. A man-shape of woven vines and leaves, green and growing. His hair was grass, flowing to his shoulders; his eyes, huge hazelnuts; his fingernails, acorns. Green leaves made his tunic and trousers; seamless bark, his boots. Butterflies swirled around him, lighting on his fingers, his shoulders, his face. Only one thing spoiled the verdant perfection. A deep fissure ran up his cheek and temple across the top of his head, and in that the vines were brown and withered.

"The Green Man," Egwene whispered, and the scarred face smiled. For a moment it seemed as if the birds sang louder.

"Of course I am. Who else would be here?" The hazelnut eyes regarded Loial. "It is good to see you, little brother. In the past, many of you came to visit me, but few of recent days."

Loial scrambled down from his big horse and bowed formally. "You honor me, Treebrother. *Tsingu ma choshih, T'ingshen.*"

Smiling, the Green Man put an arm around the Ogier's shoulders. Alongside Loial, he looked like a man beside a boy. "There is no honoring, little brother. We will sing Treesongs together, and remember the Great Trees, and the *stedding,* and hold the Longing at bay." He studied the others, just now getting down from their horses, and his eyes lit on Perrin. "A Wolfbrother! Do the old times truly walk again then?"

Rand stared at Perrin. For his part, Perrin turned his horse so it was between him and the Green Man, and bent to check the girth. Rand was sure he just wanted to avoid the Green Man's searching gaze. Suddenly the Green Man spoke to Rand.

"Strange clothes you wear, Child of the Dragon. Has the Wheel turned so far? Do the People of the Dragon return to the First Covenant? But you wear a sword. That is neither now nor then."

Rand had to work moisture in his mouth before he could speak. "I don't know what you're talking about. What do you mean?"

The Green Man touched the brown scar across his head. For a moment he seemed confused. "I . . . cannot say. My memories are torn

and often fleeting, and much of what remains is like leaves visited by
caterpillars. Yet, I am sure. . . . No, it is gone. But you are welcome
here. You, Moiraine Sedai, are more than a surprise. When this place
was made, it was made so that none could find it twice. How have you
come here?"

"Need," Moiraine replied. "My need, the world's need. Most of all
is the world's need. We have come to see the Eye of the World."

The Green Man sighed, the wind sighing through thick-leafed
branches. "Then it has come again. That memory remains whole. The
Dark One stirs. I have feared it. Every turning of years, the Blight
strives harder to come inside, and this turn the struggle to keep it
out has been greater than ever since the beginning. Come, I will take
you."

CHAPTER
50

Meetings at the Eye

Leading the bay, Rand followed the Green Man with the other Emond's Fielders, all staring as if they could not decide whether to look at the Green Man or the forest. The Green Man was a legend, of course, with stories told about him, and the Tree of Life, in front of every fireplace in the Two Rivers, and not just for the children. But after the Blight, the trees and flowers would have been a wonder of normality even if the rest of the world was not still trapped in winter.

Perrin hung a little to the rear. When Rand glanced back, the big, curly-haired youth looked as if he did not want to hear anything else the Green Man had to say. He could understand that. *Child of the Dragon.* Warily he watched the Green Man, walking ahead with Moiraine and Lan, butterflies surrounding him in a cloud of yellows and reds. *What did he mean? No. I don't want to know.*

Even so, his step felt lighter, his legs springier. The uneasiness still lay in his gut, churning his stomach, but the fear had become so diffuse it might as well be gone. He did not think he could expect more, not

with the Blight half a mile away, even if Moiraine was right about
nothing from the Blight being able to enter here. The thousands of
burning points piercing his bones had winked out; at the very moment
he came within the Green Man's domain, he was sure. *It's him that
winked them out,* he thought, *the Green Man, and this place.*

Egwene felt it, and Nynaeve, too, the soothing peace, the calm of
beauty. He could tell. They wore small, serene smiles, and brushed
flowers with their fingers, pausing to smell, and breathing deep.

When the Green Man noticed, he said, "Flowers are meant to
adorn. The plants or humans, it is much the same. None mind, so long
as you don't take too many." And he began plucking one from this
plant and one from that, never more than two from any. Soon Nynaeve and Egwene wore caps of blossoms in their hair, pink wildrose
and yellowbell and white morningstar. The Wisdom's braid seemed a
garden of pink and white to her waist. Even Moiraine received a pale
garland of morningstar on her brow, woven so deftly that the flowers
still seemed to be growing.

Rand was not sure they were not growing. The Green Man tended
his forest garden as he walked, while he talked softly to Moiraine,
taking care of whatever needed care without really thinking about it.
His hazelnut eyes caught a crooked limb on a climbing wildrose, forced
into an awkward angle by the blossom-covered limb of an apple tree,
and he paused, still talking, to run his hand along the bend. Rand was
not sure if his eyes were playing tricks, or if thorns actually did bend
out of the way so as not to prick those green fingers. When the towering shape of the Green Man moved on, the limb ran straight and true,
spreading red petals among the white of apple blossoms. He bent to
cup one huge hand around a tiny seed lying on a patch of pebbles, and
when he straightened, a small shoot had roots through the rocks to
good soil.

"All things must grow where they are, according to the Pattern," he
explained over his shoulder, as if apologizing, "and face the turning of
the Wheel, but the Creator will not mind if I give just a little help."

Rand led Red around the shoot, careful not to let the bay's hooves
crush it. It did not seem right to destroy what the Green Man had
done just to avoid an extra step. Egwene smiled at him, one of her
secret smiles, and touched his arm. She was so pretty, with her unbound hair full of flowers, that he smiled back at her until she blushed
and lowered her eyes. *I will protect you,* he thought. *Whatever else
happens, I will see you safe, I swear it.*

Into the heart of the spring forest the Green Man took them, to an arched opening in the side of a hill. It was a simple stone arch, tall and white, and on the keystone was a circle halved by a sinuous line, one half rough, the other smooth. The ancient symbol of Aes Sedai. The opening itself was shadowed.

For a moment everyone simply looked in silence. Then Moiraine removed the garland from her hair and gently hung it on the limb of a sweetberry bush beside the arch. It was as if her movement restored speech.

"It's in there?" Nynaeve asked. "What we've come for?"

"I'd really like to see the Tree of Life," Mat said, not taking his eyes off the halved circle above them. "We can wait that long, can't we?"

The Green Man gave Rand an odd look, then shook his head. "*Avendesora* is not here. I have not rested beneath its ungentle branches in two thousand years."

"The Tree of Life is not why we came," Moiraine said firmly. She gestured to the arch. "In there, is."

"I will not go in with you," the Green Man said. The butterflies around him swirled as if they shared some agitation. "I was set to guard it long, long ago, but it makes me uneasy to come too close. I feel myself being unmade; my end is linked with it, somehow. I remember the making of it. Some of the making. Some." His hazelnut eyes stared, lost in memory, and he fingered his scar. "It was the first days of the Breaking of the World, when the joy of victory over the Dark One turned bitter with the knowledge that all might yet be shattered by the weight of the Shadow. A hundred of them made it, men and women together. The greatest Aes Sedai works were always done so, joining *Saidin* and *Saidar,* as the True Source is joined. They died, all, to make it pure, while the world was torn around them. Knowing they would die, they charged me to guard it against the need to come. It was not what I was made for, but all was breaking apart, and they were alone, and I was all they had. It was not what I was made for, but I have kept the faith." He looked down at Moiraine, nodding to himself. "I have kept faith, until it was needed. And now it ends."

"You have kept the faith better than most of us who gave you the charge," the Aes Sedai said. "Perhaps it will not come as badly as you fear."

The scarred, leafy head shook slowly from side to side. "I know an ending when it comes, Aes Sedai. I will find another place to make things grow." Nutbrown eyes swept sadly over the green forest. "Another place, perhaps. When you come out, I will see you again, if there

is time." With that he strode away, trailing butterflies, becoming one
with the forest more completely than Lan's cloak ever could.

"What did he mean?" Mat demanded. "If there's time?"

"Come," Moiraine said. And she stepped through the arch. Lan
went at her heels.

Rand was not sure what he expected when he followed. The hair
stirred uneasily on his arms, and rose on the back of his neck. But it
was only a corridor, its polished walls rounded overhead like the arch,
winding gently downward. There was headroom enough and to spare
for Loial; there would have been room enough for the Green Man.
The smooth floor, slick to the eye like oiled slate, yet somehow gave
a sure footing. Seamless, white walls glittered with uncounted flecks in
untold colors, giving a low, soft light even after the sunlit archway
vanished around a curve behind. He was sure the light was no natural
thing, but he sensed it was benign, too. *Then why is your skin still
crawling?* Down they went, and down.

"There," Moiraine said at last, pointing. "Ahead."

And the corridor opened into a vast, domed space, the rough, living
rock of its ceiling dotted with clumps of glowing crystals. Below it, a
pool took up the entire cavern, except for the walkway around it, perhaps five paces wide. In the oval shape of an eye, the pool was lined
about its rim with a low, flat edging of crystals that glowed with a
duller, yet fiercer, light than those above. Its surface was as smooth as
glass and as clear as the Winespring Water. Rand felt as if his eyes
could penetrate it forever, but he could not see any bottom to it.

"The Eye of the World," Moiraine said softly beside him.

As he looked around in wonder, he realized that the long years since
the making—three thousand of them—had worked their way while no
one came. Not all the crystals in the dome glowed with the same intensity. Some were stronger, some weaker; some flickered, and others
were only faceted lumps to sparkle in a captured light. Had all shone,
the dome would have been as bright as noonday, but they made it only
late afternoon, now. Dust coated the walkway, and bits of stone and
even crystal. Long years waiting, while the Wheel turned and ground.

"But *what* is it?" Mat asked uneasily. "That doesn't look like any
water I ever saw." He kicked a lump of dark stone the size of his fist
over the edge. "It—"

The stone struck the glassy surface and slid into the pool without a
splash, or so much as a ripple. As it sank, the rock began to swell,
growing ever larger, larger and more attenuated, a blob the size of his
head that Rand could almost see through, a faint blur as wide as his

arm was long. Then it was gone. He thought his skin would creep right off his body.

"What is it?" he demanded, and was shocked at the hoarse harshness of his own voice.

"It might be called the essence of *Saidin*." The Aes Sedai's words echoed round the dome. "The essence of the male half of the True Source, the pure essence of the Power wielded by men before the Time of Madness. The Power to mend the seal on the Dark One's prison, or to break it open completely."

"The Light shine on us and protect us," Nynaeve whispered. Egwene clutched her as if she wanted to hide behind the Wisdom. Even Lan stirred uneasily, though there was no surprise in his eyes.

Stone thudded into Rand's shoulders, and he realized he had backed as far as the wall, as far from the Eye of the World as he could get. He would have pushed himself right through the wall, if he could have. Mat, too, was splayed out against the stone as flat as he could make himself. Perrin was staring at the pool with his axe half drawn. His eyes shone, yellow and fierce.

"I always wondered," Loial said uneasily. "When I read about it, I always wondered what it was. Why? Why did they do it? And how?"

"No one living knows." Moiraine no longer looked at the pool. She was watching Rand and his two friends, studying them, her eyes weighing. "Neither the how, nor more of the why than that it would be needed one day, and that that need would be the greatest and most desperate the world had faced to that time. Perhaps ever would face.

"Many in Tar Valon have attempted to find a way to use this Power, but it is as untouchable for any woman as the moon is for a cat. Only a man could channel it, but the last male Aes Sedai is nearly three thousand years gone. Yet the need they saw was a desperate one. They worked through the taint of the Dark One on *Saidin* to make it, and make it pure, knowing that doing so would kill them all. Male Aes Sedai and female together. The Green Man spoke true. The greatest wonders of the Age of Legends were done in that way, *Saidin* and *Saidar* together. All the women in Tar Valon, all the Aes Sedai in all the courts and cities, even with those in the lands beyond the Waste, even counting those who may still live beyond the Aryth Ocean, could not fill a spoon with the Power, lacking men to work with them."

Rand's throat rasped as if he had been screaming. "Why did you bring us here?"

"Because you are *ta'veren*." The Aes Sedai's face was unreadable. Her eyes shimmered, and seemed to pull at him. "Because the Dark

One's power will strike here, and because it must be confronted and stopped, or the Shadow will cover the world. There is no need greater than that. Let us go out into the sunlight again, while there is yet time." Without waiting to see if they would follow, she started back up the corridor with Lan, who stepped perhaps a bit more quickly than usual for him. Egwene and Nynaeve hurried behind her.

Rand edged along the wall—he could not make himself get even one step closer to what the pool was—and scrambled into the corridor in a tangle with Mat and Perrin. He would have run if it had not meant trampling Egwene and Nynaeve, Moiraine and Lan. He could not stop shaking even when he was back outside.

"I do not like this, Moiraine," Nynaeve said angrily when the sun shone on them again. "I believe the danger is as great as you say or I would not be here, but this is—"

"I have found you at last."

Rand jerked as if a rope had tightened around his neck. The words, the voice . . . for a moment he believed it was Ba'alzamon. But the two men who walked out of the trees, faces hidden by their cowls, did not wear cloaks the color of dried blood. One cloak was a dark gray, the other almost as dark a green, and they seemed musty even in the open air. And the men were not Fades; the breeze stirred their cloaks.

"Who are you?" Lan's stance was cautious, his hand on his sword hilt. "How did you come here? If you are seeking the Green Man—"

"He guided us." The hand that pointed to Mat was old and shriveled to scarcely human, lacking a fingernail and with knuckles gnarled like knots in a piece of rope. Mat took a step back, eyes widening. "An old thing, an old friend, an old enemy. But he is not the one we seek," the green-cloaked man finished. The other man stood as if he would never speak.

Moiraine straightened to her full height, no more than shoulder high to any man there, but suddenly seeming as tall as the hills. Her voice rang like a bell, demanding, "Who are you?"

Hands pushed back hoods, and Rand goggled. The old man was older than old; he made Cenn Buie look like a child in the bloom of health. The skin of his face was like crazed parchment drawn tight over a skull, then pulled tighter still. Wispy tufts of brittle hair stood at odd places on his scabrous scalp. His ears were withered bits like scraps of ancient leather; his eyes sunken, peering out of his head as if from the ends of tunnels. Yet the other was worse. A tight, black leather carapace covered that one's head and face completely, but the front of it was worked into a perfect face, a young man's face, laughing wildly, laughing insanely, frozen forever. *What is he hiding if the other shows what he shows?* Then even thought froze in his head, shattered to dust and blew away.

"I am called Aginor," the old one said. "And he is Balthamel. He no longer speaks with his tongue. The Wheel grinds exceedingly fine over three thousand years imprisoned." His sunken eyes slid to the arch; Balthamel leaned forward, his mask's eyes on the white stone opening, as if he wanted to go straight in. "So long without," Aginor said softly. "So long."

"The Light protect—" Loial began, his voice shaking, and cut off abruptly when Aginor looked at him.

"The Forsaken," Mat said hoarsely, "are bound in Shayol Ghul—"

"Were bound." Aginor smiled; his yellowed teeth had the look of fangs. "Some of us are bound no longer. The seals weaken, Aes Sedai. Like Ishamael, we walk the world again, and soon the rest of us will come. I was too close to this world in my captivity, I and Balthamel, too close to the grinding of the Wheel, but soon the Great Lord of the Dark will be free, and give us new flesh, and the world will be ours once more. You will have no Lews Therin Kinslayer, this time. No Lord of the Morning to save you. We know the one we seek now, and there is no more need for the rest of you."

Lan's sword sprang from its scabbard too fast for Rand's eye to follow. Yet the Warder hesitated, eyes flickering to Moiraine, to Nynaeve. The two women stood well apart; to put himself between either of them and the Forsaken would put him further from the other. Only for a heartbeat the hesitation lasted, but as the Warder's feet moved, Aginor raised his hand. It was a scornful gesture, a flipping of his gnarled fingers as if to shoo away a fly. The Warder flew backwards through the air as though a huge fist had caught him. With a dull thud Lan struck the stone arch, hanging there for an instant before dropping in a flaccid heap, his sword lying near his outstretched hand.

"NO!" Nynaeve screamed.

"Be still!" Moiraine commanded, but before anyone else could move the Wisdom's knife had left her belt, and she was running toward the Forsaken, her small blade upraised.

"The Light blind you," she cried, striking at Aginor's chest.

The other Forsaken moved like a viper. While her blow still fell, Balthamel's leather-cased hand darted out to seize her chin, fingers sinking into one cheek while thumb dug into the other, driving the blood out with their pressure and raising the flesh in pale ridges. A convulsion wracked Nynaeve from head to toe, as if she had been cracked like a whip. Her knife dropped uselessly from dangling fingers as Balthamel lifted her by his grip, brought her up to where the leather mask stared into her still-quivering face. Her toes spasmed a foot above the ground; flowers rained from her hair.

"I have almost forgotten the pleasures of the flesh." Aginor's tongue crossed his withered lips, sounding like stone on rough leather. "But Balthamel remembers much." The laughter of the mask seemed to grow wilder, and the wail that left Nynaeve burned Rand's ears like despair ripped from her living heart.

Suddenly Egwene moved, and Rand saw that she was going to help Nynaeve. "Egwene, no!" he shouted, but she did not stop. His hand had gone to his sword at Nynaeve's cry, but now he abandoned it and threw himself at Egwene. He thudded into her before she took her third step, carrying them both to the ground. Egwene landed under him with a gasp, immediately thrashing to get free.

Others were moving, too, he realized. Perrin's axe whirled into his hands, and his eyes glowed golden and fierce. "Wisdom!" Mat howled, the dagger from Shadar Logoth in his fist.

"No!" Rand called. "You can't fight the Forsaken!" But they ran past him as if they had not heard, their eyes on Nynaeve and the two Forsaken.

Aginor glanced at them, unconcernedly . . . and smiled.

Rand felt the air stir above him like the crack of a giant's whip. Mat and Perrin, not even halfway to the Forsaken, stopped as if they had run into a wall, bounced back to sprawl on the ground.

"Good," Aginor said. "A fitting place for you. If you learn to abase yourself properly in worship of us, I might let you live."

Hastily Rand scrambled to his feet. Perhaps he could not fight the Forsaken—no ordinary human could—but he would not let them believe for a minute that he was groveling before them. He tried to help Egwene up, but she slapped his hands away and stood by herself, angrily brushing off her dress. Mat and Perrin had also stubbornly pushed themselves unsteadily erect.

"You will learn," Aginor said, "if you want to live. Now that I have found what I need"—his eyes went to the stone archway—"I may take the time to teach you."

"This shall not be!" The Green Man strode out of the trees with a voice like lightning striking an ancient oak. "You do not belong here!"

Aginor spared him a brief, contemptuous glance. "Begone! Your time is ended, all your kind but you long since dust. Live what life is left to you and be glad you are beneath our notice."

"This is my place," the Green Man said, "and you shall hurt no living thing here."

Balthamel tossed Nynaeve aside like a rag, and like a crumpled rag she fell, eyes staring, limp as if all her bones had melted. One leather-clad hand lifted, and the Green Man roared as smoke rose from the vines that wove him. The wind in the trees echoed his pain.

Aginor turned back to Rand and the others, as if the Green Man had been dealt with, but one long stride and massive, leafy arms wrapped themselves around Balthamel, raising him high, crushing him against a chest of thick creepers, black leather mask laughing into hazelnut eyes dark with anger. Like serpents Balthamel's arms writhed free, his gloved hands grasping the Green Man's head as though he would wrench it off. Flames shot up where those hands touched, vines withering, leaves falling. The Green Man bellowed as thick, dark smoke poured out between the vines of his body. On and on he roared, as if all of him were coming out of his mouth with the smoke that billowed between his lips.

Suddenly Balthamel jerked in the Green Man's grasp. The Forsaken's hands tried to push him away instead of clutching him. One gloved hand flung wide . . . and a tiny creeper burst through the black leather. A fungus, such as rings trees in the deep shadows of the forest, ringed his arm, sprang from nowhere to full-grown, swelling to cover the length of it. Balthamel thrashed, and a shoot of stinkweed ripped open his carapace, lichens dug in their roots and split tiny cracks across the leather of his face, nettles broke the eyes of his mask, deathshead mushrooms tore open the mouth.

The Green Man threw the Forsaken down. Balthamel twisted and jerked as all the things that grew in the dark places, all the things with spores, all the things that loved the dank, swelled and grew, tore cloth and leather and flesh—Was it flesh, seen in that brief moment of verdant rage?—to tattered shreds and covered him until only a mound remained, indistinguishable from many in the shaded depths of the green forest, and the mound moved no more than they.

With a groan like a limb breaking under too great a weight, the Green Man crashed to the ground. Half his head was charred black. Tendrils of smoke still rose from him, like gray creepers. Burned leaves fell from his arm as he painfully stretched out his blackened hand to gently cup an acorn.

The earth rumbled as an oak seedling pushed up between his fingers. The Green Man's head fell, but the seedling reached for the sun, straining. Roots shot out and thickened, delved beneath the ground and rose again, thickened more as they sank. The trunk broadened and stretched upward, bark turning gray and fissured and ancient. Limbs spread and grew heavy, as big as arms, as big as men, and lifted to caress the sky, thick with green leaves, dense with acorns. The massive web of roots turned the earth like plows as it spread; the already huge trunk shivered, grew wider, round as a house. Stillness came. And an oak that could have stood five hundred years covered the spot where the Green Man had been, marking the tomb of a legend. Nynaeve lay on the gnarled roots, grown curved to her shape, to make a bed for her to rest upon. The wind sighed through the oak's branches; it seemed to murmur farewell.

Even Aginor seemed stunned. Then his head lifted, cavernous eyes burning with hate. "Enough! It is past time to end this!"

"Yes, Forsaken," Moiraine said, her voice as cold as deep-winter ice. "Past time!"

The Aes Sedai's hand rose, and the ground fell away beneath Aginor's feet. Flame roared from the chasm, whipped to a frenzy by wind howling in from every direction, sucking a maelstrom of leaves into the fire, which seemed to solidify into a red-streaked yellow jelly of pure heat. In the middle of it Aginor stood, his feet supported only by air. The Forsaken looked startled, but then he smiled and took a step forward. It was a slow step, as if the fire tried to root him to the spot, but he took it, and then another.

"Run!" Moiraine commanded. Her face was white with strain. "All of you run!" Aginor stepped across the air, toward the edge of the flames.

Rand was aware of others moving, Mat and Perrin dashing away at the edge of his vision, Loial's long legs carrying him into the trees, but all he could really see was Egwene. She stood there rigid, face pale and eyes closed. It was not fear that held her, he realized. She was trying to throw her puny, untrained wielding of the Power against the Forsaken.

Roughly he grabbed her arm and pulled her around to face him. "Run!" he shouted at her. Her eyes opened, staring at him, angry with him for interfering, liquid with hate for Aginor, with fear of the Forsaken. "Run," he said, pushing her toward the trees hard enough to start her. "Run!" Once started, she did run.

But Aginor's withered face turned toward him, toward the running Egwene behind him, as the Forsaken walked through the flames, as if what the Aes Sedai was doing did not concern Aginor at all. Toward Egwene.

"Not her!" Rand shouted. "The Light burn you, not her!" He snatched up a rock and threw it, meaning to draw Aginor's attention. Halfway to the Forsaken's face, the stone turned to a handful of dust.

He hesitated only a moment, long enough to glance over his shoulder and see that Egwene was hidden in the trees. The flames still surrounded Aginor, patches of his cloak smoldering, but he walked as if he had all the time in the world, and the fire's rim was near. Rand turned and ran. Behind him he heard Moiraine begin to scream.

CHAPTER 51

Against the Shadow

The land tended upward the way Rand went, but fear lent his legs strength and they ate ground in long strides, tearing his way through flowering bushes and tangles of wildrose, scattering petals, not caring if thorns ripped his clothes or even his flesh. Moiraine had stopped screaming. It seemed as if the shrieks had gone on forever, each one more throat-wrenching than the last, but he knew they had lasted only moments altogether. Moments before Aginor would be on his trail. He knew it would be him that Aginor followed. He had seen the certainty in the Forsaken's hollow eyes, in that last second before terror whipped his feet to run.

The land grew ever steeper, but he scrambled on, pulling himself forward by handfuls of undergrowth, rocks and dirt and leaves spilling down the slope from under his feet, finally crawling on hands and knees when the slant became too great. Ahead, above, it leveled out a little. Panting, he scrabbled his way the last few spans, got to his feet, and stopped, wanting to howl aloud.

Ten paces in front of him, the hilltop dropped away sharply. He knew what he would see before he reached it, but he took the steps anyway, each heavier than the one before, hoping there might be some track, a goat path, anything. At the edge he looked down a sheer hundred-foot drop, a stone wall as smooth as planed timber.

There has to be some way. I'll go back and find a way around. Go back and—

When he turned, Aginor was there, just reaching the crest. The Forsaken topped the hill without any difficulty, walking up the steep slope as if it were level ground. Deep-sunken eyes burned at him from that drawn parchment face; somehow, it seemed less withered than before, more fleshed, as if Aginor had fed well on something. Those eyes were fixed on him, yet when Aginor spoke, it was almost to himself.

"Ba'alzamon will give rewards beyond mortal dreaming for the one who brings you to Shayol Ghul. Yet my dreams have always been beyond those of other men, and I left mortality behind millennia ago. What difference if you serve the Great Lord of the Dark alive or dead? None, to the spread of the Shadow. Why should I share power with you? Why should I bend knee to you? I, who faced Lews Therin Telamon in the Hall of the Servants itself. I, who threw my might against the Lord of the Morning and met him stroke for stroke. I think not."

Rand's mouth dried like dust; his tongue felt as shriveled as Aginor. The edge of the precipice grated under his heels, stone falling away. He did not dare look back, but he heard the rocks bounding and rebounding from the sheer wall, just as his body would if he moved another inch. It was the first he knew that he had been backing up, away from the Forsaken. His skin crawled until he thought he must see it writhing if he looked, if he could only take his eyes off the Forsaken. *There has to be some way to get away from him. Some way to escape! There has to be! Some way!*

Suddenly he felt something, saw it, though he knew it was not there to see. A glowing rope ran off from Aginor, behind him, white like sunlight seen through the purest cloud, heavier than a blacksmith's arm, lighter than air, connecting the Forsaken to something distant beyond knowing, something within the touch of Rand's hand. The rope pulsed, and with every throb Aginor grew stronger, more fully fleshed, a man as tall and strong as himself, a man harder than the Warder, more deadly than the Blight. Yet beside that shining cord, the Forsaken seemed almost not to exist. The cord was all. It hummed. It sang. It called Rand's soul. One bright finger-strand lifted away, drifted, touched him, and he gasped. Light filled him, and heat that should have burned yet only warmed as if it took the chill of the grave from his bones. The strand thickened. *I have to get away!*

"No!" Aginor shouted. "You shall not have it! It is mine!"

Rand did not move, and neither did the Forsaken, yet they fought as surely as if they grappled in the dust. Sweat beaded on Aginor's face, no longer withered, no longer old, that of a strong man in his prime. Rand pulsed with the beating in the cord, like the heartbeat of the world. It filled his being. Light filled his mind, till only a corner was left for what was himself. He wrapped the void around that nook; sheltered in emptiness. *Away!*

"Mine!" Aginor cried. "Mine!"

Warmth built in Rand, the warmth of the sun, the radiance of the sun, bursting, the awful radiance of light, of the Light. *Away!*

"Mine!" Flame shot from Aginor's mouth, broke through his eyes like spears of fire, and he screamed.

Away!

And Rand was no longer on the hilltop. He quivered with the Light that suffused him. His mind would not work; light and heat blinded it. The Light. In the midst of the void, the Light blinded his mind, stunned him with awe.

He stood in a broad mountain pass, surrounded by jagged black peaks like the teeth of the Dark One. It was real; he was there. He felt the rocks under his boots, the icy breeze on his face.

Battle surrounded him, or the tail end of battle. Armored men on armored horses, shining steel dusty now, slashed and stabbed at snarling Trollocs wielding spiked axes and scythe-like swords. Some men fought afoot, their horses down, and barded horses galloped through the fight with empty saddles. Fades moved among them all, nightblack cloaks hanging still however their dark mounts galloped, and wherever their light-eating swords swung, men died. Sound beat at Rand, beat at him and bounced from the strangeness that had him by the throat. The clash of steel against steel, the panting and grunting of men and Trollocs striving, the screams of men and Trollocs dying. Over the din, banners waved in dust-filled air. The Black Hawk of Fal Dara, the White Hart of Shienar, others. And Trolloc banners. In just the little space around him he saw the horned skull of the Dha'vol, the blood-red trident of the Ko'bal, the iron fist of the Dhai'mon.

Yet it was indeed the tail end of battle, a pausing, as humans and Trollocs alike fell back to regroup. None seemed to notice Rand as they paid a few last strokes and broke away, galloping, or running in a stagger, to the ends of the pass.

Rand found himself facing the end of the pass where the humans were re-forming, pennants stirring beneath gleaming lancepoints. Wounded men wavered in their saddles. Riderless horses reared and galloped. Plainly they could not stand another meeting, yet just as plainly they readied themselves for one final charge. Some of them saw him now; men stood in their stirrups to point at him. Their shouts came to him as tiny piping.

Staggering, he turned. The forces of the Dark One filled the other end of the pass, bristling black pikes and spearpoints swelling up onto mountain slopes made blacker still by the great mass of Trollocs that dwarfed the army of Shienar. Fades in hundreds rode across the front of the horde, the fierce, muzzled faces of Trollocs turning away in fear as they passed, huge bodies pulling back to make way. Overhead, Draghkar wheeled on leathery pinions, shrieks challenging the wind. Halfmen saw him now, too, pointed, and Draghkar spun and dove. Two. Three. Six of them, crying shrilly as they plummeted toward him.

He stared at them. Heat filled him, the burning heat of the touched sun. He could see the Draghkar clearly, soulless eyes in pale men's faces on winged bodies that had nothing of humanity about them. Terrible heat. Crackling heat.

From the clear sky lightning came, each bolt crisp and sharp, searing his eyes, each bolt striking a winged black shape. Hunting cries became shrieks of death, and charred forms fell to leave the sky clean again.

The heat. The terrible heat of the Light.

He fell to his knees; he thought he could hear his tears sizzling on his cheeks. "No!" He clutched at tufts of wiry grass for some hold on reality; the grass burst in flame. "Please, nooooooo!"

The wind rose with his voice, howled with his voice, roared with his voice down the pass, whipping the flames to a wall of fire that sped away from him and toward the Trolloc host faster than a horse could run. Fire burned into the Trollocs, and the mountains trembled with their screams, screams almost as loud as the wind and his voice.

"It has to end!"

He beat at the ground with his fist, and the earth tolled like a gong. He bruised his hands on stony soil, and the earth trembled. Ripples ran through the ground ahead of him in ever-rising waves, waves of dirt and rock towering over Trollocs and Fades, breaking over them as the mountains shattered under their hooved feet. A boiling mass of flesh and rubble churned across the Trolloc army. What was left standing was still a mighty host, but now no more than twice the human army in numbers, and milling in fright and confusion.

The wind died. The screams died. The earth was still. Dust and smoke swirled back down the pass to surround him.

"The Light blind you, Ba'alzamon! This has to end!"

IT IS NOT HERE.

It was not Rand's thought, making his skull vibrate.

I WILL TAKE NO PART. ONLY THE CHOSEN ONE CAN DO WHAT MUST BE DONE, IF HE WILL.

"Where?" He did not want to say it, but he could not stop himself. "Where?"

The haze surrounding him parted, leaving a dome of clear, clean air ten spans high, walled by billowing smoke and dust. Steps rose before him, each standing alone and unsupported, stretching up into the murk that obscured the sun.

NOT HERE.

Through the mist, as from the far end of the earth, came a cry. "The Light wills it!" The ground rumbled with the thunder of hooves as the forces of humankind launched their last charge.

Within the void, his mind knew a moment of panic. The charging horsemen could not see him in the dust; their charge would trample right over him. The greater part of him ignored the shaking ground as a petty thing beneath concern. Dull anger driving his feet, he mounted the first steps. *It has to be ended!*

Darkness surrounded him, the utter blackness of total nothing. The steps were still there, hanging in the black, under his feet and ahead. When he looked back, those behind were gone, faded away to nothing, into the nothingness around him. But the cord was yet there, stretching behind him, the glowing line dwindling and vanishing into the distance. It was not so thick as before, but it still pulsed, pumping strength into him, pumping life, filling him with the Light. He climbed.

It seemed forever that he climbed. Forever, and minutes. Time stood still in nothingness. Time ran faster. He climbed until suddenly a door stood before him, its surface rough and splintered and old, a door well-remembered. He touched it, and it burst to fragments. While they still fell, he stepped through, bits of shattered wood falling from his shoulders.

The chamber, too, was as he remembered, the mad, striated sky beyond the balcony, the melted walls, the polished table, the terrible fireplace with its roaring, heatless flames. Some of those faces that made the fireplace, writhing in torment, shrieking in silence, tugged at his memory as if he knew them, but he held the void close, floated within himself in emptiness. He was alone. When he looked at the mirror on the wall, his face was there as clear as if it *was* him. *There is calm in the void.*

"Yes," Ba'alzamon said from in front of the fireplace, "I thought Aginor's greed would overcome him. But it makes no difference in the end. A long search, but ended now. You are here, and I know you."

In the midst of the Light the void drifted, and in the midst of the void floated Rand. He reached for the soil of his home, and felt hard rock, unyielding and dry, stone without pity, where only the strong could survive, only those as hard as the mountains. "I am tired of running." He could not believe his voice was so calm. "Tired of you threatening my friends. I will run no more." Ba'alzamon had a cord, too, he saw. A black cord, thicker by far than his own, so wide it should have dwarfed the human body, yet dwarfed by Ba'alzamon, instead. Each pulse along that black vein ate light.

"You think it makes any difference, whether you run or stay?" The flames of Ba'alzamon's mouth laughed. The faces in the hearth wept at their master's mirth. "You have fled from me many times, and each time I run you down and make you eat your pride with sniveling tears for spice. Many times you have stood and fought, then groveled in defeat, begging mercy. You have this choice, worm, and this choice only: kneel at my feet and serve me well, and I will give you power above thrones; or be Tar Valon's puppet fool and scream while you are ground into the dust of time."

Rand shifted, glancing back through the door as if seeking a way to escape. Let the Dark One think that. Beyond the doorway was still the black of nothing, split by the shining thread that ran from his body. And out there Ba'alzamon's heavier cord ran as well, so black that it stood out in the dark as if against snow. The two cords beat like heartveins in countertime, against each other, the light barely resisting the waves of dark.

"There are other choices," Rand said. "The Wheel weaves the Pattern, not you. Every trap you've laid for me, I have escaped. I've escaped your Fades and Trollocs, escaped your Darkfriends. I tracked you here, and destroyed your army on the way. You do not weave the Pattern."

Ba'alzamon's eyes roared like two furnaces. His lips did not move, but Rand thought he heard a curse screamed at Aginor. Then the fires died, and that ordinary human face smiled at him in a way that chilled even through the warmth of the Light.

"Other armies can be raised, fool. Armies you have not dreamed of will yet come. And you tracked me? You slug under a rock, track me? I began the setting of your path the day you were born, a path to lead you to your grave, or here. Aiel allowed to flee, and one to live, to speak the words that would echo down the years. Jain Farstrider, a hero," he twisted the word to a sneer, "whom I painted like a fool and sent to the Ogier thinking he was free of me. The Black Ajah, wriggling like worms on their bellies across the world to search you out. I pull the strings and the Amyrlin Seat dances and thinks she controls events."

The void trembled; hastily Rand firmed it again. *He knows it all. He could have done. It could be the way he says.* The Light warmed the void. Doubt cried out and was stilled, till only the seed remained. He struggled, not knowing whether he wanted to bury the seed or make it grow. The void steadied, smaller than before, and he floated in calm.

Ba'alzamon seemed to notice nothing. "It matters little if I have you alive or dead, except to you, and to what power you might have. You will serve me, or your soul will. But I would rather have you kneel to me alive than dead. A single fist of Trollocs sent to your village when I could have sent a thousand. One Darkfriend to face you where a hundred could come on you asleep. And you, fool, you don't even know them all, neither those ahead, nor those behind, nor those by your side. You are mine, have always been mine, my dog on a leash, and I brought you here to kneel to your master or die and let your soul kneel."

"I deny you. You have no power over me, and I will not kneel to you, alive or dead."

"Look," Ba'alzamon said. "Look." Unwilling, Rand yet turned his head.

Egwene stood there, and Nynaeve, pale and frightened, with flowers in their hair. And another woman, little older than the Wisdom, dark-eyed and beautiful, clothed in a Two Rivers dress, bright blossoms embroidered round the neck.

"Mother?" he breathed, and she smiled, a hopeless smile. His mother's smile. "No! My mother is dead, and the other two are safe away from here. I deny you!" Egwene and Nynaeve blurred, became wafting mist, dissipated. Kari al'Thor still stood there, her eyes big with fear.

"She, at least," Ba'alzamon said, "is mine to do with as I will."

Rand shook his head. "I deny you." He had to force the words out. "She is dead, and safe from you in the Light."

His mother's lips trembled. Tears trickled down her cheeks; each one burned him like acid. "The Lord of the Grave is stronger than he once was, my son," she said. "His reach is longer. The Father of Lies has a honeyed tongue for unwary souls. My son. My only, darling son.

I would spare you if I could, but he is my master, now, his whim, the law of my existence. I can but obey him, and grovel for his favor. Only you can free me. Please, my son. Please help me. Help me. Help me! PLEASE!"

The wail ripped out of her as barefaced Fades, pale and eyeless, closed round. Her clothes ripped away in their bloodless hands, hands that wielded pincers and clamps and things that stung and burned and whipped against her naked flesh. Her scream would not end.

Rand's scream echoed hers. The void boiled in his mind. His sword was in his hand. Not the heron-mark blade, but a blade of light, a blade of the Light. Even as he raised it, a fiery white bolt shot from the point, as if the blade itself had reached out. It touched the nearest Fade, and blinding canescence filled the chamber, shining through the Halfmen like a candle through paper, burning through them, blinding his eyes to the scene.

From the midst of the brilliance, he heard a whisper. "Thank you, my son. The Light. The blessed Light."

The flash faded, and he was alone in the chamber with Ba'alzamon. Ba'alzamon's eyes burned like the Pit of Doom, but he shied back from the sword as if it truly were the Light itself. "Fool! You will destroy yourself! You cannot wield it so, not yet! Not until I teach you!"

"It is ended," Rand said, and he swung the sword at Ba'alzamon's black cord.

Ba'alzamon screamed as the sword fell, screamed till the stone walls trembled, and the endless howl redoubled as the blade of Light severed the cord. The cut ends rebounded apart as if they had been under tension. The end stretching into the nothingness outside began to shrivel as it sprang away; the other whipped back into Ba'alzamon, hurling him against the fireplace. There was silent laughter in the soundless shrieks of the tortured faces. The walls shivered and cracked; the floor heaved, and chunks of stone crashed to the floor from the ceiling.

As all broke apart around him, Rand pointed the sword at Ba'alzamon's heart. "It is ended!"

Light lanced from the blade, coruscating in a shower of fiery sparks like droplets of molten, white metal. Wailing, Ba'alzamon threw up his arms in a vain effort to shield himself. Flames shrieked in his eyes, joining with other flames as the stone ignited, the stone of the cracking walls, the stone of the pitching floor, the stone showering from the ceiling. Rand felt the bright thread attached to him thinning, till only the glow itself remained, but he strained harder, not knowing what he did, or how, only that this had to be ended. *It has to be ended!*

Fire filled the chamber, a solid flame. He could see Ba'alzamon withering like a leaf, hear him howling, feel the shrieks grating on his bones. The flame became pure, white light, brighter than the sun. Then the last flicker of the thread was gone, and he was falling through endless black and Ba'alzamon's fading howl.

Something struck him with tremendous force, turning him to jelly, and the jelly shook and screamed from the fire raging inside, the hungry cold burning without end.

CHAPTER
52

There Is Neither Beginning Nor End

He became aware of the sun, first, moving across a cloudless sky, filling his unblinking eyes. It seemed to go by fits and starts, standing still for days, then darting ahead in a streak of light, jerking toward the far horizon, day falling with it. Light. *That should mean something.* Thought was a new thing. *I can think. I means me.* Pain came next, the memory of raging fever, the bruises where shaking chills had thrown him around like a rag doll. And a stink. A greasy, burned smell, filling his nostrils, and his head.

With aching muscles, he heaved himself over, pushed up to hands and knees. Uncomprehending, he stared at the oily ashes in which he had been lying, ashes scattered and smeared over the stone of the hilltop. Bits of dark green cloth lay mixed in the char, edge-blackened scraps that had escaped the flames.

Aginor.

His stomach heaved and twisted. Trying to brush black streaks of ash from his clothes, he lurched away from the remains of the Forsaken. His hands flapped feebly, not making much headway. He tried to use both hands and fell forward. A sheer drop loomed under his face, a smooth rock wall spinning in his eyes, depth pulling him. His head swum, and he vomited over the edge of the cliff.

Trembling, he crawled backwards on his belly until there was solid stone under his eyes, then flopped over onto his back, panting for breath. With an effort he fumbled his sword from its scabbard. Only a few ashes remained from the red cloth. His hands shook when he held it up in front of his face; it took both hands. It was a heron-mark blade— *Heron-mark? Yes. Tam. My father* —but only steel for that. He needed three wavering tries to sheathe it again. *It* had *been something else. Or there was another sword.*

"My name," he said after a while, "is Rand al'Thor." More memory crashed back into his head like a lead ball, and he groaned. "The Dark One," he whispered to himself. "The Dark One is dead." There was no more need for caution. "Shai'tan is dead." The world seemed to lurch. He shook in silent mirth until tears poured from his eyes. "Shai'tan is dead!" He laughed at the sky. Other memories. "Egwene!" That name meant something important.

Painfully he got to his feet, wavering like a willow in a high wind, and staggered past Aginor's ashes without looking at them. *Not important anymore.* He fell more than climbed down that first, steep part of the slope, tumbling and sliding from bush to bush. By the time he reached more level ground, his bruises ached twice as much, but he found strength enough to stand, barely. *Egwene.* He broke into a shambling run. Leaves and flower petals showered around him as he blundered through the undergrowth. *Have to find her. Who is she?*

His arms and legs seemed to flail about more like long blades of grass than go as he wanted them to. Tottering, he fell against a tree, slamming against the trunk so hard that he grunted. Foliage rained on his head while he pressed his face to the rough bark, clutching to keep from falling. *Egwene.* He pushed himself away from the tree and hurried on. Almost immediately he tilted again, falling, but he forced his legs to work faster, to run into the fall so that he was staggering along at a good clip, all the while one step from falling flat on his face. Moving made his legs begin to obey him more. Slowly, he found himself running upright, arms pumping, long legs pulling him down the slope in leaps. He bounded into the clearing, half-filled now by the great oak marking the Green Man's grave. There was the white stone arch marked with the ancient symbol of the Aes Sedai, and the blackened, gaping pit where fire and wind had tried to trap Aginor and failed.

"Egwene! Egwene, where are you?" A pretty girl looked up with big eyes from where she knelt beneath the spreading branches, flowers in her hair, and brown oak leaves. She was slender and young, and frightened. *Yes, that's who she is. Of course.* "Egwene, thank the Light you're all right."

There were two other women with her, one with haunted eyes and a long braid, still decorated with a few white morningstars. The other lay outstretched, her head pillowed on folded cloaks, her own sky-blue cloak not quite hiding her tattered dress. Charred spots and tears in the rich cloth showed, and her face was pale, but her eyes were open. *Moiraine. Yes, the Aes Sedai. And the Wisdom, Nynaeve.* All three women looked at him, unblinking and intent.

"You *are* all right, aren't you? Egwene? He didn't harm you." He could walk without stumbling, now—the sight of her made him feel like dancing, bruises and all—but it still felt good to drop down cross-legged beside them.

"I never even saw him after you pushed—" Her eyes were uncertain on his face. "What about you, Rand?"

"I'm fine." He laughed. He touched her cheek, and wondered if he had imagined a slight pulling away. "A little rest, and I'll be newmade. Nynaeve? Moiraine Sedai?" The names felt new in his mouth.

The Wisdom's eyes were old, ancient in her young face, but she shook her head. "A little bruised," she said, still watching him. "Moiraine is the only . . . the only one of us who was really hurt."

"I suffered more injury to my pride than anything else," the Aes Sedai said irritably, plucking at her cloak blanket. She looked as if she had been a long time ill, or hard used, but despite the dark circles under them her eyes were sharp and full of power. "Aginor was surprised and angry that I held him as long as I did, but fortunately, he had no time to spare for me. I am surprised myself that I held him so long. In the Age of Legends, Aginor was close behind the Kinslayer and Ishamael in power."

"'The Dark One and all the Forsaken,'" Egwene quoted in a faint, unsteady voice, "'are bound in Shayol Ghul, bound by the Creator. . . .'" She drew a shuddering breath.

"Aginor and Balthamel must have been trapped near the surface." Moiraine sounded as if she had already explained this, impatient at doing so again. "The patch on the Dark One's prison weakened enough to free them. Let us be thankful no more of the Forsaken were freed. If they had been, we would have seen them."

"It doesn't matter," Rand said. "Aginor and Balthamel are dead, and so is Shai'—"

"The Dark One," the Aes Sedai cut him off. Ill or not, her voice
was firm, and her dark eyes commanding. "Best we still call him the
Dark One. Or Ba'alzamon, at least."

He shrugged. "As you wish. But he's dead. The Dark One's dead.
I killed him. I burned him with. . . ." The rest of memory flooded
back then, leaving his mouth hanging open. *The One Power. I wielded
the One Power. No man can.* . . . He licked lips that were suddenly
dry. A gust of wind swirled fallen and falling leaves around them, but
it was no colder than his heart. They were looking at him, the three
of them. Watching. Not even blinking. He reached out to Egwene,
and there was no imagination in her drawing back this time.
"Egwene?" She turned her face away, and he let his hand drop.

Abruptly she flung her arms around him, burying her face in his
chest. "I'm sorry, Rand. I'm sorry. I don't care. Truly, I don't." Her
shoulders shook. He thought she was crying. Awkwardly patting her
hair, he looked at the other two women over the top of her head.

"The Wheel weaves as the Wheel wills," Nynaeve said slowly, "but
you are still Rand al'Thor of Emond's Field. But, the Light help me,
the Light help us all, you are too dangerous, Rand." He flinched from
the Wisdom's eyes, sad, regretting, and already accepting loss.

"What happened?" Moiraine said. "Tell me *everything!*"

And with her eyes on him, compelling, he did. He wanted to turn
away, to make it short, leave things out, but the Aes Sedai's eyes drew
everything from him. Tears ran down his face when he came to Kari
al'Thor. His mother. He emphasized that. "He had my mother. My
mother!" There was sympathy and pain on Nynaeve's face, but the
Aes Sedai's eyes drove him on, to the sword of Light, to severing
the black cord, and the flames consuming Ba'alzamon. Egwene's arms
tightened around him as if she would pull him back from what had
happened. "But it wasn't me," he finished. "The Light . . . pulled me
along. It wasn't really me. Doesn't that make any difference?"

"I had suspicions from the first," Moiraine said. "Suspicions are not
proof, though. After I gave you the token, the coin, and made that
bonding, you should have been willing to fall in with whatever I
wanted, but you resisted, questioned. That told me something, but not
enough. Manetheren blood was always stubborn, and more so after
Aemon died and Eldrene's heart was shattered. Then there was Bela."

"Bela?" he said. *Nothing makes any difference.*

The Aes Sedai nodded. "At Watch Hill, Bela had no need of me to
cleanse her of tiredness; someone had already done it. She could have
outrun Mandarb, that night. I should have thought of who Bela car-

ried. With Trollocs on our heels, a Draghkar overhead, and a Halfman the Light alone knew where, how you must have feared that Egwene would be left behind. You needed something more than you had ever needed anything before in your life, and you reached out to the one thing that could give it to you. *Saidin*."

He shivered. He felt so cold his fingers hurt. "If I never do it again, if I never touch it again, I won't. . . ." He could not say it. Go mad. Turn the land and people around him to madness. Die, rotting while he still lived.

"Perhaps," Moiraine said. "It would be much easier if there was someone to teach you, but it might be done, with a supreme effort of will."

"You can teach me. Surely, you—" He stopped when the Aes Sedai shook her head.

"Can a cat teach a dog to climb trees, Rand? Can a fish teach a bird to swim? I know *Saidar*, but I can teach you nothing of *Saidin*. Those who could are three thousand years dead. Perhaps you are stubborn enough, though. Perhaps your will is strong enough."

Egwene straightened, wiping reddened eyes with the back of her hand. She looked as if she wanted to say something, but when she opened her mouth, nothing came out. *At least she isn't pulling away. At least she can look at me without screaming.*

"The others?" he said.

"Lan took them into the cavern," Nynaeve said. "The Eye is gone, but there's something in the middle of the pool, a crystal column, and steps to reach it. Mat and Perrin wanted to look for you first—Loial did, too—but Moiraine said. . . ." She glanced at the Aes Sedai, troubled. Moiraine returned her look calmly. "She said we mustn't disturb you while you were. . . ."

His throat constricted until he could hardly breathe. *Will they turn their faces the way Egwene did? Will they scream and run away like I'm a Fade?* Moiraine spoke as if she did not notice the blood draining from his face.

"There was a vast amount of the One Power in the Eye. Even in the Age of Legends, few could have channeled so much unaided without being destroyed. Very few."

"You told them?" he said hoarsely. "If everybody knows. . . ."

"Only Lan," Moiraine said gently. "He must know. And Nynaeve and Egwene, for what they are and what they will become. The others have no need, yet."

"Why not?" The rasp in his throat made his voice harsh. "You will be wanting to gentle me, won't you? Isn't that what Aes Sedai do to men who can wield the Power? Change them so they can't? Make them safe? Thom said men who have been gentled die because they stop wanting to live. Why aren't you talking about taking me to Tar Valon to be gentled?"

"You are *ta'veren*," Moiraine replied. "Perhaps the Pattern has not finished with you."

Rand sat up straight. "In the dreams Ba'alzamon said Tar Valon and the Amyrlin Seat would try to use me. He named names, and I remember them, now. Raolin Darksbane and Guaire Amalasan. Yurian Stonebow. Davian. Logain." The last was the hardest of all to say. Nynaeve went pale and Egwene gasped, but he pressed on angrily. "Every one a false Dragon. Don't try to deny it. Well, I won't be used. I am not a tool you can throw on the midden heap when it's worn out."

"A tool made for a purpose is not demeaned by being used for that purpose," Moiraine's voice was as harsh as his own, "but a man who believes the Father of Lies demeans himself. You say you will not be used, and then you let the Dark One set your path like a hound sent after a rabbit by his master."

His fists clenched, and he turned his head away. It was too close to the things Ba'alzamon had said. "I am no one's hound. Do you hear me? No one's!"

Loial and the others appeared in the arch, and Rand scrambled to his feet, looking at Moiraine.

"They will not know," the Aes Sedai said, "until the Pattern makes it so."

Then his friends were coming close. Lan led the way, looking as hard as ever but still somewhat the worse for wear. He had one of Nynaeve's bandages around his temples, and a stiff-backed way of walking. Behind him, Loial carried a large gold chest, ornately worked and chased with silver. No one but an Ogier could have lifted it unaided. Perrin had his arms wrapped around a big bundle of folded white cloth, and Mat was cupping what appeared to be fragments of pottery in his two hands.

"So you're alive after all." Mat laughed. His face darkened, and he jerked his head at Moiraine. "She wouldn't let us look for you. Said we had to find out what the Eye was hiding. I'd have gone anyway, but Nynaeve and Egwene sided with her and almost threw me through the arch."

"You're here, now," Perrin said, "and not too badly beaten about, by the look of you." His eyes did not glow, but the irises were all yellow, now. "That's the important thing. You're here, and we're done with what we came for, whatever it was. Moiraine Sedai says we're done, and we can go. Home, Rand. The Light burn me, but I want to go home."

"Good to see you alive, sheepherder," Lan said gruffly. "I see you hung onto your sword. Maybe you'll learn to use it, now." Rand felt a sudden burst of affection for the Warder; Lan knew, but on the surface at least, nothing had changed. He thought that perhaps, for Lan, nothing had changed inside either.

"I must say," Loial said, setting the chest down, "that traveling with ta'veren has turned out to be even more interesting than I expected." His ears twitched violently. "If it becomes any more interesting, I will go back to Stedding Shangtai immediately, confess everything to Elder Haman, and never leave my books again." Suddenly the Ogier grinned, that wide mouth splitting his face in two. "It is so good to see you, Rand al'Thor. The Warder is the only one of these three who cares much at all for books, and he won't talk. What happened to you? We all ran off and hid in the woods until Moiraine Sedai sent Lan to find us, but she would not let us look for you. Why were you gone so long, Rand?"

"I ran and ran," he said slowly, "until I fell down a hill and hit my head on a rock. I think I hit every rock on the way down." That should explain his bruises. He tried to watch the Aes Sedai, and Nynaeve and Egwene, too, but their faces never changed. "When I came to, I was lost, and finally I stumbled back here. I think Aginor is dead, burned. I found some ashes, and pieces of his cloak."

The lies sounded hollow in his ears. He could not understand why they did not laugh with scorn and demand the truth, but his friends nodded, accepting, and made sympathetic sounds as they gathered around the Aes Sedai to show her what they had found.

"Help me up," Moiraine said. Nynaeve and Egwene lifted her until she was sitting; they had to support her even then.

"How could these things be inside the Eye," Mat asked, "without being destroyed like that rock?"

"They were not put there to be destroyed," the Aes Sedai said curtly, and frowned away their questions while she took the pottery fragments, black and white and shiny, from Mat.

They seemed like rubble to Rand, but she fitted them together deftly on the ground beside her, making a perfect circle the size of a man's hand. The ancient symbol of the Aes Sedai, the Flame of Tar Valon joined with the Dragon's Fang, black siding white. For a moment Moiraine only looked at it, her face unreadable, then she took the knife from her belt and handed it to Lan, nodding to the circle.

The Warder separated out the largest piece, then raised the knife high and brought it down with all his might. A spark flew, the fragment leaped with the force of the blow, and the blade snapped with a sharp crack. He examined the stump left attached to the hilt, then tossed it aside. "The best steel from Tear," he said dryly.

Mat snatched the fragment up and grunted, then showed it around. There was no mark on it.

"Cuendillar," Moiraine said. "Heartstone. No one has been able to make it since the Age of Legends, and even then it was made only for the greatest purpose. Once made, nothing can break it. Not the One Power itself wielded by the greatest Aes Sedai who ever lived aided by the most powerful *sa'angreal* ever made. Any power directed against heartstone only makes it stronger."

"Then how . . . ?" Mat's gesture with the piece he held took in the other bits on the ground.

"This was one of the seven seals on the Dark One's prison," Moiraine said. Mat dropped the piece as if it had become white-hot. For a moment, Perrin's eyes seemed to glow again. The Aes Sedai calmly began gathering the fragments.

"It doesn't matter anymore," Rand said. His friends looked at him oddly, and he wished he had kept his mouth shut.

"Of course," Moiraine replied. But she carefully put all the pieces into her pouch. "Bring me the chest." Loial lifted it closer.

The flattened cube of gold and silver appeared to be solid, but the Aes Sedai's fingers felt across the intricate work, pressing, and with a sudden click a top flung back as if on springs. A curled, gold horn nestled within. Despite its gleam, it seemed plain beside the chest that held it. The only markings were a line of silver script inlaid around the mouth of the bell. Moiraine lifted the horn out as if lifting a babe. "This must be carried to Illian," she said softly.

"Illian!" Perrin growled. "That's almost to the Sea of Storms, nearly as far south of home as we are north now."

"Is it . . . ?" Loial stopped to catch his breath. "Can it be . . . ?"

"You can read the Old Tongue?" Moiraine asked, and when he nodded, she handed him the horn.

The Ogier took it as gently as she had, delicately tracing the script with one broad finger. His eyes went wider and wider, and his ears stood up straight. *"Tia mi aven Moridin isainde vadin,"* he whispered. "The grave is no bar to my call."

"The Horn of Valere." For once the Warder appeared truly shaken; there was a touch of awe in his voice.

At the same time Nynaeve said in a shaky voice, "To call the heroes of the Ages back from the dead to fight the Dark One."

"Burn me!" Mat breathed.

Loial reverently laid the horn back in its golden nest.

"I begin to wonder," Moiraine said. "The Eye of the World was made against the greatest need the world would ever face, but was it made for the use to which . . . we . . . put it, or to guard these things? Quickly, the last, show it to me."

After the first two, Rand could understand Perrin's reluctance. Lan and the Ogier took the bundle of white cloth from him when he hesitated, and unfolded it between them. A long, white banner spread out, lifting on the air. Rand could only stare. The whole thing seemed of a piece, neither woven, nor dyed, nor painted. A figure like a serpent, scaled in scarlet and gold, ran the entire length, but it had scaled legs, and feet with five long, golden claws on each, and a great head with a golden mane and eyes like the sun. The stirring of the banner made it seem to move, scales glittering like precious metals and gems, alive, and he almost thought he could hear it roar defiance.

"What is it?" he said.

Moiraine answered slowly. "The banner of the Lord of the Morning when he led the forces of Light against the Shadow. The banner of Lews Therin Telamon. The banner of the Dragon." Loial almost dropped his end.

"Burn me!" Mat said faintly.

"We will take these things with us when we go," Moiraine said. "They were not put here by chance, and I must know more." Her fingers brushed her pouch, where the pieces of the shattered seal were. "It is too late in the day for starting now. We will rest, and eat, but we will leave early. The Blight is all around here, not as along the Border, and strong. Without the Green Man, this place cannot hold long. Let me down," she told Nynaeve and Egwene. "I must rest."

Rand became aware of what he had been seeing all along, but not noticing. Dead, brown leaves falling from the great oak. Dead leaves rustling thick on the ground in the breeze, brown mixed with petals dropped from thousands of flowers. The Green Man had held back the Blight, but already the Blight was killing what he had made.

"It is done, isn't it?" he asked Moiraine. "It is finished."

The Aes Sedai turned her head on its pillow of cloaks. Her eyes seemed as deep as the Eye of the World. "We have done what we came here to do. From here you may live your life as the Pattern weaves. Eat, then sleep, Rand al'Thor. Sleep, and dream of home."

CHAPTER
53

The Wheel Turns

D awn revealed devastation in the Green Man's garden. The ground was thick with fallen leaves, almost knee-deep in places. All the flowers were gone except a few clinging desperately to the edge of the clearing. Little could grow in the soil under an oak, but a thin circle of flowers and grass centered on the thick trunk above the Green Man's grave. The oak itself retained only half its leaves, and that was far more than any other tree had, as if some remnant of the Green Man still fought to hold there. The cool breezes had died, replaced by a growing sticky heat, the butterflies were gone, the birds silent. It was a silent group who prepared to leave.

Rand climbed into the bay's saddle with a sense of loss. *It shouldn't be this way. Blood and ashes, we won!*

"I wish he had found his other place," Egwene said as she mounted Bela. A litter, fashioned by Lan, was slung between the shaggy mare and Aldieb, to carry Moiraine; Nynaeve would ride beside with the white mare's reins. The Wisdom dropped her eyes whenever she saw Lan glance at her, avoiding his gaze; the Warder looked at her whenever her eyes were averted, but he would not speak to her. No one had to ask who Egwene meant.

"It is not right," Loial said, staring at the oak. The Ogier was the only one still not mounted. "It is not right that Treebrother should fall to the Blight." He handed the reins of his big horse to Rand. "Not right."

Lan opened his mouth as the Ogier walked to the great oak. Moiraine, lying on the litter, weakly raised her hand, and the Warder said nothing.

Before the oak, Loial knelt, closing his eyes and stretching out his arms. The tufts on his ears stood straight as he lifted his face to the sky. And he sang.

Rand could not say if there were words, or if it was pure song. In that rumbling voice it was as if the earth sang, yet he was sure he heard the birds trilling again, and spring breezes sighing softly, and the sound of butterfly wings. Lost in the song, he thought it lasted only minutes, but when Loial lowered his arms and opened his eyes, he was surprised to see the sun stood well above the horizon. It had been touching the trees when the Ogier began. The leaves still on the oak seemed greener, and more firmly attached than before. The flowers encircling it stood straighter, the morningstars white and fresh, the loversknots a strong crimson.

Mopping sweat from his broad face, Loial rose and took his reins from Rand. His long eyebrows drooped, abashed, as if they might think he had been showing off. "I've never sung so hard before. I could not have done it if something of Treebrother was not still there. My Treesongs do not have his power." When he settled himself in his saddle, there was satisfaction in the look he gave the oak and the flowers. "This little space, at least, will not sink into the Blight. The Blight will not have Treebrother."

"You are a good man, Ogier," Lan said.

Loial grinned. "I will take that as a compliment, but I do not know what Elder Haman would say."

They rode in a single file, with Mat behind the Warder where he could use his bow to effect if needed, and Perrin bringing up the rear with his axe across the pommel of his saddle. They crested a hill, and in an eyeblink the Blight was all around them, twisted and rotted in virulent rainbow hues. Rand looked over his shoulder, but the Green Man's garden was nowhere to be seen. Only the Blight stretching behind them as before. Yet he thought, just for a moment, that he saw the towering top of the oak tree, green and lush, before it shimmered and was gone. Then there was only the Blight.

He half expected they would have to fight their way out as they fought their way in, but the Blight was as quiet and still as death. Not a single branch trembled as if to lash at them, nothing screamed or howled, neither nearby nor in the distance. The Blight seemed to crouch, not to pounce, but as if it had been struck a great blow and waited for the next to fall. Even the sun was less red.

When they passed the necklace of lakes, the sun hung not far past its zenith. Lan kept them well away from the lakes and did not even look at them, but Rand thought the seven towers seemed taller than when he first saw them. He was sure the jagged tops were further from the ground, and above them something almost seen, seamless towers gleaming in the sun, and banners with Golden Cranes flying on the wind. He blinked and stared, but the towers refused to vanish completely. They were there at the edge of vision until the Blight hid the lakes once more.

Before sunset the Warder chose a campsite, and Moiraine had Nynaeve and Egwene help her up to set wards. The Aes Sedai whispered in the other women's ears before she began. Nynaeve hesitated, but when Moiraine closed her eyes, all three women did so together.

Rand saw Mat and Perrin staring, and wondered how they could be surprised. *Every woman is an Aes Sedai,* he thought mirthlessly. *The Light help me, so am I.* Bleakness held his tongue.

"Why is it so different?" Perrin asked as Egwene and the Wisdom helped Moiraine to her bed. "It feels. . . ." His thick shoulders shrugged as if he could not find the word.

"We struck a mighty blow at the Dark One," Moiraine replied, settling herself with a sigh. "The Shadow will be a long time recovering."

"How?" Mat demanded. "What did we do?"

"Sleep," Moiraine said. "We are not out of the Blight yet."

But the next morning, still nothing changed that Rand could see. The Blight faded as they rode south, of course. Twisted trees were replaced by straight. The stifling heat diminished. Rotting foliage gave way to the merely diseased. And then not diseased, he realized. The forest around them became red with new growth, thick on the branches. Buds sprouted on the undergrowth, creepers covered the rocks with green, and new wildflowers dotted the grass as thick and bright as where the Green Man walked. It was as if spring, so long held back by winter, now raced to catch up to where it should be.

He was not the only one who stared. "A mighty blow," Moiraine murmured, and would say no more.

Climbing wildrose entwined the stone column marking the Border.

Men came out of the watchtowers to greet them. There was a stunned quality to their laughter, and their eyes shone with amaze, as if they could not believe the new grass under their steel-clad feet.

"The Light has conquered the Shadow!"

"A great victory in Tarwin's Gap! We have had the message! Victory!"

"The Light blesses us again!"

"King Easar is strong in the Light," Lan replied to all their shouts.

The watchmen wanted to tend Moiraine, or at least send an escort with them, but she refused it all. Even flat on her back on a litter, the Aes Sedai's presence was such that the armored men fell back, bowing and acceding to her wishes. Their laughter followed as Rand and the others rode on.

In the late afternoon they reached Fal Dara, to find the grim-walled city ringing with celebration. Ringing in truth. Rand doubted if there could be a bell in the city not clanging, from the tiniest silver harness chime to great bronze gongs in their tower tops. The gates stood wide open, and men ran laughing and singing in the streets, flowers stuck in their topknots and the crevices of their armor. The common people of the town had not yet returned from Fal Moran, but the soldiers were newly come from Tarwin's Gap, and their joy was enough to fill the streets.

"Victory in the Gap! We won!"

"A miracle in the Gap! The Age of Legends has come back!"

"Spring!" a grizzled old soldier laughed as he hung a garland of morningstars around Rand's neck. His own topknot was a white cluster of them. "The Light blesses us with spring once more!"

Learning they wanted to go to the keep, a circle of men clad in steel and flowers surrounded them, running to clear a way through the celebration.

Ingtar's was the first face Rand saw that was not smiling. "I was too late," Ingtar told Lan with a sour grimness. "Too late by an hour to see. Peace!" His teeth ground audibly, but then his expression became contrite. "Forgive me. Grief makes me forget my duties. Welcome, Builder. Welcome to you all. It is good to see you safely out of the Blight. I will bring the healer to Moiraine Sedai in her chambers, and inform Lord Agelmar—"

"Take me to Lord Agelmar," Moiraine commanded. "Take us all." Ingtar opened his mouth to protest, and bowed under the force of her eyes.

Agelmar was in his study, with his swords and armor back on their racks, and his was the second face that did not smile. He wore a troubled frown that deepened when he saw Moiraine carried in on her litter by liveried servants. Women in the black-and-gold fluttered over bringing the Aes Sedai to him without a chance to freshen herself or be brought the healer. Loial carried the gold chest. The pieces of the seal were still in Moiraine's pouch; Lews Therin Kinslayer's banner was wrapped in her blanketroll and still tied behind Aldieb's saddle. The groom who had led the white mare away had received the strictest Orders to see the blanketroll was placed untouched in the chambers assigned to the Aes Sedai.

"Peace!" the Lord of Fal Dara muttered. "Are you injured, Moiraine Sedai? Ingtar, why have you not seen the Aes Sedai to her bed and brought the healer to her?"

"Be still, Lord Agelmar," Moiraine said. "Ingtar has done as I commanded him. I am not so frail as everyone here seems to think." She motioned two of the women to help her to a chair. For a moment they clasped their hands, exclaiming that she was too weak, that she should be in a warm bed, and the healer brought, and a hot bath. Moiraine's eyebrows lifted; the women shut their mouths abruptly and hurried to aid her into the chair. As soon as she was settled she waved them away irritably. "I would speak with you, Lord Agelmar."

Agelmar nodded, and Ingtar waved the servants from the room. The Lord of Fal Dara eyed those who remained expectantly; especially, Rand thought, Loial and the golden chest.

"We hear," Moiraine said as soon as the door shut behind Ingtar, "that you won a great victory in Tarwin's Gap."

"Yes," Agelmar said slowly, his troubled frown returning. "Yes, Aes Sedai, and no. The Halfmen and their Trollocs were destroyed to the last, but we barely fought. A miracle, my men call it. The earth swallowed them; the mountains buried them. Only a few Draghkar were left, too frightened to do else but fly north as fast as they could."

"A miracle indeed," Moiraine said. "And spring has come again."

"A miracle," Agelmar said, shaking his head, "but. . . . Moiraine Sedai, men say many things about what happened in the Gap. That the Light took on flesh and fought for us. That the Creator walked in the Gap to strike at the Shadow. But I saw a man, Moiraine Sedai. I saw a man, and what he did, cannot be, must not be."

"The Wheel weaves as the Wheel wills, Lord of Fal Dara."

"As you say, Moiraine Sedai."

"And Padan Fain? He is secure? I must speak with him when I am rested."

"He is held as you commanded, Aes Sedai, whining at his guards half the time and trying to command them the rest, but. . . . Peace, Moiraine Sedai, what of you, in the Blight? You found the Green Man? I see his hand in the new things growing."

"We found him," she said flatly. "The Green Man is dead, Lord Agelmar, and the Eye of the World is gone. There will be no more quests by young men seeking glory."

The Lord of Fal Dara frowned, shaking his head in confusion. "Dead? The Green Man? He cannot be. . . . Then you were defeated? But the flowers, and the growing things?"

"We won, Lord Agelmar. We won, and the land freed from winter is the proof, but I fear the last battle has not yet been fought." Rand stirred, but the Aes Sedai gave him a sharp look and he stood still again. "The Blight still stands, and the forges of Thakan'dar still work below Shayol Ghul. There are many Halfmen yet, and countless Trollocs. Never think the need for watchfulness in the Borderlands is gone."

"I did not think it so, Aes Sedai," he said stiffly.

Moiraine motioned for Loial to set the gold chest at her feet, and when he did, she opened it, revealing the horn. "The Horn of Valere," she said, and Agelmar gasped. Rand almost thought the man would kneel.

"With that, Moiraine Sedai, it matters not how many Halfmen or Trollocs remain. With the heroes of old come back from the tomb, we will march to the Blasted Lands and level Shayol Ghul."

"NO!" Agelmar's mouth fell open in surprise, but Moiraine continued calmly. "I did not show it to you to taunt you, but so that you will know that in whatever battles yet come, our might will be as great as that of the Shadow. Its place is not here. The Horn must be carried to Illian. It is there, if fresh battles threaten, that it must rally the forces of the Light. I will ask an escort of your best men to see that it reaches Illian safely. There are Darkfriends still, as well as Halfmen and Trollocs, and those who come to the horn will follow whoever winds it. It must reach Illian."

"It shall be as you say, Aes Sedai." But when the lid of the chest closed, the Lord of Fal Dara looked like a man being denied his last glimpse of the Light.

Seven days later, bells still rang in Fal Dara. The people had returned from Fal Moran, adding their celebration to that of the soldiers, and shouts and singing blended with the pealing of the bells on the long balcony where Rand stood. The balcony overlooked Agelmar's private gardens, green and flowering, but he did not give them a second look. Despite the sun high in the sky, spring in Shienar was cooler than he was used to, yet sweat glistened on his bare chest and shoulders as he swung the heron-mark blade, each move precise yet distant from where he floated in the void. Even there, he wondered how much joy there would be in the town if they knew of the banner Moiraine still kept hidden.

"Good, sheepherder." Leaning against the railing with his arms folded across his chest, the Warder watched him critically. "You are doing well, but don't push so hard. You can't become a blademaster in a few weeks."

The void vanished like a pricked bubble. "I don't care about being a blademaster."

"It's a blademaster's blade, sheepherder."

"I just want my father to be proud of me." His hand tightened on the rough leather of the hilt. *I just want Tam to be my father.* He slammed the sword into its scabbard. "Anyway, I don't have a few weeks."

"Then you've not changed your mind?"

"Would you?" Lan's expression had not altered; the flat planes of his face looked as if they could not change. "You won't try to stop me? Or Moiraine Sedai?"

"You can do as you will, sheepherder, or as the Pattern weaves for you." The Warder straightened. "I'll leave you now."

Rand turned to watch Lan go, and found Egwene standing there.

"Changed your mind about what, Rand?"

He snatched up his shirt and coat, suddenly feeling the cool. "I'm going away, Egwene."

"Where?"

"Somewhere. I don't know." He did not want to meet her eyes, but he could not stop looking at her. She wore red wildroses twined in her hair, flowing about her shoulders. She held her cloak close, dark blue and embroidered along the edge with a thin line of white flowers in the Shienaran fashion, and the blossoms made a line straight up to her face. They were no paler than her cheeks; her eyes seemed so large and dark. "Away."

"I'm sure Moiraine Sedai will not like you just going off. After . . . after what you've done, you deserve some reward."

"Moiraine does not know I am alive. I have done what she wanted, and that's an end to it. She doesn't even speak to me when I go to her. Not that I've tried to stay close to her, but she's avoided me. She won't care if I go, and I don't care if she does."

"Moiraine is still not completely well, Rand." She hesitated. "I have to go to Tar Valon for my training. Nynaeve is coming, too. And Mat still needs to be Healed of whatever binds him to that dagger, and Perrin wants to see Tar Valon before he goes . . . wherever. You could come with us."

"And wait for some Aes Sedai besides Moiraine to find out what I am and gentle me?" His voice was rough, almost a sneer; he could not change it. "Is that what you want?"

"No."

He knew he would never be able to tell her how grateful he was that she had not hesitated before answering.

"Rand, you aren't afraid. . . ." They were alone, but she looked around and still lowered her voice. "Moiraine Sedai says you don't have to touch the True Source. If you don't touch *Saidin,* if you don't try to wield the Power, you'll be safe."

"Oh, I won't ever touch it again. Not if I have to cut my hand off, first." *What if I can't stop? I never tried to wield it, not even at the Eye. What if I can't stop?*

"Will you go home, Rand? Your father must be dying to see you. Even Mat's father must be dying to see him by now. I'll be coming back to Emond's Field next year. For a little while, at least."

He rubbed his palm over the hilt of his sword, feeling the bronze heron. *My father. Home. Light, how I want to see. . . .* "Not home." *Someplace where there aren't any people to hurt if I can't stop myself. Somewhere alone.* Suddenly it felt as cold as snow on the balcony. "I'm going away, but not home." *Egwene, Egwene, why did you have to be one of those . . . ?* He put his arms around her, and whispered into her hair. "Not ever home."

In Agelmar's private garden, under a thick bower dotted with white blossoms, Moiraine shifted on her bedchair. The fragments of the seal lay on her lap, and the small gem she sometimes wore in her hair spun and glittered on its gold chain from the ends of her fingers. The faint blue glow faded from the stone, and a smile touched her lips. It had no power in itself, the stone, but the first use she had ever learned of the One Power, as a girl, in the Royal Palace in Cairhien, was using the stone to listen to people when they thought they were too far off to be overheard.

"The Prophecies will be fulfilled," the Aes Sedai whispered. "The Dragon is Reborn."

The End
of the First Book of
The Wheel of Time

GLOSSARY

A NOTE ON DATES IN THIS GLOSSARY. The Toman Calendar (devised by Toma dur Ahmid) was adopted approximately two centuries after the death of the last male Aes Sedai and recorded years After the Breaking of the World (AB). Many records were destroyed in the Trolloc Wars, so much so that with the end of the Wars there was argument about the exact year under the old system. A new calendar was proposed by Tiam of Gazar, celebrating the supposed freedom from the Trolloc threat and recording each year as a Free Year (FY). The Gazaran calendar gained wide acceptance within twenty years after the Wars' end. Artur Hawkwing attempted to establish a new calendar based on the founding of his empire (FF, From the Founding), but this is now known and referred to only by historians. After the widespread destruction, death and disruption of the War of the Hundred Years, a fourth calendar was devised by Uren din Jubai Soaring Gull, a scholar of the Sea Folk, and promulgated by the Panarch Farede of Tarabon. The Farede Calendar, dating from the arbitrarily-decided end of the War of the Hundred Years and recording years of the New Era (NE), is currently in use.

Adan, Heran (ay-DAN, HEH-ran): Governor of Baerlon.

Aes Sedai (EYEZ seh-DEYE): Wielders of the One Power. Since the Time of Madness, all surviving Aes Sedai are women. Widely distrusted and feared, even hated, they are blamed by many for the Breaking of the World, and are generally thought to meddle in the affairs of nations. At the same time, few rulers will be without an Aes Sedai adviser, even in lands where the existence of such a connection must be kept secret. Used as an honorific, so: Sheriam Sedai; and as a high honorific, so: Sheriam Aes Sedai. *See also* Ajah; Amyrlin Seat.

Age Lace: See Pattern of an Age.

Age of Legends: The Age ended by the War of the Shadow and the Breaking of the World. A time when Aes Sedai performed wonders now only dreamed of. *See also* Wheel of Time.

Agelmar; Lord Agelmar of House of Jagad (AGH-el-mar; JAH-gad): Lord of Fal Dara. His sign is three running red foxes.

Aiel (eye-EEL): The people of the Aiel Waste. Fierce and hardy. Also called Aielmen. They veil their faces before they kill, giving rise to the saying "acting like a black-veiled Aiel" to describe someone who is being violent. Deadly warriors with weapons or with nothing but their bare hands, they will not touch a sword. Their pipers play them into battle with the music of dances, and Aielmen call battle "the Dance."

Aiel Waste: The harsh, rugged and all-but-waterless land east of the Spine of the World. Few outsiders venture there, not only because water is almost impossible to find for one not born there, but because the Aiel consider themselves at war with all other peoples and do not welcome strangers.

Ajah (AH-jah): Societies among the Aes Sedai, to which all Aes Sedai belong. They are designated by colors: Blue Ajah, Red Ajah, White Ajah, Green Ajah, Brown Ajah, Yellow Ajah, and Gray Ajah. Each follows a specific philosophy of the use of the One Power and purposes of the Aes Sedai. For example, the Red Ajah bends all its energies to finding and gentling men who are attempting to wield the Power. The Brown Ajah, on the other hand, forsakes involvement with the world and dedicates itself to seeking knowledge. There are rumors (hotly denied, and never safely mentioned in front of any Aes Sedai) of a Black Ajah, dedicated to serving the Dark One.

Al Ellisande! (ahlehl-lih-SAHN-dah): In the Old Tongue, "For the Rose of the Sun!"

Aldieb (ahl-DEEB): In the Old Tongue, "West Wind," the wind that brings the spring rains.

al'Meara, Nynaeve (ahl-MEER-ah, NIGH-neev): The Wisdom of Emond's Field.

al'Thor, Rand (ahl-THOR, RAND): A young farmer and sheepherder from the Two Rivers.

al'Vere, Egwene (ahl-VEER, eh-GWAIN): Youngest daughter of the innkeeper in Emond's Field.

Amyrlin Seat (AHM-ehr-lin): (1.) The title of the leader of the Aes Sedai. Elected for life by the Hall of the Tower, the highest council of the Aes Sedai, which consists of three representatives from each of the seven Ajahs. The Amyrlin Seat has, theoretically at least, almost supreme authority among the Aes Sedai. She ranks as the equal of a king or queen.

(2.) The throne upon which the leader of the Aes Sedai sits.

Andor (AN-door): The realm within which the Two Rivers lies. The sign of Andor is a rampant white lion on a field of red.

angreal (ahn-gree-AHL): A very rare object which allows anyone capable of channeling the One Power to handle a greater amount of the Power than would be safely possible unaided. Remnants of the Age of Legends, the means of their making is no longer known. *See also sa'angreal.*

Arafel (AH-rah-fehl): One of the Borderlands. The sign of Arafel is three white roses on a field of red, quartered with three red roses on a field of white.

Aram (AY-ram): A young man of the Tuatha'an.

Avendesora (Ah-vehn-deh-SO-rah): In the Old Tongue, "the Tree of Life." Mentioned in many stories and legends.

Aybara, Perrin (ay-BAHR-ah, PEHR-rihn): A young blacksmith's apprentice from Emond's Field.

Ba'alzamon (bah-AHL-zah-mon): In the Trolloc tongue, "Heart of the Dark." Believed to be the Trolloc name for the Dark One.

Baerlon (BAYR-lon): A city in Andor on the road from Caemlyn to the mines in the Mountains of Mist.

Barran, Doral (BAHR-rahn, DOOR-ahl): The Wisdom in Emond's Field prior to Nynaeve al'Meara.

Bel Tine (BEHL TINE): Spring festival in the Two Rivers.

biteme (BITE-me): A small, almost invisible biting insect.

Black Ajah: See Ajah.

Blasted Lands: Desolated lands surrounding Shayol Ghul, beyond the Great Blight.

Blight, the: See Great Blight, the.

Blue Ajah: See Ajah.

Borderlands, the: The nations bordering the Great Blight: Saldaea, Arafel, Kandor, and Shienar.

Bornhald, Dain (BOHRN-hahld, DAY-ihn): An officer of the Children of the Light, son of Lord Captain Geofram Bornhald.

Bornhald, Geofram (BOHRN-hahld, JEHF-rahm): A Lord Captain of the Children of the Light.

Breaking of the World, the: When Lews Therin Telamon and the Hundred Companions resealed the Dark One's prison, the counterstroke tainted *saidin*. Eventually every male Aes Sedai went horribly insane. In their madness these men, who could wield the One Power to a degree now unknown, changed the face of the earth. They caused great earthquakes, leveled mountain ranges, raised new mountains, lifted dry land where seas had been, made the ocean rush in where dry land had been. Many parts of the world were completely depopulated, and the survivors were scattered like dust on the wind. This destruction is remembered in stories, legends and history as the Breaking of the World. *See also* Hundred Companions, the.

Bryne, Gareth (BRIHN, GAH-rehth): Captain-General of the Queen's Guard in Andor. Also serves as Morgase's First Prince of the Sword. His sign is three golden stars, each of five rays.

Byar, Jaret (BY-ahr, JAH-ret): An officer of the Children of the Light.

Caemlyn (KAYM-lihn): The capital city of Andor.

Cairhien (KEYE-ree-EHN): Both a nation along the Spine of the World and the capital city of that nation. The city was burned and looted during the Aiel War (976–978 NE). The sign of Cairhien is a many-rayed golden sun rising from the bottom of a field of sky blue.

Carai an Caldazar! (cah-REYE ahn cahl-dah-ZAHR): In the Old Tongue, "For the honor of the Red Eagle!" The ancient battle cry of Manetheren.

Carai an Ellisande!: In the Old Tongue, "For the honor of the Rose of the Sun!" The battle cry of the last king of Manetheren.

Cauthon, Matrim (Mat) (CAW-thon, MAT-rihm): A young farmer from the Two Rivers.

channel: (1) *(verb)* To control the flow of the One power. (2) *(noun)* The act of controlling the flow of the One Power.

Charin, Jain (CHAH-rihn, JAY-ihn): See Farstrider, Jain.

Children of the Light: A society holding strict ascetic beliefs, dedicated

to the defeat of the Dark One and the destruction of all Darkfriends. Founded during the War of the Hundred Years by Lothair
Mantelar *(LOH-thayr MAHN-tee-LAHR)* to proselytize against
increasing numbers of Darkfriends, they evolved during the war
into a completely military organization, extremely rigid in their
beliefs and completely certain that only they know the truth and
the right. They hate Aes Sedai, considering them, and any who
support or befriend them, Darkfriends. They are known disparag-
ingly as Whitecloaks; their sign is a golden sunburst on a field of
white.

Covenant of the Ten Nations: A union formed in the centuries after the
Breaking of the World (circa 200 AB). Dedicated to the defeat of
the Dark One. Broken apart by the Trolloc Wars.

cuendillar (CWAIN-deh-yar): *See* heartstone.

Damodred, Lord Galadedrid *(DAHM-oh-drehd, gah-LAHD-eh-drihd):*
Only son of Taringail Damodred and Tigraine; half-brother to
Elayne and Gawyn. His sign is a winged silver sword, point-down.

Damodred, Prince Taringail *(DAHM-oh-drehd, TAH-rihn-gail):* A
Royal Prince of Cairhien, he married Tigraine and fathered Galadedrid. When Tigraine disappeared and was declared dead, he
married Morgase and fathered Elayne and Gawyn. He vanished
under mysterious circumstances and has been presumed dead for
many years. His sign was a golden, double-bitted battle axe.

Dark One: Most common name, used in every land, for Shai'tan: the
source of evil, antithesis of the Creator. Imprisoned by the Creator at the moment of Creation in a prison at Shayol Ghul; an
attempt to free him from that prison brought about the War of
the Shadow, the tainting of *saidin,* the Breaking of the World, and
the end of the Age of Legends.

Dark One, naming the: Saying the true name of the Dark One
(Shai'tan) draws his attention, inevitably bringing ill-fortune at
best, disaster at worst. For that reason many euphemisms are
used, among them the Dark One, Father of Lies, Sightblinder,
Lord of the Grave, Shepherd of the Night, Heartsbane, Heartfang, Grassburner, and Leafblighter. Someone who seems to be
inviting ill fortune is often said to be "naming the Dark One."

Darkfriends: Those who follow the Dark One and believe they will gain
great power and rewards when he is freed from his prison.

Daughter-heir: Title of the heir to the throne of Andor. The eldest
daughter of the Queen succeeds her mother on the throne. Without a surviving daughter, the throne goes to the nearest female
blood-relation of the Queen.

Dha-vol, Dhai'mon (DAH-vohl, DEYE-mon): See Trollocs.

Djevik K'Shar (DJEH-vihk KEH-SHAHR): In the Trolloc tongue, "The Dying Ground." The Trolloc name for the Aiel Waste.

Domon, Bayle (DOH-mon, BAIL): The captain of the *Spray.*

Dragon, the: The name by which Lews Therin Telamon was known during the War of the Shadow. In the madness which overtook all male Aes Sedai, Lews Therin killed every living person who carried any of his blood, as well as everyone he loved, thus earning the name Kinslayer. A saying is now used, "taken by the Dragon," or "possessed of the Dragon," to indicate that someone is endangering those around him or threatening them, especially if without cause. *See also* Dragon Reborn.

Dragon, false: Occasionally men claim to be the Dragon Reborn, and sometimes one of them gains following enough to require an army to put it down. Some have begun wars that involved many nations. Over the centuries most have been men unable to channel the One Power, but a few could. All, however, either disappeared, or were captured or killed, without fulfilling any of the Prophecies concerning the Rebirth of the Dragon. These men are called false Dragons. *See also* Dragon reborn.

Dragon Reborn: According to prophecy and legend the Dragon will be born again at mankind's greatest hour of need to save the world. This is not something people look forward to, both because the prophecies say the Dragon Reborn will bring a new Breaking to the world, and because Lews Therin Kinslayer, the Dragon, is a name to make men shudder, even more than three thousand years after his death. *See also* Dragon, the; Dragon, false.

Dragon's Fang, the: A stylized mark, usually black, in the shape of a teardrop balanced on its point. Scrawled on a door or a house, it is an accusation of evil against the people inside.

Dreadlords: Those men and women who, able to channel the One Power, went over to the Shadow during the Trolloc Wars, acting as commanders of the Trolloc forces.

Easar; King Easar of House Togita (EE-zar; toh-GHEE-tah): King of Shienar. His sign is a white hart, which according to Shienaran custom is held also to be a sign of Shienar along with the Black Hawk.

Elaida (eh-LY-da): An Aes Sedai who advises Queen Morgase of Andor.

Elayne (ee-LAIN): Queen Morgase's daughter, the Daughter-heir to the Throne of Andor. Her sign is a golden lily.

Else; Else Grinwell (EHLZ GRIHN-wehl): A farmer's daughter met on the Caemlyn Road.

Eyeless, the: See Myrddraal.

Fade: See Myrddraal.

Fain, Padan (FAIN, PAHD-ahn): A peddler who arrives in Emond's Field just before Winternight.

Far Dareis Mai (FAHR DAH-rize MY): Literally, "Maidens of the Spear." One of a number of warrior societies of the Aiel; unlike any of the others, it admits women and only women. A Maiden may not marry and remain in the society, nor may she fight while carrying a child. Any child born to a Maiden is given to another woman to raise, in such a way that no one knows who the child's mother was. ("You may belong to no man, nor may any man belong to you, nor any child. The spear is your lover, your child, and your life.") These children are treasured, for it is prophesied that a child born of a Maiden will unite the clans and return to the Aiel the greatness they knew during the Age of Legends.

Farstrider, Jain (JAY-ihn): A hero of the northern lands who journeyed to many lands and had many adventures; the author of several books, as well as being the subject of books and stories. He vanished in 994 NE, after returning from a trip into the Great Blight which some said had taken him all the way to Shayol Ghul.

Father of Lies: See Dark One.

First Prince of the Sword: Title normally held by the eldest brother of the Queen of Andor, who has been trained since childhood to command the Queen's armies in time of war and to be her adviser in time of peace. If the Queen has no surviving brother, she will appoint someone to the title.

fist: The basic military unit of the Trollocs, varying in number; always more than one hundred, but never more than two hundred. A fist is usually, but not always, commanded by a Myrddraal.

Five Powers, the: There are threads to the One Power, and each person who can channel the One Power can usually grasp some threads better than others. These threads are named according to the sorts of things that can be done using them—Earth, Air, Fire, Water, and Spirit—and are called the Five Powers. Any wielder of the One Power will have a greater degree of strength with one, or possibly two, of these, and lesser strength in the others. Some few may have great strength with three, but since the Age of Legends no one has had great strength with all five. Even then this was extremely rare. The degree of strength can vary greatly between individuals, so that some who can channel are much stronger than others. Performing certain acts with the One Power requires ability in one or more of the Five Powers. For example, starting or controlling a fire requires Fire, and affecting the weather requires Air and Water, while Healing requires Water and Spirit. While Spirit was found equally in men and in women, great ability with Earth and/or Fire was found much more often among men, with Water and/or Air among women. There were exceptions, but it was so often so that Earth and Fire came to be regarded as male Powers, Air and Water as female. Generally, no ability is considered stronger than any other, though there is a saying among Aes Sedai: "There is no rock so strong that water and wind cannot wear it away, no fire so fierce that water cannot quench it or wind snuff it out." It should be noted this saying came into use long after the last male Aes Sedai was dead. Any equivalent saying among male Aes Sedai is long lost.

Flame of Tar Valon: The symbol of Tar Valon and the Aes Sedai. A stylized representation of a flame; a white teardrop with the point upward.

Forsaken, the: Name given to thirteen of the most powerful Aes Sedai ever known, who went over to the Dark One during the War of the Shadow in return for the promise of immortality. According to both legend and fragmentary records, they were imprisoned along with the Dark One when his prison was resealed. Their names are still used to frighten children.

Galad (gah-LAHD): See Damodred, Lord Galadedrid.

Gawyn (GAH-wihn): Queen Morgase's son, Elayne's brother, who will be First Prince of the Sword when Elayne ascends the throne. His sign is a white boar.

gentling: The act, performed by Aes Sedai, of shutting off a male who can channel from the One Power. This is necessary because any man who learns to channel will go insane from the taint upon *saidin* and will almost certainly do horrible things with the Power in his madness. A man who has been gentled can still sense the True Source, but he cannot touch it. Whatever madness has come before gentling is arrested by the act of gentling, but not cured by it, and if it is done soon enough death can be averted.

gleeman: A traveling storyteller, musician, juggler, tumbler and all-around entertainer. Known by their trademark cloaks of many-colored patches, they perform mainly in the villages and smaller towns, since larger towns and cities have other entertainments available.

Great Blight, the: A region in the far north, entirely corrupted by the Dark One. A haunt of Trollocs, Myrddraal, and other creatures of the Dark One.

Great Hunt of the Horn, the: A cycle of stories concerning the legendary search for the Horn of Valere, in the years between the end of the Trolloc Wars and the beginning of the War of the Hundred Years. If told in their entirety, the cycle would take many days.

Great Lord of the Dark: The name by which Darkfriends refer to the Dark One, claiming that to use his true name would be blasphemous.

Great Pattern: The Wheel of Time weaves the Patterns of the Ages into the Great Pattern, which is the whole of existence and reality, past, present and future. Also known as the Lace of Ages. *See also* Pattern of an Age; Wheel of Time.

Great Serpent: A symbol for time and eternity, ancient before the Age of Legends began, consisting of a serpent eating its own tail.

Halfman: See Myrddraal.

Hawkwing, Artur: A legendary king who united all the lands west of the Spine of the World, as well as some lands beyond the Aiel Waste. He even sent armies across the Aryth Ocean, but all contact with these was lost at his death, which set off the War of the Hundred Years. His sign was a golden hawk in flight. *See also* War of the Hundred Years.

Heartfang; Heartsbane: See Dark One.

heartstone: An indestructible substance created during the Age of Legends. Any known force used in an attempt to break it is absorbed, making heartstone stronger.

Horn of Valere (vah-LEER): The legendary object of the Great Hunt of the Horn. The Horn supposedly can call back dead heroes from the grave to fight against the Shadow.

Hundred Companions, the: One hundred male Aes Sedai, among the most powerful of the Age of Legends, who, led by Lews Therin Telamon, launched the final stroke that ended the War of the Shadow by sealing the Dark One back into his prison. The Dark One's counterstroke tainted *saidin;* the Hundred Companions went mad and began the Breaking of the World.

Illian (IHL-lee-ahn): A great port on the Sea of Storms, capital city of the nation of the same name. The sign of Illian is nine golden bees on a field of dark green.

Ingtar; Lord Ingtar of House Shinowa (IHNG-tahr; shih-NOH-wah): A Shienaran warrior met at Fal Dara.

Kandor *(KANH-dohr):* One of the Borderlands. The sign of Kandor is a rearing red horse on a field of pale green.

Kinch, Hyam *(KIHNCH, HY-ahm):* A farmer met on the Caemlyn Road.

Ko'bal *(KOH-bahl):* See Trollocs.

Lace of Ages: See Great Pattern, the.

Lan; al'Lan Mandragoran *(AHL-LAN man-DRAG-or-an):* A warrior from the north; Moiraine's companion.

Leafblighter: See Dark One.

league: A measure of distance equal to four miles. **See also** mile.

Luc; Lord Luc of House Mantear *(LUKE; MAN-tee-ahr):* Tigraine's brother, who would have been her First Prince of the Sword when she ascended the throne. His disappearance in the Great Blight is believed to be in some way connected to Tigraine's later disappearance. His sign was an acorn.

Lurk *(LUHRK):* See Myrddraal.

Machera, Elyas *(mah-CHEER-ah, ee-LY-ahs):* A man encountered by Perrin and Egwene in the forest.

Mahdi *(MAH-dee):* In the Old Tongue, "Seeker." Title of the leader of a Tuatha'an caravan.

Malkier *(mahl-KEER):* A nation, once one of the Borderlands, now consumed by the Blight. The sign of Malkier was a golden crane in flight.

Mandarb (MAHN-dahrb): In the Old Tongue, "Blade."

Manetheren *(mahn-EHTH-ehr-ehn):* One of the Ten Nations that made the Second Covenant, and also the capital city of that nation. Both city and nation were utterly destroyed in the Trolloc Wars.

Maradon *(MAH-rah-don):* The capital city of Saldaea.

Merrilin, Thom *(MER-rih-lihn, TOM):* A gleeman who comes to Emond's Field to perform at Bel Tine.

mile: A measure of distance equal to one thousand spans. Four miles make one league. **See also** span.

Min *(MIN):* A young woman encountered at the Stag and Lion in Baerlon.

Moiraine *(mwah-RAIN):* A visitor to Emond's Field who arrives just before Winternight.

Morgase *(moor-GAYZ):* By the Grace of the Light, Queen of Andor, High Seat of House Trakand *(TRAHK-ahnd).* Her sign is three golden keys. The sign of House Trakand is a silver keystone.

Myrddraal *(MUHRD-draal):* Creatures of the Dark One, commanders of the Trollocs. Twisted offspring of Trollocs in which the human stock used to create the Trollocs has resurfaced, but tainted by the evil that made the Trollocs. Physically they are like men except that they have no eyes, but can see like eagles in light or dark. They have certain powers stemming from the Dark One, including the ability to cause paralyzing fear with a look and the ability to vanish wherever there are shadows. One of their few known weaknesses is that they are reluctant to cross running water. In different lands they are known by many names, among them Halfmen, the Eyeless, Shadowmen, Lurk, and Fade.

One Power, the: The power drawn from the True Source. The vast majority of people are completely unable to learn to channel the One Power. A very small number can be taught to channel, and an even tinier number have the ability inborn. For these few there is no need to be taught; they will touch the True Source and channel the Power whether they want to or not, perhaps without even realizing what they are doing. This inborn ability usually manifests itself in late adolescence or early adulthood. If control is not taught, or self-learned (extremely difficult, with a success rate of only one in four), death is certain. Since the time of Madness, no man has been able to channel the Power without eventually going completely, horribly mad; and then, even if he has learned some control, dying from a wasting sickness which causes the sufferer to rot alive—a sickness caused, as is the madness, by the Dark One's taint on *saidin*. For a woman the death that comes without control of the Power is less horrible, but it is death just the same. Aes Sedai search for girls with the inborn ability as much to save their lives as to increase Aes Sedai numbers, and for men with it in order to stop the terrible things they inevitably do with the Power in their madness. *See also* channel; Time of Madness; True Source.

Pattern of an Age: The Wheel of Time weaves the threads of human lives into the Pattern of an Age, which forms the substance of reality for that Age; also known as Age Lace. *See also* ta'veren.

Questioners, the: An order within the Children of the Light. Their avowed purposes are discovering the truth in disputations and uncovering Darkfriends. In the search for truth and the Light, as they see it, they are even more zealous than the Children of the Light as a whole. Their normal method of inquiry is by torture; their normal attitude that they know the truth already and must only make their victim confess to it. The Questioners refer to themselves as the Hand of the Light, and at times act as if they

were entirely separate from the Children and the Council of the
Anointed, which commands the Children. The head of the Questioners is the High Inquisitor, who sits on the Council of the An-
nointed.

Red Ajah: *See* Ajah.

sa'angreal *(SAH-ahn-GREE-ahl):* An extremely rare object which
allows an individual to channel much more of the One Power than
would otherwise be possible or safe. A *sa'angreal* is like unto, but
much, much more powerful than, an *angreal.* Remnants of the
Age of Legends, the means of their making is no longer known.

saidar; saidin *(sah-ih-DAHR; sah-ih-DEEN): See* True Source.

Saldaea *(sahl-DAY-ee-ah):* One of the Borderlands. The sign of Saldaea is three silver fish on a field of dark blue.

Sea Folk: Inhabitants of islands in the Aryth *(AH-rihth)* Ocean and the
Sea of Storms, they spend little time on those islands, living most
of their lives on their ships. Most seaborne trade is carried by the
Sea Folk's ships.

Second Covenant: *See* Covenant of the Ten Nations.

Shadar Logoth *(SHAH-dahr LOH-goth):* In the Old Tongue, "the
Place Where the Shadow Waits." A city abandoned and shunned
since the Trolloc Wars. Also called "Shadow's Waiting."

Shadowman: *See* Myrddraal.

Shai'tan *(SHAY-ih-TAN): See* Dark One.

Shayol Ghul *(SHAY-ol GHOOL):* A mountain in the Blasted Lands,
the site of the Dark One's prison.

Shepherd of the Night: *See* Dark One.

Sheriam *(SHEER-ee-ahm):* An Aes Sedai, of the Blue Ajah.

Shienar *(shy-NAHR):* One of the Borderlands. The sign of Shienar is
a stooping black hawk.

shoufa *(SHOO-fah):* A garment of the Aiel, a cloth, usually the color
of sand or rock, that wraps around the head and neck, leaving
only the face bare.

Sightburner: *See* Dark One.

span: A measure of distance equal to two paces. A thousand spans
make a mile.

Spine of the World, the: A towering mountain range, with only a few
passes, which separates the Aiel Waste from the lands to the west.

stedding *(STEHD-ding):* An Ogier *(OH-geer)* homeland. Many *stedding* have been abandoned since the Breaking of the World. They
are portrayed in story and legend as havens, and with reason.
They are shielded in some way, no longer understood, so that

within them no Aes Sedai can channel the One Power, nor even sense that the True Source exists. Attempts to wield the One Power from outside a *stedding* have no effect inside a *stedding* boundary. No Trolloc will enter a *stedding* unless driven, and even a Myrddraal will do so only at the greatest need and then with the greatest reluctance and distaste. Even Darkfriends, if truly dedicated, feel uncomfortable within a *stedding*.

Stone of Tear: The fortress guarding the city of Tear. Said to be the earliest fortress built after the Time of Madness, and said by some to have been built *during* the Time of Madness. *See also* Tear.

Sunday: A feastday and festival in midsummer, widely celebrated.

tabac *(tah-BAHK):* A weed, widely cultivated. The leaves of it, when dried and cured, are burned in wooden holders called *pipes,* the fumes being inhaled.

Tallanvor, Martyn *(TAHL-ahn-vohr, mahr-TEEN):* Guardsman-Lieutenant of the Queen's Guard; met in Caemlyn.

ta'maral'ailen *(tah-MAHR-ahl-EYE-lehn):* In the Old Tongue, "Web of Destiny."

Tanreall, Artur Paendrag *(tahn-REE-ahl, AHR-tuhr PAY-ehn-DRAG):* *See* Hawkwing, Artur.

Tar Valon *(TAHR VAH-lon):* A city on an island in the River Erinin. The center of Aes Sedai power, and location of the Amyrlin Seat.

ta'veren *(tah-VEER-ehn):* A person around whom the Wheel of Time weaves all surrounding life-threads, perhaps *all* life-threads, to form a Web of Destiny. *See also* Pattern of an Age.

Tear *(TEER):* A great seaport on the Sea of Storms. The sign of Tear is three white crescents on a field of red and gold.

Telamon, Lews Therin *(TEHL-ah-mon, LOOZ THEH-rihn):* *See also* Dragon, the.

Thakan'dar *(thah-kahn-DAHR):* An eternally fog-shrouded valley below the slopes of Shayol Ghul.

Tigraine *(tee-GRAIN):* As Daughter-heir of Andor, she married Taringail Damodred and bore his son Galadedrid. Her disappearance in 972 NE, shortly after her brother Luc vanished in the Blight, led to the struggle in Andor called the Succession, and caused the events in Cairhien which eventually brought on the Aiel War. Her sign was a woman's hand gripping a thorny rose-stem with a white blossom.

Time of Madness: *See* Breaking of the World, the.

Tinkers: *See* Tuatha'an.

Traveling People: *See* Tuatha'an.

Trolloc Wars: A series of wars, beginning about 1000 AB and lasting more than three hundred years, during which Trolloc armies ravaged the world. Eventually the Trollocs were slain or driven back into the Great Blight, but some nations ceased to exist, while others were almost depopulated. All records of the time are fragmentary. *See also* Covenant of the Ten Nations.

Trollocs (TRAHL-lohks): Creatures of the Dark One, created during the War of the Shadow. Huge in stature, vicious in the extreme, they are a twisted blend of animal and human stock, and kill for the pure pleasure of killing. Sly, deceitful and treacherous, they can be trusted only by those they fear. They are omnivorous and will eat any kind of meat, including human flesh and the flesh of other Trollocs. Largely of human origin, they are able to interbreed with humankind, but the offspring are usually stillborn, and those which are not often fail to survive. They are divided into tribe-like bands, chief among them being the Ahf'frait, Al'ghol, Bhan'sheen, Dha'vol, Dhai'mon, Dhjin'nen, Ghar'ghael, Ghob'hlin, Gho'hlem, Ghraem'lan, Ko'bal, and the Kno'mon.

True Source: The driving force of the universe, which turns the Wheel of Time. It is divided into a male half (*saidin*) and a female half (*saidar*), which work at the same time with and against each other. Only a man can draw on *saidin,* only a woman on *saidar.* Since the beginning of the Time of Madness, *saidin* has been tainted by the Dark One's touch. *See also* One Power.

Tuatha'an (too-AH-thah-AHN): A wandering folk, also known as the Tinkers and as the Traveling People, who live in brightly painted wagons and follow a totally pacifist philosophy called the Way of the Leaf. Things mended by Tinkers are often better than new, but the Tuatha'an are shunned by many villages because of stories that they steal children and try to convert young people to their beliefs.

Village Council: In most villages a group of men, elected by the townsmen and headed by a Mayor, who are responsible for making decisions which affect the village as a whole and for negotiating with the Councils of other villages over matters which affect the villages jointly. They are at odds with the Women's Circle in so many villages that this conflict is seen as almost traditional. *See also* Women's Circle.

War of the Hundred Years: A series of overlapping wars among constantly shifting alliances, precipitated by the death of Artur Hawkwing and the resulting struggle for his empire. It lasted from

FY 994 to FY 1117. The war depopulated large parts of the lands between the Aryth Ocean and the Aiel Waste, from the Sea of Storms to the Great Blight. So great was the destruction that only fragmentary records of the time remain. The empire of Artur Hawkwing was pulled apart, and the nations of the present day were formed.

War of the Shadow: Also known as the War of Power, it ended the Age of Legends. It began shortly after the attempt to free the Dark One, and soon involved the whole world. In a world where even the memory of war had been forgotten, every facet of war was rediscovered, often twisted by the Dark One's touch on the World, and the One Power was used as a weapon. The war was ended by the resealing of the Dark One into his prison.

Warder: A warrior bonded to an Aes Sedai. The bonding is a thing of the One Power, and by it he gains such gifts as quick healing, the ability to go long periods without food, water or rest, and the ability to sense the taint of the Dark One at a distance. So long as a Warder lives, the Aes Sedai to whom he is bonded knows he is alive however far away he is, and when he dies she will know the moment and manner of his death. The bonding does not tell her how far he is, though, nor in what direction. While most Ajahs believe an Aes Sedai may have one Warder bonded to her at a time, the Red Ajah refuses to bond any Warders at all, while the Green Ajah believes an Aes Sedai may bond as many Warders as she wishes. Ethically the Warder must accede to the bonding, but it has been known to be done involuntarily. What the Aes Sedai gain from the bonding is a closely-held secret. *See also* Aes Sedai.

Web of Destiny: A great change in the Pattern of an Age, centered around one or more people who are *ta'veren*.

Wheel of Time, the: Time is a wheel with seven spokes, each spoke an Age. As the Wheel turns, the Ages come and go, each leaving memories that fade to legend, then to myth, and are forgotten by the time that Age comes again. The Pattern of an Age is slightly different each time an Age comes, and each time it is subject to greater change, but each time it is the same Age.

White Ajah: *See* Ajah.

White Tower: The palace of the Amyrlin Seat in Tar Valon.

Whitecloaks: *See* Children of the Light.

Wisdom: In villages, a woman chosen by the Women's Circle to sit in the Circle for her knowledge of such things as healing and foretelling the weather, as well as for common good sense. A position of great responsibility and authority, both actual and implied. She is generally considered the equal of the Mayor, and in some villages his superior. Unlike the Mayor, she is chosen for life, and it is very rare for a Wisdom to be removed from office before her death. Almost traditionally in conflict with the Mayor. *See also* Women's Circle.

Women's Circle: A group of women elected by the women of a village, responsible for deciding such matters as are considered solely women's responsibility (for example, when to plant the crops and when to harvest). Equal in authority to the Village Council, with clearly-delineated lines and areas of responsibility. Often at odds with the Village Council. *See also* Village Council.